City of Dreams

A Novel of

Nieuw Amsterdam

and Early Manhattan

BEVERLY SWERLING

SCRIBNER PAPERBACK FICTION

Published by Simon & Schuster

New York London Toronto Sydney Singapore

SCRIBNER PAPERBACK FICTION
Simon & Schuster, Inc.
Rockefeller Center
1230 Avenue of the Americas
New York, NY 10020

First Scribner Paperback Fiction edition 2002
SCRIBNER PAPERBACK FICTION and design are trademarks of
Macmillan Library Reference USA, Inc., used under license by
Simon & Schuster, the publisher of this work.

For information regarding special discounts for bulk purchases,
please contact Simon & Schuster Special Sales at 1-800-456-6798 or
business@simonandschuster.com

Designed by Katy Riegel

Manufactured in the United States of America

1   3   5   7   9   10   8   6   4   2

The Library of Congress has cataloged the Simon & Schuster edition as follows:
Swerling, Beverly.
City of dreams : a novel of early Manhattan / Beverly Swerling.
p. cm.
1. New York (N.Y.)—History—Colonial period, ca. 1600–1775—Fiction.
2. Manhattan (New York, N.Y.)—Fiction. 3. British Americans—Fiction.
4. Dutch Americans—Fiction. I. Title.

PS3619.W47 C58 2001
813'.6—dc21   2001020669

ISBN 0-684-87172-6
0-684-87173-4 (Pbk)

For Michael, our forever darling boy.

Hasta la proxima, entonces, mi niño.

Author's Note

THE PHYSICAL HISTORY of New York City and, more specifically, Manhattan is accurate as presented here, with one exception: Hall Place never existed. It's a composite of what's known about many small, nondescript Nieuw Amsterdam lanes in the vicinity of the old Stadt Huys.

I have attempted to be accurate, as well, in the matter of New York's complex political and social history. In fact, the most barbaric events are the truest, lifted whole from the diaries and letters of people who lived through them. Again, however, there's an exception. The decree against inoculation was actually issued in 1747, under Governor Clinton, ten years later than it occurs in this book. Evidence indicates that attitudes were exactly the same a decade earlier, and certainly the practice was already being hotly debated. I changed the date of the law to suit the story's need.

Finally, and perhaps this is hardest to believe, the descriptions of medical techniques and practices are historically correct. People did endure such surgeries without anesthesia, and sustain such extraordinary, exhausting, and excruciating treatments. Hope, after all, is more attractive than despair. And by however roundabout a path, their hope has led to our certitudes. Those caregivers of the past, with their lust for knowledge and their thirst to cure, were often uncommonly brave and strong. This is their story.

Acknowledgments

THIS BOOK WOULD not have been written without the loving support of my wonderful husband. You would not be reading it but for the exemplary skill of my agents, Henry Morrison and Danny Baror—I am even more grateful for their friendship. The excellent editing of Sydny Miner made the book considerably more than it would have been without her.

Beyond those bedrock fundamentals, my greatest debt is to the authors of countless books lodged in the city's many and mighty political and social and medical collections. The New York Public Library can, I think, have no equal. I'm particularly indebted to its Schomburg Center for Research in Black Culture, a truly remarkable resource. The library of the New-York Historical Society and the vast library systems of the city's colleges and universities were equally invaluable. For the historical novelist, New York on New York is as good as it gets.

The research was made immeasurably easier by endlessly helpful and patient archivists and librarians. Two deserve special mention: Adrienne Millon, archivist of the Ehrman Medical Library at NYU Medical Center, who made available the records of Bellevue Hospital back to its arguable and misty origins in Nieuw Amsterdam; and Caroline Duroselle-Melish, reference librarian of the Historical Collection of the New York Academy of Medicine, who unlocked for me a seventeenth- and eighteenth-century world of wonder preserved in pages so fragile one hesitates to breathe while examining them.

An army of other people offered their wisdom and their guidance. My special thanks to Hope Cooke, urban historian extraordinaire. And to Ted Burrows and Mike Wallace, whose Pulitzer Prize–winning history of the city, *Gotham,* was published when I was halfway through the writing of *City of Dreams*. *Gotham* became my polestar, the navigational aid that could always be relied on, and the authors were unfailingly generous in their writerly willingness to share speculation.

While many women, I'm sure, have reason to thank their gynecologists, mine is possibly unique. Dr. Judith Morris de Celis mentioned seaweed, and sent me down a path that led to a wholly unexpected twist of the tale.

And whom does one thank for the Internet? This book and my life have been enriched by the people I met there, all so ready to make their expertise and their information available at the click of a mouse. I wish in particular to thank Lee Salzman, whose award-winning histories of the First Nations, including the first Manhattanites, shaped my thinking and framed my story. They are available to all at dickshovel.com.

Lastly, any errors of fact that crept in despite the best efforts of so many are entirely my fault and certainly not theirs.

Beverly Swerling
The High Hills Island
2001

Contents

BOOK I: THE LITTLE MUSQUASH PATH
June 1661–October 1664
17

BOOK II: THE SEEING FAR PATH
December 1711–June 1714
111

BOOK III: THE HIGH HILLS PATH
August 1731–February 1737
187

BOOK IV: THE SHIVERING CLIFFS PATH
August 1737–November 1737
275

BOOK V: THE CLAWS TEAR OUT EYES PATH
September 1759–July 1760
333

BOOK VI: THE PATH OF FLAMES
July 1765–December 1765
427

BOOK VII: WAR PATH
August 1776–March 1784
475

EPILOGUE: THE PATH OF DREAMS
June 1798
577

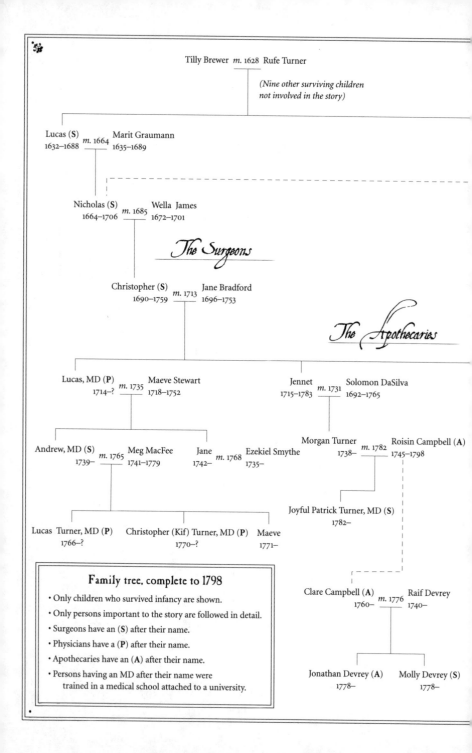

Tilly Brewer *m.* 1628 Rufe Turner

(Nine other surviving children not involved in the story)

Lucas (**S**) *m.* 1664 Marit Graumann
1632–1688 — 1635–1689

Nicholas (**S**) *m.* 1685 Wella James
1664–1706 — 1672–1701

The Surgeons

Christopher (**S**) *m.* 1713 Jane Bradford
1690–1759 — 1696–1753

The Apothecaries

Lucas, MD (**P**) *m.* 1735 Maeve Stewart
1714–? — 1718–1752

Jennet *m.* 1731 Solomon DaSilva
1715–1783 — 1692–1765

Andrew, MD (**S**) *m.* 1765 Meg MacFee
1739– — 1741–1779

Jane *m.* 1768 Ezekiel Smythe
1742– — 1735–

Morgan Turner *m.* 1782 Roisin Campbell (**A**)
1738– — 1745–1798

Lucas Turner, MD (**P**)
1766–?

Christopher (Kif) Turner, MD (**P**)
1770–?

Maeve
1771–

Joyful Patrick Turner, MD (**S**)
1782–

Clare Campbell (**A**) *m.* 1776 Raif Devrey
1760– — 1740–

Family tree, complete to 1798

- Only children who survived infancy are shown.
- Only persons important to the story are followed in detail.
- Surgeons have an (**S**) after their name.
- Physicians have a (**P**) after their name.
- Apothecaries have an (**A**) after their name.
- Persons having an MD after their name were trained in a medical school attached to a university.

Jonathan Devrey (**A**)
1778–

Molly Devrey (**S**)
1778–

The Physicians

Sally (**A**) *m. 1664* Jacob Van der Vries (**P**)
1637–1697   1630–1670

Lisbetta (Red Bess) (**A**) *m. 1688* Moses Smythe
1665–1714   1662–1694

Willem (Will Devrey) *m. 1698* Susannah Hawks
1667–1740   1681–1742

Tamsyn (**A**) *m. 1712* Zachary Craddock, MD (**P**)
1695–1754   1687–1778

Bede *m. 1730* Nancy Mariah Howe   Lorene   Caleb, MD (**P**)
1702–1779   1710–1785   1704–1759   1708–1765

Paul S   Marit   Cecily   Wella
1720–1754   1721–1789   1722–1800   1726–1785

Raif   Samuel, MD (**P**)   Susan   Celeste
1740–   1740–   1742–   1745–

Persons Held as Slaves and Indentures

Hetje
c.1647–1719

Selma
c. 1659–1722

Cuffy
1700–1759

Shirley
1702–1746

Chassy
1703–1766

Robin
?–1712

Tom
1684–1712

Kinsowa
?–1712

Amba   *m. ?*   Quaco
c. 1693–1755   ?–1712

Phoebe A
1712–1774

Tilda
1710–1777

Flossie O'Toole
1690–1770

Cuf
1738–?

Clemence
1712–1738

Bridget Hagan
1740–

Laniah
1768–

City *of* Dreams

Book One

The Little Musquash Path

JUNE 1661–OCTOBER 1664

Manhattan. In the Algonquin language, the High Hills Island. Before the coming of the Europeans it was the summer home of the Canarsie people, who in winter returned to the place they called Metoaca, the Long Island. Werpoes, the main Canarsie village on Manhattan, was at the narrow southern end of the island, and was where people from many clans came to trade for the exquisitely made Canarsie wampum, intricately carved shells that were prized by all who saw them.

Not far from Werpoes was the special place the women went during their menses, and again when they gave birth. There the blood spirits protected the women and hid them from the eyes of the men, who would be angry if, having looked upon a female when she was unclean, they thereby lost their manly power to hunt and fish and kill their enemies.

To get from Werpoes to their sacred compound, the women traveled the path they called the Little Musquash.

Chapter One

ELEVEN WEEKS IN a ship thirty-seven feet long by eleven wide, carrying a crew of nine as well as twenty passengers. Lurching and lunging and tossing on the Atlantic swells, the sails creaking night and day, spread above them like some evil bird of prey. Hovering, waiting for death.

The dung buckets on the open deck were screened only by a scanty calico curtain that blew aside more often than it stayed in place. For Sally Turner the dung buckets were the worst.

She was twenty-three years old—small, with dark hair, bright brown eyes, and a narrow, pinched face—from a Rotterdam slum by way of a rodent-infested corner of a Kentish barn. The crossing had turned her insides to water. She went seven or eight times a day to the dung buckets. The flimsy cloth almost always blew aside and she saw the grizzled, hungry-eyed crewmen watching, waiting for her to lift her skirts. As if all the battles between Kent and now had been for nothing.

Her brother suffered more from the seasickness. Lucas Turner was a big man, like his sister only in his dark coloring, and in the intelligence that showed behind his eyes. Until now most would have called him handsome; the journey had reduced him to a shell. From the start Lucas hung day and night over the side of the wooden ship, vomiting his guts into the sea.

The voyage was beyond imagination, beyond bearing. Except that there was no choice but to bear it. One small consolation: the April day when the *Princess* left Rotterdam was exceptionally warm. A premature summer rushed toward them as they sailed west. Most of the food spoiled before the end of the first three weeks. Constant illness prevented hunger.

A crossing longer and more miserable and more dangerous than anything they had talked about or prepared for, and when they got there—what? By all reports bitter cold in winter and fierce heat in summer. "And savages," Sally Turner said the first morning of June, when they were nine weeks into the voyage, and she and her brother were hanging on to the rail in the ship's bow. The swells were stronger in that position, but Lucas was convinced he could be no worse. And there was a bit of privacy. "There are red men in America, Lucas. With painted faces and feathers and hatchets. In God's name, what have we done?"

Lucas didn't answer. They had decided the risk was worth the taking while they were still in Holland. Besides, he had to lean over the rail and puke yet again. There was nothing in his stomach to come up, even the bile was gone, but the dry heaves would not leave him.

For as long as Sally could remember, it was Lucas who made such security as there was in her world. She felt every shudder of his agony-racked frame as if it were her own. She slid down, using the wooden ship's planked bulkhead to keep her steady, and pawed through her basket. Eventually she drew herself up and pulled the tiny cork of a small pewter vial. "Chamomile powder, Lucas. Let me shake some onto your tongue."

"No, that's all you've left. I won't take it."

"I've more. With our things down below."

"You're lying, Sal. I can always—" He had to stop to heave again.

His sister leaned toward him with the remedy that promised relief. Lucas eyed the small tube with longing. "You're sure you've more?"

"In our box in the hold. I swear it."

Lucas opened his mouth. Sally emptied the last few grains of the chamomile powder onto his tongue. It gave him some fifteen minutes of freedom from nausea.

Below decks, in the sturdy box that held all their belongings carefully wrapped in oilskin, she did indeed have more chamomile, but only in the form of seed. Waiting, like Lucas and Sally Turner, to be planted in Nieuw Amsterdam and thrive in the virgin earth of the island of Manhattan.

There was a wooden wharf of sorts, but two ships were already moored alongside it. The *Princess* dropped anchor some fifty yards away, and a raft carried them to shore. It wasn't big enough to take everyone in one trip. Lucas and Sally were dispatched on the third.

They clung together to keep from being pitched overboard, and listened in disbelief to one of the crewmen talk about the calm of the deep, still harbor. "Not too many places on this coast you can raft folks to land like this. But here the bay's flat as a lake when the tide's with you." Meanwhile it seemed to Lucas and

Sally that they were sliding and rolling with each wave, unable to lift their heads and see what they'd come to after their eleven weeks in hell.

At last, land beneath their feet and they could barely stand on it. They'd experienced the same misery three years before, after the far shorter crossing between England and the Netherlands. "Give it a little time, Sal," her brother said. "We'll be fine."

Sally looked at what she could see of the place. A piece of crumbling earthworks that was a corner of Fort Amsterdam. A windmill that wasn't turning because there was no breath of air. A gibbet from which was suspended a corpse, covered in pitch and buzzing with flies. And the sun beating down on them. Relentless. "Lucas," she whispered. "Dear God, Lucas." Her brother put a hand on her arm.

"You there," a voice shouted. "Mijnheer Turner. When you get your legs under you, come over here."

"There's some shade over by that tree," Lucas murmured. "Wait there. I'll deal with this."

A couple of rough planks had been spread across two trestles made from saplings. The man seated behind this makeshift table was checking off names on a list. Lucas staggered toward him. The clerk didn't look up. "Turner?"

"Aye. Lucas Turner. And Sally Turner."

"English?"

His accent always gave him away. "Yes, but we're come under the auspices of . . ."

"Patroon Van Renselaar. I know. You're assigned to plot number twenty-nine. It's due north of here. Follow the Brede Wegh behind the fort to Wall Street. Take you some ten minutes to walk the length of the town, then you leave by the second gate in the wall. The path begins straightaway on the other side. You'll know your place when you get to it. There are three pine trees one right behind the other, all marked with whiting."

Lucas bent forward, trying to see the papers in front of the Dutchman. "Is that a map of our land?"

"It's a map of all the Van Renselaar land. Your piece is included."

Lucas stretched out his hand. The clerk snatched the papers away. At last, mildly surprised, he looked up. "Can you read, Englishman?"

"Yes. And I'd like to see your map. Only for a moment."

The man looked doubtful. "Why? What will it tell you?"

Lucas was conscious of his clothes hanging loose from his wasted frame, and his face almost covered by weeks of unkempt beard. "For one thing, a look at your map might give me some idea of the distance we must go before we reach those three pine trees."

"No need for that. I'll tell you. Half a day's walk once you're recovered from the journey." The clerk glanced toward Sally. "Could take a bit longer for a woman. Some of the hills are fairly steep."

This time when Lucas leaned forward the map wasn't snatched away. He saw one firm line that appeared to divide the town from the countryside, doubtless the wall the clerk had spoken of, and just beyond it what appeared to be a small settlement of sorts. "Our land"—Lucas pointed to the settlement beyond the wall—"is it in that part there?"

"No, that's the Voorstadt, the out-city, a warehouse and the farms that serve the town." The clerk seemed amused by the newcomer's curiosity. He placed a stubby finger on an irregular circle a fair distance beyond the Voorstadt. "And that's the Collect Pond as gives us fresh water to brew beer with. Anything else you'd care to know, Englishman? Shall I arrange a tour?"

"I was promised land in the town," Lucas said. "But I'll take a place in this Voorstadt. I'm a barber. I can't earn my keep if—"

"Your land's where I said it was. You're a farmer now. That's what's needed here."

"Wait." The voice, a woman's, was imperious. "I wish to speak with this man." A slight figure stepped away from the knot of people standing a little distance from the clerk. Despite the heat she was entirely covered by a hooded cloak of the tightly woven gray stuff the Dutch called duffel. She freed a slender arm long enough to point to Lucas. "Send him to me."

"*Ja*, mevrouw, of course." The clerk jerked his head in the woman's direction. "Do as she says," he muttered quietly in the Englishman's direction. "Whatever she says."

Lucas took a step toward the woman. He removed his black, broad-brimmed hat and held it in front of him, bobbed his head, and waited.

Her hair was dark, shot with gray and drawn back in a strict bun. Her features were sharp, and when she spoke her lips barely moved, as if afraid they might forget themselves and smile. "I heard you tell the clerk you could read. And that you're a barber."

"Both are true, mevrouw."

"Were you then the surgeon on that excuse for a ship?" She nodded toward the *Princess* riding at anchor in the harbor. "God help all who cross in her."

"No, mevrouw, I was not."

"A point in your favor. We are cursed with so-called ship's surgeons in this colony. Ignorant butchers, all of them. You're English, but you speak Dutch. And that miserable craft sailed from Rotterdam, not London. So are you a member of the English Barbers' Company?"

"I am, mevrouw. But I've lived two years in Rotterdam, and I was told I'd be allowed to practice here exactly as . . ."

"I have no reason to think otherwise. And if you know your trade—" She broke off, chewing on her thin lower lip, studying him. Lucas waited. A number of silent seconds went by; then the woman pointed toward Sally. "I take it that's your wife."

"No, mevrouw, I am unmarried. That is my sister, Sally Turner." Lucas motioned Sally forward. She didn't come, but she dropped a quick curtsy.

The woman's eyes betrayed a flicker of amusement. "The *juffrouw* does not seem particularly obedient, Lucas Turner. Is your sister devoted to you?"

"I believe she is, mevrouw."

"Good. I, too, have a brother to whom I am utterly devoted. I am Anna Stuyvesant. My brother is Peter Stuyvesant. He is governor of Nieuw Netherlands. And right now . . ."

Sweet Jesus Christ. Bloody Stuyvesant and his bloody sister. When the only thing Lucas wanted, the thing that had made him come to this godforsaken colony at the end of the world, was to be where the authorities would leave him in peace.

Either his reaction didn't show, or she chose not to notice it. "Right now my brother is in need of a man of great skill. And I am trying to decide, Lucas Turner, if you might be he."

He had no choice but to seize the moment. "That depends on the nature of the skill your brother requires, mevrouw. I know my trade, if that's what you're asking."

"It is part of the question. The other part is the precise nature of your trade. Is it true that, though they belong to the same Company, London barbers and surgeons do not practice the same art?"

Lucas heard Sally's sharply indrawn breath. "Officially yes, mevrouw. But the two apprenticeships occur side by side, in the same hall. A man interested in both skills cannot help but learn both. I am skilled in surgery as well as barbering. What is it the governor requires?"

The woman's eyes flicked toward Sally for a moment, as if she, too, had noted the gasp. A second only; then she dismissed the younger woman as of no importance. "I believe my brother to be in desperate need of a stone cutter, barber."

Lucas smiled.

Finally, for the first time in weeks, he felt no doubt. "Pray God you are correct, mevrouw. If it's an expert stone cutter your brother needs, he is a fortunate man. He has found one." Lucas turned to Sally. She was white-faced. He pretended not to notice. "Come, Sal. Bring my instruments. I've a patient waiting for relief."

Word was that Peter Stuyvesant ruled with absolute authority and that any who questioned him paid a heavy price. Right then, ashen, sweating with pain, the man lying in the bed looked small and insignificant.

Lucas put his hand on Stuyvesant's forehead. The flesh was cold and clammy. "Where does it hurt, mijnheer?"

"In my belly, man. Low down. Fierce pain. And I cannot piss for the burning. My sister is convinced it's a stone."

Anna Stuyvesant was in the room with them, huddling in the gloom beside the door. Some mention had been made of a wife, and when they arrived Lucas had heard the voices of children, but none had appeared. He'd seen only a black serving woman—from what he'd heard of this place she was probably a slave— and the man in the bed. And, in control of all, the sister. Obviously married, or had been, since the clerk at the dock had called her mevrouw, but one who, following the Dutch fashion, hadn't taken her husband's name. Looked like the type who wouldn't take willingly to his cock, either. Lucas was conscious of her fierce glance drilling a hole in his back.

He leaned closer to the patient, observing the clouded eyes, the pallor, the sour breath that came hard through a half-open mouth. "Judging from the look of you, mijnheer, Mevrouw Stuyvesant may be right. And if she is, if it's a stone, I can help you. But . . ." He hesitated. Afterward, some men thought of the relief, and were grateful. Others remembered only the agony of the surgery, and those hated you forever. God help him and Sally both if the governor of Nieuw Netherland hated him forever.

"But what?" Stuyvesant demanded.

"But it will hurt while I do it," Lucas said, choosing not to dip the truth in honey. "Worse than the pain you're feeling right now. After the operation is over, however, you will be cured."

"If I live, you mean."

"The chances are excellent that you will, mijnheer."

"But not certain."

"In this world, Mijnheer Governor, nothing is certain. As I'm sure you know. But I've done this surgery dozens of times."

"And all your patients lived?" Wincing with pain while he spoke. Having to force the words between clenched teeth.

"Perhaps six or seven did not, mijnheer. But they were men of weak constitution before the stone began plaguing them."

Stuyvesant studied the Englishman, even managed a small smile. "I am not a man of weak constitution. And you, you're a strange one, barber. Despite your mangled Dutch, you speak like a man with his wits in place. But the way you look, not to mention how you smell . . . Ach, but then my sister tells me you only just got off the *Princess,* so per—"

The pain must have been savage. The Dutchman gritted his teeth so hard Lucas thought he might break his jaw. The sweat poured off him.

Lucas leaned forward and wiped the governor's face with a corner of the bedding. Half a minute, maybe less. The wave of agony abated. Stuyvesant drew a few deep breaths. "This operation . . ." He whispered the words, his strength sapped by the pain. "How long will it take?"

"Forty-five seconds," Lucas said. "Start to finish. You can time me."

The governor stared into Lucas's eyes. "I will. Forty-five seconds? You're certain of that?"

"I am."

Stuyvesant flung back the covers. "Took them forty-five minutes to do this." His right leg had been cut off at the knee.

Lucas looked down at the stump, then at the face of the man in the bed. Pain had hollowed his cheeks, but when their eyes met Stuyvesant did not look away. Finally Lucas nodded. He turned to the woman beside the door. "Bring some rum, mevrouw. He must drink as much as we can get down him."

Anna Stuyvesant stepped out of the shadows. "There is no rum in this house."

"Then send someone to get some. Your brother cannot—"

"Yes, I can." Stuyvesant's voice, sounding firmer than it had, trembling less with agony. "I must. I take no drink stronger than ordinary ale."

"But under the circumstances . . ." Lucas looked again at the stump of leg.

"Not then, either," Stuyvesant said quietly. "I fear the Lord more than I fear pain, barber."

"As you wish. But perhaps I can satisfy both masters. If you will excuse me for a moment . . ."

Lucas stepped into the narrow hall. Sally was there, sitting at the top of the stairs, clutching her basket and the small leather box that contained his instruments. She jumped up, pressing her bundles to her, her narrow face shriveled with anxiety. "How is he? Can you help him without cutting?"

"No." Lucas was sweating. He wiped his forehead with the sleeve of his black jacket. The accumulated filth of the journey left a dark mark. "God help me, I must remove the stone."

"But—"

"There is no 'but.' If it doesn't come out, like as not he'll drown in his own piss."

"What if he dies of the pain of surgery? What if he bleeds to death?" Her voice was an urgent whisper.

"This man can bear suffering." Lucas looked anxiously toward the bedroom door. "He's had one leg cut off at the knee, and he doesn't take more than an ale to quench his thirst. No strong spirits, not even to dull the onslaught of the knife and the saw. As for bleeding to death, I must see that he does not. Say your prayers, girl, and give me my instruments."

"Lucas, if anything happens, what—"

"Nothing is going to happen. Except that mijnheer the governor will think I'm the greatest surgeon since Galen."

"But you're a barber, Lucas. In heaven's name, your surgeon's instruments are what got us hounded out of London in the first place."

"I know. But we're in Nieuw Amsterdam, not London. We must take our chance when it presents itself. See if you've any stanching powder in your basket."

Sally hesitated.

"Do it, Sal. Otherwise I'll go ahead without it."

A few seconds more. Finally she began pawing through her things. "Yes, here it is." She held up a small pottery crock. "Stanching powder. A fair supply."

"Excellent. Now some laudanum."

Sally shook her head. "I have none. I swear it, Lucas. I only brought a little aboard, and we used—"

"Damnation! Look well, Sal. If any's left, I can use it to advantage."

After a few moments groping, she produced a tiny pewter vial of the kind she'd used to store the last of the chamomile powder. "This held laudanum. But it's empty."

Lucas snatched the container, uncorked it, sniffed, squinted to peer inside. "A drop, perhaps. It will be better than nothing. Aye, I can see a drop or two at the bottom." He recorked the vial and slipped it into the side pocket of his breeches, then turned back to the bedroom. "Wish me luck, Sal. And stop up your ears. But don't worry, the shouts won't go on for long."

Sally went again to sit on the top step, clutching her basket in her lap, as if her simples were the only thing she had to remind her of who she was and how she came to be in this place.

The house at the corner of the fort built for the governor of Nieuw Netherland was nothing like as grand as places she'd seen from afar in London and Rotterdam, but it was the grandest she'd ever been inside. Two stories, and both of them for the living of this one man and his family and his servants. Brick outside and polished wood within. Even the wooden steps were buffed to such a gloss that when she leaned forward she could see her reflection, her face peeking over the toes of her scuffed boots.

Lucas had bought her the boots before they left Holland; he said clogs wouldn't do for such a long and perilous journey. The boots had pointed toes and laced to well above her ankles. She'd thought them incredibly grand at first, but less so now. And the sturdy Dutch folk in gilt frames looking down at her from the walls seemed unimpressed. God knew, they were not the first.

Back in Kent, in the barn behind their father's Dover taproom, the eleven Turner brats had slept tumbled together in the straw because all the beds were rented for a penny a night to travelers. There Lucas had protected her from the despicable things that befell their sisters and brothers (often with their father's connivance). There Sally believed in Lucas's quest to be better than he'd been born to be. When he taught first himself to read, then taught her, she believed. When he wrangled a barbering apprenticeship to the Company of Barbers and Surgeons by showing a member of the gentry the sketch Sally had made of the men, bare arse in the air, rutting with a boy of six beside the stable (and never mind that the child was a Turner), Sally believed. When Lucas sent for her to come to London to join him, and two years later the wrath of the Surgeons drove them both into the street, his sister believed in the rightness of her brother's aspirations. Now, when they had come so far to this strange place, and he was yet again rushing headlong into conflict with authority; now, she was less sure.

Lucas returned to Stuyvesant's bedroom. His patient lay silent in his bed, rigid with pain. The governor's sister was leaning over him, bathing his face with a cloth dipped in scented water. Lucas leaned toward her. "Send word to the barracks that we'll need three strong men," he said softly. "Make sure they're young, with—"

"No." Stuyvesant's word was a command. "I'll not be held down."

"I didn't intend for you to overhear me, mijnheer. But I don't mean you to be held down, only held in position. It is through no lack of courage that a man twitches under the knife."

"I will not twitch, barber."

"Mijnheer—"

"Get on with it, man. Else I'll have you hanged as a charlatan who offers hope when there is none."

Lucas hesitated, looked at Anna Stuyvesant. She shook her head. Lucas took the pewter vial from his pocket. "Very well. Please open your mouth."

"I told you, I don't take strong drink."

"This isn't drink. It's a medicinal draught made by my sister." Stuyvesant still looked wary. "Consider the size of it, mijnheer." Lucas held the tiny pewter tube in front of the other man's eyes. "Could this hold enough rum or geneva to satisfy even an infant's thirst?"

The governor hesitated a second longer, then opened his mouth. Lucas shook the single remaining drop of laudanum onto his tongue. The argument had been pointless; there wasn't enough of Sally's decoction to do any good. On the other hand, sometimes what a patient believed to be true was as good as the reality.

"That will make things very much easier," Lucas said. He even managed to sound as if he meant it. "Now, mijnheer, in a moment we must get you out of your bed and over to that chest by the window where the light's best. I'll want you to lean on the chest, support yourself on your elbows. But first"—he turned to Anna Stuyvesant—"bring me a bucket, mevrouw. And some cloths. And a kettle of boiling water."

She left. Lucas checked the contents of his surgeon's case. A dozen ties made of sheep's intestines. Three scalpels of different sizes, a couple of saws, a needle threaded with catgut, and, for stone cutting, a fluted probe and a pair of pincers with a jointed handle that could be opened to the width of four spread fingers.

The sound of flies buzzing in the sun beyond the window was the only noise. The man in the bed gritted his teeth against the agony and said nothing, just kept looking at Lucas. Lucas looked back. Finally Anna Stuyvesant returned. "Hot water, you said, and clean cloths and a bucket. It's all here."

"Thank you." Lucas stood up and removed his jacket. He began rolling up the sleeves of his shirt. "Now, mijnheer, may I assist you from the bed?"

"Yes, but first . . . Anna, go. Leave us alone."

"I do not like to go, Peter. If you should—"

"This is nothing for a woman to see. Go." And after she had gone, "Very well, barber, let's get this over with. If you hand me my stick I can—" Stuyvesant broke off, gritted his teeth against another wave of the pain. "Do it," he whispered finally. "I don't care how much it hurts or for how long. For the love of God, man, do it now."

"Forty-five seconds," Lucas promised again. "From the first cut. I swear it."

He helped Stuyvesant hobble to the chest beside the window. The governor leaned forward, taking his weight on his elbows as Lucas directed. In fact Lucas would have preferred that his patient stand on the chest and squat, but a man with one leg couldn't be asked to assume such a position. Bent over like this was the next best thing. Lucas pushed up the governor's nightshirt, exposed the Dutchman's plump buttocks, then, a moment before he began, "There is one thing, Mijnheer Governor."

"What one thing, barber?"

"My fee."

"Are you mad? I'll have you horsewhipped. Of course your fee will be paid. What do you take me for?"

"A strict man but a fair one. I'm told your word is absolutely to be relied on."

"It is. I take it you mean to ask for something other than money." The words came hard, with wheezing breath, limned by pain. "Ask then. Quickly."

"A homestead closer to the town than the one my sister and I have been assigned. And a place inside the town to practice my trade."

Stuyvesant turned his head, looked at Lucas over his shoulder. "There is no place inside the town. In Nieuw Amsterdam the one thing even I can't control is the roofs over people's heads. Fifteen hundred souls between the wharf and the wall, and all of them building where they . . . For the love of the Almighty, barber, this is an odd sort of conversation to be having with a man when your arse is in his face."

"I do not need much space to practice my craft, mijnheer, a small room will do." Lucas still hadn't touched his instruments.

"But I tell you . . . Very well. We'll find a corner for you. Now—"

"And a different piece of land for my sister and myself. As I said, it need not be inside the town, only close to it. In the Voorstadt, perhaps."

Stuyvesant looked into Lucas's eyes for a second more. "Get on with it," he said finally. "You'll have what you ask. A barber shop this side of the wall and a homestead in the Voorstadt. But only if I live to issue the orders."

"I expected you'd see that part of it, mijnheer." Lucas pushed his rolled sleeves further up his arm. "This is only the examining part of the surgery. The forty-five seconds doesn't start until I'm done."

He inserted his finger deep into Stuyvesant's rectum. The governor grunted, but he didn't move. The soft wall of the intestine yielded to probing. Lucas could feel the bladder, and when he pressed a little harder, the stone. "Ah, a pebble of some size, Governor. No wonder it's causing such trouble." Stuyvesant's only answer was his labored breathing. "Now, mijnheer, the forty-five seconds begins. You may start counting."

Lucas yanked the bucket into position below his patient's dangling genitals. He withdrew his finger from the governor's body and took up his scalpel. One quick cut between testes and rectum. Two inches long. Deft and swift, with his arm wrapped around the man's waist to hold him in position. Stuyvesant's body jerked once, but in a second he was again rigid, and he made no sound except for a soft groan.

Blood was obliterating the cut. Lucas grabbed the pincers and inserted them into the wound. One quick snap and the handle opened wide, spreading the flesh apart. He could see the wall of the bladder. He chose another scalpel, smaller than the first, made another quick cut. Less than half an inch, but the sharp reek of urine told him he'd opened the right place. And through it all, Peter Stuyvesant neither moaned nor twitched.

Piss gushed into the leather bucket. And a second later, clearly, a sound that could not be mistaken in the silence broken only by his patient's wheezing breath, the ping made by the stone as it fell. Thanks be to God, he wouldn't have to probe for it.

Lucas had three ligatures ready, thin strands of sheep's intestine. He tied off the blood vessels and mopped the wound with the cloths Anna Stuyvesant had given him. A slow but steady flow of blood was oozing from some vessel he'd cut but couldn't see. There was nothing for it but to lengthen the original opening and tie off the vessel. A lesson he'd learned from bitter experience. Fail to do that and no matter how tightly and neatly you sewed together the flesh, the patient died.

Thirty-five seconds were gone. If he was to live up to his boast he must begin to stitch, but he dared not.

He reached for the smaller scalpel, made the wound half an inch longer at each end. There, the source of the blood was near the top of the cut, close to the kidneys. Lucas grabbed the vessel with his probe, pulled it forward, and tied it off. Forty-two seconds. And not a sound or a movement from the man who was bent over the chest. If anything, the silence was deeper than it had been.

Sweet Jesus Christ, maybe Stuyvesant had stopped breathing. "Mijnheer Governor," Lucas whispered, "can you hear me?"

"Ja." The voice was weak.

Lucas felt a moment of triumph. He and Sally—finally, fate was smiling on them. "Just checking on you, mijnheer, almost finished." He sponged the wound with hot water, sprinkled on some of Sally's stanching powder. Finally he released the spring on the handles of the pincers, removed the instrument and tossed it aside, then grabbed the needle threaded with a thin strip of sheep's intestines and began to stitch.

"Done," he said a few seconds later. "It's over, Governor. The stone is out. Such pain as you'll have for the next few days is from the wound, and when it heals you'll be cured. Meanwhile you must have a bran and salt enema every day. There is to be no straining at stool."

Lucas helped his patient back to bed while he spoke, supporting the other man with an arm around his waist. "I'll call your sister, shall I," he said when the governor was back in bed and the covers were drawn up over him. "Perhaps you'll sip some ale to restore your—"

"Fifty-two seconds," Stuyvesant said. "I counted." There was a thin line of blood along the margin of his lower lip. And tooth marks. He'd bitten through his own flesh rather than cry out. "It took you fifty-two seconds, barber, not forty-five."

Lucas nodded. "You had a high bleeder. I had to make a second cut to find it. If I had not, Governor, though I sewed you well up, you would bleed inside your body and be dead before morning."

For a moment he thought Stuyvesant might denounce him as not the stone expert he claimed to be. Instead, "Go down to the waterside. Tell Heini the clerk I said to let you sleep inside the fort tonight, in the storehouse. And that he should come see me in the morning. Tell him I mean to change your land appropriation."

II

It turned out the pitch-blackened corpse hanging near the dock was a kind of scarecrow, a warning to potential wrongdoers, but there were plenty of tall trees in the colony and no lack of real hangings. Inside the fort there was a stockade open to all weather that served as the town jail, and two whipping posts.

Nieuw Amsterdam was not, however, as desolate and forbidding as Lucas and Sally imagined at first sight. Apart from the crumbling earthworks of the fort—forever in need of repair—and the macabre display at the waterfront, there was much to please the eye.

Thirty-five years had passed since Peter Minuit bargained with the local tribes for the island. Now the compact settlement occupied about a third of the narrow southern tip of Manhattan, running a scant half-mile from the fort to the wall and sheltered by the hilly, thickly wooded landscape of the rest. To be sure, Nieuw Amsterdam's streets were crooked and narrow, created by simply widening the footpaths of the red men, and it was not long since the settlers were living in pits roofed with reeds, but by 1661 proper houses had been erected. Stuyvesant and his council, the burgomasters and schepens, had outlawed thatched roofs because of the fire hazard they presented, and had begun importing enough glazed yellow bricks to allow the wealthier residents to duplicate the sturdy, cheerful dwellings of Holland.

To Lucas's eye, even the simpler wooden houses built of local materials were unmistakably Dutch. Most were small two-story structures with steeply pitched roofs and dormered windows, nestled side by side and built gable end to the road so there might be more of them in a row. The Netherlanders had long considered it a sign of affluence to live in a populous city.

Doubtless thoughts of home also inspired the tidal canal that had been dug from the beginning of the curve of the eastern shore northwest for some eight hundred of a tall man's strides. When it froze the locals used it for skating. Those who had neglected to bring their blades to the New World strapped beef shinbones to their shoes instead.

The rest of the year the canal made it possible for cargo ships to offload directly into the warehouses of the richest merchants. They were the ones who built their substantial yellow brick residences along the canal's banks, and found space for a garden in front of each house. There were gardens as well in front of the brick homes on the street called Pearl that ran beside the waterfront (almost the first thing the Dutch did when they arrived was to pave the river road with shells from the nearby oyster beds) and still more gardens adjoining the prosperous dwellings lining both sides of the Brede Wegh.

If Lucas put his back to the sea and stood on a high point such as the middle of the three bridges crossing the canal, his strongest impression was of a neat little town hugging the tip of the island, protected by the mountainous and wooded terrain to the north. It was "a brave and a pretty place," as the pamphlet encouraging immigration had put it. What the view from the bridge concealed was the rowdy and raucous life that made this town unlike any other in the New World.

Boston and Providence and the rest had all been founded in pursuit of some high ideal of philosophy or religion, and were occupied by English folk of like mind. Nieuw Amsterdam was created by rich Dutchmen who wanted to become richer. Any who could further that aim were welcome. On a given day you might hear eighteen different languages at the intersection of the Brede Wegh and Wall Street.

Lucas did not find here the huddled poor who were such a fixture in Dover and London and Rotterdam. There appeared to be money to be made in every lane and at every crossing. All you needed was an eye for a trade. And courage. And, of course, luck and a strong stomach.

In New England a shared theology created order. In the seething mix of nationalities, beliefs, and nonbeliefs that the Dutch West India Company had created in Nieuw Amsterdam, not even an iron fist like Stuyvesant's could alter the fact that the making of a quick fortune was a disorderly and a boisterous affair. Once they had money, men—particularly the trappers and traders and sailors who crowded the town's narrow streets—craved pleasure. A good number of the upstanding Dutch burghers liked something on the side as well.

Whores were tolerated as long as they kept themselves to Princes Street and did not mingle with the good Netherlander *huisvrouwen*. There were twenty-one taverns, taprooms, and alehouses in the little town. The mix pleased Lucas: fucking and boozing led to arguments and mayhem. A man of his skills was bound to be kept occupied.

Stuyvesant had assigned him a tiny shop built against the easternmost end of the wooden palisade that gave Wall Street its name. Lucas's place was really a lean-to, no more than five long strides in each direction. There was no window, only a fireplace against the back wall, and across from it a door split horizontally in the Dutch fashion. "The wily bastard just barely managed to keep his promise," Lucas told Sally. "It's almost inside the town." Nonetheless, a steady stream of customers found him from the first day he banged the striped red-and-white pole into the summer-parched earth outside the door.

A good many came to be bled, often for the aftermath of drink. Lucas was not entirely sure that opening a blood vessel in the temple of the sufferer, or even setting the leeches to him, really would relieve the nausea and the pounding headache, but it could do no harm.

Large quantities of rum and geneva could also be counted on to result in broken bones that needed to be set. Lucas built a sturdy wooden frame to assist him in carefully aligning fractured arms and legs before forcing them back into position. The ship's surgeons who were his only competition in the colony—mostly men who stayed a short time, then got restless and went again to sea—set bones by brute force, using as many vicious yanks as the patient could endure. The pain was equally intense using Lucas's frame, but the results were far more satisfactory. He put the apparatus to use three or four times a week.

Also thanks to drunkenness, he was twice asked to trepan a man's skull. Desperate *huisvrouwen* hoped that boring a couple of holes in a husband's head might rid him of his craving for alcohol. Lucas knew that was unlikely, but he had recently made himself a new drill and was interested in refining his trepanning techniques. Those two operations were among the most interesting he performed during his first few months in Nieuw Amsterdam. They occupied a page each in his journal.

From the day he set up shop, Lucas made copious notes about every procedure, even ordinary barbering—delousing and shaving and bleeding and lancing boils—but he took special pains to write in detail about the more intricate surgeries, cutting away fistulas and tumors and removing stones. He did a great deal of the latter. Since the operation on Stuyvesant he'd become famous for it. Sufferers made the journey to his little room beside the wall from remote farms on the long island and Staten Island. Some arrived from as far north as Nieuw Haarlem. One came from a large holding, a *bouwerie,* in Yonkers.

At first it was Lucas's speed that mattered. He knew it didn't hurt his reputation when he had whoever accompanied the patient stand on one side of the room and count the seconds between the initial cut and the last stitch. But in the autumn, after Sally's first crop of poppies bloomed, Lucas was best known for the fact that he could, with a few spoonfuls of one of his sister's decoctions, make the patient so groggy and fill his head with such soporific dreams that he felt considerably less pain.

As in the case of the barber shop, Stuyvesant had almost kept his word about their land assignment. The Turner homestead was small, what the Dutch called a *plantage* rather than a *bouwerie,* and it was beyond the Voorstadt, nearly a mile from the town, not far from the Collect Pond. But it took them twenty minutes to walk to Wall Street, not half a day. And, after a lifetime of being misfits and almost three years of wandering, here in the wilderness of Manhattan Lucas and Sally had a place of their own.

They planted before they built, and all that first summer they slept rough with a musket between them, though so far the natives they'd seen weren't hostile. "A little sullen and withdrawn," Sally said. "As if they needed a good purging, but harmless enough."

Lucas wasn't so sure. Even when their cabin was finished—hewn timber walls and a thick roof thatched with reeds and grasses, as was permitted north of the wall—he went every night to his bed with the musket loaded and at hand. People in the town told endless stories of women who'd been raped, children murdered, men tortured before they were killed, and years of work gone up in flames when a homestead was burned to the ground.

One good thing: the Dutch had never been greedy enough or stupid enough to sell guns to the tribes living closest to them. In the vicinity of Nieuw Amsterdam, superior weapons gave the Europeans an advantage, though they were outnumbered. In the far north, near Dutch Fort Orange, there was constant fighting with the marauding Catskill and Wawarsink tribes who had been armed by the French and the English, desperate to have the Indians take sides in their wars over colonial territory. It seemed an idiotic policy to Lucas. If you had to choose between trusting a savage or trusting your gun, the weapon won every time.

Sometimes, long after dark, when he heard the sounds of strange night birds calling to one another in the surrounding woods, he remembered the stories he'd heard about ritual fires where death came after hours of screaming agony, and about mutilation that began with the toes and moved slowly upward. Lying awake in the night, Lucas put his hand to his head and wondered whether a man was always dead before some savage peeled off his scalp. And whether Sally had heard as many stories of rape and torture as he had.

They were too busy to speak of such things. The earth around their cabin was black and rich. The first season, despite how late she was getting things in the ground, nearly all the seeds Sally brought with her sprouted and thrived. She planted local vegetables as well, the pumpkins and Indian corn the settlers had adopted as basic foods, and at Lucas's urging she gave over a large field at the edge of their cleared land to poppies. "I need enough laudanum, Sal, so I can perform any surgery I want and the patient will not run screaming from the knife."

"For the patient's sake, of course," Sally said.

"Of course."

"You're a liar, Lucas Turner. You want the people you're cutting to be all but senseless because that way, once you cut into them, you can take your time and study how they're made."

"Aye, there's some truth in that." Lucas spoke without looking up. It was October, five months after their arrival, and he was sitting by the fire in their cabin, using the light to write by. "Truth, but no harm."

"You're a barber, Lucas, not a surgeon. Only surgeons are permitted to perform an anatomy."

"You're contradicting yourself, Sal. It's not an anatomy if the patient is alive. Only if you cut open a corpse."

"Don't lecture me, Lucas. According to Company rules, you are not a surgeon. If they were to discover what you're doing, we—"

"Are you entirely mad, girl? We're in Nieuw Netherland, not New England. And the Company is on the other side of the ocean. Do you think any English magistrate is going to live through eleven weeks on one of those hell ships just to come and see whether Lucas Turner is being a good boy?"

"I suppose not." She finished wiping clean the pewter bowls they'd used for their stew of rabbit and corn, and placed them neatly on the shelf above the hearth.

The pewter bowls had come from a gentlewoman in England. Lucas had moved away the veil that made her blind in her right eye. The literature on the subject went back to the great practitioners of the mystic East, but it was an operation so delicate—only the very tip of the lancet could be used, and the amount of pressure applied was critical—that three English surgeons had refused to attempt it. After he said he would, and did so successfully, Lucas was expelled from the Company on the grounds that he, a barber, possessed surgical instruments. If the woman had died, perhaps he would have been dealt with more leniently. Since she lived and thrived, the jealous surgeons hounded Lucas and Sally from London.

He watched Sally put away the pewter bowls. A penny to a pound the surgeons who made such grief for him still ate their suppers off wood.

Sally caught his smile and saw her chance. "Lucas, things are going well for us here, are they not? Your business is doing well?"

"They are and it is. And if you'd stop worrying about me so I could stop worrying about you, everything would be perfect."

"I'll try, Lucas. Meanwhile"— she turned away, so she wouldn't have to look at him—"I've been meaning to ask you . . ."

"What? Go ahead, Sal, ask."

"Since we're here and you have so much custom . . . Is there enough money to put some by for a dowry?"

It was something they'd talked about before they left Rotterdam. With a dowry, Sally might find a husband who was worthy of her. It was the only chance at marriage she'd have, since she wouldn't accept a man of the class they'd come from, and Lucas had sworn he wouldn't force one on her. "I've thought of it, Sal. But often as not I'm paid in wampum rather than guilders, and—"

"Everyone uses wampum here. It's as good as money. I'm sure wampum would do for at least part of a dowry."

"Perhaps you're right. I'll do some asking, Sal. And keep my eyes open for someone who wouldn't mind—" He broke off.

"Wouldn't mind what, Lucas?"

"That you're nearly twenty-four. And . . ."

"And not comely."

"I didn't say that."

"You may as well have."

"No. What I was going to say was 'Nearly twenty-four, and more clever than any man I'm likely to find in need of a wife here in Nieuw Amsterdam.'"

Three years earlier, during the typhoid epidemic of 1659, Stuyvesant had established a hospital for those who had not long to live. The worst of the town's whores and drunkards, most of them. Decent folk died in their homes. The hospital had five beds in which, at no cost and purely for the love of Almighty God, the undeserving indigent were allowed to die.

The good women of the town saw it as their duty to care for the dying, however unworthy. Anna Stuyvesant was frequently seen at the hospital. Occasionally the governor's wife also came. Judith Bayard (though a French Huguenot, she followed the Dutch custom of retaining her own name after marriage) was beautiful, but also a woman of strict rectitude. Even the dying were less likely to scream and curse when she was present. So, too, when the wife of the rector of the Dutch Reformed Church did some of the nursing. Sally Turner, on the other hand, inspired no awe. She got the full brunt of the patients' misery and discontent. Nonetheless, she appeared the most consistently of all the nursing women.

Nearly every day the juffrouw Turner and her basket could be seen walking along the narrow woodland path between her brother's *plantage* and the town, entering through the west gate in the sturdy wooden wall, hurrying along the wide Brede Wegh, skirting the small offshoot of the main canal known as Bever's Gracht, then crossing by the narrow bridge that led to Jews Lane.

That was the only part of the walk Sally disliked. The Jews were fairly recent arrivals, a remnant from a settlement in Brazil. Stuyvesant was known to loathe them, but he'd been forced to let them in because there were Dutch Jews among the directors of the West India Company.

Just walking past the Jews' yellow brick houses below the mill made the back of Sally's neck prickle. All those stories of strange rituals involving the blood of Christian children . . . She could never get through the lane fast enough. Sally was glad to gather up her skirts for the passage through Coenties Alley, always slick with mud, toward the three-story stone building that stood at the water's edge.

Until the year before, the structure had been merely Nieuw Amsterdam's largest tavern and its only inn. When Stuyvesant needed somewhere big enough for all the townspeople to meet, he made it the Stadt Huys, the city hall, as well. Coenties Slip, leading to the town wharf, was in front of the Stadt Huys. Nearby were the town storehouses. Above them, in five workshops that had formerly been leased to the shipwrights, was the hospital.

There were two windows in the hospital. The dying stank, so the windows were kept open except in the worst of weather. While she went about her duties Sally could look out and see the short street called Hall Place, and the door to the butcher's house Lucas visited so frequently.

To buy the pig bladders and sheep intestines he needed in his craft, Sally told herself. That's why her brother was so often at the butcher's on Hall Place. And never mind that it was a ten-minute walk from Lucas's shop. After all, he came to the hospital a few times a week to see if anyone needed bleeding or surgery, so naturally—

"Juffrouw . . . Please, juffrouw . . ." A woman's voice. A few hours earlier, weeks before her time and squatting in the alley behind the Blue Dove alehouse on Pearl Street, she'd given birth to twins—dead, and that was a blessing. One had no legs, the other a huge hole in the top of its head. The woman, a notorious whore, had been bleeding since the birth. Sally figured she'd be dead within the next hour or two.

"Please, juffrouw, can you give me something as stops the burning in my chest? Him over there"—the woman nodded toward the man in the next bed, a drunk who the previous day had had the lower half of his body crushed by a falling barrel but refused to allow Lucas to saw off his legs—"he says you can."

Sally reached into her basket for a salve of saxifrage and egg yolk, and made herself stop thinking about her brother's too-frequent visits to the butcher's on Hall Place.

"Good day to you, mevrouw." There was no one else in the shop. Lucas didn't have to keep the twinkle from his eye or the laughter from his voice.

"And to you, barber. I've something put by just for you. The intestines of a large cow. Come in the back and see."

Marit Graumann, wife of Ankel Jannssen, stepped from behind the wooden block. Her husband was one of the town's twelve "sworn butchers," permitted to slaughter cattle inside the wall. He paid the tax for a stall in the Broadway Shambles, the market across from the fort, and was required to be there every morning except Sunday. In the afternoon he was permitted to do business from his home. All well and good, except that after Marit gave him his dinner Ankel always stumbled off to bed in a drunken stupor. She herself had to hack apart the meats and poultry sold from the house on Hall Place.

A curtain of burlap separated the front from the rear of the shop. Marit pushed it aside and waited for Lucas. As soon as he brushed past her he felt himself get hard. She had a special smell. A woman smell. He'd had countless whores in London and Rotterdam, even a few here, but none had ever smelled like Marit. Neither did the women who came to him for treatment. They reeked of illness, often of filth. Mevrouw Marit Graumann smelled of flowers. And her lust had a dark and seductive fragrance of its own. Lucas had never before been with a woman who actually desired him. The experience was intoxicating.

It was foolhardy to visit the Hall Place house as often as he did, he knew, but he didn't stop. The butcher's wife was as blond as he was dark, and almost as tall. Her body was lush and full. When he held her, Marit's flesh yielded to him, seemed to melt against his. What he could see of it in the dimness behind the butcher shop where all their meetings had taken place was pink and white, and always, when he was near, flushed with longing.

She led him past the hanging carcasses to the corner of the room they used and that she kept clear for the purpose. The floor of the storeroom, like that of the shop, was covered in sawdust, and she dared not make her husband suspicious by sweeping it clean. They had to couple standing, but that didn't inhibit them. When Marit turned to him she'd already loosed the ties of her bodice.

Lucas put both hands on her full breasts. He stroked them gently. He'd never known such softness; only the nipples were hard. "Suck them," she whispered. "Lucas, please, suck them. I cannot wait another moment."

He buried his face in her breasts, sucking both nipples, one after another. Dear God, the smell. And the velvet skin that burned wherever he touched it. She was trembling in his arms.

"Lucas, ah Lucas . . . I dream about you every moment. Waking and sleeping. I live only to feel what I feel when I give myself to you."

He began fumbling himself out of his breeches. She started to lift her skirts. Suddenly there was a clattering above their heads. They froze. Another sound, louder than the first. Then silence.

"It's all right," Marit whispered after a few seconds. "The bedroom is just above. He must have knocked something over. He drank three mugs of geneva and two of rum with his dinner. He will not wake for hours."

Lucas stared up at the splintered wooden planks and the rough timbers that formed both the ceiling above his head and the floor of the Jannssen's bedroom. Ankel Jannssen was a hulking brute of a man, a drunken animal. He had no right to a woman like Marit, but he had her nonetheless. God help them. If the butcher found out he could go to law, have Marit whipped and turned into the streets with only the clothes on her back. And everything Lucas owned would be forfeit to him.

Sweet Jesus, this was insane. Why did he continue to do it? Because even now, after that moment of stomach-churning fear, he was again hard as a rock and raging for her.

Marit was breathing through her mouth, the tip of her tongue tracing the outline of her lips. "Lucas," she whispered, and lifted her skirt and her petticoats, held them above her waist, and leaned aginst the wall and spread her legs. "Take me, Lucas. Do whatever you want to me. Only kiss me while you do it. Let me feel your tongue in my mouth."

He put his lips on hers and sucked her breath into his body. His hands were on her buttocks, squeezing the hot flesh, pulling her toward him. His cock knew where to go. It had learned the way these past three months. She began to moan. He thrust deeper into her, squeezed harder. She trembled more. Her moans came faster. The sounds she made grew louder.

The bell on the shop door rang. "Mevrouw Graumann, are you serving?"

They had long since decided that locking the door would arouse more suspicion than Marit's absence from the front of the shop. Lucas took his mouth from Marit's. She turned her face to the flimsy curtain that separated them from the waiting customer. "I'll be with you immediately, mijnheer—a moment only."

"*Ja*, fine. I'll wait."

Marit leaned her head back. Lucas could see her face in the dim light. Her cheeks were flushed, her skin dewy with the sweat of her passion. He could smell her. She looked into his eyes. He began thrusting again. Slowly at first, then faster. She closed her eyes and bit her lips to stifle the sounds of her delight. Watching her, feeling her shiver and tremble in his arms, was the most exciting thing he had ever experienced. He finished in a burst of such indescribable pleasure it left him hungry for more, knowing full well he could never have enough.

A moment later she'd laced her bodice and adjusted her skirts. Marit patted her hair into place and went out into the front room. Lucas heard her discussing the relative merits of pork and venison and soon after, the sound of her cleaver hacking apart the meat the customer had chosen.

From his corner of the storeroom Lucas could see a side of beef hanging from a hook in the wall, still dripping blood onto the sawdust. A pig's head hung from a second hook, a large and formless drape of cow's intestines from a third. Lucas had mentioned that he'd like to try making ligatures from that rather than the intestines of a sheep. There were a couple of pig bladders as well. They were probably also for him. Lucas could never have too many pig bladders.

"Lucas, come out front now. He's gone."

Marit was standing in the storeroom of the doorway, beckoning to him. Lucas went to her, but he drew her to his side of the curtain. "Marit, we must stop this. It is insane. What if you were to find yourself with child? Or—"

"In seven years of marriage, Lucas, I have not conceived. But if I were with child, people would assume it was my husband's."

He felt the rush of blood to his head, knew his face was dark with anger. "I cannot bear the thought of that pig touching—"

"Ssh, calm yourself. He almost never does. Ankel prefers drink to me."

He took her face between his hands, began kissing her cheeks and her nose and her forehead. "Ah, Marit, Marit . . . We are mad. This is incredibly dangerous. The consequences are—"

"I want to go to the woods with you." It was as if she hadn't heard him. "I have been thinking of it for days and days. I want to take off all my clothes and all your clothes, and lie down on the clean earth and have you lie atop me."

"Marit, we can't. What if—"

She lifted his hands to her lips and began kissing them, sucking his fingers. Drawing each deep between her pursed lips, keeping her gaze locked on his all the while. "You would not believe the things I want to do to you, Lucas, to have you do to me. I do not believe them. They come into my head and I do not know from where. Think of a way, my darling. It will have to be a Sunday when the shop is closed. Ankel sleeps all Sunday afternoon. You live far from the town. Find a place we can meet and tell me how to get there."

Sally also had secrets. Hers, too, involved women. Indian women.

The contact began the first autumn, when they had been only a few months in Nieuw Amsterdam. Sally came across a little Indian girl gathering rose hips in the woods near the cabin. The child ran as soon as she saw the white woman standing nearby, but apparently the bushes near the Turner homestead were specially prized, because she kept returning. There was another accidental meeting, and soon a third. Each time the girl and the woman came a little nearer to trust.

Finally the moment came when the youngster stood still long enough for Sally to point to the rose hips she was collecting and to simulate a loud sneeze.

The child giggled. Then she also pretended to sneeze. Next she, too, pointed to the contents of her basket and made an exaggerated wiping motion across her face.

"Yes, exactly," Sally said, "rose hips ease the winter sickness. And do you, I wonder, make them into a tisane as I would?" She made the motions of pouring water from a jug to a pot and placing it over a fire. The little girl nodded furiously in agreement, an enormous smile on her face. "Ah, so you do! How I wish you could tell me what else you gather from these woods and how you use it."

The child looked puzzled and shook her head.

"No, of course you don't understand a word I'm saying. But perhaps . . . Sally." Sally pointed to herself. "I am Sal-lee."

The child smiled. "Tamaka," she said. "Ta-ma-ka." Then she grabbed her basket and ran.

A few days later the child appeared again, this time at the edge of the clearing surrounding the cabin. She was carrying two ears of Indian corn. Sally went out to meet her with a mug of homemade root beer.

Sally and Tamaka communicated mostly by signs at first; then each learned a few words of the other's language. Finally they developed a shared language of their own—part signs, part English, part the tongue of the child's people—in which they communicated with ease.

Tamaka told Sally about how once, long ago before the white people came to this island, the place the Turners' cabin stood had been special. It was where women went to give birth; that was why the healing plants here were filled with so much power. Another day the child led her new friend to a thicket where the blackberries grew larger than any Sally had ever seen. And yet another time she showed Sally a shy yellow iris that grew in hidden places beside streams, and explained that the root of the plant could be made into a paste that was good for burns.

In return Sally showed Tamaka the sweet-smelling pink gillyflowers whose seed she had brought with her from Holland. They could be steeped in honey and the syrup used to treat sore throats, as well as made into a poultice to ease bruises of the ankles and wrists. She gave Tamaka some seed to take back to her village. A few days later Tamaka brought her mother and her aunt to see the gillyflowers growing in Sally Turner's garden.

That first winter Sally saw Tamaka many times, but she didn't see the older women again until the following summer. Not until Tamaka brought her to the outskirts of the Indian village, and the women who had visited Sally came to meet them. On that occasion, looking grave and purposeful, they led Tamaka's friend to see the gillyflowers growing in their fields among the pumpkins and the squash and the corn.

Sally never mentioned any of this to her brother. It was the first real secret she'd ever kept from him, but she knew what would happen if she told. Lucas would rail at her about savages. He'd make her swear she wouldn't again go to the Indian village. This little corner of her life, Sally decided, she would keep from her brother. In the interest of peace.

She kept that promise to herself for two years, until a summer's day in 1663 when she staggered screaming into the barber shop, carrying Tamaka's limp body. "Lucas! Are you here? Lucas!"

"Sally, what's wrong? What— In Christ's name, girl, who are you bringing me?"

"Tamaka. She . . . in the woods . . . Oh, God . . ." Sally had carried the child all the way from the cabin to the town, and she was so exhausted she was barely coherent. "Tamaka." She put the girl on Lucas's surgical table and, relieved of her burden, leaned against the wall, panting. "Tamaka."

Lucas stared at his sister. He made no move toward the child.

"Her hand. Look." It was all she could manage. Sally slid down the wall and huddled in a heap on the floor, hanging her head between her splayed knees, sucking air into her lungs, waiting for the fiery pain in her chest to subside and her legs and arms to stop quivering.

Lucas glanced at the girl Sally wanted him to examine. The front of her deerskin skirt was soaked in blood. She lay perfectly still. Only the faint rise and fall of her bare chest told him she was alive. Lucas went to his sister, bent over her, put his hand on her shoulder. "Here, girl, you're half dead with fatigue. Hang on a minute. I'll run across the road and get you a draught of ale."

"Not me. Tamaka." The words came a little easier now. "Look at her hand, Lucas."

He turned his head and glanced at the girl on the table. "Sally, she's a squaw brat. An Indian. One less of them means a few less of us to be murdered in our beds."

Lucas had adopted the colonial summer fashion of wearing a tightly belted leather jerkin in place of a coat. Sally reached up and grabbed its hem. "It's not like that. Don't turn away, Lucas. Look at me. For the love of Jesus Christ, she is a child! And she's my friend."

"Your what?"

"My friend. I've known her almost as long as we've been here. We were gathering orris roots in the swamp. She was using a tomahawk. It slipped and she cut her fingers off. I brought them to you. I brought you Tamaka's fingers, Lucas, so you can sew them back on. The ancient Egyptians did it. You told me so. You can do it, too. Please, Lucas. Please."

Despite himself, Sally's words thrilled him. He'd read of such operations. Back in London he'd even heard of a case in Prussia where a foot was sewn back on, though later it turned black with gangrene and the patient died. But a child's fingers . . . Small, malleable, an excellent place to practice such surgery. And this was a squaw brat, so it didn't matter if she lived or died.

Sally was still clinging to his jerkin. Lucas detached her hands and turned to the treatment table.

Above the blood-soaked skirt he could see the child's budding breasts. She did not move. Lucas thought she was still unconscious; then he looked into her face. She was wide awake and staring at him. Her large dark eyes gave away nothing of what she might be feeling, not even her pain.

She was holding her left hand with her right, both clasped over her belly. Lucas touched her hands. She did not relax her grip and her eyes never left his face. "She won't let me touch her."

Sally struggled to her feet and came to the table. She stood beside Tamaka, stroked her forehead and her cheeks. "It's all right, my dear. Brother, mine." She linked her thumbs in one of their private signs. "He can help you." She turned to Lucas. "You can examine her now."

Lucas peered at the damage to the left hand. Sally had bandaged the wound with sumac leaves and wrapped her shawl around it, but the blood had soaked through everything. He took the shawl and the leaves away. Three small fingers fell to the floor.

Lucas knelt down and reclaimed them. They were cut clean, but on an awkward slant. "A challenge," he murmured.

Sally remained beside Tamaka, stroking her face.

Lucas studied his sister. "Your friend," he said again. "A squaw brat."

"She's a child, Lucas."

"It's a fascinating surgery." Lucas had made up his mind. "Come, Sal, assist me."

She had helped him before and knew exactly what he'd want. She rushed to pour wine into a pot hanging over the fireplace. Lucas always kept a fire going, though in these hot days of August it was well banked. Sally poked at the logs, making them flare, then rushed back to the other side of the room for his instrument case and opened it. Finally she went to the store of simples for the jug of laudanum.

"No." Lucas was cleaning the wound, swabbing the bloody stumps.

"For the pain," Sally whispered. "She will suffer so much less."

"And appreciate less what we're doing for her. No laudanum, Sal. I can't spare it." The child's hand had largely stopped bleeding. "How did you know to pack the wound with sumac leaves? It seems they're excellent for the purpose."

"Tamaka showed me. The Indians use sumac for hemorrhage."

"Kept her wits about her, did she? After her mischance with the tomahawk."

"No, she fainted. I mean she'd told me about the sumac before."

"Ah, yes, I forgot. You've known her since we arrived. Though you never thought to mention it before now."

"Lucas, I—"

"It doesn't matter. I forgive you, Sally. We need not discuss it again." He was examining the severed fingers while he spoke. "Won't be a great deal left of these after I even them up. But worth trying all the same."

"You must succeed, Lucas. If she's missing fingers, she'll be rejected for marriage. The Indians believe—"

"Good God, you're an expert on what they believe as well?"

"Of course I'm not. I simply— Can you do it, Lucas? Sew her fingers back on?"

"I don't know. But it's interesting to try."

Lucas began working on the detached fingers. Sally took up her post beside Tamaka, stroking her head, murmuring soothing words. Lucas paid no attention to his sister and the child. He was intent on sawing the splintered bone from the severed fingers, leaving a clean cut, then using a razor to clip the mangled flesh. Finally he dropped the fingers in the wine that was simmering over the fire.

It was one of Lucas's distinctions as a practitioner that he used wine the way the ancients had, to wash wounds and to soak bandages before applying them. He wasn't entirely sure why, but he was convinced that wine often helped the healing. And it really would be more interesting if this girl lived with her fingers sewn back on than if she took his handiwork to an early grave. "Now let's see about the hand, shall we?"

Lucas put a piece of board beneath Tamaka's hand. He strapped it to her arm. "Hold her down," he told Sally. "If she moves she's liable to have no hand as well as no fingers."

"She won't move," Sally said.

Lucas looked up. "Hold her," he said. He chose his smallest saw, the one with the finest teeth, and bent over his patient.

Lucas could make no attempt to reunite the bones or the sinew. All he could do was stitch the fingers back in place and hope nature would somehow nourish them. The books spoke of the body leaking blood into the once-severed part, enough to keep it from turning gangrenous and sending poison through the entire system. The best he could do was create a clean place for the join. He must trim away the damaged flesh and bone on the hand exactly as he had on the fingers.

He began to saw. Slow, careful strokes, as if he were paring toenails. The girl didn't move. Lucas lifted his head, glanced at his patient and his sister. Sally's face was screwed up in a grimace, as if she suffered the child's pain. Tamaka had not changed her expression.

A few more minutes, then the sawing was finished. Lucas took his most delicate scalpel and began trimming the shredded flesh. Each time he raised his head and looked at Tamaka she was looking at him. She made no sound.

"Tough," Lucas said when he was done preparing for the surgery. "Very tough, your friend. No wonder she and her kind are so hard to get rid of."

Sally swallowed her rage. Lucas was simply repeating what he'd heard. "Indian women don't utter a single cry when they give birth, Lucas. It's a matter of honor with them. Do you know any white woman who can do the same?"

"Couldn't say." He didn't look at her. "Birthing's not my line of country. Get me the stanching powder."

She got it and Lucas applied it liberally to the wounded hand. Then he took up the index finger and began to sew. Small, dainty stitches, close together, making an overlap of the skin from the stub of the hand so that there would be strength enough to hold in place the finger that was not attached by bone. It took him nearly four minutes to sew on the first finger. Then he moved on to the second.

"They're at least a third shorter than they were," he said when he was finished. "But that's her doing, not mine. And she won't be able to move them, of course."

Sally dismissed this with a shake of her head. "That doesn't matter. It's missing parts that would make her unacceptable. To the braves."

"How nice to know that if she lives, your little friend can make more Indians to come and burn us out."

"Tamaka would never do such a thing. Neither would her people. Lucas—she will live, won't she?"

"Truthfully?" Sally nodded. "I can't say. But I've done my work carefully and she's young and strong. I suspect she will."

"You've done a great thing, Lucas. You and I, we'll have nothing to fear from the Indians after this."

A week after the surgery, two of Tamaka's restored fingers had turned black. "Too bad," Lucas said. "Still, it was interesting to try."

"Lucas, what about Tamaka? If she—"

"If the black fingers don't come off, she'll die. I've seen it many times. First the blackened flesh signaling the gangrene. Next the fever. Then death."

"And if I can get her to agree, will you take off the black fingers for her?"

Lucas hesitated only a moment. "Why not? But it will have to be here in the cabin, not at my shop in town. We were lucky last time. I don't want to chance it again."

"Chance what?"

"Being seen operating on a squaw brat."

As it turned out, Lucas needn't have worried. Sally went to the village. Tamaka's aunt appeared. "Tamaka," Sally said, "please, I must see her. My brother has agreed to help her. It's very important that she—" The Indian woman lifted her finger and put it over Sally's lips. Then she turned and walked away.

Another week went by and Tamaka didn't appear. Finally, Sally screwed up her courage and returned to the Indian village. At first no one came to meet her. She stood at the edge of the cluster of bark-covered huts and waited the way she always did. A couple of the women glanced toward her on their way to work in their fields, but no one approached. Sally could think of nothing to do except stay where she was and wait. Eventually an old woman walked over to her. "Tamaka," Sally said, pointing to her own hand. "How is she?"

Apparently the woman had been chosen as emissary because she had a few words of English. "Tamaka dead," she said.

III

"Good afternoon, barber. I am Jacob Van der Vries."

Lucas looked up and saw a thickset man, not tall, but with an air of importance. He had startlingly red hair, a small red beard, and an exceptionally full red mustache. And though he'd spoken in English, his accent was plainly of the Low Countries. "Good afternoon, mijnheer. I presume it's shaving you were wanting?"

"No, not shaving."

"Delousing, then?" Lucas rose from the stool beside the fire—it was a dark day in early December and he'd been using the light to write by—and carried his journal to the surgical table.

"Not delousing either," the Dutchman said. "What do you have there?"

"Some notes on various ailments. Nothing for you to worry about, I imagine. You do not look ill."

On the contrary, Van der Vries looked particularly healthy. Rich, as well. The cuffs of his shirt were ruffled lace. His belt was buckled with polished silver and strained to keep his coat together over his well-fed paunch. "I haven't seen you in the town before," Lucas said. "Does that mean you've just arrived?"

"A few days past. And you are right, I am not ill. But your notes do interest me, barber." Van der Vries held out his hand. "May I see?"

"No. They are simply notes, so someday I can make a fuller account of what I've observed in two and a half years in Nieuw Amsterdam." Lucas locked his journal away. "Now, if you don't want shaving or delousing, and you don't need bleeding, what brings you to me, Mijnheer Van der Vries?"

"Actually, I am Jacob Van der Vries, Practitioner of Physic."

"Ah, I see." Lucas pocketed the key to the drawer in the surgical table. "A physician."

"Indeed. I was apprenticed to the most fashionable practitioner in The Hague. And for a time I served the sick in your fine city of Cambridge. Now I am in the employ of the Dutch West India Company. So we shall be seeing quite a bit of each other, barber. I shall call on you when my patients require bleeding. And now that there is someone to oversee your activities here, you will perhaps no longer feel it necessary to make notes of—"

The door swung open so hard both halves thwacked against the wall. "Business for you, barber! Bring 'em here, lads!" Four soldiers trotted behind the sergeant, carrying two stretchers. "Savages—attacked the Bronck *bouwerie* and the little *plantage* of old man Heerik. Burned them to the ground. Left seven dead. Fortunately one of our patrols happened to be passing. Ran the bloodthirsty animals off Heerik's land before they finished the job. Two of the wounded seemed worth bringing to you."

One of the stretchers carried a young woman, unconscious, an arrow still in her gut. Her pale blond hair dragged on the ground, because her scalp was half off. The second victim was an old man. He had three arrows in him, but he was awake and his hair was still tight on his head. "Forget me," he whispered as the soldiers put his stretcher down. "See to my daughter."

"*Ja, ja,* be calm. I will see to you both." It was Van der Vries who answered, and Van der Vries who was bending over the young woman, examining the remarkable head wound.

Lucas was more interested in the soldier. "My sister, Sergeant! She is alone. Our *plantage* isn't far from—"

"It's all right. We've already sent patrols to bring the families from the nearby farms into the fort until we catch the war party."

"Soldier!" Van der Vries again. "Send someone to my quarters immediately. Tell him to bring my bag. My servant will give it to him. Hurry!"

"*Ja,* mijnheer. Right away."

Van der Vries removed his jacket and held it out to Lucas. "Here, barber. Put this somewhere it will stay clean. Then put another log on that fire. I will have to get the cauterizing iron good and hot to deal with this wound."

Lucas took the other man's coat and slung it over his shoulder. "I don't have a cauterizing iron, Mijnheer Physician. In fact, I don't believe in cauterizing. Though logs we have aplenty, and I'm happy to put as many on the fire as you wish."

Van der Vries leaned forward and squinted. He seemed to be studying Lucas. "You don't believe— What can you possibly know about medical treatment?"

"I am a surgeon as well as a barber."

"Ach, so that's it. A surgeon. I gave you the benefit of the doubt, since everyone calls you barber. Instead I find you are one of those butchers who practice their foul trade on human flesh. Well, I am here now, surgeon or barber or whichever you are, and—"

"And the patient is weakening while we argue." Lucas took a step closer to the woman on the stretcher. "The skull is not injured, and there hasn't been overmuch bleeding. If we are quick and use some of my sister's stanching powder, and bathe the wound with wine and sew the scalp back on, then get that arrow out of her gut, she might even survive."

"Stanching powder. Now, that is something interesting. Where does your sister get this stanching powder?"

"She—"

"I make it from the root of the plant the herbalists call *Achillea,* mijnheer. You probably know it as yarrow." Sally was removing her shawl as she came into the surgery. "The soldiers brought me, Lucas. They told me what happened. And about the good physician being here." She was already at the dispensing bench, shaking the dried and powdered yarrow root onto a sheet of birch bark. "Good day to you, mijnheer."

Van der Vries looked in her direction. The squint remained in place. "Interesting," he murmured. "The cutter has his own resident apothecary. Tell me, what part of England are you from?"

"Dover in Kent," Lucas said, "originally."

"Ah, the provinces. I thought so from your accents." The Dutchman turned to the patient, bent over her, and began squinting at her wound. "But of course you'll have studied your trade in London, no?"

"Yes," Lucas said. "In London."

Sally caught her breath. She covered by quickly handing her brother the piece of bark containing the stanching powder. "Here, Lucas, it's ready."

Lucas moved toward the young woman lying on the stretcher. Her breathing was very shallow. There wasn't a great deal of time. "Sally, have you some stimulating tonic?"

"I think so. If not here, then in my bas— Yes, here it is." She was unstopping a small flask as she spoke, reaching for her dosing spoon.

"So now," Van der Vries said softly, "you must tell me about your stimulating tonic, Juffrouw."

"A decoction of *Digitalis purpuria*. Foxglove to you, mijnheer. Gerard and Culpepper are both—"

"Foxglove. Please, you must refresh my memory. The flowers are shaped like the heart? Or is it perhaps the lungs?"

Sally stared at him. Lucas made a sound somewhere between a snort and a laugh and got ready to dust the patient's head wound with stanching powder. Van der Vries darted forward. He moved with astonishing speed for a man of his bulk. Before Lucas could begin sprinkling the yarrow on the wound, the Dutchman had pushed his hand away. The precious powder was scattered on the floor.

"Good God, man! Do you see what you've done? How can—"

"I am a physician in the Company's employ. That means I am responsible for these poor people, barber. And apparently both you and your sister are ignorant of the doctrine of signatures. The juffrouw Sally tells us she makes her stimulating tonic from a plant the flowers of which look neither like a heart or a lung, and her stanching powder from, of all things, yarrow. Yellow flowers, not red. Yarrow cannot, therefore, be effective in anything to do with bloody wounds."

"You're not serious, man?" Then, after a few seconds, "Sweet Jesus, you are. I don't believe— C'mon, Sal, simpling's your line of country. Tell him. The doctrine of signatures was disproved . . . what? Thirty years past?"

Sally was still holding the decoction of foxglove and the dosing spoon. "Lucas, the woman, she's barely breath—"

"Tell him, Sally. Gerard, wasn't it? Gerard disproved the doctrine of signatures."

"Yes, he did. Over forty years ago. It took time for his ideas to be accepted, but now every apothecary agrees."

"Thank you. Here, Sal, give me that." Lucas took the tonic from her, and the spoon. The woman was unconscious, but he managed to get a few drops between her lips. "Let's see how she responds to that before we give her more. And we have to deal with the head wound, or it won't matter."

Van der Vries looked at Sally; indeed, he seemed to be studying her, but he spoke to Lucas. "Since there has not before been a practicing, I might say a practical, physician to take charge of your activities, I will ignore your dosing of my patient without my permission. And since you have no cauterizing iron, I assure you there is nothing to be done for her head wound until the soldier returns with my bag."

Lucas began threading a needle with catgut.

"I swear, barber, you will not sew up this woman's head before I have cauterized her skull."

"Fried her brain, more like."

"Wounds burn the body. Fire is needed to treat fire. A first principle of medicine. Though of course you know nothing about that, either. I will not— Ah."

A young corporal came in. He handed a fair-sized leather satchel to Van der Vries. The physician snapped it open and pulled out a long iron rod with an ivory handle. He went to the fire and shoved the metal part of the device deep into the red-hot embers. "It needs to be as hot as we can make it. Nothing else will do. We must wait."

Lucas looked at Sally. She shrugged. He looked at the young woman, whose breathing was if anything even shallower. He thought of giving her more of the stimulating tonic, but by the time he finished Van der Vries would be ready to burn her alive. Lucas turned to the old man still lying on the stretcher on the floor. "You said she was your daughter. What do you want done? Do you want this Van der Vries here to burn her skull, or me to sew her scalp back on?"

There was no answer.

Sally crouched beside the old man. She put her hand beneath his shirt and over his heart and waited a few seconds. "He's dead, Lucas."

The soldier meanwhile had been staring at the half-scalped woman, fascinated with her extraordinary wound. "So's this one. Leastwise, she don't seem like she's breathin'."

Lucas went to the table and put his hand on the woman's chest, then leaned down and pressed his ear to her heart. Nothing. Sally appeared beside him, holding a shard of silvered glass. Lucas took it and held it to the woman's lips, then leaned toward the light of the fire to study the result. There was no haze of moisture. "She's dead. Damn your eyes, Van der Vries, we've lost her. The old man as well."

Van der Vries took the cauterizing iron from the fire and laid it carefully on the hearth to cool. He became for a moment entirely preoccupied with his lace cuffs, examining first one then the other. When he spoke, his voice was very soft.

"So much for your stimulating tonic, Mistress Sally." Then, to Lucas, "From now on my instructions will be followed without question. Do you understand?"

"I understand that you're a—"

"A practicing physician. And in England, as in my country, physicians oversee surgeons and barbers, not the other way around. Is that not so? Come, Mijnheer Turner, the barber who also practices surgery: this soldier and I are waiting for your answer."

"It's so."

"Good. An honest man, however ignorant. I hoped that would be the case." Van der Vries continued to adjust his lace cuffs. "Corporal, you must tell your superiors that in the future any injured are to be brought directly to me. If I need the barber's services, I will send for him."

The worms were black, many-segmented, each about three inches long. Van der Vries had nearly a pint of them. They made a throbbing black aggregation inside his large glass jug stoppered with thick cork. From the shadows where he stood Lucas saw the squirming mass as a single entity, but he knew what he was looking at. *Hirudo medicinalis.* Leeches.

Customarily Lucas checked the hospital once every day or two. In the week since the Indians attacked, since Van der Vries arrived in the colony, he'd been too busy. Treating arrow wounds, mostly. The Canarsie and the Shinnecock and the Raritan—all local tribes—were on the warpath.

Only once had Indians breached Nieuw Amsterdam's defenses. In 1655 a Wappinger war party managed to land their canoes a short distance from the fort and rampage through the streets. On that occasion Stuyvesant had been far north, at Fort Orange. This time he was at home. The southern shore was bristling with men-at-arms, and there were sentries every ten feet along the wall. Naturally enough, every colonist living in the Voorstadt and beyond had sought protection in the town. The settlement was heaving with people. In response the savages had mounted a siege.

And in the midst of all this, Lucas had Jacob Van der Vries to deal with. A man who believed in the doctrine of signatures three decades after every sensible physician had discarded the theory, and who had apparently provided himself with a supply of the black worms that did a barber's job without the necessity of a scalpel.

Lucas left the protection of the doorway. "Good afternoon, Mijnheer Van der Vries. I take it your patient needs bleeding."

"Ah, barber. Yes, I believe bleeding would profit this poor creature. But I won't be needing you. I have my little friends." Van der Vries held up the glass jar. The leeches that had been trying to climb the slick sides had given up. The black mass was still. In the parlance of the trade, the leeches were relaxed: meaning they were in the optimum state to attach themselves to human flesh and suck blood.

Lucas nodded toward the jar. "Found them here, did you? They're too big to be from Holland."

"Indeed they're not. Came from a pond not five minutes' walk from my house. Remarkably large, don't you agree?"

"I do. That's the difficulty with them. Leeches suck until they're full before they drop off. Those we grow here in Nieuw Netherland take a lot of filling."

"All to the good." Van der Vies was busy opening his bag. "Going to do something, you might as well do it right, I always say. Never saw any point in half measures."

Lucas leaned toward the patient. The woman was unconscious, perhaps forty and gaunt to the point of emaciation. There was a protrusion almost the size of his fist on her neck. Lucas palpated the tumor. It was cold and hard as rock. He used both hands to finger the throat on either side of the growth. The flesh was of a normal temperature and yielded to his touch. Finally he looked again at the woman's face. This time, despite the disfigurement of illness, he recognized her. "The Widow Kulik. Lives near the fort. Not the sort usually to be found in this place. How long has she been here?"

"Couldn't say." Van der Vries had ignored Lucas's uninvited examination of the patient. He was preoccupied with pawing through the contents of his satchel. "Don't know what I did with my cupping tool. I'm sure it was in here . . ."

"Your cupping tool," Lucas said quietly. "You mean to blister her, then?"

Van der Vries was still pawing through his bag. "The thought had occurred to me, yes."

Lucas looked around. Sally was usually at the hospital, but not today. Since the siege began they'd been living in the one-room barber shop. His sister hated it. Sally spent all her time trying to get the place as clean as she kept the cabin. It was a battle she'd never win, but she refused to give in.

The siege had not, however, made Anna Stuyvesant desert her nursing duties. The governor's sister was standing at the opposite end of the little ward watching them. If it had been Sally, Lucas would have summoned her. As it was, he walked the few steps. "I see the Widow Kulik has been brought to your care, mevrouw. May I ask why? And how long she has been here?"

"Since yesterday. Neighbors brought her. There was no one at home to attend her dying. Her last surviving son was killed two days past."

"Savages?"

"Of course. What greater plague do we know in this place?"

Lucas nodded. "I seem to recall there were children."

"Three. Babies still. The Widow Kulik was caring for them since their mother died last year in childbirth. The good folk who lived nearby have taken the children. They could not be expected to take the dying grandmother as well."

"So now she's Van der Vries's patient," Lucas said quietly. "And he means to bleed and blister her. Is that his usual way, mevrouw?"

"How could I know? He's been here less than a fortnight."

"Long enough for one with your astuteness to make a judgment." Anna Stuyvesant didn't meet his eyes.

"He's a practicing physician, barber. He learned his art with men who served the most fashionable society. It is fitting that he be put in charge of the hospital."

And earn the twenty-guilder-a-year stipend that went with the appointment. "You've seen the lump on Widow Kulik's neck?"

"It would be difficult not to see it."

"Indeed." Lucas's voice was soft but insistent. "The entire medical world recognizes such goiters, mevrouw. They must be surgically removed. Raising a blister with the cup is sure to do nothing but add to the patient's misery. As for bleeding, in these cases it is of no value whatever."

"And if the Widow Kulik had come to you, you'd have cut away this goiter?"

"Yes. I could not guarantee— Sweet bloody Jesus!" Lucas turned and dashed back to the woman in the bed. Jacob Van der Vries had given up on finding his cupping tool. Instead he had removed the cork stopper from the wide-mouthed glass jar and upended it above the woman's head. "Are you insane! You can't apply leeches in that fashion. For the love of God, you'll kill her!"

"That's a strange philosophy for a barber, isn't it? Thought bleeding was your answer to everything." Van der Vries watched the leeches tumble from the jar. A number fell on the bedding, but many more landed on the woman's face. And at least six attached themselves to her neck. "Good," the Dutchman whispered. "Excellent. Do your work, little friends. Suck the poison out of the swelling."

Lucas was nearly sputtering with rage. When he spoke his voice trembled. "The swelling, as you call it, is a tumor. Not a boil that will profit from bleeding or lancing."

Van der Vries chuckled. "Jealous, are you, Englishman? These creatures, after all, ask no fee for their services. Only to fill themselves with the evil blood that is causing this poor woman such distress."

Lucas swallowed a protest. It was too late. Nearly every leech was now well attached. The woman's face and neck had become a black mass, a writhing thing that grew ever larger as the jointed, hairy bodies of the worms became engorged with her blood. "You are a fool," Lucas whispered. "Worse, you're a criminal and a murderer. Four leeches at a time. Perhaps five. And applied to the inside of the arm, not—"

"I seem to have forgotten my cupping tool. Careless of me, I admit." Van der

Vries was studying the fingernails of his left hand. "But hardly cause for consternation, given how far advanced this woman's illness is. And it would do little good to take blood from her arm when any fool, even a barber who believes himself to be a surgeon, can see that the evil humors have lodged themselves in the poor creature's throat."

Lucas drew a long breath. The enormity of the error was stupefying. He all but choked on it.

Anna Stuyvesant had stayed out of their argument. Now she took a few steps toward them. Lucas took a step to his right so she could get a good look at the black and writhing thing on the bed. She gasped. "So many, Mijnheer Van der Vries." None of her famous bossiness. She sounded as if she were pleading. "I have never . . . Perhaps, barber, you and the physician can possibly remove a few of the—"

"No. We cannot." Lucas watched one last sluggish worm make its way across the bedclothes and crawl over the bodies of its relatives until it found a bit of exposed skin behind the woman's ear. He could have prevented that one from attaching itself, but there was no point. "Leeches have to be allowed to fill themselves until they drop off, mevrouw. Otherwise they leave their sucking tool inside the patient and the wound becomes poisonous." He looked at Van der Vries. "Is that not correct, mijnheer?"

"Yes, of course." Van der Vries was leaning over his patient, staring at the worms. "But see, at least six are fixed on the goiter. It will be drained of the evil blood that—"

"Tell me, Van der Vries, when you were healing the sick with the fashionable practitioner of physic in fashionable Cambridge, England, did you not hear of the English king's extremely fashionable personal physician, William Harvey?"

Van der Vries didn't look up. "Harvey," he murmured. "Yes, I seem to recall the name."

"I'm pleased to hear it. Because over thirty years ago Harvey proved that the blood circulates in the human body. The Widow Kulik's goiter is a growth, a struma made of tissue and fed by blood from the whole body. It is not depend—"

"At last we have reached the nub of the argument." The Dutchman looked directly at Lucas. "You wished to cut, did you not, barber?"

"I could have removed the goiter, yes. There is no guarantee of success, but—"

"But definitely a guarantee of excruciating pain. Look at the size of this swelling. As big as two pullet eggs. Do you not agree it must have been growing on the woman's neck long before my arrival in the colony?"

"Of course."

"Indeed. And despite the fact that you were here and I was not, this poor creature never consulted you."

"Some are afraid of the knife. You know it as well as—"

Anna Stuyvesant put herself between the two men. "Look, the leeches . . . They are starting to fall off."

"Ah, yes." Van der Vries bent over the bed and began scooping the fat black worms into his jar. "Thank you for recalling me to my duty, mevrouw. These beauties will serve some other patient as well. Be ready for a new meal soon, won't you, my little friends?"

The face of the Widow Kulik began to emerge from the curtain of leeches. Her skin was ghostly white, her eyes open and staring, her mouth relaxed. Lucas put his hand on the woman's chest. "She's dead."

"*Ja, ja.* I thought so already." Van der Vries was intent on gathering up the leeches. It was not difficult; they weren't only stiff with blood, they were stupefied with it. They tumbled happily into the glass jar and made no effort to attach themselves to the Dutchman's pudgy hands. "Her case, as you just admitted, was well advanced. Nonetheless, it is the duty of the true physician to try all possible remedies until the very end."

IV

Having known her naked in the woods, Lucas found it difficult to once again have Marit only in the storeroom of the butcher shop.

Still, any way was better than no way. Over a year now, and their lust hadn't cooled. Marit still moaned and gasped in delight when he entered her, and trembled like a leaf in a tempest when finally she was overcome by ecstasy. Seeing her that way had always made Lucas feel like a god. It still did. But it was not the same.

Sometimes when he thought about the things they had done to each other in the cave—a mere twenty minutes' walk from Wall Street—he blushed. Both of them naked as Adam and Eve, surrounded by nothing but the forest, bathing naked in the cool fresh water of the Collect Pond.

Lucas desperately missed the freedom of those precious hours. So did Marit. While he was deep inside her in the storeroom, she would whisper her memories in his ear. "Ah, yes, do that, Lucas. Put your fingers inside me there and rock them back and forth. When we went to the cave you used to put your cock inside that place. Do you remember, my darling Lucas, putting your cock in my arse? Do you remember?"

When she said those things he went wild. Who would imagine a woman would speak such words? Not a whore—a respectable woman who had a husband and went to church on Sundays, and sometimes caught his eye when she came out of the service, and just from the way she looked at him made him know what she was thinking. What she would say aloud as soon as they were together in their secret cave. *I want to suck your cock, Lucas. I want to take it in my mouth and suck it dry.*

No more. They dared not risk it. Aside from the threat posed by Ankel Jannssen asleep upstairs, there were the customers, more of them than ever before.

Normally Nieuw Netherland was a place of incredible plenty, much of it free for the taking. Now, with overland access to the farms and the surrounding countryside cut off, all the town's provisions had to arrive by ship. Stuyvesant inaugurated a rationing system. It should have meant less business in Jannssen's shop.

But the atmosphere of danger bred rumors faster than maggots on a dung heap. A story made the rounds that Ankel and Marit had a secret supply of meat hidden in the cellar beneath their house. That it would have long since become putrid didn't stop people from coming and asking to buy some of the hoard. They seemed to think if they could just catch the mistress butcher on her own and offer her a bit of extra money, she'd find them something over their ration.

Marit turned them all away. "Even if I had extra meat, which I do not, I wouldn't dare sell you more than your share. The fine for cheating on the rationing is a fortune, three guilders."

The first time Lucas heard her say it he was hiding in the storeroom, his still-unsatisfied cock stiff as a broom handle inside his breeches. When he thought about the penalty for what they were doing—far worse than a three-guilder fine—he marveled at their foolhardiness. But he didn't leave. And he didn't stop visiting the butcher shop at every possible opportunity. Neither did the customers who continued to believe the rumor because they wanted it to be true.

It was rare that Lucas and Marit could be together the way they were that January Thursday, over a month into the siege. For once they hadn't been interrupted, and when he was done Lucas could chance staying inside her for a few seconds. He smoothed Marit's golden hair back from her forehead. He kissed her cheeks and her lips and her eyes.

"I miss the woods," she whispered between his kisses. "I long to be naked with you."

"Me, too. But I don't long to lose my scalp, or see you lose yours."

He eased out of her. Marit sighed. "Each time you part from me it's like a little death."

"I know. I feel the same."

"Do you, Lucas?"

"Dear God, Marit, of course I do. How can you ask?"

"Because if you are as unhappy apart from me as I am from you, then we must do something about it."

Lucas adjusted himself and buttoned his breeches. He leaned forward and kissed her forehead. "Dearest Marit, there is nothing to be done."

"We could go away, Lucas."

He pulled back, stared at her. "What are you saying?"

"We could go to New England. To Boston."

Lucas chuckled. "Wouldn't we have a fine time with the Puritans in Boston! A nonbelieving barber and a runaway wife. They'd hang us ten minutes after we arrived."

"Then we could take a ship back to Europe. To England."

"I can't return to England. Anyway, I can't leave here. I have my sister to look after."

"Ah yes." Marit began lacing her bodice, easing her heavy breasts back into their restraint. "The saintly Juffrouw Sally who goes so frequently to the hospital to care for the stinking vagabonds brought there to die. Your sister is how old, Lucas?"

"Twenty-five," he admitted. "Nearly twenty-six."

"Yes. And she's a dried-up old prune. It is long past time you found her a husband."

"We can't afford a dowry. And I promised Sally I wouldn't—"

The footsteps of the butcher were heavy on the stairs. "Marit! Damn you, woman, where are you? Marit!"

Heart pounding, Lucas ran from the storeroom to the front of the shop and positioned himself in front of the wooden counter.

Marit was right behind him, adjusting her skirt and smoothing her hair as she took her place on the other side of the chopping block. "*Ja*, I am here, Ankel. I am talking to a customer." Her red mouth sent Lucas a silent kiss.

Ankel Jannssen shoved aside the burlap curtain and peered into the shop. He was a big man, as tall as Lucas and twice as broad. A lifetime of meat-eating had packed flesh onto his frame. He filled the doorway. "Listen, woman, I want— Who's this?"

"The barber, Ankel. Lucas Turner."

"*Ja*, Turner. The English. So what are you doing here, barber?"

Lucas thought his mouth too dry for speech, but the words came. "Your good wife provides me with sheep's intestines and pig bladders for my trade, butcher. I was hoping she had some put by for me today."

"Not today. We have nothing like that now. Everything but the smell, they eat. Pretty soon even the sawdust from the floor."

Jannssen stepped up to the chopping block, leaned on it, and looked hard at Lucas. The stench of stale drink came off the man in waves. It almost overcame the reek of his unwashed body. He had small close-set eyes, pig eyes. "*Ja*, Turner the English." He sounded as if he'd been thinking a lot about it. "Don't come any more here, barber. Go somewhere else for your guts and bladders. There are butchers closer to your place. Plague them. Even though their wives don't have tits quite so big."

Marit flushed dark red and turned away from her husband. Lucas looked directly at him. "It will be exactly as you say, Mijnheer Jannssen. Good day to you. And to you, mevrouw."

Lucas turned and walked out of the shop. He heard the unmistakable soft thwack of a fist striking flesh before he'd closed the door. And Marit's voice. "No, Ankel. No. I told you . . . you are imagining—" A second blow cut off her words.

Lucas froze in the doorway. There were at least a dozen other people on the short street. More than enough to rush to the butcher's aid if they heard him being beaten to pulp by the much younger and stronger barber, Lucas Turner. Plenty of respectable witnesses to testify that Ankel Jannssen had been exercising his legal right to discipline his wife when the Englishman, for no good reason, turned on him.

God alone knew what suspicions Ankel Jannssen would testify to in a court of law, but Lucas didn't need any messages from God to tell him what would happen to Marit if she were branded an adulteress and divorced.

He turned and walked the length of Hall Place, past the tidy wooden houses with their calico curtains and their small pots of flowers standing either side of every front door. Until he cleared the large open space in front of the fort he was sure he could hear the sound of Jannssen's fists pounding Marit's soft, yielding flesh.

Lucas didn't go to the butcher shop on Friday or Saturday. On Sunday he considered attending church, but decided against it. Unlike New England, Nieuw Netherland imposed no penalty for nonobservance. The wrath of Stuyvesant and the burgomasters was reserved for those who attempted any form of public worship other than that prescribed by the Dutch Reformed Church. Even the Jews were known to conduct their rites in a room above the mill on Beaver Street. As long as they made no public show about how they prayed or to whom—and as long as no Christian children were reported missing—they were left alone.

For his part, Lucas had no particular beliefs. God knows he was no Jew, but one sort of Christian or another seemed to him to make little difference. He'd felt safe from God's wrath and Stuyvesant's when—only to get a look at Marit—he'd gone a few times to the Sabbath liturgy at the Church of St. Nicholas. But the Sunday after Ankel surprised them, he contrived to arrive when the service was almost over.

The church was within the walls of the fort. A brutal wind whistled cold and icy across the parade ground, carrying the promise of snow. Lucas sheltered in the doorway of a storehouse a few steps from the church. He heard the last notes of the closing hymn, the drone of the minister's final blessing. A few moments later the worshipers began to leave the building. Everyone moved swiftly, anxious to get home to their fires. Marit and Ankel always occupied a pew toward the rear. They were among the first to appear.

Lucas huddled in the shadows. The butcher and his wife got closer. Ankel was talking to the man on his right. Marit was on her husband's left, the side closer to Lucas. She walked with her head down, one hand clutching the hood of her gray duffel cloak tight beneath her chin. When she drew level with Lucas, she turned her face in his direction.

Lucas gasped. Her eyes were swollen nearly shut. There was a cut on her right cheek, and her left was black and blue. And Jannssen had added shame to Marit's punishment by making her go to church so everyone would know she had done something to displease him, and he'd given her the discipline she deserved.

Lucas had to make a conscious effort to keep from lunging forward and throwing the butcher to the ground.

Marit turned her head so she could continue to see him as she and her husband walked on. Finally she turned away.

Lucas stayed where he was, trembling with rage. When he finally dared move, the church was empty, the last of the congregation had left the fort. He was alone.

The threatened snow began before he was halfway home. When he opened the door of the barber shop and smelled the dinner Sally was cooking, he gagged. For a time he stood where he was, the wind raging behind his back, blowing snow into the barber shop.

"Lucas!" Sally turned from the fireplace. "For heaven's sake, have you lost your senses? Shut the door before all the fire's warmth escapes."

He did as she asked, but he felt no difference in the temperature. His fury was an inferno. Having nothing else to feed on, it consumed Lucas himself.

Chapter Two

"I'M GOING HOME." Sally made her announcement while squatting over the narrow hearth in the barber shop, poking at the logs, though the fire didn't need tending. Lucas stood by the open top half of the door, gazing into the frozen street.

It was the last week in January. Seven weeks into the siege. Nine days since Lucas had seen Marit after church. Twelve days since he'd touched her. He burned. He was in no mood for Sally's nonsense. "Sweet Christ, woman, you can't go to the cabin. How long do you think you'd survive?"

"The Indians know I'm their friend. That's why our place is still standing and everything in it is untouched. Please, Lucas, close the door. I'm perishing with cold."

The icy air was a small relief from the fire raging inside him, but Lucas swung the door shut.

"Thank you. Now, please look at me."

Lucas turned. "Very well, I'm looking at you."

"Everything I'm saying is true. Our cabin is untouched. No Indian has gone near it. You heard that young soldier tell me so this very day."

"I heard. All it means is that the savages haven't gotten around to our place yet."

"No, it means that the Indians trust me. You never knew how many wounds I treated for them, Lucas. And I always traded fairly with the women and children. Besides, Tamaka used to tell me that our cabin stood on ground only women could go, a place that was forbidden to braves."

"My God, Sal, you have a brain. How can you possibly believe the babble of a squaw brat? There are thousands of them and we have a few hundred soldiers.

This is a war to the death, Sally. Those savages we don't kill will try to kill us. Without exception."

"I don't believe you. Anyway, I cannot stay here any longer. I cannot." She returned to poking at the logs, making the sparks fly. "Look at us, crammed together in this little room with the lice and the fleas, breathing the stink of blood and sweat day and night. I cannot bear it, Lucas."

"Yes, you can." Lucas's tone softened. "You and I, Sal, we know all about bearing what we must."

"Only until it can be changed. In Dover, you were the one to change things. Now it's my turn."

"Sally, believe me, as bad as that vile barn may have been, it was safer for us as children than our cabin in Nieuw Netherland is right now."

"Then in God's name, Lucas, why do we stay? Why don't we just leave this wretched colony?"

Sweet Jesus, where did these women get such notions? "Where is there for us to go, Sal? Tell me, for I should very much like to know."

Sally pushed her hands into her hair and lifted the temples as if she'd remove her own scalp. The gesture raised the corners of her mouth and her eyes, and she looked almost pretty. Certainly much younger. As soon as she took her hands away she was the same as always. Homely Sally, growing swiftly old. "We can go home, Lucas," she said. "We can go home."

Lucas crossed to the fire and kicked back a log that had fallen forward. The sparks chased themselves up the chimney. "Where's home? London? So the surgeons can throw me in jail? Or Dover, perhaps? The old man may be dead, but if he isn't, there's probably enough strength left in his arm to lift the horsewhip. Rotterdam? Our places on that crowded piece of earth must be taken by now."

"The cabin we built with our own hands. Spring will come. I must prepare to plant. If I don't, there'll be no physics for the year to come."

"We've precious little need of physics now that Jacob Van der Vries has taken charge."

"Exactly! And what are you doing about it, Lucas? You simply let him—"

"I spoke with Stuyvesant's sister, after Van der Vries murdered old Widow Kulik with his damned leeches."

"You did? Lucas, you never told me. Mevrouw Anna knows how skilled you—"

"She knows that I'm an English barber and Van der Vries is a Dutch physician."

"But surely, after what you did . . . The governor must—"

"Must nothing. I made a bargain with Stuyvesant. I kept my part, and he kept his. As Mevrouw Anna so succinctly put it, that was the end."

Sally shook her head. "Still. You can't just sit there night after night yearning over—" She broke off.

Lucas stared at her. "Yearning?" Sally didn't reply. "Finish what you were saying. Yearning over what?"

"Not what, who. Marit Graumann."

An icy hand gripped his bowels and twisted. "And where did you get that idea? Is the subject of my affections a matter of discussion for the *huisvrouwen* of Nieuw Amsterdam?"

"Dear God, no. I would have told you at once if anything so dangerous were happening. It's my own notion, Lucas. Because I can see Hall Place from the hospital windows. I see how often you call at Jannssen's butcher shop."

"To get the things I need for my work." He bit out the words between clenched teeth. "Pig bladders and sheep intestines. From the butcher I pass on my way to the hospital."

"Very well. It's your affair. I didn't mean to pry." Sally put both hands on the surgical table and leaned over it as if she needed the support to stay upright. She did not lift her head when she spoke. "Lucas, about going back to the cabin . . . I cannot stay cooped up here like this. I cannot bear it. Whatever you say, I cannot."

"You will bear it as long as you must." He ran a hand through his hair and kicked at the logs again. "Enough, damn it! I forbid you to speak of this again."

Sally stared at him. In all her life Lucas had never spoken to her in that tone or used such words. "You forbid me?" she whispered.

"Yes. Because you leave me no choice. You won't listen to reason, so you must yield to authority. I forbid you to ever again mention leaving the town until *I* say it is safe."

Sally went to the corner and lay down on the pile of skins that served as her bed. She stared dry-eyed at the rough timbered ceiling of the squalid little room.

Lucas took one of the journals from the locked drawer in the surgical table and began refining his account of a fistula he'd cut away six months before. He went on writing until the fire died. Then he banked the embers and went to his own makeshift bed.

In the morning, when he woke, Sally was gone.

The night was bitter, so cold the air seemed to crackle. Sally breathed deep and felt cleansed. Moonlight splashed across the path. She took long, unhampered strides, her boots crunching on the frozen earth. After all those weeks of confinement, her sense of freedom left no room for fear. Twice she heard the sound of an owl, once the cooing of a dove. They were sounds she knew, and they did not alarm her.

Pappitan made the cooing-dove sound one more time. He waited for the owl hoot, expecting it to be closer. It came, but from farther away. Pappitan was Shinnecock; his native lands were deep on Metoaca, the long island. He was fourteen and this was his first time on the warpath. Those were the reasons he had become separated from the war party when he went deeper into the woods to relieve himself. They did not make him less ashamed.

Before he returned to his village, Pappitan promised himself, he would cover his tomahawk in blood and take many scalps. That way, when the other braves told the story of how Pappitan had been lost for hours because he could not smell his own camp, only his own dung, the laughter would be friendly.

He cooed again. Again the owl answered. This time the sound seemed to come from a different place.

Pappitan clutched the fox totem that hung on the leather thong around his neck. *Lead me from this place that I may not disgrace myself. Help me to take many scalps to cover my shame.* The owl hooted again, from yet a third direction. Pappitan turned to follow where he thought it led. He had taken only a few steps when he heard the whiteface. It had to be a whiteface. No brave would make such thunderous noise simply by walking in the woods.

The enemy was coming toward him. Pappitan hid himself and waited. His heart thudded with joy and he sent many prayers of thanksgiving to the fox totem who had answered his prayer. When he returned to the war party he would bring his first scalp. The tale of Pappitan's dung would be a man's tale of valor, not a boy's tale of shame.

How quiet the woods were. How sweet the fresh, cold air. Sally almost didn't want this short journey to end. But she was anxious to see the cabin, to assure herself that everything was exactly as they'd left it, the way the soldiers said. She'd make a fire and sleep beside it. In the morning, when she woke, she'd check the root cellar and see if that big pumpkin was still sound. She'd cook a piece of it over the fire for her breakfast. Then she would see if she could snare a squirrel, so when Lucas came there would be a hot stew waiting for him.

She was pretty sure he would be with her by midday. He'd be furious, of course. But once she'd shown the way he'd be too embarrassed not to follow. He'd understand how stupid it was to linger in the stinking town when he could live in his own cabin. Yes, she was certain of it. Lucas would come. And the pair of them would be perfectly safe.

Pappitan could hardly believe that one small woman could make so much noise. He was disappointed. He had pictured himself returning to the war party carrying a soldier's scalp and wearing the soldier's clothes. Instead he was faced with a short, ugly woman.

Pappitan could see her clearly. Hatred for her rose in Pappitan's heart. Not just because she was a whiteface, one of those he had vowed to drive from the lands of the People. He hated her because she was not what he had wanted her to be.

Pappitan hefted his tomahawk. His uncle had made it for him and it fit perfectly in his hand. If she were a man he would throw the tomahawk right now and it would divide the shoulders of his enemy and kill him. There was no brave young or old in his village who could throw a tomahawk more accurately than Pappitan of the Fox clan. But the thought of killing this woman in that swift way, as if she were his equal in battle, did not please him.

He watched her shift the split log that barred the door of the cabin. He waited. Perhaps inside was the man, maybe even the soldier, the fox totem had brought to Pappitan's tomahawk.

Sally left the door of the cabin open behind her. She needed the moonlight until she could locate some dry kindling and find the tinderbox and get a fire going. Funny, she wasn't a bit tired. It must be two of the clock, but—

The hand that went around her neck was the only thing that kept her upright. In that first moment her shock was such that if the Indian—she couldn't see, but she knew instantly that her attacker was an Indian—hadn't been holding her she'd have fallen.

Her hands fluttered in the air. She grabbed at his arm, trying to get free. The grip tightened. She was choking. The room was spinning. Sally fought the release of oblivion. She knew it meant death. But to live she must speak, and to speak she must breathe. Sally clawed at the arm around her neck, dug her nails into the skin. Suddenly her attacker released the stranglehold and threw her forward onto the ground.

Her face smashed into the dust covering the floorboards. She lay gasping, struggling for air. She was half unconscious, almost unaware that her hands were being tied behind her back.

Pappitan did not desire her. Her smell was terrible and the many layers of clothes she wore on her body were thick with filth. He had to suppress his disgust as he cut them away and exposed her flesh. He prayed to the fox totem to give him a hard tool to do what he must do: use the woman before he killed her, so her kind would know he was the master and she could only submit.

When he was finished he would slice open her woman part. Then he would cut off her breasts. Only then would he slit her throat and take her scalp. And maybe after all that he wouldn't be so angry that there was no soldier, no whiteface man, anywhere near this cabin to honor his tomahawk with its first enemy blood. Only this stupid, ugly woman with the whiteface stench thick upon her.

Because her hands were tied behind her, Sally had no means to support herself when the Indian lifted her legs. Her upper body bounced on the floor, her face was dragged and scraped across the rough, splintered boards. She gagged on her own vomit even while she struggled to speak. "No. You don't understand. I'm your friend. I've always—"

She could not suppress her scream. It was as if a white-hot poker had been thrust inside her, reaching up into her belly and searing her guts.

Pappitan was astounded at the resistance his tool met. Perhaps whiteface women were made differently from women who were of the People. Maybe the tools of whiteface men were different. No, he was inside her now. The woman hole was very small and tight. His thrusts began to give him pleasure, but it ended quickly. In a few seconds he felt the last shudders of enjoyment come and go.

Then he felt the arm that circled his neck.

The brave who pulled Pappitan from the whiteface woman was the leader of the war party and Pappitan's uncle, the man who had made the boy's first tomahawk and taught him to throw it. It was that tomahawk the uncle now raised above his nephew's head. "You have wakened the blood spirits," the older man said. "You have come to a place where in the old days the women came to bleed and give birth, and you have wakened the blood spirits they left behind."

Pappitan opened his mouth. Before he could speak the tomahawk came down with all his uncle's weight behind it. The boy's skull was split almost entirely in two.

His sister's child. A member of his clan. But the law must be obeyed. The uncle took the knife from his belt and opened his nephew's chest and cut out his heart. Then he carried it to the door of the cabin the whitefaces had built on the forbidden ground of the blood spirits.

"Hear me, holy ones," he cried out. "I have killed my sister's son in your honor. Do not make evil and defeat come to the war parties of the People. The warpath will never again cross the Little Musquash Path." Then he flung Pappitan's heart into the woods beyond the clearing. "Sleep, holy ones. You have blood to drink." Finally he returned to where the woman still lay on the ground.

He knelt over her and listened. Her spirit had flown, but she still breathed. Perhaps because she was a female the blood spirits would save her; it was not for him to decide if she was to live or to die. He used the same knife with which he'd cut out Pappitan's heart to cut the leather thong that bound her wrists. Then he hoisted the body of his dead nephew and ran silently and swiftly from the cabin.

It was soon after dawn when Lucas reached the clearing in front of the cabin. He'd run all the way, relying only on his musket for protection. His first thought had been to get a couple of soldiers to accompany him, but by the time he woke and saw that Sally was gone the patrols had all left the fort, and the few soldiers who stayed behind were needed to man the guns that protected the town.

Even as he ran across the clearing Lucas saw that there was no smoke coming from the chimney. A bad sign. But if she weren't there, where could she be? Dead and scalped somewhere in the woods. He wouldn't let himself think such thoughts. "Sally! Sal! For the love of God, Sally, where are you?"

The log that held the front door shut had been removed and the door was open enough so Lucas knew it wasn't bolted from the inside. Thanks to his shouting he'd already given up any chance of surprise. God, what a bloody fool. The musket was primed and ready. He raised it to his shoulder, then lunged forward, kicking the door open the rest of the way.

Silence. And blood. It seemed to be everywhere. The floor and the walls were covered with it. Something else as well. Clots of gore in a trail leading from the door to somewhere near the cold hearth. He recognized it almost at once. Parts of a human brain. "Oh, my poor Sal," he whispered. "My poor, foolish sister."

He heard labored breathing. Lucas turned, swinging the musket in a wide arc, searching the gloom of the cabin. She was huddled in the corner, her back to the timber wall, her skirts wrapped around her and her knees drawn up nearly to her chin. "Sal! Thanks be to God, you're alive! I thought . . . Are you all right? Is there some wound that—"

His sister didn't seem to know he was there.

He set down the musket, leaning it against the table, and went to Sally and knelt beside her. Her face was scraped and bruised, one eye half closed with swelling. Worst of all she stared past him. "Sally, in God's name, tell me what . . ."

He pulled her upright. Her body was limp in his hands and she made no move to cover herself when her clothing fell away. Her skirts and petticoats had been slashed and ripped apart, exposing her from the waist down. Lucas stared at that evidence of what had happened in the cabin. Dear God. Dear bloody God. "Come, Sally," he whispered. "I'm taking you home. We won't speak of this again. It never happened. Do you hear me? It never happened."

She still didn't look at him, but she was docile enough when he led her away.

It was the one time Lucas was grateful for the location of his barber shop. He was able to get Sally into the town with no one seeing her except the sentry who waved them through the gate as soon as he saw they were white, and went back to scanning the countryside for Indians.

A few steps brought them to the shop. "Come inside." He led her to the stool beside the fire. "Now sit. I'll poke up the blaze." He prodded the embers and when they reddened put on another log. "There, that's better. Are you cold? Sal, you have to say something. You can't just—"

A loud knock interrupted his words. Lucas went to the door but opened only the top half. It was a child. Sent to fetch something "as will loosen my pa's bowels and sweeten his spirits."

"Wait where you are. I'll give you something." Lucas shut the door, turned back to the shop. "Your laxative draught, Sal. The bitter licorice. I don't know where—"

She was no longer sitting by the fire. Lucas felt the beginnings of alarm. With the door shut the small room was dark, the blackness relieved only by the spiked shadows cast by the fire, dancing in the gloom. "Sal, for God's sake, where are you? I've got to get rid of the lad before— Ah, yes." His voice softened, lost the edge of panic. "That's wise. Rest is the best thing."

She'd crawled in between the skins and wool coverlets that made her bed. Lucas knelt beside her, drew the top blanket up to her chin. "Rest," he said again. "But first tell me where you store the tincture of bitter licorice."

Sally stared into space. The lad knocked again on the door. "I'm coming!" Lucas called. "Don't be so bloody impatient!" He got up and fetched one of his precious pig bladders and a handful of the bran-and-salt mix he prescribed after stone cutting or any other surgery involving the bottom half of the patient.

The child had brought a drawstring bag made of gingham. He held it open and Lucas put the bran mix at the bottom and dropped the bladder on top. "Tell your ma I said to give the old man a warm enema. Say I said to make sure she gets the liquid well up inside. Keep him sitting on the stool for hours. Fix him up and give your ma some peace besides." The little boy gave him a wicked grin and a handful of wampum.

When he turned back to his sister she hadn't moved. Lucas wished he could prescribe as easy a remedy for what ailed her. "Your own fault, Sally," he whispered into the dark. "But dear God, what a price to pay for your disobedience."

Next morning when he woke she was tending the fire. "Sal, are you well? Is there anything—"

"I've made corn cakes for your breakfast. There is no meat."

Her voice sounded almost normal. And she was poking repeatedly at the logs, insistently, with more strength in her arm than he'd have imagined her to have at the best of times. "What are you doing? Will the wood not burn?"

"Aye, it burns fine."

Lucas rose and stood behind her, peering into the fireplace. He could just make out the last shred of one of her petticoats. When he looked down he saw that she was wearing her other skirt, the dark red one she normally kept for Sunday best. She'd burned everything else. She was, he realized, following his advice. She would put what had happened behind her. So would he. "I'm ready for my corn cakes," Lucas said.

Sally served him without a word, but at least her hair was tidy, drawn into its customary bun, and she was no longer staring into space.

II

Though Van der Vries had left instructions forbidding any surgery without his permission, Lucas took to visiting the hospital daily. It gave him an excuse to walk the length of Hall Place. Past the butcher shop.

Occasionally the shop door was open and he managed to glimpse Marit behind the wooden counter. Sometimes the old magic worked and she knew he was nearby, and glanced toward the street at the precise moment he passed. At such times their eyes locked, but it was always Marit who looked away first

Those moments of connection told Lucas what he needed to know. He dare not try and see her. She was terrified, warning him off. Small wonder. Each time he saw her she seemed to have some new bruise.

The marks on that lovely face haunted him. He lay awake most of every night, imagining Ankel Jannssen taking his belt to Marit. Or lying over her. Lucas could not decide which was worse.

The next week the door of the butcher shop was closed whenever he passed. Lucas knew that there were customers and Marit was serving them, but he never saw her.

The following Sunday morning he again hid himself in the doorway near St. Nicholas's Church. The butcher and his wife didn't appear. Monday afternoon, when Lucas turned into Hall Place on his way to the hospital, Jannssen was waiting for him. The butcher stepped into the road, blocking his path.

"You. English. Why do you come this way so often? I told you to take your trade to another butcher."

"I have. I come this way because I visit the hospital to see if any need my services. Let me pass." Lucas's hands balled into fists. In his head he was sitting astride Ankel Jannssen, pounding his face into a shapeless pulp. Like one of the sides of beef he used to see hanging in the butcher's storeroom.

Jannssen didn't move. Lucas's nails bruised his palms. He could feel the pulse in his arms. He started to shove past the other man. "Go back to your trade, butcher, and let me get on with mine."

The man put out a hand and planted it in the middle of Lucas's chest. "Hold your bye. I've something to say."

Waves of alcohol poured off Jannssen. Talking to him was like hanging your head over a still. "Very well. Say it, then."

The Dutchman looked around. There were four or five people in the street. The door to his shop opened and two women came out. Everyone was looking with some interest at the butcher and the barber standing in the middle of the narrow road. "Not here," he said. "At the Wooden Horse. Tonight. Right after sundown."

The Wooden Horse was filled with customers. The air was thick with pipe smoke, and the smell of ale and rum was overpowering. The tavern drew its trade mostly from transients—trappers and sailors and Indian fighters. Lucas never drank here: the look and the din and the smell of the place reminded him of his father's taproom in Kent. He stood at the door for a moment, looking for Jannssen, half expecting to see his father come out from behind the bar. Carrying his horsewhip, most likely.

"English. Over here."

Jannssen was sitting at a wooden table in a corner near the door. Lucas took a seat across from him. The smoke was so thick he could hardly see the other man. The smell of the place made him want to puke.

"Good ale in the Horse. And the best geneva and rum." Jannssen kept his pipe clenched in his teeth and nodded toward the bar at the far end of the crowded room. "Go get what you want. I'll wait."

"No thanks. I didn't come here to drink with you." Lucas had considered not coming at all, but he'd been afraid Marit would pay the price. "Speak your piece, butcher. Then I'll leave."

Jannssen took a long pull from his tankard. Rum: Lucas could smell it. Jannssen kept staring at Lucas over the rim. Finally he put the drink down and wiped his mouth. "So, tell me, where are you hurrying to, English? A whore over on Princes Street, maybe? Got a stiff cock, have you? Of course, if you were married, like me, that wouldn't be a problem. All you'd have to do is roll over in your own bed and there she'd be. Big tits, nice soft pink belly. And her thighs . . . You should see my Marit's thighs, English. Round, with dimples. And her skin is like—"

Lucas leaned over and grabbed the front of Jannssen's shirt. He spoke very softly. "Butcher, I am going to say this once, so listen carefully. If you don't speak respectfully of your wife I am going to beat you until your face looks like a piece of meat you've hacked apart in your shop. Do you understand me?"

Jannssen smiled. "I understand you, English. And I am not frightened. Everyone can beat someone who is older or younger or weaker or smaller. That's how the world works. You can beat me, and I can . . ."

He didn't finish the sentence. He didn't have to. Lucas released his hold.

"So now," Jannssen said, "it's my turn. Do you understand me, English?"

"I understand you."

"Good." Jannssen drank again. "I have a proposition for you. Sixty guilders."

Lucas was sweating. "I don't know what you're talking about."

"Money. Guilders. Or pounds if you like. Only no wampum."

"Money for what?"

"So I can go away." Jannssen hunched forward. His pig eyes were narrow slits. "Give me sixty guilders and you can have her. I'm off south to the islands. Barbados, maybe. Maybe Curaçao. Warm. All the rum a man can drink for a quarter of what it costs here." He jerked his head toward the port. "There's ships leave here for the islands every week. Sixty guilders and I'm on the next one going."

"I haven't got sixty guilders."

"Pity," Jannssen said. "Till you do, she's mine to fuck or flog."

Lucas stood up. He was sure he was going to vomit. A man was coming toward him. His father. Same thin strands of greasy black hair plastered over a mostly bald head. Same evil expression.

"That's mine host," Jannssen said smiling. "Owns this tavern. Rich. Maybe I should make the same offer to him. He's always had an eye for Marit." Lucas turned to go. "One thing," Jannssen said to his back. "Don't come near my place again. Not without the money. If you do I'll take a horsewhip to her. That's a man's right, you know. With his lawful wife."

Lucas took to walking the town, in fair weather or foul, trying to think of some way he could get sixty guilders. Two weeks went by. In all that time he saw Marit only once. It was a late February Saturday and she was carrying her basket and hurrying across the Brede Wegh. Delivering one of the scarce Sunday joints to a member of such as fancied themselves Nieuw Amsterdam's gentry.

She saw him at the same moment he saw her. They stopped and stared at each other across a distance of maybe ten yards.

Lucas took a few steps toward her. Her face was unbruised. For the space of two heartbeats she stayed where she was, then walked on.

"Wait," Lucas called softly. "Wait." In these days of warpath and siege when almost the entire colony was sheltering behind the wall, the street was full of people. "Mevrouw, please, if I might speak with you a moment . . ."

Marit turned. She looked at him—so much love and longing in that look, though only Lucas could see it—then shook her head and hurried on.

Sixty guilders. It might as well be six hundred. Or six thousand. It was a fortune and he had no means of getting it.

The summons came the following Wednesday at midnight. "Barber! Barber! Are you in there? Open up."

Lucas stumbled half asleep to the door. "Yes, what is it?" He flung open the top half of the door but could see nothing. "Who's there, what's—"

"It's me, barber, Stuyvesant's Micah. The governor sent me."

Lucas blinked, looked again. It was a night of heavy cloud, without stars or moon. Only the whites of the black slave's eyes showed in the dark. "What's wrong?"

"The governor wants you, barber. He says you're to come right away. He's waiting."

Lucas did not need to be told to bring his instruments. There was no other reason for Peter Stuyvesant to summon him.

Judith Bayard's bedroom was across the hall from the room where Lucas had operated on her husband. She lay in a traditional Dutch bed, built into the wall, framed by the paneled doors of many cupboards. There was a small log fire, and a single candle stood on the table beside the door: light enough for Lucas to see her pale blond hair spread across her pillow, and to see how flushed she was. He put his hand on her forehead. The skin was exceptionally dry and hot to his touch. "She's burning up with fever."

"I know." Stuyvesant used his silver-topped stick to support his weight while he lowered himself to the edge of the bed. He reached for his wife's hand. Her fingers lay unmoving in his. "She cannot seem to hear me. I talk to her, we all do, but she makes no reply."

Every breath first rattled in her chest, then came harsh and whistling from her nose. Lucas had heard such breathing before, always from patients near the end. "How long has she been like this?"

"Two days. The sickness came on so suddenly. . . . She was well, a hoarse throat, nothing more."

"I see. And what's been done for her?"

"Anna has been at my dear wife's side all the hours of the day and night. She has tried to get Judith to take some nourishing broths, but she will not."

"Listen to her breathing. Her lungs are full of fluid. You must not force her to drink broth or anything else in such a condition, mijnheer. She could choke to death."

Stuyvesant nodded. "I know. Anna knows, as well. But we are at a loss. I thought perhaps you . . ."

Lucas bent over the woman a second time. Then straightened. "I presume you have consulted Van der Vries. What's his opinion?"

"I have not called on Van der Vries."

Lucas folded his arms and leaned against the wall. "Ah, how interesting. A physician specially dispatched by your employers, but the governor of the colony does not summon him to treat his wife's terrible fever?"

"Stand up straight, man. And stop your baiting. It doesn't matter what you think of me. Or of Van der Vries, for that matter. My wife has grave need of your skills. As a Christian you have no choice but to lend her what assistance you can."

Lucas shrugged. "I would not refuse to help your wife if help were in my power. It's not."

The Dutchman used his stick for leverage to stand, and took a few paces toward the fireplace. Each move was accompanied by the double tapping made by the stick and the peg leg strapped to his right knee. A man of few vanities, they said. Only his unshakable belief that he was always right, and the elaborately worked silver that topped his cane and formed his peg. In the taverns and the slop shops there were endless jokes about Peter Stuyvesant tapping a jig in hell while the devil piped the tune on a silver flute. Lucas had heard them all.

Apparently so had Stuyvesant. "I'm not popular," he said softly, his back to the Englishman. "I know that. But I try to serve my God and my employers with all the loyalty and wit at my command. I know no way to do things except my own way. Few women could live happily with such a man. I am blessed with two. My sister and my wife. Are you telling me, barber, that I am to lose one?"

"I did not say that. Only that I cannot help her. I know of no surgical treatment for what ails the mevrouw Bayard."

Stuyvesant turned around. Bathed in the red glow from the fire he looked like a demon summoned from the nether world. "Tell me only this," he whispered. "Is it scarlatina?"

Lucas lifted the candle and carried it closer to the bed. Judith Bayard's mouth hung slack, half open. Lucas put his fingers below her chin and turned her face to his. He bent forward, studying her in the light of the candle flame. Finally he put two fingers in her mouth and pried her jaw wider apart. Her fevered breath was hot on his hand. "Not scarlatina," he said. "Her tongue is neither red nor pimpled."

"Anna says the same. She says strawberry tongue is the only reliable sign of scarlatina." Stuyvesant sounded more despairing, then relieved. "I can but pray you are both correct."

"Calm yourself, Governor. The mevrouw Anna is correct. Your wife does not have scarlatina." Lucas carried the candle back to the table beside the door, put it down next to his instrument case. "I think perhaps it is a distemper of the throat."

"What can you do for it?"

"Nothing." Lucas did not meet the governor's glance. "I can do nothing."

"She's dying." Stuyvesant's voice was harsh with pain. "I summoned you because you're my last hope. My wife is dying and you—"

"Keep her warm," Lucas said. "Make sure there is always someone with her, and—" He didn't have a chance to say they must wait for the breaking of the fever and pray she survived it. Judith Bayard's labored and hollow breathing turned to a loud wheeze, almost a whistle. A terrible sound. Both men hurried to the bed. "Judith," Stuyvesant called. He sounded impatient with her, even angry. "Judith!"

The wheezing was louder and at the same time more shallow as she struggled for breath. Lucas put his hand behind the woman's shoulders and lifted her forward. "For God's sake, stop shouting. Here, help me raise her head. More pillows. Hurry."

Stuyvesant piled pillows behind his wife's back. They didn't seem to help. Her face, a moment ago so hot and dry, poured sweat. The fever was breaking, but that hardly mattered if she could not breathe. More wheezing, faster, louder, and at the same time more gasping and ineffective.

The governor took a backward step. "Do something," he whispered. "Do something."

Lucas continued to hold the dying woman. "I can do nothing for distemper of the throat," he said softly. "I'm sorry, I know no surgery for—"

"Don't tell me that! I won't listen. You're a man of exceptional skill. You can save her, Englishman. For the love of Jesus Christ, do it!"

"I tell you, there's nothing . . ." Lucas stopped.

Nothing. Except for one thing. It had been in the back of his mind from the moment he'd walked into the sickroom and heard those struggling breaths. In London, years before, at the very beginning of his apprenticeship, the surgeons had spoken of a man named Severino, a surgeon in Naples. During an epidemic of the throat sickness he had saved countless lives by opening the trachea, creating a temporary airway.

They talked about the successes. God alone knew how many had died under Severino's knife. And Lucas had never seen it done, had never even seen a drawing of it in a book. He had only heard the story at age sixteen from surgeons he wasn't supposed to be listening to, since he was an apprentice barber.

"Dear God, Turner," Stuyvesant's voice was a harsh whisper, "I'm begging you. Don't let her die."

Lucas still had his arm behind Judith Bayard's frail shoulders. He could feel her agony as if it were his own. Her fight to draw breath was becoming a death throe: her face was turning blue. There were only moments left.

Lucas flung the pillows aside and lowered her head. "My instrument case! Over there by the door!"

Seconds later the small lancet was in his hand.

Stuyvesant had thought to bring the candle as well. He held it above his wife's head. Lucas used his free hand to draw the skin of her throat taut. He heard yet another of the woman's high-pitched, wavering attempts to breathe. His blade hovered over the depression between the throat and the clavicle. For the first time ever he could remember, his hand trembled.

Nonetheless, he cut.

The blood oozed. He had not, thank God, severed any of the major arteries that lay so dangerously close to the trachea. The wheezing stopped. Lucas dropped the knife on the bedclothes and used both hands to spread the wound. Four air bubbles, one right after another in rapid succession, then more, in a slow but steady rhythm.

"What's happening?" Stuyvesant's voice was weak. "Judith," he whispered. "My dear . . . Englishman, is she gone?"

"Your wife is alive, Governor. And a little more comfortable." The light of the candle grew brighter as the other man leaned forward. "Look right there," Lucas said. "Between my fingers. Those air bubbles. They are caused by her lungs taking in air directly through the windpipe."

"God in heaven. It's a miracle."

"No, Governor. Distemper of the throat chokes the patient to death. I have bypassed the throat and opened another airway. The lungs are designed to take in and expel air. They will do so by whatever passage it arrives."

"Then," Stuyvesant said softly, "I repeat: the design is a miracle. A gift from Almighty God." He put a hand on his wife's forehead. "She is much cooler."

"Indeed. It was the breaking of the fever that caused the crisis."

"Barber, this opening in her throat . . . Must she always breathe so?"

"No, of course not. We will close the wound in a few days. When the distemper has passed and the mevrouw is fully recovered. For now I must find some way to keep the passage open. Severino, the Italian who devised this technique"—Lucas was speaking more to himself than to the Dutchman—"they say he designed as well an ivory tube to insert . . . Governor, send someone to fetch me some of the tall reeds that grow over by the waterfront. The ones with hollow centers."

It was Anna Stuyvesant who saw Lucas to the door. "We are once more in your debt, Englishman," she said quietly. "On behalf of my brother and my sister-in-law, I thank you."

"I am glad I was able to help, mevrouw."

"So am I. Now you must tell me the fee for your services. That way we can have it ready when you return tomorrow to attend my sister-in-law."

He thought of asking for sixty guilders. But he knew he wouldn't get it. The most he'd ever been paid for an operation was two. "There is no fee."

Anna Stuyvesant raised her eyebrows. "Yes, there is." A suggestion of a smile, but she didn't allow it to form. "We have experience of your 'free' services, barber. Will you tell me what you wish to have, or will you wait and discuss it with my brother?"

"I'd as leave tell you, mevrouw. If you promise to pass on the request."

"Of course."

"The hospital. I wish to—"

"The governor will not put the hospital under your charge, barber. To be frank, I suggested it earlier. After the leeches ki— After the Widow Kulik died. The governor believes in tradition as a guide to behavior. Physicians are above surgeons. Certainly above barbers."

"I know. But will you ask him?"

"If you wish."

"I do. Remind him what he said about my skills. And that his wife is breathing."

Anna Stuyvesant was waiting for Lucas when he returned to the house later that same day. "Your patient is doing remarkably well. The fever is gone. And she breathes with ease through the reed."

"Excellent. I shall insert a fresh reed today and another tomorrow. Then I can probably stitch the wound. Mevrouw, is the governor here?"

"No. He is at the fort. They are discussing new ways to deal with the savages."

"In the town they say New England may be willing to help."

"Pray God that is so. For my part, I leave such things to my brother. And he left this for you."

The envelope she passed him was heavy. "Money," Lucas said.

"Three guilders. A very generous payment, but as I said, we are all in your debt."

"And the hospital remains—"

"In the charge of Mijnheer the Physician Van der Vries. Custom and usage, barber. The governor knows no other way."

III

"Sal, would you believe it? They say the English king has given us to his brother. As a gift." Lucas shut both halves of the barber-shop door and slid the bolts in place. "As of this moment, back in London they believe Nieuw Netherlands belongs to the Duke of York. Because His Royal Highness Charles II says it does. Did you ever hear such bloody nonsense?"

When he went out he'd wrapped himself in an Indian blanket against the pelting March rain. He carried it across the small and squalid room and set it to dry by the fire. "Not that we're much of a gift. Damned mud's everywhere. The streets are swimming in it."

Sally was already sweeping away the filthy trail her brother's boots had left between the door and the hearth. She did that constantly, but the dirt sank deep into the splintered boards and no amount of scrubbing could wash it away. Lice and fleas made happy homes in the dried mud Sally Turner could never get rid of, but she went on trying.

There was a pot of something aspiring to be a proper stew hanging over the fire. A handful of dried corn and the eighth part of a squirrel's haunch. "Smells vile," Lucas said, sniffing his supper. "Not your fault. I know you do the best you can with little. Anyway, about this gift business, old man Doncke's going around saying war should be declared on all the English settlers in the colony. Fortunately every other man in the alehouse thought the idea was—"

He broke off. She wasn't listening to him. Sally had slipped the bolts and opened the door. She was pushing the mud into the street with a worn straw broom. Fighting the gale that tried to blow it back in. Something about the way she performed that futile task terrified Lucas. Her whole body was rigid. She seemed to quiver with tension.

"Leave it, Sally. It's clean enough for now. Come, rest by the fire. We'll treat ourselves to a tot of geneva."

She didn't turn around, just went on pushing the broom against the gale, struggling to overcome the invincible rain and the wind and the mud. "Sal, leave it. You've done enough. For God's sake, woman, are you hearing one word I'm saying?"

She swung around to face him, but she didn't close the door. A gust came along and blew it wildly open, then almost shut, then open again. A torrent of dirt, and last autumn's leaves, and small pebbles, and clots of what was probably dung blew into the room. Sally ignored it. She stood framed in the opening, both halves of the door banging behind her. "I am with child, Lucas."

He rushed to shut the door and pull her back inside. For a few seconds he could pretend he hadn't heard.

In the weeks since she'd run away, in between his pain over the loss of Marit, his fury over Van der Vries taking from him the opportunity to perform all but the most debased and menial surgical tasks, Lucas had told himself that his worst fear would not come to pass. Nearly two months now and he'd watched Sally day and night, fretted over her silences, over how withdrawn she was, how dark her mood, but rejoiced that she was if anything thinner than ever. To Lucas, because he so desperately wanted it to be so, that proved the savage could not have visited a half-breed bastard on his sister, and ruin on Lucas Turner.

"Come inside, Sal! Come! It's blowing up a gale. Far worse than when I—"

"Lucas, did you hear me?" Her voice became more shrill with every word. "I am with child, Lucas. I shall have a little papoose of my very own. What have you to say, now that you're about to be an uncle?"

Lucas shot the bolts. When he turned to her it was he who trembled.

"You can't know for sure," he said. "You can't, Sally. It's only a little over a month since—"

"Two." She spoke more quietly than before, but with the same tone of total despair. "Two months, Lucas. And always before now my flow was as regular and as certain as sunrise."

"Look at you, look how thin you are. If—"

"I am thin, aren't I?" She smiled. "That's because of all the purges I've taken these past weeks. Have you not noticed, Lucas, how I have run outside to use the stool night and day? And every emetic my physics can yield. Cramping poisons so strong they should certainly force a babe to be born. All to no avail. The papoose in my belly grows stronger every day. It will be neither shat out, nor vomited out, nor forced untimely between my legs."

She crouched beside the fire and began poking absently at the logs. Lucas had never seen her like this. She was a stranger to him, this creature who had abandoned all hope, who would not trouble to preserve even a tiny particle of her dignity. He could only stand and stare at her.

"Such a strong little papoose," Sally whispered. "Can't you see me carrying it up the Brede Wegh in a few months' time? Strapped to a board on my back the way the Indian women do? Won't that be a sight, Lucas?"

Sweet Jesus, what in God's name were they to do? If Sally really was pregnant, she might not live long enough to strap an Indian papoose to her back. The code still allowed stoning for a woman who conceived a child out of wedlock. Unlikely that the burgomasters would go that far. But she would be put in the stockade for a few days. And quite possibly tied to the ducking stool and plunged into the cistern near the Stadt Huys. Propriety demanded no less. Custom and usage, bloody Stuyvesant would tell Lucas. Never mind that he had saved both the governor's life and his wife's. As soon as Sally's belly swelled and they knew, they'd drag her off to—

On the other hand, they were nothing if not a clever pair. There was bound to be a way. And could be if he gave Stuyvesant a face-saving gesture, a way out . . . "Sal, listen to me. I've an idea."

She didn't even raise her head. Lucas went to where she was and grabbed her shoulders and pulled her to her feet. "Listen to me, girl! Are you listening?"

At last Sally lifted her gaze. "Yes."

"Good. Here's what we'll do. We'll say you have a tumor. We'll tell everyone it's a growth inside you. And after the bastard's born we'll find some way to deal with it. Give it back to the Indians, maybe. Or . . . We'll worry about that when we must. Meanwhile, you'll be safe. How can they fail to believe us? I'm a surgeon, after all. With an excellent reputation. The townspeople trust me to—"

"They'll make Van der Vries examine me," Sally said. Her tone had changed. She sounded more like her old self. And she was looking at him with some of the old affection. She even put her hand up to stroke his cheek. "My poor, dear brother. Do you not think I know that this is as bad for you as it is for me, that I have not considered all the possibilities? We can say I have a growth, but the good people of Nieuw Amsterdam will not be deprived so easily of a chance to enjoy a mighty scandal. Nor will they for one single moment entertain the notion that I did not invite this loathsome conception."

Sally shook free of her brother's grip. She began whirling and dipping and curtsying in steps Lucas would never have believed she knew, a caricature of the aristocratic ladies of London and Rotterdam. "Think of it, brother dear. Jacob Van der Vries of the red hair, and the red mustache, and the red beard, and the pea-sized brain will be called upon to decide what is truth."

Sally grabbed on to the chair Lucas used for tooth pulling, gripped the high back with both hands, and leaned toward him. Her face glowed red in the firelight. "Consider, Lucas. Even a fool like Van der Vries will know enough to listen for the heartbeat of the child and put his fingers inside me and feel the child. Even stupid, stupid, stupid Jacob Van der Vries will know that I am pregnant. So, short of murdering him in his sleep, there's no way to avoid the single time the drooling idiot will make a correct diagnosis."

Lucas walked to the fire and leaned his arms on the split log that served as a mantel. For a long time he said nothing. When at last he turned back to his sister she was still standing behind the chair. Watching him.

"There's one other possibility, Sal." He whispered the words because he knew she'd already thought them. Because by saying them aloud he was making them real. "I could try and—"

"—and cut the child out of me," she finished. "I've thought of that as well."

"We can do it this very night, Sal," Lucas said. "Have it over and done with before—"

"No, Lucas."

"How can you say no? What other choice remains? Sally, do you not know what the so-called respectable people of this settlement will do?"

"I know. They can stone me, but I don't think they'll go that far. They'll put me in the stockade for a few days, give me a few lashes, maybe a ducking. Then they will banish me. I will be put outside the wall and told to make my own way. Which, given the present state of affairs, is a death sentence more sure than stoning."

Lucas could not reply.

"Do you think I mistake the way it will proceed, Lucas? Have you another suggestion for how our little mummery will unfold to entertain the good folk of Nieuw Amsterdam?"

"Yes, Sal, I do. I will cut this abomination out of you, and in a few days you will be well again and no one will be the wiser." He was pushing everything on the table to the floor as he spoke, readying it for surgery. "Take all you've left of laudanum. Right now. Every drop, Sal. And give me all your stanching powder. I'll start heating the wine and—"

"No, Lucas."

"In God's name, Sally! Are you mad? Why do you resist the one chance to survive this horror?"

"Because the chances of surviving your surgery are so very, very small, my dearest Lucas. Come, don't look at me like that. You know it's true. Women do not survive such attempts to take the babe from them. They bleed to death, Lucas."

He looked at her for a moment but finally nodded. "Aye, Sal. That's true. But we must take the chance."

"I will not, Lucas. I know you can use force. I don't think you will."

"No, Sally, I won't. But I will never understand why—"

"Because I am the one who trusted and was proved wrong, Lucas. If as a result I am to be turned into the wilderness to die, then so be it. What I will not allow is that you spend the rest of your days blaming yourself for my death."

"Home! It's over, you can all go home!"

Lucas was at the mill that early April day when the soldier sent to bring the news of the treaty rode through Nieuw Amsterdam crying the words everyone wanted to hear. The war with the savages was over. The Indians had made peace.

The colonists could return to their homesteads. Now, in spring, while there was still time to plant.

Lucas ran from the redbrick mill clutching the small bag of corn, yet warm from the grinding, and began shouting Sally's name when he was fifty yards from the barber shop.

She had been some better in the weeks since she confessed her condition to him: having shared her burden, she seemed to find it easier to bear. Now, Lucas realized as he pelted toward Wall Street, they had been offered a way out.

"Sal! Sally! Where are you? Come to the door, I've news. Sally!"

The door of the shop opened. Sally was already wearing her shawl, and carrying a parcel wrapped in the piece of oilskin that served for transporting those things they wanted to keep safe and dry. Lucas smiled when he saw her. "I take it you've heard."

"Yes. The Indians have sworn peace. Everything we need is in here." Sally lifted her bundle. "I even gathered up all your surgical notes. I want to go home right now, Lucas. This very instant. Please, we must."

"No reason we can't, Sal. None at all."

The cabin was exactly as they'd left it that last terrible morning.

Every surface was thick with dust. Spiders had spun webs wherever they could find purchase. The blood that had been splashed on the floor and the walls had dried into dark brown splotches.

Sally stood in the doorway a moment, surveying the scene. Lucas watched her. After a few seconds she turned to him. "What happened in this place, Lucas? Why was I was allowed to live?"

"I don't know, Sal, though I've tried many times to understand."

Sally removed her shawl and hung it in its customary place on the nail beside the door. "Have you, Lucas? You've never said."

"I didn't like to remind you."

She laughed. "No fear of that. I carry a permanent souvenir."

"Not permanent. Only until October."

"And then?"

"Ah, Sal, I don't know. I thought we agreed we would address that when we had to."

A visible shudder passed over her. "So we did, Lucas. When we come to it. Meanwhile I must address this."

She turned in a circle as she spoke, looking at every corner of the cabin. "And address it I will. I've had enough of filth to last me three lifetimes. Fetch us a meal, Lucas. Go see if your traps in the stream are still there. Perhaps there's a beaver or a duck. Otherwise, bag us a squirrel. Give me an hour and you'll come home to something worth calling by the name."

She waited till he'd gone, then rolled up her sleeves and went to the rain barrel. It was full to overflowing. Over and over Sally plunged the leather bucket to its depth and hauled up gallons of fresh clean water and sluiced the walls and the floor of the cabin. The blood of her child's father ran out the door and soaked into the ground, a rust-colored libation to appease whatever gods had preserved her life and taken his.

At the end of May the child quickened.

The first time it kicked, Sally was working in her physic garden thinning a patch of yarrow. When she felt the movement within her she put down her trowel and clasped her hands over her belly. It was still only a small mound, easily concealed beneath her clothing. And inside that swelling, a life. Her child.

No. What was she thinking? Not a child: a bastard papoose. Born of a brutal attack by a savage.

The baby kicked a second time. Sally moaned. Tears filled her eyes and trickled down her sunken cheeks.

Lucas had never permitted her a husband. She had never let herself think of it exactly that way before, but deep in her heart she'd always known the truth. Her brother enjoyed having her around to tend his house and cook his meals and look after his garden and prepare his remedies. That's why he'd never managed to find enough money to provide her with a dowry. And because she owed Lucas so much, Sally had accepted that her fate was to be a spinster.

But now, as a result of events so terrible she could not bear to think about them, she was to have a child.

Lucas meant to take the babe away from her after it was born. Probably he meant to kill it. And she had allowed him to hint at his plan and never told him that she would not permit such an evil.

Oh, my baby, my sweet child. Forgive me. Forgive me for thinking such a thing with even a tiny corner of my mind. I have been out of my senses. But I am sane now. And I swear to Almighty God that I will see you come to no harm.

The weeks passed. It was June, then July. Unlike many pregnant women, Sally did not grow plump and rosy; only her belly was swollen. No one who saw her from a distance would guess at her condition. To be sure no one got close enough to guess, Sally stopped accompanying her brother to the barber shop and going to the hospital. Sometimes she fretted that staying away would draw the town's attention as surely as letting them see her.

"There's nothing to worry about," Lucas insisted. "I tell everyone the same thing. After the siege you have no physics left to dispense, and all your time is spent tending the garden and preparing new remedies. And to any as don't seem satisfied with that I say that besides you've a cough and sometimes a fever."

"And they seem to believe you?"

"Of course they believe me. Who is not ill after the winter we've had? Anyway, almost everyone's busy trying to rebuild, harvest a few crops and plant new ones. They haven't time to worry about me and you, only themselves."

Sally knew him too well. "Almost everyone. But not all. I'm right, aren't I, Lucas? Who isn't too busy to think about me?"

"Van der Vries. He's come to the shop three times in the last five days. He keeps asking me for physics. Laudanum, particularly. Today he specifically asked where you were."

"And what did you tell him?"

"The same as I told the others."

"I see. And have you told him that there's no laudanum left and there won't be more for two months?"

"I have. He seemed satisfied. Not happy, mind you, but ready to take my word. I promised we'd share our stores with him as soon as we had any."

"And why would we do that?"

"If you believe what I told him, because his patients feel pain the same as the few I have left. If you prefer the truth, because if I hadn't made the promise he'd never have finished going on about what he called our secret supply."

"We have no secret supply."

"I know that, Sal, and you know it. The fat physician doesn't."

"The fat, stupid physician. Don't forget 'stupid,' Lucas. It's the most noteworthy thing about him." There was a touch of the old Sally in that remark, a glimmer of the quick-witted companion she used to be. "Lucas, why does he come now for laudanum? He never—"

"Laudanum and other physics," Lucas corrected. "He says he had his own stores, brought with him from Holland. Now that they've run out, he needs to share ours. Says he'll pay, by the way, either guilders or wampum. As we like."

They'd finished eating. Sally stood up and carried their bowls to the rain barrel beside the door. "Tell him when we have physics we'll take wampum for them. Much better than guilders around here."

She squatted and began rubbing the bowls with a handful of grass to remove the last of the pigeon fat from the surface. "Tell him I'll prepare him some physics when the plants are full-grown, and we'll agree on a fair price then." Sally dipped her hand into the rain barrel and sprinkled the bowls with water, then dried them on her skirt.

"I'll tell him. Somehow I don't think it'll keep him from coming back."

"He hasn't enough to do," Sally said. "When you've a house inside the town and haven't been burned out like all the farmers in this benighted colony, you've time to waste bothering other folk." She set the bowls on the shelf above the fireplace, then remained with her back to her brother. "Lucas, I've been thinking . . . after the baby comes." She heard his sharply indrawn breath, but forced herself to continue, "We must do nothing evil, Lucas. Nothing we will spend our lives regretting."

"And what was done to you," Lucas said softly. "Was that not evil?"

"Yes, but that's not to say—"

"What the burgomasters will do to you if they find out you are with child, is that not evil?"

"Lucas, I know all that. But—"

"What will happen to me if you are found out, that I will be forced to forfeit all I possess in reparation for your wrongdoing, does that not qualify as evil?"

Sally turned to face him. She put her hands over her ears. "Stop! I know all these things, Lucas. I think of them night and day. But I cannot—" There was no reason to say more. Lucas had left the cabin.

IV

High summer. Fierce heat and no rain. The air was full of mosquitoes and flies and gnats and wasps. Lucas left for town by dawn. Sally was in the garden well before seven and by ten she was back in the house, hiding from the heat and the bugs until the sun went down. It was a routine that went on day after day without change.

Until the second Friday of July, when Sally was pulling weeds from among the barley plants.

"Good day to you, Juffrouw Sally."

She knew instantly who it was. She took a deep breath, and tried to compose herself. "And to you, Mijnheer Van der Vries." She did not stand up. She was almost seven months along. These days she had to kneel beside her plants, because squatting was no longer possible. And from any position, getting to her feet was an awkward and difficult chore.

The Dutchman's plump, stockinged legs came level with her eyes. Sally raised her face so she could see the rest of him. "If you're looking for Lucas, he left for town two hours past. I'm sure you'll find him there."

Van der Vries was breathing hard; drops of sweat trickled down the red mustache and hung from the pointed red beard. He took a handkerchief from his sleeve and began wiping his face. "I apologize, Mistress. The path is very narrow. I had to leave my wagon a distance back and walk."

"And you've missed Lucas. I am sorry for your trouble, mijnheer." She still hadn't figured out a way to stand up without calling attention to her belly. Dear God, make him leave.

"Actually, I was looking for you." The Dutchman put away his handkerchief. "Here, juffrouw, allow me to help you up." He extended his hand.

She had no choice but to take it. His flesh was moist, soft, the palm sticky with sweat. Sally hauled herself to her feet. She exerted every scrap of will to make the movement seem lithe and easy, but judging from the way he was looking at her, she hadn't succeeded.

Van der Vries spoke slowly, looking her up and down with every word. "Your brother tells me you have not been well. Indeed, that's partly why I called. Perhaps you are in need of my care?"

His eyes continued to study her. Sally could feel that some strands had come loose from her bun and were hanging beside her face. The dress she wore was one she'd made seven years before in Rotterdam, from a length of calico Lucas had given her as a present for her twenty-first birthday. Once pretty, it was now faded and worn. Shapeless as well. Sally had discarded the dress's sash. The garment hung loose from her neck, covering her swollen belly. But not entirely hiding it.

That's what Van der Vries seemed most interested in, the bulge where her waist had been. She spoke quickly, without thinking. Anything to get his eyes to leave her stomach and look at her face. "You are kind to be concerned for me, mijnheer. But I am not ill, only tired after our hard winter. You said my health was partly your reason for calling. What, then, is the other part?"

He was still holding her hand. "You are sure, juffrouw? You are entirely well?"

"Entirely." Sally took her hand from his. "If you came here to treat me, mijnheer, I thank you for your concern. But I'm in no need of your services."

"*Ja,* so I see." He was speaking very softly, looking into her eyes now. As if he dared her to flinch or look away. "I think I begin to understand that you and your brother have everything you need out here in the woods. Mostly, of course, you have each other."

She felt the fury rise like bile in her throat. "You are correct, mijnheer. Everything we need." She spoke the words with studied innocence, like a woman with no secrets. "Now, please. Tell me the second reason you have come."

"Ah, yes. The second reason. Apart from my concern for you, of course. That is precisely it, juffrouw. I treat so many in Nieuw Amsterdam that I have run through the physics I brought with me. I am in need of more. And while there are others in the colony who grow all the signature herbs, none compound the receipts with skill approaching yours. What is your English word for the art? 'Simpling,' is it not?"

"Simpling, yes. And I thank you for your compliment, but just now I have no physics to give you."

"Sell me, juffrouw. I told your brother I would pay, and I will. Guilders or wampum, as you choose."

"Yes, so he said. But I believe my brother also told you that our stores ran out during the winter and we've not yet replenished the supply."

"But you have been here now since April. You and your brother only. In this fastness where none come and trouble you." He was looking directly at her again. Much as she wanted to, Sally would not let herself be the first to look away.

It was Van der Vries who finally turned and pointed to the far field at the edge of the clearing. They stood among the barley and the peas. Nearby were the corn and the squash and the pumpkins. Beyond them the saladings, the green pot herbs that made up much of their diet and all of their medicine. And beyond the saladings, the field of flowers that held the attention of Jacob Van der Vries. Poppies in full bloom, red heads nodding.

"Those look well grown to me. Ready to pick. So you are making laudanum, are you not?"

"I am not. It is too early. First the petals must drop. That will occur in a few days, perhaps a week. Then I harvest the seed capsules. After which I do my simpling."

Van der Vries nodded. "So we must wait a little longer. A few more days perhaps."

"A few more weeks, maybe a month."

"Impossible. You just said those flowers would drop their petals in—"

"A week or less. Yes. But laudanum takes time to prepare. It can't be rushed."

"I see. Well, I am sure you and your brother will work as hard as you can to get some ready quickly." This time he was staring not into her eyes but at her belly. "All things considered, I'm sure you agree that would be wise."

"And all this time, while he was going on about the laudanum, the pair of you were just standing out there in the garden?" Lucas demanded incredulously. "In the hot sun?"

"It wasn't so long. Ten minutes, perhaps."

"But why didn't you take him into the cabin, give him some of your root beer or a draught from the ale barrel? For God's sake, Sally, if you could have distracted him, charmed him even, perhaps he—"

"Charming gentlemen is not among my talents, Lucas. As you well know. And distracting him by taking him inside and dosing him with beer of any sort was not possible."

"Why not, Sally? You're clever enough to—"

"And you are a fool. Look at me, Lucas. Watch me." They were in the big room—big only by comparison with the rest of the cabin. Sally took four paces to the south wall, then turned and strode six paces to the north. After that she stopped and waited for her brother to comment.

"So?" Lucas asked.

"Are you blind? I don't walk, Lucas. I waddle. If I were standing absolutely still, wearing a loose garment like this one, you might not be sure I am with child. See me walk, with my belly thrust out before me, and you would have no doubt."

"I see. You're right, of course. But you think that even though you didn't walk, Van der Vries guessed."

"I know he did."

"You can't know."

"Yes, I can. I do. And I know something else, Lucas." Sally turned away so he would not see how her face burned. "Jacob Van der Vries believes you fathered this child upon me."

A young black woman opened the door. Lucas had frequently seen her around the town. She was Van der Vries's Hetje, a girl some eighteen years old, born not in Africa but in the slave compound up in the woods north of the wall. Van der Vries had bought her soon after he arrived. Lucas pushed past her. "Where is your master? Is he here?"

"Yes, but—"

"Which door? This one?" Lucas threw open the door to his left. He saw a large room with chairs ranged around the walls. It was empty. "Where is he? Come, do you mean me to beat it out of you?"

"He be over there." The woman pointed to a door at the rear of the hall. "You wait here. I'll tell him you—"

"I'll tell him myself." Lucas shoved her aside and walked the length of the hallway. The door gave at his touch. The windows were open to the summer twilight and the room was full of the sweet smell of tobacco. Van der Vries was sitting in a chair beside the empty fireplace, puffing on a large, curved pipe, cradling the bowl in his pudgy hand. He looked up. "Lucas Turner the barber," he said softly. "Come in, man. I've been expecting you. Though perhaps not quite so soon."

"You went to see my sister."

"*Ja.* Today I saw her. This morning. I was concerned, since you said she was ill. Then, when I saw her, of course I realized . . ."

Lucas balled his hands into fists, but he kept them at his sides. "What did you realize? That's what I came here to ask about."

"*Ja.* I know. But first we must have a glass of something. What do you prefer, barber? Ale, perhaps? Yes, I think so. It's too hot for rum or geneva. Even for wine. Hetje! Come!"

The girl appeared in the open door, got her instructions, then left. The physician turned back to Lucas. "Now, please, sit. Do you smoke, barber? I can offer you a pipe if you did not bring your own."

"I prefer to stand. And I don't use tobacco."

"Ah, I see. Well, we all have our own pleasures, do we not? The things we enjoy, whatever the upright citizens might— Ah, here is Hetje with our ale."

The slave brought two pewter tankards filled to the brim. Lucas had run all the way from the cabin to Van der Vries's house on Pearl Street. He drank half the ale on the first go.

"You are thirsty, barber. It is a long way to town from that isolated cabin of yours. Hetje, bring us a jug of brew and leave it here." Then, after she had gone, "Isn't this cozy, Lucas Turner? Where but in the New World would a barber and a physician have a drink together as if both were gentlemen?"

Lucas drained the last of the ale, then put the empty tankard on a table. "I am thinking of beating you senseless, Jacob Van der Vries," he said quietly. "You might do well to curb your tongue while I consider the matter."

"Beating me? In God's name, why? And if you do, how will that help you?"

"You know why. Because of the foul things you have implied and—"

"The foul things, as you call them, are not my doing but yours, barber. And you can beat me as much as you like, but it will make your unmarried sister no less pregnant, no less a woman about to be branded as a fornicator and stoned for her crime."

Lucas lunged forward and grabbed the other man by the lapels. He yanked him out of the chair. The Dutchman was at least a head shorter than his attacker. Lucas looked down at the red hair, the small red beard, the flowing red mustache. "You are wrong. Do you understand me, you gross and stupid pig, you are wrong. Now, ask me why I am not afraid to come here like this and tell you so to your face, even though you are a man of power and influence in Nieuw Amsterdam and I am the barber. Go ahead, you bloody fool! Ask me!"

"Let me go. I will—"

"Ask! If you don't, I'll hurl you through that window." Lucas tightened his grip and raised Van der Vries higher. The fat legs dangled in the air. Lucas took a couple of strides toward the window. It faced a newly planted orchard. "I imagine your apple trees will survive, mijnheer. But you may break your neck. At the very least a few bones. And I assure you, I will have no interest in setting them."

Van der Vries was kicking furiously, but connecting with nothing. "Wait! Wait! What do you want me to ask? I don't understand what—"

"I want you to ask why it is that I am not afraid of you, worm that you are,

Jacob Van der Vries. Why I am not troubled by your filthy accusations. Now, go ahead, you idiot, ask!"

"*Ja*, very well. I am asking. Why? Why do you come here and—"

"Say it!" Lucas roared. "Filthy mind and filthy accusations. Say it!"

"Filthy mind and filthy . . . whatever you said."

Lucas dropped him. The Dutchman went down on his knees and stayed there. "Now I will tell you why," Lucas said softly. "But first I will drink."

Lucas turned back to the table. Hetje was standing beside it, holding the jug of ale her master had ordered, but she was looking at Lucas, not Van der Vries. She was thin, but tough and wiry. Hetje, Lucas knew, could have come to her master's aid. She could have used the heavy pewter jug as a weapon. Or picked up the poker beside the fireplace. She'd done neither. She approved of anything that put Jacob Van der Vries on the receiving end of a little discomfort.

Hetje and Lucas looked at each other. Lucas held out his tankard. Hetje filled it. "Thank you," he murmured. "Now, leave the rest of the ale and go."

Hetje hesitated. She looked toward her master. He was still kneeling on the floor, wiping his face and trying to catch his breath. She looked once more at Lucas. He understood.

"Get out," Lucas yelled. "Go or I'll kill the both of you!" The slave set the jug of ale on the table. Lucas winked at her. Hetje ran from the room, slamming the door shut behind her.

Lucas refilled his tankard and drank again. Finally he turned to Van der Vries. The Dutchman had stood up and moved away from the open window. He seemed to be edging toward the fireplace. The heavy brass poker gleamed in the half light.

"Now, to return to our discussion, mijnheer." Lucas spoke with studied calm. "The reason I am not afraid of your filthy mind or your filthy accusations is because I realize that you are unable to be happy without laudanum. And my sister and I are the best—nay, the only—source of supply in Nieuw Amsterdam. Quite possibly in all of Nieuw Netherland."

"I see," Van der Vries said softly.

"Indeed. I thought you might. I presume you see as well that it is not in your best interest to stir up trouble for Sally. Or for me. The making of first-quality laudanum takes a great deal of skill. My sister has no equal."

"*Ja*, I am sure she does not."

"Good, then there is nothing more for us to discuss. I'll be going."

Lucas started toward the door. "Barber," Van der Vries called. Lucas hesitated, then turned to face him. "Do not be in such a hurry, barber. Since you are here . . . I have a proposition for you."

"I'm not interested."

"Ach, not so quick to make up your mind."

Lucas's gut told him to walk out the door, that no good would come of talking longer to the Dutchman. His head told him to listen to what the man had to say. He stayed where he was.

"Very good," Van der Vries said softly. "Now, there is one thing I must ask you. Since you insist it is not you who fathered—" Lucas made a move toward the physician. Van der Vries held up his hand. "For God's sake, calm yourself. I believe you. But if not you, who?"

Lucas stared at him. He made no reply.

"Come, what harm can it do to tell me? We have agreed that everything that transpires will go no further because that is contrary to our best interests. Who, barber? Which one of our upstanding neighbors has been frolicking with your—"

"Hold your tongue or I'll rip it out. She was . . ." Lucas choked on the word. "She was raped."

"Ach . . . A terrible thing. The poor creature." Van der Vries reached for his pipe, began filling it. "Who did this? A trapper, perhaps?"

"A savage. Don't look so surprised, man. God knows she's not the first."

"No, of course not. Only . . . To be outraged by an Indian and still have her scalp . . . I thought they either took the women captive or killed them."

"We quarreled, and she went back to our cabin. I followed and got there in time to kill the savage." He hadn't told it that way to make himself look like a hero. His version of the story was easier to believe.

"How fortunate," Van der Vries said softly.

"Yes. Now, why did you want to know? What difference does it make?"

The Dutchman took a couple of long puffs on his pipe. Lucas could smell the smoke, but he couldn't see it. The room was growing dark. "Because," Van der Vries said at last, "I am proposing to marry the juffrouw. So the father of her bastard is of some interest to me."

"Marry! You're insane. Sally would never accept you."

"It is not necessary that she accept me, barber. Only that you do. You are truly her brother, are you not? Her sole guardian."

"I am." Even those two words were difficult for Lucas. His mouth had suddenly gone dry and his tongue felt thick.

"Good. Then we need discuss only what you and I wish to do in this matter. The juffrouw will surely obey the brother who is her lawful guardian."

"No. She won't. Not when—"

"Stop talking like a child, barber. The woman is unmarried, and she is pregnant by, she claims, a savage who attacked her. Under the circumstances, do you not think the burgomasters might conclude that you are lying to protect her, and that she was the Indian's willing companion?"

"It doesn't matter what they might think." Lucas was coming to himself again.

"Or what Sally might or might not want. I won't permit you to marry my sister. Spoiled goods she may be, but she's still worth ten of you, Van der Vries. And as you say, I am her sole guardian. Good night to you, mijnheer." Lucas turned to go.

"Barber. Lucas. One moment more. Consider this. I might be tempted to report the facts to the authorities. I admit the juffrouw Sally's proficiency in her art sways me, but after all, I am a physician, a man of standing. So you can see . . . And there is one other thing for you to take into account."

Lucas did not move. "What other thing?"

"If you will give me your sister in marriage, I am prepared to pay you forty guilders."

Lucas's hand was still on the door, but he didn't push it open. "Why?" His voice was a harsh whisper. "Why do you want her? How can she possibly be worth such a sum to you?"

"Under the circumstances, dear future brother-in-law, I do not think you should concern yourself with such questions. But if you must know, I am extremely fond of the juffrouw. From the first moment I saw her."

"Fond."

"*Ja*, fond. Forty guilders. It is a great deal of money. The measure of my feelings."

For long seconds Lucas did not turn around. When he finally did, more seconds went by without his saying a word. The two men stared at each other.

Finally Lucas spoke. "Sixty guilders, not forty," he said. "Make it sixty guilders, and you have a bargain."

V

Dear God, what would she say to him? What could he say to her? That it was the only solution. That otherwise Van der Vries was going to turn them over to the authorities. That if she didn't marry the Dutchman she was as good as dead, Lucas was a bankrupt, and both their lives were finished. This way both had a chance.

All those things. More things. He would think of more convincing arguments. But not now. Now he had to find Ankel Jannssen.

It wasn't yet nine of the clock. There was still a faint light in the sky, and when it was gone the watchman would make his rounds and call the curfew. But no one even pretended to enforce that law down by the docks.

Lucas heard the revelry from the Wooden Horse halfway down the street. When he pushed open the tavern door, the noise was deafening and the smoke blinded him. Just like the last time.

Lucas blinked a few times, looked toward the table where Jannssen had been sitting when they met before. He recognized no one.

"Barber!" someone called. "Over here. I'll buy you a drink, man. Rum or geneva?"

Lucas turned. A trapper was shoving his way through the crowd, waving his tankard at Lucas. He'd deloused the man a few days previously. "Haven't felt this good in years," the trapper shouted over the din. "First time I can remember not itching. Name your pleasure, barber."

"Thanks, but I'm not come to drink. I'm looking for Ankel Jannssen, the butcher. We've business. Do you know the man?"

"Aye. But I haven't seen him tonight." The trapper turned to some men standing nearby. "Jannssen the butcher, who's seen him?"

Someone said that Jannssen had been in earlier, but he'd left. And no one could suggest any other tavern he might be drinking in. "Probably went home to that fat and sassy wife of his," a voice shouted. "If I had something like that waiting for me, I wouldn't waste my time drinking with the sort you find here."

Lucas escaped to the street.

It was full dark now. The waves slapped rhythmically against the pilings of the wharf. The clouds parted for a moment and Lucas saw three brigs riding at anchor, their tightly furled sails like white fingers pointing to the sky. He put his hand over the pouch hanging from his belt. Sixty guilders. All he had to do was find Ankel Jannssen, give him the money, and the butcher would sail away in one of those ships. Sweet Jesus, what was he waiting for?

Lucas broke into a run. Apparently the watchman had already come by. The streets were empty, the houses mostly dark. Lucas made straight for Hall Place.

The butcher shop was tightly shuttered. Lucas stepped into the road and craned his head, searching for a crack of light from the windows above. Nothing. He studied the houses across the way. Every door was closed and every window dark, but it wasn't yet ten of the clock; there might easily be eyes watching him from behind some of those closed shutters.

After he gave Jannssen the money, after the man went away—what were he and Marit going to do then?

Forget it. Put it away. The problem was to get to Jannssen, to make sure he was going to keep his word. Thirty guilders only, at first. That will have to be the arrangement. The second thirty he gets when—

"Lucas. Thanks be to God."

The words were a soft whisper on the hot and humid night air. Lucas couldn't tell where they'd come from, only that Marit had spoken them. He spun around to face the shop. The clouds completely covered the moon now. Lucas tipped his head back, straining to see her in one of the windows.

"Not up there, Lucas. Over here. Look."

She was in the alley beside the building, close to the wall, a black-on-black smudge in the night. Lucas went toward her. When he got close he saw that despite the heat Marit had wrapped herself entirely in her dark gray cloak and pulled the hood forward over her hair and face. "Come." Her whisper was hoarse and urgent. "Stay by the wall and follow me."

She led him along the alley, then around a corner to the rear of the shop. Lucas had no idea where she was taking him, or to what end. "Marit, what are we doing here? Where's—"

"Ssh. Later. Come."

One moment Lucas was squinting at her shrouded form, struggling to see her in the darkness, the next she was gone. He looked around, panicking at the thought that he'd lost her.

"Lucas, look down. By your feet. There's a door." Lucas crouched. He had the impression she was holding open some sort of overhead hatch. "Sit on the ground and slide in feet first," she whispered. "Quickly."

He sat down, pushed his long legs through the opening and slid forward on his back. The drop was only a few feet; then he was standing on something firm, but cushioned. Sawdust, he realized. They were in the storeroom.

The darkness was total. He heard her closing and bolting the half-door half-window by which they'd entered. Then he felt her turn to him. He was at once conscious of the exquisite scent of her, the warmth of her flesh. He reached for her. Marit put up her hands on his chest and held him away. "Wait, Lucas, first I must tell you—"

"I cannot wait." The words came from somewhere deep inside him, from the place where all these endless weeks he had buried the pain of his loss. "But you're right, for now we must. Where's Ankel? I have to see him, Marit. He made me a prop—"

"I prayed, Lucas. Since maybe two hours I have been walking around this place and praying. Then I looked out the window and there you were and I knew God had sent you to me."

She was no longer whispering. So Jannssen must be unconscious with drink. Damn the man to hell, the one time Lucas wanted him sober and awake he . . . The intoxicating scent of Marit surrounded him. He could not bear not to touch her. This time when Lucas reached for her she allowed him to take her in his arms. Their mouths met. He drank in her honeyed sweetness. "Marit . . . Sweet Jesus, how I've longed for you. I've been mad with missing you."

He began fumbling with his breeches. She put her hand over his. "Wait, my darling. Please, I beg you, not now. But soon. I swear it." Once again she was gone.

Lucas waited. A few seconds went by. He heard the sound of a tinderbox opening, of a flint being struck. He saw the faint red glow when the wadding caught. Then the flare of a candle lit the walls of the storeroom. Marit turned to him. She still wore the all-enveloping cloak, but the hood had been thrown back. The candle flame illumined her face. It was streaked with blood. Her hair was crusted with it.

"Sweet Jesus! What has he done to you?"

"Tonight nothing. I am not hurt, Lucas."

"What do you mean you're not hurt? I can—"

"Come." She turned. The candle flame began moving away. Like a moth drawn forward, with no thought for anything except that tiny blaze, Lucas followed.

The stairs were steep and twisted, the passage narrow and cramped. The woman he hungered for was always a few steps ahead of him, just out of his reach.

They reached the upper hall. There were two doors, both closed. Marit went to one of them and stood in front of it.

"Lucas, do you love me?"

"Dear God, woman, do you not know the answer to that?"

"I believe I do," Marit said softly. She reached behind her and opened the door and thrust the candle into the room.

Ankel Jannssen lay half on and half off the bed. Staring at the ceiling. With his brains hanging out of his split skull. The meat cleaver that had killed him was buried in his head, and there was a pool of blood beside the bed, already dried by the heat of the summer night.

For some seconds neither Lucas nor Marit moved. He did not need to ask who had done this thing. At last he touched the pouch at his belt. Sixty guilders. "If only you had waited," he whispered.

"I could not." She turned to a table beside the door and set down the candle; then she turned back to him. "Make no mistake, Lucas. Much as I love you, and God knows I am crazed with loving you, that is not why I did this."

His hand was still on the pouch at his belt. Sixty guilders. He'd sold Sally to buy Marit, and the money had been put in his hands two hours before. Perhaps at the very moment when she had lifted the cleaver and split her husband's skull. "Only a little while longer," he whispered. "If you'd endured one more night, I could have saved you."

"Lucas, look at me."

He turned to face her. Marit raised her hands to the neck of her cloak and released the single button that held it closed. Then she dropped the coarse gray garment to the ground and stood naked before him.

Her pink-and-white flesh gleamed in the candlelight. Lucas looked at her full, dark-tipped breasts, the curve of her hips and her gently rounded belly, and despite the carnage a few feet away his breath caught with longing. He wanted her as much as ever. More. But he was paralyzed; held in place by the spell cast by a corpse.

Marit held up her hand. "Wait," she whispered. "Wait." She turned around.

The windows were tight shut and there was no breeze in the room. Only Marit's movements made the candle flicker. As soon as she was still again it burned bright and steady. The light shone on the long blond hair hanging in a single plait down her back. And on the welts that covered her from her shoulders to her ankles. Most were gnarled and knotted scars that had already healed. Many were red and raw and still crusted with blood.

Lucas gasped. Marit swung around to face him. "When he used his fists I could endure," she said. "When he began tying me to the rail in the storeroom and using a horsewhip, I could not."

"Sweet Jesus, Marit. Oh, God . . . Why didn't you . . ."

"Why didn't I what? I am—I was—his lawful wife. No one could stop him. Only if he beat me to death would he be in conflict with the law. Ankel never used the whip where it would show. He used only his fists on my face. He said he didn't want to spoil my beauty, only mark me enough so all would know I was his property."

She bent down and retrieved the cloak and wrapped herself in it, as if she needed protection even from him. "I did the only thing I could do, Lucas. Tonight, when Ankel came home from the tavern I knew from the way he looked at me what he was planning. He would sleep for a time. Then wake. Then he would take the whip to me. It had become his custom. So I brought the cleaver upstairs and waited until he slept. Then I killed him. And I prayed, Lucas. I begged God to help me. And you appeared. So I know God forgives me for what I have done. Only one question remains, Lucas. Do you?"

For answer he took her in his arms. He had her there. On the floor. With Ankel Jannssen's dead eyes watching them. While she was yet streaked with her husband's blood. It had never been better.

Lucas considered burning the body, but that wasn't practical. On a hot night such as this every fire was banked and the smell of roasting flesh close to midnight would announce the deed. The only way to rid themselves of Ankel Jannssen's corpse was to bury it, and for that they had to get him to the woods beyond the Voorstadt. In broad daylight, when all went about their travels. In packages small enough to rouse no suspicion.

Lucas removed his coat and hung it on a peg in the hall outside the bedroom. He began rolling up his sleeves. "Bring me the saw from downstairs," he said quietly. "The big one you use for disjointing a side of beef."

Sally heard the cart soon after dawn, while she was still sitting at the table. She had sat there since three in the morning. Since she had wakened and realized Lucas had not come home.

In the almost three years they'd lived in this place, this was the first time she'd heard the sound of wooden wheels trundling over the narrow path that led to the cabin.

She stood up, moving slowly, heavy with fatigue and heat and worry, and the weight of her belly. Sally put one hand over her stomach. "Do not fear, little one. Whatever happens, I will not let you come to any harm."

She walked to the door, opened it, and waited. The approaching vehicle grew louder, then stopped for a time. She heard men's voices complaining, but she could not make out the words. Apparently the wagon, or whatever it was, had become stuck.

She couldn't remember any time before now when Lucas had stayed away all night. Always, no matter what he did or where he went, at some point he returned and slept in his own bed.

She'd known no good would follow, known it as soon as he stormed out of the cabin like a man possessed, shouting to her to bolt the door and stay inside until he returned, then began running toward the town as if the demons of hell pursued him.

It was all her fault. She'd told her brother of Van der Vries's suspicions to warn him, so he'd be on his guard. If instead Lucas fought with the Dutchman, punished him for the terrible thing he seemed to believe, the law would come down on him with all its might.

Dear God, what was she going to do if he was in the stockade? The authorities might insist she couldn't stay in the cabin by herself, that she should live in the barber shop until Lucas was freed. In town. Where all the *huisvrouwen* could look at her and—

The wooden wheels were turning again. The sound grew louder, it was coming toward her. The morning was already stifling, but Sally reached for her shawl and wrapped herself in it. She thought of hiding, but it seemed pointless. She could not hide forever. Not even for the two months until her baby was born.

A small cart pulled by a single horse drove out of the woods and into the clearing. "Ah, juffrouw, I am pleased that you are already awake. Waiting for me, perhaps. Eagerly. As a bride should."

Van der Vries. And Minister Goos from the church. Whatever Lucas had done to the Dutchman, it had addled his brain. The physician was babbling like an idiot. Holding the shawl close around her, Sally stepped out of the cabin. "Where is my brother? Why are you both here?"

"Where else should a groom be but with his bride? And the minister is here to marry us, of course." Van der Vries climbed down from the wagon. "Are you quite ready? If you are, the ceremony will be performed right here. This very minute."

"You're mad. Reverend Goos, I am not a churchgoer, but I appeal to—"

"All in Nieuw Amsterdam are my flock, juffrouw. And since Jacob here has informed me of the circumstances, I am in total agreement that the wedding should take place at once. You will be forgiven your moment of folly by both God and man, my dear. You must have no doubt about that. Once the two of you are husband and wife, no one can judge the passion that caused you to sin."

"Passion? I assure you, sir, I have no passion for Jacob Van der Vries. I despise the man. I—"

"I am sure you feel that way now," the minister said softly. "But even if he did take advantage once, you cannot quarrel with the fact that Mijnheer Van der Vries is making full restitution. You are to be his wife, have his protection before the law. I do not think you have any choice in this matter, juffrouw." Goos nodded toward her belly. Apparently, since he'd been told what to expect, its small bulge was enough for him. "Under the circumstances," he added.

Sally turned to Van der Vries. "In God's name, what have you told him?"

"The truth. Having repented of my sin, I knew I must confess it."

"The truth . . . That you and I . . . Reverend Goos, he is lying. I swear it."

"My child, I have seen many women in your condition. There is no point in further prevarication."

"Where is Lucas? I must see my brother. He would never permit—"

"Calm yourself, juffrouw." Van der Vries reached inside his coat and brought out a piece of paper. "The matter has been dealt with. Perhaps you'd like to see this." He held the paper out to her, but spoke to the minister. "A remarkable woman, as I told you. She writes as well as reads. She even draws. Is that not so, my dear?"

Sally snatched the paper from him. "I, Lucas Turner, being the sole and lawful guardian of my sister, Sally Turner, do give my complete and unfettered agreement to the marriage . . ."

"Where did you get this?" Her voice was weak and her breath came in hoarse gasps. She thought she might faint. "Where is Lucas? Sweet heaven, what did you do to him to get him to—"

Van der Vries flicked at a piece of lint on his lapel. "I did nothing to him. I paid him sixty guilders. To be frank, I offered forty, but he refused and insisted on twenty more. Your brother values you highly, juffrouw." He looked at her and smiled. "As, indeed, do I. Now, it is growing hotter by the minute. Let us get on with it."

The minister looked a little confused, perhaps a little sad. Sally turned to him. "Reverend, I implore you. I do not wish to marry this man. Surely I cannot be forced to do so."

"Juffrouw, I ask you to answer me two questions. Truthfully. With God as your witness. Are you with child?"

Sally stared straight at him. "I am. But this—"

Goos held up his hand. "The second question. Is the signature on that document truly that of your brother and sole guardian, Lucas Turner?"

Despair came over her in waves, as if she had been thrown into the sea and knew that she must drown. She could not breathe. She was dying, and there was no one to help her.

"I am waiting for your answer, juffrouw. As God is your witness, is that the signature of your brother?"

"It is."

"Then, since your brother consents and Mijnheer Van der Vries wishes it, we will proceed at once with the ceremony."

Chapter Three

SHE'D BEEN HIS WIFE for nearly three days, but Van der Vries hadn't touched her. "I will not claim my marital rights until after you're rid of your . . . embarrassment," he told her. "I'm sure you will appreciate my consideration and act accordingly."

Sally wasn't sure what acting accordingly meant until he showed her the room at the front of the house. "Prepared especially for you, my dear. If there's anything you need that you do not have, tell me."

Crocks, vials, jugs, jars—a few even of rare and precious glass—dosing spoons and scales, a brazier for heating small quantities and a fireplace for large ones . . . there was nothing lacking in the manner of equipment. "I have need of plants to simple with." Sally had made no attempt to keep the scorn from her voice. "Perhaps you have forgotten that, mijnheer."

"No, mevrouw. I have not. Hetje, come."

The slave came in carrying a bushel basket filled to the brim with the seed capsules of poppies. "I wish you to make as much laudanum as you can, but be sure and save enough seed for further planting. I'm thinking of buying a field at the end of the road for the purpose. If that is not possible, we will uproot the orchard."

Laudanum. That's what this was all about. Her skill in making it and Jacob Van der Vries's lust for the strange and compelling dreams it induced. As long ago as Roman times herbalists such as Pliny had written of the dangers of sipping the juice of the poppy. *Sweet pleasure that leaves pain and destruction behind . . .* Laudanum had set them on this road to hell, but Sally saw no choice except to follow it.

At least until the child was born.

Sally knew Van der Vries's mind as she'd known Lucas's. Her husband, God help her, intended to kill the baby the moment it left her body. She knew, too, that she would defeat them both. Her child would live. The answer lay in the practice of her craft. The room at the front of the house on Pearl Street would be her refuge.

Lucas tried three times to see her. He picked his moments, watching until he saw Van der Vries leave the house, but twice his knock went unanswered. He was sure Sally was inside and that she knew it was him, but short of breaking in there was nothing he could do. The third time, Hetje came to the door.

"Hetje, thank God. I wish to speak with my sister. Tell her I'm here."

The slave shook her head. "Mevrouw tell me no, barber. Mevrouw say you can't come in."

"She's got to see me, Hetje. I have to explain."

"Mevrouw told me to tell you she's the physician's wife now. Doesn't matter to her what a barber thinks about anything. Mevrouw say every barber in Nieuw Amsterdam can drop dead this very minute and it means nothing to her."

"Indeed. Well, you can tell her the message is clear. How is she, Hetje?"

"Mevrouw be a little tired, barber. She got the ague."

"So that's the story Van der Vries is putting about, is it? She has the ague."

"Mevrouw be well soon. See everybody then." Hetje spoke the words as if by rote.

Lucas leaned toward the black girl. "Hetje, you and I, I believe we understand each other. We both know that sometimes you have to do things you hate. Tell my sister for me this was one of those times. Say I'm sorry. That I'll do anything I can to make amends. Swear you'll tell her."

Hetje nodded. "I be—"

"Hetje! Shut the door and come inside."

Sally's voice. She was probably sitting on the stairs, listening to every word. Lucas tried to push past the slave, but she was ready for him, stiffened against his assault. "Mevrouw say you can't come in, barber. She say I'm not to let you in."

Although Hetje was strong, Lucas could easily have overpowered her. But he saw no point. Not until Sally's attitude softened. After she was rid of the savage's child. "You're sure she's all right? That sod's not abusing her in any way? If he ever does, Hetje, you must tell me immed—"

"Mevrouw a little tired from the ague." Hetje was staring past him, looking at some point in the air over his left shoulder.

Lucas turned to go. He was halfway down the path when he turned back. The black girl was still standing in the door, but this time she was looking directly at him. "Hetje, the poppies that grew on my land, near my cabin . . . After the petals dropped, the seed capsules were all harvested in the middle of the night. That was a few days after my sister married your master. You wouldn't know anything about that, would you?"

"Mevrouw be a little tired from the ague."

"Very well," Lucas said softly. "Tell her what I said. Tell her I'm sorry." He walked down the long path between the apple trees and let himself out Van der Vries's front gate and onto Pearl Street.

Hetje watched until the gate closed behind the barber, then turned to look for her mistress. Mevrouw Turner was no longer in the hall. The slave went to the simpling room. "The barber be gone, mevrouw. He told me to tell you he—"

"I know what he told you. I heard every word. And believed not one of them. Pass me that ladle."

The laudanum was almost ready. The poppy seeds had been steeping fifteen days with ripe apples and dried currants. The brew was semi-liquid and covered in froth. Sally dipped the ladle to the bottom of the crock and lifted a bit of the mixture to her nose. The smell was perfect, rich and heady, with the distinct odor of yeast. "It's ready for straining. You'll have to help me with this part. Carry the crock over there to that table. Hetje, where do you buy the doctor's meat?"

"At the shambles market on the Brede Wegh, mevrouw. I be going early in the morning. Get the very best. You want me to pour this stuff into that cloth?"

"Into the straining muslin, yes. Carefully, so you disturb the sediment as little as possible. From now on you are to buy meat in the afternoon. From the butcher on Hall Place, Hetje. And tell me everything you observe when you're there."

Sally had never before made such a quantity of laudanum at one time. When she finished decanting it she had four crockery jugs of the pale gold liquid. And one more jug made of glass, tightly corked, carefully wrapped, and hidden beneath a loose board in the floor of the simpling room. She was careful to put it there when she was sure none could see her, not even Hetje.

From the first day she'd arrived at this place as Jacob Van der Vries's lawful wife, she'd known that the young slave was prepared to be her ally. But if there was one thing the last few months had taught her, it was to trust no one. Not the Indians she'd thought were her friends. Not the minister who said he served Almighty God. Not the brother who had protected her all her life, until he sold her for sixty guilders. *But you, my darling child, can trust me. I will not fail you.*

Jacob Van der Vries had no reason to look for a hidden supply of laudanum. He looked instead at the jugs lined up on the counter in the simpling room he'd prepared for his new wife and trembled with delight. "Excellent, my dear. Excellent. I take it the quality is up to your standards?"

"I've made none better."

"Excellent," Van der Vries repeated softly. "Perhaps after the midday meal I will sample a bit. Just to be sure it is fit for my patients."

They ate early, at Van der Vries's insistence; it was just past two when Sally took her place opposite him at the table. The meal was silent. Sally had initiated no conversation with Jacob Van der Vries since the moment the minister pronounced them man and wife. When he spoke, she answered; otherwise she kept her lips clamped shut. Mostly, he was silent, too, except to inquire after the laudanum. Now that it was made neither had anything to say to the other.

Hetje brought the food and set the dishes in front of them. They ate.

Sally took only as much as she needed to keep the baby healthy and strong, and gagged even on that. She had to force each mouthful past the lump of rage and misery that lodged somewhere between her heart and her throat. Normally Van der Vries was a hearty eater. Today he had a few mouthfuls of venison and pumpkin and beans, then jumped to his feet. "I have eaten more than enough. I believe it is a good moment to test your laudanum, wife. Bring me some."

"A spoonful?" She made herself sound chastened and compliant. "In some hot water perhaps?"

"Two spoonfuls." Van der Vries smiled. "And I require no water. A fair test."

She went to the simpling room and came back with a small tin cup containing the viscous yellow liquid. He grabbed it from her and gulped it down. Ten minutes later he was sitting in his study, puffing dreamily on his pipe, staring into the empty fireplace and smiling a vacant, happy smile.

Sally stood in the door and watched him for a bit, keeping her hands clasped over her belly all the while. Finally she turned away.

She went to the kitchen. It was small, dominated by the fireplace and the bake oven built into the wall beside it. Hetje was there, cleaning up after the meal. Sally sat down on the stool beside the table in the middle of the room. "The venison you served for dinner was excellent, Hetje. Did you get it at the butcher shop in Hall Place as I told you to?"

"Yes, mevrouw. I always be doing everything you and the master tell me to."

"I think not," Sally said softly. "Only when it suits you."

"Hetje be a good slave." The girl set to wiping the table with long sweeps of her strong arms. "Mijnheer and mevrouw never have no cause to beat Hetje."

"I will never beat you," Sally said quietly. "You have my sworn oath on it. And I will do everything I can to see that"—she could not bring herself to say "my husband"—"that he doesn't beat you either. In return, Hetje, will you help me?"

"Hetje be a good slave. Hetje do everything mevrouw tells—"

"Enough, Hetje. I am in this place because I have no choice. Exactly as you are.

And I am going to have a child." Hetje stopped cleaning the table. She carried the crumbs to the wooden barrel in the corner and disposed of them. Finally she turned around. "What you be wanting me to do, mevrouw?"

"Tell me what you discovered at the butcher shop."

"There be a lot of talk in that place, mevrouw."

"What kind of talk? Is my brother—"

"I hear nothing about the barber. It be the butcher they talk about. He went away last month and no one seen him since. His poor wife be doing everything by herself. And her eyes be all red from weeping."

"Weeping? Marit Graumann? Over Ankel Jannssen? I don't believe it. Everyone knows that pig was a drunk who treated her abominably."

"I don't know nothing about that, mevrouw. But her eyes be half closed with crying. That's plain enough. And she look ill."

"And no one truly knows where her husband has gone?"

"That's what I be hearing in the town, mevrouw. No one knows. Two of the burgomasters and the sheriff search the whole house up and down and find nothing. They say the butcher's clothes be gone as well. And that he be saying for years he be going to sail away on a rum ship. Going to the islands, maybe."

"And my brother, the barber? What do they say of him?"

"Nothing, mevrouw. I don't be hearing nothing about the barber."

Sally drew invisible lines on the table with one finger. She didn't look at the other woman. "Shall I tell you something, Hetje? A secret? I think I shall. My brother, Lucas, and the butcher's wife are lovers. They have been lovers for well over a year. I thought it for a time, but I wasn't sure. Then one day, before the siege, I followed Lucas to a secret place in the woods up near the Collect Pond, Hetje. I saw the things they did to each other, my brother and the butcher's wife. You would not believe them."

Sally stopped speaking. Hetje was staring at Sally with her great black eyes and it was as if she could see into her soul. "You be poisoning your heart with what you watched," she whispered. "You watch another couple loving and it poisons—"

A loud and insistent pounding cut off Hetje's words. The two women rushed to the hall. "It must be him," Sally said breathlessly. "The laudanum's made him mad."

"Not the master," Hetje said. "Somebody be beating on the front door."

"Dear God, maybe it's a patient. He's in no condition . . . Answer it, Hetje. Tell whoever it is the physician is not here. Say he won't return until this evening." Sally stepped back into the shadows near the kitchen. "Very well, now, Hetje. Open the door."

A man stood on the stoop, back lit by the late afternoon sun. Sally had to squint to see him, but she could hear him plain enough. "English warships!" he shouted. "Four of them. Just sailed into the harbor. Tell your master. And stay inside with your doors well bolted."

Colonel Richard Nicolls demanded the town in the name of Charles II, King of England. Stuyvesant presented him with a letter reviewing the Dutch claim to the territory. Nicolls refused to read it. "You may write what you wish, sir. If the town is not surrendered in two days' time it will be shelled."

The fort was crumbling. After the latest Indian war, there were fewer than sixty soldiers; no replacements had come from Holland. There was a reasonable amount of ammunition for the soldiers' muskets, but almost none for the town's cannon. The English terms were generous. The residents of the town could retain their property and worship as they chose. The governor hesitated, tormented by his fierce loyalty to the Dutch West India Company. The colonists had no such scruples. They demanded capitulation.

There were well over two thousand people in Nieuw Netherland. Not even Peter Stuyvesant could stand against the will of so many. He signed the terms of surrender on the eighth day of September, 1664, then retired to his extensive *bouwerie* beyond the Voorstadt, north of the wall. Nearly everyone else stayed where they were and went on with their lives, the only differences being that now they were ruled by the brother of the English king, James, Duke of York; Fort Orange had become Albany; and Nieuw Amsterdam was New York. And being English was suddenly an advantage. Of sorts. Under some circumstances.

"Been living with the Dutch for some time, have you, barber?"

"Three and a half years here in the colony. Since June of 1661. Before that I was in Rotterdam."

"I see. Get on with them, do you? Speak the language?"

"Well enough."

The Englishman turned a few more of the papers on his desk. The two men were in the former Stadt Huys. It was now called the City Hall, but the window at the far end of the room still looked out toward Hall Place. Not close enough for Lucas to see anything, but he kept gazing over the other man's shoulder nonetheless, in the direction of Marit's shop.

"They tell me you're a surgeon as well as a barber." Witherspoon, the man asking the questions, wore the latest fashion—a powdered wig and a pale blue satin waistcoat and dark blue velvet breeches. Called himself secretary to Nicolls, who was now the governor of New York. "I hear you're an expert stone cutter. And that you are, as well, adept at setting broken bones and cutting away tumors."

"I am well trained in my craft, Mr. Witherspoon. And you seem to know a good deal about us for a man who's been here less than a week."

"The value of taking a census, Mr. Turner. One hears so much."

"Yes, I suppose that's so. Now, if that is all, I'll—"

"Of course, mustn't keep you. Just one last thing. Did you learn your trade in Rotterdam? Among the Dutch?"

"No, sir. In London. With the English Barbers' Company." There was no doubt in Lucas's mind that Witherspoon already knew as much. The Company published lists of its members every year, had been doing so for nearly a century. Men who became secretaries to colonial governors were the sort who made themselves familiar with such lists.

Witherspoon smiled. "Rare in these modern times, isn't it, to be both a barber and a surgeon? I mean, if one is apprenticed to the English Company?"

"Extremely rare."

"Then New York is indeed fortunate," Witherspoon said softly. "One barber who is also a surgeon, and a physician as well. Who, as luck would have it, is married to the barber's sister. That's correct, isn't it?"

"It is."

"And you, sir—as yet, you are unmarried?"

"As yet."

"I see." Witherspoon put down his pen. "Very well, you may leave." Lucas turned to go. "There's just one other thing, Mr. Turner. Since you're an Englishman by blood and birth . . . In some ways Governor Nicolls finds this a strange place. One would expect the Dutch church to hold sway, but it appears there are, as well, Sabbatarians, Antisabbatarians, Singing Quakers, Ranting Quakers, Jews . . . It boggles a man's mind. I'm told there are even a few Papists."

"I believe that's true."

"But Stuyvesant . . . The word is that he's as stubborn a believer in his own religion as any you'll meet. Do you not, barber, find that a strange combination of circumstances?"

Lucas took a few steps toward the other man's desk and pointed at the window. "Out there you have a town founded with one intent: the earning of money. If whatever God you pray to assists you in that aim"—Lucas shrugged—"then the Dutch West India Company made you welcome. Believe what you like, and keep quiet about it. More important, get on with business."

"And you find that acceptable?"

"I find it less unacceptable than some other creeds. There are none starving in this place. And in general, the peace is kept."

Witherspoon smiled. "A fair measure. The general peace. You are intelligent, barber. And as I said, an Englishman. That is a fortunate combination. I think you will not mistake my meaning when I ask you to keep your eyes open. And to have a quiet word with me if any here in New York seem to be particularly unhappy about His Grace's rule."

"What I have been trying to explain, sir, is that the people of New Ams—New York are not much interested in who rules back in Europe. They will be content if you can keep the savages in their place, do not tax them unduly, and let them get on with their lives."

"Which, according to you, involve largely the creation of wealth."

"Yes."

"Fair enough. But if you should note anything else—anything you judge untoward—you will find Governor Nicolls to be most accommodating to his friends, Mr. Turner."

Lucas calculated rapidly. Seize the opportunity when it presents itself; the concept had served him well before. "There is one man you might wish to keep an eye on. Name's Jan Doncke. A few months back he was suggesting the Dutch colonists declare war on the English."

"Thank you. We shall be wary of Mr. Doncke."

Fair enough. It was something to keep them occupied until they found out Doncke was a doddering old fool and no one paid him any mind. "One other thing as well, Mr. Witherspoon. A question about English legal practice." The man behind the desk nodded, waiting.

"If a man deserts his wife," Lucas said softly, "disappears with no warning, and no provision made for her well-being, how long must it be before the woman is declared a widow and free to marry again? The Dutch say seven years. Is English law the same?"

Witherspoon made a tent of his fingers and peered at Lucas over the top of them. "An interesting question, Mr. Turner. Personally, not being schooled in the law, I have no idea what the answer might be back in London. Of course, Governor Nicolls is in complete charge in New York. Here the law is what he says it is."

The sweat poured off Sally. The contractions were still quite far apart, but when the sharpest of them came she gritted her teeth to keep back the screams. In between she swallowed her moans and clung to Hetje's hand. The slave never moved from her side. She wiped Sally's brow and murmured comfort. "You doing just fine, mevrouw. That baby going to be just fine."

"What about him?" She looked toward the hall.

"I keep telling you, mevrouw. Master not be back yet. He say he not be back until it be time for his dinner."

"That's two hours from now," Sally whispered. "Maybe the baby will be born before then."

"No," Hetje said. "You be just at the beginning, mevrouw. A first baby takes a while to get itself born. But you don't be worrying. Hetje be doing everything exactly like you said."

"You made the pie? The way I told you?"

The other woman chuckled. "I made a beautiful pie, mevrouw. With pigeon and apples and currants. And good and plenty of mevrouw's special sauce. The master going to enjoy his dinner today. Oh, yes."

Sally squeezed Hetje's hand. "And sleep for hours after it. Enough time to . . ." Sally couldn't speak the words. Her eyes filled with tears.

Hetje stroked her forehead with a damp cloth. "Don't worry, mevrouw. Everything going to be fine. This baby's going to be fine."

"Hetje, have you . . . have you ever had a child?"

"Three, mevrouw. I be eleven first time they put me with a man."

"They put you. Did you care for him, Hetje?"

"Never saw him except for that one week up in the slave compound. He did it to me, and then they took him off someplace and I never laid eyes on him again. Nine months after, I be having me a little girl."

"Where is she? What did—" Another contraction took Sally's breath away. She clung to Hetje's hand and bit her lips to keep back any sound.

"You got to breathe, mevrouw. Breathe deep each time the pain comes."

Sally gulped air. Twice, three times. The pain ebbed. "What about your little girl?" she asked. "Where is she, Hetje?"

"Never saw her after she was four," Hetje said. "That be when they sold her. I never knew where."

"Oh, God. Hetje, I'm so sorry."

"Had two little boys, too. One died of the cholera when he be two. The other one got sold when he be five."

"And each time . . . The fathers . . . You didn't . . ."

"It always be like the first time. They put me with men when they wanted me to have a baby. That's how it be in the compound, mevrouw. Men and women live separate. Everyone do their work by day, and by night—" Hetje broke off. The two women looked at each other. " 'Course, it might have been different with me," Hetje added. "I be born to free folk."

"Truly?"

The black woman nodded. "My mama and papa be having a little farm up in the woods. In them swamplands around Minetta Brook. Governor before this one, Kieft, he wanted folks not be Indians to be living between the town and the trouble. Kieft gave my mama and papa a little ground to work and build a cabin on. Gave 'em papers, too. Said they could live free long as they gave the governor a fat pig once a year. And came into town to work whenever he needed them."

The slave wiped Sally's face with a cool cloth. "Thank you, Hetje. I don't understand. If your parents were free, why—"

"The papers don't say nothing about children, mevrouw. A man and a woman living free with old Governor Kieft's papers, their children got to go to the slave compound if that's where they be needed. That's what happened to me. I be needed. They said eleven was time enough. They said they needed more stock, so I couldn't just be let stay fallow."

Sally squeezed the black woman's hand. "I'm sorry for all your troubles, Hetje—" She gasped at the next contraction. "Hetje, what if my baby is—"

"You stop worrying yourself, mevrouw. Your baby going to be fine. Sure to be a woman with enough milk for your baby in the compound. They won't let your baby die. Babies in the slave compound be valuable. Worth a lot of money once they got a few years behind 'em. That be the important thing, mevrouw. You keep thinking on that. Your baby going to live."

At four A.M.—after Hetje tied a sheet to the head of the bed so her mistress could cling to it and scream only silently, after Sally had labored nearly seventeen hours—she pushed her child into the world.

"Be a little boy, mevrouw!" Hetje put the infant on his mother's stomach. "A beautiful little boy!"

Sally struggled to raise her head. "A boy . . . Is he all right, Hetje?"

"He be perfect, mevrouw." The child gave one sharp cry as she spoke.

Sally struggled to sit up. "Hetje, don't let him make any noise. He mustn't—"

"You quiet yourself, mevrouw. Everything be exactly how it should be. This baby be fine. Got everything he's supposed to have, and he can shout besides." Hetje was tying off the cord in two places as she spoke. "I be going to cut this thing now, but don't you worry. Ain't be hurting none." Hetje put her heavy shears between the two knots and snipped. "There, that be done. You didn't feel nothing, did you?"

"Nothing." Sally's voice was weak with exhaustion. She put her hand on the infant's back. "A boy," she whispered. "My son. Hetje, where is the master? Maybe he heard the child cry. Run out to the hall and check."

"I be out to the hall ten times in the past hour, mevrouw. Mijnheer be sleeping before and he be sleeping now. I told you, he ate that whole pie all by hisself. Didn't leave even one crumb on the plate."

"Yes, yes, you told me." Sally laid her head back. She knew she wouldn't be able to fight the exhaustion much longer. Hetje reached for the child. "Got to take him now, mevrouw. Got to get him cleaned up and wrapped up."

"Hetje, is he . . ." She was too tired to see. Too frightened to trust her judgment. "What color is his skin, Hetje?"

"Nice dark little boy, mevrouw. Blackest hair you ever saw."

"Good," Sally whispered. "That's good. Dark. It will be better for him."

A few moments later Hetje placed the swaddled child in Sally's arms. Sally pressed him to her. She could feel his heartbeat against her heart. The way it had been for these nine months. "My sweet baby son," she whispered. "My darling boy." The baby was tightly wrapped. Only his face showed, red and wrinkled, and a fringe of straight black hair. Sally kissed his forehead. She hugged him close.

Hetje peered into the dark beyond the window. "Mevrouw, the watchman passed this way a little while past. He be coming again soon. Better if I go before it starts getting to be morning."

"Yes, I know. Only a few minutes more." She held the child close. Dear God, how could she let him be taken away?

Hetje went to the door of the bedroom and cracked it open. The only sound was that of the snores coming from the study. "He still be sleeping, mevrouw. This be the best time for Hetje to leave."

"Yes," Sally whispered. "The best time." She kissed her son once more. "Have your life, little one. I cannot raise you, but I swore I would not let them kill you and I have kept my promise." Then, without another word, weeping silent tears, she gave the boy to Hetje.

"Well now," Hetje whispered to the child she had hidden beneath her shawl, standing on Pearl Street as the muffled dark gathered itself to fight off the dawn. "Looks like you and me be all alone out here. Only thing has to happen now be for Hetje to decide where to take you."

There was no moon, only starlight. Hetje opened her shawl a bit and peeked at the face of the infant. The redness of birth was already starting to fade. "A little white boy," she whispered. "I be telling mevrouw you were a dark baby, because that be what she wants to hear. That be what we were counting on, the mistress and me. Since you had a white mama and a red papa, you were going to be a dark baby and I could slip you into the slave compound and no one ever be sure where you came from. But now . . . What Hetje be doing with this little boy nobody be wanting? You got any answers for me, little white baby?"

The child continued to sleep.

Lucas stared at the infant in Marit's arms. "He's *what*?"

"A foundling. Sent to us by God. I'm sure of it. I've never conceived, Lucas. I doubt if I—"

"Where did you get him? When? How are you feeding him?"

The baby cried. Marit leaned forward and kissed the tiny face. She held the child close and began rocking back and forth. "Hush," she whispered. "Your voice is too loud, Lucas. You are making him cry."

"Marit, I have to know what—"

"I opened the door and there he was. First thing this morning. It was barely dawn. And I am feeding him with milk from my neighbor's cow. Look, I'll show you." Marit dipped a corner of a piece of cloth into the bowl of milk on the table beside her. She put the cloth to the infant's lips. He sucked eagerly. "See, he is a smart boy, our Nicholas. He knows—"

"Our Ni— Marit, listen to me. We are to be married this afternoon, less than three months since . . . since you are without a husband. That is already a huge concession. Since no minister will perform the ceremony, a justice of the peace will preside. That is a second huge concession."

"You told me Governor Nicolls has made it legal anywhere in New York for a couple to be married by a justice of the peace."

"Yes, he has. That doesn't mean the people are going to accept it."

"The English are in charge now." She dipped the cloth in milk a second time and gave it to the baby. "The people have to accept what the English say."

"They have to act as if they accept it, but they don't—"

"Look, Lucas, at his eyes. Wide apart like yours. And his forehead is like yours. I think he looks like—"

"Marit, what are we going to do if people stop coming to me for treatment?"

"You are the only real surgeon in New York, the only one people trust."

"There will be many more now that we are an English colony. Marit, please, we cannot keep this child. It is madness."

Marit held the baby closer. When she looked up at Lucas her large blue eyes were shiny with tears. "Whatever Ankel did to me," she whispered, "whatever he threatened to do to me, I would not stop loving you. I risked everything because I love you so completely, Lucas. Now I love this child the same way. He is the only son I will ever have. How can you ask me to give him up?"

Lucas knelt beside her. "Only because it's so dangerous, my love. Because it will put us in so much peril."

Marit reached for his hand and placed it on the baby's chest. The infant was entirely swaddled in flannel; only his tiny face showed. Lucas could feel the small heart beating beneath the soft cloth. The child seemed strong, healthy. "Your son," Marit whispered. "Sent to you by God." Lucas knew what she wanted him to feel but he did not feel it. There was for him nothing but risk in this tiny creature Marit had so quickly come to love. "No," he whispered. "Not my son, Marit."

He stood up and walked to the window. It was nearly three. Most people had gone home for their dinner. Hall Place was deserted. "Have you considered whose child he might truly be?"

The Seeing Far Path

DECEMBER 1711–JUNE 1714

In the days before the coming of the Europeans, when each autumn the Canarsie departed the High Hills Island of Manhattan and crossed the Sun-Coming River to spend the winter on the long island of Metoaca, they left behind two women. That way the manetuac, the blood spirits of Manhattan, would not feel deserted.

The older of the staying-behind women was she who was most skilled in making medicine; the younger was her apprentice. At least once during each winter the older woman would lead the younger along what the Canarsie called the Seeing Far Path, up and down the steep and icy hills, and across the frozen streams and rivulets to the side of the island that faced the Sun-Going River. There, where the frigid wind never ceased to blow and you could see over the water to the land of the distant mountains, was the place of the holy stones the medicine women wore around their necks.

The stones were red.

Red was for healing.

Also for blood.

Blood was for life. And for the most sacred oaths.

Chapter Four

ON THE LAST NIGHT of the year of 1711 they came to Peter the Doctor with a red hen.

Kinsowa the Ibo had stolen the hen from his master's coop. It was a feat of great daring. The colonists prized their chickens, most knew exactly how many they had, and everyone knew the role the birds played in the making of West Indian magic. That was why the freed slaves, men like Peter the Doctor living on the Negro plots around Beekman's Swamp, were not allowed to keep chickens. Kinsowa the Ibo was a brave man.

They were all brave.

The word had passed in whispers. Among those who had been born in the old slave compound in the woods. To two of the Indians who'd been left behind as slaves when the rest of their clan were driven north. To a dozen Africans not long off the ships. To the very few who were what New Yorkers called seasoned slaves, blacks bought from the West Indies, though it was hard to talk rebellion to the seasoned slaves with their permanently welted backs and their dead eyes.

Altogether they were thirty-six converging on the cabin that night. All slaves except for Peter the Doctor, who had been given his freedom according to the terms of his master's will. Peter the Doctor had promised to help them. If they could bring him a hen.

The thing was possible only because they were in New York where there were no plantations, no overseers, no guards. In New York most slaves lived two or three together, under their master's roof or adjacent to it, and went freely about doing their master's business. A few could easily meet and talk. And those few could meet and talk and scheme with a few more. But it was also possible—easy—to be betrayed in New York. That's why they had come to Peter the Doctor.

He was not a West Indian, but his woman had been. She had drowned in the swamp, but people said her spirit had gone into Peter the Doctor and now he had her West Indian magic. He had the *obeah.*

Singly and in pairs they came, avoiding the light of the full moon, dangerous, yet so auspicious for their undertaking, staying in the shadows, saying nothing, barely breathing. Until they were all together. With free Peter the Doctor. With brave Kinsowa the Ibo who had stolen the red hen. With the old white man with the sick arm.

The white man was hidden by the brambles that surrounded the swamp. He watched the blacks assemble and he shook with fever and with fear. He stayed only because he was too terrified to run.

The light in the cabin came from a small fire in a pit in the middle of the single room. Peter the Doctor stood beside the fire holding the hen, the others around him in a circle of silent power. Peter raised the hen above his head. The bird clucked fiercely and tried to beat its wings and peck at Peter's hands. But when he spoke to the bird it became silent and docile in his grip. "*Coo-ha,*" Peter whispered. "*Jaba, jaba, jaba. Coo-ha.*"

Slowly, holding the hen high, Peter made a full revolution, showing the bird to everyone in the room. Showing everyone to the bird. He sang out the strange words that only he and the hen understood. "*Coo-ha! Tami! Tami! Tami!*"

One of the West Indians remembered being a small child on a sugar plantation where once someone had managed to find both a hen and the courage to perform the ancient ceremony. He remembered when the overseer discovered what was happening and put the man of courage into a pit with his hands chained behind him and his ankles chained together and let the dogs tear out his throat, then tried to whip the memory out of the rest of them. But now, all these years and all these whippings later, the child was a man who still remembered. "*Tami,*" he chanted softly, blending his voice with that of Peter the Doctor. "*Tami, tami, tami.*"

Deep in their bowels, wherever they were from, all the Africans understood. Kinsowa the Ibo and the two Fantis and the nine Ashantis who were among the latest to have come from the slave fortress off Guinea. Even the one woman in the group, an Ashanti lucky enough to have been sold with her man and taken with him to the home of a family in the town. This was a faraway place with its own spirits, who nonetheless served the one great spirit. This ceremony said the same thing as their ceremonies. The same with different words. "*Tami, tami, tami,*" they chanted with Peter and the West Indian man. "*Tami, tami, tami.*"

The Africans began to move their feet. Back and forth, back and forth. Holding themselves upright, only their feet shuffling on the cabin's dirt floor. *"Tami, tami, tami."* The words and movement drawing in the New York blacks, the ones cut off from their roots, turned into beasts of burden, made ignorant up there in the slave compound in the woods. The Ibo and the Ashantis and the Fantis made them all part of one thing. One freedom prayer. *"Tami, tami, tami."*

"Coo-ha!" Peter the Doctor sang out the ritual words. *"Jaba! Jaba! Jaba!"* Again he raised the hen toward the sky. *"Coo-ha!"* Then he turned to face the woman and thrust the hen toward her. *"Coo-ha!"*

The woman looked into Peter's eyes. She clasped her hands over her protruding belly, offering the child inside to the great spirit. *"Tami, tami, tami."* The child would be born free. Or it would die.

Peter moved closer to the woman. The others parted and gave them room. The hen made a sudden clucking sound. Peter held the bird tighter, stretched it toward the woman. She knew what he wanted, what the bird wanted. She parted her lips and opened her mouth wide. Her sharp white teeth gleamed in the firelight. Peter the Doctor put the head of the hen into the woman's open mouth. Without hesitation she snapped her jaws shut and bit through its neck.

The chicken blood ran down the woman's chin and she reached up and wiped it away with her two hands; then she spat the head of the bird into the fire and licked her palms clean.

The Doctor carried the red hen to each of them, and one after another they sipped its blood. "For strength," Peter said. "To bring good fortune. To bring you free." Then he held the carcass of the dead bird by its crossed legs and swung it three times above his head before flinging it into the fire.

The old man outside could watch no more. Even though he'd come out to the swamp because folks said you could cure an arm like his by dipping it in swamp water and he hadn't done that yet. Sick as he was, bad as the fever was, much as his arm ached and throbbed, he turned and began running back toward the town, propelled by terror.

In the cabin Peter the Doctor took a knife smeared with the entrails of the hen and cut the wrist of each of the thirty-six. They sucked one another's blood. "Now we cannot fail," Peter told them. "If any one of us betrays the others his spirit will never be free. After he dies, he will still be a slave."

The bellman discovered the old man at five in the morning on the first day of the new year of 1712. He lay on his back among the deserted stalls of Fishmongers' Alley, in a pool of mud and slush in which floated coagulated nuggets of vomit.

At six the fish stalls would open. Soon after the alley would be filled with the good people of New York. The four bellmen who patrolled the streets by night were hired to announce the weather, the hour, and to see that the waking residents were not bothered by sights that wouldn't please them. "Here, you. On your feet."

The man opened his eyes and blinked a couple of times. "Leave me be . . . not harming anyone."

"C'mon, old man, you know you can't stay here."

"Why not? Told you, not harm—"

"The decent folk will be abroad soon, that's why not. On your feet. Fetch a bucket of water from the well round the corner and clean up the mess you've made, then be on your way."

"Leave me be and I'll tell you what I saw. Out by Beekman's Swamp. They was—"

"I'm not interested in Beekman's Swamp. Just you, right here in Fishmongers' Alley. Now, will you move before or after you've tasted my fist?"

The bellman was young and strong, and he carried a heavy brass bell that would do for a weapon in a pinch. The old man staggered to his feet and managed a few steps before the dizziness and nausea overcame him again and he fell facedown in the same noxious puddle.

"Here! You can't do that. I told you—" The bellman turned the drunk over with his booted foot. Mud and vomit coated the man's stubble of gray beard and clung to his mouth and his nose.

The bellman leaned down. Something was wrong with the man's left hand; it looked as if he'd had some sort of accident. "Burning up with fever," he muttered. "And upchucking your rum-rotted guts. Well, you can't die here." He grabbed the man under the arms and began hauling him over the cobbles, away from the waterfront and toward the corner of Dock Street and Broad.

The old man regained consciousness for a moment as he was being dumped into the bellman's two-wheeled barrow. "Not the hospital," he whispered. "For the love of Jesus Christ, lad, for the souls of your own father and mother, not the hospital."

The hospital the Dutch had created from five tiny workshops down near the docks had been abandoned in 1700 when the old Dutch Stadt Huys and a number of surrounding buildings were judged unfit. The mayor of the time was charged with finding some new place to put the dying indigent. Meanwhile temporary arrangements were made: three beds in a portion of the attic of a seldom used warehouse well north of what used to be the Voorstadt, at the outer limits of what was, by royal decree, no longer New York Town but New York City, near the intersection of the Broad Way and the King's High Road to Boston. Now, twelve years after the decision to find something better, the makeshift hospital was still in use. But only by those who could not manage to avoid it.

The various churches—Anglican, Dutch Reformed, and Scots Presbyterian—all had charity boxes beside the doors, and all assigned wardens to visit every household and identify the deserving poor. When such people were ill the churches paid for them to be cared for in their homes like decent folk. The rest—a handful of incorrigible drunks and whores—died where they lived, hidden from view in the narrow streets and back alleys. Unless, like the old man, they had the bad luck to be picked up by one of the bellmen and carted off to the hospital.

He was the only patient that day, and he was all but incoherent with fever by the time Christopher Turner unlocked the attic door and found him. The first thing the young man did was throw open a window to the cold, gray damp of the New Year's morning. Then, holding a cloth over his nose, he went closer.

No matter how badly they stank—and this one made him gag—vagrants always interested Christopher. People who came to the barber shop on Hall Place could say no if he suggested a surgery they thought too drastic, and often they did. The paupers brought to the hospital were subject to his authority.

He laid a hand on the patient's shoulder. "What's wrong with you, old man? Where does it hurt?"

The old man opened his eyes. His breath came in wheezing gasps, and he struggled to sit up. "Listen, lad. You let me out . . . Tell you what I saw."

"Is it your belly? Are you in pain?"

"Tried to tell the bellman. . . . Wouldn't listen. . . . They was drinking chicken blood."

"How long have you been ill?"

The old man fell back, exhausted. "Out by Beekman's Swamp," he mumbled. "A chicken . . . And the moon was full."

"It was full as well right here in the town, my friend. And I trust a chicken or two could be found if we looked." The cot was covered by a sheet of rough burlap stained with the excretions of countless previous patients. Christopher saw fresh additions close to the patient's head. "Been vomiting, have you? When was the last time? Any blood?"

"That's it. They drank blood. Did the chicken dance. Saw it with my own eyes."

Without touching him Christopher could feel the scalding heat of the man's fever. Small wonder the old geezer was crazed. Christopher pressed the cloth tighter over his nose and mouth and leaned closer. He thumbed up one of the man's eyelids. The part that should have been white was sickly yellow, and the skin of the forehead felt dry and taut.

The man tried to sit up, and his good hand grabbed at Christopher's arm. He was too weak. "They drank the chicken's blood," he whispered, sinking back on the filthy cot. "Saw it. Didn't do nothin' else. Shouldn't be in this place only for that."

The bellman who'd brought the man in had covered him with a stiff horsehair blanket. Christopher pulled it back, looked for a moment, then sighed with satisfaction. The source of the man's fever and delirium was at last obvious.

The lower half of the left arm was liverish, swollen to three times normal size. The hand and the fingers were badly mangled. Christopher had seen such wounds many times before: the old man's hand was half eaten. One of the hazards of being a falling-down drunk was providing the city's rats with a meal.

Christopher ignored the foul smell, shoved up his sleeve the cloth he'd been holding over his nose, and used both hands to palpate the swollen arm. It was rock-hard and, if possible, hotter than the rest of the body.

The man began to whimper. "Chicken blood. Truth, I told you. Chicken blood."

Christopher bent closer. "Here, old fellow, look at me. Now, try to understand. You have two choices. Lose the arm or lose your life. Which is it to be?"

The old man was weeping. Big tears rolled down his filthy cheeks. "Not lying, lad. I swear it. Saw the chicken dance."

The entire arm had to come off. *In the Case of a Blackened Limb, the Amputation must be made at the unaffected Joint closest to the Torso. If none such Presents Itself, it is Already too late.* Such surgeries weren't easy at the best of times. Under the brutal conditions of the hospital, where Christopher worked entirely alone, the preparations took the better part of the morning.

He had his instruments with him, and he knew there was a coil of strong rope in the locked cupboard under the stairs. Six months before, when he had been put in charge of this makeshift facility—the job was worth eight pounds a year—he'd been given a bunch of keys. He found the one that opened the stair cupboard, hoisted the rope, and took it up to the attic. Next he tied the old man's torso and his legs to the cot, and made sure to tie the right arm firmly in place as well. The left, the one that was to come off, he bound to a sturdy board.

The authorities had done little to make this place suitable for medical care, but they had remembered to sink a few metal hooks in the wall. He was able to tie the board into position at a right angle to the body. Finally, despite how often the old man gagged and retched, Christopher managed to pour nearly an entire flask of rum down his throat.

His grandfather, Lucas Turner, had used laudanum, at least until Lucas's sister, Sally, married Jacob Van der Vries. That's when she had stopped speaking to Lucas and he couldn't get any more. According to his journals laudanum didn't make for painless surgery—*that is a Hope for Fools and Children*—but it was far more effective than liquor.

Christopher agreed. He often sent his patients to buy laudanum from the apothecary shop Great-aunt Sally had opened on Pearl Street. Christopher would have liked to lay in a supply of the stuff for himself, but he could not go to the shop. For reasons having nothing to do with surgery, it wasn't prudent for him to go anywhere near Pearl Street. So, since he had no wife to simple for him, he bought his stanching powder and other ordinary remedies from the housewives of the town. Few of them, however, knew how to make good laudanum. For this old man rum was the best Christopher could do.

When the flask was empty he pulled a chair up to the side of the bed, hiked up his sleeves, opened the leather case he'd inherited from his grandfather, and made a choice from among his knives.

His amputation technique was Lucas's, learned from the journals, like almost everything else he knew of surgery. *I recommend to Begin with a Shallow Incision made through the* Membrana Adiposa *with the small Triangular Scalpel.* Christopher leaned forward and considered for a moment, seeing the procedure in his mind. Finally he lifted the hand holding the scalpel and with no hesitation drew the blade in a swiftly descending curve from the upper part of the shoulder across the pectoral muscle and down to the armpit.

Apparently the rum hadn't helped much. The screams began instantly. "Stop! For the love of Jesus, stop!"

The old man's underarm flesh was wrinkled and dry, each crease filled with a lifetime's accumulated grime. It flaked away in the knife's wake. *Then, saving as much Skin as possible, turn the Knife with its Edge upwards and Divide part of the Deltoid, which may be done without Danger of Wounding the Great Vessels, which will be Exposed by these openings.*

"Jesus help me! Stop!"

He'd found some rags in the cupboard with the rope. He used them to sop up the flow of blood, then tied off the artery and the vein, as Lucas recommended, with a strong ligature of sheep's stomach. Finally he reached for the broader, more spatulate scalpel and inserted the thin blade between the muscle and the skeleton and carefully—*with neither Undue Haste nor Wasteful Lingering*—began to scrape away the connective membrane and bare the bone.

The old man's shrieks were ear-piercing.

In less than a minute the muscles were a floppy formless mass, disconnected from the shoulder and easily pushed aside. The bone was exposed. Christopher stopped scraping.

His patient's screams became sobbing whispers. ". . . love of Jesus, stop. Telling the truth. Saw the chicken. Saw them drinking blood."

"Sure you did, old friend. I know you're telling the truth." Once more

Christopher used the rags to mop up the blood oozing into the wound from the vessels below the ligatures. "Listen to me, old man, no one's punishing you for anything. I'm trying to save your life." He reached for the saw. "I swear to you, it's for your own good."

For this he must stand. He did so, and began.

The patient arched and bucked, as much as the ropes allowed.

The soft cartilage parted. Christopher started on the bone. It was much harder work. He had to put his back into it. Ignore the old man's screams, though they filled his ears and echoed in his brain. Think only about the saw. Back and forth. Back and forth. Back and forth.

"Jeeeeesusssss . . ."

Down to the marrow now. A little easier, but only for a short time. Then the hard stuff again. He was dripping with sweat by the time the arm tied to the board dropped away and swung free from the hook in the wall.

The old man was silent.

He might well be dead.

That was common enough with any surgery, more so in the case of amputation. Christopher was still struggling to catch his breath, and mopping his sweaty face when he bent his head to the man's chest. The heart was beating at a much accelerated rate, but it was thumping strongly. The old derelict had been lucky for once in his life. He'd fainted.

In his journals Lucas boasted of keeping count of the passing seconds while he operated. Christopher didn't know if his father had been able to do the same thing. After Chris's mother died—the boy was eleven—Nicholas bought a slave to act as housekeeper for his son, and became a ship's surgeon. He was lost at sea when Christopher was sixteen. But even when he'd been home Nicholas Turner had been a dark and forbidding man. A silent man. Christopher had never asked about the counting. All he knew was that he couldn't manage the technique. Performing the surgery and observing the anatomy took all his attention. He could estimate only that amputating the arm had taken him something under an hour. And he still wasn't finished.

He stitched the flap of skin over the empty shoulder socket, applied stanching powder, and bandaged the wound. Then he set three relaxed leeches to the man's chest and another two to his neck to suck out any poison that had crept up from the affected lower arm. Finally, though he'd missed his dinner and it was already growing dark, he sat and watched the man for at least another hour. Possibly two. There was a well nearby, but like most on Manhattan it gave only brackish, virtually undrinkable water. A bucket of ale kept in the back of the room yielded a more potable liquid. Before he left Christopher saw to it that his patient took a few sips. "There, you daft old bugger, you couldn't have had better care if you were a gentleman in a mahogany bed with damask hangings."

The King's High Way to Boston was well maintained, but narrow, like the old Indian path it followed. Completed thirty years earlier, it accommodated post riders carrying mail between New York and the New England colonies. The road went north as far as the small village of Harlem, then crossed to the mainland by way of the King's Bridge.

The widened section of the Broad Way (only the few old Dutch speakers who hadn't learned English still called it the Brede Wegh) ended where it joined the post riders' road. North of that point it was a path through the woods, with a rope railing. There was talk of grading and widening that section as well, but it wouldn't happen unless more people wanted to live so far from town, and up to now few did. Christopher made his way through a dense winter dark broken only by the distant glow from the windows of a few isolated farmhouses. Only the sound of his sturdy boots on the packed-dirt road broke the silence.

He crossed Washerwomen's Creek and, beyond that, Maiden Lane. He was approaching the cobbled streets of the proper town when he realized he hadn't soaked the bandages in wine. Hell, he'd had no wine, and the nearest tavern was still a few minutes' walk away. Besides, Lucas himself had not been entirely sure the practice was salutary. *Sometimes I think I cling to the use of Wine for reasons more of Superstition than of Science*, he'd written. *Perhaps, in the end, I am as suggestible as I believe my Patients to be.*

Nonetheless, Christopher was still fretting when he turned into Broad Street, a wide thoroughfare that ended in a stone-lined basin between West Dock and East Dock and the long wooden bridge that joined them. The houses of wealthy merchants—all redbrick and white pediments and perfect symmetry—faced one another across carefully laid cobbles. Such splendid houses made it difficult to remember that Broad Street was built over the infill of the old Dutch canal.

In its last days, when not even the tide was strong enough to carry away the quantities of garbage and slops tipped into it, the canal had become a festering sewer. Today it was the most fashionable street in the town. Elsewhere, every seventh house was obligated to hang a lantern from a pole and suspend it from an upstairs window as soon as it grew dark. Here on Broad Street a number of the wealthy residents had erected permanent standards by their front gates, each topped with a lantern, and every week a slave was appointed to tend to their lighting.

Progress, the mark of science. Wine be damned. He'd done well by the old souse.

The blood dripped slowly, drop by drop from the distended pig bladder into the thin glass tube that had been fitted with a hollow needle and inserted into an open vein in the old man's right arm.

It was forty-eight hours since the surgery and the man's fever hadn't broken. However uncertain blood transfer might be, Christopher told himself, it was this patient's final hope. Such thoughts answered the prick of doubt that said his own need to live up to Lucas's legacy played as much a part in the decision as the survival of the man in the bed.

His grandfather (Christopher never thought of Lucas as his adoptive grandfather, though he knew that to be the legal truth) had died at age fifty-six, peacefully, with Marit holding his hand. She went a year later. Christopher knew them only from the portraits painted toward the end of their lives by an itinerant artist—a phizmonger, as folk called them.

Marit was said to have been a beauty. In the portrait her hair was white, but her eyes had still been large and blue, and there was a smile in them. Lucas looked more stern. Though he'd died three years after sitting for his portrait, his hair and his beard were still entirely black. The pictures hung on either side of the front door on Hall Place, looking down at the spot where, until their marriage transformed the butcher shop into a barber shop, Marit stood behind the wooden counter and hacked apart the haunches of venison that fed old Nieuw Amsterdam.

Christopher was sure Lucas would have been fascinated by this practice of putting fresh blood into a human body. His grandfather's journals were proof of his concern with every conceivable surgical practice, though quite possibly, cut off from the medical literature that was available in Europe, Lucas had never heard of transfusion.

Christopher had heard. His education in surgery began with his grandfather's journals, but it was completed by the books Nicholas brought home after he went to sea. Long after others were in bed, Christopher Turner sat at the kitchen table, reading his father's books until the candle burned down to a guttering stub. No single thing had made a greater impression than the description of blood transfusion.

That was the real reason he'd accepted this thankless job as the hospital surgeon. Far more important than the stipend was the opportunity to have the sort of patients on whom he could try new things.

For the good of humanity, Christopher told himself. To further the interests of science.

He'd made four previous attempts at putting blood into a person. All had failed. Nonetheless, he'd come to the hospital that morning prepared to try again with the pig bladder, the glass pipette fitted with its hollow iron needle, the bandages, and the scalpels. And the blood.

He'd found the old man delirious, with a raging fever. He began the procedure immediately. It went well for the first twenty minutes; then the man's breathing started to come harder and louder. Now each respiration had a little wheeze in it.

Christopher began adjusting the neck of the pig bladder and looked anxiously at his patient. The man was ashen, and his eyes were open but staring unseeing at the ceiling. "Don't die, damn you. After all my hard labor, don't you dare die."

Behind him the door opened.

Christopher stiffened. Almost no one came here except himself, the half-dozen constables who acted as police by day, and the four bellmen who did the job at night. "Who is it? Who's there?"

"It's me. Jeremy. I thought I'd find you here."

"Damn your eyes, Jeremy. You frightened the bejesus out of me. I'm busy. What do you want?" Christopher spoke without turning around, preoccupied with the pig bladder. The blood poured down the tube so fast it was oozing between the needle and the old man's skin.

The problem seemed to be in the brass valve he'd had made at the smith's. It had a nozzle at either end and was divided by a movable partition made of lead and controlled by a thumb screw. Meant to regulate the flow of blood between the pig bladder and the glass tube, the partition was proving totally ineffective. Christopher turned the screw as far as it would go, but still the blood gushed forth. The old man was struggling to breathe. His skin had gone from pasty white to ghostly blue. "Bloody hell! Don't die, you daft old bugger. Don't you dare die."

"Sorry, Chris." Jeremy had moved in closer and was looking over Christopher's shoulder. "Looks to me as if this one's spent as much time with you as he cares to. And sweet Jesus, does he stink."

"The flow is too fast. If I can slow it down, he—"

"Good God, man, you never give up. What is it this time? More calf's blood?"

"No." The valve wouldn't close. The thumb screw was jammed. "Bloody smith. Can't do a damned simple thing like—"

"Squirrel and pigeon? That was the mix about three corpses back, wasn't it?"

"Four. This is neither. Dog."

"Dog!"

"Yes."

"Whose dog?"

"Does it matter?" Christopher gave up on the screw and began pinching the bladder, trying to decrease the rate of flow at the source. There was a chattering sound from the throat of the man on the bed.

"No," Jeremy said, "actually it doesn't matter. Your patient is no longer with us, Mr. Turner."

Christopher looked from the pig bladder to the man on the burlap-covered cot. Jeremy was right. Dead. Definitely. He shrugged. "Poor old bugger. But he didn't have a chance anyway. Though God knows, I did everything I could." He began dismantling his apparatus, being particularly careful of the valve. It was still usable, though he'd need to get the smith to make some changes. "What are you doing here, anyway? Why were you looking for me?"

"To take you to the Nag's Head. The new year is two days old. It's time we drank its health."

"I have no interest in going to the Nag's Head, and not much interest in the health of the new year. I'm a surgeon, remember. Illness makes my living."

"It's liable to make your jailing. At the very least, a trip to the whipping cage. I wonder how the town fathers would take to the idea of your experiments in their hospital. Or the clergy. They'll be denouncing you from every pulpit in New York if they get the chance, Chris. You'll be famous."

"'Infamous' is the word. Look, Jeremy, I know you don't approve of my experiments, but you wouldn't say any—"

"Don't be a jackass. Of course I wouldn't. I simply want you to take an interest in something besides your odd ideas about putting blood in people rather than taking it out. Come with me, Chris. You'll have a fine time once you do. You know you will."

Christopher shook his head. "No, I won't. Not today." He looked at his dead patient. "I don't think he ever realized I really was doing the best I could for him. Damn it, Jeremy, this should work. It does work. They were transfusing blood successfully in France nearly seventy-five years past."

"But they're not doing it now. Not in Paris or anywhere else."

"I can't say. Perhaps—"

"Perhaps nothing, Chris. It was a disaster. You told me so yourself."

"Not entirely. Of course there were a few deaths. Such as I've had. It's inevitable that any new technique—"

"It's not new. You just said as much. It's a failed technique, Christopher. Come on, man. Let's get out of this charnel house. There's a good time waiting to be had."

"Hang on a minute." Christopher leaned over his patient, lifted the arm that had not been amputated, and began palpating the vein in the crook of the elbow.

"He's dead, Chris."

"I know."

"Then why—"

"Something's just occurred to me. Jeremy, after a man's dead, until the body stiffens, his blood is still liquid in his veins, is it not?"

"I presume it must be. Where could it go?"

"Nowhere. So one could collect it—draw it out exactly as I've drawn the blood of the various creatures I've been using until now."

"Sweet Jesus. You're not serious, Christopher. You can't be thinking of using human blood?"

"I am serious. And it's been done before. Pope Innocent I think it was. Somewhere around fourteen-ninety-something. They put the blood of four little boys into—"

"Of course! What black arts wouldn't they practice in Rome? We're Protestants. We're supposed to know better."

"I think Denis used human blood at the Sorbonne as well. When he successfully transfused three people. And why not? Give me one reason why it wouldn't work."

"Because it's unnatural. It's like . . . like cannibalism. Some savage eating the heart of his enemy. What do you propose, Chris? Putting the blood of a Quaker or an Anabaptist into the veins of an Anglican bishop? Good God, man, don't you see how contrary to nature that is?"

"Calm down." Christopher bent forward and closed the old man's eyes. "It was just a thought. It's difficult enough getting animal blood. I've no idea where I'd get the human variety. Very well, let's go before the rest of your rowdy friends have drunk the Nag's Head dry."

When he stood Chris almost touched the attic ceiling. At twenty-two years of age he was just under six feet. Easily the tallest man in New York. That and his straight, coal-dark hair had earned him a nickname: the Black Giant. Mothers were known to point him out on the street when their children misbehaved. But when he stretched out one long arm to reclaim the tricorn hanging on a nail in the wall, clamped the hat on his head, and draped the other arm around his friend's shoulders, Christopher Turner looked like any other young man concerned with having a good time. He even smiled. "Listen, I was thinking. Perhaps we might go by way of Pearl Street."

"I might. You might not. Red Bess will spot you."

"Yes, probably. I meant you could go that way. Put your head into the apothecary shop. Only for a moment, Jeremy. Before we go on to the tavern."

"The Nag's Head is more than a tavern, my lad. It's a palace of supreme pleasure. It is not, however, best reached by way of Pearl Street."

"I know, but Red Bess doesn't know where we started from. Besides, she has no reason to suspect you."

"Wrong. She does suspect me. Because I'm your friend."

"But she can't—"

Jeremy chuckled. "Earnest Chris. Don't know when you're being teased. Never have and never will. Of course I'll stop by the apothecary shop. I'll march myself in the front door and ask for Mistress Tamsyn and say her cousin Christopher is wanting to arrange a tryst. Will tonight do? Sometime after dark, of course. After her mother—"

Christopher grabbed his friend by the arm and began dragging him toward the stairs. It wasn't difficult: Jeremy Clinton was small, fair, of a delicate, almost frail build. The youngest son of one of a pair of lawyering brothers, Jeremy was apprenticed to the firm, but it was hard to imagine him arguing a case before a jury. He would never be taken seriously.

They were nearly out the door when Christopher remembered he hadn't raised the black flag. Unless he did the bellmen would have no way of knowing there was a corpse to be collected and buried in the potter's field out by the Common. He got the banner, unfurled it, and pushed it firmly into the holder by the window. A strong wind snapped it into a stiff, familiar statement of death. "There, no way they can miss that. Maybe for a change they won't leave the body here until it rots."

II

Red Bess. That was what the whole town called her. She was forty-seven, the elder of the two children Jacob Van der Vries had fathered on Sally Turner. Bess had Jacob's red hair, but she had Sally's wit and Sally's grit. She was a woman afraid of nothing and no one, certainly not of a toothless old slave who stayed in her tiny room at the top of the house on Pearl Street, not doing much except sitting and dreaming and waiting to die.

Hetje was sixty-five, possibly older—she wasn't entirely sure what year she'd been born—and Bess's great fear was that the slave would die before she told the truth. That was why once or twice every day she stomped up to Hetje's room and slammed the door and threatened the old woman with all kinds of mischief, not just here but in the hereafter.

"You took an oath and you broke it, so you're going to hell. Going to burn for all eternity, you are, Hetje. Forever and ever. In fires so hot you can't even imagine them."

"Hetje never swore no oath."

"Yes, you did. Doesn't matter whether or not you knew. You swore. The governor said so—he wrote it down in a law." She had quoted that code to Hetje so many times Bess knew it by heart. " 'No woman shall exercise the employment of midwife until she have taken oath.' That's what the law says, Hetje. So you are sworn, and you broke your oath and you're going to hell."

"Hetje be no midwife. Hetje be a good slave who—"

"You're a lying slave, Hetje. You birthed me, didn't you? And my brother, Willem, and my three dead sons, God rest their souls, and my daughter, Tamsyn. Well, didn't you?"

"Yes, but only because the mistress—"

"See, you're convicted out of your own mouth. You're a midwife because you birthed us all. Including the one you took away. And it says in the midwife's sworn oath that she will not 'suffer any woman to claim any other woman's child for her own, nor collude to keep secret the birth of a child, nor keep secret the birth of bastards.' So it's eternal fire for you, Hetje. Forever and ever and ever."

"Never swore no oath. Only did what the mistress—"

"All her life my mother grieved over that child, and you never told her what happened to him."

"Yes I did. I told Mistress Sally and I'm telling you. Hetje be doing exactly what Mistress said. Took that baby up to the compound. Had to. He don't be a white baby. The master wouldn't let—"

"But there wasn't anyone at the compound the right age. Mama went there. She asked. She tried to buy a little boy who'd been born when her baby was born, but there wasn't any such boy, Hetje, because—"

"Because they be selling him to someone else first. How many times I need to tell you the same thing, Miss Bess? That little boy, he be five by the time your mama went looking for him. Lots of times by then they be already sold."

That was true enough. Mama had waited for five years after her first child was born, when Bess was four and Willem was three. A short time after Papa was found hanging from the old scarecrow gibbet down by the waterfront, covered in pitch.

Killed himself, people said. Jacob Van der Vries climbed up on a stack of wooden crates, put the noose around his own neck, and kicked the crates away. They said the devil got into him and made him do it. Must have been the devil that poured black pitch over his corpse, as well.

So after she had him cut down Sally had to bury Jacob in the potter's field well north of the town, near the burying place for Negroes and Jews. All because the churches said Jacob Van der Vries was a suicide, and not one of them would let him lie in hallowed ground. Which didn't bother her overmuch, considering everything else.

After it was done, that was when Sally began trying to buy a little boy slave.

She said she was looking for a child born in the autumn of 1664, right after the English came, but she was never able to find exactly what she wanted. For a long time she haunted the compound and went to every slave auction in New York. Later, when the little boy she'd been looking for would have grown up into a man, she took to stopping slaves in the street and looking deep into their eyes. "When I find the one I want, I'll know him," she used to say. But she never did.

The night Bess's first child was born, Sally confided her secret grief to her daughter. After Hetje helped Bess deliver her son and Sally laid the child in her daughter's arms, her mother sent Hetje from the room. She told Bess the tale of the rape, of why she'd had no choice but to send her son to the slave compound. And, she said, she would never stop looking for him.

Sally rested her palm on the head of her newborn grandson, and looked into her daughter's eyes. "Never," she whispered. "As long as I draw breath, I'll never stop grieving and looking." And, in 1697, when Sally was sixty years old and on her deathbed, she held Bess's hand and made her promise to continue the quest. "Find your half brother. Tell him I'm sorry. Swear you will."

Bess swore.

Hetje knew something. Bess was sure of it. Sally had been devoted to her slave and had never questioned Hetje's word. Bess did. She had four slaves of her own, left to her when her husband died. They lived in a shed out behind the house, but Hetje she kept under the family roof. Bess fed the old woman and clothed her, and looked after her as Sally would have wished. And every day she demanded the truth. It was a war of wills between mistress and slave, and any weapon was permitted. "You swore an oath, Hetje."

"Never swore no oath. Not a midwife. Just be doing what Mistress Sally say."

The bell on the shop door rang. Even here, at the top of the house, Bess heard it. No matter if she'd left one of the slaves or even her daughter, Tamsyn, minding the old simpling room that had become an apothecary shop; like Sally before her, as soon as she heard the bell Bess rushed to see who had come and what they might wish to buy.

She'd already pulled open the door of Hetje's room and gathered up her skirt and her petticoats in preparation to run down the stairs, but she had to have the final word. "You swore an oath, Hetje, and unless you tell what you did you'll go to hell and burn for all eternity."

Moses Smythe died of the pox and left Bess a widow when she was twenty-nine and pregnant. She lost their three young sons in the same epidemic. Soon after her daughter was born, Bess sold the small Smythe farm in Yonkers and took herself and the baby back to her mother's house. Within two years, the simpling room where Sally dispensed her special Health-Giving Tonic—a penny a pull from the barrel on the wooden counter—had become a proper apothecary shop, the first in New York. Eighteen years later it remained the only one.

Bess had learned much of her mother's art of compounding simples, but she was by nature a woman of business who saw no reason to be content with a penny if you could have a shilling.

The shop still sold Health-Giving Tonic and it was still made according to Sally's receipt, laced with laudanum she'd first added from her secret supply. The only difference was that customers could no longer bring their own containers and have them filled for a penny no matter what their size. Bess had found a potter to make her small crockery jugs, each of which held about a gill, as much as a man might swallow in a gulp. She filled the little jugs from the barrel and sold them for a penny each. People still got the tonic for the price they'd always paid; they just got less of it. And came back with their pennies more often.

Tamsyn was putting a jug of Health-Giving Tonic in the hands of a purchaser when Bess opened the door that led from the house to the shop. "Here, you," she called out, "that's a penny. We don't give credit or take barter."

"He knows, Mama. Jeremy's already paid."

"Oh, it's you, is it? I don't wonder you're feeling poorly, what with all your drinking and carousing. You should buy two of those. You probably need them."

"One will do me for the moment, Mistress. That way when I need more I'll have an excuse to return and bid good day to Miss Tamsyn."

Bess narrowed her eyes. "Like as not you'll find me or one of my Negroes to serve you. Miss Tamsyn has other things to do. And you'd best not bring your friend with you. I told you that months past, Jeremy Clinton, and I haven't changed my mind. No Turner is welcome here. Christopher Turner least of all. And if he—"

"Mama, you're getting yourself worked up over nothing. Cousin Chris isn't here. He never comes to the shop."

"No, he sends this one instead. I know exactly what the pair of you have in mind, young man, and—"

Jeremy turned to her and held his coat wide open. "Look, Mistress Bess. I am as you see me. You may check my pockets if you like. I swear I don't have Chris Turner hidden anywhere on my person."

Tamsyn put her hand over her mouth to hide a giggle. She was tall and slender, like her father. Her hair was dark like her father's, too, and a few curls escaped from her drawstring cap. And when she tried that way to suppress her laughter, Tamsyn looked so much like Moses that Bess had to look away lest anyone see she was an old fool who could still weep for the man she'd lost. "If you want nothing else, you'd best be going." Her voice was rough.

"I am, Mistress Bess, that's exactly what I'm doing. Going. See, I'm gone." Jeremy pulled the door closed behind him. The bell jangled, then was silent.

Bess turned to her daughter. "Is that all he bought, the tonic?"

"Yes, Mama. Only that."

"And were there no other customers this past hour?"

"Two, Mama. One bought a tincture of chamomile for the gout, the other four jugs of tonic."

Bess pulled open the money drawer and peered inside. Six pennies; two were even proper coins from England. The other four were wood, but in New York that made no difference. Queen Anne was said to be truly interested in New York, and she'd been a dozen years on the English throne, but she was no more inclined to grant the colony a mint than had William and Mary before her. Among New Yorkers wooden pennies were as much legal tender as those made of copper. Nonetheless, Bess frowned when she saw the accumulation in the drawer. "This means I didn't hear the bell. According to you, Tamsyn, I missed the bell twice."

"It doesn't matter, Mama. I was here."

"Yes, you were." Bess was still staring at the money. And calculating. "But if you sold a tincture of chamomile for tuppence, and four jugs of tonic . . . no, five including Jeremy's, you're a penny shy."

Tamsyn dropped Jeremy Clinton's copper coin on top of those already there. It made a satisfactory ping. "All accounted for, Mama."

Bess nodded. "Yes, now so it is."

Tamsyn folded her hands and looked demure, giving no indication of the quickly scrawled note she'd tucked up her sleeve.

High up in her room under the eaves, Hetje stood by the window. All her teeth were gone and her hearing wasn't what it had been—she blamed Miss Bess's screaming for that—but her eyes were as sharp as ever. She'd watched Jeremy Clinton from the moment he left the simpling room and walked down the path and out the front gate.

She was watching him now. He crossed the road and turned up Coenties Alley, walked past the Jews' houses, approached the redbrick mill facing Stone Street. A gust of wind came along and nudged the broad blades atop the mill's tall tower. Braked they must be because they didn't spin, only shuddered a bit. Master Jeremy hunched forward, clutching his hat. In a moment he'd round the corner and she wouldn't be able to see him.

He hadn't cleared Jews' Lane before the other one came to join him. Hetje squinted to see better, but Christopher Turner was hard to miss. The Black Giant, they called him; showed you what white folks knew. If he'd been black—at least, if his father'd been black—a lot of things would be different. For one thing, Hetje wouldn't have Miss Bess screaming at her all the time. Telling her she was going to hell for breaking an oath she never took.

If Mistress Sally's firstborn had been born black—or even brown—Hetje could have taken him to the slave compound the way she planned, and maybe Mistress Sally could have bought him back and spared them all a lot of tears.

But it wasn't that way. And it wasn't Hetje's fault the mistress's baby had black hair but white skin. And it surely wasn't Hetje's doing that, after she'd lived almost six years with the master, Mistress Sally couldn't face any more.

"Help me, Hetje. You have to help me."

Hetje was a good slave. She'd helped Mistress Sally do almost anything she wanted until the day Sally died. Some things though, Hetje took no part in. Putting that length of twine around the master's neck while he slept, and twisting it around and around on a wooden darning egg until his eyes fairly popped out of his skull—Hetje just watched while that happened. The only thing she helped with was stuffing him into a burlap sack and, when night came, dragging the sack from Pearl Street to the gibbet down by the fort. And piling up the boxes and hefting the master up, and putting the old noose around his neck and leaving him hanging there. Hetje did do that with the mistress, but Hetje hadn't poured any pitch. Mistress Sally did that all by herself. And afterward, when Mistress started searching for the little boy she'd made Hetje take away, Mistress did that alone as well.

Hetje had thought on all those things plenty of times. Decided there wasn't any point in telling it. It was just how life had worked itself out. If she hadn't given the baby to Mistress Marit and Master Lucas, for sure the old master would have killed him. And Christopher Turner would never have been born. So Mistress Bess could shout and scream as much as she liked. Old Hetje, she wasn't saying anything different from what she'd said before.

III

Singly or in pairs, they went to the special place. For weeks after the night of magic out by Beekman's Swamp, one or another would move silently through the night to the chosen place, and kneel down and say the *obeah* words Peter the Doctor gave them for protection, and begin to dig.

It was Peter who thought of using the field behind the Crooke orchard. The Crooke place was out at the edge of town, one of the last you could get to from the paved part of the Broad Way, and so far back from the road no one would see them. House and field were separated by a barn as well as an orchard. They could bury their stolen knives and clubs in Crookes' field.

Just to make sure, Peter the Doctor had brought the *obeah* to the chosen place. He brought strong magic to make the ground always soft for digging, and to make it certain that no one of the people living in the house would come out to use the stool while a hole was being dug. The *obeah* was why not a single one of the Crookes' six slaves ever spotted the freshly turned earth, or reported anything suspicious to their masters.

The *obeah* kept their secret. Nearly six weeks and they had not been betrayed, nor were they tempted to betray one another. That was how strong was the magic of Peter the Doctor. He made them invincible. The oath-takers thought of freedom coming soon, and they rejoiced.

Later, Bess always insisted that the bell on the shop door had jangled with a different tone that February morning. She swore it had been more forceful. Tamsyn thought that was nonsense, but she never said. When you grew up with Red Bess you learned to keep some things to yourself.

"Good afternoon, ladies. I can't tell you how glad I am to find you here. In truth, I am overjoyed."

Bess had been pouring a large jug of freshly made Health-Giving Tonic into the barrel. She stood on the wooden counter; Tamsyn's arms wrapped around her legs to steady her. Seeing the fine-looking young man who had expressed such pleasure in meeting them, the girl let go long enough to gather up her skirts and drop a quick curtsy. "Good day to you, sir. Is there something you wish to purchase?"

"I have no doubt that sooner or later I shall wish to purchase every remedy you stock." The young man took off his hat and bowed in Tamsyn's direction. Without the tricorn he looked even better. He wore no wig—his faint accent marked him as a Scot, and Scots seldom indulged in such frippery—and his hair was a warm golden brown, much the same color as his eyes. It was tied neatly at the back of his neck with a black grosgrain ribbon. "You are Miss Tamsyn, are you not? And this must be the lady the whole town calls Mistress Bess."

"Red Bess is what they call me. And you can't have been here long or you'd have heard that."

"Mistress Bess," the man said firmly. "And if your task is finished, will you allow me to help you down?" He didn't wait for an answer, just reached up, put his two hands around Bess's waist, and despite her substantial bulk, swung her easily to the floor.

"Considering how fond of my dinners I am, young man, that was most impressive."

"Nay, Mistress, I'm the one that's impressed. Back in Edinburgh they told me it was foolhardy for a trained physician to come to New York. They said there wasn't a proper apothecary to be found, that every housewife fancied herself adept at simpling, and that as a consequence one must bear the burden not only of prescribing one's chosen remedies, but of preparing them. Yet the moment I landed I heard of your shop, and here I see a truly amazing array." He waved his hat at the display of tall glass jugs with their carefully lettered labels.

Bess nodded. "Well, Edinburgh's not a surprise. Your burr is well hid, but it's there nonetheless. But a trained man of medicine? As young a one as you? Are they apprenticing physicians straight from the birthing bed in Scotland these days?"

"Mama!" Tamsyn's cheeks were bright pink. "What will our visitor think if—"

"Nay, please, Miss Tamsyn, you must not trouble yourself. I take no offense. Your mother's question is entirely to the point." The young man turned to Bess. "I know that long years of apprenticeship are still the fashion here in the colonies, Mistress, but we have more modern methods at home. I have spent three years studying at the university in Edinburgh, with professors skilled in every kind of medicine. I am, in fact, not simply a physician. I am fortunate enough to hold the degree of Medical Doctor." He made a second bow, considerably deeper than the first, and meant to include both women. "Zachary Crad-dock, M.D., ladies. And I am, as I said, most powerfully content to make your ac-quaintance."

Hours later Bess could still feel his hands gripping her waist. Dear Lord, what a long time it had been.

Four babies in five years Moses Smythe had fathered on her. By the time she was bearing Tamsyn she thought her belly would burst, so tender and tired of baby weight had it become. But the getting of them . . . ah, that had been so sweet. If Moses had lived she'd have gone on bearing him children until she dropped in her tracks. As many a woman had before her, except for some who were wiser. And more daring.

Tincture of nux vomica, mixed with a decoction of black bryony and a few grains of powdered aconite. Deadly poisons all, but if combined in exactly the right proportions and taken before the second month passed with no effusion of blood, cramps would occur that were terrible enough to make a woman scream aloud with the pain, and ofttimes strong enough to expel the babe from the womb.

Nux vomica was the dried seed of the poison nut tree and came from the East. It had to be bought from the spice dealers. The other herbs grew in the gardens Sally had made when she ripped out the old orchard and surrounded the house with the plants of her craft. As for the receipt, that, too, was part of Sally's legacy. "Sometimes it works and sometimes it does not, as I know full well" had been the cryptic comment that went with the lesson. "But you should know the making of it, nonetheless. Only be careful, Bess. When it comes to this particular receipt, take exceptional care."

She'd been a child of twelve at the time and she'd replied earnestly, "I will, Mama. I know those herbs are all poisons."

"I'd have taught you nothing if you didn't know that. It's not the herbs you must guard against. Listen to me, child; all men are terrified of women who know this manner of expelling their seed. It means they cannot entirely control us. And mark my words, Bess, frightened men can be vicious beyond telling."

How right Sally had been. The very midwifery oath Bess was constantly recit-ing to Hetje contained the clause "No midwife shall administer any medicine to produce miscarriage . . ." But clearly some did. And sometimes the decoction worked.

Take her brother Willem's wife, for instance. Susannah had borne Willem no more than five children in the fourteen years they'd been wed, and only three of those survived. Must be she knew how to stop a babe growing inside her when that was what she wanted. Susannah with her laces and frills and fans hadn't produced a brood so large they sucked her tits down to her belly. At thirty-one the bloody woman still had the high, firm pappes of a girl, not a sagging shelf like Bess's. Of course that might be because Willem was such a dried-up fig of a man.

Her brother had been a skinny, pimple-faced youth who didn't look as if he knew how to use the gift between his legs. Probably he'd never learned. Else, with a man to sleep beside her and all she had of this world's goods, why would Susannah always look as if she needed a strong purge?

This Scotsman, however, he was something different.

Just remembering the feel of his hands on her waist when he swung her off the counter made Bess sure of it. Good. She wouldn't wish a dried-up fig on her Tamsyn. Not when she thought of the hot sweetness of being abed with the girl's father. But a virile young man with a degree in medicine, who would have cause to avail himself of every remedy that could be simpled in the only apothecary shop in New York City . . . And had she not heard that there were a few such university doctors in Philadelphia, and that they charged ten shillings a visit while a physician who had been apprenticed was paid only five . . . ?

A match worthy of serious thought. Not least because once she had Tamsyn wedded and bedded, she could stop worrying about the way bloody Christopher Turner mooned over the girl.

"I've had no truck with any that live under Lucas Turner's roof," Sally had whispered in her last minutes, holding tight to her daughter's hand. "Not ever, Bess. Lucas sold me so he could have her. Not Ankel Jannssen's seed, either. No truck. And nor must you."

She had yet to find her half brother, but the means of fulfilling her second promise might have finally presented itself.

The day was chosen by Peter the Doctor. According to the *obeah,* the auspicious moments occurred during the first hours of the first day of April, which fell on a Thursday. Peter advised the time right after moonset, around two in the morning.

Kinsowa the Ibo made the plan. They would attack in the way his people had always made war on their enemies: create a distraction that would draw the warriors out of their stronghold, then kill them.

Finally, to make success absolutely certain, Peter the Doctor gave them a magic powder to rub on their bodies before they left their masters' homes that night. And he promised to bring the fire, red-hot coals transported from his cabin in a covered tin bucket.

Seven of the original oath-takers had been sold to owners in other towns, even other colonies. One had died of an illness. Twenty-nine kept their word. They met in the field behind the Crooke house. It was the first time since the night they had sucked one another's blood that they were all together. In the dark and the silence they dug up the butcher knives and the hatchets and the clubs they had buried. Three of them, the two Indians and one of the Africans, had even managed to steal their masters' muskets. When they were all armed and ready, they made a circle around Kinsowa.

Quaco stepped forward. He was one of the Ashantis, the one whose woman had bitten off the head of the chicken. She was near to giving birth now, but she stood with them in the field beside her man, who didn't look at her but thought instead of the son to come. The son who would be born free.

Quaco took the fire from Peter the Doctor. He had prepared a number of cloths soaked in pitch and he distributed them to six of the fastest runners. Amba, his woman, had wanted to be the first. She said it was her right because she had been the one to bite off the chicken's head. Quaco agreed with her reasoning, but in her present condition it was not practical. The runners, he told her, had to move like the wind passing over the earth.

Quaco crouched down close to the earth and uncovered the fire brought by Peter the Doctor. His face shone in the red glow of the coals. "Come," he whispered, looking around the assembly. "Come now. Rise up and come."

For long seconds no one moved. So far everything they'd done would get them nothing but a whipping. This was different.

"Come," Quaco repeated. In his homeland he had been the son of a king, born to rule. Here he had only his conviction to persuade them that having braved so much they must take the final step. "Come and make you free."

Amba started to step forward, to again offer herself for the task. The first runner, shamed by the courage of a woman, pulled her aside and went to where Quaco squatted. He leaned down and held his pitch-soaked rag above the coals. A tongue of fire shot up and the cloth burst into flame. The man held it above his head and turned and raced toward the outbuilding they had chosen. His flaming torch was a shooting star crossing the sky. In seconds he had flung it into the timber barn. No sooner had he turned to run back to the others when the second torchbearer came. And after him the third. Six in all.

By the time the third fire carrier reached the small wooden building it was ablaze. Quaco, the son of an Ashanti king, had done his part. Kinsowa, the Ibo warrior chief, was again the leader. He motioned to the others and they began moving closer, padding silently across the field and into the orchard.

"Fire!" someone screamed. The sound came from the direction of the Crooke house. "Fire! Sound the alarm!"

Moments later the great bell by the side of the road started clanging. At the same time the family ran out of the house and began streaming toward the orchard. The Crookes' slaves came as well, roused from their sleep by the cry of fire.

"Kinsowa, listen to me," Peter the Doctor whispered urgently. "We don't kill our own." He grabbed the other man's arm. "You hear me, African? We don't kill our own kind. It's bad magic."

Until they put him in the slave fortress in Guinea, Kinsowa had never seen a white face. He was captured by black men, sold by other black men, from tribes that had always been the enemies of his people. But in the year since he was brought to the slave fortress, since he was stuffed into the Guinea ship and chained in one tiny space where he must always stand, never sit or lie down, and eat and sleep and relieve himself without moving in the stifling dark, in the time since he was hauled out of that ship and put on the block and sold, in those twelve months Kinsowa had learned to recognize the enemy who was above all other enemies. That's why he had been willing to drink the blood of Fantis and Ashantis and all the rest who were not his people. Because he had learned that the true enemy was white.

"No black," he whispered, using the few words of English he'd learned since coming to this terrible place. "Kill no black."

"Good," Peter the Doctor whispered. "Good. Pass the word."

The people hurrying to fight the fire were all in the orchard now, babbling and shouting and trying to organize themselves into a line for passing buckets of water from the well to the burning barn. The Crookes naturally, but also people who lived in houses close enough to see the flames before they heard the alarm. They came with their own buckets, ready to help with putting out the fire. And since every live body was required, they had brought their slaves.

There were twenty-odd whites—including five women and three children—and eleven blacks among the firefighters. And still hidden, the twenty-eight oath-takers. Who alone were armed.

Kinsowa stepped forward and raised his fist to the sky. There was no moon, but the light from the burning building gleamed on the butcher knife he held. "Hah-noooo," Kinsowa cried in a single, breathless yell that came from somewhere deep in his belly. "Hah-fawaaah." Those were the war words his people had used for as long as anyone knew, and even those who did not recognize their meaning heard menace in the sound.

"What the bloody hell!" The white who was standing closest to Kinsowa saw the slave materialize like a spirit out of the black night. "Hey, boy! Who do you belong to? What do you—"

Kinsowa slashed the white's throat before he could finish the sentence. The man fell.

It was not enough.

An orgy of killing had erupted all around him. Kinsowa could smell the hot blood as it spilled and the stink of bowels loosened by terror. Still it was not enough.

He plunged his knife into the heart of the man whose throat he'd slit. For the time in the slave fortress. He ripped open the man's belly. For the horror of the Guinea ship. He slashed at the man's genitals. For making him stand on a block and be sold with a collar around his neck like an ox yoked to a plow.

A woman at the top edge of the orchard, up near the house and the well, was the first of those not in the thick of the mêlée to realize what was happening. She heard the tone of the shouts change, and she smelled the fear and the blood rising on the breeze, overcoming the smell of smoke and cinders. The woman grabbed a young boy standing frozen with terror beside her. He, too, had begun to realize that this was not a fire like any other he had seen. This was Armageddon, come to claim them all, just like the preachers said.

"Get to town," the woman screamed. "Here you, Joe Crooke! You do what I say. Get to town. Run fast as you can! Tell them to send the soldiers. Tell them the slaves are killing their masters. Go!"

The boy hesitated, transfixed by the horror of the scene. A gunshot rang out as the African who had stolen a musket managed to fire it. "Go!" the woman screamed, grabbing the boy's shoulder and shaking him until his teeth chattered in his head. "You hear me, Joe Crooke? If you don't, every Christian in New York will be dead before morning. Go!"

Finally the boy turned and ran.

In the orchard the ground was soaked with blood. Eight white men were dead and seven more were dying of their wounds. Amba dispatched one of those when she heard him groan. She knelt beside him and took a two-fisted grip on her club and brought it down on his head and heard his skull crack open, and screamed with joy when she reached in and with her bare hands tore out his brains.

The eleven slaves who were not part of the rebellion, who'd been brought by their masters to help fight the fire, fell back and stayed among the trees and watched those who claimed to own them being slain and did not know what to do. They had no weapons. They knew nothing of any planned revolt. They had been slaves so long they did not know the meaning of free.

Only one understood. When he saw the woman whose belly was swollen with a coming child club a man to death, he ran forward and wrested the weapon out of the woman's hands and turned on the nearest white man. It was his master's teenage son, a boy he'd known since he was born. The slave who had only that instant become a rebel beat the boy's face and his shoulders and his chest with the club, and the boy fell down at his feet and the slave howled with the emotion that had only just been born inside him and turned to find the next white man he could kill.

The men who had run back to their houses to get their muskets returned to the orchard. "Fire at will!" someone shouted. There were no commanders in this battle, only seven muskets in the hands of seven white men who knew how to use them and twenty-eight slaves armed with clubs and hatchets and knives, and two muskets that had run out of shot, and one that was held by a man who had never before fired such a weapon.

Peter the Doctor had a hatchet. He had used it well. The blade dripped blood and was flecked with chips of bone. But the plan had been to kill all the whites quickly, to let none get away and spread the alarm. When he saw the men running toward the orchard with their muskets, Peter knew they had failed. "Run!" he screamed. "Run! Into the woods!"

Amba could not run, at least not very far, and Quaco would not leave her. The two Indians would not shame their ancestors by running. Most of the others didn't move fast enough. Nine men followed Peter the Doctor in the direction of the woods to the north. Four more—the slave who had clubbed his master's teenage son among them—ran toward the town to seek a place to hide there. The rest, including the slaves who had been brought to the orchard to fight the fire, were captured.

It was done before the red-coated detachment from the garrison could be heard coming down the road, their booted feet pounding the cobbles at double time.

"To arms! To arms!"

Christopher had been up half the night reading and it was still dark when the alarm was cried. He had to shake himself awake when the bellman ran by his window shouting the command. "To arms! To arms!"

Indians perhaps. Or the damned Dutch back again. Or maybe the French. God alone knew what the threat was this time, and it didn't matter a great deal. He'd find out soon enough. He swung his long legs off the bed and began pulling his breeches on over the underwear he slept in. His boots next, and after that his shirt and his coat. All without the need of a candle and in less than forty seconds.

Christopher could hear the cries of the bellmen outside his window as they passed down other roads, and the muffled calls of the men of New York City as they ran into the streets, prepared to defend their homes and families.

It had been so since the colonies were founded. No government thousands of miles away could send sufficient troops to guard the New World settlers. Every colonial assembly charged the able-bodied men in its jurisdiction with the duty to own a musket and be prepared to fight in the common defense. The only exemptions were ministers and magistrates.

Christopher was neither. His weapon was in the cupboard beside the front door. He grabbed it, then found his powder horn and slung it over his shoulder.

"You going out there, Mr. Christopher? You got any idea what's happening?"

"None, Selma. But don't worry, whoever's come to make mischief will be leaving soon enough." He raised his musket in the direction of the old black woman who had looked after him since he was eleven. "A taste of this and I'll be back by sunup for some of your johnnycakes."

In the streets, listening to the whispered stories of his friends and neighbors, Christopher knew it wouldn't be that simple. This time the enemy was within the gates.

Sweet Jesus. A slave revolt. A cold chill gripped his bowels. He had only old Selma, and clearly she was part of no rebellion, but others . . . Nearly every household in the town owned three or four blacks. Many had more. They were as necessary to ordinary, decent life as chairs and tables and bedding.

The men around him were thinking the same thing. They stood with their muskets at the ready, waiting for orders to proceed somewhere and do something, but you could see by the way they turned and looked back at their own front doors that they were considering whether the wisest course was to run back inside and protect their families from the blacks who'd been bought to serve them.

One man made a move in that direction, but before he could start a stampede a redcoat ran into Hall Place, shouting, "You there! Come with me! I need a dozen musketmen to relieve the soldiers posted at the ferry slips."

The men peppered him with questions. Whose slaves? Where? How many? What had they done?

"Don't know much more than you do. Only that there's a pile of corpses out at the edge of town. Hacked apart, they were. Come this way. The governor wants every regular soldier for searching the woods, so you're needed to relieve the sentinels."

The redcoat waved the men forward, and the majority followed him. Christopher did not. He looked after the others for a moment, then turned and ran in the opposite direction, toward Pearl Street. Tamsyn and Red Bess lived alone, with no man for protection, and Bess had four or five slaves at least. Maybe more.

"What are you doing here? You're no more welcome now than ever you have been." Bess had opened the apothecary shop in answer to his wild beating on the door. Her drawstring cap was askew and under her wrapper she clearly wore no corset. Surplus flesh seemed to tumble around her, all of it quivering with fury.

"I came because I'm kin," Christopher said, pushing past her and kicking the door shut behind him. "I have a duty to you and Tamsyn."

"I can look after myself and my daughter." It appeared she could. Red Bess was holding a musket that looked every bit as fit for service as Christopher's, and she was pointing it straight at him. "I'll thank you to leave."

"Not until I'm sure you're all right. It's a slave revolt. They've already murdered God knows how many."

"I know what it is. My slaves are not part of it. They're all well fed and well sheltered and well looked after. They've no cause to revolt."

An old black woman had come to the door between the shop and the private house. She stood there and said nothing, listening to her mistress, but staring at Christopher with particular attention. Or so it seemed to him.

Christopher stared back. Bess saw the direction of his glance and swung around. "Oh, it's you, is it? You've been with this family longer than any of the others, Hetje. Tell him there are no rebels here. Then perhaps he'll leave and take the Turner stench with him."

Hetje continued to look at Christopher. She began nodding, but she didn't say a word.

"Do as I say!" Bess shouted. "I won't put up with your insolence forever, Hetje. I can't be responsible for keeping my temper if you—"

"That Tom who be tending the fires and driving the wagon," Hetje said. "He be gone."

"Tom? But he's . . ." Bess's face was suddenly as white as her cap. "You must be mistaken. My husband bought Tom when he was a boy," she whispered. "He has been with us for over twenty years."

"Well, he don't be with you anymore." Hetje turned to go.

"Wait," Christopher commanded. Hetje stopped walking. Been a long time since there had been a man giving orders in this house. "Where's Miss Tamsyn? Have you seen—"

"I'm right here, Christopher. And I am perfectly fine."

Unlike her mother, Tamsyn was properly dressed. The bodice of her yellow calico frock was carefully laced, the width of her skirt evidenced a series of stiff petticoats, and her dark hair was neatly tucked under her cap. "It was good of you to come to protect us, Christopher, but Mama and I are surely in no danger from any rebellious slaves."

"Tom's gone." Bess whispered the words, staring straight ahead. "Hetje just told me. Tom's one of the rebels. "

Tamsyn gasped. Hetje went on nodding. And looking at Christopher.

There was something remarkable in the way she was studying him. Christopher had to force himself to look away. "If one of your own slaves is with the rebels, that surely makes it clear you need a man here. I'll stay until—"

The door opened. Christopher swung around to face whoever was coming in, musket cocked and ready.

The man was white, and he clearly did not consider himself in any danger from Christopher's weapon. He carried one of his own, but lowered it as soon as he saw the two women. "Mistress Bess, Miss Tamsyn. I give thanks you're both unharmed."

It occurred to Christopher that the stranger might be someone sent by Willem. In an emergency, the responsibility for his widowed sister and orphaned niece was clearly his. But Chris had picked up the hint of a Scots accent in the other man's words, and nothing of a servant's tone. "May I know your name, sir?"

"Zachary Craddock. And yours?"

"This is Christopher Turner, Zach." Tamsyn took a step forward, put herself between the two men. "Chris is my second cousin. He came to protect us."

Craddock nodded, a brisk movement that was minimally polite but could not be mistaken for a bow. "Ah yes, Turner the surgeon. I've heard of you."

"Zachary's a trained physician, Chris. He has a degree in medicine from Edinburgh University."

"Indeed. I am honored, sir. I haven't—"

Bess was oblivious to the two young men standing in her apothecary shop who had just now recognized each other as rivals and declared a private war of their own. "Tom's joined the rebels. I can hardly credit it."

"That is alarming news, mistress. It makes me more than happy I've come to take you away."

"Take us away where, Zachary?" Despite the gravity of the situation there was a lilt of sudden pleasure in Tamsyn's words. She knew she was the prize both men sought, and in all of her entirely sheltered life she'd never been taken away anywhere. "Whatever do you mean?"

"The King's Arms Tavern, Miss Tamsyn, in the countryside beyond Trinity Church. A number of the women and children are being sheltered there until the villains are caught and the rebellion safely put down." Craddock turned to the older woman. "Mistress Bess, I believe it's wise to take you both at once to that safety."

Bess still wasn't listening. "Tom. He's been with us since he was eight."

"If it makes you feel better," Craddock said, "I heard there was witchcraft involved. Magic from the islands. They gave your slave chicken blood to drink. Small wonder he—"

"Sweet God in heaven." Christopher whispered the words, but they were spoken with such shock it was as if he'd shouted. "The chicken dance out by Beekman's Swamp."

Craddock turned to him. "Am I to understand you know something of this business, Turner?"

"I didn't realize it until this very moment. Sometime back, New Year's day it was, I had a patient, a pauper in the hospital. He was crazed with fever and poisoned blood so I paid little attention, but he went on about seeing the chicken dance, and seeing people drinking blood out by Beekman's Swamp."

"Where is he? You must bring this man to Governor Hunter. He may have valuable intelligence that—"

"I'm afraid I can't oblige. He died a few days after I first saw him."

"Aye," Craddock said. "I might have guessed. Put the old man to the knife, did you?"

"His arm was rotting with gangrene. I took it off. The pity is that I didn't get to him sooner. If I had, he might still be alive to contribute his intelligence to this action against rebellion."

"Or you might have recognized the importance of what he was saying before you did your cutting."

Christopher paled with fury, but he managed to sound civil. "Unfortunately, sir, I did not. Perhaps in the fine city of Edinburgh you have time to pay attention to every rant inspired by illness and fever. Here in the colonies we must spend our energies on making people well."

"Aye, until they are corpses moldering in the ground." Craddock turned to the women. "Perhaps you might help your mother to dress, Miss Tamsyn. Before all the best places at the King's Arms are taken."

"Yes, of course. Come, Mama. Zachary has a sound plan." Tamsyn took Bess's arm.

The older woman allowed herself to be led toward the door. "Tom," she murmured. "All those years . . . Never whipped, not once. You know that, Tamsyn. You know no slave is ever whipped in this house."

"I do, Mama. Everyone knows it. Now, come." Tamsyn had guided her mother as far as the door from the shop to the house before she turned back to look at Christopher. "Thank you for coming, Cousin Chris. It was kind of you to think of us. But as you can see, we are in excellent hands."

The job of the sentinels posted at the landing places of the Long Island ferries was to prevent any slave escaping by that route. None were foolish enough to try. By mid-morning the garrison had been supplemented by regular militia from the towns of White Stone and Jamaica. By noon the governor had ordered the combined forces to beat a drive up Manhattan.

A long thin line of bright redcoats and drab colonial militia marched out of the city and through the farmlands and the orchards. They crossed Minetta Brook and the swamplands, went around the Collect Pond, which was too deep to ford, then headed over the Old Kill, which carried the waters of the pond out to the East River, up Potters' Hill and down the other side, and past the Powder House to the flat Common. Finally into the woods. It was a hard slow slog, and that first day they had nothing to show for it.

The armed men of the town conducting a house-to-house search had better luck. They found Robin, the slave who had murdered his master's boy, hiding in a cellar on Stone Street. A survivor of the massacre identified him.

Two more rebels were found nearby, in the storeroom behind the mill in Jews' Lane. Both were Africans, and each had a knife. When they heard the whites coming for them each man slit his own throat.

Six slaves who were with the group the soldiers eventually discovered in the woods also killed themselves. They'd been there nearly two weeks by then and were half crazed with starvation. Those who didn't choose suicide seemed almost glad to give themselves up.

Kinsowa, Quaco, and Amba had been among those taken alive the first day. In the end they also got Peter the Doctor and Red Bess's boy, Tom. By the fifteenth of April there were seventy blacks in custody. It was well known that there hadn't been that many in the Crookes' orchard, but the whites were convinced that nearly every slave in New York had been aware of the plot to murder, as they put it, "each Christian man, woman, and child."

There had never been such terror in the city. In the coffeehouses and the taverns and the alehouses men spoke of what might have happened if the plotters had been better strategists. Over their back fences and at the markets the women whispered the same thing. "What if they had come into the town? Would our own slaves have risen from their beds and murdered us in our sleep?"

New York was the largest slaveholding colony north of Chesapeake Bay. The city at the tip of Manhattan island had an enormous stake in the "peculiar institution." Of the total population of just over five thousand, nearly two thousand were slaves. Three days of bloody vengeance was the minimum catharsis required for such soul-destroying dread as was caused by this rebellion.

New York had become too important to be governed from the back room of a tavern. There was a new City Hall going up on Wall Street, halfway between the East River and Trinity Church. The City Hall wasn't entirely finished, but among the first projects completed had been the leveling of the bit of ground in front of the entrance, and the installation of the pillory, stocks, and whipping cage. Next to those devices they erected the gallows.

On an April Monday fourteen of the rebels—the two Indians, some of the locally born blacks, and the handful of "seasoned slaves" from the islands—were brought to the place of execution and hanged. The huge crowd that had gathered to watch cheered each opening of the trapdoor and every snap of the noose, but when it was finished they went away grumbling. Their hatred and their fear were too powerful to be satisfied by such easy deaths.

Tuesday was better. Three of the blacks were racked: Robin and two of the African Fantis. After two hours of half-inch by half-inch stretching and almost constant screaming Robin and one of the Fantis were broken on the wheel and died. The other man was not granted such a speedy end. They stretched him until it seemed he could take no more but was still alive. Then a Dutch sailor who had learned the technique in Rotterdam stood above Claus's racked body and used a club to break all his bones one by one. It took hours and he stopped occasionally to quench his thirst at a nearby alehouse, then returned to his task. Meanwhile the soldiers brought out Kinsowa.

The Ibo had been whipped repeatedly and many of his wounds still bled. In the last few days of captivity he'd been well fed, but that had nothing to do with mercy. They stood Kinsowa beneath the gallows, but they did not put the noose around his neck. Instead they wrapped chains around his arms and his legs and hauled him to the top of the gibbet and fixed him in place crosswise.

Kinsowa's sentence was to hang on the gibbet until he starved to death. It was sure to take many days. As for Claus, he died at two in the morning. Most of the onlookers had left by then and the sailor's arm was getting tired. He finally bashed in the black man's skull.

Wednesday promised to be the most satisfying day of all, so the crowd came early.

The three poles and most of the logs had been soaking in water for many hours, so the fire would take longer to catch hold. The lower halves of the men would be well incinerated before their upper bodies began to char. That was the sentence, burned alive in a slow fire. It was calculated by those who knew about such things that the screams would go on for eight or nine hours.

For Governor Robert Hunter's purposes—edification of the whites and terrorizing of the blacks—the wind was right, a stiff sea breeze blowing east to west. Everyone in town would smell the burning flesh.

Everyone who wasn't already there to watch.

In 1699, when the old wooden palisade came down, the plan had been to make Wall Street into a wide boulevard. It turned out the governor of the time had bought the parade ground to the north, divided it into building lots, and made a fortune selling them off. As a result Wall Street was what it had always been, a thirty-six-foot-wide trench. That day it was packed solid with people. The lucky ones were above the crush, hanging out the windows and clinging to the steeply pitched roofs of the grand residences that now lined the street.

The man who styled himself Will Devrey—Willem Van der Vries was both too Dutch and too obviously connected with the sordid family history—owned one of them. His was a square mansion of dark red brick, with long, elegant windows, four tall chimneys, and a steep slate roof topped by a gleaming white ornamental balustrade.

Devrey got the money to build his house the same way the owners of most of the other fine houses on Wall Street got theirs: from the Guinea ships. Will had seven. Mostly they plied the Middle Passage, the most profitable leg in the Triangle Trade. Some Devrey ships brought grain and meat from the English colonies to the West Indies, and rum and sundry goods from the Caribbean to Africa. Most had been built solely to bring slaves back from the forts along the Guinea coast. The trade had made him very rich, but it occurred to Will that after this episode he might become much poorer.

Already, since it was widely believed they had led the insurrection, there was talk of forbidding the direct importation of African slaves. Will planned to argue against so rash a law. In fact, as a man of substantial means and a member of the governor's council, he should have been on the arcaded porch of the City Hall with Governor Hunter and the other dignitaries. It would have been an excellent opportunity to make his case. Instead he was forced to stay up here with his wife and the twittering ladies she'd invited for the occasion. Because, of course, his damned sister was bound to make a spectacle of herself.

"She's coming! Red Bess is coming!"

The cry came first from those standing at the intersection of the Broad Way and Wall Street, crowded ten deep on the bit of fenced grass at the rear of Trinity Church. Though Devrey and the other shipowners fancied themselves the economic backbone of the city, the small brownstone-and-brick church dedicated to saving the souls of the English elite gave them its backside. Trinity looked west, across the open countryside between the Broad Way and Hudson's River. Indeed, Queen Anne had recently granted the church ownership of a wide swath of that rural landscape, but today all that was of interest lay in the opposite direction.

"Red Bess is coming!"

She'd chosen to wear a black shawl and a black dress, and to cover her red hair almost entirely with a black straw bonnet. Bess walked up the Broad Way at a leisurely pace, acknowledging no one and looking neither right nor left. She wasn't in any hurry. They would not start without her.

Governor Robert Hunter was a man who understood the importance of ritual. Red Bess had taken her mother's place: if it concerned slaves, she had to be there.

Sometimes Sally had actually put herself between the lash and a slave who was to be whipped. At least for as long as it took for her to look into the slave's eyes, then shake her head and turn away. Bess was sometimes equally bold, but during the hangings she'd done nothing, nor had she done anything when they broke the three on the rack. And she hadn't gone near the Ibo they'd gibbeted. Everyone hoped for better sport at the burnings.

The crowd fell back to make room for her. Bess turned the corner and walked undisturbed half the length of Wall Street. When she faced the execution site she had her back to her brother's mansion. She swung around, raised her head toward Will and Susannah's windows, then turned again and looked at the governor.

They'd made a special place for Governor Hunter on the porch of the half-built City Hall, an elevated stall draped with a cloth of state and a cushion for him to lean on. Hunter had come to it the way he went every Sunday to church, with the gentlemen of his council behind him on foot, and following them half a company of red-coated musketeers and a drummer beating the march. The mayor, the sheriff, and the aldermen had all been there to welcome him and were standing beside him now. But as she knew he would, Hunter had waited for Red Bess.

She looked up. He looked down. The governor did not quite nod, but their eyes met. After that he lifted his hand.

A contingent of redcoats broke ranks and trotted into the building. Though the debtors' cells planned for the attic were not yet built, the criminal dungeons below City Hall were already stout and secure. It took only a few moments for the soldiers to reappear with the last of the condemned, Quaco, Peter the Doctor, and Bess's boy, Tom.

All three were manacled and shackled. They marched to the waiting stakes with a clanking of chains that could almost be heard above the hubbub of the throng. They were chained to the posts.

Everything was ready. The crowd was a single creature drawing one expectant breath.

This time Bess did not disappoint. She pushed through the ring of guards and walked toward the black men. A collective sigh was released. This was what they'd been waiting for. It was exactly what crazy Mistress Sally would have done.

A member of the militia, a boy brought over from the long island who knew nothing of the city, stepped into Bess's path and raised his musket.

"Hold your fire!" A redcoat snapped out the order, then looked toward the governor. Hunter nodded. "Let her pass."

The boy stepped out of Bess's path. She approached the black man chained to the central stake and for a few seconds simply looked at him. Finally she spoke. "Why, Tom? Tell me only that, why?"

He'd been beaten so badly his face was distorted almost beyond recognition. All his teeth were gone, and his lips were swollen and cracked to the point where speech was difficult. But not impossible. "To make me free."

Tom's body was crisscrossed with lash marks. Bess reached out and touched his shoulder. "I never . . . You were never beaten under my roof. Never abused. Wasn't that enough?"

"Free," Tom whispered. "Free."

The crowd had begun jeering her on.

"Give him the evil eye, Red Bess."

"Talk to him the way crazy Mistress Sally did. Tell him the secret."

"C'mon, Red Bess, tell him whatever it is your mother used to tell 'em. Loud enough so's we can all hear."

The usual remarks, laced with catcalls and whistles, except that this time was not like any other. The hatred had never been this intense.

"Get out of the way, Bess. Let him get what's coming to him."

"The bloody bastard would have watched us all murdered in our beds. Get out of the way and let him burn."

Bess ignored them. "I can't believe you're a murderer," she whispered. "Not you, Tom."

"Didn't kill nobody." The words were a faint whisper that only Bess could hear. "Wanted to, but couldn't."

Bess smiled. "I didn't think so. Swallow this." Her hand moved quickly; in less than a second she'd shoved the ball of pine resin mixed with the powdered seeds of nux vomica into the back of his mouth. "Strychnine," she murmured. "Not easy, but easier." Bess saw the thanks in Tom's eyes. More important, she saw him swallow.

"What'd she do?"

"Gave him something. Some bloody witch thing."

"Red Bess gave the bastard some potion. He's going to disappear."

Bess ignored the shouts and turned and walked back to her place. The people closest to her began shoving and pushing. Someone made a grab for her bonnet.

The governor raised his hand. The militia men started bringing the logs, piling them at the foot of the poles.

Quaco began to sing.

Amba, his woman, had been tied to a fourth stake a little distance apart. Not to burn, only to watch. Against the wishes of practically everyone, Hunter insisted she be spared because she was so heavily pregnant. Her voice joined Quaco's.

Peter the Doctor didn't know their chant, but he could feel it with his belly. He keened along with them.

And from the gibbet, knowing how much longer he must hang there and how much worse it was yet to be, Kinsowa began his Ibo death chant.

It was enough of a diversion. The crowd turned its attention from Bess to what it was they'd come to see.

One of the redcoats poured a little pitch over a few logs in each pyre, just enough to get things going. A second brought the torch.

Bess watched only Tom. She held her breath. The first flames were licking at his shins when she saw him begin convulsing. Minutes later she knew he was dead. No one else seemed to notice. Perhaps because that was about the time Peter the Doctor stopped singing and began to scream. Quaco's chant continued for another thirty minutes. Then he, too, began to whimper, and finally to howl.

Kinsowa stopped chanting after five hours. The heat of the fires and the terrible thirst took his voice away. Amba alone sang the slowly burning men to their deaths. It took nearly ten hours for first Quaco, then Peter the Doctor to die, and she didn't stop once in all that time. Not until they came and untied her and led her away.

Much of the crowd had long since left. Bess stayed until the end. Finally, when it was only she and the few redcoats detailed to guard the slaves who'd been sent to clean up the mess, she walked over to the soldier who was in charge. "Tell the governor Red Bess wants to buy the woman. He won't get any kind of a price for her as she is, especially not considering what she is, but tell him I'll pay whatever he asks."

The soldier said he'd pass on the message. Bess walked home through the pall of greasy black smoke that hung over the town and filled it with the stench of burning flesh.

Chapter Five

THE WINTER OF 1713–1714 was the harshest in a long time. There was a dispute between the city and the colony's agricultural land to the north, and far less grain than was needed reached New York's mills. Flour was so scarce that bakeries charged a shilling a loaf for bread.

Such exorbitant prices strained both the resources of the churches, and the paupers' relief fund established by the city to supplement them. Even the deserving poor went hungry.

The situation was exacerbated by worse cold than any but the oldest could remember, and so much snow the oyster banks between Manhattan and Long Island became inaccessible. Oysters were normally a steady source of free food for the indigent. Without them times were hard.

It was snowing yet again on the Friday night in February when Bess left her house. She'd wrapped herself in one of Sally's old duffel cloaks and pulled the hood over her head, but the cold penetrated even the thick gray wool. No matter. The weather couldn't compete with the bone-deep chill she felt inside.

For the first time Bess could remember, there were paupers in plain sight along the road. She counted eleven on the short walk between Pearl Street and Hall Place, huddled in the doorways and leaning against the lampposts. A few were still alert enough to watch her passage with hungry eyes; others were too wretched to bother. Two she judged to be already dead. Bess was too troubled to care, too intent on her own pain to be sensible of theirs, and given the sort of woman she was, certainly not afraid.

All the same, it was prudent to avoid the dark expanse of the White Hall wharf, where she was sure to come across still more loiterers. She walked, instead, up Dock Street, where a few of the old-fashioned wooden houses had so far survived the fashion for brick, and turned finally into Hall Place. Born and raised in the city, she could never remember being on this short and narrow street. Sally used to walk her children as far out of the way as necessary to avoid Hall Place. Bess had continued the custom. Until she saw the red-and-white-striped pole beside the door—it was just visible behind a thick veil of flying snowflakes—she wasn't sure which house she wanted.

Useful as a landmark, the pole was in some ways an anachronism. Lucas Turner had erected it when he married Ankel Jannssen's widow and moved into her house. It had stayed ever since, but strictly speaking Lucas's grandson did no barbering. Christopher was too much in demand as a surgeon to bother with shaving or delousing or pulling teeth.

Word was that, busy as the town kept him with his knives, Christopher slept less than most men. True apparently. It was nearly midnight, but Bess could make out the shimmer of candlelight behind the ground-floor shutters. No matter, she'd have roused him from the sleep of the just if that's what was required.

She took a deep breath. Normally she wasn't much of a churchgoer. Sally stopped taking her children to any church after they refused to bury her husband. Bess had made her peace with the clerics when she married Moses. Now high days and holy days saw her in a pew at Trinity Church, singing the Anglican hymns with gusto. The rest of the year she minded her business and let the good Lord mind his. Still, before she lifted the brass knocker she whispered a prayer. It was something she'd done frequently of late. "Please. For the sake of Jesus Christ thy beloved son. Amen."

Christopher himself came to the door, carrying a candle that he shielded from the wind with his hand. The masked flame did little to dispel the dark. "Yes? Can I help you?"

"It's me. Cousin Bess. May I come in?"

"Bess . . ." Christopher was startled by the sound of the midnight bell tolling over the city from the high square steeple of Trinity Church. As if it would have been less extraordinary had Red Bess come calling at noon. "Yes. Well, I suppose . . . I mean . . . Is something wrong?"

"Of course. Would I be here otherwise?"

"No, you would not. I'm sorry. You startled the wits from me. Come in. Here, let me take your cloak."

She shook the snowflakes from it before she gave it to him, and wiped her boots on the scraper beside the front door. Bess carried no muff, and he noticed that her hands were red and chapped with the cold. And she had lost considerable weight. "Tamsyn," he said, turning to hang the duffel cloak from a carved peg set into the wall. "Is she well?"

"Very. Though the birth of the child left her tired. Bearing them's an exhausting business, as you're soon to discover. How is Mistress Jane?"

"My wife is well. And we've almost two months before the baby is due to be born."

"I know."

He smiled. "Yes, I expect you do. Come, let us go in to the fire. You look cold."

"I'm perishing. It's bitter out there. I counted a number of poor fools who'll be lucky to survive until dawn."

"There's talk of building an almshouse where they might be looked after and taught better habits."

"I know. My son-in-law Zachary Craddock sits on the committee considering the matter."

Christopher opened the door to his sitting room, but Bess paused before following him. "That's them, isn't it?" She nodded to the pair of pictures on the wall. "Lucas and Marit?"

He raised the candle so she could better see the portraits. "That's them."

"He sold my mother to buy her, did you know?"

"I'd heard a version of the story."

Bess sighed. "I expect they're all 'versions of the story.' The family resemblance is hard to deny, whatever affection might be lacking. Willem looks much like him. While you . . ." She shot a quick glance from the pictures to Christopher, then back again. "You don't look a thing like her. For all she was your blood grandmother. And if I didn't know it wasn't possible, I'd say you had Lucas's eyes."

"Sometimes," Christopher said softly, "it has seemed to me you had forgotten that I'm a Turner only by adoption."

"No, I never did. That's not why I wouldn't let you have Tamsyn."

"Why, then?"

Bess glanced toward the stairs. "Your wife is asleep up there, I take it."

"She is."

"She's a good woman, is Jane Bradford. I've known her since she was a child. Count your blessings, Christopher, and stop mooning over what was never meant to be. Now where's that fire you promised me?"

"In here." He opened the door wider and held the candle for her to see the way.

In essence the room was as it had always been when Christopher lived alone but for old Selma—a table, a few chairs, the floor covered by a Turkey carpet that Nicholas had brought back from one of his earliest voyages—but Jane had added those touches lacking since his mother died. The brasses shone, there was a freshly laundered cloth on the table, even some sprays of pussy willow cut a few days before and about to erupt into bloom forced by the warmth of the fire.

"Pleasant enough," Bess said, giving everything a frank appraisal.

"It is now," Christopher said. "Jane's brought the place to life. Selma was always willing, but I never knew what to tell her. Besides, she's old. My mother-in-law gave us two young house slaves as a wedding present. They have made a difference."

"Indeed. They always do. May I sit?"

"Good God. Of course. I'm sorry. Would you like something? A toddy, perhaps. I can rouse someone to—"

"No. Let them sleep. You'll get a better day's work out of them tomorrow. Besides, if it were only a toddy I wanted, I'd not have come."

"No, you wouldn't."

Bess had taken a chair beside the fire. Christopher put the candle on the table next to her and took the chair opposite. She wore no cap. He noted that her hair was still bright red, laced with only a few strands of gray, but her face was pale, the skin drawn tight over bones that seemed sharper than he remembered. "Very well, tell me."

"They say that young as you are, you're the finest surgeon in the city." She sat back, studying him as if she'd never seen him before. "Is it true?"

"I try very hard to do the right thing for my patients."

He should have known it was to do with illness. He'd hoped it was somehow connected to Tamsyn. Foolish. His skill with the knife: stupid of him not to have realized earlier. "Your color is not good," he said bluntly. "I thought it was the cold, but you've been by the fire for some minutes and it has not brought a flush to your cheeks. What other symptoms have you?"

"I'm not a very red Bess these days," she said with a small chuckle. "And no surprise. I've been so much bled it's a wonder my veins aren't empty."

Christopher sat forward. "When was the last time?"

"The Sunday five days past."

"The blood thins in cold weather. I thought everyone knew it was unwise to bleed at such times. Even medical doctors from Edinburgh."

"Everyone does know, Zachary Craddock included. But in some instances, when the need seems great . . ." Without any warning, Bess began unlacing the bodice of her dress. "It's best you see for yourself."

Christopher was startled for only a moment. Then he sat back in his chair, looking not at her but at the fire.

Bess understood his courtesy. "All right," she whispered after a few moments. "Now."

She was not corseted and had opened her chemise as well as her bodice. The breasts she bared were huge and pendulous. She seemed shamed not by the showing of them, but by the way they looked. "You may not believe it, but time was when I had pappes a man would find exceeding pleasing. But that was before I suckled four babes. And before this." She reached up and with her left hand lifted her right breast and pulled it aside. The lump she exposed was the size of a large, lopsided egg. It stood out from the taut flesh.

Christopher leaned forward and put out his hand. "May I?"

"I wouldn't have come if you might not."

The growth was hard and unyielding. That could be a good sign, but the lump was also very smooth and that was definitely not good. Christopher had learned not to show his concern, and his face gave nothing away. *Encysted Tumours borrow their Names from a Cyst or Bag in which they are contained. If the Matter forming them resembles Milk-Curds it is an* Atheroma; *if it be like Honey,* Meliceris; *if composed of a fatty Substance,* Steatoma, *which unlike the first Two is decidedly Firm to the touch. Suety Tumours, are also recognized by being Pock-Marked and full of Indentations. They cause no Illness to the Patient and are easily Excised, even from the Breast.*

"Well," Bess said, "what opinion have you?"

"None yet." Christopher stood up and palpated the growth with the fingertips of both hands. Bess winced. *The* Scirrhus *may be distinguished by its want of Inflammation in the Skin, its smoothness and slipperiness deep in the Breast, and generally by its pricking Pain. As the Tumour degenerates into a Cancer, which is the worst degree of* Scirrhus, *it becomes unequal and livid and, the Vessels growing varicose, at last ulcerates.* "How long have you had this?"

"I first noted it when Tamsyn was two months with child. The wee babe, as her father calls her, is a month old."

"Lift your arm, please." He prodded the soft underarm flesh gently but firmly. There were at least three knots, possibly more. "I take it Craddock's been treating you?"

Bess nodded. "I went to him when no simples of mine proved effective. I think the thing had been with me some three months by then."

"And growing all the time?"

"Yes. Considerably more in recent weeks."

"And what does your son-in-law prescribe?"

"Frequent bleeding and strong purges. And for some time he cupped it every second day until the lump was blistered all over. When that did nothing, he used the lancet four times. He tells me medical doctors from Edinburgh do not require barbers for such things. They are themselves schooled in what he calls the benign use of the knife. Anyway, it makes no matter. The thing does not burst. It only oozes a small amount of liquid and blood, then dries at once."

"Clear liquid or cloudy?"

"Clear. A drop or two, no more. The poison will not be drawn, though

Zachary started at once with poultices of mustard and flax and has continued the prescription. In fact I'd been using poultices before I consulted him. Hog dung. There is no more powerful drawing medicament."

"Does Craddock know you are come to me?"

Bess shook her head.

"So I thought."

"I'm my own woman, Christopher Turner. Fatherless since the age of four and husbandless these twenty years. Zachary Craddock is married to my daughter, not to me."

"Yes, of course." He started to draw her chemise closed. "There's nothing more examination can tell me. You may restore your clothing, Cousin Bess."

"The question," she said brusquely, "is whether you can restore my health."

There are some surgeons so disheartened by the ill-success of this Operation that they decry it in every Case, and even recommend certain Death to their Patients, rather than a trial. "It is rather late for surgery. The likelihood of a successful outcome is burdened by the length of time—"

"Christopher: can you cut it out of me, or can you not?"

He drew a long breath and looked not at her but at the fire. "I cannot excise a tumor such as this. It is embedded too deep. It would be a cruel lie to say otherwise."

"And if it continues to grow, it will kill me, will it not?"

His mouth was too dry for speech. Christopher nodded.

"Sooner rather than later?"

He nodded a second time.

Bess finished lacing her bodice. She stood up. "Very well. Thank you for giving me your opinion. I take it . . ." She hesitated. "I presume your refusal to cut is based on no ill will."

"It is not, Bess, for I bear you none." Craddock had been Tamsyn's choice as much as her mother's. Christopher had not fooled himself about that. "Besides, I've never refused any as I thought I could help."

She nodded. "The whole town says as much. Forgive me."

They walked together to the door. Christopher took the old cloak from the wall and wrapped it around her. "I'll walk with you, shall I?"

"No, you shall not. Thank you, but I prefer my own company at the moment." Bess pulled up her hood. Christopher opened the door.

The snow had stopped falling and the wind had died; the cold seemed yet more intense. It stung the nose and the throat to breathe it. He watched her take a step into the night. Red Bess. There was none like her; quite possibly there never would be. And even if only by adoption, they were kin. "Cousin Bess, wait a moment."

She turned back to him and he saw on her face something he had come to recognize, sometimes to dread. The look of intense, almost unreasoning hope with which so many patients confronted him. "Yes?"

"There is a chance. It's very small." *The Success of this Operation is exceeding precarious, from the great Disposition there is in the Constitution to form a new Cancer in the Wound or some other Part of the Body. There are those who will not recommend this surgery for Fear that their Reputations will be harmed by the low Rate of good success. But the Instances where Life and Health have been preserved by it, are sufficiently numerous to warrant the Recommendation of it.* "Almost no chance at all. I'd be lying if I didn't tell you that."

"My granddaughter Sofie Craddock is a month old," Bess said softly. "Yesterday I held her and she seemed to smile. A touch of the colic, no doubt, but the real smiles are coming. I am forty-nine years old. With luck I might expect a few more years. Any chance is worth the taking."

"You may not think so when you hear what I'm suggesting."

Bess waited.

"I can cut off the whole breast," Christopher said.

II

Have no truck with the Turners. Sally's nearly last words. And here Bess was readying her bed for one of them.

"I'd no choice, Mama," she whispered as she gave a final pat to the embroidered coverlet that had been a part of her trousseau. "I do not wish to die if it can be avoided. The thing is that simple."

Bess heard a noise behind her. She'd sent Cuffy, the youngest house slave, after extra bedding and clean rags. "Good," she said without turning around. "Put them down beside the fireplace near that old pail. That way they'll be warm and dry and to hand if Mr. Turner wants them. And I think you'd better get some—Oh, it's you. I was expecting Cuffy."

Amba still spoke little English, but she had come to understand most of what was said to her. She lay the pile of cloths and coverlets beside the fire, then waited for another instruction. She looked eager but uncomfortable. Since her daughter was born, Amba had taken the place of Tom, driving the wagon, tending the fires, and doing some of the heavier work in the garden. Those things suited her better than fussing with the household linen.

She was built like a man, Bess thought, with muscles rippling beneath her sleek ebony skin. Or perhaps some strange but beautiful African beast. Amba had been broken to domestic service more easily than Bess might have imagined, but there was still a wild and foreign quality to her. She looked entirely unsuited to the plain gingham dress Bess insisted all her women slaves wear. That veneer of New York respectability didn't cover much. Bess never looked at the girl but that she remembered her singing the Ashanti death chant for ten hours while her man burned slowly to death in front of her eyes.

"Thank you, Amba. Is Cuffy seeing to the hot water?"

The girl nodded. "Much water," she said. "Plenty hot. Amba make big fire."

"I'm sure you did. That's everything, then. You may go. There's work in the shed for you. I want those hoes sharpened before— Oh, my . . . I never . . ." The slave had gone down on her knees before Bess and was kissing her hand. "Get up, Amba. This is entirely unnecessary. You are to obey my orders, not worship me like some Roman prince. Is this what you do in your—"

"Mistress Red Bess not die," the young woman said fiercely. "Amba make strong magic so Mistress live."

She pushed something into Bess's hand while she spoke. A lump of chicken feathers from the look of it, held together with what appeared to be dung. "Thank you, Amba. I appreciate it. I really do. Now, on your feet. Surely it's time to feed that daughter of yours. I think I can hear her crying."

The child, Phoebe, was past two years, and still avid for her mother's breast. She'd been born less than a week after they burned her father, a few days after Amba was brought to Bess's house. Bess stayed beside the girl throughout her labor, bathing her sweating face, giving her sips of a feverfew and henbane tea that somewhat eased the pain. She'd made the brew with her own hands. She delivered the babe as well.

That had been a bloody business. Amba was not formed as were women, black or white, born here in the colony, including Amba's own newborn daughter. Bess didn't understand that, and she and Amba didn't have enough common language to discuss it. But the agony of labor and the joy of birth, those were things women required no words to communicate. Only after the babe was delivered and the cord cut and the swaddling seen to did Bess turn over the care of Amba and her child to the other blacks.

It was no less than she did for any slave she owned, but Amba saw only the fact that these were the first white hands to offer comfort rather than pain. "Mistress Red Bess not die," she said again, then sprang up and ran from the room.

"Let us hope not," Bess whispered after her. "I'd count it a great pity to be buried with one pappe when I might have gone to my maker with two."

The lump of chicken feathers and whatever it was that glued them together was sticky in her hand, and it emitted an unpleasant smell. Having long been accused of practicing witchery, Bess had little confidence in it. She started to throw the fetish in the fireplace, then thought better of the notion. She went back to the bed instead and tucked the thing under her pillow. In these circumstances any assistance was welcome, and any chance, however remote, worth the taking.

"We shall need more help than this old one can provide," Christopher said brusquely, not looking at Hetje when he spoke. "Tell me whom else to summon. Younger and stronger."

Red Bess lay on her back, her hair spread out on the white linen pillowslip, her eyes half closed. "Hetje will do," she murmured sleepily. "I can't . . ." The words trailed away. A small smile played about her lips.

Christopher himself had instructed her to take as much laudanum as she was sure wouldn't kill her a few minutes before his arrival, and to drink a couple of tots of rum after that. But he was sure he'd also told her he would need a couple of young slaves to help. "Cousin Bess, listen to me, I told—"

"I birthed her," Hetje said. "And her brother and all her children. Hetje be a good slave. Do whatever the master says."

She was looking at him with the same intent gaze he had noticed the night of the slave uprising. Something about this old black woman made his skin prickle, but that wasn't why he was disturbed by her presence. "You can stay if your mistress said you could. But I need a couple of young helpers with strong arms and stronger backs."

"And strong stomachs," Hetje said bluntly. "Nobody gonna come. Every one of them be afraid. They say you be a torturer."

"It doesn't matter what they say." Recalcitrant blacks who would not obey without argument seemed to Christopher a great deal more trouble than they were worth. Far better to hire them out if they had useful skills, or sell them on if they did not. He glanced at Bess. Magnificent to be able to sleep before going under the knife, and in his experience, a degree of relaxation impossible to achieve with strong drink alone. He'd seldom seen the benefits of laudanum so clearly demonstrated; but she was of little use to him at the moment.

He'd promised he wouldn't tie her down. "That's the one thing I can't bear the thought of," she'd confided, "being roped into place like a mule on a tether."

"I would not consider it," he'd told her. "It isn't seemly." Being tied to the bed was all right for patients in the hospital, but not acceptable for a decent woman being treated in her own home. Unfortunately she had not left him with many options.

"The mistress gave instructions that everyone was to do exactly as I say," Christopher lied. "Now, go get two of your strongest young house slaves. And if you're not back in ten seconds I'll have you whipped for gross disobedience."

Hetje looked at him. She seemed not in the least impressed with his claims to authority, and certainly not frightened by his threats, but after a few moments she grunted and left the room. She returned in under a minute, accompanied by two younger women.

One hung back, hovering by the door with her hand pressed over her mouth, her dark eyes wide with fear. The other went immediately to the bed and looked down at her mistress. "She be fine." The mutterings were aimed more in Hetje's direction than Christopher's. "Amba make strong medicine."

"Amba," Christopher murmured. "Yes, of course, I thought I recognized you. I remember from the day of the bur— Good God, Bess bought you, did she?"

"Amba make strong medicine. Mistress Bess not die."

"I hope not," Christopher said. He swung around to face the other girl, the one still cowering near the door. "You, what's your name?"

"Cuffy, master."

"Very well, Cuffy, come here."

The girl approached. She was maybe fourteen and looked plenty strong. "You'll do, Cuffy. Position yourself there at the bottom of the bed and get a good, steady grip on your mistress's legs. I don't want her to kick and thrash about, do you understand? If she does it could be very dangerous for her. I need her to stay still. Come on, girl, say something. Do you or don't you understand?"

The girl nodded and moved to where she could get a solid hold on Bess's ankles. "Good. Now, you." Christopher turned to face Amba. "You'll have to steady the top part of her body. Her head and her shoulders mustn't move. Is that clear?"

Amba sprang onto the bed. Christopher made a move toward her, but Hetje was there before him. She stretched out both hands, grabbed Amba's arm, and began to yank. "You get off that bed, girl. You be altogether too familiar. I be telling you how it got to be. You don't—"

Bess opened her eyes. "Hello, Amba," she murmured, then drifted off again. The young woman meanwhile had shaken off Hetje's grip and hitched up the skirt of her gingham frock. Christopher could see the sleek ebony thighs, muscles taut beneath the skin. Amba set Bess's head on her lap and leaned forward, supporting the older woman's shoulders on those muscular thighs, twining her young black arms around Bess's old white ones. "This be what you want?"

"You supposed to say 'master,'" Hetje railed. "I been telling you that right along. And you can't—"

Christopher held up a restraining hand. "Yes, that's fine," he told Amba. Then, to Hetje, "It's all right. Let her do it in that fashion. It will work very well, and I don't think your mistress minds."

Bess was sleeping again, still smiling.

"Hetje be a good slave," Hetje grumbled. "Know better than—"

"It's all right," Christopher said again. "All of you are to stay exactly where you are. The pair of you"—he glanced at Cuffy positioned by Bess's ankles, and at Amba cradling her torso—"remember that your job is to hold your mistress absolutely still. Hetje, you will stay right where you are and get me anything I ask for. Instantly, do you understand? With no grumbling and no questions. And the three of you remember this: whatever you see—or hear—never doubt for one moment that I am doing exactly the right thing for your mistress. Exactly what she wanted. Now, let us begin."

Christopher drew a chair up to the right side of the bed, sat down, and folded back the coverlet. Following his instructions, Bess had put herself to bed naked above the waist. Her huge breasts hung slack to either side. Christopher lifted the one on the right and gently prodded the tumor. It was only three days since she'd come to him at Hall Place and exposed the growth, but it seemed larger. Still slick and smooth and rock-hard, however. And even in her dreamy, half-sleeping state, when he palpated the protruding mass she gave a little gasp of discomfort.

He moved his fingers up to the armpit. This time he counted four tight knobs, or knots, as Lucas had called them. *When the* Scirrhus *is attended by Knots in the Arm-pit, no service can be done by Amputation unless the Knots be taken away as well, for there is no sort of dependence to be laid on their subsiding by the discharge of the Wound of the Breast.*

He was sweating. Christopher had to stop to wipe his face with one of the cloths that had been laid beside the bed in preparation for his needs. "Have you told them what you intend?" he'd asked the day after Bess's first visit, when she came back to tell him of her decision. "Tamsyn and her husband, do they know?"

"They do not."

"Bess, I don't think—"

"You are not to tell me how to run my life, Christopher Turner." She'd looked straight at him in that way she had. "You are to prevent my losing it. Zachary Craddock and my daughter will know soon enough what I have done. Either they will come to bury me, or to drink a toast to my restored health."

"Cousin Bess, I have to tell you, I can give no guarantees."

"I ask none. Only your best efforts."

The possibility of extirpating these Knots, without wounding the great Vessels, is very much questioned by Surgeons; but I have done it when they have not laid backwards and deep.

A manual examination gave him a fair certainty that they were upstanding, not lying backward, but he wouldn't know how deep they were until he cut. Christopher opened his instrument case.

In extirpating the Scirrhus, *if it be small, a longitudinal Incision will dilate suf-*

ficiently for the Operation, if large, an oval piece of Skin must be cut through first, the size of which is to be proportioned to that of the Tumour.

He had sharpened every one of his scalpels before he left the house that morning. Jane had watched him perform the ritual. "You seem more than usually agitated," she'd said. "You must not fear this surgery, my dearest. You are well up to the doing of the thing."

"Thank you for your confidence. Though I rather think if I told you I was to cut off the head of a man and put it on a pussycat, you'd tell me I was 'well up to the doing of the thing.'"

"Indeed, because you are. Though I can't think why anyone would want to perform so strange an alteration. Pussycats are on the whole much nicer than men. With some exceptions, of course." She'd come close to him then, and lifted her face for his kiss, and he'd bestowed it, and patted her distended tummy and put the knives back in their case and brought them here. And now it was time to see if he was, as his adoring wife insisted, well up to the doing of the thing.

He selected the long, curved scalpel. To be sure there were no filings clinging to it from the recent honing, he wiped it across the fabric of his breeches. Then he leaned forward. *In taking off the whole Breast the Skin may be very much preserved by making the Wound of it a great deal less than the Basis of the Breast, which must be carefully cleared away from the Pectoral Muscle.*

The first cut made her moan, but nothing like as loudly as she would have if only rum had been administered. Christopher heard Cuffy moan as well. "You there," he said without lifting his head or turning around, "Cuffy. Don't you dare move or I'll see you're caged and whipped, and whatever else I can think of on the day." He glanced up at Amba. She was looking not at him but at Bess, and she hadn't budged.

The shallow cut he'd made was oozing blood. "Give me one of those cloths," Christopher murmured. Hetje held it out. He took it, swabbed at the red puddle on Bess's white skin, then gave it back to her. "You saw what I just did. Can you do that, Hetje? Move in a little closer beside me and keep mopping up the blood whenever it comes. Even if there's quite a lot of it. Just sop it up. I need to see what I'm doing. Have you got that?"

"Hetje be a good slave. Do whatever the master say."

"Right. Fine. Then do it." He was conscious of her looking over his shoulder when he selected a second scalpel. This one was broader, more triangular in shape. Christopher used his left hand to spread the wound he'd made, then inserted the blade between the pectoral muscle and the fatty breast tissue and, working inside the skin, began separating the two.

Bess screamed again. Louder this time, longer, and she was trying to jerk away from the knife. Behind him Christopher heard Cuffy sob, but she held steady. Amba had still not moved so much as an inch. Bess continued to scream, and to try and arch her back, but the black girl who cradled her upper body did not allow her to pull out of Christopher's reach.

He worked from right to left, away from the tumor. *It is Imperative not to pierce the Tumour itself, for great Harm can come to the Patient if the evil in the thing is spread throughout the Body. Indeed, a decent Practitioner can easily follow this Advice because, all these* Scirrhuses *being enlarged Glands, are encompassed with their proper Membranes, which make them quite distinct from the neighboring Parts, and easily separable.*

The left side of the breast was free of the rib cage. Christopher eased the knife between the skin and the muscle and loosened the top half of the breast from its covering.

The screams were much louder now, and she'd opened her eyes. Bess was staring at him, and yelling so that it seemed everyone in New York must hear. Blood was flooding the wound. "Hetje! Come, do as I told you. Mop it up!"

The old woman reached across his hand with the wadded cloth and began swabbing at the flow. Christopher waited until she'd gone some way to reducing the inundation. It gave him a few seconds to make up his mind.

It was still entirely possible he would have to sew up the wound and declare the operation a failure. *In cases where the Tumour adheres to the subjacent Muscle and that Muscle to the Ribs, the Operation is impracticable.*

He was almost entirely certain that was not Bess's case. On her second visit, when she said she wanted him to take off her breast, he'd examined her again. The growth had seemed to him then entirely free of the parts beneath it, a creature of only her offending pappe, as she called it. However, if he was wrong, he had shortened her life rather than preserved it. Worse, he had put her through this agony for no reason whatever.

She was screaming steadily now, all her strength seeming to go into that one sustained screech of torment that patients uttered toward the end of a surgery, when all their courage and endurance were exhausted. And he was only just begun.

There was, however, a slightly different quality to these shrieks. They seemed to issue almost as an involuntary reaction. Bess's eyes were open and looking at him, but they did not accuse; they seemed filled with a dreamy indifference. Christopher was an expert on the screams of surgery, and he'd neither seen nor heard anything quite like this before.

The quantity of laudanum, perhaps. Bess would have access to far more than any ordinary patient. Could be she'd taken enough to create this odd disconnection between her self and her pain.

Cuffy, however, couldn't see into her mistress's eyes, only hear her agonized yells. The girl was sobbing almost as loud as Bess. Even Hetje, standing by Christopher's side, was whimpering. Only Amba remained silent.

Christopher looked at the African girl. She seemed to sense his glance and looked from Bess's face to his. She smiled, as if . . . No, that was absurd. A black savage, what did she . . . The smile, however, was definitely one of encouragement. Suddenly she opened her mouth and emitted a kind of hoot punctuated by a clicking noise. And she never stopped staring into his eyes. The noise she made was strange, but not terrifying. It had the sound of joy in it, the promise of hope.

Black savage or no, she helped him decide. He and Bess had agreed to the operation. Bess was in no position to change her mind. He had no excuse for doing so.

With one downward plunge of the scalpel Christopher severed two-thirds of Bess's right breast from her torso. What remained was held in place only by the section containing the tumor. And thanks to the technique learned from his grandfather's journals, there was a good-size flap of skin left with which to cover the wound when he was done.

Bess continued to scream, Cuffy to sob, and Amba to hoot. Hetje was silent. Christopher ignored them all and concentrated on his task. "Hand me that threaded needle from my case." He had to shout twice to get Hetje to hear him over the din, but finally she pressed something into his hand. Christopher did not look away from his patient.

He'd prepared the ligature earlier, while mentally rehearsing Lucas's instructions. *The Bleeding of the large Arteries is to be stopped by passing the Needle twice through the Flesh, almost round every Vessel, and tying upon it, which will necessarily include it in the Ligature. In order to discover the Orifices of the Vessel, the Wound must be cleansed with a Sponge wrung out of Warm Water.*

Hetje was still sopping with the blood-soaked rags she'd been using right along. "Use a fresh cloth," Christopher snapped. "Dip it in that water by the fireplace first." As if by following Lucas's advice down to the last comma he could assure himself of his grandfather's brilliant skills.

Amba was still hooting, and Bess was thrashing with more force than before. Her screams were somehow different as well, more heartfelt. The rum and the laudanum were starting to wear off. And the worst was yet to come. "Hold her tight," Chris said. "And damn it, girl, stop that extraordinary wailing. No one can hear my instructions and I can't hear myself think."

Amba fell silent. Now all he had to listen to were Cuffy's sobs and Bess's agonized yells. The one piece of advice he'd gotten from Nicholas rather than Lucas was that a surgeon must stop his ears against his patient's cries, however heartrending.

He had come, as Jane would put it, to the doing of the thing: it was time to remove the cancer that was stealing away Bess's life. Christopher chose his longest and narrowest scalpel. *It is Imperative not to pierce the Tumour itself* . . . He lifted the bloody lump of formless flesh that had once been what Bess had called "a pappe any man would find exceeding pleasing." The growth moved with it.

Thanks be to God. His diagnosis had been correct. The tumor did not adhere to the muscle underneath or to the ribs.

With one sure and swift cut Christopher released that part of the breast from her body. Next the knots in the underarm. *The possibility of extirpating these . . . very much questioned by Surgeons . . . done it when they have not laid backwards and deep.* He didn't think they were backward and deep, but God help him, he could be wrong. He'd know soon enough.

He chose the smallest blade so he could efficiently cut around the hardened knobs. The first cut he made no deeper than a quarter-inch. The knot lifted easily on the tip of his scalpel. So did the second. The third and the fourth were joined. Both came free in one cut.

Christopher sighed with pleasure. It was done. The entire bloody mess lay on the bed beside Bess. She and her pappe were separated. The cancer was no more with her.

For the past few moments it was as if he'd been attached to his instruments, as if he felt and heard and thought and smelled only through them. Now he was once more in the room, with his patient and her three black slaves. He heard Bess's cries of torment—more whimpering than screaming, now that he'd stopped cutting—Hetje's stertorous breathing, and Cuffy's terrified sobs.

Only Chris and Amba were silent. He lifted his eyes. This time he discovered the African girl already staring at him. "Hallelujah," Chris said. Amba smiled. He smiled back. "Hetje, get me an empty bucket." He spoke without turning his head. "I believe there's one over there by the fireplace." Amba nodded at him meanwhile, as if she wanted him to know he had earned her approval. Then, deliberately disobeying his instructions, she opened her mouth and gave one more tongue-clacking hoot. She stopped before he could again reprimand her. She was still smiling. He lowered his gaze.

Hetje brought him the old tin pail. Christopher took it from her and with his hand swept the formless mass of fat and skin and muscle and cancer off the bed and into it. The large round ball of the tumor could be easily distinguished atop the pile of discarded flesh.

Christopher wasted no time examining the growth. "Fetch me some wine," he instructed. "Be quick."

Hetje did as he said, but this time he washed the wound himself, trusting no one else to be sufficiently thorough. When it was as clean as he could make it, he dusted the area with stanching powder and began to stitch. Finally he dressed the whole with bandages soaked in wine. Only then did he allow Cuffy and Amba to move from the positions they'd held for over an hour.

Chris moved as well. He gave in to the great need to stretch his legs, even extended his arms above his head, linked his fingers, and pushed at the sky. Truth was, at that moment he felt he might be able to touch it.

The pair of young slaves were standing beside the door, waiting for instructions. "You may go," Chris told them. "But first, you both did exceptionally well. Your mistress has an excellent chance of being restored to health. I shall be sure to tell her—"

"Master! Come!"

Hetje's voice. Christopher turned back to the bed. Bess had been barely conscious when he finished operating; now he expected to find her sleeping with exhaustion. Instead she was half sitting in the bed, leaning on Hetje's arm. "She ain't but barely breathing, Master. I be sitting her up to make it better, but it don't be helping a whole lot."

Bitter as it is for the Surgeon who has done his Best, it must be faced that a kind of Cyanosis oft follows on a successful Surgery, as if the Body has borne too much, lost too many of its vital Fluids. The Skin turns blue and the Breath comes only with great Difficulty, though there is no apparent Obstruction. This Condition inevitably leads to Death and Sadly, short of never Operating on any but those who are Young and in the Prime of Health, I know of no manner of Preventing it.

Sweet bloody Jesus. After all this. To lose her now, after all they'd both been through . . . Damn it, he wouldn't! Not without a struggle. Lucas might not have known a way of preventing Cyanosis *due to loss of Vital Fluids,* but he bloody well did.

The pipette and the hollow needle were always at the bottom of his case. There was a pig bladder in there as well. Even the latest version of the succession of brass valves he was forever having the smith make for him. What he did not have was blood.

Bess kept chickens out back in a coop at the far end of her garden. He seemed to recall there was a pig out there as well. He took a step closer to the bed and put his hand over her heart. The beating was very fast, a peculiar, almost hollow thump he'd come to recognize. She had seconds left, not minutes. There was no chance he could get an animal slaughtered and bled in the time she had left.

Though he'd dismissed them, Amba and Cuffy had stayed when they heard Hetje's cry. They were staring at him, waiting for him to do something. Hetje as well. Three black women, all of whom apparently held their mistress in true affection. All required to follow his instructions without hesitation. Christopher looked at each of them in turn.

No, he could not do it.

It was impossible to even consider, far worse than Jeremy Clinton's chidings about the blood of a Quaker being put in the body of an Anglican bishop. Negro blood in a white woman. Unthinkable.

There was only one option available. Christopher tore off his jacket and began rolling up the sleeve of his shirt.

"What do you mean, she's resting and cannot be disturbed? My mother does not rest. And she has never once in her life refused to see me." Tamsyn pushed by the slave standing in the door. A young black girl followed on her heels. Tamsyn turned to her. "Here, take the babe"—she handed little Sofie to the young slave—"and wait for me here."

There was a strange smell outside Bess's room. Tamsyn caught the scent before she was halfway up the stairs. A dark earthy odor, not so much unpleasant as unfamiliar. And the door to the bedroom was closed. "Mama, are you in there? Are you unwell?"

That Zachary had been treating her mother for something, Tamsyn knew. But she was not sure for what. "Nothing to bother you with," he'd said repeatedly.

"I'm old, I've the usual aches and pains" had been Bess's response to questions. "What profit in having a son-in-law who is a trained medical doctor from Edinburgh if you never consult him?"

Tamsyn looked at the closed door for a moment. Then she tapped on it. "Mama, you must answer me. I am becoming very feared that something is seriously amiss."

When there was no response she turned the knob.

The transfusion had been in progress for just under five minutes. The change it had wrought was truly extraordinary. Bess's cheeks were a healthy pink. Her breathing was easy and natural. Her eyes were closed, but you had only to look at her to know that she was sleeping, not senseless. Chris was lightheaded. He put it down to exultation. He wanted to shout out loud for the sheer joy of it. He knew how to do it now. He could put blood back in patients, not merely take—

"Oh, dear God! What is happening here?" Tamsyn stood in the open door, paralyzed. "Christopher, in the Lord's name . . . what unholy thing are you doing?"

"Close the door, Tamsyn. Your mother needs warmth. Then come closer and I will explain. I cannot, as you perhaps recognize, stand to greet you just now."

He was sitting beside Bess's bed, exactly as he had for the hour it took him to perform the operation, but this time his bare arm was extended over hers. And between the two, the wasted arm of the patient who had been ill for some months and the young muscular arm of the surgeon in his prime, there was a glass pipette through which blood could drip from his open vein into hers.

Tamsyn took a few hesitant steps. She looked at Hetje, standing on the other side of the bed, at Cuffy and Amba over by the fireplace. "What has happened here?" she whispered. The slaves looked back at her and did not reply. "Please, Christopher. You must tell me what you are doing."

"I am giving your mother some of my blood. To replace the large quantity she lost when I cut off her breast."

Though she covered her mouth with her hand, Tamsyn's gasp was audible. Christopher chose to ignore it. "There, I think that is sufficient for the moment. Hetje, you will find a few more ligatures in my case. Not threaded. Bring me one. And some of the lint I use for packing wounds." Then, to Tamsyn, "Hetje assisted me during the surgery, as your mother insisted. And I must say, she proved wise in the matter. Hetje did excellent service."

The old woman meanwhile had brought him the things he asked for. Christopher disconnected the makeshift apparatus from his arm first. He was careless of the wound he'd made when he opened his own vein, as he'd have time to treat it more thoroughly later, but he used the ligature to tie a tourniquet above the cut. He was, he realized, a little dizzy from loss of blood, not simply lightheaded with success.

Tamsyn watched him in silence for a moment or two, then found her voice. It was a whisper, hoarse with pain. "How could you do such a thing?"

"With more ease than I imagined, if you must know." He was removing the needle from Bess's vein while he spoke, packing a soft scrap of cotton sprinkled with stanching powder into the small wound he'd opened to receive it. "I have known for some time that blood transfusions were possible. I have, however, only today proved that success lies in using human blood."

"No," Tamsyn whispered. "No."

For the first time since she came into the room, Christopher turned to look at her. He was prepared to argue his case but she did not seem capable of listening. Tamsyn was swaying. He wasn't finished with Bess's wound, and for the moment she had first call on his skills. "Amba," he said coolly. "Catch Mistress Tamsyn. I believe she is about to swoon."

His words had the effect of revitalizing her. Tamsyn shook off the arm of the black woman. "No, I am not going to swoon." Her voice was charged with rage. "How dare you submit my mother to such abuse? What gives you the right to—"

"Bess herself gave me the right. For the love of God, Tamsyn, do you imagine I came here and knocked her down and proceeded to work my will upon her? You've a brain, woman. Use it."

"Whatever ill feeling you bore her because of me, I cannot imagine—"

"You prize yourself more highly than is perhaps warranted, my girl." Christopher grabbed up the pail with Bess's breast and covered the distance to where Tamsyn stood in two long strides. "Here, if you can do so without retching, take a look at this. It's the part of your mother's body that was rushing her to an early grave. I cut it off and saved her life."

He thrust the thing under her nose. Despite herself, Tamsyn looked. The stuff in the bucket was recognizable as a breast only by the nipple that remained upstanding. And next to that was a noxious lump that clearly was not a normal part of a woman's body. Tamsyn gagged. She again put both hands over her mouth. And began to sway. This time she truly might have fainted had Amba not cried out.

Throughout the exchange between Christopher and Tamsyn, Amba's attention had remained riveted on Bess. When she suddenly let out a piercing scream and lunged toward the bed, Christopher's heart sank. Before he ran to Bess's side, he knew.

Unlike every other corpse he'd seen, Bess was not white and drained. Her face was almost the color of her hair, the effect made more dramatic by the whiteness of the pillowslip. Red Bess indeed. Dead Red Bess. Christopher put his hand over her heart, but he knew what he would find. "Sweet Christ!" He could not keep himself from crying out. "How did this happen?"

"How could it not?" Tamsyn trembled with rage; her voice shook with the power of her feeling. "Answer me that, you butcher! How could any human being survive the tortures you put my poor mother through? I'll see you hanged, Christopher Turner. Damn me for eternity if I do not."

Christopher sat by the fire, staring at the smoldering logs and ignoring the book on his lap. Four days since Bess's death and he was still drained, still considering what he might have done differently, why, when success had been so close, he had failed.

The door from the hall opened. "Mr. Craddock to see you, Christopher." Jane's voice was as soft and as temperate as ever.

In all the years he'd known her—and they'd grown up side by side—Christopher had never heard his wife sound any other way. Even when he bedded her it was no different. When he was done she sighed a little sigh and bade him goodnight in much the same tone she now used to inquire if he would like her to bring some mulled wine for himself and Zachary Craddock.

"I do not think the doctor has come to drink my health," Chris said. "Come in, Craddock. Jane, leave us, please."

Her curtsys were awkward with her belly so large, but Jane did her best, then withdrew. The Scotsman stood in front of the door she'd closed behind her, staring at Christopher.

"I'd suggest you come closer and take advantage of the fire," Christopher said. "It is a bitter evening, is it not?"

"No more bitter than the pain my wife and I feel at the loss of her mother, Turner. But I don't imagine you can understand that."

"And why wouldn't I understand it? I too have known loss, sir. And for all our differences over the years, I admired many of Red Bess's qualities."

"Might I ask why, then, you performed such atrocious acts upon her?"

"I do not accept the description of my actions, but I did what I did because she was dying. Because I was her only hope. And I deeply regret, sir, that it was a hope unfulfilled." A small table with a glass decanter half full of brandy stood beneath the window. Christopher walked to it. "I told my wife you had not come to drink my health. Perhaps you will, however, take a tot against the cold."

Craddock waved away the offer. "I was treating Mistress Bess. She was my patient. I alone was in a position to decide if she was indeed dying."

"Good God, sir, did they teach you nothing in that famous school of medicine in Edinburgh? Have you ever seen a Scirrhus so hard and deep respond to any simple known to man? Have you ever lanced a thing so huge and had it discharge nothing but a drop of clear liquid and not realized that it was not a boil of the usual sort, but—"

"I know exactly what sort of growth plagued my mother-in-law. I do not question your diagnosis, surgeon. It is your cruel insistence that your precious scalpels are the answer to everything which fills me with rage. Have I not seen enough corpses carried into the churches of this town with the mark of your knives hidden in their coffins to know how fallacious that prescription is?"

Christopher poured himself a pony of brandy. He turned to Craddock and lifted the small pewter cup in his direction. "Are you quite sure you won't join me?"

"I bloody well will not. You're a barbarian and a mutilating heathen to boot. God forbid I should drink with a man who after he butchers a patient puts his own blood into her. You're a practitioner of evil sorcery, Turner. Burning is too good for you."

"First, I must ask you to keep your voice down. As you saw, my wife is soon to give birth. It is not good for her to be upset. Second, I am for what it's worth, a baptized Christian like yourself. Third, there is no sorcery whatever in the matter of blood transfusion. It has been used by men of science in both Paris and Rome. Finally, as to the corpses you mentioned, there are, I believe, more New Yorkers who carry the marks of my surgery on their living bodies than have taken them to the grave. Now, sir, have you said everything you came to say?"

This time Craddock spoke without bluster. "You're a cool one. I'll say that for you."

"I daresay I'm warmer than you, for all you've not removed your cloak, nor taken advantage of my brandy or my fire." Christopher tossed back the last of his drink and turned to put the empty cup on the mantel. "Since you're obviously not interested in my hospitality, are we done?"

"Not quite. I came to tell you I intended to bring an action for murder."

Christopher swung round to face him. "You're entirely mad. The magistrates would refuse to hear your case. There could be no healing done in this town ever again if a surgeon were held to a charge of murder when his patient died."

"If it made you cutters less quick to cut, then it would be an act of Christian charity to prove you wrong in a court of law." Craddock pursed his lips. "But it is not within my power to do so. I said I *intended* to bring an action. I have discovered I cannot."

Despite his scoffing Christopher felt some relief. Mad as the notion might be, if such a case were actually tried and went to a jury of ordinary men, there was no saying how it might come out. "I see. Well then, it seems pointless to discuss the matter. Though I admit, I'm curious. If it's not the fear of ridicule that stops you, why can't you bring your preposterous suit?"

"Because the final clause in my mother-in-law's will plainly states that it was her choice to submit to your inhuman ministrations. And that you are to be held in no way responsible for the outcome."

"Good Bess," Chris said softly. "After all that had been between us. That was kind of her."

"Far kinder than you deserve."

"I will say it one more time, Craddock, and then we are done with this discussion. In the case of a Scirrhus tumor as large and deeply embedded as was hers, removal of the part of the body wherein it is lodged is the patient's only chance of survival. And mark my words, before too much longer, blood transfusion will be recognized as the savior of hundreds."

"That is utter rubbish, an unspeakable libel on decent humankind. But I have not come here to argue with you."

"Fair enough. And not, if I correctly understand you, to tell me you are taking me to court for murder. So perhaps now we truly are done."

"Not quite yet." Craddock had left his hat in the front hall. He had removed his gloves; now he began pulling them on. "Before I go there are two pieces of information I wish to pass on."

"Very well, I'm listening."

"First, you are discharged from your post as surgeon in charge of the paupers' hospital on the Broad Way. I have been able to convince the governor that it is scandalous to allow such a proven incompetent, not to say a vicious madman, to continue in that responsibility. I'll thank you, sir, to give me the keys to the place."

Christopher walked to the large square table in the middle of the room and pulled open a drawer. He lifted out the ring of keys and dropped it into Craddock's outstretched hand. "Pity. I shall miss the old duffers. I was on occasion able to restore one or another to a semblance of health. Perhaps I will have a word with Hunter about this, now that you've had your say."

"Frankly, unless you fancy humiliation, I would not advise it." Craddock closed his gloved hand over the key ring. "You have been much discussed of late among the powerful of this town. I sit, as you may know, on the committee seeing to the arrangements for an almshouse. We have reached a decision. We are to build such a place, and to incorporate under its roof a substantially larger hospital for the indigent. My colleagues and I have, however, passed a resolution forbidding you from entering the premises, much less treating the patients."

III

Parliament permitted no mint anywhere in America; but the colonists created wealth in plenty. In the province of New York it grew in the holds of the single-masted sloops and twin-masted brigantines that sailed in and out of the harbor.

Thousands of miles south, in the West Indies, the English and Dutch settlers had covered the land with the greatest cash crop the world had thus far seen, the thing Europe craved beyond surfeit: sugar. Cane ruled on the Caribbean islands. As a result, virtually every morsel of food the islands' residents ate—grain, vegetables, meat—was shipped from the English colonies. Moreover, the tending and harvesting of the cane in the tropical heat was a job so hellish no white man would do it. A steady stream of black slaves hauled west from Africa were required. The Triangle Trade—New York to the islands to Guinea and back—had made men like Will Devrey and John Burnett enormously rich.

The right to build a new wharf beyond what had been the old East Gate of Wall Street had been granted to Burnett and Devrey in 1708. A ten-yard extension of the land was to be achieved by sinking ships to act as cribs for rubble and scree. That meant progress waited on the pair having ships they were willing to scrap. Since both men ran their vessels until the last possible moment of seaworthiness, it was not something that happened often. It took them nearly two years to build the wharf. In 1710 they at last got the job done and each wondered why he'd been so foolish as to tolerate the other's delay.

The new wharf—it became Burnett's Key when Burnett won the toss after an evening at the Blue Dog Tavern—had space for six ships to lie alongside: three berths for each partner. As for the newly created land behind the moorings, the pair rented it to the grain merchants for sixty pounds a year. The place became still more profitable when another set of tenants joined the Meal Market. In 1711 a consortium of the owners of Guinea ships opened the Slave Market on Burnett's Key. After that Will Devrey had only to walk a hundred yards from his elegant Wall Street front door, to the now widened place where Wall Street and Pearl Street met, to see his ships riding at anchor, and their cargos being sold.

On the tenth day of March, 1714, Devrey had other business to attend to: the final disposition of his sister's estate. Bess had written her will the day before she died, but she'd taken no legal advice in the matter and it turned out only some of the provisions were lawful. The now famous final clause holding Christopher Turner harmless was the talk of the town for some weeks, but none could see any way around it. The rest of the provisions were, with one exception, more or less what had been expected.

"To my beloved daughter, Tamsyn, I leave my house, all my furnishings and personal effects, and the entire contents of the simpling room and apothecary shop. I call to her particular attention her obligation to impart the skills she has learned from me, and by indirection from her grandmother Sally Turner Van der Vries, to her daughter, Sofie Craddock.

"There are, however, two things I do not leave to my dearest Tamsyn. I do not burden her with the obligation to pursue any quests or hold sacred any feuds, and I do not bequeath to her my slaves. Having come to believe that the danger of uprising and its terrible consequences will not depart this colony until we no longer affirm the peculiar institution, with this my last will and testament I manumit them all."

That last could not be done.

Naturally enough, being a woman, his sister was unaware of the finer points of the laws of the colony. Will sat on Hunter's council. He knew exactly how the statutes passed two years before were worded. Indeed, he'd been instrumental in making the argument that brought them into being.

It was not, he and a few others had advised the governor, so much the African blacks who were to blame for the revolt of 1712. The cause of the trouble was the presence of freed blacks, who owned land and lived where there were no decent Christian men and women to keep an eye on their behavior. They roamed the streets and gathered down by the waterfront and formed themselves into such gangs as the Smith Fly Boys and the Free Masons.

Blacks were not capable of looking after themselves. Every slave owner in the colony knew they were lazy and stupid. Manumission was bestowed by those who, against all logic and experience, held to the sentimental belief that savages could be made equal to whites.

Thanks to such arguments, the law Hunter finally signed did not forbid the direct importing of slaves from Africa as Massachusetts had done, nor place such a huge tax upon them that the trade was made entirely unprofitable, as had been the solution in Pennsylvania. New York's new law forbade freed slaves to own real estate, however far from the populous part of the city it might be. The old Negro plots that surrounded the various swamplands were abolished. Moreover, every person who wished to manumit a slave was to pay twenty pounds a year to the slave for life, to insure that the freedman would not prove a burden on the public charity. Otherwise the manumission was null and void.

Under the circumstances, Bess's attempt to free her slaves failed.

Old Hetje would soon be dead, but Bess's estate would not cover the hundreds, nay thousands, of pounds involved in keeping the others to the tune of twenty pounds a year each for the rest of their lives. Will did not see that he was under any obligation to assume such a huge expense, nor did he have any reason to take in his sister's slaves. He had five of his own. Tamsyn and Zachary were likewise completely provided for, and as a young couple newly starting out they certainly could not afford to pay the upkeep for Bess's slaves. Tamsyn insisted she and her husband must make a place for Hetje, and in the interest of domestic peace Craddock agreed. The rest were to be sold.

There were five altogether: the three surviving blacks Bess had inherited from her husband, the African woman Bess had bought after the executions, and the child the woman had borne.

Damn Bess. Will had warned her back then it was a foolish purchase. Now he was saddled with trying to get rid of not just an obviously brooding wench (most buyers considered that a disadvantage) but a child not yet three, who would need food and a place to sleep for at least another two years before any useful work could be had from her.

The more he thought about the way Bess never listened to anything he told her, the angrier Will became. Anger always made him sweat. He was drenched in perspiration by the time he reached the slave market.

"Morning, Mr. Devrey." The black who looked after the day-to-day operation of the holding pens and the washing sheds belonged to Burnett, who in turn hired him out for the job and charged the consortium a shilling a week for his services. Jebbo not only knew all the shipowners, he had a fairly clear idea of their financial dealings. "I hear how you got special business with us this day."

"I do, Jebbo. Family business. My late sister's slaves are to be sold. I believe they were brought to you last night."

"They were, Mr. Devrey. And I seen to it that they were kept good and quiet and all proper like. And they was washed already this morning. Bring you a fair price, they will. Jebbo can promise you that."

"Slaves! Black slaves! Prime slaves! Sale today! Slaves for sale!" The cry of the auctioneer echoed up Wall Street. "Slaves for sale! Gentlemen all come! Special today. Seasoned slaves today! And a cargo of prime Fantis just landed. Come and place your bids."

The men leaving the Merchants' Coffee House on their way to the auction did not move quickly. Though many were not New Yorkers—they came from all over the northern colonies—most had been before and knew the procedure. Slaves for rent would be offered first. The men of property from the upper reaches of New York colony as well as Rhode Island and Connecticut and Massachusetts had no interest in bondsmen for hire. That was strictly a local affair.

"Here's Tom, a skilled cooper. Belongs to the Widow Drummond, who since her husband died has no need of his services. Offered for three pounds the year. Ah, a hand raised. Done, sir." The hammer cracked on the table in front of the auctioneer.

"Belle now, a fine wench and a fine cook. Absolutely positively proven not to breed." A wink followed on that remark. And ripples of laughter. "Rentable for six months only, while her master is away visiting his family in Providence Town. When he returns it'll be nearing winter and cold and he'll want her back." Gales of laughter this time. "Four shillings the whole hundred and eighty days for Belle. A bargain, gentlemen. Am I not— Fine, sir, I see you. Done."

The auctioneer's voice droned on, punctuated by the smack of his hammer. And there were side deals being made all the while, men arranging among themselves the rental of slave bootmakers and bakers and carpenters and tanners and blacksmiths and chimney sweeps. Every conceivable trade was represented. The slave market did a brisk business in the hiring of workers trained by their owners in various skills, and hired out when those skills were no longer required.

"No surgeons, I note," Christopher murmured to Jeremy. "At least I'm safe from that competition."

"Hmm, it's an interesting thought. Could you train a black to surgery? How about it, Chris, a wager? You try to—"

"Quiet, they're about to start."

"What do you mean? They have started. Oh, I see. That motley crew they're marching out now. That's what interests you?"

"Yes."

Jeremy made a face. "Good God, why? There's not a one of them looks as if— Hey! that woman at the end, the one carrying the child. Isn't she the one who sa—"

"That's her. Amba."

"How do you know her—"

"Red Bess bought her the day after they burned the others. She was there when I did the operation."

Jeremy winced. "I can't bear to think of it. Cutting off the old girl's tit like that, it makes my flesh creep."

"Your flesh creeps all too readily, Jeremy. Now please shut your mouth for a few moments."

The rental business was done with. The auctioneer was moving into the next phase of the sale. "Here we have an interesting assortment, gentlemen. Something you're not likely to see many times again. A team of seasoned slaves all trained to work together to the highest degree of perfection, by a lady who demanded no less, as anyone in this town will tell you. Who will make me a bid for the lot of them? Come now, how often do you get such an opportunity? Five slaves who—"

"Hey!" A voice from the rear of the throng. "If we want to buy whole cargoes we'll deal with the Queen's slavers. Sell 'em off separate and let's have done with it."

The crowd laughed, but a few other voices chimed in. "He's right. One at a time. That's the point of this place, isn't it?"

Indeed. Will Devrey and his colleagues sold their blacks individually, not by the cargo the way the English Royal African Company insisted on doing. Deal with the Crown's own slavers, and you paid for the contents of the hold and took every one they unloaded, dead or alive. That was all right for southern plantation owners growing mostly rice, and for the Caribbean kings of sugar. They required huge crews of blacks for gang labor. Northern gentlemen came to the New York slave market at the foot of Wall Street for household help and farmhands. Frugal descendants of the Puritan pioneers, every one of them, not your New York free spenders. Upstanding and virtuous men who cared for their accounts with the same strict rectitude that informed their church. They expected to see what they were getting before they parted with their cash.

The slave trade underpinned the city's entire economy. At least a thousand slaves a year were required in the colony of New York alone, and a prime black sold for as much as a skilled craftsman might earn in a lifetime. The slave trade was an enterprise worth hundreds of thousands of pounds annually, and the profits of the importers seeped down to the insurers, lawyers, clerks, and scriveners who handled the paperwork. Members of every class and profession supplemented their incomes with the part-time buying and selling of blacks. Those who made it their main endeavor, men like Devrey and his fellow shipowners, were growing fabulously rich from the Middle Passage. And in true New York fashion, they did not hoard their wealth, they spent it. Which in turn kept the town's various merchants and craftsmen in business.

No one knew all this better than the auctioneer, whose job depended on running a smooth sale. It was midmorning by now, and when he was at last done with this small consignment of Red Bess's leavings—used goods or seasoned goods, depending on your point of view—there were two pens full of recently landed Africans to get through. The auctioneer gave in to the desire of the crowd. Bess's slaves would be sold one by one.

Cuffy went first. No surprise, for she was young and strong, had years of work left in her. A Connecticut gentleman paid four hundred pounds for Cuffy. A present for his newly married daughter, someone heard him say.

Bess's cook was sold next, then her gardener. One went to Boston, the other to New Haven. They brought lesser sums. The auctioneer didn't say that they were husband and wife, or that they were Cuffy's parents, nor did anyone ask. Notions of family had no weight where slaves were concerned.

"Moving on, gentlemen." The hammer slammed down. "Pay attention now. Here's one you don't want to miss."

Amba stood on the block in the respectable dress Bess always made her wear. She held Phoebe in her arms and stared straight ahead. As if she were not there, Chris thought. As if this weren't happening.

"She's prime, gentlemen! Prime!" The auctioneer's voice was filled with enthusiasm. "A wench strong as any man. Years of labor left in her. Come, gentlemen, what am I bid?"

"She's the one was involved in the revolt!" a voice shouted from the rear. "Shame on you, Will Devrey, for putting her on the block. She should've died with the rest of the murdering bastards."

Will had been standing at the rear of the crowd. His goal was to be rid of the slaves; whether the estate realized the last possible farthing on each was not important. Craddock was Tamsyn's lawful husband; the proceeds of the sale would all go to the Scot in any case. But it wasn't possible to ignore a challenge like the one that had been issued. Will was being accused of undermining the good repute of the market, a danger to them all and a crime the other importers might not forgive.

"The wench has been trained by my sister these two years," Will shouted. "I can promise you she is entirely seasoned and well—"

The heckler wasn't convinced. "She should've burned! Everyone knows as much."

"Prime, gentlemen. Absolutely prime." The auctioneer again, trying to calm the ruckus. "Come now, what am I offered? Seven hundred pounds? Six hundred?"

Standing as he was at the back of the crowd, Christopher could see the tops of the heads of all the buyers. Amba had to be purchased by someone who would treat her with some decency. She wasn't a run-of-the-mill black. She was special. That was why he'd come today. To see if whoever bought her was someone who might recognize that fact.

The auctioneer was still soliciting bids. "Five hundred, gentlemen, a bargain at the price. Come now, start me off. What am I offered?"

"Two hundred," a voice called out.

Christopher strained to see where the bid came from, spotted the raised hand toward the front of the crowd. He elbowed Jeremy. "The man who's made the offer, who is he?"

"Comes from Massachusetts. Has a large estate on Cape Ann, owns fishing boats."

"Is he a decent sort?"

"I suppose so. I never heard otherwise. Why do you—"

"Quiet. I want to hear."

The auctioneer still held his gavel in the air. "Any advance on two hundred, gentlemen? No? Well, sir, looks like you've got a bargain."

"Two hundred and I'll take the wench," the New Englander called out, "but not the child, mind you."

Christopher sucked in a long breath. Sweet Jesus, they wouldn't let that happen, would they? Surely the auctioneer was instructed to make the buyer take both.

The auctioneer tried. "The girl's three, sir. Only another year or two and she'll begin to earn her keep. After that you can look forward to a long life of hard work. I'm authorized to accept two-fifty for the pair of them. A bargain, sir. What say you?"

The potential buyer dropped his arm and shook his head.

The situation was the one the auctioneer had most hoped to avoid. The breeding of slaves was a business with little profit; children had to be fed and sheltered for too many years before they became productive. Most buyers paid a premium for any black proven sterile. A few, however, dabbled in what they called stock farming, breeding selected slaves and raising up the offspring until they were old enough to sell. Such men never bid until the very end of a transaction. They bought cheap and sold dear, and they showed their money only after every other option had been exhausted.

Every auctioneer in New York knew the breeders and located them in the crowd well before the sale began. This day there was only one present, standing alone to the right. The auctioneer looked straight at him. Waited. The man let a few seconds go by. Then, slowly, with an air of not caring much how things came out, he raised his hand. "Very well, I'll do you all a favor. I'll take the little girl for five pounds. Not a penny more, and you're lucky to get it."

The auctioneer grinned. "Thank you, sir, you have solved all our problems. Done, gentlemen. Well and properly done." The hammer fell.

"Good God." Christopher clutched Jeremy's arm. "Look at her. She doesn't know what's happening."

Amba hadn't moved throughout the bargaining, and she was still motionless, still staring impassively straight ahead.

Jebbo took a step forward and reached for Phoebe. The little girl turned away and buried her face in her mother's neck. Amba tightened her grip on the small body. Jebbo got hold of one tiny arm and yanked it toward him. Phoebe screamed in pain, then started to wail. Jebbo tried again. This time Amba twisted out of his reach, hissing at him while kicking fiercely at his shins.

"Told you! She's a witch." The voice of the original heckler was heard again. "Damn bitch should be ashes by now."

Jebbo darted back, out of the range of Amba's leather boots, and cracked his whip with a vicious snap.

"Give her a couple, Jebbo," someone shouted. "Long overdue. Let's see the color of her blood."

Jebbo raised the arm holding the whip.

"Wait! Hold up!" Christopher shoved forward, shouting at the top of his lungs. "Let me pass! I've a better offer!" The crowd was surging, closing behind Christopher, sucking him into its depths. Jeremy made a futile grab at his sleeve. "Chris, are you mad? There's already enough talk about you to—"

Christopher shook off his friend's hold and kept moving forward. "Five hundred for the pair," he shouted. "Five hundred pounds for the woman and the child together!"

The auctioneer shook his head. "Can't be done, sir. The hammer went down on the other offers. Them's the rules."

"Yes," came another faceless voice. "And the rest of us are waiting to do some real business. For God's sake, man, get on with it."

Jebbo had managed to get Phoebe away from Amba, and two of his assistants had hold of the woman. They pinned her arms behind her and held her suspended above the wooden platform of the auction block. Her kicking feet were of no use, and the curses she hurled at them had no effect.

Christopher was close enough now to actually look into her face. "Amba," he called out. "Over here. Look at me."

She heard her name called, turned her head. Their eyes met. "Quiet," Christopher commanded. "Be quiet. You're not doing yourself any good."

She held his gaze only for a moment, then looked away, toward her child. For a moment her customary mask of stoicism disappeared and every bit of her anguish showed.

Christopher spun around and looked toward the rear of the crowd. "Cousin Will Devrey! I saw you back there. You're one of the owners of this market, and you have a duty to your sister's estate, and to your own kin. I'm offering double what the other two paid. What say you?"

Will swabbed at the sweat pouring down his face. He was standing near the holding pens, frantically waving at the man waiting to bring on a group of chained Fantis. "Get them up on the block," he screamed. "Now."

The Fantis began moving through the crowd, urged on by the cracking whips of the pen guards.

Christopher refused to be distracted. "What about it, Will? Five hundred pounds for the girl and her child. That's more than twice what you've been offered. You can pay each buyer a premium for his disappointment and still make a bigger profit for the estate. How can there be anything fairer than that?"

A few of the men murmured their approval. The Massachusetts man who had originally bought Amba shouted that considering what he'd just seen he'd accept twenty-five pounds ill-use money and consider himself well out of the bargain. The stock breeder raised his hand. "Twenty-five will do me fine as well. If I get it, the hammer never came down."

"Yes, very well!" Will shouted. "You'll both get your money. Jebbo, give Mr. Turner the girl and the child. And for God's sake, let us proceed."

"Aye, that's what we all say," came a voice. "Let's see some real slaves."

The Fantis had reached the block and were starting to climb the stairs. Jebbo and his assistants prodded them into position.

"Prime!" the auctioneer shouted, turning to point to the new offerings now arrayed before the waiting buyers. "All prime! Come, gentleman, what am I bid?"

He'd all but beggared himself buying her, and now he was . . . What? Christopher was not quite sure.

Amba and Phoebe had been part of his household for three weeks, but this was the first time he'd been alone with the African woman, without Jane having first provoked the meeting, then lurking nearby trying to hear what Christopher made of it. This time, though he and Amba were in the kitchen in the rear of the small house, Jane was otherwise engaged. Christopher could hear her screams.

His wife had been in labor for nineteen hours. Tess Hancock was in attendance. According to Jane and her mother, Tess was the finest midwife in New York. Christopher had no reason to think otherwise, but the thought that it was his fault such a sweet and gentle thing as Jane was in such agony, and that he could do nothing to help, was driving him mad. Not to mention that while his wife labored he was sitting in his kitchen watching a black savage heat a kettle of water and thinking about the way her breasts rose beneath her calico frock. It was . . . Sweet Jesus, there was no name for it.

"You got that water ready yet?" The young woman burst into the kitchen already speaking, breathless from her race down the stairs, but she saw Christopher sitting at the kitchen table before Amba could answer. "Oh, Master. I didn't—" The girl had been seasoned by Jane's mother. She knew enough to drop a quick curtsy.

"It's all right." His mother-in-law had given them a pair of slaves for a wedding present. Shirley and Chassey were sisters who looked so much alike Chris could never keep them entirely straight. "Shirley, isn't it?"

"That's right, Master. Chassey, she be upstairs with Selma and Midwife Hancock."

"Tell me, Shirley, how is your mistress?"

The youngster did not meet his glance. "She be doing 'bout as well as she can, Master."

"Good God, what does that mean? Is there any sign—"

"Water," Amba said, thrusting a steaming jug in Shirley's direction. "You go now."

Shirley grabbed the jug and turned to leave.

"Wait!" Christopher said. "What's Midwife Hancock doing with all this water? Is your mistress bleeding? If she is losing much blood I must be in—"

"Go!" Amba said, waving both her hands at the girl. "You go. Now."

Shirley ran from the room.

Amba stood by the door watching her.

"How dare you?" Christopher said. "You interrupted me when I was speaking to another slave, and you took it upon yourself to dismiss her. That is gross disobedience, Amba. You deserve to be whipped."

She turned to him and smiled. "Mistress Jane make you son. He big and strong, fight hard. That's why take long time to birth him."

She always knew he wasn't really angry with her.

Christopher gave up the pretense. "Very well. If you say so." For once he stared not at her breasts but at her head. He liked the form of it. He had, he realized, never before seen the actual shape of a woman's head. Amba's was on display because two days after he brought her and little Phoebe home from the slave market, she had cut off all her hair.

"She's hacked off every lock, Christopher." The first of the bitter complaints Jane brought him. "With a kitchen knife, I'm told. I can't believe Selma let such a one as Amba get to the knives, but she did. Now Amba truly looks like the half-tamed savage she is. You must discipline her. And have a word with Selma, too."

Chris never told Jane that he quite liked the look of Amba's very short and curly hair clinging to her skull. He found another excuse. "She says it's the fashion among the women of her clan back in Africa," he reported. "I can't see that it does any harm, my dear. Amba does her work as well with or without hair, does she not?"

Perhaps, but Amba's shorn head was one more thing that set her apart, one more thing that unsettled Jane, like the presence of the child. Amba, however, settled Christopher. That's why he'd come to the kitchen looking for comfort when Jane's screams became more than he could bear.

"You make me feel better," he told her. "There's no reason for it, but you do. Make me a toddy, Amba. Bring it to the sitting room. Midwife Hancock has Selma and Shirley and Chassey to assist her. Surely you can be spared."

"Take off everything. I want to see you naked." Dear God, what was he doing? "You have to do what I say, Amba. I'm the master and you're a slave." Christopher reached behind him and turned the key in the lock of the sitting-room door.

"Amba not a slave. Amba a queen."

"Really? In your country you were a queen?" The notion went straight to his crotch. Everything about this exotic creature did.

"Amba woman of the son of king. Amba a queen."

"Yes, I suppose that's how it would work. But you're a slave here. Now do as—" He broke off because there was no need to say more. Whether or not she believed herself to be a slave, Amba was removing her dress.

Her camisole came next. She pulled it off and threw it aside and paused a moment, long enough to smile at him. Then she stepped out of her petticoats. She was naked. And when she kicked aside the heap of discarded clothing the muscles rippled beneath her taut black skin. "You're magnificent," Christopher whispered. "Like . . . Like a queen. Yes, I can believe it."

Amba stood very still.

He heard Jane's voice. From the room directly over his head, where she was struggling to give birth to his child. "Noooo. . . . Help me! I can't bear it! No!" Amba was almost as tall as he was, and incredibly sleek, like a painting of a leopard he'd once seen. There was no womanly softness about her. Her breasts were perfectly formed; they looked as if they were carved out of marble. He stretched out his hand and stroked them lightly, with only the very tips of his fingers. The flesh was more yielding than he expected, but her nipples grew hard and erect the moment he touched her. "You desire me," he whispered. "That's true, isn't it?"

She didn't answer but he knew it was true. Christopher put both his hands on Amba's shorn head. It was as if he could feel her thoughts through his palms. In some ways the vulnerability of the almost naked skull was the most exciting thing about her. "I like your hair in this outlandish fashion," he murmured. "There's no reason I should, but I do."

"Amba cut hair for you," she said softly. "Show master she is queen."

"So only royalty get to cut off their hair. I see. And do kings and queens among your people also do this, Amba?" He bent his head and kissed her.

Above them Jane shrieked, a long, wordless cry of anguish. "Push, child!" the midwife could be heard yelling. "Keep pushing!"

Christopher went down on his knees. His face was inches away from the curly black hair of her mound. He reached up, ran his hands over her midriff, her hips, her buttocks, her thighs. She stood very still and let him do whatever he wanted. Christopher bent his head back and looked up at her. She was smiling. "Lie down here," he whispered, "beside the fire. Yes, that's it. I like to look at you like that. My very own beautiful black jungle cat."

There were things he'd experienced once or twice with the Princes Street whores, things he would never do to Jane or expect from her. But with Amba . . . Still kneeling beside her he leaned forward and tangled his fingers in the lush thatch of her pubic hair, then, using both his hands, he opened her legs.

She had no vulva.

The labia, both major and minor, had been entirely removed, sliced away in what appeared to be a single sweep of the knife. And afterward, judging from the scar, the wound had been sewn tightly shut, leaving only a tiny opening for the demands of nature. God knows how she must have been torn when she gave birth. Now she had healed into a wide and gnarled ridge of flesh stretching from her mons pubis almost to her rectum.

Christopher stared at the brutal disfigurement. It was many seconds before he could look at her and be sure his face did not betray his horror.

Horror apparently didn't enter into it for Amba. Certainly not shame. She was smiling at him again, a broad smile of immense satisfaction. Her large dark eyes and her white teeth gleamed in the firelight. "Amba a queen," she said softly. "Master see proof now. Amba a queen."

Someone was knocking on the door of the study. "Master, you come now. Midwife Hancock, she say to tell you it's time to come. Baby's here, Master! Baby's here!"

Christopher staggered to his feet, ran his hands through his hair, swallowed hard, and finally found a somewhat normal voice. "I'm coming. Tell your mistress I'll be there in a moment."

"Come quick, Master! Mistress make you a little boy. Midwife Hancock say you come—"

"Yes, yes. I heard you. I'll be right there."

"Well, is it working out?" Jeremy asked.

Chris raised his tankard and took a long pull of ale before he answered. "It's wonderful of course, but it does rather change the character of a man's household."

For a moment Jeremy stared at him, uncomprehending; then he grinned. "Ah, I understand. You mean the birth of young Luke. I was referring to the purchase of your expensive black pigeon and her fledgling."

"Oh, that."

"Yes, that."

"Frankly, it's not. Working out, as you put it. I'm thinking of sending her away."

"For God's sake, man, you paid a fortune for the wench! Not that I have the least idea why."

"Nor have I, to be perfectly honest. It just seemed unbearably cruel to separate her and the child like that. But she unnerves Jane. She says just looking at Amba curdles her milk. I'll have to do something. I need to find somewhere she's wanted, and where they'll let her keep her daughter."

"You never will, Chris. And if you did, you'd never get your money back."

"I know. I don't expect to. Not that I couldn't use it."

Jeremy looked away. They were in the place where his father and his uncle did most of their legal business, a large and comfortable room in the front of the Clinton mansion on the corner of the Broad Way and Little Queen Street. "Am I to take it that the purchase of the Hanover Square property is . . . Well, you know . . ."

"At a loss for words, Jeremy? You? Allow me to say it for you. My plan to elevate my station is now out of the question. Buying Amba has beggared me."

Jeremy lifted a document from the corner of the small desk his father and uncle had assigned him, rolled it tightly, and shoved it into a pigeonhole. "Pity. I was quite looking forward to actually lawyering a transaction. And the grand place would have suited you. Did I tell you I'm now absolutely certain that it, not the house next door, is the property Captain Kidd occupied for a time? Sixteen-eighty-one to 'eighty-two, I think. Something like that, anyway."

"Pity. Jane will be doubly disappointed. She was all set to have the slaves digging up the garden looking for buried treasure."

Equally a pity for him. Christopher had set his heart on the Hanover Square house. He'd already made a sketch to take to the smith and planned the inscription of the sign he would order. Christopher Turner, Surgeon. A simple proclamation that Lucas Turner's grandson lived with his wife and his child in fashionable Hanover Square, in a four-story, twelve-room brick house overlooking the leafy greenery of the small park in the middle, among the most prosperous of the gentlemen of New York City. In, if anyone cared to notice, a rather better house than was occupied by Zachary Craddock, M.D., even now that he'd moved into his mother-in-law's substantial old place on Pearl Street.

Jeremy saw his friend's disappointment. "Chris, are you quite sure? I mean, there are ways these things can be managed. You know I've no money my father doesn't control, but perhaps your cousin Will . . . Some sort of mortgage loan."

"Out of the question. For one thing, I doubt he'd do it. The family is still in at least a theoretical state of war, whatever good Bess wrote in her will. For another, it's not just the sum I paid for Amba that's left me scratching. I've seen barely ten patients all this month. And not many more the month before that."

"Yes, well . . ."

"Well what? Damn it, Jeremy, is the entire city of New York so bloody stupid they think I killed the woman because she gave me the rough side of her tongue when I was a lad trying to court her daughter? Does a preposterous tale become less so when it's told with a Scots burr?"

"Fair questions, I suppose."

"Good. Then tell me the answers."

Jeremy went to the window and opened it. The soft June evening was sweet with the smell of honeysuckle from the King's Arms across the road. The sound of music—a hammer dulcimer and a flute—drifted on the breeze. People in the town said Jeremy Clinton's fondness for wine and song were the result of his growing up in direct view of the most fashionable tavern in the city. But when his father built the house a quarter-century before, Little Queen Street was a bucolic retreat. Back then people said the attorney was mad to move his young family so far north of the wall.

Then, when Jeremy was five, the country inn and tavern had gone up across the way. And this past May the Broad Way had been graded from Maiden Lane to the flat land known as the Common, once so far from the town it had seemed safe to put the powder house there and declare it a burial place for Jews and Negroes.

The grading made it official: the city of New York stretched a generous mile from the fort. The Clintons' front door no longer opened on a wide dirt path at the top of a steepish rise. The house looked out on a broad and flat cobblestone road bordered on either side with a prim row of newly planted shade trees. At the moment the road was empty, but the tavern sounded as if it was doing a lively business. Jeremy turned back to his friend. "Do you fancy going over the way for some punch? I daresay if we're careful we can get across the cobbles without being knocked down by old man Beekman's coach. That's why they did this bit of stonework, you know. So fat old Beekman could drive his grand imported rig from the fort to his farm without having to—"

"What I fancy, Jeremy, is for you to tell me what's on your mind."

"I already have. A mug of punch and a song or two. Maybe even a sight of—"

"Fat old Beekman's coach whizzing over the cobblestones. Yes, Jeremy, so you said. But that's not what you're thinking. Come, I know you too well. We're not done with the subject of poor Bess's tit, are we?"

"I'd as leave be done with it. But as for the rest of the town, no, they are not." Jeremy returned to his desk. "Look, it's not killing Bess by cutting off her pappe that folks hold against you."

"I didn't—"

Jeremy held up his hand. "All right. I know. And you've made such a reputation with the knife that nearly everyone would give you the benefit of the doubt on that score. But the other—" He broke off, shrugged. "You know how people are."

"I take it," Christopher said softly, "you're telling me that what disturbs the good folk of New York City is the notion of the transfusion of blood."

"Exactly. Damn, Chris, I did warn you. I can't count the times I told you it was a fool's idea."

"It nearly saved her, Jeremy. No, don't look at me like that. It's the truth. When I infused my blood into her veins she was remarkably revived. I saw it with my own eyes."

"Listen to yourself! Chris, you're the stubbornest man in America, I swear it. The woman's dead. She died with her own daughter looking on, watching you do that . . . that despicable thing you did."

For most of the conversation Christopher had watched Jeremy pace back and forth between the desk and the window while he sat in his chair, with his ale in his hand and his long legs stretched out in front of the cold fireplace. Now he got up and deliberately walked the length of the room and restored the empty tankard to the tray on the sideboard. It gave him a few seconds to think. "Despicable," he said finally. "Is that what you really believe, Jeremy? That I am to be despised for what I did?"

"No, of course not. I mean . . . I know you don't see it that way." Only a slight hesitation in the words, but enough.

"I see. Very well; acting as my lawyer, then, advise me."

"I can't."

"Why in bloody hell not? Tell you what, I'll advise myself. I suggest I make a statement and have it cried from every corner of the town. I, Christopher Turner, have done nothing to countermand the surgeon's oath to do no violence or cruelty to the body of any. That should do it. What say you, lawyer?"

"That your statement won't do any good. It's a bloody waste of time, and the money you'd pay the scriveners and the criers. Tamsyn and her husband are two voices. You have only one."

"And the fact that I was born and raised in this place, that everyone who knows me also knew my father and grandfather before me . . . You're telling me that counts for nothing against the accusations of a medical doctor from Edinburgh?"

"It doesn't. Not when—"

"When what? Sweet Jesus, Jeremy. You've something else on your mind. Spit it out."

"Craddock says it's not just what you did to his mother-in-law that so disturbs him. It's what you did to the whole of the city, particularly to the Crookes and their unfortunate neighbors."

"The Crookes? Jeremy, what new madness is this? What am I supposed to have done?"

"The revolt. Craddock says you had word of it before it happened and you warned no one. He says you admitted as much in front of him and Tamsyn and their old slave Hetje."

Christopher stood where he was for some long seconds. "The old man," he whispered finally. "The chicken dance."

"Exactly. Chris, I don't know what to make of that myself. I was with you the day the old duffer died. You never gave hint of what you'd heard. Not even to me. You were so full of your thoughts of blood transfusing that you never so much as mentioned a word of anything the man told you."

"For the love of Christ, Jeremy, that's because he didn't tell me anything. He was delirious with fever, ranting. How can you think I'd—"

Jeremy had been looking straight at him. Now he looked away. As if he could no longer stand the sight of his oldest friend.

"Very well," Christopher said softly, "you make your feelings quite clear. And I'm in your debt. At least now I understand the true dimensions of the problem. It appears that if my family is to eat I had best polish up my grandfather's pole and see to my delousing skills."

The High Hills Path

AUGUST 1731–FEBRUARY 1737

The Canarsie people who lived on the long island of Metoaca in winter and on Manhattan, the island of hills, in summer knew that truth was a thing men saw with different eyes. To discern what was reality and what was not, they devised tests. If those were passed, then all people could know that a thing was proven and it was no longer necessary to doubt.

If a speaker could hold fire and not be burned, the speaker's words were true.

If a speaker who had been tied into an overturned canoe, which was then pulled across the Sun-Coming River from Manhattan to Metoaca, was alive when the journey ended, the speaker's words were true.

If a speaker could jump from the tall cliffs at the end of the High Hills Path, in the place of the tree that had been divided by sky fire, and soar like a bird rather than sink like a stone to be smashed on the rocks below, the speaker's words were true.

In the case of a disputed truth, those whom the tests killed were known to have been liars. If, however, a person did not wish to submit to the test, they too were proven to have lied. Such a one was made to leave the places of the People and live like an animal in the forest, without friends or kin. The clan no longer knew him.

Chapter Six

AUGUST 1731. Smoke hung over the city. It clogged the nostrils and made the eyes tear and choked the throat. There was no escaping it.

A bonfire burned on every corner. Every hour patrols of redcoats marched double time down the New York lanes and streets and byways, bringing fresh logs. The flames soared and the sparks flew as the desperate townspeople and their equally desperate government tried to burn the smallpox out of the air. It was the only thing they knew to do.

Official New York had a tenuous hold on this pestilence. The last Royal Governor had died quite suddenly the previous month, and his replacement hadn't yet arrived. The responsibility for ruling the colony fell to Rip Van Dam, simply because he was the eldest member of His Majesty's Council for the Province of New York. Van Dam, canny and shrewd, had grown rich from the Caribbean trade. But the smallpox was beating him.

The disease had spread to every part of the town, from the fort on the southern tip of the island—renamed Fort George II, for the present king—to newly built streets like Franklin and Cherry a mile north. Beekman's Swamp had been drained to make room for the new streets. Some said that was how the smallpox got started, rising up from the depths that were exposed when the old swamp was emptied. Even if that was true, there was no way to put the swamp back.

The bonfires were supposed to protect the people, but they extracted a high price. Seven houses caught fire in one August week. Five people were burned alive. That same week the city's first newspaper, the *New-York Gazette*, announced the smallpox tally. Twenty-two Church of England, eleven Dutch Reformed, six Presbyterians, five Quakers, and two Negroes had died of the disease. Nearly fifty victims in seven days, a new record. The fires burned on.

The pox was God's scourge, the preachers ranted. Let the people mend their ways, and this plague would pass as it had passed before.

Van Dam left church one Sunday morning after a particularly passionate sermon and declared the following Wednesday a day of humiliation and public penance. And an occasion for the renunciation of evil practices, cures that amounted to little more than witchcraft.

"It is strictly prohibited and forbidden to all and every of the Doctors, Physicians, Surgeons, and Practitioners of Physick, and all and every other person within this Province, to inoculate for the smallpox—variolation as the detestable practice is called—any person or persons within the City and County of New York. On pain of being prosecuted to the utmost rigor of the law."

Christopher Turner thought of that while he made his way to the home of a Dutch family living on Stone Street, with the tools of variolation tucked in his pockets. Stupid bastards. They made him almost as sick as the choking smoke and the August heat, as the gritty cinders that made his eyes sting until he was practically blind.

God knew he was in no position to ignore the law. He could never have paid their poxed fines. Nine people were crowded into his little house on Hall Place, all depending on him.

Nearly twenty years since the business with Red Bess's tit, and he was still treated like a bloody leper. He kept his household fed and clothed and off the streets only by giving a few private classes in surgical practice. To idiots, mostly. Might as well invite them to murder as put a scalpel in their hands. He also got a few pence for the medical articles he wrote for the *Gazette*. Couldn't use his own name, of course. That galled him as much as anything, but he needed the money. Thank Christ for the occasional braver-than-most patient. The only time he truly felt alive was when he operated. Now, God help him, he was putting that miserable living at risk.

He kept patting his pockets every few minutes, in between coughing and wiping his eyes. Of course everything was exactly where he'd put it. Lancets, vials, blades . . . Where would it have gone? He was almost as bad as Van Dam and the rest of the politicians.

Like every other street, lane, and alley in the town, the cobbles of Stone Street had a thick coating of brick dust and quicklime. That was another of their idiotic remedies. He'd wager anything it had been Zachary Craddock's idea. Craddock had Van Dam's ear. Probably he'd been the one to . . . *Ah, sweet Christ, be fair.* The damned government had been doing the same thing as long as anyone could remember. Every time some filthy plague came, be it the smallpox or the yellowing fever or any other kind of pestilence, it was the same. Prayers and penance and fire, brick dust and quicklime over the cobbles, and violent blistering, bleeding, and purging for the patient. But God knew the smallpox was the worst. And the fools wouldn't take a chance on variolation, the one thing that could help. Craddock, damn his soul, carried a large part of the blame for that.

The Scot wasn't alone. The great objections to variolation came mostly from university-trained medical men. Christopher ground his teeth just thinking of it. Sweet Christ, if he could make Van Dam look at the simple, straightforward results of the thing . . .

The house he wanted was at the far end of Stone Street, almost facing what used to be known as Jews' Lane. It was Mill Street now, though the Jews' synagogue had been built there a year before. The door he was looking for was a few steps away from the place the Hebrews called Shearith Israel, the Remnant of Israel. Probably the good Dutch Reformed people in the small yellow brick house believed that was why this disaster had struck them. Probably thought the Jews put a curse on them.

As soon as he was inside Christopher knew it wasn't likely. Anyone living like this was beyond thinking.

The stench was unbelievable. It took all his will not to gag. The hunched crone who led him through the tiny front hall to the small sitting room didn't seem to notice.

She walked with a cane. Her clothes hung limp and neglected around her sticklike frame. The wood floors of the house were covered with remnants of the powder that had been tracked in from the streets, and the old woman's skirts had trailed so much through the mess they'd developed a dark, orange-red hem.

"Can't nothing do," she muttered as she led him from the sitting room to a kind of back hall. "Can't nothing do more for my grandboy. Not neither for my girl and her man." She made a vague gesture to a rag-covered hump on the floor beside what appeared to be a back door.

The reek was worse in here. Christopher gagged and hoped she hadn't seen. His eyes began to adjust to the dim light. Sweet Christ, two bodies lying on the floor, covered with burlap sacking. He put out a hand and touched the woman's arm. "Mevrouw . . ."

She turned to him. The old Dutch courtesy made her eyes flicker with something left over from a time before the pox came. The light died quickly. "Did all what I could," she repeated. "Can't nothing do more."

He started to say something, but she stopped him by raising her face—it was the first time she'd looked at him full-on—and pushing back her lank and dirty white hair. The skin of her left cheek was badly pitted, an ugly hole that stretched as far as her ear.

She let him look for a while, then pulled the hair back over the scars. "That's why I'm still here, no?"

He swallowed, but he couldn't answer. The stink would choke him if he opened his mouth.

The woman had lived with it so long she didn't seem to notice. "I knowed you when a boy you were, Christopher Turner. Knowed your papa. And your mama, God rest them both. Smart, all you Turner people. So you tell me, is that why I'm left and they be all gone? Because already I had it? In 1702, last time it came." She nodded toward the corpses under their covering of sacks. "Afore they were born."

He summoned all his grit, and told himself it was like taking the saw in his hands and starting to cut. "That's why, mevrouw. But you shouldn't stay here like this. With these . . ." He nodded toward the rotting corpses. "There must be somewhere for you to go."

She shook her head. "Born in this house. Die here I will. Soon, please God."

"Mevrouw, your church, they'll come and bury your dead. You must let me inform them."

She shrugged her hunched shoulders. "Do what you want. But . . ." She drew away, gave him a sly glance. "What you promised you will give me, no? You won't refuse because of them?"

"No, mevrouw, I won't refuse. The child, he's still alive?"

"Last time I looked he was." She took a step toward a door, opened it. "In here he is. See for yourself."

Christopher went through the narrow door. Following the lay of the land, the room had been built slightly below ground level. He had to step down to cross the threshold. The light was no better than in the back hall, and the atmosphere still more foul. There was a tiny window, but it was high up, and closed tight. Considering the smoke and ash and cinders flying about in Stone Street, he dared not open it.

The boy lay in an old-style Dutch bed built into one wall. Christopher steeled himself to the stink of rotting flesh and stepped closer to the patient. "I'm going to take a look at you, son," he murmured. "See if I can—"

He broke off. In the face of so much misery the lie wouldn't come. He wasn't here to see if he could help the boy. It was far too late for that. The child—nine or ten, Christopher guessed—was past hearing or reacting. He was still alive, but only barely. Death would come in a few hours, perhaps. And it would be a mercy.

He bent nearer. The acrid smell of vomit mingled with the stench of putrefying flesh, and he spotted rust-colored stains on the covers. Blood. The internal hemorrhage that often accompanied the final stages of the disease. Gingerly he touched a corner of the bedding and moved it aside.

"You're not feared of the pox, are you?" The old woman's voice came out of the shadows beside the door where she still stood. In her mind, Christopher realized, she'd already said good-bye to her grandson. This stinking thing on the bed bore no relation to the child she'd loved. "Already you had it, yes?" the old woman persisted. "In 1702?"

"I had it," he said curtly.

"But your face is unmarked. How can that be, Christopher Turner?"

"I was lucky, mevrouw. Now, if I can get on with what I came for . . ."

"*Ja*, of course. A shilling, you said." She stuck out a bony hand.

Christopher reached into his pocket and found the coin and gave it to her. The old woman closed her fist around it.

"How are you eating? The farmers refuse to come into the town, and the markets are empty by nine of the morning. Do you go early and stand in the lines?"

She chuckled. "Not me. Pompey, he goes. Brings me back things."

"Pompey's your slave?"

"Not mine. Ain't got no slaves. Sold them years ago to make a dowry for my daughter. A foolishness that turned out to be." She nodded in the direction of the back hall and the corpses. "Pompey, he be my neighbor's boy. Went to the country, they did. To the village of Greenwich to get away from the pox. Left Pompey to look after things. He don't get it neither. The blacks don't, most of 'em. That did you know, smart Christopher Turner?"

"I knew it, mevrouw."

"Why? That you know, too?"

"I'm not sure. A natural immunity, maybe. A gift from God to make up for their black skin. Mevrouw, I have to . . ." He gestured to the boy.

"*Ja, ja*, of course. Do it and go and leave me alone."

Christopher returned to the boy and rolled back the covers. A new wave of stink rose from the bed. The child was naked and his entire body was so thickly covered with the pox it was impossible to see clear skin. He had the confluent form of the illness, the most deadly. A factor to be reckoned with.

Christopher took a lancet and a small glass vial from one of his pockets. The boy was so far gone in the disease that most of the pustules, the variola, had long since scabbed over and fallen off, taking the skin with them. The child's entire body was a suppurating wound. He could be of no use to Christopher if all that was left was this hunk of rotting butcher's meat. No, there on the lad's left thigh, a few fresh pox.

He pricked each one with the lancet. Then, with the forefinger and thumb of his left hand, he squeezed gently to expel the yellow pus. As each drop appeared he used the broad side of the lancet to scrape it up and transfer it to the glass container.

After a minute or two he had enough. He took a last look into the face of the dying boy. The child hadn't moved. His head was like a skeleton's, the skin taut over the bones, sunken eyes open, staring at the ceiling.

Then, slowly and with enormous effort, the wasted face turned toward his. The boy's mouth opened as if he wanted to speak. Christopher bent nearer; he heard nothing but an ominous rattle. There were maybe minutes left, not hours. He straightened and turned away.

The old woman went with him as far as the sitting room, then left him to find the front door by himself. Thank Christ for that. He couldn't get out of the house fast enough. When he stepped into the street and yanked the door closed behind him he had to fight the urge to draw a deep breath of the smoke-poisoned air.

His name was Solomon DaSilva, and though he'd been born in Brazil he spoke perfect English tinged with a faint Irish lilt, the result of having learned the language as a small boy from a governess born in Tipperary. But in ten years in New York he had never been taken for Irish. He was short and stocky, flesh and muscle tightly packed on a squat frame, and very dark. He always wore a black satin coat and white satin breeches with diamond buckles, and carried an ebony walking stick topped with the head of a golden horse with ruby eyes.

The girl's name was Jennet Turner, and she liked the walking stick best. Of all the remarkable things there were to look at and wonder about when she was with Solomon, the golden horse was the most appealing. "Here," he said, knowing she fancied it. "You may hold it if you care to."

"Yes, thank you, I will." She took the stick in her elegant, long-fingered hands. "But I'm not a child any longer, Solomon. You can't keep me entertained with geegaws."

"That geegaw was made in Paris for the King Louis, who is now known as a saint."

"Ah, well, that makes it far too old for me." She gave it back to him with a quick and taunting grin. "I like young, fresh things."

DaSilva took the walking stick and crossed his legs, relaxing against the velvet-covered cushions of his recently imported carriage. "If that's so, why do you bother with me?"

"You know why."

"Yes, but tell me again. I like to hear it."

"Because I want you to give me money."

He exploded in laughter. It was her honesty as much as her rare beauty that kept him meeting this extraordinary child. (He still thought of her as such, though she'd turned sixteen the previous winter.) DaSilva lived in a world where few said exactly what they meant—least of all, women. The directness of this girl he'd known since she was twelve was as refreshing as clear springwater. "I do give you money. And what does it buy me?"

"You don't give me enough. And it buys you the knowledge that you are laying up treasure in heaven by giving to the poor here on earth."

"Ah, yes, the Christian charity argument."

She drew her supple fingers through the silk fringes that edged the carriage windows. They were tightly closed today, against the smoke and the fetid winds from the swamps. Everyone said that was where the pox came from. Never mind. Solomon's swarthy face had a scattering of pockmarks that showed he'd already had the disease, and she knew she was immune. "Do Jews not believe in charity?" she asked.

"I suppose they do. I haven't been near a synagogue in so many years, I can't be sure."

"Then you're not afraid of going to hell?"

He shrugged. "I count on being able to make my peace before I die. But I don't believe that will be any time soon."

It was her turn to laugh, a low throaty chuckle. That was another thing he liked about her. She never giggled or twitted; her pleasure was always as direct as her speech. And dear God, she was beautiful. But her moods changed more quickly than the weather. Suddenly she was serious, looking at him with a remarkable intensity. "Tell me again what you said last week."

"Which bit of my wisdom do you want repeated?"

"Don't tease me, Solomon. You remember."

"Yes, I expect I do. About a woman not being able to be a surgeon." He sighed. "It's impossible, Jennet. You know it is."

"I do not know any such thing." She looked away.

DaSilva touched her defiant chin with the head of the horse stick. "It's not practical, my dear. You must put aside such notions. Society can be thwarted in some things, Jennet. This they won't tolerate."

"But why?" A whisper, slightly hoarse with the pain of frustration and disappointment.

"If I knew why people were narrow-minded I would tell you," he said gently. "I don't." Then, very softly, "Jennet, do something for me." She turned to him. "Take off your cap so I can see your hair."

He'd asked for that favor many times. She did what he wanted quickly and without much thought. Her long, straight black hair was twisted into a heavy, silken braid that fell over the bodice of her simple calico dress.

DaSilva reached out, then pulled his hand back. He had never taken advantage of her innocence. Sometimes he wondered if she knew what that cost him. "Why do you never use the money I give you for a pretty new dress?"

"For one thing, there are better ways to spend it. For another, how would I explain a pretty new dress to my parents?"

"I don't know. But they seem remarkably unconcerned about where you go and what you do." He'd met her when a man at the Fly Market tried to say she'd only given him two coppers for her skinned hare, not the shilling she insisted she'd paid. Solomon had no idea which of them was telling the truth, but he made the man give Jennet change for a shilling—DaSilva was the man's landlord—and drove her home in his carriage. When he asked why she'd been sent alone to shop she explained that she was the eldest daughter among six children, that her family had few slaves, and that her mother was again with child. So of course she had to help.

After that DaSilva saw her at least once a week, always like this—in the privacy of his carriage, parked outside his front door because she refused to set foot in his house.

"About your parents," he said, "haven't they ever questioned you about your meetings with me?" The city insisted that Christopher Turner was a scoundrel. DaSilva wasn't entirely sure. But only a fool would fail to see the economic potential of a daughter who looked like Jennet, and no one ever said Christopher Turner was a fool.

"How could they? They don't know I meet you." She spoke without taking her eyes from his face. Remarkable eyes. A blue so dark it was almost violet. "I don't wish to trouble them with such a small thing."

"Is that how you think of our meetings? As a small thing?"

She shrugged. "Yes, of course. That's what they are, aren't they?"

"If you say so." He didn't know whether he wanted to smack her or kiss her. Both, perhaps. It was the urge to touch her that was almost overwhelming. But not quite. Patience, he reminded himself. Patience. "Some people would say keeping secrets makes you a disobedient daughter."

"I don't care what some people would say."

She was still looking straight at him. DaSilva couldn't bear it. He glanced out the carriage window and smiled. "Turn your head, my dear. That's your father, isn't it? Coming down the road toward us."

Sweet Christ, it was like walking through a charnel house. Damned smoke had driven everyone off the streets. Only a few black-clad mourners scurrying about, coming and going from burials, the poor bastards. The only exception seemed to be this shiny black carriage with two white horses, sitting in front of a grand three-story redbrick mansion.

Hard to remember that not long ago Nassau Street had been the winding path through the woods that led to old man Kip's farm. It was graded and cobbled now, paved up to the edge of the town where it joined the King's High Road to Boston. Splendid houses either side. He could remember when they'd called this stretch Pie Woman's Alley.

The mansion Christopher was approaching was set well back and fronted by an orchard. The leaves of the trees were grimy with soot and smoke, but the branches were so heavy with fruit they hung over the road. A pear dangled directly over the head of the driver of the carriage, a black man wearing a tall black hat and white livery with shiny gold buttons.

The driver ignored the fruit and remained motionless on his high perch, staring straight ahead. Had to mean the carriage was occupied, that he was waiting for the command to move on. Heading for one of the docks, most likely, so whoever was rich enough to own the mansion and the orchard and the carriage and the splendid white horses could get out of New York.

Christopher kept walking. He was almost abreast of the carriage when he saw a female hand reach up and draw a curtain over the window, and heard a male voice call out a command. The black man cracked his whip and the white horses began moving down the road, their hooves sending up little puffs of brick dust as they struck the cobbles.

God knew they'd left it late enough. Most who could afford to escape had already gone. The first few days, as soon as people heard there was smallpox in the town, the ferries couldn't cope. Private craft took up the slack. The single-masted sloops and two-masted brigs usually used for goods transport to the Caribbean carried fleeing New Yorkers across the narrows to Brooklyn, or farther up the long island's coast to Jamaica and Flushing. Some took the westerly route around the tip of Manhattan and went northward up Hudson's River to the village of Greenwich, or went beyond it to the yet more isolated village of Harlem. Nearly eight thousand inhabitants in New York City, and just about all of them, for the time being at least, wanting to be somewhere else.

Christopher watched the elegant black carriage turn the corner and disappear, then walked on.

Nothing to see except smoke until he reached the intersection of the Broad Way and Little Queen Street, where his path was blocked by a swaybacked black nag pulling a black wagon that carried a black coffin. Christopher took off his hat and bowed his head. The shabby rig was followed by a sobbing woman dressed entirely in black. She was flanked by two men who had to hold her arms to keep her from collapsing. Sweet Christ, so much grief. The funeral cortege passed out of sight. He crossed the road and lifted the brass knocker of Jeremy Clinton's front door.

Age hadn't been kind to Jeremy. He and Christopher were both forty-one, but

Jeremy looked older. Most of his fair hair was gone, his once slight build had turned to fat, and worst of all, the spirit had gone out of him. Jeremy had become a whiner. "Come in. What took you so long? I've been waiting."

"I had to stop by the Dutch church on my way." Christoper used the iron scraper beside the front door to remove the brick dust from his boots. "The old Dutch widow lady on Stone Street I told you about . . . Turned out she's living alone surrounded by corpses."

"Corpses? But you said you had to have a live donor, that the—"

"A figure of speech, Jeremy. There was a child with enough life left in him for our purposes." His boots were as clean as they were going to be. Christopher stepped inside and hung his tricorn on a peg in the hall. "For God's sake, close the door. We'll choke to death on the smoke."

"Personally I thank God for the smoke. It's the only thing keeps me from thinking we're all just sitting here waiting to die."

"The fires do no bloody good at all. There's absolutely no evidence they affect—" He broke off. Jeremy had never been interested in scientific argument. "Tell me something. Why do you stay? You could move the family to the country until the pox plays itself out."

"A household of eight—five if I left the slaves behind: it would still be a considerable expense."

Jeremy's father and his uncle were both dead, and Jeremy wasn't much of a lawyer. It was true he had little money. Still, "It's not finances, old friend. It's Marjorie, isn't it?"

Jeremy shrugged. "She can be difficult. Particularly out of familiar places. She's calm today, though. I did what you suggested and got a large supply of syrup of red poppies from Tamsyn's shop. By the way, the black who served me was your Phoebe."

"Yes. I hired her out to Tamsyn these past two years." What a ruckus that had caused. Jennet, his eldest daughter, was closer to little black Phoebe than to her own sisters; she'd howled for days when Christopher sent Amba's daughter away. But it hadn't changed his mind: he needed the cash too much. "Made the arrangement as soon as old Hetje died and Tamsyn had room for another slave."

"I didn't know. Anyway, she seemed able enough for the work. Gave me exactly what I asked for and made the proper change. Not that there's much left of a shilling when you buy a flagon of poppy syrup. But it quiets Marjorie a great deal. In fact, she begs for it when there's none in the house."

Christopher did not find that a surprise. Poppy syrup wasn't as strong as laudanum, but he'd long since noted that both created cravings. No matter, Marjorie had to have it. Jeremy's wife had lost her wits after they'd been married ten years, when her ninth child was born dead. Anything that dealt with her screaming frenzies was justified. "I'm glad to hear the syrup still has an effect.

Perhaps it would be wise to begin with Marjorie, then. Before she . . . While she's calm."

The Clintons' bedroom was spacious, but since the stillbirth Marjorie slept in it alone. Christopher had known it for years. "Off to visit holy ground I am," Jeremy confided at the end of an evening's drinking. Trinity Church owned the land between it and Hudson's River, and on that land most of the city's whores could be found; so everyone called the brothels holy ground. "Care to come and pray with me, Chris? For old times' sake."

"I won't, thanks. But say hello to any as remember me." He hadn't been unfaithful to Jane since he married her. Unless you counted his unconsummated encounter with Amba. Which he didn't. "I wouldn't have thought you'd find the expense worthwhile, Jeremy. Marjorie's still a fine-looking woman."

That's when he'd heard about the constant screaming, and the raving, and the fact that on one occasion, when Jeremy tried to climb into bed beside his wife, Marjorie had attacked him with a pair of scissors. Ever since, Christopher hadn't been able to look at his old friend without pity. Probably that was why he was taking this risk today. That, and his fondness for the three living Clinton children, and the knowledge that not one of the Clintons, Jeremy included, had ever had the smallpox.

Marjorie was sitting in a chair beside the window, staring dreamily into space. Christopher went to her, but she looked straight through him. He'd stood witness at her wedding and he was godfather to two of her children, but he might have been a stranger. "I'm delighted to see you looking so well, my dear Marjorie. This heat doesn't seem to trouble you."

The slave who never left Marjorie's side reached over to tuck a strand of light brown hair into her mistress's cap. "Mistress Marjorie don't mind hot or cold. Long as we give her what she wants, she be nice and peaceful like."

"Well, then, let's do what we've come to do quickly, and not disturb her." Christopher took his lancet and a small pewter dish from one pocket, and the vial containing the smallpox pus he'd extracted from the dying boy from another.

"That's it, then?" Jeremy stared at the little glass container and whispered as if the pox might jump out and attack him if it heard his voice.

"That's it."

There was a tall mahogany bureau against one wall. Exactly the right working height for Christopher. He took a step toward it, then stopped to wipe the sweat from his face. Damned heat was insufferable. "God, can't you open a window? It's stifling in here. The smoke would be better than this."

"The pox," Jeremy murmured. "I don't . . ."

"Sweet Jesus, man. How many times do I have to tell you? The pox is not a bloody bird. It doesn't fly through the air. A window, Jeremy. I cannot bear it."

The window was opened. Christopher grunted his thanks and went on with his task. Jeremy continued to watch his every move. Sweat was pouring off him as well—not only from the heat. From fear. "Chris, listen." He nodded toward the vial. "If the disease doesn't fly through the air, how does it infect so many?"

"I'm not sure. I think it's because we touch things that have touched . . . God help us, things that have touched that."

Jeremy shook his head. "If it were only that, we in this house would be safe. We've nothing but our own things, and none of us have the pox."

Christopher sighed. "I know. I can't entirely explain it. I can tell you one novel idea, however. You've heard of Mather, up in Boston?"

"Cotton Mather? The minister? Isn't he the one who started all this agitating for variolation?"

"The very same. Mather claims he's looked at the variola through one of the latest microscopes. Says he saw tiny worms. Says they crawl among us without our ever seeing them, and that's how the disease is spread."

"Good God, what useless nonsense."

Christopher shrugged. "Probably. But that"—he nodded toward the window and the smoke now wafting into the bedroom—"is worse than useless nonsense. It's never been shown to do any good, and God knows we've seen the harm."

"Perhaps. But what you're doing is harmful as well."

"A controlled harm. A small dose of the disease to make you immune to a larger one, and—" Christopher stopped in midsentence. "Listen, Jeremy, I told you there are no guarantees. And it was you who asked me, remember? I don't want—"

"I know you don't. I'm the one who wants. I want the same protection for my family and myself that you have arranged for yours. I trust you, Christopher. And I know you're taking a risk in doing this for us in the face of the Council's proclamation. I'm grateful. Now get on with it."

Christopher picked up the dish and a lancet. It was not the same one he'd used to puncture the boy's eruptions. Though the invisible worms probably existed only in the minister's imagination, there was no harm in taking the extra precaution. He had no desire to infect Jeremy's wife with twice the dose he intended.

A decade earlier, when the practice was first advocated by Mather and a few like-minded progressives, out of every hundred variolated some sixty or seventy died. Christopher was convinced the deaths occurred only because the victims had been given too much of the disease.

So far he'd been lucky: he'd never lost an inoculation patient. But how much of the noxious matter was enough rather than too much was guesswork. Christopher based his guesses on the variables of health and constitution and the potency of the diseased serum. It was a leap in the dark, an act of faith. And in the main, Christopher Turner was not a believing man.

His hand shook. He shot a quick glance at Jeremy, who was looking at Marjorie with something between pity and fury and . . . terror, Christopher decided. Like all mad people, Marjorie mirrored the secret demons inside others. That was why lunatics were feared, because they made others see the thin line between themselves and insanity.

The thought steadied him. Christopher carried his instruments to Marjorie's chair and sat down beside her and took her hand. "Now, my dear, I'm only going to prick your finger." It was done before he'd finished speaking. Christopher squeezed a few drops of her blood onto the pewter dish, then returned to the bureau, and, very carefully, working with the absolute concentration that had once marked his practice of surgery, he lifted a drop of the pus on the tip of his lancet and added it to the blood.

It took only a few seconds to thoroughly mix the two together. He went back to Marjorie. She still didn't look at him. "Roll up her sleeve," he told the slave. "Good. Now hold her arm steady."

Christopher looked for a moment at Marjorie's milk-white skin. Not a mark anywhere. Marjorie Clinton did not have smallpox. She might never get it. Many, after all, would not. But he was about to give it to her, and he damned well knew it was the right, the kind, the medically sound thing to do. Whatever bloody Zachary Craddock and his friends with their medical degrees said or did, and however much influence they had over those who ruled New York.

He swiped the scalpel quickly and repeatedly across a small patch of skin on the inside of Marjorie's elbow, making shallow cuts. The blood oozed, a faint red haze on her thin, pale arm.

Jeremy took a step closer and bent his head to see. Christopher didn't turn around. "You're sure?" he asked. "There's still time to stop."

"I'm sure."

Christopher dipped a fresh lancet into the mix of blood and pus in the pewter dish. He lifted a tiny quantity on the tip of the blade, then tapped off a portion. Only a pinhead of the mixture was left. Too little to do any good, perhaps. No, the correct amount. The boy had confluent pox. An absolutely lethal form of the disease.

Still he hesitated.

A second or two more passed. He felt Jeremy's eyes boring into him. Even the slave was looking puzzled. Christopher smeared the tiny bit of infected matter on the cuts on Marjorie's arm. "Done," he said softly.

Jeremy let out his breath loudly. "Me next," he said. "Then the children. After that the slaves. But let's go across the hall to my room to do it."

Christopher stood up, began gathering his things. "Your mistress may feel

poorly for a few days," he told the black woman. "She may raise a slight fever, perhaps even a few pox. Don't be alarmed. It won't be bad."

"I know, master."

"You know? How?"

She was an old Ibo who'd been brought to America in one of the Guinea ships
when she was a girl of eighteen. For answer she lifted her skirts and showed him
her leg. The smooth dark skin of her thigh was marred by one puckered scar,
very like the scars that Christopher and Jane and their children all had on their
upper arms. He knew instantly what it meant. "You were variolated?" he said in
astonishment.

"When I was a little girl," the woman said. "Soon as the pox came to a nearby
village. Always, master. Long as anyone can remember, in my village they always
be doing this."

"In Africa. Among the black seed of Cain. Well, I'll be damned. I only hope
Craddock and his crowd don't hear about it. It'll be one more reason for them to
reject the procedure as heathen wickedness."

II

Shreds of September fog drifted in and out of the pall of smoke.

A young man walked alone through the bleak and deserted streets. He was tall
and moved with the natural grace of a man who had been born knowing his elevated place in society. When he reached the corner where Dock Street joined
Hall Place he stopped and hid himself in the shadows. A few minutes went by. A
quarter-mile away, the clock at the City Hall on Wall Street tolled twice. The
deep, resonant gong was muffled by the fog. A few seconds later the door to the
house beside the barbering pole opened and Jennet Turner appeared.

He'd been watching for a week, and it was always the same. After she'd pulled
the door shut behind her Jennet paused a moment on the stoop, long enough to
pull the hood of the old gray duffel cloak well forward so her face was deeply
shadowed. In one hand she carried a large wicker basket; the other held her cloak
tightly closed and lifted her skirts above the powdered streets. The young man
was quite sure she had no idea she was being followed.

The first time he'd stayed quite close, afraid he'd lose her in the fog of smoke.
Now he knew where she was going, and he could hang back. His boots made a
hollow echo on the cobbles. Once or twice he thought he heard the drumming of
horses' hooves.

Jennet headed up the Broad Way as far as Trinity Church, where she paused.
The full length of the wide street was lined with trees. The man hid himself be-

hind the thick trunk of an oak. Across the way Jennet unlatched the gate to the churchyard and made her way among the graves. In seconds she had disappeared into the gray mist.

He looked up and down the road—once, in a fog not as thick as this, he'd seen a man run down by a horse and carriage that seemed to appear from nowhere—then darted across the cobbles, which were slippery with red dust. The churchyard was surrounded by a wooden post-and-rail fence. He gripped the top bar and leaned forward, straining to see.

Jennet had met the other women. They were six altogether, all cloaked and hooded just as she was, and that day all clustered around what looked like a freshly dug grave. They put their baskets on the ground at their feet and joined hands. Their heads were bowed and they seemed to be praying, though they made no sound. Then, one by one, they threw back their hoods, gathered up their baskets, and left.

The man stepped back a few paces, disappearing again into the fog and the shadows of the trees, but he was close enough to see the women's faces as they walked out the gate. One had no nose, another only one eye. Three had skin so pocked and pitted it no longer looked human. They wore their disfigurements like a badge of honor.

He had read of such sisterhoods, beginning back in the fourteenth century, the time of the Black Death in Europe. Alliances of women who had walked through the fire of the plague and lived. In Spain, for a time, they had been the only people permitted by law to bury the dead.

Jennet was the last to leave the graveyard. No sign of the pox on her. At first he'd thought that was what these afternoon journeys meant, that Jennet had contracted the pox while he was away and was ugly and maimed. Not so. Despite her association with the plague women, Jennet was still as beautiful as he remembered her. Christ, there was little he had remembered better in the three years he'd been away studying medicine in Edinburgh. Caleb Devrey, Will Devrey's youngest son, had not stopped thinking about his cousin, though when he saw her last, he was a man of twenty and she was a child of thirteen.

Back then Caleb had found nothing about her mysterious. Now each day he followed her raised more questions. Jennet walked the streets with total confidence. Perhaps she knew she was naturally immune. Caleb was sure that was the case with him. He'd gone through two visitations of the pox while he was in Scotland and succumbed to neither. Which didn't make him glad to have returned to New York in the midst of yet another epidemic. He'd come back to an empty house. His parents and his brother and his family had fled to the long island. His sister had married an Albany man and lived in the upper reaches of the province.

That was why he could spend his time following Jennet.

Who was, more was the pity, his second cousin—but only by adoption, he reminded himself. So he need feel no shame in the thoughts he had about her.

Caleb could no longer see the women who'd left the graveyard, but he knew they were bringing food and medicine and such comfort as they could offer to the sick and dying. He admired all of them for their charity, Jennet as well.

Obviously Jennet carried food in her basket, perhaps some salves for the afflicted, and quite probably some potpourri to relieve the pox stench. She spent some ten minutes in each house she visited. But then, when she was finished, his cousin did not return to the graveyard for a final rite with the other nursing women, and she did not go back to her father's house on Hall Place. She walked north.

Each time he'd followed her, Jennet had finished her errands of mercy in the city, then pulled her hood back over her head and hurried past the cobbled streets to those made of hard-packed dirt. There the houses were sparse and built of wood, not brick, and almost the only tradesmen were the tanners who had been forced to take their evil-smelling occupation to the very edge of the town, to the new-made neighborhood surrounding the remains of Beekman's Swamp.

There was only one other business this far from the town. Dolly's Shipyard was considerably east of the tanneries. It had spread itself over the area abutting a recently built wharf on the East River. Normally a hive of activity, these days the shipyard was empty. Those who did not have the pox cowered, terrified, in their homes; those already stricken were too ill to work. The only sign that Dolly's wasn't a ghost yard was the small cluster of people waiting for the girl in the gray cloak.

They were nearly a dozen people, women and children, paupers who lived in the old shacks the freed blacks had built around the swamps before they were forbidden to own land in the aftermath of the revolt of 1712.

What could she do for them? Caleb had heard his father say often enough that Christopher Turner was practically a pauper himself, so Jennet couldn't be giving them money. And there was no way she could have enough food left to feed these people.

All those years in Edinburgh . . . Endless nights he'd lain awake dreaming of Jennet, thinking of how she must be growing up. Taller, her breasts a little fuller. He'd wondered whether her waist was still as tiny. And he had dreamed of her hair. Jennet's glorious hair would still be shining ebony. And her eyes would stay as big, and as dark a blue.

This past week his reveries had changed. Instead of rejoicing that Jennet was still the most beautiful creature he'd ever seen—and, God be praised, still not married—he'd lain awake trying to figure out what she was doing in Dolly's Shipyard.

The routine never changed. As soon as Jennet arrived she opened the door of an old shed. The misbegotten children and their haggard mothers crammed themselves into it. Jennett went in after them and pulled the door shut. Soon after that the women and their children started leaving, a few at a time, sneaking off into the shadows as if they were afraid to be seen.

In God's name, what was she doing in there?

Caleb had made up his mind. Today he'd have the answer.

Fourteen people had ducked into the shed when she arrived. He waited until eleven of them had gone, then walked boldly up to the door and threw it open.

The windowless shed was lit by a couple of candles. He could see Jennet quite clearly. She was seated on a low stool, and one of the two remaining urchin children stood between her splayed knees. She held the boy's bare arm in one hand. In the other she held a lancet.

"So, Cousin Caleb."

"So, Cousin Jennet."

It was the morning of the next day. They were standing on the wooden bridge that spanned the old canal basin at the foot of Broad Street, looking out to an inner harbor that was as deserted as everywhere else in the city. They might have been, as Jennet had said, on the moon. Caleb said that perhaps if they had been, what she was doing would not be so horrifying.

"Truly detestable. And that's quite apart from the fact that it's against the law and does no good." He kept staring at the water, because if he looked at her he could not be as stern as he must be. For her sake. "It is entirely unnatural."

"How can you say variolation is unnatural? It's—"

"I didn't mean that."

"What, then?"

"I meant it is deeply offensive to see a young woman with a lancet in her hand. That is what goes against nature."

"Against nature!" She held up her two hands, the long slim fingers spread so that each was lit by the sun that managed to show itself down here where the sea breeze had blown away the smoke. "Please do not think me immodest, Cousin Caleb. I can work magic with these hands. Surely that is a gift from God and it is meant to be used."

He was unmoved by her passion. "You are a female. To see you hold a lancet is disgusting and unnatural."

She dropped her arms to her sides. "That is certainly an opinion shared by many people."

"By every decent person. Jennet, you must promise me you will stop this thing. Swear you'll stop it. If you do not, I . . . I shall have no choice but to tell your father what I know."

"My father would not object."

"You can't believe that."

"I do."

"Then have you told him what you're doing?"

She looked away and didn't answer.

"I knew you hadn't. Your father is a highly intelligent man, for all—" he broke off.

"My father never did any of the things they accused him of. And he believes in variolation."

Caleb had removed his hat and tucked it under his arm. When he shook his head, the red hair he'd inherited from his aunt Bess and his grandfather Jacob Van der Vries glinted in the sunlight. Jennet liked the fact that he did not wear a wig, and that he was a head taller than she was. His stubbornness was less appealing.

"I am sure your father would not approve of a young woman administering variolation, even if he truly believed in it," he insisted. "And I refuse to accept that your father would advocate such a dangerous and heathen practice."

Jennet's green-and-white dress had long sleeves that tied at the wrist with a green ribbon. She stretched out her left arm and with her right hand undid the bow. Then, slowly and carefully, she started to roll up the sleeve.

Caleb stared, unable to take his eyes from the vision she was revealing. Her wrist was as delicate as a flower stem. The skin of her arm was as white as her face, and flawless. There wasn't so much as a freckle. Was it true of all of her? Were her thighs as white and firm, her midriff, her breasts . . . He swallowed hard. "What are you doing? I don't think you ought to—"

"Be quiet, Cousin Caleb. I don't care what I ought to do. I would have thought you realized that by now. I care about two things only. The first is showing you this."

She had rolled back her sleeve as far as her shoulder. Its curve was as perfect as any he'd ever seen. He could imagine her in a ball gown like the ones worn by the grand ladies of Edinburgh society. Blue satin, perhaps, the same color as her eyes, with her shoulders entirely bared and her bosom swelling above . . . "What's that?"

She was tapping the upper portion of her right arm with one finger of her left hand, drawing his attention to a scar about two inches across and an inch long. "That is the mark left by the variolation my father performed on me."

He kept looking at her white skin, at the puckered, distinctive scar. "Are you telling me that's where you got the idea? From your father?"

"No. I got the idea from reading the exchange of views between Mr. Mather and Dr. Douglas. And it seemed to me that the minister made a great deal more sense than the physician in this regard." She rolled down her sleeve as she spoke, with the same care she'd taken in rolling it up. "I learned to do it properly from watching my father, however. He is a very skilled practitioner, as I'm sure you know."

"I don't believe you." Caleb spoke in a whisper. Damn her, she took his breath away as well as his wits.

"What don't you believe? You must believe that I've been variolated, since I've just shown you the scar. As for the variolation protecting one from the pox, you admit to following me around the town for a week, so you know that I go where I will, without fear and without infection. It therefore follows that the variolation is effective, and you must—"

"No! Some people have a natural immunity. I do myself. We have always known—"

"Cousin Caleb." She held out her arm to him and smiled so sweetly that it seemed impossible the same red mouth had just been saying such provocative things. "Will you tie my sleeve for me? I cannot make a proper bow with one hand."

"Yes, of course." Easy to say. His fingers felt swollen to twice their normal size as he fumbled with the thin strand of ribbon that pulled the cuff tight around her slender wrist. He was terrified his hat would come loose from under his arm and he'd make a fool of himself chasing it up Broad Street. "Look, dear Jennet, I don't blame you for wanting to believe in something magical like var—"

"You mean, as opposed to the cures the doctors and physicians and apothecaries offer?" she said, so gently that it didn't seem as if she'd interrupted him. "The strong purges twice a day, and the constant bloodletting? The broth made of sheep's purslane and sugar syrup to sweeten the internal humors, followed by a vigorous emetic, nux vomica perhaps, to bring forth the dangerous fluids in the belly?"

"We do what we can." He was finished with the bow. Caleb let her go. "I admit it's not perfect, but the pox is a disease of the most virulent nature. That's why deliberately spreading it, even among the poor beggars you're trying to—"

"Not one of the 'poor beggars' has sickened with the pox after I variolated them. Nor have I, nor has my father or my mother, nor my two brothers, nor my three sisters. We are all of us here in this plagued place, breathing the wretched smoke the stupid government bids us rely upon in place of a real cure, and we are none of us ill. How do you explain that, Caleb Devrey? What did they teach you in Edinburgh that is stronger than the evidence of your own eyes?"

He could think of nothing to do except clap his hat back on his head. Jennet was still looking at him. "I can't explain it," he said finally. "I admit to knowing nothing to disprove your ideas."

Jennet sighed. "I am so glad. You cannot know how glad I am, Cousin Caleb." The intensity with which she spoke was startling. "You are? Why?"

"Because that tells me that you're an intelligent man. Only a fool insists on believing what he's believed before when contrary evidence is presented to him."

"And that's what pleases you, that I'm not a fool?"

"Indeed. Caleb, do you remember my telling you there were two things that interested me? You never asked me what the second was."

If he could keep her talking it didn't matter what she said. As long as she spoke she must stay here with him in the sunlight on the bridge overlooking the still and silent harbor, with those few strands of her jet-black hair escaped from her white cap and fluttering around her face, and her blue eyes looking directly at him. "Did I not? Very well, Cousin Jennet, I am asking now. What is the second thing?"

"That although I am a woman, I mean to practice surgery and open an infirmary to serve the poor. And it strikes me, dear cousin, now that you've returned from Edinburgh with a degree in medicine: the simplest way to accomplish that would be to marry you. So that's what I shall do."

III

"It appears that the young people have quite made up their minds." Will Devrey was plainly uncomfortable entertaining his cousin Christopher, but determined to do his duty. "And now that the pox seems to have left the town, I suppose we may as well arrange for the banns to be cried."

Susannah Devrey had been shocked at the suggestion that Christopher Turner should be invited to the Devrey home, but indifferent to the engagement of Caleb and Jennet.

Bede, the Devreys' older boy and the one who would take over his father's business, had always been his mother's favorite. She'd tried to feel more for Caleb, but when he announced his desire to go to Edinburgh and study medicine she had washed her hands of him. Susannah could not imagine wanting to be around sick people all the time. So Caleb could marry whom he liked, even the daughter of the family black sheep, and she would not trouble herself. But Susannah found it unthinkable that Christopher Turner should be invited to sit in her Wall Street drawing room and take tea.

Will compromised by meeting his cousin in his ground-floor office. The charts detailing the voyages of his eleven ships were pinned to the walls, and there was a jug of brandy on the desk between them. Will poured a glass for each of them. "Considering that the children are only second cousins, it doesn't seem we need—"

"They aren't related by blood in any case." Christopher took his drink, got up from his chair, and began studying one of the charts on the wall. An excuse to turn his back on Will. A supercilious bastard, and rich as bloody Croesus. "Lucas Turner adopted my father. Nicholas was Ankel Jannssen's son."

"Yes, quite. Odd, wasn't it, the way Ankel Jannssen disappeared? I've always wondered if—"

"My ancestor was a stumbling drunk who could barely walk for the amount of liquor he poured down his gullet daily." Christopher was willing to shame himself just to rub Will Devrey's nose in the cesspool his son would marry into. "Ankel Jannssen probably wandered off into the woods and was killed by a savage, or drowned in a swamp."

"Yes, probably. And as you say, since there is no blood shared, we have not those grounds to object to the desires of our young."

"Some other grounds perhaps, Cousin Will?"

"No, of course not. I just meant—"

"Yes, I know." One reason he hadn't argued more strongly when Jennet insisted she wanted to marry Will Devrey's boy was because he took some pleasure in thinking how the bastard would squirm at the thought. "Have to be honest with you. I can't give Jennet much of a dowry. Thanks to your nephew-in-law."

"I realize that. Zachary Craddock means well, but he can be intemperate at times. As for dowering your daughter, under the circumstances I should think we might . . ."

"Yes?"

"We might overlook that formality. Here, have another drink."

"No, thanks. Don't let me stop you, however."

"I shan't." Will poured his fourth brandy. His forehead was beaded with sweat and he made a conscious effort to change the subject. "That chart you're looking at, it's the route of my latest ship. The eleventh. Making her maiden voyage. She's called the *Susannah*. After my wife, of course."

"Of course. I take it you expect her to be profitable." Susannah was well known to spend money faster than even Will Devrey could make it.

Will didn't take offense. He'd never curbed Susannah's extravagances because it gave him pleasure to be seen as a man who could afford them. "Very profitable. See here"—he got up and went to stand beside Christopher and tapped the chart with a stubby finger—"that's the first leg of the journey. New York to the Indies, carrying timber and flesh and fish and butter and biscuit."

"The first leg. The *Susannah*'s not coming straight back, then? I thought the West Indies ships always brought back rum. Or at least sugar for the making of it."

"Not this one. She's going on to Newcastle, where she'll unload her cane and take on coal for ballast. Then to London, where she'll lade some of the mother country's pleasures for us poor colonials." Will allowed himself a wry grin.

"Nothing but the best for the *Susannah*. She'll be bringing back choice furniture and cloth, the finest satins and laces. All the made goods that fill our best markets. Named her well, didn't I?"

"So it seems. But why no trip to Africa for blacks? Is that not the better part of your trade?"

"Was once. Less so now. No, the *Susannah*'s not a Guinea ship. No point in building more of those at the moment. Van Dam and the Council insist we lessen the proportion of blacks in the province. Safer to bring in white servants, they say. Indentures. You ask me, it's not how many slaves we have but how well we discipline 'em that matters. However"—he tapped the chart again—"we are His Majesty's obedient servants. Now sir," returning to his desk and upending the brandy decanter into his glass one more time, "to get back to the business at hand. Shall we say three weeks hence for the wedding?" He had no idea why Caleb wanted to marry a pauper's daughter, but there it was. Susannah wanted the boy out of the house, getting on with his life. As for Will, anything that made for peace under his roof was welcome. "How about it, Christopher? Three weeks."

Christopher glanced at the calendar on the wall. "That would make it . . . January tenth. A few weeks before Jennet's seventeenth birthday. I can see no objection."

Will smiled a small smile that didn't seem to reach his eyes. "The tenth of January in the year of Our Lord 1732 for the wedding of Miss Jennet Turner to Mr. . . . . No, no, I'm told that the fashion now is that I must say 'Doctor.' To Dr. Caleb Devrey. That should please them. Please Caleb, at any rate. I expect three weeks is about as long as he's willing to wait."

"I have news for you." Jennet was holding the walking stick, stroking the gold horse's head. "I'm to be married."

Merda! He felt as if he'd been punched in the belly. *Filho da puta!* DaSilva clenched his fists until the knuckles whitened. But what could he expect? Her father was a virtual beggar, but she was a young woman and a rare beauty. Of course she'd marry. But *merda!* Not so soon. "Does your father not think you're too young?"

"He did at first. But Caleb and I insisted. We told him we would run off if he didn't agree."

"I see." She was looking out the window, avoiding his direct glance. "You are a headstrong child, Jennet Turner. I think if I were your father I would put you over my knee and give you the spanking you deserve."

"Well, I'm not."

"Not what?"

"Not your daughter. And my father has never beaten any of us. He does not approve of beating."

"I said 'spank.' It's entirely different."

She shrugged. "Perhaps. Anyway, it doesn't matter what you think. Caleb's papa and mine have agreed. The first banns are to be cried this Sunday. The wedding will be on the tenth of January in the new year."

"And who is this Caleb?" The first shock had passed; he could breathe a little easier now. His words did not sound quite so strained in his own ears. She, of course, had noticed nothing. Whatever she thought of him, it would not occur to her that he would be distraught by the thought of her marrying. "Is he in any position to support a wife?"

"Oh that." She waved her hand as if such considerations were of no importance. "He is Caleb Devrey, and his father is Will Devrey. So there is plenty of money."

Filho da puta! "Will Devrey. I see. Well, you are right, there is plenty of money." Something else occurred to him, another straw to grasp. "But you and Devrey's son . . . are you not cousins?"

"Second cousins, and that by adoption. There is no objection. So it's all settled."

She turned to face him. "I haven't told you the best part. Caleb is a doctor of medicine, just returned from studying at the University of Edinburgh. After we're married we shall devote our lives to bringing medical care to the poor."

"An interesting plan." DaSilva reached over and took his walking stick from her hands. "Does your husband-to-be agree with it?"

"Of course. Caleb always does whatever I say." He snorted and she blushed. "Well, he does after a bit. Sometimes I must persuade him first."

"I think you will be miserable—"

"What a terrible thing to say! Why would you wish misery upon me, Solomon?"

"I don't. You didn't let me finish. I was going to say I think you'll be miserable if you marry a man who always does everything you say."

Jennet shook her head. "No, you are quite wrong about that. Caleb suits me perfectly. We shall be blissfully happy. On January tenth my life begins. And what of you, Solomon, shall you give me a fine wedding present?"

"Perhaps"—he held up the walking stick—"I shall give you this."

When Marit and Ankel Jannssen lived in the house on Hall Place, the front room had been the butcher shop. After Lucas married Marit it was his barbering room and surgery. When young Christopher Turner became the most celebrated cutter in the city he took his tools to his patients' homes and was welcomed as a savior. In those days, the front room of the little house was the family parlor, and Jane had dreams of being a fine lady and entertaining New York City society. Since Christopher's fall from grace, the room was once more a place of sweaty labor. He wrote there, taught there, and, when he had the chance, saw patients there.

That December night he'd brought every candle in the room to the small table beside the fire, concentrating all the light into a single yellow pool. In the middle of the light a woman sat alone, shoulders hunched, fair head bowed. Her name was Martha Kincaid, and she'd kept her shawl over her hair until Christopher insisted she remove it. Now it was clutched in her lap and trailing on the floor, ignored in her general misery and shame.

Hezekiah Jackson, far and away the cleverest of the three students who had answered Christopher's latest advertisement offering instruction in surgery, hovered behind the patient he had brought to his teacher. Christopher stood to her side. Both men stared intently at the woman's face.

She had a growth on her jaw the size of two plump Christmas oranges. A series of uneven mounds set one on the other, it spread from her earlobe to the corner of her mouth. The thing was pocked and pitted and covered in what appeared to be black boils. It was so grotesque she refused to be on the streets except after dark, and then only with the black shawl covering her head and most of her face.

"The tumor extends to the larynx below and the pharynx behind," Hezekiah Jackson said. "So it's not operable, is it?"

Christopher made no reply. Instead he stretched out his hand and gently fingered the lumps.

"According to the three physicians she's seen," Hezekiah continued, "it's an osteo-sarcoma, and they cannot be treated."

The woman winced. Not, Christopher thought, because of his feather-light touch. "Mr. Jackson, your patient has a facial tumor. In my experience, that does not make her deaf. It's a lesson worth remembering."

"Yes, I know, but—"

"Be quiet, Mr. Jackson. At least until I have completed my examination."

Christopher leaned a little closer, probed a bit more deeply. The gesture brought his face out of the shadows into the candlelight. The woman looked into his eyes. Hers were brown, and her skin, apart from the tumor, fair. In her twenties, he guessed, healthy except for this repulsive thing on her face and quite possibly pretty without it. He returned to his study of the tumor, running his fingers over it repeatedly, using his sense of touch to plumb the thing's secrets. Aware that she was staring at him all the while.

Christopher ended his examination, but he didn't immediately straighten up. "You are married, mistress?"

"Aye. To Tom Kincaid the miller. At least, I s'pose I must still say as I'm married to him."

"I'm sorry, I don't—"

"Ain't what most folks mean when they says 'married.' Tom Kincaid won't have me in his bed these five years past. Not since this thing began growing."

Her directness startled him. Christopher pulled back, out of the light. "Yes, well, sometimes—"

"Sometimes," she finished for him, "a woman's so ugly a man can't be blamed if lookin' at her face turns his stomach."

A little gasp followed that statement. Not from Martha Kincaid. She spoke as if she were discussing the day's weather, or the eggs her backyard chickens had produced that morning.

Christopher looked toward the sitting-room door. Could be that Jane had come to see what was keeping him so late. The shadows were deep and still. He took a step toward the door. Martha Kincaid's voice stopped him. "This thing. It's something as will kill me, ain't it?"

Christopher returned his attention to his patient. "I will not lie to you. An osteo-sarcoma is usually fatal." She winced again. It seemed to be the only response she made to any sort of pain. "But for that to be the result you must first have the thing. And you, I think, do not."

There was an audible gasp of dissent from Hezekiah Jackson. "But three practitioners said—"

"Donkeys are popular in New York, Mr. Jackson. There are at least that many jackasses to be found on the city streets on any given day. For God's sake, man, feel right here." He grabbed his student's hand and put it on the woman's cheek. "No, don't bear down like that. You eliminate any chance to know what the thing has to tell you. Lightly. Only run your fingers over it."

"It moves."

"Exactly. And an osteo-sarcoma does *not* move. It is a cancer anchored in the bone. This is a cyst attached to muscle and skin." Christopher looked from Jackson to the patient. "I can help you, mistress. Do you wish me to proceed?"

He expected her to leap at the chance. Instead she hesitated. "You gonna cut?"

"Yes, some cutting is involved."

Martha Kincaid said nothing.

"I have saved a great many more than I ever lost," Christopher said softly.

Sweet Christ. He was reduced to this, to begging for the chance to use the scalpel and the lancet. Because his hands itched to do so. Because it was what he'd been born to do. "In any event," he added, "you shall eventually die, Mistress Kincaid, as must we all, but not because of the growth on your face. You can go on living, with or without it. The choice is yours."

She raised her hand and touched the tumor. "It moves, you say."

"It does."

"I don't feel it move."

"You are a woman. Females are not inclined by nature to be successful in such an exploration."

She nodded. "But three practitioners," she whispered, "and all of 'em said—"

"What did they do for you, these three? Blistering? Bleeding? Purging?" She nodded again. The deformity moved up and down with her head. "And did any of those affect the growth?

She shook her head. "No."

Christopher reached a long arm to the table behind him where his instruments waited. He fumbled till he found a hand glass in a tortoise frame, then grabbed it and shoved it at her. "Look at yourself. Go on. You came here for help. This is the best I can offer."

She lifted the glass for a moment, then dropped it to her lap.

"Now," Christopher said. "Sit very still. And don't worry, I won't cut until I have your permission. Jackson, come closer. Watch me. That's what you come for, isn't it? To learn something. Well, learn this."

He put his long fingers on either side of the largest of the black, boil-like eruptions on the tumor's surface, midway on a point between her earlobe and the tip of her nose. The head of the apparent boil was faintly indented, resting in a pit in the skin. Fair chance the entire growth had begun in the scars left by a brush with the pox. Probably when she was a small child.

"What we have here, Mr. Jackson, is a benign sebaceous cyst, a sac below the skin that is constantly filled and refilled. And see, right here where I'm pointing? That black mark, like all the others, is one of the outlets. So if I compress the sides like this . . ." He pressed hard. The dark point shot out first, followed by an undulating thread of white.

"Worms . . ." Hezekiah breathed the word on a long sigh. "There are live maggots below the surface of her skin." Martha Kincaid gasped. "It's not maggots, you idiot," Christopher snapped at Jackson. "It's fatty matter. Your patient has a disease of the skin." He squeezed while he spoke, extracting a nearly six-inch length of the white, grainy substance. "The sac fills with these fatty particles and flakes of the dead epidermis. And while we may squeeze as much as we like—even empty the whole lump of its contents—the sac, unless cut away, will soon fill again."

Christopher reached behind him once more. This time he retrieved a flat pewter dish and a small spatulate probe. He used the probe to scoop the sebaceous matter from the woman's face and deposit it on the dish. There was at least an ounce of it. Possibly two. "Here, mistress, examine this. Then raise the glass again and take a very close look at your face. Tell me if you find the lower part of the lump somewhat decreased in volume."

She spent only a moment on the substance in the dish, a little longer studying herself in the tortoise-framed mirror. "It is smaller," she said finally. "You can't know how many nights I went to my bed prayin' to wake up and find it so. Even by a tiny bit. Now . . ." She broke off and looked at him, plainly trying to decide whether, despite his terrible reputation, she could trust him.

"If you choose," Christopher said, "you may leave here tonight without any disfigurement. I shall not, I think, find it necessary to stitch the wound, only cauterize it, perhaps, then treat it with nitrate of silver and cover it with a small bandage of lint. You have a sac beneath your skin that has filled with solid and decaying fatty matter." Christopher gestured at the pewter dish and set it aside. "You now see it with your own eyes. It is natural for your body to continue to produce this substance. As long as the sac remains, it will keep filling. If, on the other hand, I make a small cut and extract the sac—then, mistress, you need no longer hide behind your shawl." His hands itched to pick up his weapons and begin the battle. The scalpels and the lancets were his armory. When he couldn't use them he was a knight without a sword. Useless.

"Will it hurt much?" the woman asked.

Christopher forced himself to relax. She would agree, or she would not. "It will hurt. Not, I think, as much as living with this black and ugly thing distorting your face."

She turned her head and looked at Jackson, then back at Christopher. "He said it would be three shillings. For the consultation."

"That's right."

"And for the surgery? If I agree, I mean."

However miserable his finances, Christopher missed the chance to operate, far more than he missed money. "No additional charge, mistress. The surgery is included."

"Very well. Then do it."

He stifled the yelp of pleasure that rose in his throat. "A wise decision, mistress. You will not regret it." Christopher reached for his scalpel. "Come closer, Mr. Jackson. Hold her head steady."

At the door, with her face pressed close to the tiny crack she had been peering through for the past hour, Jennet felt her hands start to tremble. She saw her father make the first incision—near the lower part of the jaw, a half-moon opening about an inch across—and she had to twine her fingers together to keep them from twitching. Soon. Only two weeks more. The very moment she was married to Caleb she would begin showing him what she could do, and convincing him she must be allowed to do it.

"Come, I will walk you home," Jackson said.

Martha Kincaid had her black shawl wrapped tightly around her face, covering the small bandage. And the absence of the lump. "Ain't no need to trouble yourself. I'm well used to going about alone."

It was late. The streets were empty and the town's four bellmen were doubtless making their rounds. "The curfew . . ." Jackson said. "You'll be—"

"The bellmen got more to do than look out for the likes of me, Mr. Jackson. Go on. These last four years . . ."

Walk her home, he said. He meant to Tom Kincaid's mill over on Cortlandt Street. Foolish waste of steps that would be. Tom Kincaid didn't care where she went, or who with, not so long as she brought him a purse full of coins once every week. Otherwise, he said, he'd report her as a runaway wife. Get her a trip to the whipping cage, that would, and thirty-nine strokes on her bare back with any as wanted to looking on. To be warned against evil ways, the preachers said. Because they liked the sight of blood, more likely. Not to mention bare tits.

She lifted a tentative hand to her face. Holy God Almighty. It still felt flat. "Don't fuss yourself none, Mr. Jackson. I knows me way about in the dark."

"Well, if you're quite sure . . ." He was glad to be let off his task. The curfew applied to loitering on the streets, but it wasn't enforced inside the taverns. Jackson was impatient to get to the sign of the Horse and Wagon over on William Street, and explain to any as would listen the vital role he'd played in the brilliant surgery. He lifted his tricorn and quickly replaced it, then turned his back on the woman and hurried up the moonlit road.

Martha heard the bellman's call. "Eleven of the clock and all is well on a dry and frosty evening." He was getting closer. It wouldn't do to be found standing here.

A bank of clouds covered the moon and Hall Place became quite dark. Behind her Christopher Turner's house was darker still, the last of the candles snuffed out. All of 'em tucked up in their beds, even whoever it was had been watching in the hall. Stupid men. So wrapped up in themselves and whatever they were doing they were blind and deaf to all else. No doubt at all that someone had been spying on the goings-on in Christopher Turner's front room.

She felt something suddenly duck beneath her skirts and begin crawling up her leg. Martha started to cry out, then clamped her mouth tight shut. A tongue was licking the inside of her thigh. "You," she whispered, lifting her skirts and pushing away an oversized bald head. "What are you doing here? Stop!"

"Thought you liked it." The dwarf crawled out from under her skirts and wiped his mouth with the edge of his battered tricorn, then clamped it back on. When he stood up he barely reached her waist. "You always be saying you like it."

"Not here I don't, you silly fool. Bellman's coming. You must be mad."

"Bellman won't be finding me. Nobody be finding Jan Brinker if he be wanting to hide. That be the good part about being three feet tall."

She'd heard that boast a hundred times. It was a lie. There was no good part of being a freak. Jan Brinker hated being a misshapen Dutch midget. Children chased him and threw the nastiest things they could find at him. Women crossed the road so they wouldn't have to pass too close to him. They knew Jan Brinker could put the evil eye on them just by looking. Anyone who was different hated it. Like she'd hated having that ugly thing on her face.

She pulled the shawl forward, grateful for the dark, not wanting the dwarf to know yet how changed she was, afraid, though she wasn't sure of what. "We best go. Bellman's nearby."

"Don't want anyone be knowing where you been, do you?" Brinker said. "Not considering what everyone be thinking about him in there."

"I don't care what everyone— It were you, weren't it? You were the one spying on us."

"In there? Not on your life! Jan Brinker ain't never been inside that murderer's house. Nothing would make me—" Somewhere a window banged shut. "Guess you be right," the dwarf murmured. "Best we go. Seems we be disturbing the peace."

He shuddered. Disturbing the peace carried a penalty of a day in the stocks. Whatever happened to ordinary folk when they were forced to stand with their head and hands imprisoned in the oak frame in front of City Hall, it was a hundred times worse for Jan Brinker.

They'd put him in the stocks once. For cavorting and begging down at the place over on Pearl Street that used to be named for an old Dutchman called Vly, until the Englishers started calling it the Fly Market. He don't be cavorting, how they called it. He be trying to get a bit of money because he was hungry.

Told 'em so, but they took him to City Hall all the same. Put him in the stocks. Gave him a chair to stand on so he could reach the openings. And before an hour went by a giggling brat kicked it away. He hung like that—taking all his weight on his neck and his wrists—for hours. Jailer finally come to release him, he be laughing himself silly at the sight. Jan Brinker didn't laugh. Both his shoulders were pulled from their sockets and his throat was swollen nearly shut. Ill for a month he be. Almost died. Would have died except for Martha Kincaid. "Come," he said. "You be right. Best we go."

The night was a familiar friend. They melted into the dark and hurried through the silent streets to the one place both knew they would be safe.

Except for a large stone chimney, the building hidden in the trees of the thick woods beyond the city's northern border, about a mile and a quarter from the harbor and Fort George, looked like a derelict shack. Inside it was comfortably furnished with wooden tables and benches, and full of the yeasty smell of ale and the rich sweetness of rum. The air was thick with pipe smoke and candle smoke, and the smoke of the roaring log fire that eased the chill of the winter night.

There were at least fifty people in the taproom. Men and women, black and white. All mixed together as equals. That was extraordinary enough in New York City, but not the most remarkable thing about this particular crowd.

"Where you two been?" a black man shouted as soon as Martha and the dwarf appeared. "We been waitin' for a song. C'mon, somebody get the midget his fiddle."

Eager hands lifted Jan Brinker and passed him over the heads of the raucous mob. Martha stayed by the door. They were all there, the people she'd come to think of as family these last few years. A few who had survived the pox and wished they hadn't. A couple of hunchbacks, any number of blind and crippled. At least five runaway black slaves with a price on their heads. And those were just the ordinary misfits.

Leaning against the wall in the far corner were fourteen-year-old twin sisters, joined at the hip since birth. By the standards of this company, they were rich. Extraordinary what some men would pay to have something different to fuck. Like the woman who'd been born with short, stubby little arms and her hands connected where her elbows should be. Or the one whose face was entirely covered by a puckered red devil's mark. And you couldn't go to the bordellos on Holy Ground if you had to be carried to the whore's bed. Two legless men were propped in a corner, banging their pewter mugs on the table to add to the uproar. Another who had a gnarled growth like a horn sticking out of the top of his skull shoved his way through the mêlée, waving a violin in the air. "Here it is! Out o' the way, you lot. Let the dwarf have his fiddle."

They all came to Martha Kincaid's. No matter what was wrong with you, you'd fit in at Martha's and find someone who'd lie with you, long as you paid. And if it chanced that you had some dealings to discuss that might not bear close scrutiny, well, at Martha's no one asked difficult questions, not as long as you put a few coins in the general purse.

She'd never planned it this way. She'd been born respectable Martha Jenson and she married Tom Kincaid when she was sixteen. She kept his house clean and helped with the milling and she bore him five children in four years, including two strong sons yet alive. He'd had nothing to complain of until the thing on her face started growing and he turned her out of his bed. One night a year or so later she tried in the dark to climb back into it—needing beyond all things to feel a human and loving touch—and he'd screamed her out of the house. She'd run sobbing through the streets until she found this abandoned shack at the edge of the woods that backed up on the farmland skirting the King's High Road to Boston.

The shack became her refuge and she returned often, fixing it up little by little with her own hands. Eventually Jan Brinker came and helped her. And the others. Until now she was what fate had made her. Martha Kincaid, proprietor of the best bawdyhouse in New York City.

Now Christopher Turner had changed everything. Martha reached up and probed beneath her shawl. The jaw had swollen some; it was tender and felt hot to the touch. Mr. Turner had told her it would be so. A reaction to the surgery. But there was no black lump. She did not have to look into a glass to know it.

Jan Brinker was standing on a stage made of abandoned wooden packing cases dragged up from the docks. He had the fiddle tucked under his chin—it was almost as big as he was—and he was bowing wildly. The crowd was singing and cheering. "Do a dance for us, Martha," someone shouted.

"Aye, c'mon, Martha, a dance!"

"No, not tonight. I don't feel like dancing tonight."

They wouldn't be put off. She was pushed forward to the makeshift stage, not able to resist because both her hands were busy keeping her shawl in place. They mustn't see. Not yet. She wasn't sure how would they'd feel now that she was no longer one of them.

Black Bento clasped her around the waist. A runaway slave from a Caribbean sugar plantation, he was wanted for hanging, on account of he'd strangled an overseer with his bare hands. Strongest hands she'd ever met. God knows she'd been glad enough to feel them the dark and lonely nights of these past winters. Not tonight, though. Not when he swung her up on the stage beside Jan, and the dwarf switched to a lively jig.

"That's our girl, Martha! Come on, show us your ankles!"

They were all shouting at once. Smiling at her. They didn't care about the black thing on her face. They had never cared. They were all freaks together here. That was the secret of the place. That's why it was home.

Martha spun around and faced the wall. Then she released her grip on the shawl and lifted her skirt and her petticoats as high as her knees and began to dance. Her clogs pounded the wooden stage in a fierce rhythm matched only by the fiddle and her wildly beating heart. She moved so fast the stripes of her knitted stockings blurred into a single flash of color. The black scarf slipped off her head and down her back and fell on the floor. Martha kept dancing.

At last, she turned around.

Bento was the first to notice. "Holy Jesus, girl," he whispered. "I never seed . . . Holy Jesus."

One by one they saw, those with eyes whispering the message to those who had none, or were too far in the back of the room to see.

The noisy clapping and yelling died away.

"The thing on her face, it's gone."

"No black lump."

"Like the rest of 'em."

"Not like us."

Martha stopped dancing. The crowd quieted. The sound of the fiddle was the last noise to die away. At last Jan Brinker stopped playing and stood on his toes so he could see better. "*Jesu Cristo.* I don't believe it. I never . . ."

Martha bent down and grabbed her shawl. She started to put it on, but Bento vaulted onto the stage and yanked it away. "Don't you do that, woman. Don't you be hidin' this here miracle. It's a visitation from Jesus Christ. You got to tell the world."

Years before, Christian missionaries had gone to the islands and begun converting the slaves, Bento among them. The law said that baptism didn't entitle a slave to manumission, but Bento remembered what was written in the holy book, *No slaves or free men, only equals in Christ Jesus.* So Bento took his freedom. Killing the overseer had been self-defense, though no one would believe it. But God knew. Jesus traveled with him. Bento had managed to get as far as Martha Kincaid's bawdyhouse, so he could be witness to this miracle. "You got to tell the world what Jesus done for you, woman."

"Your Jesus had nothin' to do with it." She couldn't hold back the words. "Your Jesus ain't never done nothin' for me. Where was he when my husband threw me into the street?" She lifted her hand and pointed at the joined twins who had shoved their way forward to get a better look at Martha's face. "Where was he when these two was born stuck together like that? Where was he when your mother was chained in a Guinea ship, then sold to some plantation owner to work herself to death hacking his sugarcane? You tell me, Bento, what has your Jesus done for any of us here?"

Bento had both his hands clasped over his ears. He was swaying back and forth under the weight of his distress. "You close your mouth, woman. You shut your mouth and go down on your knees and beg forgiveness. Otherwise I ain't sayin' what's gonna happen here in this place."

"Nothing's going to happen," Martha shouted. "It waren't your Jesus fixed my face. Not your God or anyone else's God. It was the surgeon, Christopher Turner. Him who lives over on Hall Place. He done it."

Her words shocked the crowd into silence. If an ordinary man had cured Martha Kincaid of her disfigurement, what might he be able to do for the rest of them?

On a January Sunday the banns announcing the betrothal of Jennet Turner to Caleb Devrey were cried for the second time. Will Devrey came out of Trinity

Church surrounded by well-wishers with Susannah by his side and Caleb a few steps behind them. The Devreys were too occupied by people who wanted to congratulate them on the forthcoming marriage to notice the woman standing by the door.

At first Christopher didn't notice her, either. He was busy watching New York society licking the buttocks of the rich. Sweet Christ, all of 'em toadying to Will, acting as if the fact that his son was marrying the daughter of the man they called the butcher of Hall Place wasn't the best gossip in the town. As for himself and Jane, they might as well not have been there.

That had to be painful for Jane. Even a quick glance showed she minded the snubbing. They never should have come, except that Jane insisted on doing things the "mannerly way."

By long tradition the second crying of the banns was a major social occasion, at least according to the people who attended Trinity Church. Once Christopher had dreamed of buying a fine house in Hanover Square and joining their company. He knew better now. New York society had dung for brains and cash boxes where their hearts should be. If you cut 'em they'd probably bleed pounds, shillings, and pence. Sometimes he was glad he'd never—

"Mr. Turner, Mr. Turner . . . It's me, Martha Kincaid. I been tryin' to—"

"Here, stop pulling at my sleeve, mistress. I see you."

"Please, you got to give me an answer, Mr. Turner. Them folks I told you about . . . If you could just see 'em and say whether—"

"I'm sorry, mistress." He tried to speak kindly even while he pushed her hand off his arm. "I've told you again and again, I can't help the kinds of cases you describe. Now please, let me and my family pass in peace. If you do not, I'll have no choice but to summon a constable."

Martha backed away. The surgeon and his wife and their daughter passed her by. Then the girl looked over her shoulder and fixed her dark blue eyes on Martha.

The lass was a beauty. No wonder she was marrying one of the best catches in the city. Despite what people said about her father.

"It was you, waren't it?"

Jennet looked at the woman who stood in her path. "I don't know what you're talking about. Please let me pass."

In a week she'd be married to Caleb and she'd have slaves to send to the market while she and her husband served the poor. But at the moment she was still an unmarried girl living under her father's roof, and she had to get home with the makings of the day's dinner or face the rough of her mother's tongue. Amba's, too, most likely. "Let me pass. You have no right to prevent my—"

"It were you in the hall that night. Spying on your father. I know it were you."

Jennet's heart began to thump. "You're the woman who had the lump. Martha . . ."

"Martha Kincaid. And I know it were you spying on us. I could tell by the way you was looking at me last Sunday after church."

"I told you, I've no idea what you're talking about. Now let me pass."

"You got every idea. Else how would you know my name?"

"I guessed."

"No, you didn't. You saw the whole thing and I figure that waren't the first time. I been talking to the folks who live up in the tanneries. They say you do it, too."

"Do what?" Jennet's voice was a faint whisper. Her heart beat a tattoo of fear And excitement. "What are you talking about?"

"There's some as say you're as clever with the knife as your pa is. That you can cure by cutting good as he can."

Jennet looked down and began fussing with the parcels in her basket. "A woman can't be a surgeon. It's forbidden."

"Men make the rules. That's why women is forbidden to do lots of things. But that don't mean we always got to do what the rules say."

The joined twins were the last to present themselves. By then Jennet was nearly overcome with exhaustion. She'd seen more deformities in the last two hours than in her whole life before. Even in her worst nightmares she had not imagined such things could exist. Now the worst had been saved for last: two heads on what seemed to be a single four-legged body.

The girls marched into the little room Martha Kincaid had set aside for the consultations, and stood mute before Jennet, who had so far refused to do anything for any of the people she'd seen.

The joined twins knew at once they were not going to be the exception. They could tell by her expression. And her tears.

"I'm sorry." Jennet dabbed at her eyes with a sodden handkerchief and shook her head. "I wish I could help you. I can't. I haven't the knowledge or the skill."

"Your pa," the one on the left asked, "can he do it?"

"I don't know. I don't think so. I've never seen anything— I mean, he's never talked about doing any such thing. And I've never seen it in the medical books." Not even in Lucas Turner's journals, which she'd secretly been reading since she was nine years old.

"We don't be the only ones as are born like this." The twin on the right spoke this time. "A man who comes here to . . . A learned man who visits sometimes. He says it be happening before, only usually the babes die."

"But we lived," the left twin said. "Because we strong and healthy. We be tough, miss. Tough as any man. We could stand the pain if you cut us apart."

Jennet shook her head. "I'm so sorry. If I had the least idea how to help you, I promise I would. But I—"

"We'd never tell," the right head said.

"Never," the left agreed. "You can count on it. No matter what anyone did."

"We'd never say who it was as—"

"No," Jennet interrupted, her voice firmer now. "It isn't that I'm afraid. I can't do it. Not I won't. I can't."

The twins looked at each other and, without a word, one began undoing the drawstring that tied the large skirt that covered them both.

"Please," Jennet protested. "Don't do this. It won't make any difference."

The twins ignored her. The skirt dropped to the ground. Both pairs of hands reached down and lifted their shared petticoats, revealing their plump legs in striped stockings. Above that they were naked. Jennet could see their privates, and the thick bond of flesh and skin that forever locked them together. The bridge was some nine inches long and positioned immediately below the waists of the two women. Jennet couldn't stifle her fascination. She moved a bit closer.

The twins waited in silence.

Jennet put out her hand, hesitated a moment, then touched the join. All the great surgeons insisted that the finest tool is touch. *Before he takes up the Scalpel, much less the Saw, a wise surgeon relies on his Fingertips.* Slowly, with total concentration, she let her fingers explore the connection between the two women.

The skin of the bridge was thick and rough, callused like the hands of a laborer; judging from the springy, resilient character of the link, it was strengthened by cartilage, not bone. It was warm. Blood flowed across this incredible union, and that made it impossible to operate.

Jennet shook her head for the twentieth time that afternoon. "I'm sorry. It can't be done. At least not by me. I don't think anyone could do it. Your blood is circulating through both bodies as if they were one and the same. If you were cut apart, you'd bleed to death."

"What about legs and arms, then?" the left twin demanded. "Surgeons like your father, they cut off legs and arms all the time. Those people don't bleed to death after. They gets stitched up."

"That's sawing bone, it's different."

"How's it different?"

Jennet was at a loss to explain what she'd gleaned from years of spying on Christopher, and from her secret reading. "It's done all the time. Everyone knows exactly which vessels have to be tied off. But you two, no one can say what . . . I can't explain more. You simply have to believe me. I can't do this. I have no idea what would happen if I tried."

"No one can say about freaks, that's what you mean. You can't help us 'cause we be cursed by God."

"No, please. That's not what I said. I'd never—"

The right twin sighed. "It will be all right, miss. Don't be your fault. 'Twas probably too much to hope for. But sometimes that be all you can do. Hope."

"Not even Meg and Peg?" Martha Kincaid asked. "I'd have thought that was a simple thing."

"No," Jennet said. "It isn't. It's very complicated. I can't help any of the people you sent to see me, least of all Meg and Peg."

"Pity. The women from the tanneries, they said you was kind. That you wanted to help."

"I do want to help." Dear heaven, only a heart of stone would not have responded to the way those poor souls looked at her with so much hope. "I'd give anything to help. But all your friends are beyond my skills. I don't think anyone can help them."

"Then tell me something," Martha Kincaid asked wearily, knowing quite well the girl would have no answer, "what were they made for? This just and merciful God the preachers are always goin' on about, how come He allows things like this? Does He enjoy watching people suffer?"

Chapter Seven

CHRISTOPHER HAD STOPPED looking at Amba. Twenty years since that night, and not once in all that time had he actually looked into her face. He preferred not to do so now, but she'd come into the room and closed the door and planted herself in front of it. Now she was simply standing there, waiting for him to acknowledge her.

"Yes, Amba, what is it?" he said without lifting his head, continuing to work on his article, a treatise on bleeding in cases of gout. "I didn't send for you."

"Amba knows Master didn't send for her. Amba come to talk with Master."

"I'm rather busy just now. You must discuss whatever it is with your mistress." He dipped his quill in the inkpot and scratched a few words more on the paper. Amba did not move. The piece was for the *Boston Weekly News-Letter,* the first they'd ever asked him for. He could not afford to make a hash of it. "Go, Amba. I have no time for you."

It was a bitter night and there was a coal fire in the grate; thanks to the many ships that loaded Newcastle coal for ballast, it had become cheaper to burn than wood, even in this place where there was endless forest. Amba walked across to the fireplace and positioned herself in front of the glowing coals. "This be something as matters, master. Got to talk to you, not Mistress Jane. You got to hear me."

He raised his head. That's where she'd lain after he bid her take off her clothes. Her naked black body had been stretched out on the hearth rug in front of the fire. And he had almost . . . Sweet Christ, it was impossible not to remember the way she'd looked back then. But he remembered, as well, the revulsion he'd felt at the mutilation that had been practiced on her. And how proud she'd been of it, as if such barbaric butchery were something to glory in.

Her hair was still close-cropped. In return for the favor he'd never claimed, he would not allow Jane to forbid her cutting off her hair. She continued to do so, but she was no longer beautiful. Twenty years on, Amba looked like what she was, an old, work-worn slave. "Look," he said, "if it's about Phoebe, she's hired out to Mistress Tamsyn. Anything you want to ask about her, you have to—"

"Ain't nothin' 'bout my girl. Amba got to talk to you 'bout yours."

"Jennet? Whatever have you to do with her?"

"I got plenty to do with that girl. Been lookin' after her since she was born."

Extraordinary that she'd speak to him in that tone of voice and look at him that way. "You still think you're a queen, don't you?" he said, more in surprise than in anger.

Her gaze never left his face. "Master know Amba's a queen. Master saw."

"So I did." He returned his quill to its holder and covered the bottle of ink. Finally he turned back to her. "Very well, Amba. Say what you've come to say. I'm listening."

"You not let Miss Jennet be marrying Master Caleb. Evil gonna come if that happens."

"I see. And are you going to tell me how you've reached this remarkable conclusion?"

"They is clan. It's forbidden. In Amba's place. In this place. Everywhere. All peoples know it's forbidden. Bad magic. Make bad things happen."

"Perhaps." He turned back to his work, reached again for his quill. "But in this case Miss Jennet and Caleb Devrey are officially second cousins, which is a sufficient degree of separation to satisfy both the church and the law. And they are not blood kin at all. My father was—"

Sweet Christ, why was he wasting his time explaining things to a slave? Christopher paused, looked over his shoulder. Amba remained standing in front of the fire. "I can't imagine that you understand one word of what I'm saying, Amba. And I don't in the least care. Go back to the kitchen. I'm sure there is work for you to do."

"Amba understand. But Amba knows things."

He sighed. "I see. Well, I'm sure you do know things, Amba. I'm sure you are very wise in the ways of your people and your country, but you can trust me to know how things work here. Now go and—"

"Amba knows things about Master Nicholas."

Christopher had taken up his pen and was holding it above the paper, preparing to begin the discussion of why the lancet was preferable to leeches in cases of gout. "Master Nicholas," he said without moving. "Am I to take it you mean my father?"

"Yes. Master Nicholas weren't born to that lady in the picture near the front door. The one with the white hair. He was brung here. And left outside the door. Old Hetje, before she die, she tell Amba the truth."

His fingers had started to tremble. Slaves talked, and they were privy to most of the family secrets of their owners. Considering how they lived, in the heart of the household, how could it be otherwise? But Amba had not been in New York when the child who became Nicholas Turner was born. Hell, she hadn't yet been born. Hetje, on the other hand . . . He'd seen her only a few times, but Christopher never forgot the way the old black woman had looked at him. "Exactly what did Hetje tell you?"

"She said it was a secret. She said she was giving me the secret because—"

She broke off, hesitated. That was unusual. Amba never seemed to be afraid to say anything. That was one of the things Jane so disliked about her. "Go on, Amba. Hetje gave you the secret because . . . ?"

"Because she said once you was a slave that's all you got to protect you with. Old Hetje, she tell me having secrets be what makes a slave strong."

"Stronger than your masters, you mean. Yes, I can see how it might." Christopher wasn't trembling anymore. He was suddenly very calm, entirely self-possessed. He got up from his chair, leaned against his desk, folded his arms and finally looked straight at this woman whom he had once so fiercely and so briefly desired. "Very well, tell me what Hetje told you about my father."

She still hesitated.

"Come, Amba. You no longer have a choice. You admitted to having a secret that concerns me and my family. If you don't tell me of your own free will, I'll have it whipped out of you."

"Amba knows that," she said softly. "And it don't matter how much you whip Amba, how many lashes, fifty, a hundred. If I don't want to talk, I won't."

Tied to a stake, watching her husband slowly burn to death while she was pregnant with his child, singing all the while. "Yes, I know that as well. So we both know things. But you're the one who came in here to tell me what you know."

"Ain't telling for you. Not for me, neither. Telling 'cause of Miss Jennet. 'Cause she be like my own baby girl."

"I realize that."

He waited. They looked at each other. Eventually she spoke. "Master Nicholas, he be Mistress Sally's boy. Master Lucas, he thought he was adopting a baby from another clan, but it don't be true. Baby Nicholas, he be the son of Master Lucas's sister."

His first sensation was elation. He was related by blood to the man he idolized, not to the miserable drunk, Ankel Jannssen. He was well and truly a Turner. Lucas was his . . . his great-uncle.

Then he rejected the whole notion. She was an illiterate heathen, for God's sake, a black savage. How could she possibly be relied on in a matter like this? "Thank you for telling me, Amba, but I don't believe a word of it. I'm sure old Hetje made up the entire story."

Amba shook her head. "Old Hetje, she don't be making up nothin'. She be the one put that there baby on the doorstep. Mistress Sally birthed him, but he don't be her husband's baby. One of them Indians, he be planting his seed in her. That be why she got to get rid of her baby. 'Cause otherwise her husband be killing it. Mistress Sally, she always be thinking Hetje took her baby to the slave compound, but Master Nicholas, he don't be having dark skin like they 'spect. So old Hetje, she be leaving that baby right outside the door to this place. And the man and the lady in the pictures, they make him they's son, tell everyone the lady be birthing him. Before she died, Hetje, she tell me all how it was. Said it be my secret now. Said it be making me strong. But I can't keep no secret what's gonna let Miss Jennet bring no evil spirits on her. Not my baby Miss Jennet."

"I don't believe it, Papa. I cannot believe it."

Christopher sighed. "My dear Jennet, I felt exactly the same when I first heard the tale. Then, when I spoke to Tamsyn . . ." He shrugged. "We put together what she knew, the things Red Bess had told her over the years, with what Amba reported Hetje saying, and it all fell into place."

Christopher glanced over at young Caleb, standing stiffly beside the fireplace, his face as rigid as his body, betraying nothing. "I realize this is a terrible shock to both of you. Particularly coming five days before the wedding. A great shock and a great grief. But you must think how much worse it could be. Your father, Caleb, is my uncle, not my cousin. You and I are first cousins, and you and Jennet are first cousins once removed. It is both unlawful and immoral for you to marry. Your children would be—"

"She hates you, Papa!" Jennet had been sitting beside his desk; now she jumped up and flung the words at him. "Tamsyn hates you. She'd say anything to make you unhappy. Everyone knows she blames you for—"

"For killing her mother. I know. But Tamsyn bears you no ill will, nor Caleb. Besides, she was glad to have the mystery solved. She admitted as much. Even to me. We were close once. It has helped us to understand some of what happened earlier on."

"Helped whom, Papa? You? Tamsyn? What about me? What about Caleb? Are we to sacrifice our future because of your past? We won't! We'll run away and marry. You'll never see either of us again." Jennet ran to her beloved, put her hands on his chest, and looked up at him. "Tell him, Caleb. Tell him we will be married whatever he and your father—"

"A savage." Caleb took a step backward, removing himself from her touch. His voice was barely a whisper. "You're part red savage, Jennet. That's why your hair is so black and so straight. I never thought. It never occurred to me. A filthy red savage . . ."

II

"Marry me instead," DaSilva said.

"You?"

"And why not?"

"I don't know. I just never . . ." Her eyes were red with weeping. And for once she did not seem entirely sure of herself. "I thought . . . I mean, I just assumed . . ."

"What?"

"That you were married." Jennet turned and looked at the redbrick mansion. It was the first week of January and the fruit trees were bare of leaves. The sun shone on the freshly painted white pillars beside the door, and the gleaming white roof balustrade that enclosed four tall chimneys. "It never occurred to me that you would live in a place like that alone."

"Then you were wrong, for that is exactly how I live there. Except for my servants. Marry me, Jennet. And be mistress of one of the finest mansions in New York."

She shook her head and pressed her pocket cloth to her eyes once more. The thing was tiny and sodden with tears. Solomon produced a large white linen square. "Here, use this. And forget what I said about being the mistress of a great mansion. I should have known that would hold no appeal for you. Think instead of how much you could do for the poor if you were my wife."

She stopped crying for a moment, considered, then shook her head again. "It's no use thinking about it. My father would never agree to my marrying a—" She broke off and her cheeks reddened slightly.

"Don't be embarrassed. I assure you it does not offend me to be called a Jew. And since you are, let's see, an eighth part red savage, perhaps we deserve each other."

"Papa will not see it that way."

Solomon reached over and took her hand. He had never done that before. What touches there had been between them were accidental. His flesh had burned after each one. But this time he did not allow himself to feel anything. Not yet.

"Look at me, Jennet. Good. Now listen very carefully. I am entirely serious. I want to marry you. I will give you a life far more interesting and exciting than anything you have dreamed for yourself, and I know you have more dreams than most young women your age. Moreover, if you agree—notice I say you, not your father—then his opinion is of no importance. There are other ways to marry in this colony, and they have nothing to do with the crying of banns or the approval of ministers. As for the required approval of parents, that can be avoided if one knows from whom to request the favor."

She did not reply immediately. DaSilva said nothing more. A minute passed. Two.

"The things I do at the tanneries . . . Solomon, you said I could help the poor. More than I do now. Would that truly be the case?"

"Truly," he said with a solemn nod.

More seconds passed. Then she nodded in her turn.

DaSilva had been holding his breath. He let it out. "Does that mean yes? Say it. I want to hear you say it."

"Yes." Her head was bent and the single word was almost too soft to be heard.

"You're sure? You must be sure, Jennet, for I give you my word, once you are mine I will never let you go."

If she saved a bit of money from the household account it might be possible to buy a lancet and a scalpel of her own. She could send some boy to make the purchase. He could say the instruments were for Christopher Turner. She'd never tell Solomon, of course. He would talk to her about society being intolerant and—

"Jennet, I asked whether you were sure. I'm waiting for an answer."

She raised her head, turned to him. The blue eyes looked directly into his. "I am sure, Solomon."

"Very well." Utterly calm, with nothing of his excitement showing in his voice. The last thing he wanted was to frighten her off, not now when victory was so close. He opened the carriage door on the road side and stuck his head out. "Clemence, come down. I need you."

The black driver immediately jumped off his high seat, stood at almost military attention, and waited for instructions. "Thank you, Clemence. I must go inside for a moment. I want you to stand right there where you are, beside the carriage. I wish to be sure Miss Jennet is safe."

"I won't move, Master." DaSilva had bought Clemence years before in Brazil. The black man knew exactly what he was being asked to do. He was a big man, and strong. There was no chance that this little slip of a girl would get away while he was guarding her.

DaSilva went into the house. Five minutes passed. He returned carrying two envelopes, waving them in the air so the ink would dry. "Ah, I am relieved that you are both still here. Well done, Clemence. Back to your perch. Quickly. And drive us first to Hall Place."

DaSilva needn't have worried about Jennet running away. She hadn't moved since he left her. She told herself that she was dreaming, that any moment she would wake and discover she had not truly agreed to marry Solomon DaSilva. How could she? He was an old man. Besides, she'd always known she must marry someone who adored her, someone who could be persuaded to see things her way. Solomon was the most extraordinary man she'd ever met, but never for a moment had she considered him someone she could make do her will. And she had certainly not thought of him as a possible husband.

"Hall Place," she said, as if the familiar words had jerked her back into reality. "But I told you, my father will never—"

"Hush, my dear. You have given your consent"—speaking while he climbed up into the carriage beside her, closing the door as Clemence clucked the white horses into action—"I will now take care of everything. You need think no more about it."

Clemence delivered the first note to the house beside the barbering pole. Jennet saw Amba take the envelope, and saw her look for a moment at the grand carriage waiting in Hall Place, but if she saw Jennet inside it she gave no sign. The door closed. Clemence returned. They drove on.

Ten minutes more of slow going through the narrow and winding streets of the town, threading their way among the carts and carriages and foot traffic of bustling New York at midday. In less than four months the pox had taken nearly ten percent of the population, six hundred and ninety whites and seventy-two blacks, but the crush seemed no less for that purging. Nor did the people show signs of the grief and terror they'd been through; New Yorkers were nothing if not resilient. Practically every street had a market, and each one was full of customers anxious to buy what they'd come for at the best possible price and hurry home to their dinners.

Solomon reached for her hand. Jennet jumped and stiffened, but she did not pull away.

"Tell me what you are thinking," he said.

She shook her head. "Nothing of any importance." They were out of the thick of the crowd now, almost at the edge of the town, a ways north of Trinity Church, at the corner of John Street and the Broad Way. The horses were making better time, their hooves clip-clopping merrily over the cobbles, as if they were pleased to move with greater ease. "Where are we going, Solomon?"

"To the home of a gentleman I know who is in a position to help us."

"And what is this gentleman going to do for us? And how can you be sure he'll do it?"

"He is going to marry us. It will be entirely legal, even without your father's permission. And yes, I am quite sure he will do as I ask. I can always count on my friends, my dear."

They had drawn up beside a large house, made of wood, not brick, with a wide porch running along the entire front. Clemence secured the reins and jumped from the driver's seat. Solomon opened the carriage window and handed him the second envelope; Clemence carried it to the door. "Now we wait," Solomon said. "But not for long." He smiled at her and touched her cheek with one finger. "In a few minutes, my dearest Jennet, you will be legally mine. And soon after that, truly mine."

She had no idea what he meant by the second part of that assertion. He could tell as much simply by looking at her. But as to the binding nature of a legal marriage, Jennet was an intelligent young woman; he was quite sure she understood that.

I don't have to say another word, Solomon told himself. I didn't force myself on her. I asked and she said yes. *Merda!* Then why is she looking at me like a cornered rabbit with no idea how to get away? "Jennet." He didn't know he was going to say it until the words came out of his mouth. "Listen, my dear, there is still time for you to change your mind if you want to."

She could change her mind. He'd just said so. Yes, she would. I don't want to be Solomon's wife. He's an old man. Well, almost an old man. But Amba has surely already taken the note in to Papa.

She hadn't asked Solomon what the note said, but she could guess: "I'm marrying your daughter," or words to that effect. So if she went home now they would think someone else had rejected her. And who would want her once it was known she was an eighth part red savage? Besides, Solomon was a rich man. If she married him, and if she managed her household allowance very carefully, she could ease the lives of the people in the tanneries.

Eventually she'd save enough to buy a lancet and a scalpel and a probe.

Jennet's hands began to tremble the way they never did when she was actually holding the instruments. She clasped them together in her lap.

As for the getting and the bearing of children . . . She'd not read all those medical texts for nothing. Besides, crammed together the way they were in Hall Place, she had sometimes heard muffled sounds and stirrings from the corner room where her parents slept. She had a pretty good idea how babies came to be. Well, she would simply close her eyes and endure it as her mother did, as all women learned to do.

She stared at her hands, still folded in her lap. Finally she raised her head. "I have thought about it, Solomon."

"Very carefully?"

"Yes, I assure you. With utmost care."

"And?"

"And I do not wish to change my mind."

"Being a true and valid justice of the peace, and in full and licit possession of the power invested in me by the lawful representatives of our noble sovereign, His Most Gracious Majesty George II, I hearby pronounce ye man and wife."

Jennet was not sure the man was telling the truth. At least not about what he was doing being lawful and licit.

Minutes after the carriage stopped in front of his house and Clemence delivered Solomon's note, the justice of the peace had come running out to the street to lead them inside. He had obviously left his dinner to perform the ceremony; he still had a napkin tied around his neck. His fat little wife was standing right inside the door, close enough to be a witness but plainly bored by the whole proceeding, and thinking, no doubt, that her meal was going cold in the kitchen. There had been no grand words about God joining and man not daring to put asunder. Only a lot of legal talk, and references to the king in England. As if His Majesty had the least bit of interest in what Jennet Turner did here in the colony of New York.

"My very best wishes, Mistress DaSilva," the justice of the peace said. He was speaking to her.

Jennet dropped a quick and automatic curtsy. Solomon took her arm and led her to the front door, then left her there for a moment while he had another word with the man and his wife before they climbed back in the carriage.

That was it, then. She was married. To Solomon of all people. It was simply too astonishing to be true.

"Take us home, Clemence."

"I can't go home, Solomon, I can't think what my father and mother will—"

He chuckled. "Hall Place is no longer your home, my dear. You live on Nassau Street now."

When they arrived at the front gate Clemence reined in the horses, got down, and started to open the carriage door. Solomon waved him away. "Leave us. I will call you when you're wanted." He drew the curtain on the window on his side of the carriage, then reached across Jennet and closed the one on her side. "Now," he said softly, "I am going to show you what you are, my dear, in your deepest soul. Here in my carriage, where I first came to realize it."

Caleb had kissed her a few times after they had agreed to be engaged. But those were very chaste kisses, a bare meeting of the lips. Solomon began the same way.

He took her face in his hands and put his mouth on hers. But then he forced her mouth open and put his tongue inside it.

She hated it. He tasted of tobacco and alcohol. But she did what she had promised herself she would do. She closed her eyes and endured. It could not be that he meant to do the whole thing here in the carriage. She wasn't entirely sure what was involved—the medical books were not very explicit—but she was fairly sure it required some disrobing, so they would have to go inside. This starting-out bit in his carriage was bound to be over soon.

She felt his hand on her bosom. Jennet gasped, and that drew his tongue deeper into her mouth. He was unlacing her bodice. Her corset, however, laced from behind. He could not reach the ties, but her breasts pushed up over the top of the restraint, and once Solomon had the front of her dress open he stopped kissing her mouth and lowered his head and began kissing the soft flesh of her breasts, drawing his tongue over the crease between them.

Jennet kept her eyes closed, but she wasn't enduring this part. It was quite nice. She felt her nipples swell the way they sometimes did when she had a bath and rubbed soap all over herself. All over. Even the parts that Solomon was now . . . Oh. Oh, dear God. No one had ever touched her there. She had never touched herself there. Not the way he was touching her.

Solomon's hand was under her skirt and between her legs and he was doing things she did not understand, making her feel things she had only felt half asleep in the morning, in the bed she shared with her three sisters, when she was still dreaming. Sometimes she would shiver and feel that burning and that insistent pulse between her thighs. But she always woke up and it ended. This did not end.

She groaned and slid down a bit on the seat. Solomon cradled her in one arm, the other remained busy beneath her skirt. "This is what you are, Jennet," he whispered. "You are a woman with feelings. A real woman. I've always known that about you. Now I know why. It's the savage in you. I wish you could see yourself as I'm seeing you. With your lips parted like that, moaning and gasping. And your breast heaving. And how is it if I do this?"

He had found another place to stroke, even more sensitive. Too sensitive. She could not bear it. "Stop," she moaned. "You must stop, please . . ."

"I won't stop. You belong to me. I can do what I want with you, so you must bear it. I can touch you right here, keep rubbing you right here, until . . . Ah, yes. That is what I want you to do. Let me feel all of you tremble. Yes! Exactly like that!"

A throbbing and pulsing that would not end, a great implosion of feeling. She was shaking and sobbing and crying out little cries. And afterward, when it was over, she thought she must die of shame.

Solomon said nothing to make her feel better about what had happened. Only, "Lace your bodice and put your cap back on. We must go inside now."

While he wiped his fingers with the same pocket cloth he had a short time before given her to dry her tears.

She saw it all as if through a haze: the polished wood floors covered with tightly woven canvas cloths painted in vibrant reds and blues, the chandeliers made of hammered silver and fitted with candles beyond counting, the gilded chairs with their silken cushions tied on with golden braid. It was a palace, but she felt like a scullery maid, not a queen.

"You can see the rest later," Solomon said when he had walked her through some of the downstairs. "Flossie will take you to your room."

The woman was white, and she spoke with a strong Irish accent. Another time Jennet might have been curious about who she was and how she came to be a servant in this house in New York. Now she could summon no coherent thoughts to make into words.

"Sure and it's everything you have to be taking off, child," the woman said as soon as she'd brought Jennet to the largest bedchamber she'd ever seen. "Here now, I'll help you."

"Why? It's not night. Why must I take off my clothes?"

Flossie laughed. "Just you be doing what I say. And more important, doing what himself says. It's soon enough you'll be finding out the rest of it."

She had already learned more than she wished to know. If she had ever doubted the truth of the story about her grandfather Nicholas, what had just happened in Solomon's carriage convinced her. And it must have convinced Solomon as well. Perhaps he hadn't before believed the story. Perhaps that's why he wanted to marry her. What would he do now, when he knew it was true?

"A gorgeous thing you are," Flossie said, stepping back to admire her naked form. "No wonder he's quite mad with the thought of you. And clever you must be, lass. There's many as wanted to marry Solomon DaSilva, for all he's a Hebrew and an ugly one to boot. But it's bed them not wed them has always been Solomon's way. Until now—and I can hardly credit it—here I am readying his bride."

While she spoke Flossie busily patted scented powder all over Jennet's naked body, with a large, soft cotton puff, buffing the powder into her skin. "So someday, when you've your wits about you and have stopped looking like a scared little rabbit about to be set upon by the hounds, perhaps you'll tell me how you went about the doing of it. Sure, and don't I know you will. It's great friends we'll be, lass. I can feel it in me bones."

Jennet barely heard this stream of chatter. She was too dazed to be embarrassed by the woman's attentions, or to ask what she was being prepared for. He'd already done it, hadn't he? Whatever it was that men did to women once they wedded them, Solomon had done it to her. Out in the carriage. On the street.

And she had carried on like a strumpet. Not in the shy and retiring way her father's medical books spoke of when they discussed women and their reactions to what they called "the marital act." Solomon had no need to be reminded of what the books described as "the differences between a modest, God-fearing gentlewoman, and those of cruder nature whom the groom may have known before he wed." She was one of the crude ones, with the sensibilities of a strumpet. That's what Solomon had meant when he said he was going to show her what she was.

"All right, lass, hop in." Flossie had turned back the covers of the high fourposter bed. "Come on now. It's impatient himself is. Don't keep him waiting, lass, not even on your wedding day. There's little to be gained by raising the temper of Solomon DaSilva. As I expect you'll learn soon enough."

Jennet stumbled toward the bed, too confused and frightened to argue. "I don't understand," she whispered. "I'm not sleepy. And we've had no dinner. Perhaps I should go downstairs and see about getting Solomon some din—"

Flossie hooted with laughter. "It's not food he wants at the moment, lass. In you go to the marriage bed, naked as the day you were born, with the covers drawn up to your chin. I'm off then. And you stay right here. I doubt it's long you'll be having to wait."

Flossie had left the curtains open. Solomon drew them. "I think we will leave daylight for a later pleasure, my dear. When you've a bit more experience." Bright sun crept around the edges of the curtain and created a shadowy dimness rather than the blackness of night.

DaSilva was not proud of his body. He was thirty-nine years old, more than twice as old as she, and short and thickset and covered with black hair, like an ape, he often thought. Certainly nothing like that tall slim young redhead she'd expected to marry. At least he had no cause to be ashamed of what he brought to deflower her with. His erection was enormous, and when he turned back the covers and saw what was waiting for him, it grew still bigger.

"You are very beautiful," he said softly. "Do you know that, Jennet?"

She shook her head. She was staring at his face, as if afraid to look elsewhere. He leaned over her and took her chin in his hand. "Well, it is true. You are exquisite. Now, do you know what I'm going to do to you?"

She felt she had to say something. The only thing she could think of was the punishment he'd mentioned when he accused her of being headstrong and willful. "Spank me?"

He chuckled. "No. Perhaps sometime in the future, when you are ready to be introduced to more sophisticated pleasures, but not now. Now I am going to please only myself. I am about to possess you, Jennet. And after that you will be completely and utterly mine. More so than any words spoken by a justice of the peace can make you. So much mine that your father will not dare to raise any objection to the manner in which I carried you off."

"But . . . outside," she whispered, "what you did in the carriage. I thought . . ."

"You thought that was what transpires between men and women? Oh, no, my dear, most women never feel what you felt in my carriage. Their husbands are not skilled enough to produce such feelings, and they are not capable of them in any case. But you are not like most women. I promise you will feel that way again, though perhaps not this first time. Now, enough talk. I want you to keep looking at me. Keep your eyes open, exactly like that. And spread your legs."

He clambered onto the bed and knelt over her and lifted her hips with his two hands; with one sharp thrust he was inside her, but not all the way. She made a little grunt of pain, but she kept looking at him as he had told her to. And he kept looking at her. "Now," he said softly. Another thrust, this one harder and deeper, resisted for only the briefest of moments. Then her body yielded to him.

He withdrew almost entirely, then thrust again. Slowly, and with great concentration. Prolonging for as long as he could every sweet instant of the exquisite pleasure a woman, any woman, could give only once.

DaSilva saw the way Jennet's eyes widened in shock and pain. He gloried in it. And in the knowledge that he was the first, that she was truly and in every way virgin, and that he was going to mold her to his desires, shape her to his pleasure, and that someday when he thrust in and out like this she would scream with delight. But right now he was exultant when he saw the two tears that formed in the corners of her dark blue eyes and began to slide down her cheeks.

When she bit her lip to keep from crying out the thrill was something close to bliss, perhaps madness. He was past separating the two, and he couldn't hold back any longer. DaSilva pumped wildly and screamed aloud his triumph. She was his.

III

It was close to five by the time Christopher returned from Nassau Street. He staggered into the kitchen, still reeling with shock, and found Jane waiting for him, sitting at the kitchen table, dabbing at her reddened eyes. She looked up when he appeared. "Where is she? Have you brought Jennet home?"

"No. I couldn't. I was too late. He's already . . . I mean she is no longer—" He broke off, white-faced and shaking with anger, unable to speak the words to the thin, pale, distraught woman who faced him. She'd borne him ten children, six of whom yet lived, but talk like this was never easy between them.

"Now," she said, vaguely. "But it's not yet evening. I mean . . ."

"I know what you mean. It seems, however, that at least for Hebrews, it is not necessary to wait until dark."

Jane pressed the handkerchief to her eyes again. "My poor little girl, my poor dear child."

"She may be many things," Christopher said, fetching himself a mug of ale from the bucket in the corner of the kitchen, "but poor she is no longer. Not if she is truly the wife of Solomon DaSilva."

Which Jennet surely was.

"I have arranged with Flossie to take you to the gown-maker, my dear. May I suggest you listen very carefully to her advice."

Indeed, Flossie was remarkably knowledgeable for a servant. Jennet knew it, despite the fact that she had grown up with only one black slave and no indentures. Christopher could never afford to purchase one from the sea captains, who, in return for passage to the colonies, owned the immigrant's labor for a term of ten or more years and sold it to the highest bidder as soon as the ship docked. On the other hand, her Craddock and Devrey cousins all had indentures. And since she wasn't a black slave, that's what Flossie must be. But the Irish woman called herself Solomon's housekeeper, a phrase Jennet had never before heard. She went abroad in the city streets dressed like a fine lady, with skirts held so wide on wire panniers she had to sidle through most doors, the cuffs of her sleeves made of four or five flounces of lace, and her bodice laced with satin ribbons. She was addressed as Mistress O'Toole, and the shopkeepers smiled when she walked through the door. They fawned over her and, to Jennet's observant eye, nearly turned themselves inside out trying to please her.

And the money she spent was a scandal.

At the mantua-maker—the gown-maker, Solomon had called her—Jennet felt faint when she heard the cost of the frocks that had been ordered. "One hundred and ninety-six pounds and seven pence that comes to, Mistress O'Toole."

"Fine. Himself will be seeing to it by nightfall."

"No!" Jennet objected. "We cannot spend such an amount. It is wicked."

Flossie took her arm and pulled her to the door, making some laughing remark about her being a young bride who wished to spare her husband's purse. But she wasn't laughing when she got Jennet into the carriage and Clemence started on the journey to the milliner. "You listen to me, child, for it's not another time I'll be telling you this. It's never again you're to be making it sound as if Solomon DaSilva's wife need be concerned about the price of some bit of stuff in the shops."

"But it's sinful, Flossie. I could have half as many gowns and still be as well dressed as you are, and the rest of the money could be used to help the poor."

"For the first thing, you'll not be telling me about the poor, Jennet Turner DaSilva. Not when me it was who grew up sleeping in the Dublin streets and picking crusts out of gutters to keep flesh on my bones. And you it was lived in a snug house with a blackbird to wipe your bottom, and always something on the table to put in your belly."

"Yes, but—"

"Hold your tongue, lass. It's not done I am yet. For the second part of it, your husband is quite probably the cleverest man in New York, and the kindest, as I'll go to my grave saying. But for all that, he's a Jew, a Christ-killer, and while there's plenty as will raise a mug with him in a tavern, there's not a decent Christian gentleman in this town would have him inside his home with his wife and his wee ones in the same room. So it's grand you'll look, my girl, from morning to night and every hour in between. And never the same gown you'll wear when them as saw it before might chance to see it again. He's that proud of you, is Solomon, and I mean to see he has reason to stay that way."

The bill at the milliner's was also well over a hundred pounds. A family of ten could have eaten for four years on what Flossie spent for more corsets and shifts and caps and cloaks and hoods and muffs than it seemed to Jennet she could ever wear, but she had learned her lesson and she said nothing. Until that night, when she was finally alone with her husband.

The cold had deepened considerably in the six days they'd been married. Winter had truly taken hold. And for the first time she could remember, Jennet was perfectly warm inside no matter how cold the outdoors might be.

Solomon's mansion had been built to the most exacting specifications, unlike the old Dutch wooden house in which she'd been raised. There were no cracks for the piercing winds to enter, and every room had a fire blazing day and night. Though it was nearly bedtime, the grate in their bedroom was heaped high with a mix of logs and coals, not—as was customary—burning down preparatory to damping for the night.

Jennet sat beside the fire, wearing one of Solomon's silk dressing gowns since none of hers were yet come from the shops, and brushing her black hair. Her husband stood leaning on the mantel, sipping his brandy and looking at her. And smiling.

"Solomon, I was thinking . . . I do not mean to make you angry, but you said I could help the poor if I married you."

"Indeed. And so you can." She lowered her brush. He held up a forestalling hand. "No, don't stop what you're doing. I like to watch you."

Jennet went back to brushing her hair. "Today, at the mantua-maker, and at the milliner as well, Flossie insisted we must spend such a huge amount. I can't think how—"

"My dear Jennet, you must never worry about what you spend. It is entirely my affair. Besides, I told you, you may trust Flossie completely. She'll not allow you to be cheated."

"I've no reason to think the shopkeepers cheated us. But if I'm to do something for—"

"Ah yes, something for the vagrants and beggars up by the tanneries. I have not forgotten your concerns, my dear. Here, use this to help your supplicants." Solomon took a handful of coins from his pocket. He crossed the room and, one by one, began stacking gold sovereigns on her dressing table.

Jennet's mouth formed into a tiny circle of astonishment. Seven. Eight. Nine. Solomon paused, looked at her, smiled, and added a final coin to the pile.

Ten pounds. Quite possibly more, since gold coins had extra value. Certainly enough to feed everyone in the tanneries for months. And with more than enough left over to make the other purchases she had in mind.

Solomon came to where she sat, took the brush from her hands. "Well, have you nothing to say?"

She raised her glowing face to his. "I am trying to—"

He put his fingers over her lips and bent toward her. "On second thought, be quiet. I don't want you to say anything. I want to kiss you."

He lifted her up and carried her to the bed, untied the sash of the silk dressing gown and looked for a long moment at her naked body, then began to do those incredible things that he never seemed to tire of doing. In the six days she'd been his wife he had done them so frequently Jennet had already lost count.

She was no longer sore as she had been before, and not rubbed raw each time. Indeed, now, as soon as he touched her, even so much as patted her arm with his hand, something remarkable happened. Her heart began to beat more insistently. She fancied she could feel the blood moving through her veins. And each time that part of her—which until that afternoon in his carriage she had never considered it ladylike to think about—became the center of her being.

She was moist and hot between the legs; her flesh pulsed and prickled. And she wanted him to do exactly what he did. Everything he did. With his hands and his mouth. And his cock. A word she had never dared to even think until Solomon taught her to say it aloud. The way he did. All the time. "Look how my cock stands up to greet you. Come, Jennet, don't be bashful, look. It's different from your brothers', eh?"

"Maybe." It was a small, shy whisper, but she couldn't turn away. "I only ever saw Paul's when he was a tiny boy. My brother Luke is older than I."

"Yes, but I was different from the time I was eight days old." He took her hand and guided it toward the head of his shaft. "The foreskin is cut away. Circumcision. It marks me as a Jew. The great secret is that it also makes me more sensitive. Even to a touch as gentle as this." He drew her fingers lightly back and forth.

And she didn't pull away. She smiled.

All in less than a week.

He had definitely not been wrong about her.

The lump on the knee was the size of a large walnut. It might not have seemed so big on the leg of an adult. But on a three-year-old it looked enormous.

"How long has he had this?" Jennet did not look up as her fingers traversed the swelling. Lightly, the way her father did it, but with an economy of motion that was hers alone. The lump was hot to the touch, and tight-feeling, as if the skin were stretched to thinness. "Come, tell me when this began."

"Don't know. Only ever saw it this morning."

"This morning! But a boil like this . . . it didn't start growing today."

"Never said it did, only as I ain't seen it before."

Jennet bit her lip. There were, she had long since discovered, mothers of many sorts in the tanneries. Some were devoted, others were not, just as anywhere else in the city. What was different about the women in tanneries was that practically none had husbands. They were widows, or women who had been made pregnant by someone who refused to marry them or who was already married. If the women were to feed themselves and their children, they had to resort to petty theft and whoring on the city's streets.

"So what's going to happen?" the boy's mother demanded. "Ada Carruthers told me you'd say whether or not he was going to die."

That wasn't unusual. Jennet came to the shed at the far end of Dolly's Shipyard two or three days a week—thanks to a sympathetic watchman it was never locked against her—and Ada Carruthers was usually among those waiting for her. The woman had a brood of five and it seemed there was always something wrong with one of them. If it were not one of her children that was ailing, it was one of her neighbors, or their children.

"Ada said you'd tell me, mistress. Is my wee lad going to live or die?"

Jennet stopped fingering the little boy's knee. He'd fallen asleep in her arms, and his small, pinched face was hot and flushed. "He need not die from the boil," she said quietly, her hand on his forehead. "But he's burning with fever. Have you been giving him swamp water to drink?"

The woman turned away. "I give 'em all what I have. Ale when I can buy it, water when I can't."

"All. How many children have you?"

"Five. This one here, he's the baby."

"And that's why it's important to you that he lives? Because he's your baby?"

This time the woman stared straight into Jennet's eyes. "It's important 'cause if he's gonna die, I'd best start adding his share of the food to what I give the other four. Ain't no point in wasting it."

Jennet hugged the small body to her, as if she could protect him from his mother's pragmatic cruelty. "He will live if I treat the boil," she said again. "And if he gets proper care after that."

"I'll do what I can," the woman said sullenly. "Always have. What I can. How you going to treat that thing, then?"

Jennet reached for the linen drawstring bag that lay on the ground beside her. "We are going to treat it together. You are going to hold your son quite still, and I am going to open the boil."

She had in the end chanced the buying of the instruments on her own. No one she could send to the ironmonger's in her stead would make as good a job of selecting her tools, and she did not want to involve one more person in her secret. Better to choose a purveyor in a quiet part of town, up from Lions Slip on Golden Hill, and go there dressed as inconspicuously as possible, in her old gray cloak with the hood pulled forward so it shadowed her face.

"Barbering things them is," the shopkeeper had said while she examined the display in the wooden case at the rear. "If it's knives for cutting the vegetables you're wanting, I have some up there by the door."

"No, this is what I'm after." She'd pointed quickly to a pair of scalpels in different sizes, and a lancet, and a probe, and a needle for stitching wounds. "They're for my uncle."

"I take it he's a barber."

"That's right."

"Never heard of no one sending a girl to buy his barbering tools." But while he grumbled the man took the things she'd indicated from the case, and wrapped them in a bit of newspaper. "Four shillings that comes to."

Jennet fished the coins out of her pocket, put them on the counter, grabbed her bundle, and ran.

The first thing she'd done when she got the instruments home was to lock herself in the bedroom and put the things in the soft linen pouch she'd made to receive them. After that she hid the pouch in a bureau drawer, beneath the silk undergarments that Flossie had made her buy. In the morning, after Flossie had laced her into her corset and helped her dress, Jennet went down for breakfast, then sneaked back upstairs. She reclaimed the pouch and tied it around her waist under her petticoats with the long cotton ribbons she'd attached for the purpose.

There it stayed all day, every day, lying against her hip, protected by the wire panniers that held out her skirts. Waiting until the moment when she could take out the instruments and use them to do what she was convinced she'd been born to do.

"There you have her." Bede Devrey threw out his arm as if presenting a queen to her court. "Isn't she magnificent?"

Caleb stared at the ship sitting on the ways, waiting to be fully fitted, then launched. "I suppose it is magnificent, as that sort of thing goes."

"Not it, you dunce; a ship is never an it. She's a she, a beautiful woman. The *Nancy Mariah*."

It was the name of Bede's wife, Caleb's sister-in-law. "Pretty soon all the women in this family will have ships called after them. You'll have to make a few more daughters if you aren't to run out of names."

"Not if you bring us a new possibility. Caleb, look, I know you were disappointed over Cousin Jennet, but Papa wants me to tell you—"

"That it's time I married. I know. I presumed that's why you'd brought me up here to Dolly's to see your blasted ship. So you could talk to me like a proper older brother."

"Something like that," Bede admitted.

Caleb turned from the ways and faced the rear of the sprawling shipyard. It was three of the afternoon, the dinner hour, when all the workers had gone home. The place was pretty much deserted. It seemed he never saw Dolly's under any other conditions. As far as he was concerned, this was truly a ghost yard, though the three-masted merchantman Bede was so proud of cost upwards of five thousand pounds to build. "You want to tell me I should marry," he said quietly, more to himself than his brother. "That it is the right and the proper thing to do. But this may well be the worst place you could have chosen to raise the subject."

"In God's name, Caleb, why? I know you're not interested in the business, but that doesn't mean—"

"It's nothing to do with Devrey Shipping. It's that shed back there at the far end of the yard." Caleb pointed to the neglected structure near the outer fence. "I find it rather a bitter reminder. And if I told you what I suspected went on there, I doubt you'd believe it."

The scalpel fit her hand as if it had been made for it. When she was a tiny girl, the first time Mama had placed a sewing needle in her hands, Jennet had the same feeling. She simply knew what could be done with it.

All she'd needed to do was look at a piece of embroidered goods to see exactly how the stitches were made; nothing of the intricacies of needlework were a mystery to her. When she set herself to making something like whatever she looked at, she could do so with truly astounding exactitude.

Jane bragged about her daughter's needlework to all as would listen. The house on Hall Place was filled with cushions Jennet had picked out in petit point, with curtains she'd decorated with exquisite crewel stitches, and with table coverings bordered with her hand-made lace. No one, however, would praise her mastery of surgery, for all it was a far more important craft. Instead, if she were discovered she would probably be put in the stocks outside City Hall, or tied into the ducking chair and lowered into the well until she was just short of drowned. Maybe even locked in the dungeons.

Because she was a female, and that meant she could stitch as much as she liked on cloth, but never, never on human flesh.

Papa's medical books were full of illustrations of boils and careful descriptions of how to open them, but none were clearer than Lucas Turner's handwritten instructions. *If the Boil is raised entirely above the Skin and shows no sign of having a Core that has burrowed Deep into the secondary Dermal layer, even perhaps into the Underlying Bone, then the proper examination of it will reveal a Whitened spot at the apex of the Hummock. It is there that the small Triangular Scalpel must be inserted, always being of careful Mind to Allow for the inconvenience of the spouting Poisonous Effluent such Treatment may provoke, and an X cut made that will give Opportunity to entirely empty the Wound of Noxious Matter.*

She had seen the whitened spot as soon as she examined the boy. Now Jennet held a bit of rag above the place she meant to open, and positioned her knife to do its work. "You must hold him very still. I do not wish to pierce any but the external skin."

She seated the other woman on the stool, with her son in her lap, and knelt beside them. "Very well, let us begin. Remember, he will flinch but you must not."

She lowered her hand and made the first swift, deft cut.

The child wailed as if she were slitting his throat.

"I don't understand you, Caleb. You're quite likely the most sought-after bachelor in New York, yet you—"

"Be quiet."

"No, I shan't be quiet. You're acting a total idiot. There are women just as beautiful as—"

"Shut your mouth, will you! For a moment only."

Bede stopped arguing. His brother stood where he was, staring at the fenced perimeter of the shipyard as if he had spotted the Holy Grail among the stacks of sawn lumber and trampled sawdust and barrels of pitch.

There was, however, no repetition of the sound Caleb thought he'd heard.

"Mind telling me what you're looking for?" Bede asked after almost a minute had passed.

"I'm not looking, I'm listening. I thought I heard a scream."

"A scream! Good God, Caleb, you've been too long in the highlands listening to scare stories told round the peat fire."

"Edinburgh is not the highlands. And it's Ireland, not Scotland, where they burn peat."

"Be that as it may. There's no one screaming in Dolly's Shipyard in broad daylight. Come on, we may as well go back to town. I don't fancy my chances of getting you to listen to reason wherever we are."

"I am listening," Caleb said. "And I hear everything quite clearly."

"Good. Then perhaps you'll do something about it. There's nothing to be gained by holing up and licking your wounds, little brother. Take matters in hand and do something about them. That's a man's way of dealing with setbacks."

The pus did not spout, it oozed. Moreover, Jennet had to squeeze the boil to get it to release its suppurating fluid. And when she did so the walls of the thing did not come together as she expected them to. She was instead met with some kind of resistance in the heart of the abscess.

Lucas had written that boils sometimes had a core, and she had more than once heard her father expound on the subject to a student. He called it a funnel of tissue that encompassed the nub of the infection. Tissue, however, did not feel as this did: uneven to the touch, sharp and gritty. "There's something buried inside," she told the boy's mother. "Some foreign body."

"Foreign? I don't be doin' with foreigners, mistress. Not if I can help it. I'm after doin' the best I can by my young ones, like I said, and there's none as comes to my place out here, foreign or New Yorker though he may be. I meet 'em in the town and—"

"Ssh, calm yourself." She probed the wound as gently as she could. "I didn't mean that kind of foreigner. A cinder perhaps. Or a pebble."

"In his knee? How did he get a pebble in his knee? I had a hard time when I was carrying him, but I never 'et no pebbles."

"I know you didn't. He got it by scraping or cutting his flesh on some surface where such things were present. I can easily get it out." She reached down and retrieved the scalpel from the dirt floor of the shed. "Hold tight, little man, two or three more cuts and this will be over. Now, show me how strong you are. Bite on this."

With her free hand Jennet reached into her basket and got her gold bracelet.

Flossie had put it on her when she left Nassau Street, and she'd taken it off on her way to the shipyard. Now she shoved it into the little boy's mouth.

IV

By the summer of 1732 Jane Turner had decided it was no bad thing to have her eldest daughter married to a rich Jew. God knew life had been a little easier in the following six months.

For one thing Jennet was frequently able to slip her mother a few coins to ease the running of the household. For another, Jane's eldest, Luke—his given name was Lucas but he was only ever called by the shortened version—had been able to go off to Edinburgh to study medicine thanks to Solomon's generosity. For a third, that first August after Jennet's marriage the yellowing fever came. It was called so because the victims turned yellow after death. The few who survived were left imbecile, shaking and babbling in delirium. The yellowing fever was a dreadful plague.

Solomon insisted that Jennet's family must go to Greenwich to escape the disease. And Jennet must go with them.

"But what of you? I do not want you to stay here and catch the fever, Solomon. I should be miserable if anything happened to you."

"That's true, isn't it?" With one finger stroking her cheek, gazing into her astonishing eyes. "I believe you have come to love me a little, my dear."

"I love you a great deal, Solomon." She was no longer afraid to say it. "And I want you to come to Greenwich with us, so you—"

"Hush. I cannot leave the city now. My business will not permit it."

Jennet had no idea exactly what Solomon's business might be. He owned a great deal of land, including a fair-sized piece of a few of the city's many markets, but most of his holdings were north of the Common, in the far reaches around the Collect Pond.

Flossie said that land would be worth a fortune someday but it was a wilderness of brambles now, and no one had the least interest in buying or renting it. So where did this enormous wealth come from? "He buys and sells things, does the master," Flossie said when Jennet pressed her. "Goods and services alike. Buys 'em cheap and sells 'em dear."

"What sorts of things?"

"All sorts. And if you want to know more, it's himself you'll have to ask."

But bold as she was with him, as he was teaching her to be, Jennet was still not bold enough to ask her husband what it was he bought cheap and sold dear. "I don't care a fig about your business," she said instead. "Not if it exposes you to yellowing fever."

"I have already been exposed, in Brazil when I was a boy. So I am immune. Isn't that what you tell me about these things?"

"Yes. That seems to be how it is. No one knows quite why."

"Who cares why? I am immune, and you and your family are to go to the village of Greenwich and be safe."

Jennet had never been on a boat before. This one was painfully crowded. New Yorkers were as anxious to get away from the yellowing fever as they had been to escape the smallpox. "Where do they arrive from, Papa? How do these contagions come among us?"

"I don't know." Christopher and his daughter had found themselves a place on deck, immediately beside a bulkhead. They could see the waves lapping the boat's planked wooden sides and feel the cool breeze on their face while they watched the heavily forested hills of the west coast of Manhattan slip by. "Some say they're a result of the unhealthy air rising off the swamps, here on Manhattan Island, but I am not convinced. The rest of the colonies get these pestilences as well. There's another theory that says their arrival is spontaneous, that somehow it is in our human nature to produce these things every few years."

"Do you find that more convincing?"

"I used to think so. But we know it profits any as can to take themselves to the country when the city succumbs to these plagues, and if the illness were part of our being then leaving town would do us no good." Christopher opened his coat, reached into the largest pocket, and pulled out a small, bound volume. "A case in point. Young fellow in Philadelphia, Ben Franklin, sent me this. Seems he'd read some of my articles in the press."

"I thought you never signed them with your own name."

"I don't. He found me out nonetheless. Apparently he's an enterprising sort."

Jennet nodded toward the book. "Is Mr. Franklin the author?"

"Yes. And the printer as well. He means the book to be an annual thing if the public takes to it. An amusing title."

He held the book out to her and Jennet read the words aloud. "*Poor Richard's Almanack.* Does Mr. Franklin say something in his 'almanack' about the yellowing fever?"

"Only as part of general advice about health. He reminds us that fresh air and exercise may forestall illness, and prevention is better than the blistering and purging and bloodletting that comes after it arrives."

Jennet made a face. "That's all the physicians do, isn't it? They can fairly kill you while they're curing the disease. I told Luke he was quite mad to want to go to Edinburgh and become like them. I said he should stay here and learn surgery from you."

Christopher sighed. Not much good would come from talking to Luke. Certainly not by Jennet. The boy had always been a bit resentful of his younger sister's superior cleverness and his father's reduced circumstances. Of all Christopher's children it was Luke who most detested the penury in which they'd grown up. "The Edinburgh doctors say they are trained in the 'benign use of the knife.' At least that's what Zachary Craddock said."

"I hate Zachary Craddock. It's his fault that you—"

Christopher reached out and patted her hand. "Don't trouble yourself, Nettie."

Jennet smiled. He used to call her that when she was a little girl. Using her old pet name now meant he'd truly forgiven her for marrying without his permission. "I do trouble myself. It was a grave injustice, Papa."

He shrugged. "Injustice is the way of the world. Anyway, it's nothing to do with you. As for Luke . . . Your brother likes the things that money can buy. He was right to go to Edinburgh once your kind husband gave him the opportunity. No workaday surgeon will ever earn what the grand physicians do. And Luke is handsome and charming. He'll get on well with the society ladies who call him in to see to their vapors and suchlike." He chuckled softly. "I forget, you're one of them now yourself. My little Jennet, a society lady."

"But I'm not. My husband's a Jew, Papa. Society has no room for him."

"I've wondered if that bothered you."

She shook her head. "Why should it? I never wanted to be like those idle, empty-headed women. You know that."

Christopher did know. But he doubted that his daughter had any idea how her husband earned his lavish fortune, or exactly what besides his being a Hebrew caused him to be shunned. On the other hand, he couldn't be entirely sure she didn't know. Jennet was frequently a surprise even to him. "Listen, child, I've been wanting to ask you something. Once, shortly after you were married, I chanced on Caleb . . . It doesn't bother you to talk about him, does it?"

"Not a fig."

It was said with a clear-eyed glance that told him she really meant it. Extraordinary. A man twice her age, a Jew, and in half a year he'd made her forget her youthful passion for her handsome cousin. Ah well, he'd long known how little any man understood women. "Good. Then I can tell you what he said."

"Caleb?"

"Yes. At the sign of the Black Horse over on William Street. The place was crowded and noisy, of course, so I can't be sure of his exact words. And he'd had perhaps a dram too many. But I believe he made some mention of you with . . . I know this sounds ridiculous, even offensive, but Caleb was talking about seeing you . . ."

"Yes, Papa?"

Christopher swallowed hard. Sweet Christ. He wasn't sure he really wanted to discuss this, but he'd begun so he must finish. "He said he once saw you with a lancet in your hands."

The coastline was becoming less wooded. The rolling farmlands of the small village of Greenwich, its gentle hills, even the sparkling trout stream called Minetta Water, were coming into clear focus. The crew adjusted the sails and the boat creaked as she came about and began to tack toward shore. "We're going to dock, Papa. We must join Mama and the others."

He put out a restraining hand. "Your mother can wait a moment more. Jennet, I am troubled. Have you nothing to say?"

She was wearing the gold bracelet, the one she'd given the little boy to bite on when she operated on his knee. The soft metal still showed his tooth marks, but the boy had died a week after the surgery. The wound had festered. Jennet had gotten Phoebe to give her some curative powders from Tamsyn's apothecary shop, but nothing had helped. Perhaps, if she had been able to be her father's pupil openly rather than merely catch what she could of the lessons he gave others, she might have saved the child.

"And if Caleb were not lying, Papa? If I had used a lancet, even a scalpel, and I did so to help my fellow creatures, would that be so dreadful?"

"Dear God . . . You know I am not old-fashioned in such matters. I myself taught you to read. But this . . . It isn't natural, Jennet. It's an offense against every type of human decency."

"Why? I do not understand how it is that the fact that I am a woman means I cannot be a surgeon." Close enough now to see the waving leaves of Greenwich's lush tobacco plants. The spacious white mansion that had been the first house built in the area still dominated the village from its perch atop the highest hill. Rural, peaceful Greenwich was a pretty sight, but Jennet's vision was blurred by tears. She was trembling so badly she had to clutch the side of the boat to steady herself. "I have thought about it for years, Papa. Still I cannot understand."

Christopher looked at his daughter's white-knuckled hold on the boat's railing. The passion he'd unleashed shook him more than her virtual admission that she had practiced surgery. "It is . . . Jennet, I can find no words. Does your husband know of this . . . this aberration?"

She kept her face turned to the coastline that was rushing toward them. "We are about to dock. Mama will be worried if we do not join her."

"Jennet, listen to me. Whatever I think of your activities is no longer important. You are a married woman now, your husband's responsibility. But there are things you must understand. Yours is not an ordinary situation. Your husband is . . . a Jew. And there are other matters I cannot explain that could be used against him."

"Very well. If you cannot explain these other matters, there is nothing more to say. Let us find Mama and the others."

Christopher put a hand on her arm. "There is one thing more to say. Caleb Devrey is no longer your friend, Jennet, though you were as innocent in the matter as he."

"I am not troubled by what Caleb thinks. I don't care a fig about him."

"Yes, you are very busy today telling me all the things you don't care a fig about. Including the delicacy which is supposed to be born into all females, and which is apparently missing in you. I presume, however, that you care about your husband."

"Of course I care about Solomon. I would never do anything to harm him. How can you suggest such a thing?"

"I am trying to tell you, Jennet, that Caleb has become your enemy and, by implication, your husband's enemy. And if, as you have all but admitted, you have given him such a weapon to wield against you as the fact that you actually took a surgeon's tools into your hands and used them, then you must take care. For Solomon's sake, if not your own, you must take great care."

DaSilva urged his horse into the shallow but swiftly flowing water and leaned forward, speaking softly, gentling the creature across the rocky streambed and up the steep northern bank. He'd left Manhattan behind four hours earlier, paying the three-penny toll to cross the vicious double tide at Spuyten Duyvil Creek via old man Philipse's King's Bridge. Once across, he was in the sparsely settled county of West Chester. He'd soon turned off the well-traveled road that led to the small villages and neat farms of the area—all were tenants of the eighty-six-thousand-acre Van Cortlandt plantation—and ridden deep into the woods.

Usually he made the journey with Clemence. This time, with the yellowing fever raging and the nearly empty city at the mercy of looters, he had preferred to leave Clemence to look after Flossie and Tilda, the maid, and the Nassau Street house. Jennet, thank God, was in Greenwich, safely away from all the trouble, which freed him from having to say that business would keep him away from home for a few days. Not that she'd demand an explanation yet. But she would soon enough. Every day she became more a strong-willed woman than the child he'd married. DaSilva chuckled at the thought.

The woods were quiet, but the man DaSilva was meeting could hear the falling of a leaf a quarter-mile distant. He picked up the sound of the approaching horse and stepped into the path and waited to be seen. His greasy buckskins blended into the forest. DaSilva didn't see him until he'd almost run him down. "Whoa! *Santo Deus!* Hold back, girl! Whoa, I say!" DaSilva pulled back on the reins. The mare reared, spun half around, and finally yielded to the pressure on the bit. "*Merda!* You're a bloody fool, Patrick Shea."

The other man chuckled. "Sure and didn't my old mother tell me as much when I joined King George's bloody English army? C'mon, get down. We've to go the rest of the way on foot."

DaSilva swung out of the saddle. He wore his customary white satin breeches and black satin coat, but a rifle was slung beside his saddle. It, too, was black, with a highly polished golden oak stock, shiny brass trim, and a barrel nearly five feet long.

Shea had a knife and a native tomahawk at his waist, and a musket slung over his shoulder. The gun was an ordinary seventy-five-caliber smoothbore Brown Bess. He'd probably taken it with him when he decided to part company with His Majesty's 35th Regiment of Foot. He eyed DaSilva's weapon with something akin to lust. "C'mon," he repeated. "T'others be waitin'."

DaSilva loosed the rifle, put it over his shoulder, then looked around for a place to hide his mare. Numerous treaties had been signed, and most of the natives had long since moved farther north, but these woods were still prowled by Indians traveling alone or in small groups. A horse like this in plain view would be gone in an instant. Another man stepped out of the bushes. "This here's Laktu," Shea said. "He'll look after your horse."

DaSilva eyed the savage. He was naked except for the moccasins on his feet and the breechclout tied at his waist, which was barely large enough to cover his prick. The front of the Indian's scalp was shaved clean from ear to ear, and his right cheek was tattooed with a red crescent and three blue triangles. His earlobes had been split and hung almost to his chin, weighted with carved shells and silver ornaments. Mohawk. DaSilva breathed a little easier. So far so good. But he'd been dealing with Shea for two years, long enough to learn not to trust him.

Or the Mohawks, either. This one had a tomahawk and a wicked-looking knife tucked in his waistband, and a musket slung over one shoulder and a powder horn over the other. The *bastardo* was a walking armory. Nonetheless, his eyes, like Shea's, devoured the long rifle. DaSilva handed over the horse's reins. "Thank you, Laktu. I trust my mare will be no trouble."

The Mohawk didn't answer. Shea grunted something in his language. Laktu replied with a few words; then both men nodded. Shea plunged into the thick undergrowth beside the path. DaSilva followed.

They met the others in a large clearing by a stream, some ten minutes from the path. They were seven: the Irishman and himself and five Mohawks, all looking pretty much like the one called Laktu, all carrying muskets as well as knives and tomahawks. It seemed to DaSilva that he and Shea had walked a straight line to get here, easy to retrace, but he knew that was an illusion. Left to himself he'd never find his way back. Not to worry, when the meeting was over either he'd be escorted to the path and his horse would be returned, or his scalped carcass would be left here to rot in West Chester. The rifle was the key.

DaSilva lifted the gun. The noonday sun glinted off the shiny brass fittings and the fifty-two-inch black barrel. "Here you see it, gentleman. The means of defeating your enemies."

He waited, but Shea didn't translate. Instead he spoke to DaSilva. "C'mon, Jew, sure and you said all that. 'Tis past time for words. Show 'em."

"Very well. Tell them to select their finest marksman."

This time Shea spoke a few words to the Mohawk with a long feather behind his ear, clearly some kind of chief. The man listened, then uttered what was obviously a command. The brave who stepped forward looked about fifteen.

"Excellent," DaSilva said. "Now tell this fine young man to prepare to fire his Brown Bess."

Shea spoke to the boy, who took his musket from his shoulder, expertly fingered the lock into half-cock position, and poured a bit of powder into the mechanism. He poured more powder into the barrel, then a lead musket ball, and tamped the combination home with the iron ramrod, which was then shoved back into its holder on the gun's barrel.

DaSilva had been counting. Ten seconds and the boy had the musket in position and ready to fire. Remarkable. The redcoats were drilled until they could load, fire, and reload four times in a minute. In truth, excessive speed didn't help. If you tried to fire a musket six times a minute the barrel would burst from the heat and blow you straight to hell. More important, the Brown Bess suited the British way of fighting, not the way of the savages.

"Tell him he's to fire at that red kerchief tied to the tree over there."

The tree was a hundred yards away on the other side of the stream, the red bandana had come from DaSilva's pocket. Now it was tied to a high branch, easily seen from the clearing. "Go on," DaSilva said. "Tell him to shoot down the flag."

Shea spoke out of the corner of his mouth, without looking at DaSilva. "'Tis a frigging fool you'll be making of him. It can't be done."

"Not with the Brown Bess," DaSilva said quietly. "Now do it, Irishman, or we're both wasting a fine summer's day. And likely to wind up hairless for our trouble."

"But we're the ones was after selling 'em the muskets," Shea whispered. "Have you lost your—"

"I've lost nothing. But you may lose us both our scalps." The Mohawks might not understand English, but they were plainly aware that the two white men were arguing, and judging from their looks, they didn't like it. "Now," DaSilva bit out, feeling the sweat rolling down his back. "Tell the brave to shoot at the flag."

Shea hesitated a moment more, then translated the command. The boy looked from the pair of white men to his companions. The one with the feather behind his ear nodded. The small click of the flintlock coming into fully open position could be heard in the silence. Then there was the mighty thunderclap of the musket.

The acrid smoke hung in the still air for a long few seconds. When it cleared, the red flag could be seen exactly where it had been, hanging limp and unharmed.

The Mohawks were muttering among themselves. "What are they saying?" DaSilva asked as he prepared to load the long rifle.

"Sure and what do you bloody expect they're sayin'? That the target is too far away. And that you did it deliberately. To make 'em look bad."

"Too far for a tomahawk as well, is it not?"

Shea didn't have to ask. "Aye, a bloody sight too far."

"Very well, tell them"—he was tamping home the powder and the lead ball, using the elegant brass rod fitted to the barrel—"tell them I placed the target at such a distance to demonstrate the superiority of this weapon. Tell them when the Mohawks have rifles like these they will be the finest marksmen in America."

Shea translated the message. The Indians did not look convinced.

DaSilva's weapon was ready. He knelt, hoisted it to his shoulder, sighted the flag (the Brown Bess was so ill suited for aiming it wasn't fitted with a sight), and waited until Shea had finished speaking. Then he fired.

The great length of the barrel produced an even louder roar than the musket, and unlike the musket, the rifle had a perceptible recoil. But the braves didn't notice that DaSilva had been knocked flat on his ass. They were pointing above the haze of smoke to the empty place in the sky where the branch and the red flag had been.

"Bloody hell," the Irishman whispered. "Sure I've been after hearing about the God-rotting things, but 'tis never before I've seen one fired. Bloody hell."

"Precisely." DaSilva got to his feet, brushing dirt from his grass-stained white satin breeches and adjusting his black satin coat. "Very bloody. And straight to hell for all the enemies of the Mohawk. The rifle guarantees it. A hundred of them. Probably in three months' time. Go on, tell them."

"Tell me again how much," Shea said instead.

"Same price I quoted before. Seventeen pounds each. Gold or silver. No paper money. You pay me half now, half on delivery."

"Three months, you say?"

"If we're lucky. It could take as long as six."

"Why so God-rotting long?"

DaSilva sighed. They'd been over this before. Repeatedly. "Because, Mr. Shea, getting hold of these things is a difficult and a delicate business. The patterns for building long rifles are kept locked in the Tower of London, just like those for the Brown Bess. And there's a great many fewer of them around. We cannot steal what we need. So to get any quantities they must be assembled here in the colonies."

"And who is it be after doin' the bloody assembling?"

"Ah, Mr. Shea, I'm not likely to tell you that, am I? Now, why don't you make your arrangements with these fine redmen for however many beaver skins you can get them to promise on whatever delivery schedule suits your busy trading business, and let us both leave these infernal woods with our scalps intact." The August sun was directly overhead and the sweat was pouring off him. DaSilva mopped his brow.

The Irishman's mood changed and he chuckled. "Ah, Mr. DaSilva, 'tis a hard man you are. Might you not someday learn to leave your city finery at home when you come to God's own woods?"

"Someday it may be that I will," DaSilva agreed. "But right now our hosts are waiting."

Shea turned to the Mohawks and began negotiating.

DaSilva stood where he was, using the rifle for support, blessing the man who'd had the brilliant idea of grooving the long barrel so that unlike a musket it could be aimed with accuracy. The redcoats, with their long lines of foot soldiers shooting repeated volleys of musket fire over each other's heads, were invincible in a pitched battle but virtually useless here in the colonial woods. Give the savages weapons as accurate as these and they'd do what came naturally to them: hide in the trees and pick off the officers at will. A new day was surely about to dawn, with or without him. And since he had at great cost acquired copies of the London patterns, and located craftsmen in Connecticut and Rhode Island prepared to produce the weapons, he'd be a fool not to profit by the opportunity.

V

"I want you to wear these tonight." It was February in the new year of 1733. Solomon had given Jennet the double strand of matched pearls a few days earlier, for her eighteenth birthday. Now he put them around her neck and fastened the large diamond clasp at the side, where it showed. The stones were cut in the new manner, with fifty-six facets, not the much duller sixteen facets that had prevailed until a few years earlier. "There. You look exquisite."

Jennet wore a gown of deep blue satin. "The exact color of madame's eyes," the mantua-maker said when she draped the bolt of cloth over the girl's shoulders. That fitting had given only a hint of what the woman, a French Huguenot said to be the finest seamstress in the city, had in mind. Faced with a young woman of astonishing beauty married to a man with a bottomless purse, she had outdone herself.

The bodice of the dress fastened in the back in a clever new manner that made it impossible to see the ties that held it closed. The front was cut low, inset with a tapered gusset of lace that barely veiled the rise of her breasts and ended in a point at her tiny waist. When she stood the skirt swept out, suspended from the wide and stiff wire panniers attached to the satin corset she wore tightly laced beneath the frock.

"Exquisite," Solomon said again. "I am tempted to ravish you right here and now."

Jennet no longer blushed when he said such things. Instead she curtsied and managed to look both demure and just the slightest bit wanton. "I am your obedient servant, husband. You may do with me as you wish."

"Oh, I shall," he promised, "but later." He lifted a dark blue velvet shawl embroidered with silver threads and draped it over her shoulders. "Come, we cannot be late."

"And you still won't tell me where we are going?"

"Not yet. You must trust me."

"I do, Solomon." She spoke with more seriousness than their banter warranted. "Absolutely completely."

DaSilva put his hand under her chin and drew her face forward for a gentle kiss. "I know. That gives me enormous satisfaction, my dearest Jennet. In a little while you shall perhaps understand how much."

The carriage moved beyond the lantern-lit streets of the center of the town. It was not yet six in the evening, but the early winter dark was upon them. Clemence drove the matched white horses out of the heart of populated New York, west to the rolling, uninhabited meadows that spread from the Broad Way to the shoreline of Hudson's River. It had snowed a few days before, and the way was cleared only enough for two rigs to pass each other, a straight and shining path bathed in the light of a crescent moon and passing between pristine fields of white.

"It is so very beautiful." Jennet pressed her face to the window and clasped her hands tight inside her beaver muff. "I can't think who made the path, but I am very grateful to him."

"Then you are grateful to me. I made the path. At least, I caused it to be made."

"You?"

"Of course."

"And did you do it for me? Only so that we could take this magical drive?"

Solomon chuckled. "No, I can't say that I did. I did it, my dear, for the reason I do a great many things. For profit."

"I don't understand. What possible profit can there be in making a path through the snow to a place most people only go in summer?" Hudson's River had numerous fishing places along its banks, and in the warm months half a dozen taverns, known as mead houses, opened for business in the area. In winter, as far as Jennet knew, the place was a wasteland.

"Possess your soul in patience, my love. Everything is about to become clear."

Ten minutes later Clemence reined in the horses and Jennet looked out the window at five other carriages not unlike theirs—though none quite so grand— all waiting in a field a short distance away, on the far side of a three-story building made of white clapboard with black shutters. There was a roofed porch supported on white pillars along one side. Lanterns hung from the eaves, washing the entire exterior in a golden shimmer. The shutters were all open and the flickering candles of the interior beckoned with the promise of warmth and welcome. Jennet saw shadowy figures moving inside. "Solomon, what is this place?"

He tugged her hand from her muff so he could grasp it in his. "Jennet, a while back you said you trusted me. Did you truly mean it?"

"Yes. Truly, truly. You must believe me, Solomon."

"I do. Now we shall both see if we are capable of living up to our assertions." He was carrying the walking stick topped with the golden horse. He tapped lightly on the window, and Clemence, who had been standing outside waiting for exactly that signal, swung open the door.

Solomon jumped to the ground. Clemence positioned the small stool for Jennet, and the two men handed her down. Solomon extended his arm. Jennet took it. He did not, however, lead her up the front path to the jet-black front door, topped with an elegant fanlight. Instead he guided her along the side porch, through a narrow door at the back of the building—which he unlocked with his own key—and finally up a flight of stairs to another door, this one unlocked.

The little room appeared to have been prepared for them. There were two gilt chairs with red velvet cushions. A small table held a single candle, a decanter of brandy and another of wine, two goblets, and a plate of sweetmeats. The chairs faced a red velvet curtain.

"Solomon, I am simply bursting with curiosity. You must tell me—"

"Ssh." He put his finger over his lips, then leaned very close, so he was speaking directly into her ear. "If you love me and trust me, Jennet, you must be absolutely still, no matter what you see. Not a word. Do you promise? Don't say anything, just nod."

She nodded.

Solomon poured a brandy for himself and some wine for her; then he lifted the pewter snuffer and extinguished the candle. The room was now entirely dark, but Jennet sensed her husband lean forward and open the velvet curtain.

The room she looked into was lighted by a great many candles, and separated from her and from Solomon by a heavy iron grille, in front of which hung a gossamer curtain. The curtain obscured very little of the view. Jennet could clearly see the two women in the room, one black, the other white. They were both naked.

Jennet put her hand over her mouth to stifle her gasp, and felt Solomon's eyes on her. She had given him her word. She would not break it. Whatever happened, she was going to continue to believe in Solomon, in his love for her and in his protection. But for a few moments, while she gathered her courage for whatever was to come, she closed her eyes.

When she opened them, the two women were on the bed, and a man was with them. She could hardly see him because of the way the women hung over him. The Negro seemed to be sitting on his face; the other straddled his hips, and . . . Dear God, he was . . . They were . . . She could not believe what she was seeing.

She felt Solomon's arm circle her shoulders. "Wait." He breathed the word so softly she almost didn't hear, despite the fact that his mouth was pressed to her ear. "Trust me." Jennet's face burned. It was as if a mirror had been held up to her own shameless abandon in the bedroom. She turned her face to Solomon's chest.

He did not force her to see more, but continued to hold her, and to stroke the back of her neck with one finger. Meanwhile he watched the tableau vivant on the bed.

It was a rather mild entertainment. Some things transpired in this house that he would never have asked Jennet to watch, but this fellow only wanted to take two women to bed simultaneously. The color of their skin didn't play an enormous role in his pleasure, but he was known to be fond of the black wench with the huge breasts. It was Solomon who had instructed the woman who ran the brothel that the Negro was to be sent to this customer on this particular evening.

Like Flossie, who had served Solomon in the Rio house where he began his career as a whoremaster, the woman knew it was in her best interest never to question her employer's wishes.

The noises from the bed beyond the grille were becoming louder and more animated. The women were faking, of course. Solomon was an expert in such matters. He knew to the last shuddering moan what a woman sounded like when she was truly in the grip of passion. Jennet, for instance, when she made that little mewling sound deep in her throat . . . He'd have to speak to these two. They must do better.

The man let out a triumphant yell. Nothing faked about that. The pair of whores had finished him off. Solomon felt Jennet tremble and he held her tighter. Her face was still pressed to his chest. He could smell the sweet scent of the Hungary Water perfume he had ordered for her from Paris, rising from her warm and powdered flesh. The perfume, but also her own particular smell. The one that said Jennet. He lowered his head so his lips grazed her hair, artfully up-swept and pinned with a diamond aigrette. Later it would hang free, a straight black curtain, and he would lift her so she lay over him and run his fingers through her hair while her breast was in his mouth.

Both women had rolled off the man on the bed. The dark one went to a tall stand that held a basin and an ewer. She wet a cloth and carried it back to the customer and began to sponge him from head to toe. The man lay with his eyes closed, obviously sated for the moment, enjoying the attention. Finally, after the whore had dried him all over, he stood up.

Solomon bent forward and spoke directly into his young wife's ear. "Now you must look. Only for a moment. But immediately."

She had promised to trust him. Jennet raised her head and turned it toward the grille. Solomon anticipated the gasp rising in her throat; he put his hand over her mouth to stifle the sound.

Zachary Craddock was no longer lithe and muscular. He had a paunch, and his midriff was surrounded with rolls of sagging white flesh. His hair had thinned considerably as well. It was the first time Jennet had seen Cousin Tamsyn's husband naked, fondling absentmindedly the pendulous breasts of the black woman who stood next to him, while the white woman kneeled before him trying with her mouth to coax another erection from the flaccid tool that hung between his legs.

"Well? I think it is time that you said something, Jennet. Otherwise I shall conclude you are disappointed or shocked or both."

"I'm neither. I told you I wasn't."

"I'm not entirely sure I believe you."

"I never lie to you, Solomon."

They were in the carriage again, heading back to Nassau Street. Her head was turned toward the window. He reached across and stroked her cheek with the golden horse's head. "I am sure of it. But nevertheless, unless you tell me what you're thinking I shall be worried that you are disappointed in me."

She took a hand from her muff and reached up and clasped the walking stick. It made a stiff bridge between them. "If you must know, I'm thinking it wasn't because you wanted to acquaint me with the true source of your livelihood that you took me to that place. You had another purpose in mind, Solomon. I am trying to fathom what it was."

"Clever Jennet," he said softly. "But this time you're only partly correct. I had two reasons for taking you to the brothel. I own three others, by the way. What matters is that I did want you to know how I earn our daily bread. Because if you did not hear it from me, sooner or later you'd hear it from someone else. That seemed to me a far more unpleasant prospect."

"I understand."

"Yes, I expected you would. My second purpose should be equally apparent to you. It was Zachary Craddock who ruined your father's career and deprived him of a decent livelihood, was it not?"

"Yes."

"So I understood. What I wanted you to know, my dearest girl, is that Zachary Craddock is now entirely in your power. You may hold the hoop as high as you like, and he has no choice but to jump through it. Call it a second, slightly belated birthday present."

In their bedroom, with the moonlight streaming through the open curtains, with her jet-black hair spread across the pillow, Jennet looked markedly solemn. "Solomon, I have two questions."

He raised himself on his elbow and leaned over her. "Very well, ask them."

"Why do I not fall pregnant?"

He hesitated a moment. "May I ask why you question me about this now, tonight?"

"Because it is apparently a night for revelations. And I have been thinking about the question for some time."

"Very well. You do not conceive a child because I do not wish you to. I am not ready to see your belly grow heavy and your hips spread, or to share your breasts with a squalling infant. Someday, perhaps. But not yet."

"How then do you prevent it? With that silk envelope you put on yourself?"

"Yes. And by withdrawing from your delightful and delicious cunt at the appropriate, perfect moment." He nuzzled her neck while he said it, licking the back of her ear. He'd never been sure she was aware of the sheath, but it was fairly certain her lack of experience made her innocent of the fact that there were different ways to time the act. "Are you disappointed? Do you hunger for a babe?"

"No. I all but raised my younger sisters and brother. I am in no hurry to repeat the exercise."

He chuckled. "I'm glad we're in agreement. You said two questions. What was the second?"

"The black woman, the one sitting on Zachary's face, what was she doing to him?"

This time he hooted with laughter. "What a brazen wench I'm making of you!

And if you must know, she was doing nothing to him. He was doing it to her. Come"—he put his hands on her waist and lifted her up and on top of him—"sit on my face, as you called it, and I will show you."

VI

In the spring of 1734, as if they were under some terrible indictment from the Almighty, New Yorkers were visited with the third plague in less than twenty-four months. It would later be called diphtheria. To the medical men of the day, it was known as *angina suffocativa;* bladders in the throat, or the throat distemper, to everyone else. Whatever it was called, it was misery to all. Especially the children. And Caleb Devrey.

The epidemic took hold just a few months after Will Devrey lost patience with his second son. Since Caleb's return from Edinburgh two years before and his broken engagement to his cousin, the young man had done nothing but linger about his father's house. If he bestirred himself it was to go out and drink or wench. Having invested so much money in Caleb's education, Will was determined the boy would not be a wastrel.

"Caleb, I won't force a bride on you. But you must begin to make your way as a doctor."

"I intend to, Father. But it isn't easy to attract patients in New York. There are too many—"

"Too many other physicians trained and untrained," Will finished for him. "And all advertising in the *Gazette* or in Zenger's new paper. . . . What's it called?"

"The *Weekly Journal.*"

"Yes, that's the one. Any number of physicians advertising that they can cure this, that, and the other thing. You must lift yourself above the throng, Caleb."

"I'm sure you're right, Papa. But how do you propose I do so?"

"Simple. I have arranged for you to share a practice with Cadwallader Colden."

"What an extraordinary name!"

"I can't help what he's called. You've been away too long, or you'd have heard of him. A rising star in politics, is Cadwallader Colden. He's surveyor general of New York. That's a lot of power, lad, saying who can build what where."

"But I'm a doctor. I know nothing of—"

"Exactly. And so's he."

"Who?"

Will sighed. "Cadwallader Colden. He's an Edinburgh-trained physician, same as you. But he's got a wife and children to support, and he's clever, and the governor's given him an important post. So if he's to keep his hand in medicine as well, he needs a young assistant. I've suggested that he take you on, and he's agreed."

Caleb had no money of his own, no wife, and no prospects. There was never any question but that he must comply with his father's wishes. Neither father nor son imagined that a few months after taking up his association with Cadwallader Colden, Caleb would find himself in the middle of one of the worst and most invincible epidemics the city had known.

On a single May morning Caleb watched four children die.

Each small form went through the same torturous struggle to breathe. Each one turned blue moments before the end came. Each small body arched on the bed and tore at the bedclothes with grasping fingers as suffocation progressed. In two cases the intolerable pressure popped out the victim's eyeballs before death came. Finally, painfully, slowly, in unimaginable agony, each young life ended.

Cadwallader Colden's idea of being the senior partner of a medical practice was to allow the junior partner—Caleb—to do everything medical while Colden pursued his other affairs. Visits to the homes of the sick were turned over to Caleb. He was supposed to call on two other patients before the dinner hour of the day his four small patients expired. Instead he stumbled, sweating and nauseous, back to the small office his father had made available to the two men.

The office was a tiny room on the ground floor of the Devrey house on Wall Street, next door to the rooms that served Devrey Shipping. It contained little besides a pair of desks. There was a flask of rum put by for emergencies in one of them.

Caleb slammed the door behind him, grateful to have avoided meeting his father or his brother in the corridor, and stood with his eyes shut, leaning against the wall, trembling, waiting until he'd gathered enough strength to get to the rum.

"Good God, man, what's wrong? Are you ill?"

Caleb opened his eyes and forced himself to straighten up. "Dr. Colden. I did not expect to find you here, sir. No, I'm not ill. At least I don't think so." He put a hand to his throat and drew a deep testing breath. No, he was fine.

"It doesn't often attack adults," Colden said quietly. "At least, there are few such instances in the literature."

The man was always going on about "the literature." Fancied himself more of a scientific investigator than a physician. By his lights that meant he could avoid having to stand helplessly beside little children and watch them choke to death. "I'm not afraid of catching it." Caleb crossed to his desk and set his bag on it. "But looking on and being able to do nothing while this vicious disease slaughters whom it will, that's wearying."

"Yes, I suppose it must be."

"Then you suppose correctly."

Colden had been sitting, now he stood. It didn't make a lot of difference. He was a short man, round, with little bandy legs that looked too fragile to support his body, and too much nose for his face. His short, heavily powdered wig had seen better days. It was constantly flaking and leaving a trail of white across the shoulders of the black coat he wore unbuttoned over a black vest and a white linen cravat. "How many this morning, then?"

"Four. Two in the same house. The remaining sons of a woman who has already lost her eldest boy to the bladders."

"Dear God. I take it you blistered?"

"Of course." Caleb opened his bag and pulled out the cupping tool and dropped it on the desk. "I clamped this damned thing on enough times to raise a throat blister from ear to ear. Frankly, Dr. Colden, I do not see that it did me or my patient a damned bit of good."

"It must do. The literature is quite—"

"Yes, I know. The literature is quite specific. For a malign throat, a large blister covering the larynx. I assure you, I did not neglect to cup."

What did they teach you in Edinburgh more important than the evidence of your own eyes? Jennet's words.

"And did you bleed?" the older man asked.

"Yes, Dr. Colden. I bled each of my patients. Morning and evening of every other day. *Ad deliquium* from the jugular, as the literature advises. And I administered the recommended eight grains a day of calomel. And twice daily I purged each child with a mixture of tartar emetic and cerated glass of antimony. And they shat and vomited until there could be nothing left in any part of the insides of any of them. And as far as curing *angina suffocativa* is concerned, none of it had the least effect."

"It is nonetheless the treatment advised by all the best scientific minds." Colden began gathering the papers lying on his desk. "And it certainly can do no harm. You need trouble yourself no further."

The documents Colden was so concerned about appeared to be written in Will Devrey's hand. No doubt details of property transactions he was interested in moving forward. "Dr. Colden . . . Have you lost a child to this throat distemper?"

Colden paused and looked up. "A child of my own?" Caleb nodded. The older man went back to arranging his papers. "No, sir. God has spared me that trial. And since my family lives some distance from the city, I do not fear for them in this latest plague."

"You are indeed fortunate. My sister, too, lives far from here in the north of the Province. But my brother Bede and his wife have already lost their youngest daughter and fear for the remaining girl and their twin sons."

Colden stopped fussing with the lists. "Yes, your father told me. It is a great sadness. You have my sympathies on the death of your niece, Dr. Devrey."

"Thank you. May I ask you something else?"

"Of course."

"Do you imagine, sir, that there might be . . . possibly. I mean, with great skill, enormous skill, and extra care . . ."

"Yes? What are you proposing, Dr. Devrey? Don't be shy. Science is moved forward by observation and trial. If you have noted some medicine that—"

"No, nothing like that. What I was thinking . . . Might it be possible to intervene surgically, Dr. Colden?"

"Surgically? I take it you mean with a knife?"

"With a scalpel, yes."

"Dear God, what a remarkable notion. No, of course that's not possible. I give you my word, Dr. Devrey, if you cut the throats of your young patients they will die sooner rather than later."

Caleb held up his large hands and studied them. "I didn't mean that I should do it. I'm barely able to use a lancet for bleeding. My hands shake."

"Never mind. You can call in a barber if you need to. Or use leeches."

"Yes. I can and I do." He was still staring at his hands. "But what about other people? Surgeons? Those who have skills with the knife."

"Butchers have skills with the knife." Colden had managed to arrange the papers in a manner that satisfied him and was putting them in a leather dispatch box. "I do not think any mother would thank you for bringing a butcher to her deathly ill child." The box was closed and the key turned.

"No, I'm sure you're right. But there's something else troubling me."

Cadwallader Colden had been headed for the door. He paused. "Yes? What more disturbs your peace, Dr. Devrey? It is, I may point out, almost the dinner hour. So I trust it is no important topic you are now proposing we consider."

"Not very important, Dr. Colden. Simply this. Do you believe a woman could ever be a physician? Or perhaps a surgeon?"

"A woman be a . . . You are joking, are you not, sir?"

"Frankly, Dr. Colden, I'm not sure. I suppose I must be."

In the first two years of her marriage to Solomon, Jennet saw Martha Kincaid only once, in passing on the street. Both women paused just long enough for Jennet to see that the growth hadn't returned to Martha's face, and notice the way the other woman was eyeing her fine gown and her cloak and her muff.

All the same, there was not a day since she'd visited the bawdyhouse in the woods that she wasn't haunted by the memory of what she'd seen there. The man with the horn growing out of his scalp, the woman with hands attached to her elbows, the two-headed twins . . . The memory made her more than ever determined to do what she could for those whose troubles she could treat. Her charity and her surgical skills had improved the lives of the poorest women and children of the town, but this choking illness of the throat defeated her. On a Wednesday some three weeks into the siege she came home from the tanneries with her eyes red from weeping. "Solomon, this cannot be allowed to go on."

He had been reading the *Gazette*. The paper reported a town on the long island where there were now only two children left alive. All the rest had been carried off by the bladders of the throat. "My dear girl, if it were in my power or that of anyone else in this province to stop it, the throat distemper would be gone by now. I take it you've had a particularly bad visit with your supplicants."

"Horrid. Ada Carruthers . . . I've mentioned her before, haven't I?"

"I believe so. The one with no husband and seven children."

"Five. But she only has two left. Three choked to death this week. And none of the tanneries women have husbands. You of all people should understand how it is with them, Solomon, so don't look at me in that fashion."

They were in his second-floor study and Tilda, the black maid—Solomon never permitted anyone who worked for him to be referred to as a slave; even if they had been bought, he paid them all a wage—had delivered the tea tray. While she spoke Jennet was pouring the fragrant brew into large Spode cups. She used silver tongs to put two big chunks of brownish sugar in the one meant for her husband, and added a splash of milk. Solomon took the cup from her. "Thank you. And I shall look at you in whatever fashion I choose. I'm your husband. That's my right."

"My liege lord," she said, managing a smile for the first time since she'd arrived home.

"Lord and master. Don't forget the master part."

"I shan't. The master part is delicious."

He took a swallow of the tea and smiled at her over the rim of the cup. "Jennet. Listen, my love. Don't confuse those hags you fuss over with the women who work for me. My ladies are professional prostitutes. The crones who live in those shacks by the swamp beg in the streets and fornicate in any convenient doorway. They're whores and drunks and frequently thieves. They spread disease and breed like rabbits. In any sane society they'd be locked away where they would be no threat to decent people."

"What horrid things to say! If you think that, why do you help them so much?"

"I don't. You do."

"Only through your good offices."

"Yes, but I am good for your sake. Because, as you well know, I adore you. You are good for theirs. And for the life of me, I have never figured out why."

"I've never been entirely sure myself," she admitted. "But ever since I was a child, since I knew that some people have a much harder life than I and my family did in the worst of times . . . Particularly after—" She broke off. She'd never told Solomon about Martha Kincaid's bawdyhouse, or what it contained, much less that she'd gone to visit.

"Yes?"

"Nothing." Jennet sipped her tea, didn't look at him. Solomon was looking at her with an expression that said he knew a great deal more than she'd ever told him. "Misery calls to me," she whispered. "It makes me shiver inside. And when that happens I think if I don't do something I shall die. And so I do it."

"What?" He put the cup down. "Exactly what do you do?"

"You know what I do. I bring the tanneries women food, and the salves and ointments I get from Phoebe at the apothecary shop. And I give them a bit of money so they can buy ale and not drink that terrible swamp water, or the salty stuff as comes from the wells."

"And more often than not they use the money to buy rum or geneva."

She shrugged. "I suppose they do sometimes."

"You know they do. Frequently. Jennet, you didn't answer my question. What else do you do?"

Her hand was trembling when she set down the Spode cup. "You've heard something, Solomon. You'd best tell me what it was."

"In my business I hear a great deal, not all of it true. But when a story is repeated in enough coffee shops, and taverns, and slop shops, not to mention bordellos . . . Repetition serves for truth in the end, Jennet. You know that."

"You're thinking of my father. Yes, I know it."

"Well, what about this story? The one that says you've played at being a surgeon, actually used a lancet and a scalpel." His voice softened. "On the wide arc between absolute truth and total fiction, beloved, where does that fit in?"

Jennet pursed her lips and toyed with her rings for a moment, then raised her head and looked at him. "It's absolute truth, Solomon."

"Yes, Jennet, I thought it probably was."

Her eyes widened. "You did?"

"Of course. You're clever enough. You grew up in a surgeon's house. God knows you can achieve anything with those magical hands. And I know there's a part of you that doesn't hesitate to do what you want when you want, and count the cost later."

"But I'm a woman."

"Now that is something I know to be the absolute truth."

The mood for flirting had left her. "Everyone says it's unnatural." She watched him from below lowered lashes, waiting, trying to judge his reactions. "Everyone says I shouldn't—"

"I am not usually much concerned with what everyone says." Her heart soared. Then he went on. "In this case, however, I have to be."

Disappointment was a short, sharp pain in her chest. "For a moment I thought you would understand."

"I do. I simply cannot countenance the notion of you in one of His Majesty's prisons. What you are doing is illegal, Jennet. You can be prosecuted. To the full rigor of the law, as they say." He tapped the newspaper beside him with one finger. "However desperate the state of these children, you cannot—"

She had spread a linen napkin over her lap. Now she crumpled it and flung it on the tea table. "You can stop worrying about that, Solomon. I haven't the faintest idea how to cure the bladders. If I did, I would. Whatever the law says. But I don't. As for illegality . . . In God's name, what do you call what you do?"

"Clever," he said. "I call it clever. And profitable. And necessary. And I assure you, I'm in complete compliance with the real law, the one that controls how we actually live and get by."

"I don't know what you mean."

"I know you don't. That's why we're having this discussion. Jennet, the reason my houses and I are in no danger from the magistrates is because I conduct my business properly. I pay those whose job it is to interfere with me so well and so discreetly that they have no motive to make me any trouble, and a strong one to leave me alone."

Her mouth opened in one of those little circles of surprise that always made him want to kiss her. "Oh. I see. I never thought . . ."

"No. I am aware of that. That's why I'm telling you. And have you thought about Zachary Craddock?"

"Zachary. What has he to do with any of this?"

"Everything. I gave him to you on a salver, Jennet, and you've yet to take up the gift."

"His taste for whoring, you mean. I don't know how to use it. I've thought about it occasionally, but what can I do? Even if I could make him apologize, I don't believe it would do any good at this late date. I think it would just stir up all the—"

"Hush. You are talking like a little girl. Of course it would be useless to have Craddock make some public declaration concerning your father. Revenge is not about this for that, Jennet. It is about getting a good deal more of this than however much you were made to pay of that."

She shook her head. "Solomon, I don't understand. I know you mean me to, but I simply can't see what you want me to do."

"Very well. I'll spell it out, if you give me your word that you will never again take a surgical tool into your hands."

She was silent.

"Your word, Jennet. I am offering you a bargain: help for your tanneries women and their brats, and vindication for your father. In return, you give up surgery." She didn't speak, didn't even look at him. "Come, my love, have you ever known me to make a promise and not keep it?" She shook her head. "Well, then," he persisted, "do we have an agreement?"

Jennet bit her lip and folded her hands and stared at them. He'd called them magical hands. It was almost the same thing she'd said to Caleb Devrey. *I can do anything with these hands, Caleb, I can work magic. Surely that is a gift from God and it is meant to be used.* And Caleb had shaken his head and looked shocked, and now Caleb was spreading vicious stories. The women would never tell. It was as her father had warned her: Caleb Devrey had become her enemy.

She stood up and began pacing the room, clenching and unclenching her fingers.

Solomon sat and watched her.

Since she was eight years old and happened on her father when he was removing a tumor from a man's arm, she had been transfixed by the courage it took to cut into living flesh. And when doing so could save a life . . . Even now, the thought made her breathless. Especially now. She'd gotten better and better at it the more practice she had. These days when she cut, it didn't seem that her hands were a gift from God. It felt as if she were God. She could cut away evil and leave good behind. At least sometimes.

"I am waiting for your decision, Jennet."

He spoke softly but with no attempt at persuasion, as he had spoken to her in the carriage on their wedding day. God knew she'd made the right decision that time. "I love you, Solomon."

"I know you do. The only question in my mind is whether you love me enough to give up this dangerous but apparently intoxicating practice."

"I do good, you know. I can't save everyone, but I save some."

"I'm sure you do."

She sighed. "But I do not choose to do good to others at my husband's expense." She paused, and took a deep breath, "Very well, Solomon. I will never again touch a scalpel or a lancet."

"No more adventures in the cutting trade?"

"None."

"You swear it?"

"I do, Solomon. I swear it."

He exhaled as if a great weight had been lifted from him. "Thank God. Very well, here's my part of the bargain. Your women out by the tanneries, and all the other charity cases you wear yourself out seeing to, would they not be better treated in some central place? A place like St. Bartholomew's in London, say?"

"A hospital?"

"Exactly. But not those miserable things that have passed by the name in this colony. A proper hospital. Where the poor could get proper treatment."

"Oh! Oh, Solomon, what an extraordinary idea! Could you—"

"No, I could not. What's needed is a place with public standing, not a private act of charity. It must be sanctioned by the Common Council of the Corporation and made official by the signature of the governor. And it is those authorities who must name your father to be the surgeon in charge."

Jennet pressed her hands to her cheeks. They were burning. Solomon's idea was a wonderful fantasy shimmering in the distance. "But they won't. The idea has been mentioned once or twice, and the Council has shown no inclination to build a hospital. And my father? What would persuade the Council to make such an appointment?"

"For one thing," Solomon said, "business is not good in the city these last months. Pennsylvania produces more wheat than we do in New York. Pennsylvania wheat is nowhere near as good, but the owners of the sugar plantations don't give a damn. So the Caribbean slaves eat poorer but cheaper bread, and the workmen of New York eat none. Right now, there are only two ships being built in the entire city. Eighteen months ago there were two dozen. The politicians have promised to make things better for the craftsmen. The only way they can do it is by starting some building works paid for out of the general taxes."

"But won't they build something they want rather than a hospital they don't want? How could we possibly persuade them?"

"Not we. *You.*" He saw the disbelief on her face and chuckled. "You, my darling girl, will use your power to make them do what you want."

Jennet went back to her chair, settling her wide skirts with a great rustling of silk and taffeta. Her brilliant and wonderful and always clever husband had gone mad. "I have no power on the Common Council, Solomon."

The way her breasts rose over her tightly laced bodice heated him. Later. "You do," he said. "I gave it to you."

Jennet stared at him, her lovely face a study in puzzlement. Two tears had formed in the corners of her incredible blue eyes.

"Sweet child, listen to me. You think yourself clever, and you are." He leaned forward, took her hands, and lifted first one then the other to his lips. The scent of her skin was intoxicating. "But to win in the world of men you must be ruthless as well as intelligent. Zachary Craddock has been reelected to the Council six times. It is the basis of his standing in the community. And a source of enormous pride to him and Tamsyn and their children. And you have the power to take it away."

The doing of the thing, to use her mother's favorite phrase, took nearly fourteen months, and what she got was not exactly what Jennet had set out to get. But it was close.

Luck, Solomon said, usually comes down a crooked street. Jennet's—and through her, Christopher's—arrived by a number of indirections. The latest census put the population of New York at nearly nine thousand, living in fourteen hundred houses. In a city of such size it was no longer possible to deal with the indigent from the proceeds of the church poor boxes and a small topping-up by the government.

Crime and illness went together in the minds of the public. Both were increasing in New York City, though the four bellmen had been exchanged for a dozen watchmen who patrolled the streets by night. They had been instructed to walk very softly and pause often to stand and listen. They were equipped with oak truncheons with metal tips. All the same, disease and destitution had not immediately disappeared. Nor had criminal acts.

Then there was the matter of election promises. The Council had vowed to give work to the skilled craftsmen whose incomes had plummeted so severely these last months.

Those truths helped Zachary Craddock accomplish the task Jennet Turner DaSilva set him, once she had described his most personal and secret activities in terms so accurate he was sure she must be a witch.

Craddock stood no chance of convincing the Council to appropriate the funds for a hospital as such, but the notion of one made part of an almshouse might be acceptable, even welcomed. There was such a resolution already on the books, dating from 1700, but after over thirty years it was decided that a new vote was required.

When it passed without dissent Craddock, who had moved the question, was left in such a cold sweat of relief he barely made it out the door—smiling and shaking the hands of his fellow councilors—before he had to lean over in the street and vomit.

In November 1734 a committee was established to look for a suitable house to buy. In December they reported that construction was a better idea: "We recommend using a portion of the city's unimproved Common Land." The gentleman who reported the conclusion owned land near the Common. Any development that took place in the far north of the town would put money in his pocket.

Zachary Craddock was the first to approve the proposal. Loudly enough so that when the time came to try and get more difficult ideas adopted, the resurrection of a discredited surgeon for example, what he said today would still have an echo. "A purpose-built structure on the Common's a superb suggestion. Zachary Craddock's for it, gentlemen. In fact"—slapping the table with the flat of his hand—"I think we've talked long enough. So moved, Mr. Chairman."

The owner of the adjacent land was still on his feet. "Second!" he shouted before he sat down.

The chairman had eaten a particularly large dinner that day. He burped softly before he spoke. "The motion has been made and seconded. Has anyone more to say on the subject?"

"Get on with it," someone murmured. "Call the question."

The chairman took up his gavel. "The question is called. May I hear the ayes?" A rumble of approving voices. "Nays?" A lone dissent, from an old curmudgeon who as a matter of course dissented from everything. The gavel fell. "The ayes have it. The motion is carried. Now, a name for our venture. Zachary, this all began with you, as I recall. Any suggestions?"

"Well, being a medical man . . . 'Hospital for the Poor and Needy,' perhaps?"

The name was quickly rejected. Make people too ready to depend on public charity, the Council felt. "'Public Workhouse,'" someone said.

"And 'House of Correction,' so they know we mean for 'em to change their ways."

"Aye. And add 'of the City of New York.' So's the buggers know whose bread they're eating."

The proposal carried. It would be the Public Workhouse and House of Correction of the City of New York.

Craddock jumped to his feet. "But I thought we agreed to build a hospital!"

"We did, Dr. Craddock, and we shall. But we are going to treat all the diseases of our clients, not merely the physical. Stiffen their spines, teach 'em to mend their ways. Might as well make that clear in the name. Begin as we mean to go on, as they say. Now, sir, please sit down."

They appropriated eighty pounds from the general coffers and promised fifty gallons of rum for the builder. And since construction was known to be thirsty work, they agreed to be liable for a reasonable amount more, as well as paying the cost of the beams and the raising of the roof.

The building was ready for occupancy early in the year 1736.

It stood by itself on the far northern edge of the flat, rather desolate piece of land that was east of the Broad Way and north of Nassau Street, at the very corner the post riders turned as they began the final sprint of their grueling journey and galloped toward the house of the postmaster on Dock Street. One hundred and ten years after Peter Minuit had struck his bargain with the Canarsie people for the entire thirteen-mile-long island of Manhattan, the erection of the Public Workhouse and House of Correction marked the extension of the

City of New York to a point almost exactly one and one-quarter miles from the southern tip.

The Poorhouse, as everyone would call it, was two stories high, with a usable cellar built half above ground, and a chimney topping the gables on either side. Half the cellar was reserved for those put to hard labor. The building also contained rooms for weaving and carding and spinning, and a storeroom for general provisions. The rest of the space was given over to a cage for any who required restraint. Or needed to be whipped. There was a provision in the law that said residents of the town could send their slaves or servants to the poorhouse for whipping, and whoever did the job was to be paid a shilling and sixpence.

The ground floor held the general dining room and dormitories. Above them were the quarters for the keeper and his family. And, quite apart from the rest of the facility, in a room about twenty-five by twenty-three feet on the side facing the Broad Way, was the six-bed infirmary.

The institution born in New York, on the site that was later to become known as City Hall Park, was the first real hospital in the English colonies.

"Absolutely set aside for the sick," Craddock assured the young woman who though a few days short of twenty-one had taught him what it meant to be in true, heart-stopping terror that your life was about to be terribly and unalterably changed. "Nothing punitive about it. The keeper of the poorhouse holds no sway once he steps across the hospital threshold. We've written that into the bylaws."

"Who does hold sway in the hospital, Cousin Zachary?"

"You know the answer."

"Yes, but I want to hear you say it once more."

"Your father. It's plainly stated in the Council's pronouncement. Christopher Turner, Surgeon of this City—"

"Respected Surgeon. That's what you told me it would say."

"Yes, yes. That's exactly what it says. Respected Surgeon of this City. In full and complete charge of all and whatever transpires in the manner of medical and surgical treatments. It's entirely proper."

"I am delighted to hear it."

"And can I now take it, Mistress DaSilva, that you and I have concluded our business?"

"Why yes, of course, Cousin Zachary. We're quite done. For the moment."

Later, in Solomon's arms, when her mind was clear of distractions, she asked, "Solomon, why did you make all this happen?"

"I've already told you that. Because you wanted it to happen."

"Forgive me, but I don't believe you."

He raised himself on his elbow and looked into her lovely face, lit by the candle on her dressing table. "Very well. First, I did it because of the promise I extracted from you in exchange."

"That I would never again touch a lancet or a scalpel."

"Exactly. The thought of losing you to some dungeon below the City Hall . . . I couldn't bear it, my love. I would die."

"No, you wouldn't." Kissing him little soft kisses between each word. "You would scale the walls and rescue me."

"In a manner of speaking, I probably would. But since wall scaling—or burrowing, as the case may be—is not my strength, such a rescue would be enormously expensive. I chose instead to strike first. The result being that your clients get medical treatment, and I get a wife who does not commit criminal acts."

"Not unless you count this. Or this." She was touching him as she spoke, in ways and places that she knew he adored, but she stopped before they could both become too aroused. "Solomon, you said 'first.' There's a second reason. That's the one I want you to explain."

He let go of her, lay back on the pillows, and folded his hands behind his head. "Very well, but I don't think you'll enjoy the explanation. I am a Jew, Jennet, and history is an excellent teacher. The time may come, at any moment, totally without warning, when if I am to survive I must flee."

"Why? This is New York, Solomon. It is the most tolerant place in the colonies. Everyone knows as much. Almost no one here gives a fig what church people go to. Oh, Catholics are despised, I'll grant you that, but mostly it's money that's the key to social standing in New York. I've heard Papa say so dozens of times."

"In a manner of speaking he is correct. At least for Quakers and Anabaptists and Sabbatarians and the like. Even the hatred of Catholics has more to do with politics than with religion. It's the pope they hate, and popery. But Catholics and Protestants are all one or another sort of Christian, Jennet. It's different for Jews."

"Why? There are nearly two hundred Hebrews in the city now. I heard Bilah Levy say so in the Broad Street Market just the other day."

"Indeed." He chuckled. "Are you now accepted among the Jewish matrons of quality? Taking tea with the Mistresses Levy and Franks and Simpson?"

"Not exactly. I was just standing near her and I heard . . . I wasn't eavesdropping, Solomon, you mustn't think so."

"Why shouldn't you listen to their chatter if it interests you? Besides, they're all Tudescos. Their people came from countries where they speak German. You, my dear, are married to me. That gives you greater standing in their absurd pecking order." He shifted his position, drawing her closer. "Whoremaster I may be, but I belong to the more refined segment of Jewish society, my love. I speak, God help us, Portuguese!" He shouted the last word with a hoot of triumph.

"Whatever has that to do with anything?" Jennet pounded her small fists on his bare chest. "You're making fun of me, Solomon. You're laughing at me."

"I'm laughing, but not at you. This battle between the Portuguese-speaking

Jews—the Sephardim—who were here first, and the Tudesco Ashkenazim—who are despised because they speak German—astonishes me. I'd weep if I didn't laugh. They go to war among themselves. As if Jews didn't have enough enemies."

"But that's the part I don't understand, Solomon. You have your synagogue on Mill Street. Why should you feel yourself so threatened?"

It was as if the window had been opened and a cold wind had blown into the room. Jennet felt the chill. Solomon wasn't grinning any longer. He got up and walked to the fireplace, and poked savagely at the coals a few times, then went to the small table in the corner and poured a tot of Madeira from the silver decanter that was always kept full of the nutty-brown wine he especially enjoyed.

"Solomon," she asked, softly, "have I said something to offend you?"

"I'm offended, but it's because I must explain—" He broke off, downed the wine in one swallow, then went back to the bed, sat beside her, and took her hand. "Jennet, listen to me. Jews are different because we are accused of having committed the worst crime imaginable. According to our enemies, we killed God. That's not something likely to be forgotten."

The words made her flesh go cold, and a terrible prickle of foreboding began at the back of her neck. "Solomon . . ."

"Hush, my love. If I have to flee—and you must accept my judgment that it's entirely possible—the vultures will immediately make an attempt to swoop down and carry off everything I own. If that happens, only you will be able to protect what is ours. This business with Craddock and your father and the almshouse hospital . . . I have just given you the first lesson in how it is done."

The Shivering Cliffs Path

AUGUST 1737–NOVEMBER 1737

The part of Manhattan that faced the Sun-Going River was cold and the wind always blew. The Canarsie people who spent the warm months on the High Hills Island trading their exquisitely carved wampum with the other woodland peoples did not make their villages on the Sun-Going side. But at times they visited those high cliffs, where you could look across the broad water to the land of the mountains.

The fish from the Sun-Going River were large and sweet, and in some moons the great silver-skinned beasts with the pink flesh might be caught by skillful braves who took a canoe into the swift and icy waters. Also, the medicine women's red stones came from a hidden place among the sun going hills.

The medicine women had a secret way to get to the place of the red stones. They called the way they traveled the Shivering Cliffs Path, and while they walked they sang a sad song meant to remind the gods of all they had taken from the Canarsie, of the young braves killed in war and the young women who died bearing children. That way the gods would not forget the Canarsie. They would allow the medicine women to find what they required to keep the People strong and free.

Chapter Eight

THE SIX BEDS of the almshouse hospital were filled. They had to put an extra cot in the near corner of the room to accommodate the newest patient, a nine-year-old girl. It made the ward's narrow aisle almost impassible, but the girl wasn't likely to be there long.

The child had stopped her openmouthed, noisy gasping. Her struggle to breathe was quieter now, a continuous wheezing rasp. Her skin, no longer bright red with fever, had a faint blue cast, particularly around the mouth. She was fully conscious. The dark eyes she fixed on the young doctor were filled with terror. She was slowly and painfully choking to death as less and less air got through her closing windpipe.

Luke Turner was as tall as his father; he had to fold himself almost double to get close to the girl. His hand hovered above her neck. The razor edge of the scalpel glittered in the morning sunlight coming through the twelve-paned window. Still he hesitated. He'd never done this before, but there would never be a better chance.

Pure luck that the girl had been brought in on his watch, the one morning a week he took over in the hospital so Christopher could stay home and write his notes. A marvelous opportunity. The only problem was the toothless drunk the warden had sent to assist him. The grizzled old fool wasn't putting his back into it. The girl was writhing and twisting, constantly throwing off the man's feeble grip. "I told you to hold her still, damn it! I can't do a thing if you don't stop her jerking around like that."

"I'm tryin', sir. Told you I couldn't do much with them as was doin' the death dance. Not enough strength left." That's how he'd wound up in the poxed poorhouse. Not strong enough to run from the watchmen, pox their wretched souls. Came sniffing around every corner of the town these days. Turfed folks out of whatever bit of protection the bridges and doorways offered.

"Listen, old man, it's a trip downstairs to the whipping cage if you don't do as I say. Now put some muscle into it."

Luke's scalpel hovered a hairsbreadth above the child's neck. She was bluer than she had been, fighting harder for every shallow breath, and not moving so much now. Her eyes begged for help. He put the tip of the scalpel against her thin skin.

There was a gasp from the woman who stood in the doorway. She had a large hump on her back and was bent to one side. She moaned a few times, then shuffled forward to see better. Luke didn't turn around. "I told you not to come in here."

"I won't, sir, I swears it. Only please, sir, don't cut my Tillie's throat. She ain't to blame for that loiterin'. It was me who couldn't—"

Luke turned his head long enough to bellow, "I'm trying to help her, damn it! But if you don't—" He broke off. The girl's tortured contortions were suddenly more intense. She was thrashing about, beating her clenched fists on the bedclothes. It was now or never. "Hold her still," he told the old man. "I swear you'll get twenty lashes if she moves."

The fellow almost stretched on top of the child, tried to pin her body to the cot with his meager weight. He pressed both her hands against the canvas covering. For a moment the girl stopped squirming, using all her energy to suck in air.

The end was coming fast.

Luke bent toward her again and laid the blade of the scalpel along her throat. The child opened her mouth a little, as if she wanted to scream. Her eyes remained open, staring up at him, begging for mercy. He angled the blade toward the slight indentation between the throat and the clavicle. That's what the first Lucas Turner had written, after he performed the tracheotomy that saved the life of Judith Bayard, Stuyvesant's wife.

Tilting the Scalpel slightly downward, go behind the uppermost tip of the Sternum and open the Trachea by the Width of no more than a little Finger, and that at the precise point where the Windpipe leaves the Larynx and descends toward the Bronchia. And do so in such a Careful manner as to avoid Severing the major Arteries which exist in that Exact vicinity.

Jesus. Almost seventy years ago. And the first Lucas Turner didn't have proper Edinburgh training. Do it, Luke told himself. She's all but gone anyway. Look how much quieter she is. And how her eyes are starting to glaze over.

He stretched the skin taut with his left hand, drew one long breath, then cut with his right. The very instant the skin parted, the child threw off the man holding her down and lurched up in the bed. The scalpel in Luke's hand traveled a full three inches across her throat, slitting it from the middle of her neck to the lobe of her left ear.

The first blood came in a spurt, catching the old man in the face and Luke in the chest. Then it pumped out, streaming over Luke's hands and drenching the bed coverings in a sea of red.

Behind him the girl's mother began to make soft and frightened weeping sounds. His regular patients, the rich folks he saw in their homes and sometimes in the office of his house on Ann Street, screamed when someone died. The crippled crone mewled like a wounded cat. "She's dead, ain't she? My girl's dead and you killed her."

Luke put his bloody hand on the child's heart and felt nothing. God, he was exhausted, almost didn't have the strength to answer. "Yes, she's dead. The throat distemper killed her. I tried, but . . ." He shrugged. And did not think about the way his hand had trembled at the moment he made the incision.

"She was all but gone," Luke told his father. "I tried using Great-Great-Grandfather Lucas's technique, but it was too late." His twice-great-uncle, really. But the entire Turner family kept up the fiction of the adoption being the only tie. The Devreys as well.

Christopher wasn't sure that simply because the girl was dying she deserved to be hurried along by having her throat slit, but he nodded and considered the job at hand. An anatomy. The dead child lay on the table in the little room set aside for the purpose. Dissecting the corpses of those who died in the poorhouse had turned out to be a bonus of his job. It was wonderful to have all these cadavers to examine with no relatives in a position to argue against the practice, and the churches not particularly interested when only the poorest of the poor were involved. The opportunity to learn was priceless. Still, sometimes he was troubled by how the dead came to be lying on this table. "From what you say, the girl was indeed likely to die whether or not you cut. But if you—"

"I was right to try, Papa. There wasn't time to send for you. And the tracheotomy might have saved her."

"Yes, it might." Christopher bent closer, examined the wound. It was caked in dried blood. "But as I recall, Lucas's journal says an opening the quarter part of an inch. You've given this one a gash a good bit wider."

"An accident. She jerked upward and my hand slipped."

"Were the ropes not tight enough?"

"I didn't tie her. There was a man. The warden assigned him. He was supposed to—"

Christopher turned his head and looked over his shoulder into his son's face.

"If you are to practice surgery in my hospital," he said softly, his eyes flat and showing no emotion, "you must prepare your patients in advance. And your hands, Luke, must never slip."

"I didn't mean exactly that. About the slipping. Actually, now I think about it, my hand was remarkably steady. And I'm not a surgeon. I'm a physician."

"Ah yes, how could I forget. Dr. Luke Turner, trained in Edinburgh. Where they instruct you in the benign use of the knife. Or so I'm told."

"We learn a bit, yes. Not much," Luke admitted. "Nothing like the things Great-Great-Grandfather Lucas wrote about. Or what you do."

"No." Christopher was still looking at the gash in the dead girl's throat. "It appears they didn't teach you quite so much detail. And what of anatomies, Luke? Did you watch many of those?"

"Never." Luke swallowed hard, unable to take his eyes from the scalpel his father held. As a boy he hadn't enjoyed spying on the operations performed in the front room of Hall Place. Not like Jennet. His sister always had her nose pressed to a crack in the door when Christopher cut. Luke had wanted to be a physician for as long as he could remember, but never a surgeon. Only lately had it come upon him that he was somehow less than Papa and Lucas were, because he didn't work miracles with a scalpel. There were damned few miracles to be done with calomel and cupping. At least so it seemed now that he'd started a practice of his own. "I heard there were occasional anatomies performed at the University," he said. "But it wasn't easy getting cadavers. And we weren't required to attend."

"No. Well, you're not required to attend this one either," Christopher said mildly. "But I should think it would be wise if you did. Might help you in your benign use of the knife."

Luke forced himself to be attentive.

The scalpel seemed an extension of Christopher's hand, moving with direction and purpose. There was no sign of trembling. Christopher made a lengthwise cut from beneath the chin to the middle of the chest in one swift motion, cutting through skin and the fatty tissue. Finally, he made four shorter crosswise cuts that allowed him to peel back the flesh on either side like the wrappings of a package. "Good. Now we can see what we're about. Note the condition of the esophagus, Luke. It is a bit inflamed, is it not? Redder than it should be."

"If you say so."

"I do. Definitely inflamed. And these white spots." Christopher flicked his probe lightly along the exposed organ. "Quite a few of them, aren't there? And they aren't like the pus-filled lesions of a normally bad sore throat. Come closer, lad. Take a good look."

Luke bent toward the girl lying on the table with her throat opened. There was no blood now. "Yes, I see. Tissue redder than normal. With white spots."

"Tough white spots," Christopher amended.

"Yes. Hard lesions."

"Exactly. Now we open the esophagus—carefully, so as not to damage the tissue." Again the scalpel went its delicate way, cutting just so far and no farther, an artist's touch that revealed the inner lining of the passageway. "Ah," Christopher breathed softly. "What have we here? Something interesting, wouldn't you say?"

"I . . . I'm not sure. What are we looking at?"

"This white lining in the esophagus, going as far as"—Christopher slid the scalpel downward, his perfect touch parting only the outer layer of tissue—"down the trachea and beyond. Appears to continue to where the windpipe divides and enters both lungs. Get a probe, Luke. On the table beside you. Now, lift that white part out. Very gently, mind you. We don't want it to tear."

Luke's hand shook. He could see it, so his father must as well. The trembling prevented him from getting hold of the thing he was supposed to remove from the child's throat. Looked like a piece of the caul fat the butcher used to wrap patties of chopped meat. Whitish-gray and marked with indentations. "Is it some kind of pox?"

"No, nothing of the sort. There, you almost have it. Slide the probe around to the right and lift."

In the end it was Christopher who had to remove the thing, while Luke held the tissue of the esophagus apart with two additional probes.

"There. It's free." Christopher held the tough membrane up to the window. It was late afternoon; there was not much light, but the remarkable shape was evident. "It's a perfect cast of the inside of the esophagus and the trachea."

"And you've never seen it before?"

"Never. This is no benign lining placed in the throat by the Maker, lad. This is the thing that's choking them."

"Choking who?"

"The children who die by losing their breath, *angina suffocativa*. This is the bladder, a false membrane that grows inside their windpipe and cuts off all their air."

"But how does it get there?"

"Luke, if I knew the answer to that I'd be God Almighty. I'm just a poor surgeon. Not a fancy Edinburgh-trained doctor like you are."

The younger man had the grace to flush.

The room beneath the fancy bordello over by Hudson's River was windowless, carved out of an earthen cellar. The five-foot ceiling and half-height door made it a place where no normal man could stand upright. Being a scant thirty-six inches from the top of his head to his heels, Jan Brinker entered without difficulty. He crossed the threshold, then stood in the doorway squinting.

The gloom was lit by a single candle and the reddish glow that came from a small iron brazier containing a few glowing coals. A gray-blue haze thickened the air. The smoke came from the pipe Solomon DaSilva held between his teeth. Brinker pulled the edge of his coat over his nose and his mouth. "*Jesu Cristo,*" he muttered into the cloth. "This place be worse than Hades."

He hadn't meant the words to be heard, but DaSilva looked up. "How do you know, Jan? Have you visited? I'm told you're a little devil, but I thought that was women's gossip."

DaSilva was sitting behind a rough wooden table. Its surface was entirely covered by money, mostly coins, but some bills as well. He was separating the proceeds of his various enterprises into neat piles.

Three years earlier, in 1734, the Council had issued paper money in the equivalent of twelve thousand pounds sterling. Without the security of gold or silver backing, the flood of money led to high interest rates, which contributed to inflation. That worsened the economic downturn brought on by the cheap Pennsylvania flour the Caribbean sugar planters preferred to the finer New York product. Paper money was a curse. DaSilva accepted it because he had to, but like every man of business in America he much preferred hard currency, wherever it came from.

The coins in front of him were of every denomination and represented nearly every realm under heaven. Many were gold, polished by the number of hands that had greedily clutched at them. Even in the smoky half-light of the little room, the gold shimmered.

Jan Brinker continued to breathe into the shabby fabric of his coat, but above the threadbare homespun his glance was fixed on the table. His eyes were dark and filled with longing. They were a man's eyes, no matter his height.

DaSilva went on making neat, six-high stacks of the heavy Spanish coins known as pieces of eight, each containing a full ounce of silver, worth the equivalent of the much lighter Dutch gold *daalder.* "Sit down, Jan Brinker. I'm almost done here."

There was no place to sit. Maybe the Jew meant he should squat on the floor. Won't. Not no *Jesu Cristo* animal . . .

Brinker looked around, straining to see in the dim light of the coals and the single candle. There was a three-legged stool tipped over and pushed into a corner. The dwarf got it, dragged it closer, and turned it upright. When at last he hoisted himself into position on the seat, his feet didn't reach the ground.

DaSilva went on counting. Brinker kept staring. Once or twice he licked his lips. So much money . . . Finally he cleared his throat. "I was told you be wanting me, Mijnheer DaSilva. It be the truth, no?"

"Yes, of course it's the truth. How else would you have found me here, Jan Brinker?" When DaSilva brought Jennet to this grand house on the west side of

Manhattan he'd told her it was the best bordello in the city. Every man in New York knew as much. But damned few had ever found their way to the cellar where Solomon DaSilva counted his wealth. "Is there any way you'd have got here if I didn't send for you, Dutchman?"

"Guess not," the dwarf said.

DaSilva made no reply. The seconds went by, the only sound the clink of the various coins. Along with the *daalder*s and pieces of eight there were English crowns and guineas, Danish ducats, a few Portuguese cruzados, and Spanish doubloons, and Dutch guilders—all brought by the seamen who sailed into New York harbor.

Brinker began to tremble. The chink-chink of the coins grew steadily more terrifying. *Jesu Cristo,* what did the Jew want with him?

A few more seconds. Brinker tried again. "Be a lot of money you got there, Mijnheer DaSilva. A whole big lot. All the money in New York, maybe. I think—" Brinker couldn't say what he thought. He began to cough. His little body shook and he didn't seem able to stop.

"Mind the smoke, do you?" DaSilva's tone was friendly, but he didn't stop puffing on the pipe. "A Dutchman's not supposed to mind smoke. Never heard of such a thing."

"Tobacco be doing something to me. Makes me eyes tear." Brinker wheezed, pulling his coat over his face again. "Sorry for the noise, Mijnheer DaSilva," he said through the cloth.

"So, smoking's another pleasure that's denied you, little Jan Brinker? Pity."

The dwarf was said to be twenty-some years old, but his head was entirely bald, he had no body hair, and his sweat did not stink like that of a grown man. He had balls like tiny pebbles, and his prick never grew bigger than the finger of a full-size male. DaSilva knew those things because Jan Brinker was a favorite among the women who worked in the bordellos.

The whores petted and indulged the dwarf, giving him choice tidbits to eat and cuddling him as if he were a doll, passing him from hand to hand so each in turn could offer him a plump breast to suckle. Brinker seemed to enjoy that. And snuggling between their legs and licking their twats. He liked that as well. So did the women, apparently.

DaSilva didn't give a damn what his employees did when they weren't working. He never tried to curb Jan Brinker's access to the whorehouses. He'd always known a time might come when he could use someone like the dwarf. That time had arrived.

He picked up a handful of gold sovereigns bearing the stamp of the reigning British monarch, His Most Gracious Majesty George II, and leaned on his elbows, transferring the coins rhythmically from hand to hand. The pipe expelled another cloud of smoke. "All together . . . Call it four hundred pounds," he said through teeth still clenched around the pipe stem. "I can't be absolutely accurate. I never try to count every last penny."

"*Jesu Cristo,*" Brinker whispered. He'd never dreamed of such wealth. If you had that much money you'd never be cold or hungry again.

"I've had better weeks," DaSilva said, "but times, as we know, aren't good."

"*Jesu Cristo.*" Weeks when the profit was better than four hundred pounds. Unbelievable. He knew the Jew was rich, but this . . . Brinker made a gesture with his little hands, as if he couldn't stop them from reaching toward the money.

"Go ahead," DaSilva said. "I wouldn't have asked you to come here if I didn't mean for you to have some. Take what you like." He might have been offering Brinker a mug of ale.

The Dutchman hesitated, not quite ready to believe what he'd heard.

"Don't hold back, Jan. Take it."

A few more seconds passed. Brinker put out one hand and gingerly took a wooden penny.

DaSilva removed the pipe from his mouth and chuckled. "That's it? A whore is lying here with her legs spread, and you kiss the top of her ear? Are you no more man than that, Jan Brinker? Go on, take a handful. There's nothing to be afraid of."

The penny had disappeared into the pocket of Brinker's coat. He stretched out his hand a second time, hesitated. DaSilva nodded. Brinker scooped up three New England bronze shillings, each stamped "XII" to signify its worth in pennies. "Go on," DaSilva said softly. "A bit more is in order."

Brinker removed a few Dutch guilders from the table one by one and secreted them in various pockets in his clothing. He now had more money about his person than he'd possessed in his entire life. "Good," his benefactor murmured. "Very good. You may have some more, Jan Brinker. Go on, take it."

The Dutchman waited a second or two longer, then his body jerked and he jumped off the stool. He stood closer to the table and reached up and began sweeping coins and notes toward himself with both hands.

DaSilva lunged. In one savage, swift motion he captured both Brinker's child-like wrists and yanked him forward, lifting his feet off the ground.

"I be sorry!" Brinker screamed. "Sorry I be, mijnheer. You said . . . I didn't know . . . I thought . . ." He kicked wildly, but it did him no good. The table separated the two men, protecting DaSilva's shins from Brinker's boots. The dwarf was helpless.

DaSilva reached behind him and grabbed a pair of tongs, then scooped a ruddy coal from the brazier, exactly as if he were going to light his pipe. Instead he pressed the glowing coal to the dwarf's palm. Brinker screamed.

"Be silent," DaSilva growled. "And listen well. Greed is a mistake, my small friend. Wanting too much and taking more than your due is always a mistake. Remember that."

"You said— *Jesu Cristo*, Mijnheer DaSilva, I be a white man and you be burning me alive!"

"I said to help yourself. To take some. Some, Jan Brinker. A reasoned and reasonable amount."

The little room smelled of roasted meat. The Dutchman stopped wailing and began a continuous whine of anguish. DaSilva lessened the pressure on the tongs. For a moment the coal wasn't in such close contact with the skin. The respite lasted only a second or two; then DaSilva leaned forward and attacked the same spot a second time. Brinker screamed once, then relapsed into moans. "A fair share," his tormentor said. "Accept that and you'll be better off than you've ever been. Cheat me or lie to me and you're a dead man."

"Please, mijnheer . . . Me hand. Please . . ." Tears streamed down Brinker's cheeks.

DaSilva looked at his victim a moment longer, then relaxed the pressure on the tongs and released his grip on the dwarf's wrists. The little man fell to the floor on the other side of the table. He struggled to his feet, blowing on his burned hand. "*Jesu Cristo.* Gonna be having a terrible sore. Terrible."

Solomon pushed a coin toward him. "Here, add this to your collection. It's one of those new pennies they're making up in the Connecticut colony. Says right on it, *I am good copper.* Should be enough to buy you a bit of salve at Tamsyn's apothecary."

With his good left hand Brinker scooped up the shiny copper coin. Still grasping it, he dragged his sleeve across his face, wiping away the snot and the tears. "You be telling me what this is about, Mijnheer DaSilva? What you want me to do for all this money?"

"Of course." The scuffle had upset the neat piles of coins. DaSilva began restoring them to order. "Sit down again for a moment and I'll explain."

The August sky was darkening when the pounding on the door began. It was late in the evening, well after nine. Phoebe had been sure no one else would arrive that day. She'd been working with the large containers of herbs on the shelves, dusting the pewter and glass and tin jugs and tightening the covers. The one in her hands was marked *Foeniculum dulce* and filled with black seeds.

She shoved the container back into place and turned and went to the door, but she didn't open it. She was tall, very slender, much like Amba had been when she was young. Phoebe had to bend her head to speak against the crack between the thick door cut from a single slab of oak and the brick wall. "Shop be closed. Come back tomorrow."

"Can't," a muffled high-pitched voice said. "Be needing help now. Tomorrow be too late. It be me, Jan Brinker. Please, Phoebe, open up."

Everyone in New York knew the dwarf. When she was growing up in the house on Hall Place her mother had slipped the little fellow food whenever he came to the back door. "He be *haptoa*," Amba told her daughter, using the word that signified great holiness among her own people. "Folks like that don't be growing big 'cause the spirit be entering into them. They be staying like a child because they got the *obeah*."

Phoebe had been raised a black slave in a white master's house, but she had heard about the *obeah* the same way her mama had, from the West Indians who came and went in their world. Even as a child Phoebe knew you must never let the *obeah* be turned against you. Otherwise, like Phoebe's father, you might die in a slow fire after ten hours of screaming agony.

She yanked open the door. "What you be wanting here at this hour, Mr. Jan Brinker? How come you don't be waiting till tomorrow and come do your business in the day, like decent folks?"

"Look." The dwarf held out his damaged hand.

It was almost too dark to see. Phoebe had to look closely to make out the perfect circle of red and puckered flesh in the middle of the dwarf's palm. "That's a bad burn. How did you come by a burn like that, Jan Brinker?"

"Never mind that. I got it. You got something to fix it?"

Phoebe looked up. In the dimness she could see that Pearl Street was empty as far as the corner of Coenties Alley. Judging from the muffled sound of his bell, the night watchman was just beginning his rounds a few streets away. "Best you be coming inside." She tugged Brinker into the shop and closed and bolted the door. "Wait here. I be getting something for that hand."

She knew exactly what she needed, but Phoebe went first to listen at the door that separated the shop from the part of the house where the family lived. There were only the normal sounds of a husband and wife and their three children preparing for bed. That was good. Mistress Tamsyn wouldn't like her letting the dwarf in after curfew, much less treating him for free. She'd have to do that; Jan Brinker, he never had no money. But Mistress Tamsyn, she be white. White folks didn't understand about the *obeah*. And the master, Dr. Zachary, he don't be knowin' nothin'. 'Cept the whip.

Brinker watched Phoebe and stayed where he was, with his back to the door, surveying the small shop.

It had changed little since being opened by Sally Turner Van der Vries sixty-eight years before. All the jugs and jars and bottles on the shelves still bore the labels Sally had written. The wooden counter was the one she'd installed the day after Jacob Van der Vries was found covered in pitch and hanging from the old gibbet down by the fort.

Then, as now, there was at least one slave under this roof. When Van der Vries arrived from Holland he bought Hetje from the old compound in the woods.

Red Bess kept slaves, though she'd tried to free them in her will. When Tamsyn and Zachary Craddock moved into the house on Pearl Street and took over the shop, they brought four slaves with them. Blacks had always served behind this counter. But Turner's Phoebe, as she was known even after Christopher leased her to Tamsyn, was the first who was clever in the art of simpling. That's why Tamsyn wanted her.

No one had deliberately set out to make Amba's child an apothecary. She was two when Bess died and Christopher Turner bought her and her mother and took them to live on Hall Place. In those days Jane Turner wanted to get Amba out of the house as often as possible; she frequently sent her to Pearl Street to purchase some simple Jane couldn't concoct in her own kitchen. "Take the child with you," she'd always say, wanting to be rid of both.

Phoebe liked visiting the shop. She enjoyed the opportunity to study the different containers on the shelves. As soon as one was opened she would ask to sniff it. Gradually, over time, the little girl came to know what smell and purpose were connected to each label, and what the label sounded like when spoken aloud. It wasn't exactly reading—there was a law against teaching blacks to read—but it served the same purpose.

Before she was nine, Phoebe knew the names of all the herbs on the shelves, and knew how the words looked when they were written out. After that it was easy to discover what the plant looked like when it was growing. The little girl spent every moment she could dogging the footsteps of the slaves who tended Tamsyn's gardens.

"Being born in that house be doing somethin' to you," Amba always said. "Mistress Red Bess, after she pull you out o' me, she don't be letting me give you a name like our home people. I be wanting to call you Quashee, 'cause it means Sunday and that be the day you be borned. But Mistress Red Bess, she say in this place nobody name babies for the day they be born."

"What day does Amba mean, Mama?"

"How often I have to tell you I be different, child? Amba be my marriage name. Means queen." Amba smiled at the thought that all the whites who thought themselves her masters called her queen every day of their lives.

"Mistress Red Bess, she say you be Phoebe, and giving you your name mean she be putting her spirit in you. Now you be knowing the white people's magic better than they do. You hang tight to what you know, child. It be protecting you. Old Hetje taught me that what you know, that be the only thing as keeps you safe in this white man's world."

Phoebe was in no danger of forgetting what she knew. Simpling was as much a part of her as the air she breathed or the thoughts in her deepest heart. And caution. That, too, was bred in her bone.

She stayed beside the door to the family quarters for nearly a minute. Finally, when she was satisfied that no one was coming to investigate, she went to the shelves and reached for the jar labeled *Ascrum,* St. Peter's wort.

Phoebe scooped some of the dried and crushed leaves into a small, hollowed stone; then she added a sprinkling of what Sally had called *Gallitricum,* a herb every housewife in the colonies knew as clary. She moistened the powder with some honey and a few drops of egg white beaten with geneva. Then, sniffing every few seconds to judge the progress of the remedy, she worked the mix with her stone pestle until it was a smooth paste. "Come here, Jan Brinker. Put your hand on the counter, aside this here candle."

He looked warily at the flame. "Not gonna be burning me, is you, Phoebe? Not like him."

"Who?"

"Never mind." All that money. *Jesu Cristo,* what did it matter about his hand when he be having all that money? Wait till he showed Martha Kincaid. Not all of it, mind. Waren't nobody ever gonna know how much he really be having. But if he showed Martha a gold coin or two she'd let him—

"'Course I ain't gonna burn you, Jan Brinker. Now give me your hand."

The dwarf stood on tiptoe and laid his hand palm up on the wooden counter. Phoebe bent her dark head. The candlelight showed clear liquid beading in the crevices of the angry-looking red flesh. "Burned the skin clear away," Phoebe said. "You'll have a mark for life. Nothing I can do be changing that."

"I be figuring as much. But if me hand turns black, will I sicken and die? I knowed a old woman once, burned her hand real bad in a fire down by the docks. After a bit it seemed the burn got better. But later she be having a black hand and her whole arm swelled up, and pretty soon she be dead."

"That's 'cause poison be getting into the wound and make her blood bad." Phoebe took a small tin spatula from a drawer beneath the counter and used it to smear the burn with the paste she'd made. Brinker winced at the first touch, but after that he didn't move. "Your blood don't be going bad," Phoebe said. "Not if you be doing what I tells you."

She folded a lint bandage over the Dutchman's hand. "Keep this packing dry. And every day you got to be taking it off and then be putting on some more of this healing potion. Here, you can have what I've got made up." She scraped the excess mixture into one of the small squares of oiled cloth kept for the purpose, and tied it tightly shut with a short length of yarn. "You take this, Jan Brinker. And be doing exactly what I tell you. You gonna be fine."

"Can I come back when it be time to put on the fresh stuff? Tomorrow? So's you can do it. I be here well early. Before curfew. I promise."

Phoebe was wiping her spatula and putting it away. She didn't look at him. "No, you can't."

"Why not?"

"Because I said you couldn't. Now don't you be putting the bad *obeah* on me, Jan Brinker. I be helping you all I could. And I not be asking you for so much as a wooden penny. Even though Dr. Zachary, he be taking a whip to me if he knowed I give simples away for free. So you be making sure no bad luck comes to me just 'cause I said you couldn't come back."

Phoebe went to the street door and opened it. She waited for Brinker to leave.

"I can give you something for your trouble," the dwarf said.

"Go on, get out of here. I know you don't be having any money."

"Not money exactly." He smiled, thinking of Solomon DaSilva's coins secreted in his pockets, including the Connecticut copper he'd been given to buy a simple for his burn. Brinker sidled up to Phoebe and motioned for her to lean down. "I be telling so only you can hear."

Phoebe lowered her head. Brinker stretched his neck so he could put his mouth to her ear. Seconds later she pulled away. "You've got a filthy mouth in that big head of yours, Jan Brinker. Get out of here. Right now."

Brinker chuckled. "Better be watching yerself. Any blackbird yells at a white man—even if he be a freak—she be likely to find herself in the whipping cage."

"Just go. You got what you be coming for. Now go."

"I be going. But you think on what I said, Phoebe. You can be sure someday I'm gonna do it. I always like the dark meat of the chicken. And when I do it, you be loving it, begging for more."

Phoebe closed the door behind the dwarf and leaned against it, breathing hard. She'd tried every way she knew to avoid the bad *obeah*, but in the end she'd probably gotten it. Nothing to be done about that. And much remained to be done of the job Brinker had interrupted.

She returned to the jars of herbs and simples. The house had gone utterly still, but Phoebe remained cautious. She pulled each jar forward and went through the motions of dusting it, then quickly lifted the lid and scooped a small portion of the contents into one of the tin boxes she had prepared. As each box was filled, she tucked it safely into the basket she'd stowed beneath the counter. By midnight the basket was overflowing.

Like Red Bess, the family Craddock housed their slaves in the shed in the back garden. Except for Phoebe. These days her bed was a piece of worn canvas spread on the floor in the apothecary. They'd made her start sleeping in the shop a couple of months past. Right after Jethro, the seasoned slave Dr. Zachary bought the year before, asked if he and Phoebe could be married. Jethro got sent to the poorhouse for that. On a Thursday afternoon, when the public whipper did his work for those of the town as requested it. Fifteen stripes on his bare back. Phoebe was lucky. Dr. Zachary only slapped her a few times around the face and made her start sleeping on the floor in the shop.

Phoebe knew why she'd escaped a visit to the public whipper. She was valuable goods. She knew how to simple. Like her mama always said, what you knew, that be your best protection in this white man's world.

She spread the canvas on the floor, then lay down on it fully clothed and waited without closing her eyes. After a time she heard the watchman come down Pearl Street crying, "Two of the clock and all is well on a warm and still evening." As soon as his footsteps had faded, she got up, put on her shawl, gathered up her basket, and silently let herself out.

Jethro was waiting for her by the far side of the back garden wall. He put a hand on her shoulder and looked into her brown eyes, shining in the moonlight. "You be ready?"

Ready for a lot of things. For a long, hard trek north. For the notices Zachary Craddock be putting in the paper. Even them as couldn't read knowed what them notices said: *Runaway slaves. Substantial reward paid.* Ready for how everyone be looking for them after that. Ready for what be happening if they be caught. Phoebe nodded. "I'm ready."

"Come then," Jethro said. "Time to go."

He started for the street, expecting her to follow. Phoebe hesitated. The pungent scent of the herbs rose sharp and strong on the moist and sultry night air.

Sally Turner Van der Vries had been the first to sow every inch of soil around the house on Pearl Street with the herbs of her trade. Red Bess maintained the practice. Now, in the summer, Tamsyn kept two slaves busy tending the gardens, which continued to flourish. "Burdock," Phoebe murmured. "I didn't be taking none of that."

Jethro turned back. "Get some then. But be quick."

There was a clump not a yard away. Phoebe reached it in one long stride and crouched down and snapped a dozen rough green leaves from the lush growth and tucked them into her basket.

"Good. Come now."

"There's some fine henbane over there. I could—"

"No. We have to go. Watchman be coming back." Jethro started again for the road. This time Phoebe went after him.

II

"Unbelievable!" Cadwallader Colden slammed his dispatch box onto the desk and sank wearily into his chair. "I've never seen the city so clogged. Took me almost an hour to fight my way here from the Broad Way. And every man jack on the streets shouting at the top of his lungs. You'll have quite a few patients in the days to come, Dr. Devrey. Half the town will be so hoarse they'll be braying like donkeys."

Caleb was standing by the window, but watching the tumult had lost its appeal. He let the lace curtain fall and stepped away. "That's what they look like. Donkeys. Every one digging in his heels and refusing to budge."

"I take it you're not interested in who wins the seat in the Assembly." Colden had opened the leather box. He was shuffling his papers, rolling them into narrow tubes, and tying them with the short pieces of black ribbon he kept in the desk drawer.

"Not much," Caleb admitted. "I can't see that it matters who sits in the Assembly. The governor gets to do as he likes, whatever they say."

"Well, the royal representative after all . . ."

Caleb watched the older man for a moment, wondering what went on beneath the powdered wig that constantly shed chalky dust over his shoulders. He was very busy slotting his rolled papers into separate pigeonholes. Tomorrow or next week, whenever Caleb again showed up at the office, they would be removed and other papers would take their place. None had anything to do with medicine; his so-called partner never saw a patient. The bastard took half the earnings of the practice but spent all his time being the surveyor general of the Province of New York and attending to his political future. "Tell me, Dr. Colden, leaving the royal prerogative out of it, are you passionately interested in the outcome of this election?"

Colden shrugged. "I voted, of course. Spent all afternoon the day before yesterday doing it." He grimaced at the memory. In most elections—whether for the Common Council or the Assembly—thirty men voted, perhaps fifty. This time there must have been two hundred in the field up by the Freshwater Pond, all trying to line up behind their candidate. "It's no wonder they couldn't get a proper count. Bedlam. Everyone shouting and carrying on."

"Not entirely happy with the notion of the common man electing his representatives, are you?"

"It's not that," Colden protested. "It's just that since that damned trial everyone thinks they can say what they please and bear no responsibility."

"Ah yes, Zenger. We're bound to blame everything on that, aren't we?"

"Well, what do you expect? If a jury can't see that printing calumnies about the king and the governor is actionable, what—"

"The jury said that what Zenger wrote was the truth."

Colden stared at him. "Dear God, Devrey, what's that got to do with it?"

Caleb nodded toward the ruckus outside the window. "Everything, apparently. According to you that's why they're carrying on now. Because they think they can say what they like and not be held to account. Not to your taste, is it, Dr. Colden?"

"Look here, as I said, I went to the field, and when that didn't suffice I went to City Hall and signed my name in their written poll. And you know full well I'm not happy with the result. But fair's fair. De Lancey's candidate won and we Morrisites lost. So be it."

"Only by fourteen votes." Caleb kept his voice mild. As if it didn't matter much. As if he didn't know how passionately Cadwallader Colden hated James De Lancey. Both men sat on the Common Council, and De Lancey was the major obstacle to Colden's political ambitions. "Can't blame the Morrisites for wanting a recount," Caleb said. "Not when there's only fourteen votes in it."

Sweet Christ, he knew it wasn't smart to bait Colden, but he couldn't help himself. Half the takings. Every damned month.

"They've had their recount." Colden started packing another set of papers into the dispatch box. "Now they're carrying on about whether every man who signed is a legal voter. Which question, naturally enough, only pertains to the list of the other side."

"You don't hold out much hope, then? The Morrisites won't overturn the election?"

"I really can't say. Anyway, this one seat isn't the problem. If it weren't for that damned Cosby and his greed . . . Six years of squabbling. Now he's dead and we're left to clean up the mess."

"Greed" wasn't a strong enough word for the money lust of the former royal governor, William Cosby. First thing he did on arriving from London was sue Rip Van Dam for half the salary Van Dam was paid during the year he was acting governor. Cosby said the money belonged to him, since he'd already been given the appointment. There were two papers in New York. The *Gazette* had been publishing for ten years and was the official government mouthpiece. It trumpeted Cosby's line. The *Weekly Journal* had been started two years before by the printer John Zenger. It ran articles written by supporters of Van Dam. Since the authors wrote under assumed names, it was Zenger whom Governor Cosby imprisoned for libeling the king's representative, and thus the king.

After a year in the dungeons below City Hall the printer was finally tried. And acquitted by a jury who accepted a novel argument made by a silver-tongued lawyer from Philadelphia: it wasn't libel if it was the truth. After that Chief Justice Lewis Morris threw Cosby's case out of court. The governor promptly fired Morris and made James De Lancey Chief Justice.

The feud did not fade away; it became a touchstone for wider differences. Eventually the whole town took up sides. Cosby had died a few months before. George Clark, one of the richest men in the city, was the present acting governor.

But the political rift exposed by William Cosby's avarice continued to shape the political attitudes of New York.

De Lancey's party was the voice of the establishment, of the all-powerful merchants. They spoke for taxing land, not imports and exports. In New York, owning land usually meant being a small, independent farmer. The farmers and laborers and artisans found a voice in Morris, who argued that it was absurd for such people to bear the tax burden.

The way Caleb saw it, everything the Morrisites stood for contradicted Cadwallader Colden's natural instincts, but the God-cursed fool had joined them anyway because James De Lancey had to be defanged if Colden's political future was to prosper. "Tell me, Dr. Colden, if De Lancey's candidate is held to be the winner even after the challenge, will it be the end of your Morrisites?"

"It will not. This is a battle, lad. It is not the war."

"That's not what my father says. He insists Morris wants to turn the world on its head, that he doesn't understand an Englishman's the same whether he lives in London or here in America."

Colden winced. "Indeed. I grant your father that. But none should think we Morrisites are any less His Majesty's loyal subjects on account of our difference of opinion on this matter. As I said, Dr. Devrey, this isn't about philosophy, much less loyalty. It's about one man's refusal to be fair."

My enemy's enemy is my friend. Damn the bastard. So why wasn't what was fair for Rip Van Dam also fair for Caleb Devrey? How come it was acceptable for him to do all the work for half the profit?

It was impossible to speak such thoughts. He couldn't afford to oppose his father; there were chits bearing his name in every tavern and coffeehouse in the city. But he never would dig himself out of the hole as long as he was only getting half the earnings of his labor. Will Devrey, meanwhile, ignored the political differences between himself and Cadwallader Colden, and did very well out of his son's association with the surveyor general of the province. His father and Colden, both riding on his back. The thought choked him, particularly as he had no choice but to swallow it.

Caleb stepped to the window so Colden wouldn't see the black look on his face. A group of men on horseback carrying silk banners stamped with the likeness of De Lancey's candidate were attempting to force their way through the Wall Street crowd. A gaggle of musicians, trumpeters, and violinists marched ahead of them. The procession was trying to get to City Hall to celebrate their victory, but the angry crowd of Morrisites wouldn't fall back and let them pass. Caleb opened the casement. The din was deafening.

"For God's sake, lad! Shut that damned window. We'll go deaf."

"That's your lot making all the racket," Caleb shouted over the noise.

"Shut the infernal window. I don't care whose lot it is."

No, of course not. Cadwallader Colden didn't give a whore's frozen tit for Morris and his party. Only for his own advancement. Caleb drew the casement closed.

"That's better. Now, Dr. Devrey, it's my turn to ask a question. Do you have no interest in the outcome of this fight? No—how shall I put it?—ill feeling about Cosby's actions?"

Bastard. Colden knew bloody well that Caleb fervently hoped William Cosby was burning in hell. Before he died the governor had signed the bill that gave Christopher Turner a lifetime post as chief surgeon of the almshouse hospital. The bile rose in Caleb's throat every time he thought of it. This time there was no way he could keep the hatred from showing on his face.

"Have no fear, Dr. Devrey." Colden sounded cheerful now that he'd scored. "Whatever happens, if there is any justice under heaven, in the end the Morrisites will prevail."

"So that's what they're shouting for," Caleb said softly, "justice under heaven."

"Men must act if they wish to control their destiny, Dr. Devrey. Not simply wait on divine pleasure."

"I take your point, sir." Caleb reached for his tricorn. "I shall therefore go out and add my voice to the clamor."

Colden turned back to his papers. "On behalf of the Morrisites, I presume."

"Truth to tell, I have some sympathy in that direction." For once he couldn't stifle his thoughts. "Doesn't seem right for a man to claim half another's earnings, does it?"

"I absolutely agree." Colden looked as if he had no idea of the meaning behind the words. He closed his dispatch box and began brushing flecks of powder from his shoulders. "I admire your fair-mindedness, Dr. Devrey. Personally, I've never believed a man's drinking companions should influence his politics."

The statement took Caleb's breath away, but he recovered quickly. "If you're referring to my friendship with Oliver De Lancey, I assure you he has no interest in these matters. Oliver and his brother James seldom meet."

The older man raised a placating hand. "No offense, lad. As I said, drinking's one thing. Politics are another."

"Oliver's my age, five years younger than James. And I repeat, he has no interest in politics."

Colden gave Caleb the full benefit of his thin-lipped smile. "Of course. I know that. Besides, I trust you absolutely, Dr. Devrey. We're partners, after all."

Outside the doctors' office Wall Street was in an uproar. The narrow road was nearly impassable, a frightening mêlée of horses and humans. There were wagons and barrows, even some carriages. Once the count in the Freshwater Meadow proved inconclusive, both parties commanded all the rolling stock they could find to bring in men from as far away as the village of Yonkers, up in West Chester, and Harlem, at the far northern end of Manhattan. Many were too ill or too ancient to walk or sit a horse. Still, as long as they were on the register and could be gotten to City Hall to sign their names, they counted.

In that frenzy of flesh and wheels and hooves, being three feet tall was an advantage. Jan Brinker darted between the legs of people and animals. Three or four times he got closer to his destination by ducking under a horse's belly. Finally he reached the Devrey mansion.

Brinker couldn't really see the imposing brick house. He knew where he was when a momentary break in the solid wall of humanity allowed him to spot the carved pineapples that topped the fence posts. He'd seen them many times in the last few weeks doing the job Solomon DaSilva had given him. *Watch Caleb Devrey. Let me know where he goes and whom he meets and what he does. Even what he talks about.* So far it hadn't been a difficult assignment. Today it was almost impossible.

The bodies were pressing closer, hemming Brinker in. He couldn't breathe. He'd already lost his hat. Now, simply by surging back and forth, the mob threatened to tear away his clothes. Brinker couldn't go up or sideways, so he went down. He got on his knees and began crawling through the spaces between men's legs. He was able to move again, but he had almost no air and what there was stank.

Choking and gasping, unable to avoid the ubiquitous steaming piles of manure, Brinker inched forward. His chest felt as if a great weight was squeezing it closer to his spine. He stopped crawling and tried to stand. Not a chance. The press of people was closing in. If he didn't get clear he'd be trampled. He was living his worst nightmare: all the big people were going to squash him like a bug.

Brinker's goal was the black iron fence that fronted the Devrey house. One thing kept him struggling forward: the pain in his hand. Three weeks now. The burn was almost entirely healed, but the memory still seared. Goddamn bastard. Goddamn *Jesu Cristo*–killing Jew bastard. Never going to forget what—

"Christ-killers!" the crowd shouted. "Murderers!"

Brinker stopped crawling. A terrible trembling began in his legs and moved to the top of his big head. How was it possible that the crowd had read his mind?

"The Jews killed Our Lord Jesus Christ! Hanging's too good for 'em!"

The little man started to sob. He was going mad. If anyone found out they'd lock him away in a cage somewhere and feed him bread and water. And it was all Solomon DaSilva's fault. Every fornicating terrible thing that had happened to him in the past few weeks was the fault of—

"Wait!" a man shouted. "Hear me out. I've more to say."

The crowd hushed, and—miraculously—stopped moving.

Inch by painful inch Brinker dragged himself through the filth that covered the cobbles. At last he spied a portion of the fence and reached out, stretching forward as far as he could. Bloody bastard. *Cristo*-killing Jew bastard. If he was crushed it would be— There! Got it.

Brinker hauled himself forward, head-butting his way through the crowd. Intent on the man speaking across the way, they didn't seem to notice. Brinker heard the voice but paid no attention to the words. His only concern was to keep hold of the fence. Finally he was able to use both his arms and legs to shinny up the sturdy corner post toward the blessedly fresh air. His head was level with the pineapple-shaped finial. *Jesu Cristo!* He could breathe. He could look above the crowd and see as well as hear the man standing in front of City Hall.

"I tell you, De Lancey's people are lying! They're inside insisting their man was elected by fourteen votes. That's a lie! Who elected him? Jews, by God, and that's not legal! If the God-cursed Hebrews can't vote for Parliament in England, why should they be allowed to vote for the Assembly here in New York? What will we have next? Women voters? The Jews elected De Lancey's man. That's not right or proper, and in any decent society it shouldn't be legal!"

A rumble of approval came from the men in the street. Fear and hatred of Jews was something they'd taken in with mothers' milk; it was reinforced by sermons preached from every Christian pulpit. The rumble grew into a mighty roar. "No Jew electors! Never! Not in New York!"

"What's the matter with all of you?" one of the few De Lancey supporters in the throng shouted. "Are you daft? Hebrews have been voting in New York for years! What's different now?"

The man in front of the City Hall didn't wait for the crowd to answer. "Reason, man! Can any decent Christian allow a close election like this be settled by Christ-killers? Can't you imagine yourself there in Jerusalem on that terrible day? Can't you see the brow of your Lord and Savior bleeding with the thorns the Jews braided and put on his head, the marks of the whips that tore his flesh and—"

"Was the Roman soldiers done that. Have you no Bible? Or can you not read?"

"Aye, 'twas the soldiers," another voice added. "And that bugger Pilate. They're the ones to blame."

Almost as one the Morrisites shouted down the few willing to defend the Hebrews. The mob may have been divided by their politics. They were united in their hatred of Jews.

Caleb Devrey was at the fringe of the crowd, his back to his father's front door. But he was close enough to feel what was happening. He sensed the rage starting to build, the blood hunger to rise . . . Christ! It was as if you could touch the hatred. Hundreds of people feeling what he'd felt for five years, asking themselves the question he'd asked a hundred times.

What right did an ugly old Jew like Solomon DaSilva have to a girl like Jennet? Everyone knew the Hebrews twisted and schemed and plotted to make things bad for Christians. DaSilva had used Jews' magic to align the stars and thwart an upright Christian gentleman. At last everyone in New York knew about it. At last DaSilva would pay.

"It's the Jews!" a man a few yards away from Caleb was shouting. The man was on the other side of the elaborate Devrey fence. "That's what's wrong with this city. It's why we've been getting poorer and poorer these last years. We've too much of the Jews!"

"Hang on!" another shouted. "Use your brains, all of you. It's not the Jews' fault cheap flour gets milled in Philadelphia."

The crowd didn't want to listen. "It's the Jews done it! Get rid of the Jews and we'll all be rich again!"

"It's the Jews!" Caleb didn't know he was going to join the shouting until the words were out of his mouth. He strode forward, across the strip of social distinction that made him who he was, toward the fence that separated him from the common folk. "It's the Jews that cause all our problems!"

Caleb swung open the gate and elbowed his way into the midst of the heaving throng, still shouting at the top of his voice. "We've got to rid ourselves of the Christ-killing Jews!"

Brinker was intensely conscious of the last rays of the late afternoon sun shining on his bald head. He tried to make himself unnoticeable. Devrey might have spotted him at other times in these past few weeks. Maybe seeing him here today be the final straw. Could be the Devrey influence be turning Jan Brinker over to the authorities, put him in the stocks again.

Caleb didn't so much as glance in the dwarf's direction. The crowd was looking for something or someone to tear apart, and Caleb Devrey knew who it must be. "It's the Jews!" he shouted. "Men like Solomon DaSilva, they're the ones to blame for all our ills."

Brinker's heart churned in his chest, this time with joy. DaSilva was going to get what he deserved. The scar on the dwarf's hand tingled and pulsed. Clinging to the top of the fence, he could just about see the gallows in front of City Hall. Easy to imagine himself standing on the ground below them, staring up at Solomon DaSilva's white satin breeches and shiny black boots, cheering at the snap of the trapdoor. *Jesu Cristo!* He could almost see DaSilva's legs dangling high above the gallows platform.

The image made him deliriously happy. Then he imagined what it would be like to be poor again, to have to beg in the markets and chance a trip to the stocks to keep from starving.

After the initial shower of coins in the cellar the night DaSilva burned him with the coal, the Jew paid Brinker two shillings a week. And all he be having to do was keep an eye on Caleb Devrey. Normally it be easy work, a whole big lot safer than begging. And *Jesu Christo,* better than any charity from the poor boxes.

The crowd was still screaming for blood, pushing and shoving toward City Hall. Away from the Devrey house.

The sun had gone down and the redbrick mansion cast deep shadows either side. *Jesu Cristo* . . . if he could get behind the Devrey house without nobody be seeing him, he could make his way north. Once he be away from City Hall, be easier to move.

He looked from the gallows in front of City Hall to his hand, thinking about the money. Brinker took a long breath, held it for three heartbeats, then dropped off the fence and began scurrying through the shadows of the front garden toward the house. Behind it, about half a mile north, was Nassau Street.

"And what is it you'd be wanting here?" Flossie kept a silk pocket cloth pressed to her nose while she spoke. The stench of the dwarf was horrific. There were dried bits of horse manure sticking to his clothes, and his face and his big bald head were streaked with the dirt of the streets.

"Same as I be telling the blackbird be coming to the door first. I got to talk to Mijnheer DaSilva."

"Well, you can't. And in this house we have no dealings with God-cursed freaks. Go away."

Flossie started to close the door, but Brinker had wedged his foot in it. Desperate he be. Already been to the sign of the Greased Griddle over by Queen Street, he and DaSilva met there sometimes. Right next to one of the Jew's whorehouses, the Griddle be, but no sign of DaSilva in neither place. And nearly thirty minutes gone since Caleb Devrey joined the pack of Jew-haters out for blood. He be losing much more time, be too late. "Ach, mevrouw, you be blessed if you help me." Brinker put on his best whine. That sometimes worked with women as gave themselves airs like this one did. "Me with me short legs and all, be an hour afore I be getting to Mijnheer DaSilva's . . ." *Jesu Cristo,* he couldn't say "whorehouse." The old bitch be slamming the door in his face. Close his foot right in the door, she would. "Mijnheer DaSilva's establishment over by Hudson's River. Have some charity, mevrouw. Tell if it be worth the journey. Will I be finding Mijnheer DaSilva once I be getting over by Hudson's River?"

Flossie stared at him a moment, struggling with revulsion and pity. Finally she shook her head. "No, himself isn't there. And not here, neither. It's away Mr. DaSilva is. Doing a bit of business. Now get yourself gone, you ugly little man. If you come back again I'll be after setting the constables on you, I will. 'Tis a promise."

Brinker withdrew his foot from the doorway. Flossie closed the door and leaned against it, fanning herself with the bit of silk cloth. There wasn't much she hadn't dealt with in her forty-six years, but God's truth it made her go that peculiar to have to talk to them as bore the devil's mark in their very flesh.

The mob surged from Wall Street to Broad Street, an animal with its fangs bared, looking for prey. It was full dark now. A few pitch-topped torches had appeared and been set ablaze and lifted aloft. "What about Simpson?" someone shouted. "The Jew what stamps a curse on the meat afore he sends it south to the islands. He lives near here."

"Aye, that's a Jew thing, cursing the meat afore Christians eat it. I say we—"

"Not Simpson!" came a voice. "Simpson's a Tudesco, from Germany!"

"So? He's a Jew, ain't he?"

"But what they put on the meat, it ain't a curse," the boy protested. "They says some prayers over it, and puts the stamp o' their church on it, so's other Jews can—"

The crowd turned on the lad, drawing back and isolating him in the circle of dancing light.

"How come you know so much about them heathens?"

"You got some Jew blood in you, boy?"

"Yeah, he must have! I say we take him down by the fort and string him up on the old gibbet."

Caleb's heart was hammering in his chest. He spotted a rain barrel and jumped up on it, waving his arms and yelling. "Stop! Stop! You're making a huge mistake!"

His family's wealth and social standing made Caleb a natural leader. A couple of the flaming torches were thrust in his direction, bathing him in a crimson glow. The mob quieted itself and waited.

Caleb picked up their willingness to defer to him the way he'd picked up their bloodlust. He was above them, but one with them. It was right and natural that he, an educated man, should be the general of these troops.

"Leave him be," he said, pointing toward the youth who'd made the mistake of trying to explain Hebrew ways. "He's Liam Jones. You all know he's no Jew. He works in the market where Simpson slaughters his beef. That's how he knows so much about the business."

The hostility that had been aimed at Jones eased some, but it didn't go away. The hatred was waiting to be directed.

"We don't want the Tudesco Hebrews," Caleb shouted into the night. "The ones who came from Brazil and Holland, who've been here the longest and wormed their way into our very lives, taken possession of what's rightly ours—they're the men we're after!"

"The women as well!" a voice shouted from the rear. "Cursed Jews come here and marry our women!"

"Aye, that's right!" another said. "Christian woman marries a Jew, she ain't nothin' but a whore! Any man here don't know what you do with whores?"

The response was deafening.

Sweet Christ, the thought of Jennet at the mercy of this crowd of men. At his mercy. Caleb's blood pounded in his veins. "Solomon DaSilva!" The name burst out of him, half curse, half war cry. "Solomon DaSilva's the kind of Jew we're after! Came from Brazil and made himself filthy rich with our money!"

"DaSilva's the biggest whoremaster of 'em all!"

"Aye, and he has a Christian wife!"

"C'mon, what are we waiting for?"

Caleb jumped off the rain barrel, and the horde surged forward with him at its head.

Brinker was hidden in the shadows across the road from the DaSilva place. He'd been there since Flossie O'Toole turned him away, chewing on his disappointment, thinking that whatever the women in that house got, it was no better than they deserved. All the same, he didn't leave.

'Course, there be no guarantee they be coming here. The mob might be after one of them other Hebrews by now, Levy or Gomez or Simpson. Most of 'em be closer to City Hall. Over near the place they called their synagogue, on Mill Street. *Ja*, but if Caleb Devrey be having anything to do with it . . .

Give him a lot of pleasure, it would, seeing them wreck Solomon DaSilva's fine mansion. And seeing what they'd do to his servants and his beautiful young Christian wife.

Jesu Cristo! What be the reward for someone as saved Solomon DaSilva's wife from that pack of howling wolves? Even more than he be giving for a warning about what was on the way. Five minutes went by. Ten. The September evening wasn't cold, but the dwarf shivered. The way she'd looked at him, the one who called herself Flossie O'Toole. Half pity, half disgust. He hated that kind of look. Hated her. . . .

He felt the beast before he heard it; the tramp of many feet seemed to make the earth shiver. Then came the insistent, clattering sound of men's leather boots on the stone cobbles. Finally the shouts. "Jews out! Death to the Christ-killers! Get DaSilva! Aye, him and his whore wife!"

They were coming here. And when they found DaSilva had escaped they'd be crazy, ready to tear anything and anyone apart. Him too. *Jesu Cristo!*

Candles and firelight flickered behind the tall, curtained windows on the ground floor of the elegant DaSilva mansion. Brinker kept looking at those glimmers of light as he darted across the road.

Jennet had been in the drawing room almost an hour, watching the candles burn down in their beautifully polished brass holders, trying to decide.

Not what to do, but how to do it. Solomon would have to know. Indeed, now that she was sure, she couldn't wait for him to know. She'd have to . . . Ah, there! Was that little twitch the child quickening? No, of course not. Just a bit of gas. It was too soon. She was being an idiot.

Dear God, why couldn't she concentrate? Sitting with her feet propped on a small stool, comforted by the warmth of the fire, she seemed able only to dream.

Won't you be surprised, my darling Solomon? Five years you've faithfully used those wretched silk sheaths, pumped your seed all over my belly instead of inside it, and despite that, nature won't be denied, and here I am. Almost three months gone with your child.

We must be cautious now, beloved. For our child's sake. That was what she'd say.

Solomon would see that. As soon as she told him the news, he would promise to give up selling guns to the Indians, just as she'd given up the scalpel because he asked her to. Never mind his assertions that those whose job it was to interfere with his activities were well paid to look away; Jennet wasn't reassured. The gun business terrified her, more now than before. The troubles with Canada were on the rise again, and the stories in the papers about alliances between the French and the Indians grew more and more ominous. Every week there was something about how the government would not tolerate private individuals interfering with— Dear God, what was that noise?

Jennet ran to the window and pushed aside the lace curtains. She saw the light of many torches bobbing and weaving in the dark, coming up Nassau Street, converging on—

"Psst . . . Mevrouw, it be me. Jan Brinker."

She pulled back, startled almost out of her wits by the misshapen creature leering in at her from the other side of the glass, mouthing words she couldn't hear. "Go away! What are you doing in my garden? Go, or—"

Brinker looked over his shoulder. The torches were coming closer. He raised one small fist and knocked urgently on the pane that separated him from DaSilva's wife. "Mevrouw, there be no time. Open this window and come!"

"Go away!" If only she could summon Clemence, he would get rid of this awful creature in seconds. But Clemence had gone with Solomon. She was alone except for Flossie and Tilda.

Brinker looked around. The mob was no more than fifty yards back. He had to get her out of here. If he saved Solomon DaSilva's wife, the man's gratitude would be enormous and the reward would make him safe for the rest of his days. There was a round boulder at his feet, part of a decorative edging to the flower bed beneath the window. The dwarf reached down, summoned all his strength, and hoisted the stone and threw it through the glass.

Jennet barely had time to jump out of the way. "Are you mad! I'll have you ar—"

"Mevrouw, if you value your life, come with me! Now! Listen to them!"

The sound was all around her now, a roar she had to recognize for what it was. Hatred. She heard Solomon's name and she knew it was said as a curse.

"Now, mevrouw!" Brinker reached in and tugged at her skirt. "Come. There be no more time!"

She tried to make a decision. If she ran God alone knew what would happen to this house. And what of Flossie and Tilda? She couldn't go off and leave them.

The voices in the street grew louder. The first of the torches lit the road in front of the house next to hers in a crimson flush. In seconds the shadows in her own garden would be gone.

She had one obligation above all others, to protect Solomon's child. Their child. With one hand she gathered up her skirts, with the other she thrust open the remains of the shattered casement and stepped into the garden.

"*Ja,* good! Quick, mevrouw. Follow me."

III

Martha Kincaid's bawdyhouse had changed little since the first time Jennet saw it. Men and women, black and white crowded together in the taproom. The man with the horn on his head still served the tankards of ale or rum or geneva. And the woman with the terrible red devil's mark covering her face was sitting beside a legless man who was openly fondling her half-naked breasts.

Jennet felt that mixture of fear and pity that had struck her when she visited this unholy tavern nearly six years before. But this time she was the supplicant.

"What you bringin' her to my place for?" Martha demanded of Brinker. "She ain't gonna help any what's here."

Brinker opened his mouth, but Jennet answered first. "I'm the one who needs help this time, Mistress Kincaid."

"You? Needing help from the likes of us? Not likely. Besides, why should I help you?"

The room was well lit by the fire and dozens of candles, and Jennet couldn't even see a scar from the surgery on Martha Kincaid's face. "My father served you well," Jennet said softly. "Perhaps you will help me for his sake, if you will not do so for my own."

Martha Kincaid said nothing, then turned to the wooden counter that ran the length of the room. Barrels of ale were set at intervals on the countertop, pewter tankards lined up in the spaces between. She grabbed one of the tankards, lifted it, and took a long swallow, then set it down and shouted for the barkeep. "Tom!"

The man with the horn came rushing over to get her a refill. Martha lifted her hand to her face and rested it a moment against her smooth cheek. "For your pa's sake. Aye, I expect there's something to that. What do you want?"

"Sanctuary," Jennet said.

"Her husband be away somewheres. And with the election and all . . ." Brinker's words tumbled over themselves in his anxiety to make Martha understand. "The folks in the town, crazy they be. Screaming for Jews' blood. They be murdering her if I let 'em."

"She ain't no Jew."

"No, but she be married to one. That's why I brung her, Martha. The crowd be screaming how she be a whore, and threatenin' God only knows what."

"God ain't the only one as knows." Martha Kincaid propped herself on her elbows and leaned back on the bar. "Any fool can figure out what a crowd of men would like to do to a lady like this. You thinkin' you want to work here, mistress? Lie down with Tom there, him with the horn on his head? Or maybe old Seth. He's the fellow ain't got no legs."

"I'm asking for shelter, not work, Mistress Kincaid."

"Shelter, is it? Can you pay?"

"Yes, but not immediately. We left in rather a hurry. As soon as my husband returns he'll—"

"*Ja,*" Brinker said anxiously, "her husband be Solomon DaSilva."

"I know who her husband is. So tell me somethin', Mistress DaSilva. Under the circumstances, seein' as how you're in a bit of bother, how come you didn't run to one of your husband's fancy bordellos and ask for sanctuary there? Know about 'em, do you?"

"I know." Jennet stared unflinching at Martha.

"I be bringing her here," Brinker said again, dancing up and down with impatience. "It not be her idea, Martha. I be bringing her because Solomon DaSilva, he be grateful like you never seen. Everyone knows he be mad for her."

"I know," Martha said wearily. "Stop fussing, Jan. You'll get your reward for rescuing Mistress DaSilva. She can stay long as she likes and pay when she—" Her eyes came alight. "No. Mistress DaSilva can pay for her lodging this very night."

The girl was pale and sullen, staring silently at the two women who stood beside her bed. "This here's Ellen," Martha said. "She's four months gone. She don't want the babe. Take it from her."

Jennet gasped. "I can't. And I wouldn't if I could. How can you suggest such a wicked—"

"It's her own pa as made her breed. Been doin' it to her since she was eight. She's twelve now."

"Dear God," Jennet whispered. "Her father . . . How can you know this is true, Mistress Kincaid? What if—"

"Ain't no whats in it. I been listenin' to stories like this for quite a time now. I know which ones is true."

The girl watched both women through slitted eyes, but when she spoke it was to Martha. "She got the stuff that'll make the babe come out afore time? She looks too grand to be a witch woman. Even if her dress be torn."

She'd torn it racing through the woods with Jan Brinker. And once she'd fallen in the mud beside the path. "I'm not a witch," Jennet said. "And I don't know how to—"

"Yes, you do." It was Martha who interrupted. "I talked to Ada Carruthers. All of them in the tanneries said how you could use the knife good as any surgeon or barber. Good as your pa. Till you got so high and mighty you wouldn't do it no more. Well, you ain't so high and mighty tonight. Not with half the town baying for your blood and worse. So do it. Help Ellen here and I'll help you. Fair exchange."

Jennet shook her head. "I stopped doing surgery because I promised my husband."

"Well, he ain't here to see, is he? And Jan says he ran off and left you to the mob. So—"

"He didn't! Solomon would never do such a thing. He's been gone three days. Traveling north." Jennet broke off, but not before she saw the look of calculation in the other woman's eyes.

Martha Kincaid's expression was neutral, and her voice sounded weary. "Ah, stop your blatherin'. Don't I know how a woman tells herself her man is good whether he is or not? Anyways, this ain't about you or him. It's about Ellen. A pa gives his daughter a babe, it'll be a freak. Like one of them cursed souls out there." She jerked her head in the direction of the taproom.

The girl in the bed sat up and grabbed Jennet's arm. "Please, mistress, you got to do somethin' for me. Any in the town finds out, they'll put me in the ducking chair. Flog me, even." She moaned. "I'm gonna hang myself if nobody—"

"You need do no such thing," Jennet said, removing herself from Ellen's grasp. "If you're determined not to have the child, there are powders you can take that will expel the babe." She'd heard the women in the tanneries talk about the potion. Some swore it was always effective, others said it worked only half the time, but they all knew where to get it. "I know someone who can make it."

"Sweet Christ!" Martha Kincaid's words dripped scorn. "Don't you think I know about that?"

Jennet didn't flinch at hearing the woman curse like a man. Not after all the time she'd spent in the tanneries. "Then why haven't you gotten the powder for her?"

"The black lass in the apothecary as makes it ain't there no more. The mistress won't do it. Not for the likes of us."

"Tamsyn? No, probably not. But what do you mean Phoebe isn't there?"

"She ran away, three weeks past. Christ, you rich folks; sometimes I wonder if you need someone to wipe your arse when you shit. Don't hear nothin' livin' like you do, behind them fences in your fancy houses."

"Ran away! If they catch her she'll be flogged. But why would Phoebe run away? She loves being an apothecary."

"That's as may be. But it won't keep her warm on a winter's night or give her a babe of her own to suckle. Wanted to marry, she did. One of Craddock's other slaves. Craddock wouldn't give permission. So they runned away together."

"Stop goin' on 'bout some blackbird ain't even here!" Ellen shouted. "I'm the one's in trouble. You be all I got to help me, mistress. You don't take the babe, I be cursed and I might as well be dead."

Jennet shook her head. "I can't. I'm sorry. I haven't the skill."

"You never asked me 'bout Meg and Peg," Martha Kincaid interrupted, watching Jennet. "You remember, the twins what was stuck together."

"I remember," Jennet whispered.

"Didn't see 'em out front, did you?"

"No."

"Good thing that is. 'Cause if you had you'da been seein' ghosts. Dead these past two years, are Meg and Peg. Want to know how they died, Mistress DaSilva?" Jennet shook her head, but Martha Kincaid went on. "Cut 'emselves apart. With the knife I use to butcher a pig if I can catch it. Did it together, like they did everything else. Two hands on the one handle. Only, after it was done they couldn't stop the bleedin'. None of us could."

Jennet felt the vomit rise in her throat. She swallowed and gripped the wooden bedstead.

Ellen started to sob.

Martha ignored the weeping girl. "You said your husband was away on business. And what sort of business might that be, mistress? Them Indians to the north ain't too friendly. Not the French soldiers, neither. Real dangerous it can be to go traveling these days."

Jennet's knuckles were white on the bedpost. Martha Kincaid knew. "My husband has many interests."

"He's rich as a lord, that's for sure, but them as has always wants more. That's how the world works, isn't it, Mistress DaSilva? Specially with Jews. Nothin's too dangerous if it's likely to make a profit."

"I'll need hot water," Jennet said. "Plenty of it. And rags, and a darning needle, and some yarn. And a stick or a poker long enough to reach up into her belly."

She chose a thin wooden stick, nearly two feet long, made out of dense oak so it was strong. "Black Bento," Martha explained, "he whittled that for me. To use when we boil clothes over the fire."

The end of the stick was rounded, and the whole was well smoothed. It seemed to Jennet safer than the two knives and the metal skewer that were her other options.

Martha had begun pouring rum down Ellen's throat. The girl choked and sputtered and whimpered, but she drank. When it seemed as if she'd had enough, Martha carried the empty tankard back to the taproom and returned with four women: the one with the red devil's mark, one who had lost an eye and most of her nose to the pox, one whose right leg was considerably shorter than her left, and a huge black woman.

Ellen lay flat on the bed, naked below the waist, with her knees flexed. "You hold her down," Martha told the women. "Mistress DaSilva here, she'll do what needs doin'."

The women all knew Ellen's story. They nodded and took up their positions.

Jennet began. Very slowly and gently, with great caution, she inserted the thin stick into the girl's vagina. Ellen didn't move. Passed out from the rum, probably.

The stick went in about six inches, then met resistance. Jennet knew she was at the place where the vagina joined the womb, the *uterus,* as her father's medical books called it. She had seen a sketch made by someone who'd been present at an anatomy when a dead woman's belly was cut open and a living child found inside. The text clearly said that until her time came, there was only a tiny opening into a woman's womb. Somehow she had to force her way in.

Her own babe was—

No, not now.

She pulled the stick back an inch or two, then inserted it again with more force this time. The resistance was still there. Jennet probed a second time. And a third. Still without success. Ellen came out of her drunken stupor and began to struggle against the grip of the women. Her moans grew louder. "Stop. Stop, I tell ye. I'll birth the cursed freak bastard and kill it soon as it comes out. Stop!"

"Be quiet," Jennet said through clenched teeth. "You're getting exactly what you asked for." She tried a fourth time to force the stick into the womb. And a fifth. Each thrust was more forceful than the one before. Ellen screamed.

"Mother of Jesus," the woman with the devil's mark chortled softly. "If you can't take that much shoved up your twat, Ellen my girl, you've a lonely life ahead of you."

"Aye, and lucky you are to get it so skinny," the large black woman added, bearing down on Ellen's left shoulder. "I've had a lot harder fucking than that most days since I was nine."

"Aye, me as well." The one with the short leg looked no older than Ellen; she seemed to be enjoying her part in this business. "You ought be sellin' tickets, Martha," she said with a huge grin. "There's plenty o' men would pay to watch a girl get fucked with a wooden stick."

"Watch your mouth or I'll fill it full o' ashes." Martha was standing behind the bed, stroking Ellen's forehead, making soft, wordless sounds of comfort. "How much more you got to do, mistress?"

"I can't say." Jennet concentrated on her task. This time she withdrew the stick a full four inches and rammed it back in with all the force she could muster. Suddenly it seemed to be gripped by something.

"Stop, bitch!" Ellen screamed and thrashed about.

"For God's sake," Jennet shouted to the women, "hold her still!" She had to have gotten from the vagina to the uterus. Where else could the stick go? She pushed harder. Ellen screamed again, a wordless shriek that curdled the blood.

Martha Kincaid clamped her hand over Ellen's mouth, muffling the girl's anguish. She looked up. "Mistress . . ."

Jennet was frozen. She might actually be in the uterus, but now she had no idea what to do next.

"Mistress?" Martha Kincaid whispered anxiously. "What are you waitin' on? Finish it."

An operation half done was a death sentence, she'd heard her father say so a dozen times. And Lucas Turner had written that a surgeon's first obligation was to his patient, and the second was to advance the knowledge of other surgeons. *But no matter how well Informed we Become, it is Folly to think we can ever Operate in the Black Caverns of the Belly or the Chest, or that we'll Saw our way into the Skull. Those who imagine that some day we will Perform such Atrocities on Living Flesh are as Misguided as those who believe the Time can Come when there is Surgery Without pain.*

Operating in the dark cavern of the belly, on what you couldn't see. God help her, she was doing exactly what Lucas wrote should never be done. But Martha Kincaid had left her no choice. She was doing it for Solomon's sake, and for the sake of their child.

Jennet shoved the stick in deeper. Ellen arched her back and struggled, but the women held her fast. "For God's sake," Jennet whispered, "keep her still." She began rocking the stick, twisting and turning it. The girl on the bed had developed the superhuman strength that came with agony. She tore herself out of the grip of all but the huge black woman, and jerked her mouth free of Martha Kincaid's restraining hand, shrieking. "I curses you all to hell I does!"

"For the love of Christ, child!" Martha shouted. "You're making it a hundred times worse."

Ellen had thrown them all off now. The wooden stick was still buried deep inside her body, and Jennet grimly maintained her grip on the other end. "I curse you to hell, witch!" the girl screamed as she struggled into a half-sitting position. "Forever and ever! I curse you to hell."

Martha Kincaid managed to grab Ellen's shoulders and wrestle her back to the bed. Finally she got her hand over the girl's mouth. "Quiet! Bite your tongue and bear it! Do you want every man in the taproom to know what we're doin' in here?"

The women had drawn back from the bed, looking suddenly terrified.

"Ah, for Christ's sake," Martha said turning her head so she could face them, her voice weary. "Stop lookin' like pigs about to get their throats slit. Get back where you were, all of you, and hold her down till it's over. Sooner we're done the less chance any out there will know what we be doin'."

It didn't count that every man in the taproom was himself either a freak or a fugitive. Come to something like this, they'd all make noises like gentlemen of property. A woman gets herself out of breeding, she ought to be made to feel the full rigor of the law, as they called it. As for whoever helped her to do it, flogging was too kind.

"Filling our bellies," Martha whispered, her face hanging over Ellen's, one hand stroking the girl's hair even as the other kept a stifling grip over her mouth. "Givin' us babes we love too much to leave. And us needin' the few coppers they bring home to put a bit o' bread in the wee ones' mouths, that's what makes us stay. Until they use us up, or find somethin' better and throw us out. Come the day we find a way to stop birthin' unless we wants to, that be the day we're as free as they are. Ain't a man alive can stand the thought o' that."

The women holding Ellen down were all looking sideways at the door to the taproom. "It's all right," Martha said, trying hard to sound as if she believed her own words. "Too busy fuckin' and boozin' they are to care what's goin' on in here. But holy Christ, Mistress DaSilva, are you not done yet?"

"I'm not sure." Jennet was trying desperately to feel what she couldn't see. "I can't quite—"

Ellen gave a frantic jerk that almost freed her and a loud groan wormed its way around the edges of Martha Kincaid's palm.

Jennet thrust the stick forward one last time, forcing it deeper into wherever it was. Then she twisted it around in quick circular motions. Oh God, as if she were stirring porridge.

Ellen gave another violent lurch. She still hadn't broken free, but she had managed to yank her head away from Martha's clasp, and she screamed. "Stop! Witch woman! You be killing me! I curse you! Stop!"

Jennet stopped twisting the stick and withdrew it. She'd done all she could. If it wasn't enough, so be it. Ellen's screams became whimpering sobs. Jennet's chest was heaving. The mental and physical struggle had exhausted her. She closed her eyes and fought for breath.

"Mistress." The girl who was holding Ellen's right leg jostled Jennet's arm. "Look at that, mistress." Jennet opened her eyes and glanced down. Clots of blood and globs of mucus were oozing from Ellen's vagina. The girl who'd spoken began to swipe at the mess with her apron.

"Not with that," Jennet was hoarse with fatigue. "Get the cloths and hot water from over by the fire," she whispered. "Sponge her clean."

Tired as she was, she couldn't turn away from her patient. So much blood. And those viscous lumps, was one of them the almost-child? If her baby, hers and Solomon's, were aborted, would it look the same? Was it different from this filth because it was a child conceived in love?

"Mistress," one of the women said, "can't you do nothin'?"

She couldn't seem to focus, but she had to. A bright red river covered the inside of the girl's thighs. And the bed. And the hands of all who tried to stanch the flow.

"Jesus, I ain't never thought there was that much blood in a person." That from the young girl Martha Kincaid had threatened to make eat ashes. "Bloody awful it is. You've like to killed her, mistress. Look how still she be."

Jennet rushed to the head of the bed. Ellen lay inert, her head lolling, her mouth slack. Jennet shoved the others out of the way and put her ear to the girl's chest. She picked up a weak, thready sound, raised her head, and looked closely at her patient. Ellen's breaths came short and choppy, and her skin had a faint blue pallor. "Dear God, she's lost too much blood."

"Aye, far too much blood," Martha Kincaid said quietly. "We can all see that. Can't you do nothing?"

Jennet went back to the foot of the bed. The hemorrhage had slowed, but even if she'd had proper ligatures of sheep's intenstines, there was nothing she could see to use them on. Besides, her covert practice of surgery had never extended to such art. But now, totally desperate, Jennet stretched a tentative hand toward the needle and the yarn she had requested earlier.

"You gonna sew up her twat, mistress?" This from the black woman.

"Might as well," the woman with the devil's mark said. "She'll not be needing it. Gone she is. God rest her soul."

"No!" Jennet returned to the head of the bed. She listened for a heartbeat, then put her palm to the girl's forehead. The skin was already cooling. "Get me a bit of mirror. Quickly! We can see if she's breathing and—"

"No need." Martha's voice was quiet. "The likes of us, we know death when we sees it."

"There's something else." Jennet couldn't get the words out fast enough. "I can put my blood in—"

"There's nothing you can do." Martha Kincaid put her arm around Jennet's shoulders, as if they were equals. "C'mon, lass. You've had as much trouble as one evening can bring. I'll not let you add witchcraft to whatever your sins may be. As for poor Ellen, don't go thinkin' you killed her. It's a man what done that."

The brick walls of the DaSilva mansion on Nassau Street, though darkened by smoke and soot, still stood. But the roof was open to the sky. Both the town's fire wagons had been trundled to the scene, but the volunteers had concentrated on dousing the neighboring houses to keep the conflagration from spreading.

That fierce the blaze had been. As if the many splendors of Solomon DaSilva's wealth had burned more fiercely than the ordinary things in an ordinary dwelling. The whole street could easily have gone up in flames, and the next, and possibly the one after that. Everyone's worst terror. This time it hadn't happened. A downpour had begun shortly before midnight. At dawn it was still a steady drizzle.

Christopher drew the edges of his coat closer together against the damp and ignored the water that dripped down his neck from the brim of his tricorn. A few of the city's ever present pigs were rooting around in the still-smoldering ashes. "You're sure there's been no sign of any of them?" he asked Luke for the third time. "Not Jennet or Solomon or the servants?"

"None." Luke kicked a booted foot against the blackened remains of one of the white pillars, now a dark finger pointing accusingly at heaven. "I got here almost as soon as the thing started. The mob was standing around and watching. Some of them still held the burning torches they'd used to start the blaze."

"And you held . . . that." Christopher nodded to the musket Luke carried.

"Yes. And if I'd been in time I'd have used it. Brought it because I'd heard they were going after the town's Jews."

"Bastards. Solomon's a good man. They'd no cause."

"Good to us, at any rate," Luke agreed. "Pity I was too late."

"Don't blame yourself, son. You tried. Solomon will be grateful. But you're sure you didn't see him or your sister? Or the servants?"

"Neither white nor black. Just a crowd of rabble stirred up by the election business. And, like I said, him."

"Caleb Devrey." Christopher still couldn't quite credit it. "You're absolutely sure?"

"Absolutely," Luke said.

The cousins had stared at each other in the light cast by the inferno that had been Solomon DaSilva's grand home. "Devrey was at the head of the pack." The words were bitter in Luke's mouth, but he took some satisfaction in saying them aloud. "He was the leader."

"May he rot in hell." Christopher's jaw was white with the effort not to howl his rage. And his fear. After a few seconds he regained control. "They must be safe somewhere, Luke. Solomon would never let anything happen to Jennet. And Caleb Devrey's feelings were no secret. A man like Solomon DaSilva . . . he's bound to have taken precautions."

In 1608, when the French first established a foothold in Canada, there were three thousand Wendat Island People. The French called them Huron, ruffians. By 1737 only three hundred Huron remained in the homeland they knew as Hochelaga and the French called Québec.

Those Huron who had survived the sicknesses the Europeans brought with them, and the Beaver Wars the tribes fought over the fur trade they introduced, lived as their ancestors had done for as long as anyone could remember, in long-houses surrounding a huge fire pit.

Spread-eagled on the ground, his arms and legs pegged to stakes driven deep into the earth, Solomon could smell the fire, thick wood smoke redolent with pine and crackling with pitch. "Going to burn us, are they?" he asked, turning his head to see Shea, staked out beside him. "Ritual fires to appease their gods?"

"Not exactly," the Irishman said. "The Mohawk, the Oneida, the Cayuga and the rest o' the Iroquois, they's the ones as does that kind o' burnin'. The Huron, they got ways o' their own."

DaSilva tried to raise his head and see what was happening. A moccasin slammed it back to the earth. "*Merda*," he muttered. "*Filho da puta* . . ." Seemed he could say what he liked, as long as he didn't try to move. "Shea," he said, this time without turning his head, "You can speak to them. Tell them the rifles they captured aren't the half of what we have. Say we'll bring them fifty more next week if they let us go."

"Sure and do you not think I tried that already? They ain't interested. They know them rifles they took from us was goin' to the Mohawk. Ain't nobody in this world the Huron hates more'n the Mohawk. That's a big part of it."

"What's the rest of it?" DaSilva asked.

"I ain't sure," the Irishman said softly. "Maybe huntin' ain't been so good this summer. Maybe they's hungry for a bit o' fresh meat."

Phoebe rolled herself closer to Jethro, welcoming the warmth of his body. The ground was hard and smelled of frost. It had not occurred to either of them that the farther north they went, the more mid-September would feel like the dead of winter in New York City.

"Jethro, you asleep?"

"No."

"You got any idea why we don't be seein' them Indians yet?"

"Must be they don't want to be seen."

Phoebe sighed. That's what she'd thought as well. "But everybody says they take in runaway Negro folks. Treat 'em good and let 'em live in their villages. So why they be hidin' from us?"

"Don't know." Jethro put his arm around her and drew her close. "But I figure the only choice we got be to keep goin' the way we be headed. Sooner or later the Indians will figure out we mean no harm. Then maybe they be lettin' us see 'em."

"If I can make 'em understand what be in my basket, Jethro, what I can do, I know they be taking us in. We be real useful to 'em."

"Right now," he murmured against her hair, "how 'bout you bein' useful to me?"

Phoebe giggled.

The man watching in the woods licked his lips. Christ, he was on fire. Had to have been a month or more since he had a woman. And blackbirds were sweet. Better'n white women, lots o' times. Definitely better'n squaws. On t'other hand, runaway slaves brought a bounty. Double if you took 'em alive this close to the border. Up here the redcoats were real nervous.

The rain had cooled the cinders and damped down the ash. Jennet was able to step over the broken glass and jagged brick into what had been her drawing room.

Three nights past she'd sat there safe and warm and considered how she could make Solomon promise to stop selling guns to the savages.

"T'ain't no use hangin' about here, mevrouw. Better you come back to Martha's with me. I'll keep a sharp lookout for Mijnheer DaSilva. Soon as he be anywhere near I'll—"

"What's the condition of the stairs?" Jennet picked her way across the blackened earth. "Have you been upstairs?"

"No, mevrouw. There ain't no stairs anymore." Jan Brinker followed her, speaking with quiet urgency. "No upstairs neither. I told you, mevrouw. Nothin's left. But what do you care? You're alive. Mijnheer DaSilva, he'll build you another house, mevrouw. Soon as he gets home. You just come back to Martha's with me."

"Why do you keep looking over your shoulder like that? What are you afraid of?" She was standing where the stairs should have been, looking up at the starry sky and the bright moon, and the blackened timbers that once supported the pitched roof with the shiny white balustrade that ran round the edge. Solomon was very particular about that balustrade. It had to be given a fresh coat of paint every six months. "Will the mob come back, Jan Brinker? Is that what's worrying you?"

"I don't know, mevrouw. But the way things are in the town . . ."

"Wasn't the fire enough sport for the rabble? And for Caleb, of course. My loving cousin, Caleb Devrey. He did this, didn't he?"

"*Ja,* it be him, mevrouw. I swear it. Mijnheer DaSilva, he . . ."

"Yes, you told me. He paid you to watch Caleb. That's how you happened to be here when I needed you." She heard her own voice, calm, unconcerned, and wondered where it came from. "Did Flossie and Tilda get away as well? Caleb and the rest, they got the house, but none of the occupants? Is that why they're not satisfied?"

"I told you, mevrouw. I don't know nothin'. Must be them two you mentioned got clear, since I never heard nothin' 'bout them."

"Ah, that implies you heard something about other matters. What were they, Jan Brinker?"

"Nothing special, mevrouw. Only that the Morrisites got their way in the end. They took the Jews out of the count, said they couldn't vote in New York no more. Mijnheer De Lancey's candidate ain't gonna sit in the Assembly. It's Morris's man what got elected."

"How fortunate for him. And for all the upstanding men of New York who voted for him. Like my cousin Caleb, perhaps. Do you think he voted before he led his mob here and torched my house? Do you think he did his civic duty and voted?"

"Can't say, mevrouw. But I know he be on the Morrisites' side. Even if he do be friends with Mijnheer De Lancey's brother."

"Yes, Caleb's a real man of the people. Anxious for justice for the common folk."

"Mevrouw, it's not safe to be here. The watchmen will be coming around. And the town's still all riled up. Everyone's sayin' if the rain hadn't come the whole city might have burned."

"Indeed." Jennet gathered up her skirt of rough homespun and began making her way back toward the street. Martha Kincaid had loaned Jennet clothes, and a white mobcap to cover her long dark hair. She might have been the girl she once was, the daughter of the impoverished surgeon whom everyone despised. "Tell me, Jan Brinker, if the town is so exercised about what could have happened to their property, are they about to put Caleb Devrey in the stocks? Or try him for willful arson? Have you heard anything about that?"

"No, mevrouw."

"No? Why is it I am not surprised?"

"They say it be the Jews what done it, mevrouw."

"The Jews? My husband's fellow Jews came here shouting for Jews' blood and burned a Jew's house?"

"*Ja.* That's what folks be sayin'. Now we got to go. Otherwise—"

"Yes. I know about otherwise. Be quiet for a moment, Jan Brinker. Let me think."

Martha Kincaid's bawdyhouse was out of the question. It was safe, but she couldn't bear it another minute. Solomon might not be back for four or five days. It wasn't unusual for him to be gone a week or ten days on these trips, and he slipped home in the dead of night. The dwarf might miss him. How then would Solomon find her? She had never told him about Martha Kincaid's.

Her father's house was possible. Or her brother's. Luke had a new house on Ann Street. It was less crowded than Hall Place, and she'd always gotten on well with the bride Luke brought back from Edinburgh. But if she went to either her father or her elder brother, she was placing herself once more under their authority. She couldn't bear that either. Besides, if the feeling in the town was as the dwarf said, her presence could put her family in danger. Better to go elsewhere. Once she was sure her father couldn't find her, she'd send him a note to say she was safe.

The ring of a handbell pierced the silence of the night. "Mevrouw . . ."

"Yes, very well. I've decided."

"Thank God. Now come, hurry."

"No. I'm not going back with you to the bawdyhouse, Jan Brinker."

"But, mevrouw—"

"I'm going to my husband's . . . to his establishment over by Hudson's River. I would be glad of an escort. Will you accompany me?"

Brinker hesitated only a moment. It wasn't as good as having her at Martha Kincaid's but she'd be safe. That was what mattered: keeping her safe until Solomon DaSilva got back. "*Ja,* sure, mevrouw. Why not? Only let us leave here. Now."

The bell was growing louder. Jennet turned and took one last look at the burned-out ruin that had been her home. She spotted a faint gleam amid the cinders. It was the gold horse's head with the ruby eyes, the one that had topped Solomon's favorite walking stick.

Jennet bent down and reclaimed it, wiping it clean on her skirt. It left an ugly black smudge on the homespun. Then, with great deliberation, Jennet pressed her right hand against the soot-blackened bricks of the wall beside the vanished front door.

"Mevrouw, please." The dwarf's voice was an urgent whisper. "What are you doing? We have to—"

"I'm taking a memento." Slowly, and with great care, Jennet wiped her soot-stained hand on the homespun skirt, making the black smudge even more obvious. For some seconds she looked at it, dark and ominous in the moonlight.

"Come," she said finally. "We will go now. You and I, we have a long way to travel."

IV

"Why have you brought me here, Jan Brinker?" It was three days since Jennet had seen the dwarf. Not since they arrived at Solomon's fanciest bordello and discovered Flossie and Tilda already there. Now he was leading her up a steep and narrow path to the top of a cliff overlooking Hudson's River, scurrying ahead of her on his skinny little legs.

Jennet was annoyed with herself for becoming short of breath so quickly. Time was when she could have climbed this hill with no difficulty whatever. Now, though she didn't think her belly yet betrayed her secret, she moved in a different manner, and she did not like it.

"I told you to bring the note to Hall Place and say nothing. If you expect a reward when Solomon returns, you are to tell no one where I am. So what is all this nonsense about someone wanting to see me?"

She didn't want anyone to see her. Only that morning, when she finished her bath, Flossie had eyed her with a knowing look. Jennet was determined to say nothing to anyone until she'd told Solomon . . . Ah, thank heaven. The top of the hill at last. And someone waiting over by that tree the wind had bent into such a curious position. "Amba! In heaven's name, what are you doing here?"

Jennet didn't wait for an answer. She rounded on the dwarf, shaking her finger at him. "I warned you there would be no reward if you told where—"

"I be the one made the *haptoa* tell me where you be hiding," Amba said. "I told him I'd hex him. A big hex. A lot bigger than he be. A killing hex."

Jan Brinker listened with his oversized bald head hunched down in his narrow shoulders, and one hand shielding his face, half covering his eyes. "That's what she said, mevrouw. She swore she'd hex me. And I knew she could do it."

"Go away," Jennet said. "Stop your whinging and leave us."

"But mevrouw, I couldn't—"

"Go!"

The dwarf hurried off. Jennet watched until he'd begun to slide down the cliff path; then she turned back to Amba.

It was early evening and the late-September air had developed an autumn chill. Seagulls swooped and cawed, filling their bellies from the abundant waters of the river. "Does my mother know where you've gone?" Jennet asked. Amba shook her head. "My father?" Another shake of the head. "You'll be missed. And possibly punished when you return."

"Amba not be scared of no punishment. You know that, Mistress Jennet."

"You shouldn't call me that now that I'm a married lady. I'm Mistress DaSilva now."

"Wiped your bottom until you be old enough to do it for yourself. No be changing the way I call you." The shorn head inclined toward Jennet's belly. "You be with child. Your mama been thinking you wouldn't never give her no grandbaby. Asked me to make a spell would make it happen."

"And did you?"

"What you be thinking?"

"I think you want white people to imagine that you know special African magic. But you don't, Amba. It's a fraud. Like all your talk of being a queen. You're a black slave, same as any other."

When she was little, when she and Phoebe used to sit in the kitchen and listen to Amba's tales of being royalty in Africa, she had believed every word. Now all she could think of was the way Amba always managed to make it seem as if the white people were the slaves and she the owner. And the way she'd made Jan Brinker break his promise to tell no one where Jennet was. "If you had real magical power, you'd have escaped years ago. Gone back to wherever you came from so you could be a queen again. But you're still here and you're still a slave. —Oh, Amba, don't! You mustn't cry. I'm sorry. I shouldn't have said such things. I didn't mean—"

Amba had turned away. Her shoulders were heaving though she didn't make a sound. It was the first time Jennet had ever seen her weep. "Amba, please. What's wrong? I didn't mean to make you cry."

"You be right." Amba turned. The tears had gone as quickly as they came. "When I need the magic most, I ain't got enough of it. But you do. You got more magic than your papa. I been listenin' to everything your mama and papa been saying these near six years since you ran off and got married. Solomon DaSilva, he can make anything he want happen. I need him to want to make something happen."

"My husband isn't here, Amba. And he can't send you back to your home."

"You be talking foolish. Like when you be a little girl. Amba didn't come to get herself sent back to her home people. Amba came because of Phoebe."

"Phoebe! They've found her, then?" Amba nodded. "And the boy who was with her?"

"Jethro. He be dead."

"I see. Well, he knew what would happen if he was caught. Phoebe may as well take her flogging and have done with it. She brought it on herself. Anyway, I don't think anything I'd say would stop her getting sent to the whipping cage."

"They no be going to whip my girl."

"No? Very well, I'm glad to hear it. You know I'm fond of Phoebe."

"They be going to burn my girl dead."

"Where did you get such an idea? Papa wouldn't let that happen. Phoebe's not worth a penny to him if she's dead."

"Ain't your papa going to be burning my girl. Not that Craddock man, neither. Be the redcoats." Jennet stared at her in disbelief. "My Phoebe and her Jethro, they be found near the land of the other white tribe. The ones be your enemy."

"The French," Jennet said. "Sweet heaven. They were found near the Canadian border?"

"Yes. Redcoats be saying my Phoebe and her Jethro be telling the enemy tribe secrets from this place, so they got to die. They shot Jethro. Now them redcoats be bringing Phoebe back here. Going to burn her in her home place. Front of City Hall in a slow fire. Just like what happened to her papa."

Rosa Jollette had a small parlor near the large drawing room where the gentlemen came to drink and play cards before moving on to other pleasures. Jennet knew Rosa was always there in the early evening before the guests arrived. She pushed open the door without knocking. Her entry was unexpected enough so she caught the older woman gritting her teeth at the sight of her employer's wife.

"I need to speak with you."

"I'm at your service, of course, Mistress DaSilva." All sweetness and smiles now. "But if it could wait until tomorrow, perhaps? The gentlemen will be arriving shortly."

"It can't wait." Jennet had not been invited to sit, but she did so anyway, drawing a chair with carved wooden legs and a brocaded seat closer to Rosa Jollette's elegant writing table. "There are English officers who come here, are there not? I believe I've spied men in uniform in the drawing room."

"All the most influential men of New York come to this house, mistress. I have labored hard to make it a place worthy of their—"

"Yes. Following my husband's instructions and using his money."

It was the first time she'd spoken to the woman with any hint of authority. Flossie had pressed her relentlessly to assume the role of mistress of Solomon's financial affairs and put Rosa Jollette in her place. Said she should take over such tasks as the daily counting of cash in the little room down in the cellar, and receiving the proceeds from Solomon's other interests. Jennet had refused because, she told herself, if she did those things it was an admission that Solomon was not going to return, and that it was up to her to assume responsibility for protecting what was his and her child's. Flossie had done it in her stead, but Rosa Jollette knew who was her real enemy in this time of uncertainty. She looked at Jennet with barely suppressed loathing.

Jennet pretended not to notice. "What rank of redcoat is the highest you're likely to receive of an evening?"

Rosa Jollette's eyes narrowed. "That's hard to say, Mistress DaSilva. We frequently have a number of lieutenants. Sometimes a major. Even a general or two. I can't know who will call until they arrive."

"Very well. This evening, whatever the hour, you're to send for me the moment you see any English officer who is at least a lieutenant. The very instant. Do you understand?"

"Of course I understand, Mistress DaSilva. But I assure you the master would not approve of—"

"I will be the judge of what my husband does or does not approve. And I daresay he'll be interested in my opinion of his employees when he returns." Jennet stood and looked down at the other woman. "The first redcoat who's a lieutenant or better," she repeated. "The very moment he arrives."

The redcoat turned out to be a colonel. Jennet saw him in the tiny parlor, having first evicted Rosa Jollette and spent a moment making her preparations.

The new gowns Flossie had ordered had not yet arrived from the mantua-maker, so Jennet borrowed a red lace frock from the whore closest to her size. It was decidedly tight at the waist, and her breasts were so much fuller now that she was carrying, they were barely contained by the bodice. The colonel stared at her appreciatively. "To what do I owe the honor of this meeting, Mistress DaSilva? I am, I must say, quite surprised to find you here."

"I doubt that, Colonel . . . Fenwick, did you say?"

"I did. Colonel Alden Fenwick of His Majesty's Fourth Regiment of Horse. At your service, mistress."

The uniform was splendid. Any man would have looked handsome with so much gold braid decorating his crimson coat. And that little bow of the head was most winning. Jennet had never before had dealings with a high-ranking British officer. She found the manner of his speech and the way he looked truly charming. Which had nothing to do with the fact that she despised him for his insolence.

"It's not often a man visits a bordello and is greeted by the wife of the owner."

"You mock me, Colonel Fenwick. The whole town knows that I've been burnt out of my home and made a fugitive, and for no reason except my husband's race. So why is it a surprise to find me sheltering in the one place where I'm likely to be protected?"

"I'm sure the civilian authorities are trying to discover who it was set fire to your home, mistress. And can offer you the protection of—"

"The authorities, as you call them, are trying to discover nothing. Everyone knows who torched my home. They prefer to turn a blind eye." Jennet snapped her red lace fan shut and leaned forward, giving Fenwick a still more excellent view of her all but naked breasts. "Forgive me, Colonel. You have come seeking pleasure, and it is not my intention to waste your time speaking about my personal misfortunes. I wish to discuss another matter."

Fenwick, she noted, looked intrigued. With her tits, of course, but also with her words. "Indeed. What matter is that?"

"My father's black slave Phoebe. She ran away. A foolish business involving another slave whom she wished to marry, whatever that might mean among the Negroes. Phoebe was recently captured, by soldiers as it happened. I'm told she's under sentence of death and being brought to New York to be publicly burned. As a warning to others."

"I have not heard of the matter."

"You may take me at my word, Colonel. It is as I say."

"Very well. Then it must be that she was apprehended within forty miles of Quebec. Bringing intelligence to the enemy."

"Close to Quebec, yes. But Phoebe had no intelligence to bring to anyone. She's a slave who wanted to marry and was refused permission. She is guilty of willfulness and not knowing her place, nothing more. Admittedly she is a fine apothecary and in that respect might have been useful to the French. But she knows less of military matters than I do. And, I assure you, I know nothing at all."

Fenwick cocked his head and studied her. "Somehow," he said softly, "I do not get the impression, Mistress DaSilva, that there is anything to do with men about which you're ignorant."

"You flatter me, sir. Though being married to my husband, I have of course learned some things."

Fenwick's mouth was dry. This luscious creature seemed to be offering herself to him in return for whatever he could do for some blackbird caught trafficking with the enemy. God knew she was better-looking than anything he'd find in La Jollette's drawing room. Hell, she might well be the most beautiful woman he'd seen in New York. "Tell me, mistress, how is it that we're free to have this conversation? Where is your husband this fine evening?"

"Gone to Philadelphia." The lie came easily. She'd planned it, along with everything else about this meeting. "It struck my husband that if he could negotiate a better arrangement with the Pennsylvania millers about their flour, a unified price perhaps, New Yorkers might be more inclined to leave us in peace."

"I see. That's a long journey, isn't it? All the way to Philadelphia. He might be gone a month or more."

"Indeed. At least a month."

He'd never seen eyes so dark a blue. The color of the ocean when the sun shone on it. A man could drown in such eyes. "You must be lonely without your husband, Mistress DaSilva." He leaned toward her, his face almost touching hers.

"Oh, I am," Jennet said. "But we women are accustomed to waiting for you men to conclude your affairs before you can pay attention to us." She opened her fan and slipped it between them, her eyes continuing to smile at him above the lacy edge. While he was staring at her, almost salivating, her free hand dipped into the drawer of Rosa Jollette's writing table and withdrew the stack of coins she'd placed there earlier. Thank God Flossie had taken over the finances. She'd have been hard-pressed to get a wooden penny from the madam. "Fortunately, Colonel, my husband left me well able to do whatever might be necessary in his absence."

Fenwick heard the clink of the coins. He drew back, eyes narrowed, darting from her to the money, no longer sure of exactly what was happening.

Jennet lowered her fan and let him see her radiant smile. "Fifty Dutch *daalders*, Colonel." She pushed the stack of coins closer to his side of the table. "Recompense for doing me and my family a simple favor."

Fenwick came from wealth, but like most British officers he was a second son. His elder brother would inherit, not he. The allowance his father made him was a pittance, the salary paid him by the Crown little more. And there were uniforms, and arms, and horses to be bought, and servants' wages—at least three servants, given his rank. The gold coins winked at him in the light of the candles. "A favor to do with this slave, I take it."

"With Phoebe, yes. I simply require that you see that the sentence is remanded and my father's property restored to him. I'm sure a gentleman of such high rank as you can find a way to do that." Fenwick said nothing. He did not, Jennet noted, protest that he could have no influence over the sentence. "Phoebe is no spy, Colonel Fenwick. Burning her would be a waste of a skilled slave with years of labor left."

"Carrying intelligence to the French is a capital offense. Runaway slaves caught within forty miles of the Canadian border are executed. It's very difficult—"

Too late. He'd made plain that he could step in if he wanted to. All they were discussing now was the price. A second stack of *daalders* joined the first. A hundred coins, more than his income for the next five years. "If Phoebe is returned to my father's house unharmed, I assure you there will be an equal sum waiting for you here immediately afterward."

"That is a great deal of money, Mistress DaSilva."

Jennet shrugged. "Not more than the cost of a good slave, Colonel Fenwick. Of course it would easily pay for more than one fine steed, and a fair number of splendid uniforms."

Fenwick reached out and swept both piles of coins toward him. "The balance to be paid in coin, here?"

"Yes. I will myself deliver the money, Colonel. The very day Phoebe is returned to my father. You have my word on it."

"Indeed. And what gentleman could doubt the word of a fine lady like yourself, Mistress DaSilva?"

V

Let the bowl pass, drink to the lass, I warrant she'll prove an excuse for the glass.

That she had, whoever she was. The bowl had passed Caleb Devrey so damned often he was drowning in rum punch. He staggered across the cobbles of Broad Street, catching Oliver's arm to steady himself. "Listen, I need to piss."

"Not here, Caleb. Old biddy Livingston across the way is sure to be watching from behind her lace curtains. A few more steps and you can piss as much as you like and offend no one."

Etienne De Lancey, the father of James and Oliver, was a French Huguenot who had escaped to New York in 1685, when Protestant blood ran in the gutters of Paris. Two things made him rich: he married a well-dowered Van Cortlandt daughter, and he had a head for trade. In 1719 Etienne had built the house on the corner of Pearl Street and Broad—tall, square, redbrick, with long elegant windows and a steep balustraded roof—that became the model for the home of every other wealthy New York merchant with social aspirations.

Caleb paused by the familiar front door framed by two white columns with a fan window above the lintel. "Oliver, you rotten sod, you've betrayed me. I told you my father would skin me alive if I came home one more ti—"

De Lancey grabbed his arm and urged him forward. "Don't be difficult, old man. This is my house, not yours. Come, I thought you wanted to piss."

"I do indeed. But—"

"But nothing. Just a few more steps. That's it." They were inside, in the long ground-floor room where dinner was served promptly at three every afternoon, where Etienne's sons and their wives and children were bidden to be present at the seventy-three-year-old patriarch's table if they valued their inheritance.

Oliver shoved his foot under the massive carved sideboard and kicked forward a chamber pot. "Here you go. Piss away. Only mind your aim."

"I assure you, old man, my aim is the equal—nay, the better—of any man's in the province." Caleb undid his buttons as he spoke. "In fact, I challenge you to a pissing contest. Get yourself another pot and we'll see who can fill it first. Ten-point demerit for each splash that misses the target. A guinea to the winner."

"Master Oliver, you gentlemen best be hushing yourselves some." The black man who stood in the doorway carried a candle and shaded it with his hand. "Dr. Turner, he be upstairs just now. Whole family be up there with him."

"Good Christ, Thomas, why's that? Who's ill?"

"It's Mr. James's daughter, sir. Little Emma. She's choking with the throat bladder. The doctor, he come some ten minutes past."

Caleb fumbled himself back into his britches. He sensed Oliver looking at him. "No," he said. "If they've sent for bloody Luke Turner, they've no need of me."

"Couldn't have sent for you, could they? You were with me, drinking yourself blind at the Black Horse. For the love of Jesus, Caleb, the child's not yet lived a year."

"There's not a lot can be done for throat distemper."

"There must be something. At least come upstairs and see if Turner's doing the best that can be done. Christ, Caleb, I was dandling little Emma on my knee this very afternoon. She seemed perfectly well."

"It takes them quickly sometimes. There's not a lot . . . I'm sure even a fool like Luke Turner knows enough to cup and purge."

Oliver turned to the slave still standing in the doorway. "Thomas, is that what Dr. Turner is doing?"

"That not be what I seen, Master Oliver. Dr. Turner, he be putting a pig's spirit down baby Emma. He be telling Master James and the others the pig be powerful magic for the throat bladder."

Luke had been playing with the idea for weeks now, ever since his father did that anatomy on the girl who died in the almshouse hospital when Luke tried to open her trachea. That's why he had the thing ready when the De Lanceys summoned him. A hollow tube of copper, bent to just the right angle, no bigger across than the nail of his little finger, with the small bladder of a piglet attached to one end. Elegantly simple. If it worked.

So far it seemed to be working.

He had simply instructed the others to hold her still, then forced open the child's mouth and carefully and gently inserted the copper tube down her throat. Now he was bending over her, blowing his breath into the bladder and letting it out again, squeezing and releasing in a steady rhythm. He was too busy with the apparatus to explain what he was doing, but the little girl's skin was no longer blue and she was no longer struggling to breathe. For the moment that counted as success.

"What in Christ's he doing?"

"Good evening, Oliver. We're not exactly sure." James sounded exhausted, and—unusual for him—frightened. Emma was his youngest and favorite child. "Whatever he's doing, he can't stop long enough to tell us about it."

"Caleb here says cupping's the thing. And a strong purge with calomel. Has he—"

"No," Caleb said. "He hasn't." He'd gone close enough to the bed to peer over Luke's shoulder at the patient. The child showed no evidence of a throat blister. "Look, if you want to send someone for my bag, I can try and—"

Luke turned his head just enough to see Caleb Devrey while still breathing in and out of the pig's bladder. "No," he said in the two-second interval when he allowed the bladder to deflate. "No cupping. Waste of time."

"The literature is entirely clear on the subject. Cupping and a strong purge are . . ." Caleb knew he sounded exactly like Cadwallader-Pompous-Ass-Colden. And that he was quickly becoming more sober than he'd care to be. And that Luke looked as if he'd like to murder him. Fine. Let him try. He'd like nothing better than to kill Luke Turner and have self-defense as an excuse. "You're acting irresponsibly, Turner. These people have the right to—"

"She was choking to death. Now she's not—" Luke broke off, aware that he'd let the rage that filled him at the mere sight of Caleb Devrey interrupt the far more important task of keeping little Emma De Lancey alive. Save the favorite daughter of an influential family like the De Lanceys, you'd never want for patients again. Bloody murdering bastard Caleb Devrey could be dealt with another time. Luke returned to forcing air into his patient's lungs.

"Don't turn your back on me, you sod! I say you're wrong and your patient will pay for your stupidity." Oliver put a restraining hand on Caleb's arm, but he shook it off. "You're endangering this infant's life."

"You two can settle your heats and animosities elsewhere. Not at my daughter's sickbed." James De Lancey held a lace-trimmed cloth over his nose when he turned to Caleb. "Oliver, judging from the alcohol on his breath, I think your friend's had a bit more punch than is good for him."

The child in the bed moved her hand.

Emma's mother and two of her aunts were in the room, and all three women were instantly hovering over her. "Back," Luke said in his next rhythmic pause. The women retreated. He heard James and Oliver and Caleb speaking in the background, but he shut out the sound. Breathe into the bladder. Expel the air. Breathe into the bladder. Expel the air. Breathe into the bladder. Expel the air.

And note that after the next few sequences the child started to pour sweat, and her cheeks had some normal color. Her eyes darted around the room as if she were looking for a familiar face. Slowly, with some trepidation, Luke lifted his head. Unwittingly he held his own breath while he watched the pig's bladder. It inflated, and deflated, and inflated again. By itself. Luke put a hand on Emma's forehead. She was damp, but cool to the touch. "Fever's broken," he said into the sudden hush in the room. "And she seems to be breathing on her own."

Three weeks later, in the tavern at the sign of the Black Horse where Caleb got most of his news, he heard that little Emma De Lancey had died. Her fever had suddenly shot up and she was gone before they could summon help. "Bad luck, Oliver," he said. "I know the family were all fond of the child."

"We were. All of us. Phila's quite beside herself."

Caleb looked away. It made him uncomfortable to talk about Oliver's wife. Phila De Lancey was the daughter of Jacob Franks, a Tudesco Jew. "I did warn you," he said, staring at his mug of rum punch and avoiding Oliver's glance. "Cupping and purging. Not a lot of black-art rubbish about the spirit of a pig."

"Look, I know you detest Luke Turner, but that's not what— Ah, what difference does it make? The child's to be buried tomorrow. Anyway, she seemed to have gotten over the throat bladder. Must have been something else that took her."

Caleb shook his head. "Not at all. I've seen it numerous times. They appear to recover from *angina suffocativa,* then a few weeks later they're dead. There has to be some connection."

"Perhaps." The bowl came his way and Oliver ladled himself a double helping of punch, throwing two coppers into the center of the table to pay for it. "If, as you say, it happens all the time, you can't blame Luke Turner, can you?"

Caleb did not reply.

The oars dipped silently in and out of the December-cold waters of Hudson's River, barely breaking the gray-blue surface. The canoe traveled swiftly, moving with the tide. It stayed close to the eastern bank, the coast of Manhattan, sheltered first by the overhanging cliffs, then, at the island's southern end, by the tangled shadows of the leafless trees that grew on the sloping ground that met the river's edge.

The man who lay in the bottom of the craft had no idea where they were. He was swaddled like a papoose, wrapped in blankets and tied to a long board. He could lift his head, but not high enough to see over the canoe's side. The oarsman knelt with his back to his passenger. The two did not speak. The swaddled man could not remember how long he had lain like this, drifting in and out of consciousness. He remembered very little. Except for the things he could not forget.

After a time they landed. The Indian pulled the man on the board onto dry land and left him lying there while he hid the canoe in the scrubby bushes along the shore. Then, dragging the board behind him, he moved farther inland.

The man could see only the treetops breaking the skyline. Perhaps they were different from those he'd stared up at for many weeks marked by agony and delirium. He wasn't sure, and he did not have the strength to consider the question further. He closed his eyes and gritted his teeth against the pain of his jolting passage over the rough ground.

He must have passed out. When he again opened his eyes he lay at the edge of a clearing. No, a sort of yard. With poles, and lines stretched between them. A drying yard. And bending over him a young girl, eyes wide with terror, her hand pressed to her mouth, the first white woman he'd seen since the September day he rode out of New York to meet Shea. With Clemence and the rifles. Both gone now. And if the truth be told, he, like Clemence and Shea, had gone to a distant place from which there was no return.

"Go," Solomon DaSilva whispered. A dribble of spittle came from the corner of his mouth. "Get your mistress. Bring her here. Now."

"Solomon! Oh, thank God! Thank God!" Jennet knelt beside him, right there on the kitchen floor where he lay, still tied to the board, and pressed her face to his chest. "Solomon. Oh, my dearest . . ." She couldn't stop weeping. All the time he'd been gone she hadn't allowed herself to weep. Now she couldn't stop. "I thought you were dead. I couldn't . . . Oh, Solomon."

Most of the women of the bordello were crowded around her: Rosa Jollette, four of the whores, the indentured kitchen maid who had been hanging out the wash, Flossie, and Tilda. They watched the young woman sob over a husband who now looked as if he might be her grandfather.

Jennet lifted her head. "Oh, my darling Solomon, what have they done to you?" He'd left her three months earlier with only a few strands of gray in his thick black hair; now every bit of it was white. A heavy, unkempt, mostly white beard covered the lower half of his face. Above it his eyes were dead; dark brown stones in hollow sockets. They refused to meet hers.

"Get them all out of here." He didn't look at her when he spoke, and his voice was so low only she could make out the words. "Tell them to go."

Jennet stayed on her knees beside him, staring into his ravaged face. "Leave us alone. My husband wishes it. Go. All of you."

Rosa Jollette hesitated a moment, as if weighing the authority of a man wrapped like a savage's papoose, then began herding her charges from the kitchen. Tilda went with them, casting only one last glance at the man on the floor, then pressing her hands to her mouth to stifle her sobs.

Flossie didn't follow the other women. When they were gone she took a step closer. "You don't want me to go as well, Mr. Solomon, sure you don't. Herself might need a bit of help getting you out of that thing."

Jennet wore a silk morning wrapper, and beneath it an assortment of petticoats. She wore no corset, so the clothes didn't hide the six-month bulge of her belly. "Flossie means I might need help because I'm carrying your child, my darling. I was going to tell you as soon as you returned." She couldn't speak fast enough. She wanted to see his eyes come alive, see him look at her with love. "I'm sure it's a boy. He'll be born in March. Toward the end, I think, a son to welcome the spring. Now, my dearest Solomon, we need to get you untied and into a proper bed. Flossie, help me. If we can—"

"Get away from me." He finally turned to her. The dead eyes had become burning coals. A madman's eyes. "Flossie, get her away from me."

"It's your Jennet, Mr. Solomon. Your wife—"

"*Merda!* I know who she is. Go," he repeated, staring at Jennet. "Now. Flossie will help me."

Jennet rocked back on her heels. His words came at her like knives. "Solomon," she whispered the only thing that seemed to answer his fury, "surely you know this is your child. You can't think I—"

"Go." She still didn't move. He shouted. "Go, damn you! I can't bear the sight of you. Get away and leave me with Flossie."

Jennet stumbled to her feet and stood looking down at him. "Solomon, what have I done?" He turned his face to the wall and didn't answer.

"You'd best go, child," Flossie whispered, pushing her toward the door. "I'll look after him. And sure I'll come to you soon as I can."

The other women were all jammed into the hall outside the kitchen, waiting and listening. Rosa looked triumphant.

Jennet pushed past them. She kept her head high and willed herself not to cry. Tilda was sobbing, great openmouthed gasps filled with choking tears. Jennet reached out and touched her arm. "Come with me, Tilda. I need you."

"Can you lift this thing?" Solomon asked. "Stand it against the wall?"

"Sure, I think so. But—" Flossie had a knife and was preparing to cut the leather thongs that held him to the board—"if I cut the bindings it might be easier to—"

"No. Stand me up first. Before you release the bindings."

She set the knife down, took hold of the board, and put her considerable strength into raising it. The task was so much easier than she'd expected that Flossie almost lost her footing.

"Good," Solomon said. "Now lean me against the wall."

He was featherlight. Holy God, how much of him must have melted away up there in them woods where only the angels and saints knew what else happened?

She stood the board upright against the wall, then reclaimed the knife. The leather was tough but one by one the thongs fell to the floor. Solomon was clutching the wrappings from the inside. "'Tis free you are now," Flossie said softly when the last binding was released. "Can you walk?"

"I think so, if you help me."

"Put your arm around me, Mr. Solomon. Can you be doing that?"

"Not exactly." He stuck what should have been his left arm out of the covering blankets. It ended at the elbow.

Flossie gasped. "Bloody savages," she whispered. "Cursed heathen. May they rot in hell."

"Can you put an arm around my waist to support me?" Solomon asked. "Yes, like that. Now I think we can move."

Sweet Jesus and his Holy Mother, there was almost nothing to him. She could carry him with just the one arm wrapped around his midsection. "One little step at a time," she said cheerfully. "It's home you are now, Mr. Solomon, and sure there ain't no need to rush."

"Rosa!" she bellowed. The other woman's head immediately appeared in the door. "Waitin' right outside, were you? I thought as much. Well, clear the hall. Get 'em all back to wherever they belong. And move your things out of the big bedroom. There's nowhere better, so the master will have that room now."

"His left arm's cut off at the elbow," Flossie said. "And I think he's missing most of the fingers on the right."

Jennet sat on the side of the narrow bed in the tiny attic room Rosa Jollette had assigned to her, rocking back and forth, trying to calm herself with motion, to understand why what should have been such a joyful day was turning into a nightmare. "What else? Don't hold back, Flossie. Tell me everything."

"Sure, and I don't know what else, child. I swear I don't. He kept himself wrapped in them Indian blankets. Only fell on the bed and told me to send Tilda with some hot broth, then to let him sleep."

"And that's where he is now? In Rosa's room, sleeping?"

"Aye."

"Did he say anything more about me? Why would he think it matters to me if he's lost part of his arms? Or both arms, for that matter. What do I care as long as he's here?"

"Sure, I don't know, child. I swear I don't."

"Don't ever lie to me, Flossie. I need to know I can count on you to tell me the truth. Especially now."

"You can. It's the truth I've been telling you since we got here. I said he'd come back, didn't I?"

"Yes, you did." But nothing was as Flossie had promised or as Jennet had imagined it would be.

"Perhaps I should go to him now." She whispered the words, trying to convince herself, waiting for Flossie to encourage her. "If he's sleeping I can lay down beside him and be there when he wakes."

"I don't think you'll be welcome, child. I'm sorry, but what I read in his eyes . . ."

"What, Flossie? What did you see? Tell me."

"Hatred," the Irishwoman whispered. "And terror."

"For me?" The words scorched her mouth. "My husband hates and fears me?"

"I don't know. But he hates and fears something. And one way or another, it's yourself is a big part of it."

The idea was monstrous. She clasped her hands over her distended belly. "Bring me a quill and some paper, Flossie." Her voice was firm and sure. "Then find Jan Brinker. Tell him I want him to take a note to my father."

Christopher sat beside the bed, lightly probing the mangled stump that had been Solomon DaSilva's left arm. "The lesions are not in any way inflamed. You are fortunate. The wound has been well treated. You say the Huron did this?"

"It was a Huron tomahawk that cut off the arm, but Mohawk squaws that did the healing."

For Christopher, Indians were what they'd always been: all alike and all better dead. "A skirmish, I suppose, and you got in the middle of it."

"Not exactly. I was traveling north with my coachman, Clemence, and an Irish fur trader named Shea." DaSilva's voice was neutral. "We were delivering a shipment of thirty rifles. So if you want to say I brought this on myself, you'd not be mistaken."

"I said nothing of the sort." Christopher reached for the pipe Flossie had put beside the bed. "Would you like me to fix this for you? It must be difficult with one hand."

"Everything's difficult with one hand, and that one with only two fingers. Yes, thank you, I'd like that very much."

The time he spent tamping the tobacco into the pipe and lighting it from a coal he took from the bedroom fire gave Christopher a chance to get a better look at his son-in-law. Solomon had allowed himself to be shaved by Flossie O'Toole. His face was gaunt and hollow-cheeked; that and the white hair made him look like an old man. The vigorous and clever Jew who had shaped his life to his choosing, run off with Christopher's daughter when she was barely seventeen, and managed to somehow make them all bless the day he'd bullied his way into their lives, that man was no longer here. Christopher would wager a fair sum the Solomon DaSilva he'd known was dead. But who had taken his place? "Here you go. This should be ready to yield a few puffs."

DaSilva took the pipe with his right hand, with the thumb and forefinger he had left. He was a man accustomed to adapting to circumstances, even when they were as horrific as this.

"I take it your coachman is dead," Christopher said.

"Yes. Fortunately for Clemence, he went quickly. An arrow to the heart in the first couple of moments after the Huron attacked."

"To get the guns?"

"Exactly."

"But you and this Shea, you got away?"

"There were ten of them and two of us. We were taken prisoner."

"Isn't that unusual? I thought the Huron were as murderous as any other savages."

"They are. But they have their own ways." Solomon went on sucking on the pipe stem.

Christopher looked thoughtful and tried to maintain the pretense that this was an ordinary conversation among gentlemen, an exchange of interesting information. "I see. Well, to expose my ignorance further, aren't the Huron in Canada? Does the fact that you ran into them mean you were across the border?"

"I don't think so, but I really couldn't say. Shea's the one who knew the woods. Anyway, our borders, what we whites say about who owns what, mean little to the Indians. And we didn't 'run into' the Huron. They sent a war party to intercept us and the guns before we delivered them to the Mohawk. The two tribes are bitter enemies. That mattered far more than any borders established by the English or the French."

"I see." There was a cloud of blue smoke between them now. It obscured Solomon DaSilva's face and made it impossible for Christopher to read his expression. "Are you going to tell me the rest?" he asked. "What happened to Shea, for instance?"

"What happened to Shea." DaSilva repeated the words. "What happened to Shea. Do you really want to know?"

"I expect I have to, if I'm to get you well."

DaSilva chuckled. There was little humor in the sound. "Under the circumstances, what does 'get me well' mean?"

"Have you up on your feet, not lying in bed in a nightshirt. Taking an interest in your affairs, your wife, the child you're to have."

DaSilva took another couple of puffs on the pipe, then went on as if Christopher had not spoken, "What happened to Shea? Very well. In the simplest possible words, the Huron hacked him apart bit by bit, roasted the bits over their sacred fire, and ate them."

Christopher opened his mouth, but no words came.

"They kept him alive for most of it." DaSilva's voice was calm. He might have been discussing the market price of a piece of land. "Used leather thongs to stop the blood."

"Tourniquets," Christopher whispered. "A French technique, I always thought."

"Perhaps the Huron learned it from the French. Or the other way around." He spoke in the same even tone, without emotion, the dead eyes staring up at the ceiling. "It doesn't matter. Shea was able to watch them eating his flesh, gnawing on his bones, then tossing them back into the fire. He didn't die until they cut out his heart. They ate that part of him last. Raw."

"Sweet Jesus. And you—"

"I watched, too. As it happened they ate Shea first, so I was alive when the Mohawk raiding party attacked the village. To get back the guns."

"I see. And afterward, I take it, the victorious Mohawks took you with them? To their village?"

"Yes. I'm the source of the guns. Not just muskets, long rifles. So the Mohawk decided it was in their best interest to keep me alive." DaSilva lifted the stump of his arm. "As you see, the Huron kept me from bleeding to death and the Mohawk medicine women did an excellent job of healing my wounds."

"It's a ghastly story, Solomon, I admit. But Sweet Christ, man, seems to me you should be grateful to have survived."

DaSilva flung back the covers. "Ghastly," he said softly. "Yes, that's one word for it. Not strong enough, maybe. As for 'grateful': I might be if the Mohawks had arrived a few minutes sooner. Or a few minutes later. As it is . . ."

Christopher looked at the emaciated body. DaSilva's nightshirt was twisted up around his waist. Beneath it his naked legs were like sticks, his hips as narrow as a boy's. And Sweet Jesus Christ. He had no genitals. The testes and the penis were entirely gone.

"That's the part the Huron eat first," DaSilva said. "All the braves get a bite of your cock and your balls while you watch. Raw, the way they eat your heart after you're dead. So now you tell me, Christopher Turner. How grateful should I be for my miraculous rescue?"

The first snow of the winter had begun, large, gentle flakes falling on the bare branched trees, melting into the river, melding with her tears. Jennet stood by the shore, hands clasped over her belly, face turned to the west. She was trying to understand the things her father had told her, and to consider what they meant for the future. Hers, and Solomon's. And the child's.

"Does he think it's only in the marriage bed I love him? Can Solomon be so foolish he does not—"

"You are the foolish one, Jennet. It is more than his ability to possess you that's been taken from him. It is his entire manhood. The person he was has been cruelly murdered, and a eunuch left behind."

"A eunuch . . . But, dear God, Papa, it's not my fault. I begged him to end the gun trade. Why does Solomon hate me because—"

"He doesn't hate you, Nettie." He was trying so hard to be gentle, to tell her what she must recognize and accept if she was not to torment herself into an early grave. *"It is precisely because Solomon loved you so well that he cannot bear the sight of you now. You remind him of everything he's lost."*

"I see. And do you believe he will ever feel any differently?"

He'd hesitated a moment before pronouncing her sentence. *"I think not, my dear."*

The sun set and the twilight swiftly turned to night. The cold was bitter, but Jennet felt only the heat of her anguish. Finally, unable to contain what was inside her she began to keen. The sound was primeval, a wail of sadness bred in her bone, a legacy bequeathed by the women who had gone before her. All of them forced to do the only thing possible for a female, endure.

I curse you to hell, witch woman. That was what the girl Ellen said the night Jennet bungled her abortion and killed her. The girl's father might have started the job, but Jennet had finished it, no matter what Martha Kincaid said. *I curse you to hell.* Dead Ellen had got her wish. The future that stretched in front of Jennet was impossible to imagine. So she would not try. She would simply live it day by day, however it unfolded.

Her moan rose on the wind, was carried across the river, then faded. She let it go as she let go her dreams and hopes, her love, her passion. All of it was released to the dark and the world beyond her boundaries. Jennet turned and trudged back through the snow.

The carriages were beginning to arrive, the gentlemen of New York making their way to the city's finest bordello, seeking a respite from the weighty matters that occupied them during the day. For a few moments Jennet stood in front of the house and watched. There were many faces she recognized, wellborn and important men from the town. Oliver De Lancey, Caleb Devrey's friend, was among them. She smiled.

For the first time she was aware of the cold. Jennet drew her woolen shawl tighter and started for the side entrance, the one Solomon had taken her through the first time he brought her here and began teaching her the uses of wealth and power.

Then, thinking better of it, Jennet Turner DaSilva—widow though her husband yet lived, pregnant with a child that was fatherless though not yet born— walked up the path and opened what she now claimed as her front door.

The Claws Tear Out Eyes Path

SEPTEMBER 1759–JULY 1760

Sometimes the path of war could not be avoided by chiefs of courage and honor, and the Canarsie People many times faced and killed their enemies.

The battle against those who threatened from the outside was judged to be worthy of fearless braves. But to fight within the People, blood against blood, was to be like a pair of eagles who rip out each other's eyes with their fierce talons. In the end both birds are blind.

The Claws Tear Out Eyes Path was to be avoided at all costs. Unless the manetuac, *the blood spirits, decreed otherwise.*

Chapter Nine

THE SEPTEMBER NIGHT was dark and moonless, the stars intermittently covered by fast-moving clouds. The little boat—barely nine feet from stem to stern, *Margery Dee* lettered crudely across her bow—rode the swells with confidence, her single gaff-rigged sail taut before the wind.

The old sailor had one hand on the tiller, the other controlling the lines. His rheumy eyes scanned the expanse of empty water, but once they'd cleared the roads there was little to keep him occupied. New York harbor was crammed with vessels large and small, but no other craft had left her moorings when the *Margery Dee* did.

Queer sort of nigra he was ferrying, a mulatto. Color of coffee with a squirt of fresh milk. Half and half, sort of. Must be why he sashayed around like he thought he was a white man. Leastwise on land. Wedged into the prow, long legs bent, knees almost to his chin, hangin' on to that God-cursed box, the nigra didn't look so piss proud, however much white blood he might have in him. Looked like he'd rather be anywhere 'cept where he was.

"Don't like it much, do ye?" The sailor's chuckle disappeared into the gusting wind of the black night. "Never met one of yer kind what did. Nigras only goes to sea when the press gangs catch 'em."

Cuf knew that wasn't true, but he didn't argue. The boat's pitching and chopping made him ill. All he wanted was to do what he'd come to do, and get back on land again once he'd done it. The last part might not be easy.

So she'd told him. Squaw DaSilva, as folks called her, though she'd always been

"Mistress" to him. Had to be that way, growing up in her house the way he had, belonging to her. He'd gone to the apothecary shop on Pearl Street only once every month or two, when he was sent. Phoebe—she never encouraged him to call her mama—barely spoke to him. Squaw DaSilva it was who taught him whatever he knew.

Like after she gave him the box, and the two shillings to pay for the journey to Bedloe's Island. *Make sure no one foxes you, Cuf. Getting there will be simple. Getting back could be more difficult. You're often wise. Be wise about this.*

He'd seen her blue eyes behind the black veil she'd worn as long as he could remember. A black veil covering her face, and a black dress and a black pinafore over it. Widow's weeds. Even though her husband was alive up there in that room where nobody but Tilda or old Mistress O'Toole ever went in or came out.

"There she be." The seaman eased the tiller to starboard and started the small boat tacking toward the shore. "Cursed Bedloe's cursed island. Ain't goin' no closer than them pilings off the shore. Ain't gonna get poxed. Not if you pay me twice the two shillings you promised."

Cuf peered into the darkness. He could see nothing. "Don't worry. You'll get your money."

The coins were in the pocket of his shabby leather breeches. Two iron shillings, each one hammered out by a smith somewhere up in New England. Folks said no coins made here in America were real money, but nearly everyone acted as if they were. Mistress made him an allowance of four pennies a week. Sometimes they were wood and sometimes copper. It didn't matter to him, and it would be the same with the toothless, grizzled old tar sailing this miserable excuse for a boat. "Will the sea be over my head?"

"Not a tall, strong young nigra like you. 'Course the waves be pretty high tonight. Could be . . . You swim, boy?"

"No. And you said I'd no need to swim."

The old man chuckled, louder this time. "Hold yer piss. It's me bit o' fun, that's all. 'Course ye can wade ashore from the pilings. They's there so's any who's fool enough to want to get to the poxed place can do it. Don't expect yer bothered none by the pox, though, are ye? Folks say nigras don't get it. That true?"

"What's the tide like?" Cuf asked.

The old man hadn't really expected an answer to his question. Everyone knew nigras didn't tell white folks their magic. Nigras kept their secrets. "Tide's low and gettin' lower. But it'll be turnin' in less'n an hour, boy. I ain't gonna wait."

"It won't take me long to do what I came to do."

The old man squinted into the dark. "You gonna take that there box on to poxed Bedloe's poxed island?"

"That's not your business. Not as long as you get your money."

"You keep a respectful tongue in yer head, boy. Anyways, long as yer back when ye says ye'll be back, I don't much care what in God's name ye be doin' while yer gone."

You've nothing to be afraid of from the place, Cuf. You know you won't get the pox.

The rough scar on his thigh had been there as long as Cuf could remember, and it was almost that long since he'd known that if everyone had the scar there would be no need for boats to tie up at Bedloe's Island and be inspected for smallpox before they could come into New York harbor. Mistress's brother, Dr. Luke, he'd explained it all. He also said sometimes ignorance ruled and there was nothing to be done about it. "How much longer?" Cuf asked. "Are we getting near those pilings?"

"Minute or two, no more. Not blind, are ye? Pilin's be easy to see from here. On yer feet, boy. Ye be needed to drop a line round one of 'em if I'm not to make us a heap o' splinters."

Cuf had to let go of the box to take the line. Fortunately he was able to set it on the deck in such a fashion that his body was between it and the old man.

"Right. Here we be. Drop the line over that pilin' to larboard. Come on, boy, look sharp! It ain't much of a task for a strong young— Christ! Ye blitherin' fool, ye almost missed it!"

Almost. He hadn't been able to see the pitch-blackened tree trunk standing in the choppy water until they were nearly past it. He'd had to lean over the side and toss the line rather than place it. Nothing but luck and his long arms made the maneuver succeed.

"Pull on the bloody line, boy! Tighten her down." The old man drew the tiller hard toward him, nosing the little boat farther into the wind. A wave lifted her bow high, then rolled below her and slapped her back to the surface of the water.

The box skittered between Cuf's legs along the sea-slicked deck. He reached out one arm to recapture it, but couldn't quite make it without letting go of the line. The boat was turning and tossing like a mad thing now, rising and falling on the waves. Cuf felt the icy salt spray wash over his face, almost blinding him. He still had one hand on the line, the other outstretched in a desperate gesture to get the box back.

The seaman stopped the box's precipitous slide with his knee and pinned it between his legs. "Hang on to that God-cursed line till I gets it cleated down! Bloody useless you nigras are. Keep yer dick in yer breeches. I've got yer God-cursed box." The old man let go of the tiller and the rigging lines and lunged for the prow. The sail flapped madly above their heads, and the tiller swung back and forth in a drunken dance. The old man yanked the mooring line out of Cuf's hand. "Here, gimme that!" A few swift figure-eight turns and he'd made it fast to an iron cleat fixed to the gunwale. "There we be. Safe and secure, no thanks to ye."

The boat was still pitching madly, and when Cuf peered over the side the water looked black, and cold, and very deep. "Give me my box."

"Not so fast." The tar had put the box behind him. In the dark relieved only by a few of the brightest stars, Cuf thought he saw something glinting in the man's hand. A knife? "Ye be gettin' yer box when I gets me money. Two shillings. Like we said."

Cuf reached into his pocket and brought out one of the iron coins. "Half now. Half when we're back in port."

"No chance. What's to make ye pay once yer done with needin' me services?"

"What's to make you wait for me to come back once you have your money?"

The two took each other's measure in the night. The thing in the old man's hand caught a stray shaft of starlight and glittered. Definitely a knife. "A shilling now," Cuf said, his voice steady. "The other one when I'm finished my business and I'm back aboard."

The tar thought for a moment. "Done," he said. "Gimme my money."

"I will. When you give me my box."

They made the exchange simultaneously.

The sailor kept the rough coin clutched in his hand while Cuf went over the side into the water—it barely reached his waist—and battled through the choppy surf to the shore.

The old man watched until the young one disappeared into the darkness. Light, that box had been. Too light to be money, like he first thought. Anything to do with Squaw DaSilva, figured to be something doing with money. Richest woman in New York, she was. But even mostly useless paper money weighed more than whatever was in that box. A jewel, maybe. One big diamond.

Leastwise the box was somethin' to think about, sitting here moored in the black and silent night. The sail hanging limp because the wind had dropped. Poxed Bedloe's poxed island had swallowed the wind. Cold as a witch's tit, it was, and gettin' colder. His heavy breeches, thickly coated with tar to keep out the wet, and the double layer of wool provided by his seaman's checked shirt and short jacket weren't enough to keep him warm. Too frigging cold for September. Not natural. No way he wanted to row the *Margery Dee* all the way back against the current on a night like this when God knows what was abroad. If the nigra wasn't back turn o' the tide, he'd leave alone. Take his single shilling and be glad and gone.

Up the beach, Cuf, and head to your right. After you've cleared the shingle and you're on solid land you'll see a pine tree bent like a pin by the wind.

Cuf hated every step he took. His flannel jacket and breeches were sopping and icy cold, stiffening with salt as they dried. His thighs made a scraping sound when he walked. That and the crunch of his boots on the flinted rocks were the only noises. No one lived on Bedloe's Island.

After a few moments he saw the tree, exactly where she'd said it would be and looking as she said it would look. Not likely Squaw DaSilva had ever visited Bedloe's Island. Dr. Luke must have told her about the stony beach and the tree; he was part of the committee in charge of building a pesthouse on the island. Dr. Luke called it an infirmary for those with contagions, but everyone knew it would be a place where they'd send you to die. Like the almshouse hospital. Only worse.

The tree bends to the west, Cuf. Take thirty-three full strides in that direction. No more and no less.

Cuf held the box tight under his arm and began pacing off the distance, counting aloud to be sure he got it right. "One, two, three, four . . ." When he got to thirty-three he was so far from the pine he could barely make out the bent-pin shape in the dark.

When you've gone the thirty-three full paces turn so you're facing north, back toward the city. Then take seven paces and turn east and take nine paces more.

He did everything exactly as she'd told him, making sure he took each step at the full stretch so the measurements would be the same. That had to be important. Whoever worked out the instructions meant to be able to find his way to wherever Cuf was going by doing the same things in the same way. Cuf grinned, pleased with himself because he'd figured it out. That wasn't Squaw DaSilva's kind of thinking, it was Morgan's.

Ever since they were little, when they played together as brothers ignoring who was the slave and who the son and heir, Morgan had been fascinated with the tools of navigation.

"See this, Cuf?" Morgan asked, holding out the fancy new book he'd just brought back from the bookseller in Hanover Square. "It's a drawing of a thing that lets you go to sea and sail as far as you like in any direction, and always know where you are and how to find your way back. It's called a sextant. We have to learn to use this, Cuf."

"Not me, Morgan. I'm not sailing anywhere. I hate the sea."

"Why?"

"I don't know. But I do. Anyways, I have to stay here so I can get the promise."

"Being free, you mean."

"Yes. Your mama promised. When I'm twenty-five. I'll be free."

"Then you will be, Cuf. Mama always keeps her word. But before that, you and me, we can run away to sea. Only first we have to get the hang of this sextant thing."

Cuf took the last of the nine paces east. The tree was entirely out of sight now.

Squaw DaSilva's instructions were as clear in his mind as if she were walking beside him.

There will be a large stone, Cuf, a boulder that will reach almost to your shoulder, and a shovel hidden beneath a pile of dead branches to its left. Get the shovel, and lie down with your head touching the middle of the boulder's north face and scuff a mark in the earth with your boots. Then get up and find that mark and dig a hole, as deep as from your heel to your knee.

The boulder and the shovel were exactly where she'd said they would be, and the earth soft with all the rain they'd had, so when he'd worked out the place where he was meant to dig he was able to do so without difficulty. After a couple of minutes Cuf put his left leg in the hole. It measured exactly what she'd told him it should measure. Then he did the thing Squaw DaSilva hadn't told him to do, though she must have assumed he would. Cuf opened the box.

Something gleamed in the starlight. He picked it up. A gold horse's head, with two red stones for eyes. Rubies. Cuf turned the thing over and over in his hand, held it up so he could examine it more closely. Beautiful workmanship. Each strand of the horse's mane was distinct, the features of the animal's face fully realized. Smithing gold was the most difficult part of the craft, Cuf knew. Silver required skill, as did pewter, but with something as precious as gold your hand shook holding the stylus, whoever you were. All that was part of a store of secret knowledge he was setting by against the day he got the promise.

Three years more to wait. Meanwhile there was the business at hand, here on Bedloe's Island. He took one more long look at the horse's head. It was hollow, and a coating of red sealing wax had been dripped over the opening at the base of the neck. Cuf held it to his ear and shook it. Not a sound. For a few seconds he held the golden treasure in his hand and considered. *Be wise, Cuf.*

She knew him too well. That was why she hadn't locked the box or told him not to open it. She knew he'd look inside, to satisfy his curiosity; then he'd do what she asked. Because soon she would keep the promise, and that was a lot surer than running off with a gold horse's head, however wonderfully it was made and whatever was inside.

Cuf put the gold head back into the box and put the box in the hole. He shoveled the dirt back over it and stomped it down and dragged the dead branches over to cover the area of activity. Then, shivering with cold and carrying the shovel, he made his way back to the beach.

He was glad to see that the old man and his miserable *Margery Dee* were still there. If he wasn't back by morning, Squaw DaSilva would certainly send someone to fetch him, but he'd have to spend a whole freezing night on poxed Bedloe's poxed island.

The sailor saw him coming, stood up, and began unfurling the sail. Cuf waited until the tar's back was to the shore to fling the shovel into the sea. Then, gritting his teeth against the cold, he began wading toward the boat.

His uncle Luke always said he didn't look anything like his father. "You're all Turner, Morgan."

Fair enough. Since he'd never once set eyes on the man his mother said had fathered him, the son chose not to use the father's name. Morgan Turner he was to everyone who knew him, including those who hated his guts.

The two men sheltering in the shallow doorway on Dock Street did not hate Morgan Turner. They were hired hands with no passion for the job, only for the pay it would bring. The patience required by the long wait in the cold and moonless night came hard.

"You sure he'll be comin' this way?" The taller of the two men stamped his feet to keep them from freezing.

"Sure as I need to be. They all come this way, don't they? Quickest route from the harbor to a sailor's slop shop. Soon as a tar's on land, that's what he wants, mug o' grog."

Grog. The term had come into use nearly two decades past, in 1740 when the rum ration was made law in the British navy. Cut it with water, said Admiral Edward Vernon. He always wore a coat made of the heavy silk known as grogram, so rum cut with water became grog. It was life's blood to an ordinary seaman; maybe not quite so important to the likes of the man the pair in the Dock Street doorway were waiting for.

"Morgan Turner's no tar. He's a privateer."

"Ain't no difference. Only that privateers be rich as pirates."

"Richer," the first man insisted. "And they ain't got to worry about hidin' what they got, since they took it legal like."

"Ain't many in this city hides what they got," the other said bitterly. "They flaunts it so the likes o' us can see what we be missin'."

That had been true for much of the seventeen-fifties, but in the thirties and forties times had been hard and Quaker frugality had brought greater rewards than New York daring. Back then, Philadelphia had been the most important city in the colonies. When things changed, the men of Pennsylvania didn't like losing their place to those of New York. Ben Franklin spoke for all when he wrote that New York City was raking in money faster than even her spendthrift citizens could rid themselves of it.

All because in Europe Britain made war on France and Prussia and rumbled against Spain. In America that meant the colonials were fighting the French and their Indian allies. King William's War, Queen Anne's War, King George's War—

mostly they were skirmishes that changed nothing. But the French threat was always present. In 1745, convinced they were about to be invaded from Quebec, New Yorkers had held a lottery to finance a second east–west wall across Manhattan. It went up a mile from the southern tip of the island and marked the boundary of the densely populated city with a stretch of fourteen-foot cedar logs broken only by four gates and six blockhouses. No invasion came.

The inconclusive thrusts and parries continued until in 1754 a young colonel named George Washington and a detachment of Virginia troops were forced into a humiliating surrender near the Pennsylvania frontier. The next year the British sent General Edward Braddock to put an end to the insolent French presence in the Ohio Country. Braddock was slaughtered with most of his officers and troops. Young Washington was among the few who escaped.

England had had enough; her people demanded that Canada be conquered once and for all. The aging George II bowed to public pressure and made the brilliant strategist William Pitt war minister. Pitt mobilized a huge fighting force and sent a staggering twenty-five thousand redcoats to the American colonies. The majority passed through New York. The flood of military in transit to the forts that secured the Lake Champlain corridor—William Henry and eventually Ticonderoga—had to be billeted, fed, clothed, armed, and, of course, supplied with women and drink. It was excellent trade and huge numbers of New Yorkers made a substantial living from it. But for real wealth, nothing could equal privateering.

Most of the ships clogging the city's harbor were men-o'-war sailing as privateers, seventy-some licensed pirates who scoured the seas in search of enemy shipping. It was the greatest such fleet in the colonies. The privateers brought their investors—the men who paid for the building and outfitting of the vessels and got shares of the spoils in return—nearly two million pounds' worth of coffee, cotton, sugar, wine, indigo, and every kind of comestible every year, as well as live ware (slaves) and currency—bullion, doubloons, *daalders, louis d'or,* and pieces of eight. Wealth poured from the holds of the licensed pirates into the pockets of New York's merchant kings.

The investors who backed Morgan Turner were the most daring of all, but their courage was well rewarded. In 1757, as an audacious nineteen-year-old, he raised the money to build a sleek two-masted, narrow-hulled schooner, christened her the *Fanciful Maiden,* and went to sea. The *Maiden* could do eleven knots in a stiff breeze, had a draft of no more than five feet, and carried seventy-five fighting crew as well as eight cannon and four swivel guns. In three years Turner brought home twenty-two prizes worth nearly a hundred thousand pounds. Then, at the end of her twenty-third sortie, the *Fanciful Maiden* limped into port with her hull scarred, her deck stained with blood, and her belly empty.

Six of the seven backers were philosophical. They'd been with Morgan Turner from his first voyage, and their investments had already been returned a hundredfold. The eighth had come late to the party. He lost every penny he'd put into the venture. Which was every penny he had.

Morgan Turner was delighted with that outcome. And on his guard.

He walked off the long wooden pier and turned in to the lower end of Dock Street with his hand on the hilt of his cutlass. Farther along, the customary lanterns on poles hung from the upper windows of every seventh house. This close to the harbor there were no dwellings, only warehouses and empty market stalls, and the street was as black as India ink.

The first man in the doorway saw him coming—you couldn't mistake that tall swaggering form for anyone else—and nudged the other. The second man already had his pistol in his hand.

Morgan sensed rather than saw a movement up ahead in the darkness. The hair on the back of his neck prickled. He eased the cutlass half out of its scabbard and continued walking. For thirty-six months he'd lived by close combat on the pitching decks of the merchant vessels he'd boarded and stripped, and often sent to the bottom of the sea. He wasn't about to run from the perils of a New York street.

There was the faint click of a hammer cocking in the dark. Morgan fell to his knees. The bullet whistled above his head.

He got to his feet as the attackers pelted toward him. There hadn't been time for whoever fired the first shot to reload, but he saw the shadowy form of the second killer raise his pistol arm when he was five yards away. Morgan stood his ground, waiting. A pistol was the most unreliable weapon on God's earth. The second assassin wouldn't want to repeat the mistake of the first. He'd delay firing until he was almost at point-blank range.

One second. Two. He could hear the man's labored breath and smell his unwashed stink. Three. Fear knotted Morgan's gut. The killer was too near to be fooled by a feint, and he could see his target clear enough to take aim.

Morgan raised his cutlass. Whatever happened, he'd take at least one of them with him. Finally he heard the almost inaudible sound of the weapon's hammer being drawn back. He tightened his grip on the cutlass, waited for a single heartbeat more, then slashed at his attacker with a howl of both rage and triumph.

The assailant's extended arm was opened wide from elbow to wrist, the shot went wild, and the pistol clattered to the cobbles along with the attacker's thumb and one of his fingers. The man screamed, and the sickly sweet smell of hot blood mingled with the fetid stench of his loosened bowels.

The second man lunged with a short sword. Morgan swung to meet him and thrust the cutlass straight to the heart. The assassin went down with a dull thud.

Morgan just had time to yank the cutlass from the dead man's chest before the wounded man came at him again. The cutlass sliced upward so fast it hissed.

Morgan meant to open the killer's throat and finish him, but their differing heights played him false. The deadly blade sideswiped the man's head. His ear fell to the ground. The man yowled his rage and pain, and gripping a knife in his good fist, he flung himself at Morgan in a final, suicidal bid for vengeance.

His blade nicked Morgan's shoulder, but the cutlass ripped open the attacker's belly and he staggered backward a few steps before, whimpering and weeping, he fell in a slithering mess of his own entrails, excrement, and blood.

Morgan's chest burned with the effort to draw breath. He felt the sweat pouring down his back, turning to ice in the cold night. He fought off the urge to relax. Not yet. Not until he was sure no one else would come against him. He waited and heard nothing. A few more seconds went by. A wave of triumphant elation began at his toes and traveled to the top of his skull. Two barely competent ruffians-for-hire were all the stupid bastard could afford.

Holy bloody savior! Despite the cold and fatigue and the burning pain in his wounded shoulder, the thought warmed him better than the best rum. He laughed aloud. You're a pauper now, Caleb Devrey. Or near enough as makes no difference. And since you invested in a proxy's name, you've no idea that I know. Which is exactly how it was intended to be. For a start.

The floor was covered in sawdust and the air thick with the smell of sweaty flesh, and humming with excitement. Men stood ten deep in a circle around the central pit, ladies as well. That wasn't usual. At a bearbaiting or a cockfight or a contest between a dog and a couple of dozen rats—the usual entertainments held in this venue on William Street—there might be a few sailor's doxies, but certainly no ladies. On this occasion, however, they were permitted, even invited.

"For the sake of maintaining good order and giving salutary witness to the right and wholesome conduct expected of females in this city, all are bidden to watch the just punishment meted out to women of ill repute by the authority of His Most Gracious Majesty, George II." The man in the center of the pit droned on for a few more seconds, then rolled up the scroll he'd been reading and stepped aside to make room for the public whipper.

The job was in the gift of the council. Since the usual fee was a shilling and sixpence per whipping and whippings were frequent, there were always plenty of applicants. This man had held the post for three years and seemed set to go another three. He was a big fellow, dark and burly, with arms as thick around as the legs of a small bull. He wore black leggings and was naked from the waist up, except for a long leather apron to protect his bare chest against splattered blood.

Standing to one side were the three women whose punishment for whoring in the New York streets was the event the crowd had come to witness. They were shackled together with iron chains, and each had her wrists bound in front of her with a tough leather thong.

The woman in the middle was named Roisin Campbell, and at the sight of the whipper in his black leather apron she felt her insides start to melt. She tightened her buttocks against the terror, and swallowed the bitter bile of her fear. I won't let them see me shamed. I won't. Blessed Virgin, help me.

The magistrate in charge of the proceedings wore a crimson gown, a flowing white wig, and a gold chain with a heavy medallion of office. "By the grace of Almighty God and the glory of His Most Gracious Majesty, George II, bring the first prisoner," he intoned. A pair of redcoats turned smartly and trotted in lock-step toward the three women.

They covered the distance in a few seconds, but it seemed to Roisin to take them long minutes to approach. She could see each step they took as if their pace were slow and measured. They'd almost reached her now. Dear Lord Jesus, give me courage. Holy Mother of God, strengthen me. I know I have to go through this, but don't let me shame myself or your One True Church. "Or the Women of Connemara," she added, whispering the final words aloud because they were so powerful.

The redcoats passed the woman on her right. Roisin felt a terrifying mix of dread and gratitude. She'd prayed all day to be first. She knew she could be braver if she didn't know what to expect. It wasn't to be. The redcoats passed her by and stopped beside the woman to her left.

Roisin had to bite her lip to keep from screaming aloud. Holy Virgin, all day, locked in that filthy dungeon beneath their cursed City Hall, all I asked. Only let me be first. So I don't have to watch and know what's coming. For the sake of the Women of Connemara.

The redcoats had finished unshackling the woman they'd chosen and started to lead her away. "Courage," Roisin whispered. The poor creature didn't look around.

The prisoner was brought to the center of the pit. The crowd whistled and cat-called and stamped their feet. The taller of the pair of soldiers yanked the woman's tightly bound hands upward and hung them over one of a series of iron hooks on the whipping post.

The magistrate stepped forward and lifted the woman's filthy homespun skirt and shabby petticoats so he could be sure her feet were touching the ground. That was a strict regulation in the matter of the flogging of whores: they were to be whipped standing, not suspended. British justice, the judges said, was as cruel as it needed to be, no more. The magistrate satisfied himself that the prisoner's position was correct and nodded. "You may proceed."

The redcoat took a short sword from its scabbard and with the sharpened tip nicked an inch of the back of the woman's dress. Then he sheathed his blade and used his hands to rip the bodice as far as the waist. The crowd whistled and stomped some more, and with a quick grin the soldier pushed the torn fabric far enough apart to reveal the side swell of the woman's breasts as well as her back.

Sometimes when things got this far the magistrate would nod a second time, looking as prim as he had throughout the proceedings, and the redcoat would yank the bodice all the way off so the woman would be naked from the waist up. But mostly they did that with blacks. This whore was white. And besides, there were ladies in the crowd. The magistrate shook his head and the redcoat left the dress the way it was and stepped away.

"Abigail Keene," the magistrate intoned, "you are convicted of having congress with men for money in the streets of this city and are therefore sentenced to fifteen lashes and banishment from the province. Whipper, do your duty, and for the good of all here present, do not spare your arm."

Roisin didn't want to watch, but she couldn't turn away. Ah, sweet God Almighty, look at the length of that thing. The leather whip had to be eight feet long, attached to a solid four-foot handle. The sound it made singing and snapping in the air seared itself into her soul. Dear God, dear God . . . And the whipper was simply preparing himself. He hadn't yet approached the woman fixed to the whipping post.

If this had been a hanging the man paid to do the job would have knelt and begged the victim's forgiveness before he did it. At whippings the man in the black leather apron was free to use all the showmanship he possessed. *For the benefit of all present,* the regulations said. *That they may be strengthened in Christian virtue.*

The whipper cracked his whip once more. It was a signal to the audience to quiet itself. The spectacle was about to begin.

The man in the leather apron drew back his arm a third time, raised it, and the flicking thong made its first contact with the soft, pale skin of the woman's back. The first kiss, the whippers called it. It was best if there were no old welts. A virgin kiss. Like this one.

The crowd craned forward, holding its breath, and saw the woman's body jerk. They waited, but they were disappointed. There was no sound. The whipper smiled. A strong one. But he'd have her. He had them all in the end. Melted for him, they did. Pleased with the challenge, he drew his arm back for the second kiss.

The blood drained from Roisin's face. She felt her head go light and her knees begin to buckle. No! Damn them all to everlasting hell! She wouldn't give them the satisfaction. Look away, she told herself. Pretend it isn't happening. Look at the crowd, not the poor creature in the pit. Make yourself hate them even more. Then you'll be strong.

See how the women are leaning forward as eagerly as the men. Practically licking their lips behind their fans, the heretic bitches. As for the gentlemen in their cut velvet coats and satin breeches, they probably have to keep their filthy Protestant hands in their Protestant pockets to hide how much they're enjoying it. And who was it paid women to whore, if not gentlemen like these? How come no man had ever been sentenced to a flogging for illegal congress in the streets of New York? Blessed Virgin, who is that creature in the black veil? She's staring at me. I can't see her eyes, but I can feel them.

Actually, two pairs of eyes were staring at her.

Morgan Turner stood behind his mother in the shadows of the small private gallery suspended above the pit. He couldn't be seen, but he could see everything. It was he who had drawn his mother's attention to the redheaded girl, right after he gave her a report of the fight on Dock Street. "Two of them. Both dead. Who is that luscious creature? The one in the middle with the red hair."

"I've no idea. But we shouldn't stay. You're sure there were no other attackers?"

"I'm sure."

"Then we'll go. That shoulder needs attending to."

"No, it can wait. The copperhead, I want to know what she's done."

"The same as the other two. Whoring in the streets. Making a public nuisance of themselves."

"Giving you competition, you mean."

Squaw DaSilva didn't answer. Her boy was what she'd raised him to be. Hard as granite and smarter than most men twice his age. And she had never hidden from him the fact that part of the DaSilva wealth came from running the finest bordellos in the city.

In the pit below the leather snake hissed for the seventh stroke. The woman had been mostly silent so far, only grunting and moaning when the whip made contact with her welted back. This time the first droplets of red blood appeared on her white flesh. She let out a short cry of torment. The crowd sighed with satisfaction.

"I want her," Morgan said.

"The redheaded lass?"

"Yes. Get someone to free her and bring her to me."

"It doesn't do to flaunt power, Morgan." His mother spoke softly without turning around, her voice muffled by the many folds of her veil. "Control is best exercised behind the public stage."

The crowd was stomping and cheering again, because the whipper had broken the woman. She was crying and screaming for mercy now. And she'd only had nine of her fifteen lashes. "No one's paying us any mind," Morgan said. "If you don't do it your way, I'll do it mine."

Squaw turned her head just in time to see her son ease his cutlass in its scabbard. She put out a cautionary hand, then looked away again so he wouldn't see her smile. Exactly what she'd raised him to be. She was sure he'd go to the redheaded whore's rescue in full view of the assembly. And probably succeed. That might amuse her, but it simply wouldn't do. She raised her arm and motioned to the constable stationed by the door at the rear of the gallery.

The man approached and bent near. Squaw spoke a few words. The constable bounded off, raced down the narrow stairs, then forced his way through the screaming mob at floor level. They were counting the lashes now, shouting "Ten! Eleven!" while the whore howled in agony.

Morgan took a step forward, closer to the gallery rail. He estimated the drop at ten feet, maybe twelve. He could easily make the jump. There was a door behind the magistrate's podium that led directly to the street. Yes, that would be best. He drew his cutlass half out of its scabbard. "Wait," his mother cautioned.

The constable approached the presiding official, bent down, and whispered in his ear. The magistrate looked up at the gallery. Squaw nodded. The magistrate hesitated. She nodded again. Squaw DaSilva's telling you what she wants, you old fool, and if you value the extra ten pounds that finds its way to your pocket every quarter, you'll be quick to see that she gets it.

The magistrate put his hand to the seal of office hanging around his neck, fingered it a moment, then spoke to the constable. The man set off around the edge of the sawdust-covered pit, ducking to be sure he missed both the backward flick of the whip and the blood now spurting from the whore's back.

"Thirteen!" the crowd shouted in unison. "She's passed out! Swooned she has! Wake her up, whipper, so she feels the last two!"

Someone rushed forward with a bucket of water and flung it over the woman's head and her bleeding back. The water was heavily salted; the stinging in the lacerated flesh was unbearable. The woman came to consciousness with a scream. The whip whistled again, the victim wailed in agony, and the crowd yelled "Fourteen!" in an ecstasy of pleasure.

The constable had reached the redcoat guarding the waiting prisoners. He pointed at Roisin and shouted his orders so he could be heard above the howling mob. "Unshackle the redhead. I'm to take her. Magistrate says there's been a mistake."

The redcoat tore his glance from the woman fixed to the whipping post. He looked in the magistrate's direction, got the nod, then took a key from the ring hanging at his waist.

Seconds later Roisin felt the manacles drop from her ankles. The constable took her arm and began dragging her up the aisle toward the door.

She didn't believe it was really happening until the cold night air slapped her in the face. She saw the black carriage and the veiled woman who paused and looked over her shoulder at Roisin before she climbed inside. There was a man standing beside the carriage, openly staring at her, waiting and grinning. Tallest man she'd ever seen, and handsome as a god. Or a devil. Roisin sketched the sign of the cross onto her palm with her thumb. For the sake of the Women of Connemara, she prayed, Holy Virgin, give me strength.

II

New Yorkers had to find some way to spend all that war-spawned money. No one had curbed the pigs that still ran loose in the streets, but upward of eighteen thousand people now lived in the city, in two thousand houses. Some, like the Walton house everyone talked about, were as fine as the finest London mansion. Morgan had actually been inside the Walton house once. When he was seventeen he got himself into a ball to which he hadn't been invited (there never was a New York ball to which Morgan Turner was invited) and saw the marble floors and the oak-paneled walls and the damask this and gilt that before he was recognized and evicted.

The Walton house was in the fashionable court part of town, at the southern tip, not far from the fort and the governor's mansion. The court section, indeed all the city, occupied the narrowest part of the island, where land was severely limited. Some of the richest residents had been forced to locate their elaborate houses farther north, in the outlying district that went by the name of Manhattan rather than New York.

Old man Rutgers was one. He'd made a fortune brewing beer to satisfy the boundless thirst of the redcoats, but he had to locate his grand manor on a hundred acres of East River frontage north of the second wall and south of Kip's Bay. When he was a boy, Morgan Turner had gone wherever he pleased on the Rutgers property; the fences and guards and wardens were no match for him. The same was true of James De Lancey's estate in the Bouwery, separated from the Rutgers property by what was known as Division Street.

Some years back the eldest of Etienne De Lancey's sons had left the family home to establish a three-hundred-acre country seat. The move not only symbolized James's independence, it outclassed all his rivals in the struggle for power in the city. De Lancey's impressive manor was on Bouwery Lane. His land stretched west as far as the village of Greenwich and included the old Collect Pond. The estate had a racecourse at one end and a hunting wood at the other. It always gave Morgan Turner particular pleasure to bag a rabbit or a woodcock in James De Lancey's private hunting ground, and bring it home and tell his mother where it had come from.

"The De Lanceys give him cover," his mother had explained when Morgan was still a child. "Caleb Devrey has no money of his own and, now that his father is dead and Bede has taken over Devrey Shipping, no expectations. Caleb has nothing except what his poor practice of physic brings him, and he has to share that pittance with Cadwallader Colden. It's his friendship with Oliver De Lancey, and through him James, that gains Caleb Devrey a measure of sufferance in the town."

"Is Oliver De Lancey a rich man, Mama?"

"Not as rich as his brother James. Oliver's like Caleb, a second son."

"I'm not a second son, am I, Mama?"

"Oh no, my darling boy." She'd reached out a hand to touch him, and he thought he saw her smile behind the black veil. "You are the heir to everything I have. But that means you have responsibilities as well as rewards."

"What am I responsible for?"

"Seeing that Caleb Devrey gets what he deserves."

"Do you mean for me to kill him, Mama? Am I to kill Caleb Devrey when I grow up?"

It was one of the few times he'd ever seen her anger directed at him. "Never! Never!" She'd spat the words out from behind the veil, and her fingers had dug into his shoulder like iron grips. "Killing is much too easy for Caleb Devrey. If I wanted him dead I could have arranged it myself. Swear to me that in this matter you will do exactly as I tell you, Morgan. Swear it!"

"I swear, Mama."

She still wasn't satisfied. "No matter what the provocation, you will never put Caleb Devrey to death. In fact, if he is threatened by someone else you will help him. Anything to keep him alive. Swear it, Morgan!"

"I do swear it, Mama. I said so. I swear."

She loosed her grip on his aching shoulder and drew him close. "Good, good. That is as it should be," she whispered. "Caleb Devrey must not be given the release of death. Not until he's very, very old and has suffered as much as he made us suffer."

"How, Mama? What did Caleb Devrey do to us?"

"Later, Morgan. When you are older and better able to understand, then I'll explain."

Sitting in the small carriage across from his mother and a girl whom he wasn't sure he fancied now that he could smell her, Morgan knew there were still parts of the story he didn't understand. They didn't matter. He knew what he had to know. He had just claimed the first installment of Caleb Devrey's debt.

For a time he'd worried that he wouldn't be able to pull it off. James De Lancey had become lieutenant governor of the colony six years before, when the last royal governor sent from London hanged himself. De Lancey was richer and more powerful than ever, but not as rich or as clever as Squaw DaSilva or her son. And in the end not so powerful. De Lancey never discovered their plan, and Caleb Devrey lost his patched breeches in an investment that should have been a sure thing. Merely thinking about it made Morgan smile.

Roisin thought he'd caught her staring at him and that his knowing smile was a response. She flushed and turned her head. She'd never been in this fancy part of the city before. Grand the houses were, and this was the first time she'd ever been in a private carriage. The way it swayed back and forth made her queasy.

She kept her hands folded in her lap and pretended to look at them. They were filthy, like the rest of her, the nails broken and dirty and the skin roughened by living on the street. But at least her wrists were no longer bound together. She still didn't know who he was, or who the veiled woman was, or what they wanted with her. It didn't matter. Anything was better than what she'd been expecting.

Roisin thought of the cracking whip and the screaming crowd and shuddered. The woman turned and looked at her, but said nothing.

The carriage stopped in front of a pair of tall iron gates and the driver jumped down and swung them open, then hoisted himself back to his perch and drove up to the biggest house she'd ever seen. Yellow brick, with more windows than she could count, and an entrance so wide it required two carved wooden doors.

The tall man got out of the carriage first, then turned and helped the older woman. Roisin saw how careful she was to hold her black taffeta skirts so they didn't touch any part of Roisin's ragged homespun. Not the man. He made sure his thigh rubbed hers when he handed her down. "Mind yourself," he said softly. "The step's higher than you think."

"I can manage."

"Yes, I expect you can."

The devil's own grin when he said it. And even though he was so handsome he took her breath away, she meant to tell him that some things were not as he supposed. She never got the chance. The woman cut her off. "Here's Tilda. Let her take the wench and clean her up, Morgan. You and I must talk."

Roisin was grateful that the man still gripped her arm. It was all that kept her upright. Dear God in heaven! Morgan Turner the pirate. She'd been in New York only a month, but she'd heard all about him, and his mother. The veiled woman was the one they called Squaw DaSilva, the vixen who was said to be colder and more cruel than any man, who owned the fanciest of New York's fancy houses, and who was so opposed to anyone taking her trade away by whoring in the streets that she'd arranged the public floggings as a warning. Holy Virgin, what was she going to do now?

Whatever they said, because otherwise it was the man in the black leather apron and the whip. And as Jesus would be her judge, she couldn't find the courage to face that again. The Women of Connemara strike her dead if she lied.

Tilda looked the newcomer up and down, then shook her head and sighed, but when she turned to Morgan she was smiling. "Be good to have you home, Mr. Morgan."

"Thank you, Tilda. It's good to be home."

The black woman looked again at the girl and sighed. Nothing new there. Ever since he was a little boy Morgan had been bringing home strays. Dog, cat, or urchin, it was always up to Tilda to make the newcomer presentable. "Come with me," she said and set off around the side of the house. Roisin hesitated only a moment, then trotted after her.

Morgan watched the girl go, noting the narrow waist and the curve of the hips, and imagining the shape of the ass that was hidden by the torn and filthy homespun skirt and the equally filthy petticoats. He hoped it was a generous ass. He liked a woman to have curved and soft buttocks, ready to be pinched or kissed or spanked. Tight, flat bottoms were for boys. Thing was, until you got their clothes off, it was impossible to tell. Fun to find out, though.

"Later," his mother said firmly, tugging at his good arm. "First we must talk."

The copper bath was pulled up close to the fire and a young scullery maid emptied buckets of steaming water into it under Tilda's watchful eye. "That be plenty," Tilda said after the fourth addition of water. "There not be that much to this one once we get the rags off her. All right, missy, take off them tatters what pretend they be clothes."

Roisin hated the watching eyes of the black woman and the scullery maid, but she hated the filth more. For all the nine weeks of the crossing and the four weeks she'd spent in New York after her indenture was sold, there had been nothing but a cold splash. The rising steam of the bath reminded her of her mother's kitchen. It was irresistible.

Quickly she peeled off the grease-spattered homespun skirt, the threadbare blouse, and the tattered chemise and petticoats, all of them stiff with dirt, then stepped into the copper tub. If she closed her eyes she could pretend she was alone and that no one was staring at her breasts and her belly and her knees, taking her measure as if she were a mare on market day.

"Here, missy, you be using this." The nubbin of soap Tilda gave her was ash and lye beaten into a strong brown paste and hardened in a base of tallow. Roisin knew how to make such soap. Also soap as mild and soothing as thick cream warm from the cow, sweet with the scent of grass and flowers. The knowledge was part of her legacy, handed down from one generation of Connemara Women to the next.

She'd have used the brown stuff willingly enough, but a much older woman came in just then, so heavy she waddled, with at least three quivering chins, and stray strands of iron-gray hair escaping from her mobcap. "Here." She handed Roisin a chip of something smooth and fragrant with lavender. "You best be washing with this. Sure and it's a sweet-smelling bedmate Master Morgan deserves his first night home."

Roisin's stomach churned. She was being prepared like a haunch of fresh beef turning before the fire, basted and salted until it was juicy and tender and ready to be devoured.

"I'm Mistress O'Toole," the fat one said. "That's Tilda. The young one's called Mashee, but sure and she doesn't talk enough to give you any call to use her name. Not the wits for speech. Now, missy, bend forward and I'll tip this pitcher of water over your head. Good, that's fine. How old are you? And what's your name? What will we be after calling you while you're under this roof?"

"I'm fifteen. And my name is Roisin Campbell."

"Roisin, is it? Sure and that's an Irish name if ever I heard one. How did yourself come to be Roisin when Campbell is as Scottish as can be?"

"My mother was Irish." Roisin managed to tilt her head so she could see the older woman. "From Connemara," she added, waiting to see if there was a reaction.

Flossie dug her fingers into the girl's scalp, scrubbing away the filth of weeks. "Well, Connemara's Irish enough. But didn't your mother teach you not to go selling in the street what will earn you a dozen times as much in any decent bordello? Here, tip yourself this way so I can get the other side."

Roisin did as she was told. The scrubbing continued. The scolding as well. "Look at you, child! Made as well as any girl I've laid me eyes on, you are. And this red hair will be a fine sight once we dry it by the fire. Sure and where were your Irish wits to be throwing such gifts in the gutter? Pure waste it was to spread your legs for tuppence from young bounders when any old fool with a guinea to spare would have gladly given it for no more than a cock kiss."

"I wasn't whoring. I—"

Flossie and Tilda both guffawed. Even Mashee tittered. "Saints in heaven, but all you street doxies are the same when you're caught. 'No, milord, it wasn't me was bouncing me arse off the brick wall while some drunken sailor had his willie shoved in so deep it almost reached me throat. Oh no, not me, milord magistrate. Someone as looked like me, I expect. Me twin sister, maybe it was. Or me familiar.'"

Flossie wiped the tears of laughter with a corner of her apron and returned to the business of getting Roisin in a fit state to spread her legs for Morgan Turner.

"Mashee, stop your gawping and be getting me another bucket of water. I'll not be after sending Master Morgan a doxie for a night's fuck with soap still in her hair."

Eleven! Twelve! Thirteen! She's swooned, whipper! Wake her up so's she feels the next one! Roisin clenched her teeth and said nothing.

Squaw DaSilva saw to her son's shoulder wound herself. It was superficial, already scabbing over. A shake of some stanching powder and a bit of lint was all that was required. "We've no need to trouble Uncle Luke. It doesn't need to be stitched."

"I'm looking forward to seeing him nonetheless. How is he?"

"Uncle Luke is fine, but busy. Your grandfather died this morning," she said as she patted the bandage into place.

Morgan was shocked by the news. First because he couldn't imagine a world without Christopher Turner, second because she'd waited so long to tell him. "Why didn't you say? You sent word to meet you at the pit, but nothing about— How could you have gone there tonight, knowing—"

"Would not going have brought my father back from the dead, Morgan?"

"No, of course not."

"This shirt's finished," she said, throwing it on the fire. "There's a clean one in that cupboard. Your grandfather will be buried tomorrow afternoon."

"The arrangements—?"

"Everything that needs to be done will be done. Don't trouble yourself. I told you, Uncle Luke is seeing to it."

They were in her private parlor, but she had not removed her hat or thrown back her veil. Morgan didn't expect her to. He had seen his mother's unveiled face only once that he could remember. It was the day they'd moved to this grand house on the Broad Way in the choicest bit of the court part of town, in sight of the Governor's Mansion and across from the Bowling Green where ladies and gentlemen of New York took their afternoon strolls.

Morgan was seven. In all the fuss and trouble of moving day he'd been ignored. He'd run through the enormous new house opening every closed door and looking into each room; secretly he'd been hoping he might find his father. He knew he'd been brought here earlier; Morgan had watched from the window of the house on Hudson's River where they'd all lived until that morning. He'd seen a cloaked figure, face shadowed by a broad-brimmed hat, helped into a small, two-wheeled chaise and driven away.

"He won't be after being any different in the new place, grand as it is, Morgan lad," Flossie whispered coming up from behind and putting her arms around him. "Don't be getting your hopes up."

It was true. Each closed door Morgan opened in the enormous new house had led to a room full of fancy things he'd never before seen, but they were all equally empty of people. Except for one. When he opened the door to a room on the second floor—just a crack, the way he had all the others—there was Mama. With no hat and no veil. She was holding up her black skirts and dancing across the polished parquet floor, dipping and swaying and curtsying as if she were at a ball.

He kept his face pressed to the crack in the door, watching, thinking she didn't see him, but after a few moments she said, "Come in, Morgan. And close the door behind you." And when he did she knelt in front of him and let him stare at her as much as he liked.

"You're pretty," he whispered at last. "I thought you must be ugly. I heard one of the kitchen maids say you were poxed, and that's why you wore the veil."

"No, my darling boy." She took both his hands in hers and pressed them to her cheeks. He'd felt her smooth and silken skin, and he was proud and happy because beneath her veil his mama was a beautiful lady.

"Morgan, listen to me. We are not like everyone else. I am not like them and your father is not like them. Therefore you are not like them."

"Is that why they hate us?"

"Who told you they hated us?"

"The ladies in the other house. They all say—"

"The ladies are fools. If they were not they wouldn't be whores." She'd made no apology for using the bad word, even though Flossie had washed his mouth with soap the one and only time he'd said it.

"The real reason people hate us is because we are better than they. And smarter. And richer. They call me Squaw DaSilva to shame me. No, don't look like that. I know all about the name. Don't hang your head, Morgan. I have made it a title to reckon with. That's why we are in this lovely house in the most fashionable section of the city. Because I had it built and furnished and made ready for us long before any of them had the least idea who was the true owner, and now there's nothing they can do. We are here, and we'll stay as long as we like. We will always beat them, Morgan. You and I. Always. And we will have vengeance, my darling boy. I swear to you that we will."

"What's vengeance, Mama?"

"It is getting what is rightfully yours. Restoring your pride and your honor. And causing the greatest possible suffering to the one who tried to steal those things from you."

"Did someone try to steal our honor?"

"Oh, yes."

"Who, Mama? Who did—"

"Caleb Devrey," she said, staring deep into his eyes. She took his hands from her cheeks, but she kept them clasped in hers. "Look at me, Morgan. Now say 'Caleb Devrey.'"

"Caleb Devrey," he said. And added, "The Devreys are our cousins, aren't they? Flossie said so."

"That's as may be, Morgan. It is not important. I am telling you what's important. Now, say, 'Caleb Devrey will pay. I swear by Almighty God.'"

"Caleb Devrey will pay. I swear by Almighty God."

It was the first of many times she'd made him take that oath, but the only time she kissed him. Then she made him bring her the hat and the veil that lay on the large table in front of the marble fireplace in this grand room, which was to be her private parlor, and she hid her face from him and he never saw it plainly again.

A few weeks later Morgan announced that he wished to be called Morgan Turner, not Morgan DaSilva. His mother thought about it for a moment, then nodded gravely and said it was his right to choose his own name.

Mostly she supported every other right he claimed over the next years, including his notion to become a privateer at age nineteen. Because she knew her son was besotted with the sea and would likely sail off anyway. Far better he do so as master of his own ship, under favorable arrangements made by her.

His mother was the first to invest in Morgan's *Fanciful Maiden*. And it was because she did, and because her reputation for being fiendishly clever about business was known all over the city, that others backed a nineteen-year-old who'd never been to sea. They knew the veiled witch wasn't about to lose both her son and her money, and they were right.

When she struck her bargain with Morgan her only requirement was that she choose his first mate. Morgan agreed and his mother sent him off with Tobias Carter, a man who had captained four legendary privateers of his own, then drank and gambled away most of the proceeds. "Your legs are gone, your cutlass arm won't last more than sixty seconds in a fight, and your belly's rotted with rum, but in your youth you were the best there's ever been and there's nothing wrong with your brain," she told him. "My son will supply the physical prowess. Teach him the rest."

It all went exactly as she'd intended. So far everything had. "Cuf is back from the island," she said giving the bandage on Morgan's shoulder a final pat. "Everything went well."

"The notes I sent you?"

"Safely sealed in the gold horse's head with the ruby eyes. The one that belonged to your father. Do you remember?"

"I remember." He didn't look at her. "Though I expect he doesn't." She started to say something but he cut her off. "It's not the old madman upstairs I'm concerned about. The horse's head is buried near the boulder? Exactly as I instructed?"

"So Cuf says. You know he's entirely reliable."

"I do." Morgan had found a shirt in the cupboard. He put it on, enjoying the clean white linen against his skin, then walked to the small table near the window and poured a glass of canary wine and offered it to her. She shook her head. Morgan drank it himself, quickly, appreciating the rush of warmth in his belly. God, every muscle ached and he was weary to the marrow of his bones. But, he hoped, not too tired for the girl. He pushed the thought away, knowing he had to deal with business first. That had been one of his mother's earliest lessons. Always business first.

She sensed his impatience to be gone. "What about your crew?"

Morgan poured a second glass of wine. "I paid them all off with a handsome bonus. Came to four hundred pounds each."

Squaw's eyes narrowed behind her veil. Sixty percent of the prize to the crew was standard. And generous, but only with generous pay could men be inveigled into anything as dangerous as privateering. Fully half who set out never came back, and press gangs were not permitted to do their work on behalf of any but His Majesty's navy. If you wanted pirates worthy of the name you had to pay them.

"Four hundred each to a crew of seventy-five means you handed over thirty thousand pounds. So the balance of the voyage's prize is worth . . . Dear God, Morgan, nearly twenty thousand pounds." Her voice betrayed her astonishment. "That's incredible. You've never brought back so much from a single voyage."

Morgan smiled, enjoying one of the few times he'd managed to surprise his mother. "We took four Spanish merchantmen. Not one had more than nineteen crew or three cannons. The greedy fools never learn. Reserve every inch of space for cargo and you're doing the privateers a favor."

"Doing Morgan Turner a favor," she corrected, filled with pride. "But even four cargos, Morgan . . . I don't see how—"

"The fourth was a Guinea ship stuffed to the gunwales with live ware. The blacks were on the block within minutes of our reaching Bahama Island, and the money in hand half an hour later. After that we had a bit of pure luck. There was a French East Indiaman, *La Madeleine,* in port. The best of the Quebec factors was aboard."

"Ah," she said, no longer trying to disguise the smile in her voice. "Trading with the enemy."

"Why the hell not? I'm my mother's son, aren't I?"

Squaw laughed and waited for him to tell the rest of the story, savoring the moment. If she'd been a man, she'd have gone to sea as a pirate, exactly as Morgan had done. Better still, a legal pirate who had no need to fear His Majesty's almighty navy. But then, what wouldn't she have done if she'd been a man? Surgeries so extraordinary the whole world would have sat up to take notice, for a start. "Tell me about the French factor."

"He was happy to take our sugar and indigo when I told him he could have it below the rate I'd expect at the Exchange, just so long as he paid in bullion. All in all, you're right, close to twenty thousand's left, or near enough as makes no difference. I didn't count every last doubloon. Of course the lawyers and provisioners and factors this end will need to be paid out of our pockets."

She waved that consideration away. "Of course. But what about the crew? If any of them talk it will—"

Morgan turned back to the decanter. It made a handy excuse not to look at her when he spoke. "The men won't talk. There's no profit in it for them. Anyway, most chose to stay in the islands when I told them the *Maiden* wouldn't sail again."

It was the thought of Petrus Vrinck that made him not want to look at her. The only Dutchman to sail with the *Maiden,* curse his black soul. Vrinck, drunk as a lord and screaming curses and waving his cutlass around. And Tobias Carter staying Morgan's hand when he intended to kill the drunk for his insolence. Some ancient debt between them, Tobias said, that had to be respected. Last Morgan had seen of Vrinck, the man was staggering off toward the interior swamps of Bahama Island. Probably drowned long since. "The men won't talk," he repeated.

"And the *Maiden?*" she asked, watching him.

"To be sold, of course, as we agreed."

"Of course. I meant, how did you bring her home? Since the crew remained behind in the islands."

"Most of them remained. We returned with a helmsman and a crew of four. We avoided the shore and the coves that best serve a privateer and took the open sea, navy fashion. Fortunately we were never challenged."

"I see." She nodded gravely. "I take it Tobias Carter's among those who came back with you?"

"Yes. I suggested the old sot stay on Bahama Island and be rid of the cold winters in his declining years, but he insisted on accompanying me for the last leg of the voyage. 'Sweared I'd see you home safe, lad, and by a whore's piss, that's what I'll do.'"

She chuckled at his clever imitation of Carter. It was too bad about Morgan's affection for his first mate, but she couldn't let that stand in her way. There were five witnesses walking around New York who knew what had happened on the *Fanciful Maiden*'s final voyage. They'd have to be dealt with, Carter among them. That was her job, not her son's. "Well done," she said softly. "All of it."

He flushed with pleasure at her praise.

"Go on," she said, nodding toward the door. "Claim your copper-headed prize. But mind your shoulder."

❦

She was in his bed, waiting for him with the covers drawn up to her chin.

"He's tired," Mistress O'Toole had said when she'd brought Roisin upstairs to the most elaborate bedroom the girl had ever seen. "He won't want anything fancy." She'd lent Roisin a silk wrapper after her bath. When they got to the bedroom she tugged it off and laid it carefully over the foot of the high four-poster bed. "Just get yourself between the sheets, naked as God made you. And make sure you're still awake when he comes."

She was wide awake. Green eyes staring at him as he approached. Morgan took off his shirt and dropped it on the floor. She saw the way the black hair curled over his chest and ended in a vee about his flat stomach. And how large was the bulge in his tight-fitting breeches. All the same, he looked tired. Even a bit careworn.

"I must say you cleaned up well." He smiled, and that made him look a good deal younger and less exhausted. "Your hair's a wonder." He leaned forward to touch it but winced. Unthinkingly he'd used his right arm; it was stiffening as a result of the shoulder wound.

Roisin reached up from beneath the satin quilt and gently touched his bandage. Pirate or no, she was grateful to him. The bed was clean and warm, and her back was not striped with welts. "Does your wound hurt?"

"Only a very little."

"It's been cleverly bandaged."

"By my mother. She's remarkably good at such things. We Turners come from a long line of healers."

"I know a bit about healing."

"Do you? It's an odd combination with whoring." He spoke the words unthinkingly, laughing, backing into a chair and sticking out his long legs. "Here, lass. I don't want to send for anyone to disturb us now. Come pull off my boots."

Roisin slithered to the edge of the bed and reached for the silk wrapper. "No," Morgan said. "Stay as you are. I want to see what I've got now that it's washed and clean."

She hesitated for only a moment, then lifted her chin and climbed down from the bed. Turning her back to him, she straddled his right leg.

"Lovely," he said admiring the curve of her buttocks, still flushed pink with the warmth of the bath. "That's an ass a man can truly enjoy. It's going to be a fine evening. What's your name?"

"Roisin." She tugged his right boot off, then moved to the left. "Roisin Campbell."

"Rosheen," he said, giving it the same pronounciation she had. "It's a pretty name."

"Thank you. But none spell it as it should be spelled."

She was still standing over his left boot. God, an ass to dream about on a lonely night at sea. "Know how it's spelled, do you?" he said chuckling. "Have I found a little street doxy who can read and write?"

"I can read and write, yes. My mother taught me, but—"

She'd given up on his boot and was turning to say something more, but Morgan waved her back to her task. "C'mon, lass. Get that boot off."

He liked the side swell of her tits when she was bending forward like that, and the scent of flowers that rose from her skin now that she'd been properly washed. "What's your specialty?"

"I . . . I have no specialty. I'm not—" The left boot came free; she gathered up the pair and carried them over to the wardrobe on the far side of the room.

"No specialty," Morgan said. "Too bad. But never mind, before the night's over we may have discovered what you're best at. Here, turn around and let me get a good look at the front of you."

Roisin turned and stood in front of him, waiting.

"Closer," Morgan said and she took a few steps toward him. "Now move over there into the light of the fire. Holy bloody savior, but I've got an eye! You're a flaming wonder, girl. You're wasted on the street. If you can perform anything up to the standard of your looks, I'll see to it that you get a place in the finest bordello in New York. That should be inspiration enough."

"I . . . Please, I haven't the words to say how grateful I am, but can I expl—"

"No thanks necessary, Roisin Campbell with the perfect tits and the incredible ass who knows how to read and write. And that's enough talk. I'm too damned tired to get up and walk to the bed. Come over here and service me. Make it last longer than two minutes and the bordello job is yours."

Roisin went toward him. The grate was behind her and her face was in shadow, so he didn't see the tears that streaked her cheeks.

Morgan had loosed his breeches and freed himself. He reached for her, clasping both hands around her tiny waist, and lifted her onto his lap. "Not like that, lass," he said with soft laughter when she sat back on his knees. "You're going to do the riding. I've a fine mount for you."

He squirmed until he'd gotten her kneeling over him the way he wanted her to be, then thrust upward. She gasped. "Don't," he said quickly, all hint of laughter gone from his voice. "You don't have to pretend. I grew up in a whorehouse. I know all the tricks and I hate them. Just move. No, not up and down right away. Side to side first. Yes, like that. Ahhh, it's perfect. You've a sweet, tight cunt, Roisin Campbell. It's going to take you far, but tonight it's all mine."

Outside the door, her ear pressed to the carved oak paneling, Flossie listened to Morgan's grunts and groans and smiled. Exactly what the lad needed after a long hard voyage. And the girl had seemed clean enough once they scrubbed away the surface dirt. She'd checked the child's privates for any sign of a rash or a canker and seen none. Ah, wasn't it all in God's hands in the end? There was nothing she could think of worse than having her precious Morgan get the French disease, but neither was anything going to stop a lad of twenty-two from taking a turn in the stubble. Better here in his own house, with a strumpet Flossie had herself prepared for him.

Sure and didn't all the saints in heaven know that was what she'd been doing for as long as she could remember, readying women for a fucking by one or another of the DaSilva men. So to speak. And if she died this very night she'd be after telling her savior the same thing she'd often enough told herself: And what else was I supposed to do, Lord Jesus, lie down in the gutter and starve?

The steps to the fourth floor were narrow, twisting up the side of the house at the end of a dim corridor where no one but she and Tilda were permitted to go. Flossie sometimes worried that if she got any fatter she wouldn't be able to squeeze her way up that final set of stairs. And what would himself do then? Same as he'd been doing for the more than twenty years since the murdering savages dumped him in the drying yard of the whorehouse over by Hudson's River: nothing.

Dear Lord and all the saints, she'd have sworn after that day nothing could be worse. Showed how little she knew.

She paused for a moment outside his door, preparing herself. Or trying to. Would it never get any easier? No, probably not. She'd never stop breaking her heart over what he'd become.

Flossie opened the door. Solomon was sitting by the fire. He didn't acknowledge her presence even when she stood in front of him, but he knew she was there. He had an empty pewter tankard clasped in his bony hand and he thrust it at her.

"More rum, is it?" She glanced at the tray Tilda had brought up a couple of hours earlier. It contained almost as much food as had been on it when it left the kitchen. "Sure and it's a wonder you haven't starved to death long since, it's that little nourishment you take."

Dear God and all the saints, you took so much from him in those cursed woods, sent him back to us such a small part of the man he'd been. Could you not have left the poor thing his mind?

DaSilva wore a nightshirt and a dressing gown, and a cloth draped over his head. It covered his few tufts of white hair and shaded his staring eyes and toothless mouth. If they tried to take it away from him he screamed bitter Portuguese curses, the only words he uttered these days. The remainder of his communication was a growling from somewhere low in his throat. He made it now, brandishing the tankard.

"All right! For the love of Jesus and his Blessed Mother, be easy." She took the tankard and poured another portion of rum from the decanter that was always on the table beside his bed. "It's drinking yourself into your grave you are, Solomon DaSilva. Sixty-seven and not likely to see sixty-eight the way you carry on. And sure it will be a blessing when the last day comes."

She never heeded what she said to him these days. Why should she? Hadn't they always been frank with each other? Even back when she'd loved him so much—and gone on loving him long after he'd tired of her—that simply to be near him was all she wanted from life. She was bolder still now, though she was never entirely convinced he was as mindless as he seemed to be. That was why she went on telling him things, though he never reacted to a word she said.

"Long as you're still breathing you might like to know your boy's back safe and sound."

DaSilva growled again, banging his tankard on the table hard enough so some of the rum splashed out over his wrist.

"Your son," she repeated, ignoring his agitation. "She never made you a cuckold, you old fool. Not once. Do you not think I'd have told you if she had?"

He said nothing, didn't even look at her. But she wouldn't stop trying.

"Sure your lad's downstairs," she added as she picked up a few things he must have knocked to the floor earlier. Probably in one of those silent rages he sometimes had, twisting and turning and stamping his feet until he fell down with dizziness and exhaustion. "Home safe and sound, and having a fine time. Just now he's fucking the brains out of the prettiest little redheaded doxy you've ever seen. Fifteen she is. Mother from Connemara, so she's half Irish."

She stopped what she was doing and closed her eyes for a moment, remembering how it had been. "Reminds me a bit of myself at her age, she does," Flossie whispered. "Sure, and do you remember me then, Solomon? Back when you couldn't get enough of my twat, and being in each other's arms was all we needed of heaven."

He gave her no answer, but she hadn't really expected one. "See yourself into bed, will you?" she said with a sigh. He made no move to get out of the chair. "Yes, I thought so. Good night then. Sleep well."

Flossie turned and headed for the door, pausing once before she let herself out of the attic room that contained so much hatred and misery. "Sure and everything you once loved and cared about is here under your own roof, Solomon DaSilva. That's as much as any man can ask for in his old age. It's lucky you are in spite of yourself. Same as always."

Flossie let herself out. Solomon waited until he could no longer hear her footsteps in the corridor outside his room or on the stairs, then he got out of the chair beside the fire and stretched out on the floor.

He was right above Jennet's head. He knew it. His room was over hers. The day they brought him to this house he'd noticed that arrangement and been satisfied. He could stretch out over Jennet, the way he had all those many years ago on their bed. When he lay like this, with his ear pressed to the floorboards of his room, Solomon heard nearly every word that was spoken in Jennet's private parlor. He possessed her. Just as he always had.

In the morning, when Morgan saw the blood spots on his breeches, he assumed they were from the fight with Caleb Devrey's hired killers. "Stay a day or two," he told Roisin, feeling kindly toward her because however undemanding he'd been as a result of his weariness, she had pleasured him. "Later, I promise I'll see you get work with my mother. The street's no place for anything as pretty and pleasing as you."

The cortège was impressive, made up of at least a dozen carriages draped in black. Hall Place wasn't wide enough to serve as the marshaling point for so elaborate a funeral. Six pallbearers carried Christopher's pine coffin out of the house, past the old barbering pole that still stood where Lucas Turner had installed it ninety years before, and up to Hanover Square where the others were waiting.

"God protect us," one of the watching neighbors murmured. "There's no one in the city can be trusted with a knife now."

"Not so," the man next to him said. "The way I hear it, Luke's boy Andrew is the one with the Turner touch. Holds a scalpel like he was born with one in his hand."

The first man grunted and peered more closely at the tall, fair lad shouldering his share of the coffin's weight. He was at the front, directly opposite his cousin Morgan. "Makes 'em a right twosome then, doesn't it?" the man said. "Pair of giants, both making their living by hacking away and drawing blood."

Christopher was buried beside Trinity Church, the first of the Turners to be laid to rest in that distinguished graveyard. Every important official in the city was present, and Governor James De Lancey spoke a few words of eulogy for New York's most respected surgeon.

"Full restitution, I'd say," Luke murmured to his sister.

"Never." She was looking toward the back of the crowd, at two cousins from the Devrey side who had decided they'd face less gossip by coming to the funeral than by avoiding it. Bede Devrey and Zachary Craddock stood side by side. Each wore an appropriately somber expression, and both were careful to avoid anything that might look like an acknowledgment of the notorious Squaw DaSilva.

Bede was Croesus-rich these days. Devrey Shipping had come into his hands a few years before the wartime boom began. Her old enemy Zachary Craddock didn't look anything like as prosperous. He was considerably older, of course, and for all he'd been the first Edinburgh-trained physician in the city, he'd always cared less about doctoring than about politics. He'd been bad at both, as it turned out.

She smiled behind her veil. A year or so over seventy Zachary was, a bent and feeble old man whose only income came from the apothecary shop he'd gotten by marrying Red Bess's daughter. These days there were other such shops in the city, so the old place on Pearl Street wasn't quite the gold mine it had been. Still, Zachary was dependent on Phoebe for his income. Not one of the brats Tamsyn bore him had any talent or interest in simpling, and Tamsyn herself had been dead for five years of a cancerous pappe. Like her mother.

Kitchen gossip said that a short time before she died Tamsyn went to Christopher and begged him to cut off her tit, but he refused. Squaw considered that unlikely. It wasn't in her father's nature to turn away from such a surgery. Besides, he never resented what had been done to him as much as she did. "There can't be any repayment for the years they kept him in exile," she said softly, still looking at Bede and Zachary rather than at Luke.

"You're a hard one, Jennet."

A little shiver slid down her spine like a dribble of ice water. Now that Papa was dead, who but Luke would call her by her proper name? Her mother had been gone for six years. Her younger brother, Paul, had been killed four years ago in a quarrel over a bet on a match between a fighting terrier and twenty rats. As for her three sisters, the babies she'd helped her mother raise, one had married a Boston man and moved to New England. The two others were spinsters, living still on Hall Place. They didn't seek her company and she hadn't seen them in years. Even today they stood on the opposite side of the grave from their elder sister and pretended they didn't know her. Solomon didn't count since he hadn't spoken a word to her in nearly a quarter of a century. Apart from Morgan, Luke was now her only real family. "I'm as hard as I need to be," she said quietly. Oh, yes. No one should make any mistake about that.

A bit over a mile away, at the northwestern edge of town where the paupers' burial ground had been established sixty years before, the bodies of the dead were committed to the earth without ceremony, the only witnesses to their internment the gravediggers.

"Regular plague it must be. One as only strikes Jack Tar." The first of the pair of diggers leaned on his shovel and looked at the six fresh corpses awaiting burial. Every one of them had arrived at the cemetery wearing the tarred breeches and checked shirts that marked him as a seaman. And with his throat slit ear to ear.

"C'mon," the second digger urged, "get on with it. Be here until dark we will otherwise. No call to go mournin' over 'em, has ye?"

"None. Though I knows this one." The grave digger thrust his shovel in the direction of one of the corpses. "Name's Tobias Carter. Captained a privateer of his own, time past. These last years he's been first mate to Morgan Turner and the *Fanciful Maiden*. Rich as the devil himself, was Tobias Carter."

"No privateers is rich. Spends it soon as they gets it, they do. And rich or poor, didn't keep any o' the six of 'em from bein' butchered like hogs, did it?"

"No. Anyways, this one ain't a privateer." The first grave digger prodded the final body in the row. "Knows him as well, I do. Drank at the sign o' the Dog's Head in the Porridge when he could find the price of a mug o' grog. Same as me. Had that little boat did the run back and forth to the harbor islands. The *Margery Dee*, he called her."

"Don't call her nothin' now." The second man stretched out a mud-crusted boot and rolled the old seaman's body into the freshly dug grave. It fell with a soft thud. "Dead men tells no tales. It's what they say, and it's true enough."

Chapter Ten

"YOU WEREN'T AT the funeral. I was surprised." His Excellency Lieutenant Governor James De Lancey handed his guest a snifter of brandy and put the pinch bottle as well as his elegantly shod feet on the small table between them. "A blood relative, after all. I'd have thought you'd be there."

"Everyone knows I hated the arrogant bastard." Caleb Devrey tossed back the brandy and helped himself to another. "I hope he's burning in hell."

"I've never understood what harm Christopher Turner did you. It wasn't his fault things turned out—" De Lancey saw the black look on Devrey's face. "Forget I mentioned it. Nothing worse than family discords, God knows."

"Speaking of family, it was Oliver who said you wished to see me. About a matter that was to our mutual advantage."

"Yes, I believe it is."

"Nothing to do with any Turners, I hope."

De Lancey poured another tot of brandy into both their glasses and used the opportunity to size up his visitor. Most men grew heavier with age. Devrey was even thinner than he'd been as a young man. "Gaunt" was a better word, and there was a gray, unhealthy pallor to his skin. His appearance wasn't helped by his being perhaps the only man in New York to wear a black cutaway coat whatever the season. As if he were in permanent mourning.

Mind, lately he had more than enough cause. According to Oliver, Devrey had managed to scrape together two hundred pounds to purchase shares in the last sailing of the *Fanciful Maiden*. He'd have needed a proxy to do that. Given the bad blood between Caleb Devrey and Squaw DaSilva, Devrey would never have been allowed to invest otherwise. Apparently he managed it, then proceeded to back the single barren voyage the *Maiden* ever made. Devrey's two hundred could have been expected to yield a thousand, possibly two. Instead it was gone. No wonder he looked like walking death. "Well, Dr. Devrey, I asked you here because—"

There was a quick knock. "Excuse me, Your Excellency." A servant pushed open the door and came in without waiting for an invitation. "I'll only be a moment. More wood for the fire."

"Yes, Philip, very well. But be quick."

Devrey watched the houseman deftly stack an armload of logs in the fire basket beside the hearth, feeding a few fat sticks to the flames as he worked. Man was white; probably an indenture. Since the most recent Negro revolt, nearly twenty years ago, the official line said indentures were safer for the province. Caleb didn't see it that way himself. White servants had a way about them. Arrogant. Especially when they worked in establishments like the De Lancey country seat. Even this Philip. No forehead. Black hairline that practically met his bushy eyebrows. Acted like he thought he pissed claret. Nothing he did, exactly. Just a way about him.

Neither Devrey nor De Lancey spoke while the houseman worked. The fire flared higher. The governor and his visitor edged closer to the welcome warmth. Finally Philip stood up. "Is there anything else, Your Excellency?"

"Nothing. Good night, Philip. Close the door behind you."

"Yes, Your Excellency. Of course, sir. Good night to you both, gentlemen."

The door closed. De Lancey leaned toward the leaping flames and warmed his hands. "Cold night," he murmured. "Odd for this time of year . . . As I was saying, Dr. Devrey, I've a proposition for you."

"Yes, I know. I thought we'd already gotten past that part of the discussion."

De Lancey winced at Caleb's lack of finesse. The man was an insufferable boor, and he'd never understand Oliver's fondness for him. Still, Devrey could prove useful. "Now that Christopher Turner's dead, the hospital post is available. I have been thinking that a physician would be a better choice for the position than a surgeon."

Caleb narrowed his eyes. The directorship of the poorhouse hospital carried a stipend of two hundred a year. Enough to meet ordinary expenses, keep a roof over his head, pay for a couple of servants. It might even run to a carriage and a pair of horses if he was careful. Not that he was likely to be careful. But two hundred a year for doing nothing but showing up a few times a week and administering a purge to a few diseased beggars wouldn't put a strain on the time required by his private practice. With what he got out of that—even though it was half what it should be—he might have enough to make life worth living. Particularly now that Bede had suggested it was past time his brother move out of the family home. Sweet piss on the grass, he'd jump at the directorship of the poorhouse hospital if he could get it. The only question was whether he could meet De Lancey's price. "Luke Turner's in line for the post, isn't he?"

"I suppose that's the general assumption. But it doesn't have to be so. The appointment's in my gift."

Caleb bent forward and pulled the polished glass stopper from the pinch bottle.

"Help yourself," De Lancey said dryly.

"Thanks, I will." Caleb poured half a tumbler of brandy. "What I'm wondering is whether I can afford to accept your offer."

"I haven't made it yet." De Lancey smiled his thin-lipped smile. "As I see it, we're exploring the possibilities."

"Very well." Caleb leaned back and sipped the brandy now that he had gulped enough to kill the perpetual pain in his belly. He studied the older man over the rim of the glass. "Explore away."

"Cadwallader Colden," De Lancey said.

"What about him?"

"I am interested in having . . . Let's use the French term. It's a fine language, even if it is spoken by fools. I'm seeking an *avenue*. To Colden's fine mind."

"An *avenue*. To Cadwallader's mind. Ah, yes. I see." Christ Jesus, his brains were addled. He should have known the moment Oliver told him his bloody brother the bloody lieutenant governor wanted a meeting. There was nothing on earth Caleb Devrey could bring to a trading session with James De Lancey other than a connection with that pompous ass Colden. Still surveyor general, and still the only opposing force to the power James De Lancey was gathering in the province. "An *avenue*," Caleb repeated. "But that shouldn't be a problem. Colden's daughter's married to your brother Peter, isn't she?"

De Lancey shrugged. "Indeed, but Peter's household is up in West Chester. I see little of him or his family. Besides, a man can't be too prudent, can he, Dr. Devrey?"

"No, I expect not. Though prudence, as you well know, is not one of my stronger virtues." No point in pretending they weren't both aware of his reputation as a wastrel. Besides, he was long past believing that licking the behinds of the high and mighty served any purpose other than leaving a man with the taste of shit on his tongue. "Exactly what is it I can do for you in the matter of my dear friend and partner, Cadwallader Colden?"

"Nothing exactly. Not yet. I simply thought that if something came up where Colden and I didn't see eye to eye, I might count on you to persuade him to my side of the argument."

"Not a chance," Caleb said flatly. No point in making a promise he couldn't keep and ending up with James De Lancey as his enemy. However much pain he had in his belly, and however pickled with alcohol his brain might be, he still knew that much. "I have no influence with Colden. None."

"Why not let me be the judge of that?" De Lancey said softly. "You have . . . Let's find a good English word for it. Reach. Yes, that's perfect. You have the opportunity to reach our respected surveyor general. However much time he spends away from the city, he comes in to settle his accounts with you, does he not?"

Caleb nodded. Christ, the whole bloody town knew he had to give Colden half the receipts of his practice and that that millstone had been placed around his neck by his own father. To further the Devrey fortunes from which Bede, not he, gained all the profit. Sweet piss, no wonder his gut was on fire. "He does. Come into town to settle accounts at the practice, I mean. Once a month at least."

"Good," De Lancey said softly. "Very good. I can conceive of an instance when that might be important."

Caleb stared at him, then tossed back the last of the tumbler of brandy and leaned forward to refill his glass. De Lancey nudged the bottle away with an outstretched foot. The candlelight danced on the shiny black leather and the polished gold buckle of the lieutenant governor's beautifully made shoe. "Can I take it we have an arrangement, Dr. Devrey?"

Caleb paused with his hand still reaching for the pinch bottle. Sweet piss, the only way he could affect Colden's political choices would be to murder the turd in cold blood. And he sure as Christ wasn't prepared to swing. Not for two hundred a year. "I don't see what I'd be able to—"

"I told you, you're worrying about something that's not your concern. It will be simple enough if the occasion ever arises. I promise you that. Now, once more, Dr. Devrey, do we have an arrangement?"

Caleb hesitated. Two hundred a year. For seeing a few beggars once or twice a week. He'd use it to pay his basic expenses. Everything else would be cream. Christ, half the income from his practice would seem like a fortune once his essential needs were met. And if whatever De Lancey wanted was too dangerous, he'd deal with that when the time came. There were things he knew about Oliver and his Jewess wife and her peddler kin . . . Between them the family Franks and Oliver De Lancey had taken a fortune from the quartermasters of every barracks in the province, cheating the crown right, left, and center. Oliver had boasted of it a few times. Another card to play if he needed it.

Caleb drained his glass, then put it on the table. "Yes," he said firmly. "Why not? We have an arrangement, Your Excellency."

"Good, I'm glad to hear it." The gleaming shoe nudged the pinch bottle closer. "Help yourself, Dr. Devrey. Something against the chill of the evening."

II

"Then there's nothing you can do, Dr. Turner? You're entirely sure?" The man was a candlemaker, a decent hardworking fellow whose callused hands, home-spun shirt, and leather breeches made it apparent that the shilling he'd paid for this consultation had not come easy. He'd hung back when his wife left Luke's house on Ann Street. Now, standing in the doorway, he whispered a final plea. "Are you entirely sure?"

Luke hated this part of the practice of medicine. He never could manage to say anything truly comforting after he delivered a death sentence. He shook his head, murmured, "Nothing, I'm sorry," and pressed the man's hand in a gesture of sympathy at the same time that he eased him out the door.

The man stiffened his back and walked briskly to where his wife was waiting and took her arm. Luke closed the door, took a deep breath to clear his head, and spoke without turning around. "You can come out of the shadows now, Andrew."

His eldest living son had the Turner height, but in every other way Andrew was like his Scots mother. He had Maeve's sturdy, well-padded frame, and her fair, curly hair and hazel eyes. Poor Maeve. She'd died six years earlier, birthing Luke's tenth child. A girl it was, born dead. Each of Maeve's final five deliveries had ended the same way, and they'd lost three of those who were safely born. One to the yellowing fever and two in the same instant when they were trampled by a runaway horse and wagon. It was too much for Maeve. She'd given up and died as well. Luke still missed her, but that wasn't something he could discuss with either Andrew or Jane, his two living children.

"You remind me of your aunt Jennet," he said when Andrew stepped away from the tall wardrobe that had provided his cover. "She used to spy on our fa-ther's consultations at every opportunity."

Andrew brushed some dust from the shoulder of his coat. "And did Squaw DaSilva wear a black veil back then as well?"

"Don't use that name. It's a scurrilous insult and I loathe it. She's your aunt Jennet. And no, she didn't wear a veil. She wasn't married then, much less a widow."

"She's not a widow now."

"As good as. Poor creature."

"I wouldn't have thought 'poor' was a word that applied to my aunt. Or for that matter her pirate son, my fabled cousin."

Luke sighed. "Privateering is perfectly legal. And I know you think that at age twenty you know everything in the entire world, lad, but you don't. Not yet. Per-haps in another year or two. Now come into the consulting room and tell me what you're bursting to tell me."

"I'm not bursting!"

"Yes you are. It's written all over your face. Come along."

Andrew followed his father into the room that served as Luke's study, and the place where he saw those patients he did not visit in their homes. Luke took the seat behind the large pine desk; Andrew sat opposite him. "Very well," Luke said. "Here's your chance. Get on with it."

"With what?"

"C'mon, lad. Let's have a bit of Scots directness and less Turner cleverness. You think I was wrong to send that poor woman away, don't you?"

"She's going to die."

"Of course. We all are. I don't imagine that's news to you, and I'm sure it's not news to her."

"You know what I mean, Father. She's still young, and she's going to die in a matter of months. Possibly weeks."

"Yes," Luke agreed, his mood becoming more somber. "She is. She has dropsy and it kills. We have no means of preventing that outcome."

"But we don't try. You don't try."

"For the love of Almighty God, Andrew, did you see her belly? It's as swollen as if she were nine months with child. But she is not. That's what the midwife told her and I confirmed the diagnosis. Were you close enough to hear the hollow sound when I tapped her stomach? It's like a drum, lad. Entirely full of noxious fluids. That's dropsy, and as we both agree, it's a death sentence."

"Grandfather thought a belly full of fluid like that came from a cancerated liver."

Luke paled. For a moment he couldn't answer. "A cancerated liver," he whispered finally. "Are you telling me your grandfather cut open a patient's belly and saw—"

"No, Father. Of course not. Not a live patient. In an anatomy. More than one, in fact. A few times we—"

Luke drew a deep breath. "Dear God, lad. You terrified me. I should have realized. How many anatomies did you do with your grandfather, anyway? A dozen? Two dozen?"

"More. I don't recall exactly."

"No, how could you? I don't think you were more than eleven when he began taking you into his chamber of horrors."

"It wasn't like that, Father. Grandfather was always respectful of the dead. We always put everything back and sewed them up before sending them to be buried."

"Yes. I'm sure. After you slit their bellies and examined their livers and . . . and whatever else is in those hidden places."

Sweet Christ, look at the boy, driven by a passion to heal. And I can tell him nothing about what he wants to know. Would to God we'd had a few practical lessons at Edinburgh, and not spent so much time on theories about medicine in antiquity. But in the end it would make no difference. My son has to learn what we've all learned, that no surgeon can cure what he can't see. That's where we physicians come in. Emetics and purges get into the belly. If the job can be done, they'll do it. "Whatever else," he said again. "It makes little difference."

"It does to a surgeon, Father. Please, let me show you. I've some notes and sketches in my room. I made them the last time Grandfather and I did an anatomy on a patient who'd had dropsy."

Luke held up his hand. "No, don't go running off for your notes. I'm sure they're as clever as can be, lad, and I don't for a moment doubt the accuracy of my father's observations or yours. But what difference does it make? It can't help that poor woman who came here looking for a miracle. I can't supply miracles, Andrew. And neither can you. If you're going to practice medicine, either as a doctor or a surgeon, that's something you have to accept. Miracles are not in our gift."

Andrew took a deep breath. It was now or never. "I know miracles are impossible, Father. But a cancerated liver may not require divine intervention. If a surgeon can cut off a cancerous pappe, why not remove a liver?"

Luke was speechless. Father and son stared at each other for many seconds. Then Luke exhaled and found his voice. "Why not? First, because a pappe is on the outside of the body. That's what surgery is for, lad. Things on the outside of the body, or manifested there. Second—and maybe most important—we know quite well that a woman can live with only one pappe, but we have no idea whatever that a person, man or woman, can live without a liver."

"And we never will know until we try." It was as if Andrew hadn't heard a word his father said. His voice was becoming more sure as he repeated the argument he'd made to his grandfather a few months before. "If the patient is going to die if we do nothing, isn't it better to try something? If it doesn't succeed, where's the harm?"

"The harm? Where's the harm! Are you mad, lad? Or completely insensitive to the agony you're suggesting? What in God's name do you believe the practice of surgery to be? Your grandfather didn't train you to become a torturer. We're supposed to be preventing pain and suffering, Andrew, not creating it. How in God's name do you expect any patient to withstand the torment while you calmly set about slitting open their belly? How can you dare to—"

"Stop shouting, Father. Please. I'm not going to do any such thing. I know that's the problem we've yet to solve. That's why I wanted to talk to you."

Luke fought to regain his usual calm. "Enough. That's enough. This barbaric discussion is at an end. And you're forbidden to mention the subject to anyone else. I will not have you ruining your grandfather's hard-earned reputation by suggesting he condoned the idea of such torture."

Andrew sat where he was for a few moments, battling the anger that inevitably accompanied a medical discussion with his father. And the grief of knowing he could never again talk with his grandfather, whose mind had been as open as Luke's was closed. "Very well," he said finally. "I apologize for disturbing you, Father."

"Ah, lad, you don't disturb me. At least, not the way you mean. There's no harm in having ideas. You know I still use the breathing tube to help children suffering from *angina suffocativa,* even though it doesn't always work. And I'm frequently criticized for not doing the conventional thing and raising a throat blister. Innovation is fine. Sometimes it is necessary and helpful. But you mustn't forget that you're dealing with living human beings."

Luke got up and went to the window. Too capable with his hands, the lad was; his deftness with the scalpel had run ahead of his not yet mature judgment. "I know you're remarkably skilled at cutting, Andrew. Your grandfather told me so, and there was no better judge. But go too far, further than your patients are prepared to have you go, and you will not be able to earn a living as a New York City surgeon no matter how well you do your job. Your grandfather knew that as well. I wish he'd chosen to pass on the lesson."

Andrew stood up. "He did, Father. But Grandfather was right about the transfusing of blood. And I am right about the possibility of cutting away the liver."

"Stop! I told you before, that subject is closed."

"Yes, sir. I apologize."

"I accept your apology. And I've been thinking about your future, lad. I expect I'll be notified of the official appointment to the charge of the almshouse hospital in a few weeks time, possibly less. Perhaps you'd like to have the care of the wards one day a week."

Andrew glowed with excitement. "Father, do you mean it?"

"Of course I mean it. One day a week. Give you some real experience. With people who are alive," he added dryly. "And your job will be to keep them that way."

"Thank you, sir. I'll make you proud of me. I swear it."

"I don't doubt it, Andrew. Neither did your grandfather." Luke reached down and opened a drawer in the desk. The package he withdrew was wrapped in oiled cloth and tied with strong twine. "Here. He left these to you. They're your legacy."

Andrew knew what the package contained as soon as he saw it. He reached out, struggling to keep his hand from trembling. "Lucas Turner's journals," he said, his voice quivering with emotion despite his best efforts.

"Indeed. Your twice-great-grandfather's surgical journals. And some notes made by your grandfather over the long years of his practice. Treasure them, Andrew. They're without price."

The boy's face darkened and he didn't immediately take the gift his father was offering. "Lucas Turner wasn't really my great-great-grandfather, was he? Since we're all descended from Sally Van der Vries and the savage who violated her."

"It makes absolutely no difference. Sally was Lucas's sister. He adopted my grandfather Nicholas. We are not simply Lucas's only male descendants. We're Turners by blood."

It was an argument Andrew had heard before. He leaned forward and took the precious package from his father's hands. "I will treasure the journals and Grandfather's notes, Father. With my life. I swear it."

Luke smiled at the ease with which the young took a vow. "Life is the most precious thing on earth, son. Don't be too quick to swear it away."

After the unseasonable cold snap of a few days past, the weather had turned foul. It was warmer than it had been but blowing a gale, the rain sleeting down in almost horizontal sheets. Cuf hunched into his flannel jacket and hurried up the front path of the old house on Pearl Street.

The apothecary shop looked empty from the outside. Cuf pushed open the door. The bell made its customary harsh clang and Phoebe stood up from behind the long wooden counter. "Oh, it's you, is it?"

"Yes, it's me."

"What are you come for?"

"Mistress sent me."

Of course she did, Phoebe thought. Some made-up errand same as always. 'Cause she thinks I got to see my son regular like. Thinks if I do that, someday I'll forget about the white blood inside him. Never will. I be telling her that twenty-three years ago. Right after she came and saw him in his swaddling clothes. With her belly all swollen like mine had been. "Don't worry," Jennet be telling me. "I talked with Amba. She says sometimes women of your tribe have a light-skinned baby. But after a month or two they darken right up."

Mama be telling me the same thing. Until she died she be waitin' for my boy to darken right up. Only he never did. So it didn't help that I called my boy Cuffy 'cause he be borned on a Friday and Mama said back in Africa where she was a queen and I be going to be a princess, that's what they called babies be borned on Friday. But this Cuffy don't be one of us. Not Jethro's son, much as I hoped for that. This boy's father be one of them evil white men be doing it to me night and day for a month. Either the scout what captured us and killed Jethro, or one of them redcoats that guarded the stockade where they put me after.

So I don't be having no stomach to look at my boy, and Jennet be taking him in when he be a month old, and my milk be dried up because of how much I be hating my mostly white Cuffy. Took him in and give him to the same wet nurse was looking after Morgan. And my son drank white woman's milk just like Morgan did. And grew up more white than black. And that's all fine by me. Least it would be if only she'd stop sending him around and I could be at peace. "What's the mistress want now?"

"Some of the Health-Giving Tonic." Cuf nodded toward the barrel that stood at the end of the counter as it always had, and held out the jug Squaw DaSilva had given him. "This much."

Phoebe shook her head. "A whole jug full? That's the same amount she be getting a few weeks back. What she be doin', drinkin' Tonic for breakfast?"

"Sends it to the houses. To keep the ladies in good form."

A few moments later he left the shop carrying the brimming jug. The rain had stopped but Cuf barely noticed.

There was a remarkable carriage waiting on Pearl Street, one of the grandest he'd ever seen. The two wooden wheels at the rear stood almost as tall as his shoulder. The closed coach was painted golden yellow. Pictures of cherubs and flowers and scrolls adorned every panel. The driver, a huge black man in scarlet livery, had descended from his front perch and stood beside the gate.

Cuf paused beside him. "Fine carriage you've got there. And a fine pair of horses to draw it." The geldings were matched chestnuts with red velvet ribbons braided into their manes, and tall red plumes decorating their bridles. They kept their heads down and pawed the earth, as if impatient to race away. "It's from London, isn't it? No one in New York could make a carriage looked like that."

"From London, yes." The coachman spoke with his gaze fixed on some spot over Cuf's shoulder. Cuf would have turned around to see what the man was staring at, but he knew nothing was there. Negro people often avoided looking at him. It was as if his pale brown skin offended them. As if a man had a choice about the color he was born. "My gentleman," the coachman said, still not meeting Cuf's direct glance, "he wants to see you."

"And who would your gentleman be?" The door to the coach had a glass window, but it was entirely covered by a red velvet curtain.

"My gentleman told me to tell you he was an old friend."

"Old friends come out in the open to meet. They don't hide. Not even in a fancy coach."

At last the other man looked straight at him. He was about Cuf's height, but twice as wide. His dark eyes bored into Cuf's. "Your skin's not white," he said softly, "but you got a white man's pride in your mouth. I don't know if you're one of us or one of them, boy, but unless you want to swallow a few of your teeth, you'll take yourself inside that coach the way my gentleman asks."

It wasn't the man's loosely curled fists that made Cuf go. The man was big, but Cuf figured he could hold his own in a fair fight. It was the elaborately painted carriage that attracted him. Great God Almighty, no carriage in New York was grander. What must the interior be like?

He thrust the jug of Health-Restoring Tonic at the coachman—"Here, hold on to this"—and strode to the carriage and pulled open the door.

The man waiting for him was dressed in a cutaway coat of pale blue brocade. His long undercoat was colored gold and embroidered with gold thread. Layers of lace ruffles formed the cuffs of his fine linen shirt and showed below the sleeves of his coat. His breeches were dark blue velvet, his knee-high stockings white silk, and his shoes black leather with remarkably large silver buckles. The shoes stuck straight out in front of him. Because sitting on the red velvet seat of the fine carriage, his legs didn't reach the floor.

"Hello, Cuf," Jan Brinker said. "Climb up here beside me and close the door so we be talking in private."

Cuf stared. It took him several moments to find his voice. "It's really you, isn't it?" he asked finally.

"*Ja*, of course it really be me. How many dwarfs do you be knowing?"

"None except you. Only it's been so long."

"Sixteen years. But you didn't be forgetting me, did you, Cuf?"

"No, I never forgot you."

He couldn't have. The dwarf had been a constant presence in the bordello over by Hudson's River for the first seven years of Cuf's life. Then, when Mistress moved them to the new house on the Broad Way in the court part of town, Jan Brinker disappeared from their world. Cuf had heard Tilda and Mistress Flossie talking about the terrible fight the dwarf had with Squaw DaSilva, and how she threw the little man out without giving him a penny of the reward she'd always promised him for saving her life the night Caleb Devrey and his crowd of ruffians burned her house to the ground. But Cuf had never heard any details of the quarrel, or where the little man had gone.

"Chappaqua," Jan Brinker said as if he could read Cuf's mind. "When the cheating whoremistress threw me into the street, that be where I went. Chappaqua's a lake above the Van Cortlandt plantation in West Chester County. So far in the woods, it be t'other side of hell. Almost no one be living there, 'cept a few Quakers. But it's a good place to brew beer. All the fresh cold water you need be right to hand."

"Is that what you've been doing, brewing beer?"

The little man nodded, smoothing the front of his satin undercoat and adjusting his brocaded coat. "*Ja*. Thousands of redcoats all passing through West Chester on their way to the forts. Thousands and thousands. It's thirsty they be, Cuf. Very thirsty."

Cuf grinned. The dwarf had always been good to him, and to Morgan. The pair of them had been taller than Jan Brinker by the time they were six, but he always seemed more like them than any of the other adults. "I'm glad you've got on so well, Mr. Brinker. This is a splendid carriage. And you look . . . splendid as well."

Jan Brinker nodded. "*Ja,* thirty pounds I be paying the tailor for these clothes. And to get this carriage from London, three hundred."

It was an astonishing figure. But then, it was an astonishing carriage.

The velvet curtains blocked out the daylight. A small lantern provided dim illumination. The dwarf leaned toward Cuf and squinted, as if trying to decide what kind of man the boy had grown up to be. After a few seconds he appeared to have made up his mind. He reached for the carefully folded newspaper that lay on the seat beside him. It was the latest edition of the *Weekly Post-Boy,* published just that afternoon. "You be seeing this, Cuf?"

Cuf shook his head and looked neither at Jan Brinker or the paper.

"Honest you can be with me," the dwarf whispered. "I be knowing you read. Morgan teached you years ago."

"That doesn't mean I go around the streets of New York examining the *Weekly Post-Boy,*" Cuf said quietly.

This was caution he'd learned almost before he could walk. Cuf had been barely four in 1741, when plans were discovered for a second slave revolt. Everyone said it was a conspiracy to burn down the city. The Great Negro Plot, they called it, ready to believe anything after what they'd heard about recent slave uprisings in the Carolinas and what they knew had happened in New York in 1712.

For weeks on end none of the black people who worked for Squaw DaSilva—Tilda and the other maids and a few of the whores and most of the barkeeps—could leave the house. At night they had to sleep all together in the old strongroom in the cellar. Even Cuf. Squaw DaSilva locked them in and piled stuff in front of the little door cut into the rock. So if the soldiers came, they wouldn't be found.

Mistress Flossie said no one, not even the stupidest English redcoat, could imagine that a four-year-old boy the color of sand might have anything to do with a plot to burn down New York City and murder all the whites in their beds. But Squaw DaSilva said that redcoats and, worse, magistrates, could convince themselves of anything. So Cuf was locked in the strongroom every night with the others.

He didn't mind. By then he knew what happened when one of His Majesty's judges declared you guilty of anything at all, perhaps just thinking about killing white people.

For weeks on end during the time of the Great Negro Plot the city reeked of burning flesh. The smell wafted across even the open land that bordered Hudson's River. There were some two thousand slaves in New York City; nearly two hundred were arrested. Seventeen were hanged and thirteen burned at the stake. The rest were transported to the living death of the Barbados sugar plantations.

"I know you be able to read, Cuf," Jan Brinker repeated.

"As I said, I don't announce it on the public streets."

"*Ja*, but we be private here. And Rudolf, me driver, be big and strong. We be safe."

So the coachman was a guard as well. That made sense. You needed physical protection if you were three feet tall, totally bald, and dressed as if you were going to a ball at the governor's mansion. "What do you want me to read?" Cuf asked.

"This be the story right here."

Cuf took the paper and leaned toward the dim glow of the lantern. The *Post-Boy* was reporting on a battle that had taken place a short time before in Canada, on the Plains of Abraham above Quebec City. "Though we are informed that the great General Wolfe is dead, we can also report the good news that General Montcalm has been grievously injured," the newspaper exulted. "The valiant British forces were triumphant. England has won a glorious victory. Canada must surely be ours."

"This war be all but over," Jan Brinker said when Cuf lifted his head. "The English be beating the French. Just like they be beating the Netherlanders years ago. You know the meaning of that, Cuf?"

"Canada will be an English colony. One of us."

"*Ja*, I suppose so. But that's not what be important. *Jesu Cristo*, boy, think! War be over, that be an end to all our profits. Me and my Chappaqua beer, your God-cursed mistress and her whores, Morgan Turner and his licensed piracy— we all be finished. Home the redcoats will go, to Europe to fight somebody else."

Cuf stared at the foppish dwarf. He looked ridiculous, but there was something wise in his eyes. "Why do you think that matters to me? I'm a slave. Why should I care if times are good?"

"Don't be playing the fool with me, Cuf boy. I been watching you. *Ja*, even all these years I been away, I be keeping me eye on you. I know the God-cursed Squaw promised you your freedom when you be twenty-five. And I know about the little shop you be thinking to open. Nice things you be selling. Gold things and silver things."

Cuf's heart started thumping. No one knew about the shop—it existed only in his imagination—or about the smithing lessons. No one. The dwarf could have guessed only by getting inside Cuf's head.

When Cuf was a child he'd heard Grandmama Amba use the word *haptoa*. And he knew his mother believed that the night she and her Jethro ran away, the dwarf had put a hex on her, the bad *obeah*. Phoebe thought that was why they were captured and why Jethro was killed and why she had a half-white baby.

Cuf had been doubtful about all those magical stories. But Jan Brinker was looking at him and smiling. And, God curse him, he was right about everything he'd said. "You're sure that the end of the war will mean hard times?"

"Times that ain't so good like they been. *Ja,* I be sure about that. And something else. You be a fool to trust that God-cursed hag, Squaw DaSilva. Ain't nobody knows better'n me how she be keeping her promises." The words were thick with bitterness.

Cuf took a deep breath and held it. Far better to have magic—black or white—on your side than against you. "Say you're right," he asked softly, "what do you propose?"

"A little change," Jan Brinker whispered. "You be doing the same plan, only be a little sooner than you be thinking."

Flossie had given the girl a dress of yellow calico and a few decent petticoats, and a white mobcap to cover her red hair. "Sure and ye can't be goin' around here in them homespun rags, Roisin Campbell, half-breed Scots and Irish though ye be. 'Tis not fitting."

She'd been a week in the grand house on the Broad Way, and she was glad of the clothes, for all they were probably some whore's castoffs. Her nights, however, were spent buff-naked, with Morgan Turner riding her and doing things to her she'd never imagined a man to think about, much less do. Like the night before when he'd turned her on her belly and thrust himself into her back passage. True, he'd had her put oil on his cock first. All the same, she'd had to bite the corner of the pillow to keep from screaming aloud with pain, and it still hurt to sit.

She didn't mind. The pain was slight compared to the pit and the whipper. And after the first moment it had been . . . No, she mustn't think such things. She was a decent woman, a Woman of Connemara, not what Morgan Turner and all the rest of them believed her to be. No point in arguing that now. She wasn't a virgin anymore. That hadn't been her choice, but she didn't have to give in to pleasure when he did the things he did. She need not stoop that low. Besides, that wasn't really what she felt toward him. Not that he was a source of secret delight.

She was grateful to Morgan. Still. No matter what he wanted her to do in his bed. Each time she remembered the crowd screaming out the numbers of the strokes and the man in the black leather apron drawing his arm back as far as it could go, she knew she could endure any kind of perversity Morgan Turner could imagine. And that however many sins she might be committing against the virtue of chastity (and whatever shameless pleasure she sometimes took in those sins) being here with Morgan was the Virgin's gift and the answer to her prayers. The only thing that bothered Roisin, made her sick with worry, was the conversation she'd overheard between Tilda and Mistress O'Toole:

"Mark me words, Tilda. Mistress will be after sending her away."

"Why you be thinking that?"

"Sure and it's too fond of the doxy Master Morgan's becoming. And herself, she won't be doing with a whore for a daughter-in-law. Or a whore's piglet for a grandbabe. So's it will be off to one of the houses she'll be sending pretty Roisin Campbell and her sweet twat. Sooner rather than later."

Roisin had marked those words. And she knew that like everything that had happened to her since the ship docked in New York harbor, and the captain sold her indenture to a hunchbacked old biddy who wanted a white slave because she lived alone and didn't trust Negroes, this, too, would lead to the pit unless she kept her wits about her.

The biddy had threatened Roisin with the public whipper from the moment she brought her home and set to her working eighteen hours a day. "You be doing what I tell you, slut, or it's the public whipper at the poorhouse the Thursday to come. A few licks to break your haughty spirit and teach you to be grateful you're not sleeping in the streets—that's exactly what you need."

And when on a particular Thursday she saw the woman looking at her slyly, almost licking her lips with anticipation, then putting on her cloak and announcing they were going out together, Roisin knew what her mistress planned. A few licks. Expensive at one and six, but worth it since she'd have the pleasure of watching.

They set out and Roisin walked meekly beside her mistress for a time, waiting for her chance. It came when they passed a crowd gathered around a coach that had overturned and crushed some passersby. The shattered, lifeless bodies were surrounded by curious onlookers, but it was the horse they were interested in. The animal had broken its leg in the accident and was lying on the cobbles whinnying in agony. Soon someone would come with a musket to put it out of its misery. Then a butcher would arrive and cut up the carcass where it lay. Horsemeat went cheap in such circumstances.

The old woman turned her head, checking on the arrival of the musketman and the butcher. Roisin gave her a mighty shove in the back, thrusting her into the middle of the throng. "Here!" a man shouted. "Wait yer turn, ye humped old hag!" Mistress began an indignant tirade, shaking her fist in the man's face. Roisin ran.

She'd spent her first night of freedom behind a sailors' slop shop down by the docks, listening to the street doxies who'd invited her to share the warmth of the fire they'd made with a few scraps of wood and some twigs.

"Two things you'd best be avoiding, girlie. First is gettin' picked up by the constables now you be run out on yer indenture. Ach, don't look like that. 'Course we know. Yer white, so ye can't be a slave. Ach, girlie, stop shakin'. Ain't we all in the same fix?"

"Aye, every woman here's the same. But mind ye, there's things is worse than gettin' returned to the one what buyed yer indenture, and going to the public whipper at the almshouse for a taste of leather."

"Much worse."

"No," Roisin said. "There can't be anything—"

"Stop blatherin' foolishness, girlie. Ye ain't been long enough in New York to know. The pit's much worse than the almshouse."

That was the first time she'd heard about the sawdust-covered ring on William Street, and the noisy crowd that was much larger than any gathering at the almshouse. And how after you'd been flogged until the skin was peeled from your back, they sometimes tied you to the rear of a wagon and dragged you through the streets. Then banished you from the province.

"'Course, they don't do the banishing part till whatever redcoat wants ye has ye, all bloodied and bruised though ye be. For free, o' course. Never pay for it, redcoats. Always takes what they wants with not so much as a thank-ye. And leave behind a dose o' the French disease more likely 'n not."

That was something she knew about. The syphilis. Nearly impossible to cure, even for the Women of Connemara. The sores and the terrible burning when you pissed and the stinking discharge went away, but later they came back, and far worse came with them. "But if you risk all this by whoring in the streets," Roisin said, almost unable to keep the despair from her voice, "in God's name, why do you do it?"

"'Cause we likes to eat, girlie. Same as you and every other creature put on this earth. In God's name, like ye said."

"And don't make the mistake o' thinkin' that because ye be a bit of a looker with that red hair and all, ye might be doin' better in one of Squaw DaSilva's fancy houses. Get yerself into one o' them and Squaw owns yer body and soul. Have to do it with dogs and horses, ye do, if ye be one of Squaw DaSilva's whores."

"No! I don't believe any—"

"Yer a great one for not believing what yer told. But just get took in by the Squaw and ye'll soon see the truth o' me words. Costs men a fortune jus' to step inside one o' the Squaw's fancy houses. A guinea or more. No man be paying that for an ordinary fucking. Why should he?"

A woman who hadn't yet contributed anything to the conversation edged closer to Roisin, warming her hands over the dying embers of the fire. "I heared once about a whore of the Squaw's had to suck a donkey's cock while a dog fucked her in the ass," the woman whispered, enjoying Roisin's gasp of shock and the way the others all nodded agreement. "And every man what wanted to watch had to pay two guineas."

"I'd never do that," Roisin said. "Never. As God is my judge, I wouldn't—"

"Then ye'd be sent to the pit like that," the woman said, snapping her fingers.

"Faster 'n that, even. Squaw DaSilva it was who started the whole thing. Used to be only place the whipper worked was the almshouse. But it was the Squaw suggested having public whippings on William Street. Made 'em worse. That way she figured the likes o' us wouldn't go interfering with her business. And any whore says no to Squaw DaSilva 'bout anythin', that's where she goes. The pit."

"Aye. And afterward the Squaw's pirate son, Morgan Turner, he takes the poor creature what's had the skin flayed off her back and throws her in the hold o' that pirate ship o' his, the *Fanciful Maiden* as he calls her, and sails away. And God knows what happens to the whore."

"Fucked to death," the women beside Roisin said with authority. "Don't take God to know that."

Two nights later Roisin faced her choices and knew what she had to do. She couldn't expect the women to keep sharing the food they earned at such peril. Not when she did nothing to provide for herself.

She went prowling with two of the others, hoping she'd get a kind one her first time. Not daring to tell anyone she was a virgin. Shivering with fear as well as cold. And being picked up by the constables before any man had come near her.

Even warm and clothed and fed in Squaw DaSilva's own house as she was now, she trembled every time she thought of it. The crowd screaming, the whipper in his black leather apron, the poor tormented creature sobbing and begging for mercy. It could have been her. If the Holy Virgin had let her be first, the way she'd prayed, it would have been her. So if Morgan Turner wanted to fuck her to death as the street whore had suggested, so be it. But if Squaw DaSilva put her in one of her fancy houses, she'd soon be back in the pit all over again. Because nothing could make her do it with dogs and donkeys—

"What are you doing?" Cuf asked.

Roisin looked up from the small iron pot she held over the coals of the kitchen fire. "Warming this pan."

"I can see that. Why?"

"Because when it's hot enough I'm going to put those rose petals in it." Roisin nodded toward the basket sitting on the hearth.

"I thought it was the hips were brewed to make a tea."

"It is. But it's not tea I'm making."

Cuf crouched beside her. "Then tell me what you are doing."

"Why do you care?"

"Because I care about many things. What's the point of cooking rose petals?"

"I'm not cooking them. I'm simply going to warm them enough to extract the oil." She nodded toward the basket again. "That's *Rosa gallica,* the apothecary's rose. It's the one that makes the best scent."

"Where did you find it?"

"Out back."

"In Mistress's garden?"

Roisin nodded. "The bush isn't doing well. But there were a few blooms."

"And you helped yourself. You're a bold one, Roisin Campbell."

"I do what I have to. As for being bold, you're more than that yourself, Cuf— Do you have a surname?"

"DaSilva. Like the mistress."

"Because she owns you." He didn't answer, but Roisin went on speaking anyway. "I don't think it's right that people should be allowed to own other people. Even if they buy their indentures. Even if they're black. Though you're not really black."

"I'm not going to be a slave forever," Cuf said, his words edged with urgency. "I'm going to be free soon."

Roisin raised her head. "Are you, now? And how do you come by that idea?"

Cuf didn't answer immediately. He turned his head so he was looking at the fire, not at her. "Because the mistress promised," he said at last.

Roisin realized that the answer had come a heartbeat too late to be the truth.

III

Morgan turned the black stallion in to Ann Street and pulled up at the last of the row of small but elegant brick houses. He slid out of the saddle, dropped the reins over the hitching post, strode to the front door, and repeatedly banged the brass knocker. "Uncle Luke! It's me. Cousin Andrew! Cousin Jane! Is anyone there? For the love of heaven, someone let me in!"

"Mr. Morgan, they don't be here, sir." The black woman who opened the door was called Sarah. She had been Uncle Luke's house slave as long as Morgan could remember. She was wiping her hands on her apron as she spoke, and there was a smudge of flour on her cheek. "Dr. Luke, he be going to the poorhouse hospital. Took Mr. Andrew with him. Mistress Jane, she be—"

"Never mind about Jane. How long since my uncle and Andrew left?"

Sarah puzzled over that for a moment or two. "Seems like it had to be an hour ago, Mr. Morgan. I was just getting the johnnycakes ready for the skillet and I made thirty of 'em and each one takes—"

Morgan didn't wait to hear how long it took to make a johnnycake. He turned and strode back to the hitching post. He was mounted and heading north before Sarah had closed the door.

"Luke always goes to the hospital on Wednesday afternoons," his mother had said. "You must stop him from going today." She'd been more agitated than he ever recalled seeing her, wrapping her arms around her torso the way she did when she was particularly upset. "You have to tell Luke what's happened before he goes to the hospital and finds Caleb there."

"I'll go, of course, but how can you be sure Devrey's been appointed to the post?"

"Don't be a fool, Morgan. Why else do I pay spies?"

"But if this was a private arrangement between Devrey and His Miserable Excellency . . ." He pulled on his boots while he spoke, and grabbed his cutlass not because he expected trouble, only because he felt naked without it. "Are you saying you have informants in the governor's mansion?"

"Of course. And Bouwery Lane as well." James De Lancey had bought Philip Thomas's indenture when the boy was ten. Soon after Philip had been the first recruit to her irregular army. Twopence a week if he'd keep her informed of what De Lancey was up to. She'd raised the boy's pay every year since then. A man in his early thirties now, Philip was on two shillings a month. It was money well spent. "Hurry, Morgan."

"Are you quite sure De Lancey's made Caleb Devrey the physician in charge at the poorhouse hospital?"

"I'm positive. I was told about the plan some days ago. But I only just heard that the appointment's been made official."

They hurried down the stairs, his mother in the lead and Morgan right behind her. "But if you knew some days ago, why didn't you warn—"

"I've already told you. I didn't think things would come to the boil so quickly. And I needed time to figure out how to use the information. I thought . . . Oh, never mind what I thought. Just head Luke off before he and Caleb meet. God knows how that might turn out."

Galloping north in pursuit of his uncle and his cousin, it occurred to Morgan that what really worried her was the notion that Luke might have a duel to the death with Caleb Devrey. And win. God forbid Devrey should die before Squaw DaSilva had exacted the last of her revenge.

He was instantly ashamed of his disloyalty. Why couldn't it simply be that his mother loved her only surviving brother and wanted to protect him from humiliation? He knew the answer: because she wasn't like every other female, driven by tender thoughts and family feelings. No one knew better than her son how far she'd go to get her way.

Hell, he admired her for it. Always had. And it was thanks to her that right now he had the world at his feet, not to mention the most gorgeous creature he'd ever seen in his bed. No wonder he was spending so many of his waking moments figuring out new ways to fuck her. But there were more immediate tasks at hand. Preventing his uncle and his cousin from having their dignity disturbed by Caleb Devrey, for one. For another, he had to decide what to do about Tobias and the rest.

He'd been looking for over a week for the five men who'd sailed the *Maiden* home on her last voyage. In and out of every taproom, alehouse, and slop shop in New York. No one had seen the men who accompanied him back from the islands. Not since the evening before his grandfather was buried. Meaning since the first evening they arrived in port.

It was almighty strange, but nothing to do with his mother. Stupid to think so. Why would she—

Because she trusted no one. And because Tobias Carter and the others knew that, contrary to published reports, the *Maiden* had taken plenty of plunder on her last voyage. But by God, he'd told her the men he brought back with him could be relied on. He gave her his word on it. Surely she'd have consulted him if . . .

When did she ever consult anyone?

He'd confront her with his suspicions. That very evening. Now he would put the matter aside and concentrate on overtaking Luke and Andrew.

The black stallion pounded up the King's High Road to Boston toward the outlying Common and the almshouse, overjoyed at being able to gallop flat out rather than be held to a slow canter through the city's crowded streets. Morgan flattened himself over the horse's mane and gave the gorgeous beast his head.

Holy Savior Almighty. It was like beating to windward with every inch of canvas spread and stiffened in the breeze, topsails hard-bellied, and the rigging singing.

The thrill of the wild, unfettered ride made his pulse race and his blood pound. But even as he gloried in the exhilaration, part of Morgan's mind registered that a ride like this was possible only because there were no vehicles or pedestrians ahead of him on the wide, cobbled road. And no one on horseback. No sign of his uncle or his cousin.

If Sarah had been accurate and they had an hour's head start, they were already at the poorhouse hospital. And whatever his mother hoped to accomplish by heading them off, it was long since a lost cause.

"I don't want you doing anything drastic before consulting me, Andrew. You must give me your word that you won't."

"I have given you my word, Father. Repeatedly."

"Yes, I know. Sorry. It's only that I'm not entirely comfortable letting you make the rounds of the ward in my place before my appointment's been made official. That's why I'll go with you these first few times. Simply a precaution, lad."

The almshouse and its hospital had been enlarged several times in recent years. However profitable, war also made widows and orphans who were unable to support themselves after the man of the family took a French bullet or an Indian arrow for the sake of the King. Likewise, many men wounded in battle could afterward neither fight nor work. The poorhouse on the Common was the destination of all of them, and two new wings and a new entryway had been added to accommodate the influx.

Luke took off his cloak and hung it on the peg beside the front door. Another cloak was already there; not one he recognized. Had to be a visitor. He looked around for the warden or one of the trusties who guarded the inmates, but saw no one he could ask about the caller. Not important. Keeping the lad from cutting off every finger with a splinter or toe with an ingrown nail, that's what was important.

"Very well, Andrew, let's go upstairs. Remember, don't hesitate to put any questions about the condition of the patients. And try to consider their entire well-being, not simply those bits you may be able to attack with a knife."

"A scalpel," the boy corrected, under his breath, softly enough so his father couldn't hear. Please God, let him not lose this opportunity. Having the ward of a dozen or more patients to himself one day a week, deciding what was wrong and what could be done to put it right. God Almighty, that was heady stuff.

Luke led the way to the door of the hospital, his son on his heels. Suddenly the older man stopped short. Andrew plowed into his back. "Sorry, sir. I didn't—"

Luke ignored him, concentrating on the tall, gaunt figure standing in the middle of the ward. Clad entirely in dusty black. Looking like death come to visit. "What in hell are you doing here?"

Caleb Devrey turned to face him, making no attempt to hide the glow of his pleasure. He hadn't counted on the joy of actually seeing Luke Turner get the news of how things had fallen, but he'd certainly hoped for it. "I'm earning the two hundred a year the city pays me now that I've been appointed physician in charge of the poorhouse hospital, Dr. Turner. What's your excuse for being present?"

"Your appointment? I don't believe you."

"Then allow me to convince you." Devrey reached into the pocket of his cutaway and withdrew a piece of paper. "Here's my letter of confirmation to the post, signed by His Excellency James De Lancey. Would you care to examine it?"

Luke snatched the paper from Caleb's hand, scanned it quickly, then let it drop to the floor. "This is nonsense. You are not competent to hold this position." Each word was edged with the depth of his contempt. "I shall raise the matter with the Common Council."

Caleb shrugged. "Do as you like. The Council is answerable to the governor, and this commission is in his gift. Always has been. Wasn't it that greedy fool Cosby who signed your father's appointment to life tenure? One more of the acts of misgovernment for which the entire province rightly despises him."

Luke growled, a sound of inarticulate rage, and lunged. Andrew grabbed him. "Father, no! Not here and not now. The patients . . ."

The boy's final words rather than his grip were what stopped Luke's charge. Every patient who was well enough had sat up in bed to watch the fracas at the door of the ward. It was scandalous to allow the indigent see their betters fighting like toughs in the street. Luke was still enough in command of his wits to know how the story would sound when it was repeated to the Council.

"You're right, son. The patients are ill served by this argument. You will hear from me, Dr. Devrey. But, as my son properly says, not in this place at this time." He turned to go and Andrew followed him.

"Not so brave when you don't have a musket, are you?"

Luke was halfway down the stairs. He paused, turned, and said in a loud voice, "A good deal braver than is required to set fire to a house occupied by no one but a young woman and her servants. Almighty God forbid I'd ever be that much of a coward."

"Are you accusing me of arson?" Caleb's gut was roiling. "I'll have satisfaction, Turner!" he shouted.

"Any type of satisfaction you choose," Luke shouted back, the thought of finally putting an end to the life of Caleb Devrey warming his blood. "Whenever and wherever you say. I shall await your seconds, sir."

"Father!" Andrew made himself whisper. Christ! A duel was no way to guarantee that Governor De Lancey would change his mind and rescind his order. There were other physicians in the city. Far easier to choose someone who had no part in the quarrel, even if Caleb Devrey was the one left dead. Andrew saw his opportunity to practice surgery, the beginning of the brilliant career he'd been dreaming of since he was eleven, slipping away. "Please, Father, this isn't the way."

"Silence!" Luke hissed through clenched teeth. "It's settled. The challenge is issued." He started down the stairs again, deliberately turning his back on Devrey.

"I'm not finished with you!" Caleb knew how unwise the words were, but he couldn't bite them back. The rage born the night Christopher Turner told him he'd been tricked into becoming engaged to a girl who was part savage, the injustices he'd suffered while the Turners went on to acclaim and prestige, the way Jennet ignored him as if he'd never mattered . . . Nearly three decades' worth of fury blazed inside him. The fire couldn't be contained. "You bastard, Turner! Turn around and fight like a man!"

Luke felt a rush of triumph. Devrey was digging a deeper and deeper hole for himself. The fool was probably half drunk. No, two-thirds drunk. All Luke need do was not give in to the urge to pummel the rotten bastard into the ground. Control was the sharpest sword, and a weapon only he possessed. He continued down the stairs, tossing a final challenge over his shoulder, "Your seconds, Devrey. Or if you prefer, we can tell this tale to the Council."

"Well done, Father," Andrew said quietly. "You've bested him. He's the one will be accused of creating a public row."

They were at the door of the almshouse. Luke reached up and grabbed his cloak, throwing it on as he yanked open the door, conscious that the warden and his wife and some half-dozen trusties had heard the shouting and were crowded into the front hall, watching and listening. Fine. They would make excellent witnesses to bring before De Lancey and the Council.

The moment the door was open Andrew raced down the outside stairs ahead of his father, running to get the pair of horses they'd tethered a few feet away. The best possible end to this business was for the Turners to ride to town as quickly as they could, and get their version of the tale circulating before Devrey had a chance to advance his.

Andrew had to skirt an arriving wagon carrying six huge boulders. The indigents assigned to hard labor would spend weeks pulverizing those enormous rocks with sledgehammers that often weighed more than they did.

He ran past the load, his boots thudding on the beaten-down, mud-slicked gravel. Get the horses. Get himself and his father away from the poorhouse before any further damage was done.

"Damn your miserable skin, Turner! I said I wasn't finished with you!" Devrey hurtled out the door and lunged for Luke's back. He was a madman, taking the granite steps two at a time, hands outstretched, fingers bent into claws.

Luke thrust out an arm to push him away. Caleb charged again. This time Luke stood his ground and the pair of them finished in a tangled heap, rolling about on the muddy earth at the foot of the almshouse steps.

Andrew was already astride one horse, leading the other, an aging mare, by her reins. "No! Don't fight him, Father!" He dug his heels into his mount's sides, urging the horse forward, dragging the mare behind him. "Please, Father, listen to me! A fight's the worst—"

The mare was accustomed to gentler treatment. She felt the insistent pressure on her bit and whinnied in protest and pulled back. "C'mon, damn you!" Andrew tugged harder on the reins. "Father, I beg you!" His mount, sensing the unrest and urgency in his rider's voice, snorted and tossed his mane. The mare whinnied.

The cart horse, an old gray long since beaten into submission, stood alone and untethered. The driver was trying to edge around the pair of gentleman pummeling each other at the foot of the poorhouse steps. If he wanted to be home for his three o'clock dinner he had to get inside and get the warden's permission to dump his load of boulders out back. And claim the threepence he was owed for hauling them.

Andrew tried desperately to rein in his mount, but he succeeded only in making things worse. The horse reared, nearly mauling the mare Andrew still had by the reins. At that moment a black stallion came through the gate galloping toward them at tremendous speed.

It was too much for the old cart horse. Terrified of the unfamiliar smells and sounds of confrontation, the gray tried to turn sharply and run from the danger. The wagon tilted, balanced precariously for a single moment, then cracked in two. One after another the enormous boulders crashed to the earth and began to roll toward the almshouse steps.

Morgan took in the scene the way he'd absorbed so many battles during the last three years: he was instantly aware of where his foes were and where his allies could be found. *Knowin' without knowin' how ye knows,* Tobias Carter had called it. *It's a special sense, lad. Them as is born to lead, they has it. You see what you got to do and you does it. Faster'n a whore opens her legs. And without a lot of hemmin' and hawin' 'bout where the pussy hole's to be found.*

The largest of the boulders was gathering speed, heading directly for Uncle Luke and Caleb Devrey. Each so intent on beating the other to a pulp that both were oblivious to the danger. Morgan rose in the saddle and dug his heels into the stallion's flanks, urging the exhausted animal into one final burst of speed.

The stallion thundered forward. Morgan swung sideways, hanging on with one hand, using the stirrups to secure his position and give him control. Barely a second before the boulder crashed into the two men at the foot of the steps, he swept Caleb Devrey out of harm's way. And heard his uncle Luke's scream of agony as the boulder rolled over him.

"No matter what the provocation, you will never put Caleb Devrey to death. In fact, if he is threatened by someone else you will help him. Anything to keep him alive. Swear it, Morgan!"

"I swear, Mama."

"Both his legs," Andrew said. "Crushed below the knee between the poorhouse steps and the boulder." He was white and shaking, unable to look directly at his sister.

Jane sat beside her father. Luke was stretched out on the chaise in his examining room on Ann Street. Andrew had managed to stop the bleeding, then positioned two curved barrel staves above Luke's shattered legs so the blanket wouldn't touch the terrible wounds and cause still more pain.

Luke's breath came short and hard, each inhalation rattling in his chest. His eyes were closed, his skin almost blue. "I don't understand," Jane kept repeating. "Why would Cousin Morgan save Caleb Devrey rather than—"

"I've told you over and over," Andrew said impatiently, looking at his father, not his sister. "I don't know. But that's what he did."

"No, he can't have. You must be—"

Luke's weak voice interrupted their argument. "Andrew. Are you there, boy?"

"Yes, Father, I'm here." Andrew went to the chaise and knelt beside it. "Rest, sir. Don't try to speak."

"Have to. You must . . ." He couldn't find the breath to tell Andrew what he must do.

Jane leaned forward, wiping away the perspiration that broke out on Luke's unnaturally cold forehead. "Andrew's right, Father. You should rest. We're both here."

"Andrew, come closer."

Andrew bent his head so his father's lips were almost touching his ear. "I can hear you, Father. Just tell me what you want."

"My wounds," Luke whispered. "How—" A torrent of hard dry coughs choked off his words. Jane held a mug of weak ale to his lips and Luke took a few sips. The coughing subsided. "The wounds," he repeated, "how bad?"

Andrew swallowed hard. He could say they weren't all that serious, that they'd heal, that his father might be lame, even crippled, but he'd survive. It would be kinder, but there was too much of his Scots mother in him to allow him to take such an easy course. "They're very bad, sir."

"The bones . . . All broken?"

"Every one below the patella, sir." Andrew had to struggle to get the words past the enormous lump in his throat. "I'm so sorry, Father. It's my fault. If I had stayed beside you rather than running to get the horses—"

"No one's fault. Fate, lad. Life and death. Out of our control. Except . . . except . . ."

Andrew bent closer, suspecting his father had more to say. Something about taking care of Jane, probably. "What is it, sir? Only tell me what you want and I'll do it, I swear."

"My legs," Luke said. "I want you to cut them both off."

Andrew sensed Jane staring at him and knew she'd heard the whispered words. He opened his mouth, struggled; finally the words came. "I can't, sir. I beg you, don't ask me. I've not the experience. And the pain will—"

His father was too weak and traumatized to withstand such an operation. It would kill him as surely as the gangrene that must inevitably spread from the pulverized flesh and bone. He'd die in either case, but if Andrew operated death would come during unspeakable torment. A skilled practitioner, a genius like his grandfather, might perform such a double amputation in under an hour. It would take Andrew two or three times as long. And the result? God alone knew.

Luke clutched at his son's arm. Andrew looked down and saw that his father's nails were turning blue. He could hear his grandfather's voice as if the old man were standing at his shoulder. *"Keep watch on the nails and the whites of the eyes, lad. If they're getting blue, the patient is going into shock and you don't have much time."*

Andrew couldn't bring himself to pull down his father's lower lids and check the whites of his eyes. Besides, he knew what he'd see. "I can't do it, sir. I can't put you through so much torment when it's—" He broke off. When it's pointless, he was going to say. When I'm sure you wouldn't live through such a surgery. "I haven't the experience, Father. I've never amputated on my own. Only with Grandfather standing beside me."

"He'll be beside you now, Andrew," Jane murmured. "If you do what Father wants, Grandfather will guide you."

Andrew shook his head impatiently. He's dead! he wanted to shout. Christopher Turner died less than ten days before he could have saved the life of his son. So much for all your woman's nonsense about angels and God's mercy and life everlasting. Let Jane take what comfort she could from her ideas and her church going. He ignored his sister and spoke to Luke. "I could get Hezekiah Jackson, sir. Grandfather trained him and he always said Jackson was a competent surgeon. He lives up in Yonkers, but if I left immediately I could bring him back by morning."

"Worse by morning," Luke rasped. "Maybe dead. Besides, you're the best pupil your grandfather ever had. He always told me you'd—" He was interrupted by another fit of coughing.

Jane offered the ale again, but this time her father pushed her hand away, mastering the spasm by force of will. "Andrew, listen to me. You must do this. Only you."

Jane turned and looked at her brother. He stared at his father a moment; then his gaze met Jane's. "Do you agree?" he asked. "It may not—"

"I know. It may not make any difference. But Father's right. You must try."

Andrew put a hand over Luke's heart. The beat was thready, unstable. So much rum was bound to have that effect, particularly when a man was already at death's door. Sweet Jesus Christ. He couldn't do this. But he had to. He'd given his word.

Everything was ready. Jane had poured enough rum down the old man's throat to make him unconscious. Andrew had roped him securely to the chaise, spreading oiled cloths on the floor so the flesh and bone he'd sawed off could be gathered up and discarded.

His instruments were ready. They had been given to him over the years by his grandfather, each the acknowledgment of some newly acquired skill. Four fluted probes. Three curved needles of different sizes, and plenty of carefully made ligatures. Half a dozen variously sized scalpels, all sharpened to a fine edge. Two saws, each freshly oiled to prevent snagging. He'd even read through the instructions concerning amputations of the leg in Lucas Turner's journal.

Gunshot Wounds, compound Fractures, and all sudden Accidents requiring Amputation are attended with the best Success if immediately performed. When a Leg is to be amputated the manner of doing it is this: While an Assistant holds the Leg, you must roll a Slip of fine Rag half an inch broad three or four times round it, about four or five Inches below the inferior Extremity of the Patella . . .

"Jane, can you assist me?"

She swallowed and took a breath so deep her chest heaved. "If it's necessary, I'll try."

"Of course it's necessary." It was a role he'd often filled for his grandfather. Andrew knew exactly what was required. "You have to hold the leg steady, on an even plane. If you lift it my saw will clog, and if you drop it the bone might snap. That's bad, because we need a clean break and— Jane, are you all right?"

"Of course I'm not all right." She was pressing her pocket cloth to her forehead. "Please, Andrew. Just tell me what's required as you progress. I'll do my best."

"Yes, very well."

Damned women. Ah, that wasn't fair. Jane couldn't help being a female. But what was his excuse? His hands were shaking. Both of them. He'd seen his grandfather do this at least a dozen times, and he could recall every movement and every word of explanation. But actually doing it, on his own gravely wounded father . . . Sweet Christ, he had to get control of his hands.

Andrew took a few more deep breaths, then leaned forward and rolled back the blankets, lifting them over the barrel staves. Luke groaned once, then lapsed back into unconsciousness. Andrew took the staves away and bent close to his father's shattered legs. He could feel heat rising, the beginning of the inflammation that would lead to gangrene and death. They should have delayed long enough for him to ride up to Yonkers and bring back Hezekiah Jackson.

"Hezekiah's weak on diagnosis," Grandfather always said, "but a fine hand with a knife." There was no diagnosis required here, and Jackson had been in practice these past fifteen years. Nothing but family pride made Grandfather say Andrew was the best student he'd ever had, and now that pride was going to kill his father. Sweet Christ, he'd given his word to a dying man. He had to find the strength to do what he'd promised to do.

A tourniquet around the thigh first. A strong band of leather with a slit, so he could pass one flap through the other and draw the thing as tight as his strength would allow. Luke groaned again.

"You're hurting him," Jane murmured. Then added, "I'm sorry, that's an idiotic thing to say."

"I have to compress the artery so it doesn't bleed."

"Yes, I see. Will you do both legs at once?" She was trying to sound normal, but her voice was high-pitched and breathy, and it shook.

"No, one at a time. I think that's more sensible."

"You think? Dear heaven, Andrew, are you not sure?"

"Of course I'm not sure! How could I be? I've never done this, Jane."

"Don't shout, Andrew. It will only wake him. I merely asked a question."

"Well, don't ask any more. Not until we've finished." He didn't tell her that however quiet they were, the first cut would wake the patient. He'd never seen it any other way. Alcohol might lessen the suffering somewhat, but it didn't make a man insensible of pain.

You must begin your Incision just below the linen Roller you have carefully put in place, on the under part of the Limb, bringing your Knife toward you, which at one Sweep may cut more than the Semicircle.

Luke's first shriek sent Jane reeling back from the chaise. She dropped the leg she'd been holding steady and screamed, "Stop! You're killing him, Andrew! Stop!"

Damn her! He'd been afraid of exactly this. "Get out!" Andrew shouted. "Now! Go!"

"No, please." Jane pressed both hands to her chest as if she could physically stop her heart from pounding. "I'm sorry, I want to help. It was just the shock. I'll be fine."

Andrew swabbed at the blood oozing from his first cut and didn't lift his head. "Get out," he repeated. "Send Sarah to me. Maybe she's strong enough to do what needs to be done."

He heard Jane's muffled sobs and the door opening and closing, but he didn't turn his head to see her go.

Thanks to the tourniquet he'd put in place around the thigh, the bleeding from the incision was a minor matter. In moments he could see well enough to make the second cut. *Begin your second Wound on the upper part. It must be continued from one Extremity to the other of the first Wound so the two form one line, and both must cut quite through the* Membrana Adiposa *as far as but not including the Muscles.*

The screams of suffering were relentless, like an ocean pounding at the shore. They pierced his skull. Andrew knew he must shut them out or he could not do his job. He knew, too, that they were going to get much worse when he started to saw through the bone.

His hands were shaking again, and his patient was thrashing and twisting against the ties that bound him to the chaise. If the restraints were accidentally loosened his father might move. There were times when a slip of the scalpel—or worse, the saw—could be disastrous. He could not do this without assistance. Damn Jane! Damn all women! Why were they so weak and stupid? And where in hell was Sarah?

The door behind him opened and closed. Thank God. "Sarah, come here. You must wipe away the blood so I can see what I'm doing. And hold the leg steady. Straight out. I'll show you what I mean. Just come do what I say."

Footsteps approached. Andrew didn't turn his head. A hand reached out and touched the patient's forehead. The arm was covered by a long black sleeve.

He'd been swabbing at the wound with a rag. Andrew stopped, turned. "What are you doing here?"

"I came to bring this." Squaw DaSilva held out a small brown-glass bottle. "It's laudanum, the best and most potent quality. I got it from Phoebe. I didn't know you were operating, I just thought it might help with the pain."

Andrew nodded curtly. "Give it to him. I should have thought of laudanum myself. I was so worried I forgot." No time now to charge her and her rotten son with being the cause of all their grief.

He watched his aunt pull the cork from the bottle and little by little tip the contents into Luke's mouth, waiting for the natural instinct to swallow to take over after each tiny draught. "Jane said you needed help, Andrew," she said softly, keeping her eyes on her brother rather than turning to face his son. "Will you allow me to assist you?"

"You won't swoon, or start to scream? Jane tried to help but—"

"I promise you I will neither swoon nor scream."

She spoke from behind her veil, and her tone was serious, but he could have sworn he saw a smile playing about her mouth. *Your aunt Jennet always spied on every operation your grandfather performed.* Father had said that just five days ago. "I should be glad of your help. If you will."

"Oh yes, I will," she said softly. She bent forward, inspecting the leather tourniquet around the thigh, the band of linen cloth that had been carefully tied below it, and the perfectly even, circular cut Andrew had made through the skin. She began to speak, softly, with a ring of certitude that Andrew had only ever heard in his grandfather's voice. "'Then taking off the linen Roller, and an Assistant drawing back the Skin as far as it will go . . .'" She was acting as she spoke, her hands competent, sure. They might have been his grandfather's hands. Or his own. "'. . . you make your wound from the flesh to the bone, cutting through the muscles as swiftly and decisively as you severed the skin.'"

"That's what Lucas Turner wrote," he whispered.

"Yes. I read his journals when I was a girl. I've never forgotten."

Andrew looked at the shattered mess below his father's right knee. Less than a minute had passed since he'd made the initial cutaneous cut. The bleeding was mere seepage, easily controlled, and the laudanum seemed to have helped. Father's breathing was deeper, more steady. Still Andrew hesitated.

"I can remind you of Lucas's instructions as you proceed," his aunt said. "If you like."

Andrew's throat was too constricted to allow him to answer. He nodded, then picked up the largest triangular scalpel and began the task of severing the layer of muscle and exposing the bone.

Luke's cries of anguish began again as soon as he made the first cut. Andrew kept telling himself that it wasn't as bad for his father now. The laudanum puts some kind of screen between a patient and his pain, his grandfather said. A surgeon has to stop listening and just do his job.

His aunt's voice, pitched low, was soothing and calm. It helped him block out his father's cries. "'Stand to the inside face of the leg,'" she quoted, "'so you may at the same time saw through the tibia and the fibula and there is less chance of splintering.'"

Andrew changed his position, moving to the other side of the chaise, and selected a saw. He ran a tentative finger over the edge, hearing Christopher's words once more. *Remember, lad, bones have no feeling. It's the ratcheting back and forth of the saw, all the friction you cause to the wound, that gives such intense pain. The faster and surer your movements the better. Sooner you're done, sooner it'll be over. So get on with it.* He bent over the leg, set the saw in position, and began.

Luke raised his head and shrieked. It was the wordless howl of a tortured animal. Andrew froze.

"You must not stop," Squaw DaSilva said. "The laudanum has carried away his senses. The screams are simply a reflex."

"I know, but—" Andrew looked from her to his father, then at the saw.

"Go on," she urged. "You must. Do it, Andrew and you will save your father's life."

Andrew bent to the job. *Put your back into it, lad.* It was as if Christopher were standing behind him, watching over his shoulder. *You've the Turner legacy behind you. Get it done!*

The Turner legacy. "'When the leg is taken off the next regard is stopping the blood,'" his aunt quoted. "'There is no method for this purpose so secure as tying the extremities of the vessels with a ligature. Use a crooked needle to pass twice through the flesh, almost around them, and thus hold them in stricture.'"

Andrew could no longer hear his father's screams. Only his aunt's voice. The force of her will sustained him.

"'To discover the orifice of the various vessels, your assistant must every time loosen the tourniquet.'" Her competent hands matched the words. Each time he tied off a bleeder she opened the leather binding long enough for a spurt of blood to help him locate the next one.

Six, maybe seven. He lost count. It didn't matter, the bleeding had stopped entirely, even though the tourniquet was gone. Her voice remained his anchor and his guide.

"'Now you must begin to roll the skin from the lower part of the thigh down to the extremity of the stump. This is why you put on the linen roller. Not simply as a guide for your scalpel, but so it might prevent the skin from shrinking upward as it is inclined to do. But if you have followed my instructions and made the double incision through first the skin and then the muscle, rather than cutting them both in one swift but less precise manner, you have lessened this tendency of the skin to shrink. You can stitch it well and neatly in place, which will guard the stump from ulceration.'"

The right leg was done. Now they must do it all a second time.

The tourniquet, the linen roller, the small scalpel, then the large one. The screams. The saw. More screams. His aunt's voice . . .

At last Andrew drew the final stitch, securing the skin over the second stump. "Done," he murmured.

"Well done," she said. Her words, not Lucas's. He couldn't recall how long it had been since she'd spoken her own thoughts. "How long?" he asked.

She glanced at the clock above the mantel in the small treatment room. "Since I arrived, an hour and twenty-seven minutes. Good time." She touched her brother's forehead. He'd passed out some while before, but he was sleeping normally now, and his skin was cool. "He'll raise a fever soon," she said. "I'll have Phoebe send syrup of lemon and monkshood, and instruct Jane as to the dosage."

"Yes. Whatever you say." He was staggering with exhaustion, wiping the sweat from his forehead with his own blood-soaked sleeve. "An hour and twenty-seven minutes. That's not—"

"Since I came. Had you started long before?"

"No, a few minutes only. I stopped when Jane started her yowling."

"Call it an hour and a half then. It's a fine beginning, Andrew. Your grandfather would be pleased."

He thought so too. It was as if he could feel the old man's hand on his shoulder.

"*Well done, lad. You've probably saved him.*"

"*Not surely, Grandfather?*"

"*Never that, lad. Remember, in surgery—in all medicine—there is no such thing as 'surely.'*"

They left Jane with the patient and went to the kitchen to wash the blood from their hands. Sarah was standing by with the three buckets of water she'd filled at the pump in the street. "You be wanting something to drink or eat, maybe? I got decent ale. Or my own root beer. And there be fresh johnnycakes. Thirsty work you been doin' from the sound of it."

There was a hint of curiosity in the slave's voice. Squaw DaSilva wasn't surprised. To eat or drink she'd have had to lift her veil. "Nothing, thank you, Sarah.

I left my coachman waiting outside. I shall return home at once. And don't be fooled by Master Luke's screams. They are a natural accompaniment to surgery. Master Andrew did a remarkable job. My brother has every chance of recovering."

Andrew couldn't keep back his anger any longer. "If your damned son had any loyalty or family feeling, my father wouldn't have needed surgery."

Squaw didn't turn around. It was as if she hadn't heard him. "Thank you, Sarah. That drying cloth's exactly what I need." She used the crisply ironed piece of linen with careful motions, wiping each of her fingers separately. Finally she said, "Morgan did not start the brawl between your father and Caleb Devrey, Andrew. Nor had he any role in the treachery that was behind it. Caleb made an arrangement with James De Lancey to take the hospital post that should have been Luke's. I sent Morgan to warn you and your father, but unfortunately he was too late."

She was right. Morgan had arrived long after the trouble began. And Devrey was— Christ Almighty!

Andrew realized what he was doing and shook his head as if to clear away a dream. He was agreeing to a lie simply because this damned woman said it was the truth. "That's not how it was. Morgan had a chance to pull one of them clear. He chose Devrey."

"I'm sure you're mistaken, Andrew. Morgan was guided simply by the positions of the two men."

"I am not mistaken. I saw the entire thing. If Morgan had wanted to save my father, he could have. He didn't. He chose that black-hearted bastard Caleb Devrey. Now my father's lost both his legs and Morgan is to blame."

"You are upset, Andrew. It is entirely forgivable. And of course you're very tired. We'll speak more of this when you're feeling calmer."

"Damn you! Why don't you take off that veil and look me in the eye? You won't because you're lying and you know it!"

"You must rest," she said quietly. "Sarah, see that Master Andrew eats and gets some sleep. I will send ample provisions for the household within the hour, and medicine for Master Luke. Now, you must get this young surgeon out of his bloody clothes."

Her own dress was as drenched in blood as Andrew's dark-stained shirt and breeches. She could feel the sodden, sticky cloth as she gathered up her skirts and left the house.

"What did you tell him?" Morgan was sprawled in the chair across from his mother, staring across the tops of his polished boots into the fire. It was the day after the operation—talk of which was all over New York—and he'd spent most of it going from room to room of the house studying the burning logs in a variety of fireplaces. As if the jagged flames had answers to the questions that tormented him.

"I told Andrew he was mistaken."

"It's not true."

"Yes, it is true."

"Damn it, it is not true! Andrew is not mistaken!"

"I find the ease with which your generation curses at women quite tiresome, Morgan. Your cousin does the same thing. Please learn to guard your tongue when a lady is present. What I told Andrew was the truth because I said it was the truth. No other standard is required."

He stared at her as if she were a stranger. "What kind of creature are you? What's really hidden behind that black veil?"

She had been writing a note for Jane when he came in and forced her to tell him of the confrontation with Andrew. Now she put down the pen and stood up. "The kind of creature life has made me. I thought you understood that."

"No." He stared at her. "I don't understand anything. I could have saved my uncle, whom I love and respect. I didn't. Because I heard your voice in my ears, I saved a man I despise."

"As well you should despise him." She put her hands on the desk and leaned toward him. The sour smell of her hatred overcame the lavender-scented Hungary Water she always wore. "Would you have preferred to grant Caleb Devrey the release of an early death? He cost you your father!"

"In God's name, how can it have been the fault of Caleb Devrey that my father elected to sell guns to the savages and was castrated by them?"

"All your life I've raised you to understand. How can you be so stupid now, when the sweetest revenge is almost in our grasp? How many times have you seen the skirt stained with the soot of—"

"The soot of the ruin left behind after Devrey's mob burned your house. Holy Savior Almighty, you've showed me a dozen times. The tales of that God-cursed fire were my bedtime stories. But look what you've got!" Morgan stood up, striding the perimeter of the room, possessed by a passion to make her admit the folly he had finally acknowledged.

"This," he said, using his cutlass to lift a length of the gold embroidered damask that hung at the windows. "This!" The cutlass tapped the rosewood marquetry of the table beneath the window. "And this!" He slid the blade along the edge of the ornate marble fireplace. "Is this place not a thousand times more grand than what was torched by a scarecrow coward and his band of Jew-hating rabble?"

"Do you think it's about a house? Is wealth a repayment for a stolen life? For the brothers and sisters you could never have? For the loving husband I lost to—"

"To the Huron, for Almighty God's sake! Yet you persist in this relentless pursuit of the man you've decided is your enemy. Truth is what Squaw DaSilva says it is. Disagree and you're dead."

She didn't acknowledge that for the first time in twenty-three years he'd called her by the hateful name the rest used. She tapped her fingers on the elegant, marble-topped desk in a repeated rhythm, keeping time with a melody that played only for her. "Caleb Devrey will not die until I am ready to allow him to die. If you remember nothing else in your life, Morgan, none of my lessons, remember that."

For a few seconds they stared at each other, both of them aware that they stood at the edge of a black hole of loss, and that if they once tumbled into it there would be no way to climb back out. Morgan felt a great weight bearing down on him. She was his mother; they had faced the world together as long as he could remember. When he broke the silence he spoke in a harsh whisper, his voice thick with emotion. "Tell me only one thing. Swear it. Tobias Carter, the rest of the crew who sailed the *Maiden* home with me, I can find none of them. Swear to me you had nothing to do with their disappearance."

"I swear it."

It was too swift. He knew she was lying.

He mastered the anguish and the fury that warred inside him. "Not even an oath," he said, his voice flat and his eyes cold. "Not even that stops you. The only thing that matters is getting your own way. And God forgive me, I've helped you all my life. No more." He turned and started for the door.

"Morgan! Where are you going? Wait, you must listen to me. I'll make you understand."

"I understand everything. Far too much and far too late, but I do understand."

Roisin was in the hall, pressed to the wall, hiding in the shadows and listening to every word. The oval piece of soap she'd made to give to Squaw DaSilva was still in her hands. Earlier the strong, sweet smell of roses she'd captured in it had delighted her. She'd been sure it would convince Squaw DaSilva she had other uses besides whoring. Now the scent seemed overpowering. It made her ill.

Morgan had been like an animal the night before, using her as if she could somehow absorb all his anguish, as if repeatedly exploding inside her would somehow cure his pain.

Later when she pretended to be asleep because she had no idea what to say to him to drive away his devils, he'd stood beside the bed muttering to himself. "We'll go away from here, Roisin. Why shouldn't a whore go to sea as the captain's lady when she's as pretty and pleasing as you? I'll take the *Maiden* on another voyage, and I'll bring you with me. Anywhere, as long as it's away from her."

She'd dismissed the words as part of the madness that had possessed him since the accident at the almshouse. Lying between the rumpled sheets, her flesh bruised by his mindless lovemaking, she remembered what her mother used to say: all men forgot in the daylight the things they whispered in the dark. The night before, in his frenzy, one of the whispers had included the word "love." It truly had, she'd heard it. *Ah, Roisin girl, don't be a fool. It's only yourself you can count on for protection now.*

She pressed herself to the wall outside Squaw DaSilva's private parlor, heard the tramp of Morgan's boots heading for the door, and knew he'd meant every word. He truly intended to sail off on God knew what kind of voyage, and to take her with him. But he'd tire of her sooner rather than later; and what would happen then? *Holy Virgin Mother of God, for the sake of the Women of Connemara, protect me.*

Roisin shoved the soap in her pocket and gathered up her calico skirt and her petticoats and hurried to the back stairs, a few yards away. She was out of sight when she heard Squaw's door open and bang shut, and Morgan Turner's boots clattering down the broad steps of the main staircase.

Mashee, the scullery maid, had taken Roisin with her to the root cellar a few days before, to help carry an armload of turnips. Now it was the only hiding place she could think of. Morgan Turner was unlikely to know that such a thing as a root cellar existed.

The door was cut from a single slab of maple, fitted with beaten iron hinges, and set into the ground at a slight angle. Its weight was almost too much for Roisin, but urgency gave her strength. She lifted the door.

She had no candle. She'd have to feel her way down the stairs and close the door above her head when she could no longer reach high enough. No, there was a light at the far end of the stone-lined pit. Too steady for a candle. It had to be a lantern.

Cuf's face peered at her in the pale glow. "Let the door go," he said. "Whatever you're hiding from, you're safe here."

Roisin allowed the slab of wood to settle into place. Despite the lantern, it was much darker after that. It took a moment for her eyes to adjust; then Cuf came into focus. He was sitting on the ground. A blanket was spread in front of him, piled with pewter goblets and plates. The polished metal gleamed. "What are you doing down here?" she asked. "What's all that?"

"My business. Nothing to do with you." Cuf began wrapping the treasure in the blanket. "Who's after you, Tilda or Mistress Flossie?"

She shook her head. "Neither."

"Who, then?" He produced a length of rope and started to tie his bundle.

"Morgan."

Cuf smiled. "I thought he'd already caught you."

She hated it that he knew. That they all knew. "It's not as you think." She spat the words at him. "None of you understand. It was his bed or the pit."

"I know. I wasn't blaming you. There's plenty of things worse than whoring. But what's wrong now? You look as if you've seen the devil."

Roisin shook her head. "He means to sail away and take me with him."

"No, you've got it wrong. His ship's to be auctioned."

"You're the one has it wrong. Morgan Turner's had a flaming row with his mother over what happened to his uncle. And something about his crew. He's going to sea again and he wants me to go with him."

"That's foolish. The war's all but over. Privateering is finished."

"Plain piracy, then," she said. "The way he's feeling, he'll settle for that."

"And he wants you to go with him?" Cuf asked. Roisin nodded. "But you don't want to go?" She nodded again. "Why not? What's ahead of you if you stay in New York?"

"Squaw'll either put me to work in one of her bordellos, or return me to the old biddy who bought my indenture."

"Yes," he agreed. "That's what I was thinking. So why not go to sea with Morgan? If, as you say, that's what he has in mind."

"It's in his mind, all right. And what will my future be if I sail off with him?"

Cuf stood up, hoisting his package of treasure. "Seems to me it's better than the bordellos or the biddy."

"No, it's not. When he's had enough Morgan will drop me wherever he next makes land. One of the islands, perhaps." She shuddered, remembering what she'd heard about the islands of the Caribbean, where not to be wellborn was to be condemned to the life of an animal. "And that'll be after he's told his crew they can do whatever they like with me."

Cuf shook his head. "Morgan would never do that. He's a decent man. We grew up together."

"Decent! He let his own flesh-and-blood uncle lose both his legs because a she-wolf has twisted his mind—"

"It's not like that."

"No? How is it, then? Are all the stories wrong? Will Dr. Turner be strolling along the Broad Way anytime soon?"

Cuf couldn't meet Roisin's steady gaze. He'd been sick at heart ever since he heard the story. Luke Turner had always been good to him. It was terrible to think of that tall man cut in half—if he didn't die of the surgery. "The stories aren't wrong," he admitted.

"I didn't think so. Ah, don't look like that. It's not your fault."

Roisin settled on the bottom stair, hugging herself against the cellar's chill, trying to decide what she could do.

It was just the way it had been when she was an orphan and penniless. She knew then her one hope for a better life was to go to the colonies in America, but she had no money for passage. She could only offer herself as an indenture, let the captain sell her when they arrived in New York, and work off the bondage in ten years. After all, she'd told herself, she'd only be twenty-five when it was over and she was free. Didn't she have the skills her mother had taught her? *It's never you'll die of hunger, Roisin my love, long as you remember the ways of the Women of Connemara.* The plan might have served her, except that she had never reckoned with a terror like the pit.

"Don't," Cuf said, seeing the tears that rolled slowly down her pale cheeks. "Don't cry, Roisin. None of this is your fault."

"What difference does it make whose fault it is? I'm to be his whore or hers."

"Not unless that's what you want."

"Of course it's not what I want. To be used by any man with a wooden penny . . . How could you think— Oh, go away. You don't know anything about it. You were born a slave. You can't imagine what freedom is."

"You're wrong," Cuf said. "I can imagine it very well."

Morgan's ship lay at anchor in the roads. Her canvas had been refurbished and repaired and stored belowdecks. The masts were sail-bare wooden sentinels guarding his vessel. Still his. But not for much longer.

The *Fanciful Maiden* had been readied for the auction block. Her hull was newly caulked, her decks had been scrubbed with sand, and every joint was freshly tarred. Her brass had been polished until it glittered gold in the last rays of the setting autumn sun. The distinctive smell of fresh hemp rose to meet him as he walked past the ropes, neatly coiled and ready.

He climbed the masts, checking as he went. No cracks anywhere, by God. He fingered each inch of block and tackle, hearing in his mind the whir of the lines being fed through, and the snap of the topsails taking the wind. The song sang in his heart, until he climbed to the quarterdeck above the forecastle and looked over the high wooded hills of Manhattan, and the city of New York nestled at the island's southern tip, and the ship's song died, drowned out because the city sang to him as well. It was a different melody. He'd heard it many times and been seduced by it too often. The melody was power of a different sort. Her kind of power. His legacy.

But only if he wanted it. She couldn't force him to accept any of what she willed him. He had to take it by choice. A heritage of blood and, Holy Savior, a legacy of murder.

Well, what of it? Who was he to be sickened by his mother's willingness to do whatever she must to get her way? How many men had he killed in the last three years? No, those were fair fights, not the cold-blooded murders of men who had stood by him in all weather and reckoned his life as precious as their own.

What kind of woman had borne him?

Some thirty yards away he saw a boat with eight oarsmen row alongside a frigate flying the red duster of the Royal Navy. While he watched, men newly impressed were forced to climb aboard the frigate or be shot. Morgan had seen the small drama a hundred times before. Not that frequency made it right. He couldn't imagine sailing with a crew who needed the threat of the cat or worse to make them do their jobs. Sailors were born, not made. Another thing Tobias Carter had taught him.

It's not just the spoils wot gets 'em to go with ye, lad. It's love o' the sea. Treat 'em fair, show 'em you can plan a battle wot wins the prize, and most voyages, long as you don't never let 'em question who's in charge, you can forget about gauntlet running and keelhauling and the rest.

Poor Tobias. That might well have been the best advice he ever offered. Because Morgan had listened, and not given in to the urge to prove his authority before he'd earned respect, sailing with the *Maiden* was a prized berth. Now, give him a couple of hours in the grog shops and alehouses, and he'd have a new crew handpicked from among the most able tars in the city.

Sweet God, Tobias Carter had deserved better.

If he went ashore he might find Roisin as well as a crew. Another small boat rowed by. This one had only two oarsmen, and it came close enough to the *Maiden* for Morgan to see the five doxies aboard, on their way to service the men of yet another of His Majesty's ships. All according to the regulations: women brought aboard got tuppence for every man they lay with. No encounter was permitted to last longer than seven minutes, and a hammock was provided. The location of same, by long tradition, was determined by the senior midshipman.

The wake raised by the whores' passage lifted the *Maiden*'s bow. After a few seconds she settled gracefully back into position, cradled in the gentle rocking of the upper harbor.

Morgan had taken no more than five minutes to look for Roisin before he left his mother's house. Getting away had seemed to be the greater imperative. Now he thought of her red hair and green eyes and skin like fresh cream and wished he'd spent time finding her.

The sailors were gathered on the deck of the frigate, cheering the women's approach. No more frequently than three nights out of seven, the rules said. At the discretion of the captain. For the necessary relief of concupiscence.

Otherwise the men would wind up buggering each other, or the nearest bung hole. Happened anyway on a long voyage. He never had, but he understood the need.

As for the women, poverty drove them to whoring. As it had Roisin. He couldn't blame her for that. And whore or no, there was no question but he'd not yet had his fill of her. If he had, he wouldn't be aching at the thought that he might never see her again.

The bawdyhouse in the woods had burned down years before. Now Martha Kincaid lived in a room behind the alehouse at the sign of the Fiddle and Clogs, the most popular taproom west of Trinity Church.

The Fiddle and Clogs anchored a new neighborhood, sprung up on parcels of land a hundred feet deep by twenty-five wide, leased by the trustees of Trinity Church for two pounds a year to craftsmen and artisans who could afford to pay now that work was so plentiful. The houses the workmen cobbled together on their rented ground were built of wood, not brick, and feral pigs and dogs snuffled along the dirt streets that quickly became bogs of mud, garbage, and human waste. All the same, Martha Kincaid thought her new living arrangements were paradise. "A whole room I has, all to meself." She patted Jan Brinker's arm. "Thanks to me friend here, I'm well taken care of."

"*Ja*." Brinker basked in her praise. "I be taking good care of all me friends. Leastwise them as was good to me in the old days."

Roisin looked from the dwarf in his elaborate gentleman's clothing, to Cuf in his leather breeches and flannel jacket, to the wrinkled old woman with the shawl over her head, and down at herself in a whore's bright yellow calico, half frozen because she'd neither cloak nor shawl. The four of them must look quite mad, and anyone hearing them talk would be sure of it. It seemed to Roisin insane to think they could hide right here in New York from someone as powerful as Squaw DaSilva.

"It not be really hidin'," Brinker insisted. "Squaw won't be coming after you. It's fleas the likes of you be to the likes of her. She only cares about getting even with Caleb Devrey. And now she be worrying 'bout losing her precious Morgan. And 'bout her brother with his legs cut off. The rest of us, we be fleas."

"Fleas are squashed," Cuf said.

"*Ja*, but only if they bite. Otherwise they can hop away and never be noticed."

Roisin wasn't convinced. "Cuf's her property, and I guess she thinks I am too since she and Morgan saved me from the whipper. So won't running away make her think we're biting fleas, as you put it?"

Brinker shook his head. The noisy taproom was full of men and women playing at dice and cards. The long, narrow space was lit by iron chandeliers suspended from the main roof beam. Every few moments someone was scalded by a drop of hot wax and shouted an oath, while the rest made up an instant lottery on which candle would be the next to gutter out.

"Gambles on anything, they do," Brinker said, smiling. "That be fine for me. Landlord be taking a tenth part of whatever the prize comes out. My rule. And if they be wanting to drink here, be my rules they obey."

Cuf had told Roisin that the dwarf owned the alehouse and how he came to get it. She'd never have thought brewing beer such a profitable enterprise. Particularly for someone as peculiar-looking as Jan Brinker.

"He's the strangest sight in New York," Cuf had said when he and Roisin were still hiding in the root cellar, "but Jan Brinker's my friend. He wants to help me."

"And you trust him?"

"I do."

"Very well then, but why will he want to help me?"

"Why not? If you can simple as well as you say, you'll be valuable. Anyway, I think he enjoys doing whatever he can to get back at the mistress."

"What did she do to him?"

"The way I heard the story, he saved her from a mob once. He was promised a reward but she never paid him. He's rich now anyway, no thanks to her. So he wants to get even."

"And you, Cuf, what do you want?"

"To be free," he'd told her quietly. "So if that's what you want as well, come with me."

Bad choices, that's all she ever had. This time the best of the lot had seemed to be to leave Squaw's house with Cuf. Right now all she could think of was that it was a pity she'd not had time to bring a shawl.

"Cuf says you simple," Brinker said, looking at her, thinking that with that hair and those tits he couldn't blame Squaw DaSilva for wanting to put her in one of the bordellos. *Jesu Cristo,* if the hair between her legs was as red and as curly . . .

"I do. My mother taught me. Her mother taught her. I know receipts passed down in Ireland for as long as anyone can remember. Since long before that devil Cromwell made the Boyne run red with blood, and those as was left alive all slaves to the English."

"Ah," Martha Kincaid said softly. "It's one o' them you be."

Roisin was startled. It hadn't occurred to her that an old crone in New York might know about the Women of Connemara. "Maybe I am."

Martha waved a gnarled hand. "Not here, child," she said softly. "Besides, that's not what's bein' talked about this night."

"Show Mr. Brinker the soap," Cuf said, impatient with the murmuring of the two women.

Roisin reached into the pocket of her dress and brought out the cream-colored oval. The scent of roses was strong enough to overcome the taproom reek of sweat and ale.

"You're sure she won't find me here?" Roisin asked. A single candle cast a dim shadowy light in the lean-to tacked onto the rear of the Fiddle and Clogs. Martha Kincaid had offered to share it with her for a time.

"Sure as I am about most things." Martha sat on the edge of her bed—a straw mattress spread on two trestles and some planks—rubbing absently at her thin legs in their knitted striped stockings. "You can sleep easy as that hard floor allows, lass. Mistress Jennet's a fierce one, but I think she has more to worry about right now than the likes of you."

"Jennet? Is that her real name?"

"Aye. When I first knowed her she be Mistress Jennet in her father's house. Then Mistress DaSilva in her Jew husband's. She wasn't Squaw until years later. Beautiful she be, and almost as skilled with the knife as her father. Never mind that the men of New York would have had her in the ducking chair for touching a scalpel, much less the rest of it."

"What was the rest of it?" Martha's narrow bed occupied almost the whole of the little room. Roisin lay on a bit of canvas spread on the floor beside it, propped on her elbow and looking up at the old woman. "How did she go from Jennet to Squaw?"

"Once I had a big black lump on my face," Martha Kincaid said. "Ugliest thing you ever saw. Me husband threw me out in the street jus' so's he wouldn't have to look at it. Christopher Turner, Mistress Jennet's pa, he cut that lump away and it ain't never come back. Not even now I'm a wrinkled old hag. That's how clever he was. And her, she was almost the same. Might have been the same if she weren't a woman."

"Did they catch her doing surgery?"

"No, they never catched her. Lots of things happened. But you ask me, it was Ellen what did it."

"Who was Ellen?"

"Young girl, only twelve. Her pa got her breeding, and only thing she wanted be to get rid of the babe. Three months gone Ellen was. And God help me, be me as talked Mistress Jennet into trying to help her."

"And did she help her?" Roisin held her breath waiting for the answer.

Martha shook her head. "Mistress Jennet tried, God knows. But the girl bled like a hog with its throat cut, and quicker than you can blink, she died. Suffered plenty first, though. Last words she spoke, she cursed Mistress Jennet. Wished her in hell. And the way I sees it, that's pretty much where Squaw DaSilva's been ever since."

"You're sure she was only three months gone? The babe hadn't yet quickened?"

"'Course I'm sure. Didn't she come to Martha Kincaid's the very first she knew? They all came to Martha's, come to that. Ah, lass, in the old days—"

"I could have helped her." Roisin said the words softly, watching for the other woman's reaction.

"Squaw DaSilva? No, lass. Not once a curse be spoken."

"No, the girl. Ellen."

Martha slipped off her clogs and swung her legs onto the bed. "Aye, maybe you could have, lass, seeing as how you simples. Thing is, we knowed about the potion as sometimes expels the babe."

"That's not what I'm talking about. There are many potions. None of them work for certain sure. I know another way. My mother taught me. And her mother taught her."

"Aye, so you said. But—"

"Earlier, in the taproom, you acted like you knew about me."

Martha cocked her head and smiled her toothless smile. Young ones like this, full of juice and joy whatever their troubles, they thought they knew everything. Some pleasure there be in showing them bein' old meant you knew a thing or two. "'Course I knows. Soon as I heard you goin' on about the English makin' the Irish slaves, I knew. Yer a papist, ain't you, lass?"

Every part of Roisin cautioned her to deny the charge. Her Scots father had died in the rebellion they called the '45, hanged, drawn, and quartered for fighting to put the Catholic Bonnie Prince Charlie on the English throne that was rightfully his. She'd taken in the tales of Cromwell and his heretic murderers raping and pillaging their way through Ireland along with her mother's milk. Besides, what difference did it make what she said to old Martha Kincaid?

None.

Except that she'd made a solemn promise to the Virgin when she begged for help with the plan to get to the colonies by offering herself as an indenture. The New World was sure to be as Protestant as any the treacherous English ruled, and thus a dangerous place. Nonetheless, if anyone asked her straight out, Roisin swore to the Virgin, she would not deny the true Church. "I'm a Catholic, yes. And I will be until the day I die." Defiantly she made the sign of the cross and thanked the Blessed Virgin for helping her keep her vow.

Martha Kincaid sighed. She'd had her little moment of triumph. Truth to tell, she didn't care two shits in a bucket what religion the girl claimed. Or anyone else for that matter. "Fair enough, lass. You can believe whatever you wants and pray however you pleases. Don't make no difference to me." She stretched out her hand to the candle, ready to snuff it out.

Roisin reached up and grabbed the old woman's bony wrist. "Wait. Is that all you meant? When you said I was 'one of those,' you only meant I was a Catholic?"

"What else could I have meant? What you be thinking, lass?"

Roisin shook her head, letting Martha go and sinking back to the floor. "It doesn't matter."

"You just wait, lass, you're not goin' to sleep yet. You said them potions don't always work, same as I know. So that means— Sweet God Almighty, lass, do you know how to cut the babe out?"

Roisin nodded. "I do," she said. "My mother taught me."

Martha sat straight up in the bed. "And back where yer from, the men don't punish women for doin' such things?"

"Of course they do. But that's because they're Protestant heretics."

Martha shook her head impatiently. "Religion! Men's tricks, all of it. And it be men don't want us to get rid o' their babes."

"Protestant heretics," Roisin repeated, remembering her mother's words. "They're the devil's servants. That's why they oppose a woman ridding herself of the thing that's inside her before it becomes a child of God. The True Church doesn't condemn a woman for ridding herself of a babe before she feels it move. Not before the soul is put into it. Before that she can be rid of it and commit no sin."

Impatiently Martha shook her head. "Forget about churches and all that nonsense. I want it plain, lass. Are you telling me you know how to rid a woman of whatever it is that's inside her afore it quickens? Without the poor creature bleedin' to death, or swilling up her guts until she bleeds from her belly as regularly as she does from her twat?"

"I do," Roisin said softly. "I promise you, I do."

"Holy heaven," Martha said softly. "If that's true, Jan Brinker be freeing us all, not just you and Cuf."

IV

It had been a long time since she'd walked down Hall Place. Squaw DaSilva paused by the barbering pole, touched it for the briefest moment, then lifted the brass knocker and let it fall with an insistent clatter.

Her youngest sister came to the door. "What are you doing here?"

"I'm touched by your warm greeting, Wella. May I come in, or shall we conduct our business in the street for all the neighbors to see and hear?"

Wella stepped aside and Squaw entered the house. She stood in the hall a moment, overcome with memories. The portraits painted by the itinerant phizmonger still hung either side of the front door exactly as they had for all her growing-up years. Marit Graumann and Lucas Turner. Dear God, what must they think of all they'd seen?

From the outside the entrance to her father's study and surgery looked exactly the same, but now there was no case of instruments in the corner, and no consulting chair across from the desk. "I see you wasted no time making new arrangements."

"Is that what you've come for? To inspect what's left? We sent the surgical instruments to the ironmonger on Golden Hill for selling on. To a man. Would you have preferred we give them to you?"

"Save your venom, Wella. That's an old charge. It no longer either wounds or threatens me."

"Jane says you assisted Andrew. That you stayed with him the whole time, and that you were as bloody as he was when it was finished."

"For heaven's sake, Wella, would it have been better to let the boy do it alone? Or perhaps you would prefer it hadn't been done, and we'd simply allowed Luke to die."

"It wouldn't have happened if Morgan—"

"Morgan did all he could." The *Fanciful Maiden* had sailed on the morning tide and saying his name made her heart ache, but she let nothing of her pain show. "It's Andrew I've come to speak about. And Jane."

"Very well, say what you came to say."

"I shall. But not standing here like a kitchen maid." She sat down in what had been her father's favorite chair, the one closest to the fire. After a moment or two, Wella sat across from her. "That's better. Now, here is what I propose. First, we must send Andrew away."

Wella gasped. "Away? But he's the head of the family now that Papa's gone and Luke is unwell."

"I promise you, Luke will recover and assume his proper role." She didn't bother to say that she was head of the family now that their father was gone. And if she were not, the role would fall to Morgan. Only actions mattered, not words and not titles, a lesson any woman would do well to learn. "Andrew is full of self-reproach. He blames himself for what happened to Luke."

"But that's nonsense! It was Morgan who—"

"I told you, Wella, it was neither Morgan's fault nor Andrew's. Luke was the victim of a tragic accident. It was Caleb Devrey's undeserved good fortune to be the one my son was able to save. Yet another thing for which we may despise our cursed cousin."

"But everyone says—"

"Everyone lies. Dear Lord, did you learn nothing in this house? Were the things said about Papa true because they were said?"

"No, of course not, but—"

"Andrew," Squaw said, bringing the conversation back to what she wished to discuss. "He must go to Edinburgh."

"Why?"

Heaven give her strength. "I have told you why. Because he is ill with self-blame. If he remains here he will be tormented by the sight of his father attempting to recover, feeling pain in the legs he no longer has, learning to hoist himself onto the stool with only his arms and two sticks, and in the dead of night, when he thinks no one hears, weeping over the loss of half his body."

"How terrible you make it sound," Wella whispered.

"I promise you, it will be worse than I describe it."

"If that's so, why did you do it? Perhaps it would have been better to let him die."

"I didn't do it," Squaw said. "Andrew did. And someday, when Luke is able to dandle a grandchild on what's left of his lap, or smell a joint roasting at the fire, or laugh at a jest, he will bless his son for giving him back even half a body with which to live out the rest of his days."

Wella rose and went to stand beside the window. "You're very sure of yourself. But then, you always were."

"Yes. And mostly I've been right. I'm right this time as well. Andrew is a genius with a scalpel. Someday he may be as great a surgeon as Papa, or even Great-Grandfather Lucas. If he goes to the school of medicine in Edinburgh, he can add the skills of physic to his knowledge. He'll be the first man in New York to be trained in both. Perhaps the first in all the colonies."

"Bede's son Samuel is studying medicine at the College of Philadelphia. Samuel," she said again. "Raif's twin."

"I know who Samuel Devrey is, Wella."

"And you know he's studing with Dr. Shippen."

"Upstarts," Squaw said. "Colonials. Whatever Samuel gets for himself in Philadelphia, it won't be the equal of a degree from Edinburgh."

"Andrew's very clever," Wella said, twisting her hands. "He'll learn more than Samuel wherever he goes."

"Nonsense. I always heard Raif was the dull twin. Samuel has wit in plenty. Anyway, the Devreys have nothing to do with this."

"But if—"

"If what? Speak your mind, Wella. And stop wringing your hands. You'll twist them right off the wrists if you continue."

"Andrew's a surgeon. Papa trained him. I think that's what he wants to do."

"Ah, at last. The heart of the problem. You're fond of the lad, aren't you? Stop fussing, Wella. There's nothing to prevent him from using the skills he learned from Papa."

"But no one practices both physic and surgery."

"Exactly my point. Andrew will be leagues ahead of everyone else. Because no one has ever done it, does that make it a bad idea?"

"I'm not sure. Perhaps it does."

"I am sure. It does not. Andrew must go to Edinburgh."

"The new King's College here in New York, will it not suit?"

"It's not yet finished building. Besides, I've heard nothing of plans for a school of medicine. And as I already told you, a colonial degree does not compare to one from Edinburgh."

Wella said nothing.

"Edinburgh," the eldest sister said again. "Like his father. It's the only possibility. And the suggestion must come from you. Andrew won't accept it from me. I shall pay, of course."

"What about Jane?"

"She shall nurse her father. When he is well enough so that Sarah and perhaps another slave can look after him, Jane may marry the strange little preacher I hear she fancies, and go live with him in West Chester. I'll supply an adequate dowry."

The preacher was a disciple of John Wesley, whose doctrines—called Methodism because adherents claimed to live by rule and method—were setting much of England in opposition to the established Anglican Church, and had recently spread to the colonies. "You hear a great deal," Wella said. "But then you always have."

Dear God, must everyone speak to her with the same bitterness? Even her own flesh and blood? "I survive, Wella. And so shall we all. Will you go to Andrew with the plan and see that he accepts it? I think he will be easy to persuade. Secretly he'll be longing to leave all this unhappiness behind."

"Will I tell him the money comes from you?"

Lord grant her patience. "Absolutely not. Say it's part of his inheritance from his grandfather. Tell him you found a box of *daalders* and *louis d'or* among Papa's things, with a note saying they were for Jane and Andrew. It will also save us trouble when the matter of the dowry comes round."

Wella walked with her sister to the front door. Then, just before she closed it, she said quietly, "Good-bye, Jennet. Thank you."

As soon as she got home Squaw sent Tilda to Golden Hill to buy back her father's surgical instruments.

Late that night she sat with them spread out on the writing table before her. A scalpel of her very own. How much she'd longed for that. It was quite possibly the real reason she'd married Solomon. And if she hadn't, she'd never have known passion, or love, or birthed Morgan. She'd been barely seventeen; small wonder she'd no idea she was doing the right thing for the wrong reason. Now she was forty-four; she could have scalpels aplenty if she wanted them, but she had neither husband nor son.

She picked up one of her father's well-used instruments. Her hands trembled as she fingered the exquisitely honed blade, sharp enough to cut out her own heart. Would God she had the courage.

Jennet Turner DaSilva opened her fingers and let the scalpel fall. "Good-bye, Jennet," she whispered, echoing her sister's words. Then, clasping herself as if that would ease the anguish that roiled her gut, she freed the sobs she'd stifled for over twenty-four hours. "Morgan," she whispered, "my son, oh, my son." And finally, "Your farewell came too late, Wella. Jennet died long ago."

The dwarf wore green tonight, a leaf-green brocade coat over a yellow undercoat and yellow satin breeches. He'd put on a powdered wig. Roisin liked the sight of his bald head better. The wig made Jan Brinker look like what the world took him to be, a freakish man no longer young. Without it he was neither old nor young, only himself.

"There be this one for too much wind," he said, indicating one of the closely worded notices called quackbills. Posted all over the town, they advertised treatments for various ailments. "And this one be for them as doesn't fart enough. Then there's this one. I like it best of all."

Cuf drew the third notice toward him across the scarred table at the rear of the taproom. "'Cures for every disease known to man,'" he read softly. "'A guarantee is given to all who come for a consultation.'"

Brinker turned to Roisin. "*Ja*, that be a fine idea! We can say you be giving a guarantee!"

She shook her head. "Not for everything. I can treat what I say I can. Only that."

"Not good enough." Brinker tapped a finger on the quackbill that swore to cure any disease. "Not if this woman be promising—"

"Just 'cause she promises don't make it true," Martha said. "Folks get to know the difference soon enough. If Roisin can do half what she says, she be a miracle worker."

"Oh, no!" Roisin was appalled. "Almighty God and his holy saints make miracles. I only do what my mother taught me."

Martha wasn't having it. "She can work miracles. Mark my words."

"Then that's what we'll put on the quackbills," Brinker said, tugging on the front of his green brocade coat as he did when he got excited. "We be saying miracle worker!"

"Absolutely not." Roisin was adamant. "I shan't see anyone if you do that."

"If you don't see 'em as comes with a sickness, it's back on the street you be. And in the whipping pit soon after." The dwarf leaned forward so he could look deep into her eyes. "Is that what you be wanting, juffrouw?"

"Nothing about miracles," she said stubbornly. "I won't have it."

"We don't be needing you, you know. Me and Cuf here, we still got our first plan. We be goin' back to that, you don't want to do what you said."

Cuf didn't like the direction the conversation was taking. "Roisin never claimed she could guarantee to cure every illness, Mr. Brinker, or work miracles. Besides," he added, "I like this plan better than the first one we came up with. You said yourself—folks won't have money for fancy goods when the war ends, but sickness comes whether there's war or peace."

True enough, and Jan Brinker knew it as well as any. The dwarf leaned toward Roisin. "You be having a cure for a dose?" he whispered. "Only I be asking," he added quickly, "because if you do, that be a good thing to put in one of these here quackbills."

"There's the smoke cure," Roisin said, careful not to let her voice show that she knew it was Jan Brinker who had the dose. "It does well for the French disease, some say."

Jan Brinker nodded. "*Ja*, some does. I be asking what you say?" He'd had the smoke cure years ago. Sat in a chair with a hole in the seat like a stool and had a blanket put round him, and a *Jesu Cristo* mix of something as stank worse than any shit be burned on an iron plate beneath him. Nearly choked to death. But after that it stopped burning like fire to piss, and the sore on his cock went away. Came back later on his arms and his legs. Got the red salve to rub all over himself from another quack when that happened. That be a fine cure. No trouble for years and years. Now the burning was back, and his piss stank like rotten cabbage. "I be wanting to know what you say."

"If a woman comes when the trouble first starts, I can help with that. I've never tried with a man."

Brinker grunted and turned away in disgust.

Up front a fiddler had climbed onto one of the long wooden tables. The crowd was clapping and stamping. *Ja*, a good thing. Laugh and sing when you can. Sooner or later everyone be finished the same. In the grave. The dwarf turned to Martha. "Come, we be going up front, see how they do it these days."

They took their tankards and made their way forward. Roisin and Cuf stayed where they were. All the attention focused on the noisy entertainment at the other end of the room made it seem as if they were alone. "Your first plan," Roisin said. "You meant to open a fancy goods shop."

He nodded. "I've a friend, a silversmith; he's been teaching me the craft. I made those things you saw. Paid for the metal out of the allowance Mistress makes— the allowance she used to make me. Four pennies a week." He let the words trail away, suddenly shamed by what a tiny amount of money he'd ever been able to call his own. "You thought I'd stolen the goblets and plates. I'm a slave, so how could I have them otherwise?"

Roisin shook her head. "I didn't think that. You don't strike me as the stealing sort."

He decided to believe her. "When I got the promise from Mistress," he said, "when she made me free, that's what I was going to be. A silversmith like my friend."

"But you decided not to wait."

"Jan Brinker said soon as the war with the French ends hard times will come. No one will be able to afford silver, maybe not pewter even. Anyway, Mr. Brinker thinks Mistress is lying. He says she'll never keep her word and give me my freedom. He says it will be like the reward she promised him. He never got that, either."

"Do you think Squaw was lying to you all these years?"

"I'm not sure." Cuf didn't look at her. "Maybe she was telling the truth, but I can't wait any longer. Anyway, you said yourself it wasn't right for someone to be able to own another person."

"Yes, I did."

"Well, then?" He looked hard at her, daring her to rebuke him for leaving his rightful owner.

"Well, nothing. I never said you were wrong to run away, Cuf. I was only asking why you decided things that way."

"No time to wait," he said again, still not looking at her.

Roisin fingered the quackbills still on the table between them. "How did you learn to read?" she asked softly.

"Morgan taught me."

"Good. Everything you know, it helps to keep you safe." She smiled when she said it, and Cuf felt something move deep inside him, something he wished never to feel. Not for her. Not for any white woman.

When he was a little boy and they had burned black slaves in slow fires until the whole town was filled with the greasy, sick-making smell of their roasting flesh, they said that the slaves wanted every Christian man and boy dead, so the black men would be free to vent their rapacious lust for white women.

Rapacious lust. He never forgot the phrase. White men who went to the mistress's bordellos often asked for a black whore, but if a Negro man's blood stirred for a white woman, it was *rapacious lust.* And he could be burned for it.

That wasn't Roisin's fault. "I'll keep you safe," he promised. "But that means you'll have to stay with me and Jan Brinker and do your cures."

"Yes, it does. And I will. But I won't let him say I can do miracles as if I were a saint." She had to raise her voice to be heard. The fiddler and the rhythmic clapping of the crowd had grown much more boisterous.

"I promise he won't say that." It was Brinker who had the money they needed for quackbills, and Brinker who could provide them a place to hide from the mistress and see clients, but Cuf knew he could persuade the dwarf to do things the way Cuf thought they should be done. The little man had always been in awe of the two boys. *Smart you both be as well as tall.* Brinker would listen to Cuf in the end.

"Very well, it's settled then," Roisin said, clasping his hand. "Except . . ."

"Except what?"

"How can you all be so sure we won't be found? If we stay right here in New York, why won't Squaw find us?"

Cuf shrugged. "Jan Brinker says she won't. I think he's right. She'd never come to a place like this." He waved his arm to indicate the taproom full of raucous good cheer. "Can you picture her in the Fiddle and Clogs?"

Roisin giggled. "No. I can't."

"Neither can I. Look at that." Cuf pointed to the front of the room.

Jan Brinker was scrambling up onto the table. The crowd cheered loudly when he took the fiddler's instrument and began to play. Pretty soon old Martha Kincaid was up there beside him, lifting her skirts and dancing a jig with as much energy as if she were still a young girl.

"What are you looking for?" Cuff asked.

"A special kind of plant." Roisin kicked at the sand as she spoke. The tips of her heavy, tightly laced boots sent damp clods flying, uncovering a great variety of green and black and dark red shapes.

"There are no plants here," Cuf said in astonishment. "Plants don't grow in the sand."

"What do you think these things are? And why did I make you bring me here?"

They were the same two questions he'd been asking himself all day. "Is there a beach nearby?" she'd demanded when they breakfasted on johnnycakes and coffee in the taproom. "A true beach with real sand and the sea."

Cuf had considered taking her to Bedloe's Island, but he had no desire to expose Roisin to the pox, and he'd heard they were building the pesthouse. The two might be seen. For all he knew Morgan might be there, digging up the gold horse's head. Besides, the beach on Bedloe's Island was shingle and stone. She'd asked for sand.

There were a few stretches of sandy shore at the southern tip of Manhattan, but the court part of town had become dangerous for both of them in the four days since they left Squaw DaSilva's. So he'd settled on Brooklyn.

They'd paid a penny each to be ferried from Manhattan to the place the authorities had named Nassau Island, though most of the locals still called it simply the long island. It was Cuf who got the ferry money from Jan Brinker, but he handed it over to Roisin before they left the Fiddle and Clogs. "You keep the coins and pay the fare. Everyone will think I'm your slave and no one will pay us any mind."

Now Roisin looked as if she were about to weep. The sight of the open sea, Cuf thought. Probably she was thinking of Morgan and wishing she'd gone with him when she had the chance. "What's the matter?" he asked.

"Nothing's the matter." Roisin turned and examined the deserted sweep of sand behind them, then turned again to look at the equally deserted stretch that lay ahead.

"Something is. You're almost crying. Are you missing Morgan?"

"Missing Morgan! Did you not listen to a thing I told you?"

"Ssh. I remember what you said. I wonder why we've come here, that's all. And why you're so troubled by whatever it is we've found."

"It's what we've not found that troubles me. I'm looking for a special kind of ocean plant."

Cuf shook his head. "I don't believe there can be plants in the sea."

"There are many different kinds of plants in the sea. The tide washes them up on the sand and people gather them. A gift from the Holy Virgin, my mother always said. Some are good to eat, and some are for making poultices and some for brews. But here in Brooklyn"—she kicked at another clump of wet sand—"I've not seen a single sea plant I recognize."

"My mama's an apothecary. I can ask her to tell you what they use here for whatever it is you want to do."

Roisin shook her head. Martha Kincaid had told her about Phoebe. "No. Your mother won't know about this. It's different. A secret."

She was shutting him out. Secrets were for white folks. Not Negroes like him or his mother. Cuf stopped walking and let her get a few steps ahead. The wind off the ocean was cold and sharp. It had blown most of her red hair free of her mobcap. Jan Brinker had bought Roisin a shawl and she held it wrapped tight to her body. The wind molded the woolen cloth to her hips and her breasts, and showed off the deep curve of her waist.

Cuff whirled around, turning his back to her. Roisin Campbell wasn't for him. No matter what. *Rapacious lust.* And a slow fire in front of City Hall.

"Cuf! Cuf! Come see! I think I've found it!"

He turned back, and strode up the beach toward her, unable to keep from smiling simply because she was. Roisin had both hands full of something that shone bright orange in the weak afternoon sunlight. The stuff was flat, with slightly ruffled edges, the various segments joined by little orange balls the size of a hickory nut. They felt empty when he squeezed them. "Are you telling me this is a plant that grows under the sea?" He tried to stifle his laughter, unsure whether it was the strange notion of a garden below the ocean, or simply the sight of her face, shining with delight.

"Yes, Cuf. Indeed I am. Look, you can see where the salt's dried on. Here and here."

"That's salt?"

"Of course. Lick it. You'll know for sure." Cuf hesitated. "Go on," she said, laughing at him. "It's not poison. You can trust me that much."

He opened his mouth and she rubbed a bit of the orange stuff over his tongue. He tasted the sweetness of her finger. And salt, just as she'd said. "It's salt," he conceded. "Is this the plant your mother told you about? The one that cures . . . whatever it cures?"

Roisin nodded. "I believe so, yes."

"Believe? Aren't you sure?"

"No, not absolutely. Everything's a bit different here. Many of the plants are exactly the same as we have at home, but some are not. This one . . . I'm not sure, Cuf, but I think it's the same. The same sort anyway."

There was an easy way to be certain. She could try it on herself. She had missed her monthly flow. It should have started the week before—she'd been planning to use it as an excuse to get Morgan to leave her in peace for a few nights—but it hadn't. If this was the right sea gift, it could end any worry she need have about that. Could she bear the pain? Scrape the thing out with her own hands?

Yes, if she must. But she wasn't sure she wanted it to end. Every relative she had was dead or at the other side of the ocean. She was by herself in this heretic land. And about to begin a new life. Maybe two new lives, if she birthed the babe. A part of Morgan to keep with her.

"What are you thinking?"

"What? I'm sorry, Cuf. What did you say?"

"You seemed to have gone far away." She was gazing out to sea, with an expression he didn't understand. A kind of longing. It had to be for Morgan, whatever she said.

"I was thinking about the future," Roisin said softly, beginning to stuff the sea plant into the drawstring bag she'd brought for the purpose. "Come, Cuf, help me look for more of this."

"Only if you tell me your secret," he said. Perversely, he knew. He'd no cause to torment her. It wasn't her fault if she was besotted with Morgan Turner, same as every other woman in New York. And certainly not her fault if Cuf was fool enough to have feelings to which he had no right.

Roisin looked at him. He was nearly as tall as Morgan. But so different, a creature from another world almost. Her mother had told her stories about black-amoors, but until she came to New York Roisin had never seen one. She had never seen a slave, or imagined what it would feel like to be owned. The way the biddy had owned her, or Squaw owned Cuf.

She liked the soft, pale golden color of Cuf's skin, and the way his dark eyes were so wise and yet so kind, but she had no idea what he would make of her legacy. "I can't tell you," she said. "That's why it's a secret. Come."

Roisin turned and began striding forward, head down, her gaze focused on the sand. "There must be more, Cuf. It's never you find only one bit. My mother always said that."

Five minutes later they came on a place where the ocean had thrown up so many plants the sand was entirely covered for a distance of some ten or more yards in every direction. Roisin was ecstatic. "Oh, Cuf, it's a gift from heaven! I can use this, and this." She pounced on a large clump of something bright green and another that was almost black. Finally she found a little more of the vivid orange variety and she laughed with joy as she stuffed it in her bag of treasures. "God bless Brooklyn! How many women will have reason to be thankful now!"

"Ah," he said, pleased to have discovered a bit more of the truth. "The sea plants are for a female malady. I might have guessed."

"Why might you have?" She didn't look at him when she said it.

"Because it's made you so excited."

"Yes, I guess it has. Well, you're right about that. It's for a woman's . . . malady."

He sensed something in her tone. "But that's not the secret, is it?"

Suddenly she wanted to tell him. Cuf had saved her from being Morgan Turner's whore or Squaw's. He had given her a chance to hope again. "Me. My mother," she said, "and her mother before her. And her mother before that. We're part of an ancient tribe of healers known as . . ."

"Yes?"

It was the first time she'd ever spoken the words aloud to someone who had not taken the oath. "We're known as the Women of Connemara. We make a solemn vow to heal in the name of the Holy Virgin. And never to do harm. And—"

"What else?"

"Nothing. There's nothing else." She couldn't make herself say the last part. *And never to take a babe from the womb after it had quickened and was ensouled.*

She had six, possibly seven weeks more. Time enough to make the decision, especially now that she'd found the sea gift. Except that she had already decided.

She wanted to let the babe grow and quicken and be born. She wanted it entirely, with every part of her. But a babe had to have a father. Not a pirate who was already probably murdering and robbing some poor ship full of unlucky fools. A man who would look after her and the child. Who—if the Holy Virgin was kind—might believe the child was his.

Roisin knew Cuf wanted her. She could smell the wanting on him, and see the tension that rippled through his arm when he touched her accidentally. She looked around but there was only the open sand and the crashing sea. The tide had been far out when they arrived. It was heading in now, wavelets licking ever closer to where they were, already washing away the footprints they'd earlier left in the sand.

"Say something," she whispered, moving closer to him. "I've given you my secret. What shall you give me in return, Cuf?"

"I have nothing." He ached to hold her. "I'm a slave."

"No. You must stop saying that. You and me, Cuf, we're free. Because we say we are. Not slave or indenture, free."

"Yes," he said, exulting in the word, feeling strong because she expected him to be. "Yes! We are, Roisin, we're free!"

She let the shawl fall open and reached up and put her arms around his neck, pressing her body against him, her mouth to his.

Cuf felt her breasts against his chest, his male hardness against the softness of her hips and her belly. He clasped her to him, lifting her off the ground and carrying her a few yards farther inland, away from the steadily encroaching waves. The wind didn't feel cold any longer; it was a caress, a soothing balm to his fire. He set her down. She fell to her knees, then lay on her back and lifted her skirt and her petticoats so he could see her rosy flesh, the dark red, inviting triangle between her thighs.

Groaning, Cuf lowered himself onto her, entered her, possessed her.

Roisin opened herself to him as utterly as she could, taking him deep inside her, accepting—no, inviting—his seed. Her hands gripped his shoulders and she listened to the waves breaking on the shore and waited, unmoving until he was finished. Thank you Holy Virgin for yet another gift of the sea.

Morgan. Ah, Morgan.

The woman was badly marked by the pox, and so thin you could see her bones. "You're sure you're breeding?" Roisin demanded.

"Aye. I'm sure. Why wouldn't I be? It's the twelfth time."

It was a story Roisin had heard often enough in the two weeks since Jan Brinker installed her in a room in the attic above his taproom. She slept there by night and saw those who came for cures by day. A whole stream of them had begun passing beneath the sign of the Fiddle and Clogs, climbing the stairs to consult Mistress Healsall.

That's what the quackbills Brinker circulated all over the city proclaimed her. It was a compromise between herself and the dwarf who wanted her to guarantee to cure everything. Healsall might be a name, after all, not a promise. Besides, she couldn't announce herself as Roisin Campbell and wait for the biddy to send the constables to get her. Or Squaw.

Cuf was in charge of keeping Roisin's clients in order and taking the money they paid for her services. She charged between a penny and three for most things. Martha Kincaid didn't approve of the pricing schedule. "A shilling at least if you really can rid 'em of a babe they don't want to breed," she'd advised in the dark of night when she and Roisin were in the little lean-to behind the alehouse. "And Lord knows most'll steal if they must to get it."

"They shall pay whatever they wish for that cure," Roisin had said. "Those are the rules. For ending a breeding that hasn't quickened, a woman pays whatever she can."

"And whose rules might those be, God Almighty? None as has ever done business in New York, I promise you that."

"My rules," Roisin insisted since she had no intention of explaining to Martha Kincaid about the Women of Connemara. "And if you tell Mr. Brinker, I'll leave. I swear it, Martha, I will."

"Ah, don't get yourself so upset, lass. I'll not be telling Jan. Not any man short or tall. Not about a woman ending a breeding." She'd narrowed her eyes and peered at the girl. "What about Cuf? Have you told him?"

Roisin shook her head. "No, not exactly."

"What does that mean?"

"I said I treated female maladies. All kinds."

Martha Kincaid was fairly certain that Roisin and Cuf were lying together. Didn't bother her none, though some would call it reason enough to set him burning. That's because they hadn't never felt Black Bento's kind hands in the lonely night, nor had the warmth of him like a covering quilt when everything else was ice and cold. Burned, Black Bento did, but not at no stake, thank God. In the fire took the bawdyhouse. When he was trying to help some of the others get out and a roof beam crashed down on his head. Everyone said he was dead before the flames touched him. Maybe. Either way, better than the stake.

Woman like this one Roisin was questioning now, thin as a rail she was. Sure to God, she couldn't afford a shilling to be rid of the babe growing inside her. But that wasn't what be going to decide Roisin Campbell about whether to help her or not. Martha had heard it all before. The girl had ways of her own, and the only thing to do be to accept them.

"When was the last time you bled?" Roisin demanded.

The pockmarked woman didn't look sheepish and refuse to meet her glance. Not like the last few clients who had climbed up to the attic with the same complaint. "In September," she said, her eyes steady on Roisin's face. "This be nearly November, ain't it? So's I been breedin' six weeks. Maybe seven."

Roisin remained unconvinced, unwilling to trust the consciences of the heretic Protestant women of New York. It was a problem her mother had never faced. Every Catholic knew the Church would condemn her to everlasting hell for ending a breeding after the thing inside her was a babe with a soul.

The thin woman was watching her with anxious eyes, waiting for a sign that Mistress Healsall would help her. "'Tain't quickened. I swear it," she said. "Mary Flanagan I was 'fore I was wed," she added in a hoarse whisper. "I knows the difference."

Most of the Irish in America were from Ulster. They'd been Scots originally, them as deserted the cause of Catholic Queen Mary and turned heretic and went over to the side of the she-devil Elizabeth. Their reward was land in the north part of Ireland. Roisin trusted people from Ulster less than the rest of the New Yorkers, but Flanagan wasn't an Ulster name. And the woman wasn't shamed to look at her. She'd been a Catholic once, Roisin was sure of it. "Very well. I'll help you."

It was the first time she'd agreed to end a breeding, and she could only pray that the orange sea plant from Brooklyn was truly the same as the one the Holy Virgin delivered to the beaches of Scotland and Ireland. Never England, her mother had said. *Sure and the Blessed Mary would not be giving treacherous Englishwomen the way to be safely free of a babe afore it quickened. Murderous whores that they all be.*

Roisin looked at the pockmarked woman. "Lay down right there on the floor. And spread your legs."

"How bad's it gonna hurt?" the woman asked, though she did as Roisin said without hesitation.

"This part won't hurt at all. Tomorrow when you come back it will hurt a lot. But afterward you won't be breeding."

"Thanks be to the Virgin and all the holy saints," the woman whispered, looking fearfully not at Roisin but at the old hag in the corner.

"Martha's my friend," Roisin said. "You've nothing to fear from her." She pushed up the woman's homespun skirt and her none-too-clean petticoats. Her privates smelled like fish too long ashore and her belly was distended, but when Roisin put her hand on it she felt nothing that could be a heartbeat. Hunger, most likely, not a babe grown enough to show. A diet of nothing but oysters and weak ale like all New York's poor, no wonder the creature's stomach stuck out beyond her bony hips and her dried-up, used-up twat.

Her own stomach was still completely flat. But soon her babe would quicken.

Roisin reached for the piece of the orange sea plant she'd previously cut off, twisted into a tight coil, and bound with hemp.

"Sweet God Almighty!" Martha Kincaid exclaimed, bending forward to see better. "What are you shoving into her twat?"

"What I need to," Roisin said sharply. "It must be left in until this hour tomorrow. Do you hear me, Mary Flanagan?"

"Aye, I do."

"In Jesus' name, girl," Martha demanded, "how's she supposed to piss? She can't hold her water til this time tomorrow, whatever you say."

"She can piss with no bother at all," Roisin said. "You hear that, Mary? You can piss fine with this pessary inside you. Shit as well, for that matter. Only be certain the pessary doesn't come out. If it does, use your fingers to put it back. Shove it in as far as it will go. Like this." She prodded the bit of orange stuff in farther. The woman grunted in discomfort.

She'd scream her head off tomorrow. Most of them did that. But they didn't bleed to death afterward. The pessary made of the gift from the sea would open the way to the womb. After that it would be easy to scrape out what was growing inside. Roisin had watched her mother do it many a time. It hurt something fierce. The women all shrieked as if they were being killed, but it didn't take long and nothing came out except a blob of mucus and blood. Surely to God, that could be no babe ensouled.

V

The library of James De Lancey's country seat was a spacious square room with long windows open to the freshness of the summer morning. The hour was early and nothing stirred on Bouwery Lane. The cool green canopy of shade in his front garden was irresistible.

De Lancey picked up the letter that had been delivered the night before, and the goblet of mulled wine that was his customary morning drink, and stepped outside. Stinking heat later. Nothing could prevent that in New York in July. But these few perfect moments were his to savor.

The orange lilies were coming to flower. A fine sight. He noticed beetle-browed Philip Thomas bringing them a bucket of water and nodded. "Good morning, Philip."

"Morning, Your Excellency."

"The lilies are doing well."

"Yes, Your Excellency. Very well indeed."

"Give them as much water as they need, Philip. No slacking. I brought the bulbs from home last year, you remember. I'm anxious for them to do well."

"Aye, Your Excellency, I remember. No slacking on the water. Certainly not." Born here, the man was, but when he said "home" he meant England. Damned fools all the rich was, the governor no different from the rest. Money and power addled their brains.

De Lancey wandered off, sipping his wine and holding his unopened letter. The bees were busy at a stand of lavender, and he watched their industry for some moments. Clever creatures, bees. Each one knew its job and did it. Made for a peaceful life.

His job was to read the God-cursed letter.

He'd already procrastinated longer than he should. The quarterly report from his allies in Parliament had been delivered late the previous day. It would be bad news, of course. It was always bad news. But it was the only thing that kept him one step ahead of the mad schemes the fools in London thought up to plague the colonies. Particularly now with His Gracious Majesty George III on the throne at the green age of twenty-two. God keep this province safe from the goose-traps made by greedy advisers to inexperienced boy kings.

De Lancey drank the last of the wine, then turned and went inside. He sat down at his desk and prepared to break the circle of red wax that sealed the letter.

"Grandpapa, you told me you'd read to me this morning. You said if I got up early you would."

De Lancey smiled indulgently at his youngest grandchild. She was still in her nightdress, her pudgy face flushed with sleep, one hand trailing a doll. "So I did. Very well, come and choose a book. But only for a few minutes, remember," he added trying to sound stern. "Then I must work."

He got up from the desk and went to the shelf where he kept the books that were suitable for the young. "Now, will it be—" A sudden pain. De Lancey clutched at his chest.

"Grandpapa! What is it? Grandpapa!"

The little girl dropped her doll and pressed both hands to her mouth. She watched in wide-eyed terror as her grandfather staggered a few steps and fell with a thud. For long moments she stared at the crumpled heap on the floor; then she turned and ran screaming from the library.

Summoned by the child's scream Philip Thomas rushed into the room through the long windows. She'd left the hall door open behind her and he could still hear her shouts, and the answering stir from the sleeping house. "Governor? It's me, sir, Philip."

Christ Almighty. Nothing to be done for the thing on the floor. His Excellency the Lieutenant Governor of New York was as dead as any man could be, rich or poor.

Footsteps raced toward the library. The entire household was coming. In seconds they'd all be there, setting up a wailing and a weeping, slaves and indentures and servants as well as kin. As if the frigging governor be their own blood. Not him. He'd never mistook the side of his johnnycake as had the syrup.

"Lying there on the Turkey carpet he was, mistress. Both eyes wide open and staring at the ceiling, though he couldn't see a thing. I promise you that. Dead as sure as I be breathing."

"Yes, Philip, I've no doubt you're right," Squaw said. "And you just happened to be the first to discover him?"

"No, mistress. Didn't happen like that. Watering the lilies, I was. So's I heard the little girl scream and went in and there he be." Thomas reached into his pocket and brought out the letter. "There was this as well. Gets letters like this regular, the governor does. From London. I be telling you that afore."

"Yes, Philip, you have told me. Many times."

"Right, well, I never had no chance to bring you one afore now. Saw my way clear this time, so I did it. Grabbed the letter off the desk and came straight here. Out the front gate I was, afore any of 'em had even gotten to the library to find him lying there. On the Turkey carpet. Eyes all open and staring."

"Thank you, Philip. I understand. But are you quite sure this letter won't be missed?"

Thomas drew his bushy eyebrows together and vigorously shook his head. "Certain, Mistress. Ain't nobody in the house what's to do with His Excellency's gov'mint, only the family. The letter came last night, near midnight. I let in the redcoat what brought it me own self. Brought him straight to the governor, I did. Nobody else knew nothing about it."

She was glad of the veil. He couldn't see any hint of excitement she might fail to hide. "Well, I'm pleased to have it, Philip. You did well to bring it here. Though I've little interest in politics, of course." Her voice was absolutely neutral. "But there might be something useful. And you were quick-witted, there's no denying that." She opened the drawer of her writing table and withdrew an iron shilling. "Something extra for your trouble."

Philip Thomas left looking mightily pleased.

Dear God in heaven, so was she. It almost didn't matter what was in the letter, though there was sure to be something. A personal letter from London addressed to simply J.D.L. and brought to his country residence at midnight. It was bound to discuss mischief of one sort or another. But even without that, this was a great good morning.

She got up from the desk, pressed the letter to her heart, and unable to contain her excitement any longer, spun around in a few quick turns that belled out the taffeta skirts of her somber dress. James De Lancey was dead! Dead! Dead! The best possible news she could have.

The excitement left her as suddenly as it had come. She was deflated, the anguish she'd lived with for the nine months of Morgan's absence settling like a blanket around her bent shoulders. Oh, Morgan, Morgan, how long will it take for you to realize everything I did was for you. Morgan's forgiveness, that would be the best news.

Maybe not. Maybe the best would be . . .

She glanced up at the ornate plaster ceiling, conscious of the attic room above her head where Solomon brooded on his demons. Every few months she went up there in the dead of night, when no one was awake. Praying that this time would be different.

It was always the same.

She'd listen at his door first. Then, when she heard nothing, she'd open it. Every single time Solomon instantly knew she was there. He'd sit up in his bed, and lift his one arm and point at her with the remaining two fingers. "Devil's strumpet!" he'd hiss. "Whore! Stinking cunt fishwife!"

How could he hate her so much? Once, he'd loved her as much as he hated her now.

The best news would be if Solomon and Morgan both forgave her for doing what she'd had to do. If they loved her again.

No use asking for what you could not have: another of the lessons life had taught her. But this was a fine morning nonetheless.

She went to the table that had the decanter of canary wine and poured herself a glass. Slowly, turning away from the window and facing the wall, she folded back her veil so she could sip the drink. I hope you rot in hell, James De Lancey, but I bless you for dying while Cadwallader Colden lives. Colden's the senior member of the Common Council and he will take your place as lieutenant governor. And, God willing, London will be as reluctant to send us a new royal governor as they have been these many years past, so Colden will stay in the post until he, too, drops dead.

Not long, perhaps. He was seventy-some, after all. But, pray God, long enough. Colden's connection to Caleb has never been more than easy money for him. Now he can be made to turn against my dear, dear cousin. The Devrey link will be an embarrassment to the new governor. He'll not want to show favoritism, for one thing, or be made to acknowledge the land deals he made in the Devrey interest while Will was alive. For another, Bede Devrey is one of the strongest voices among the men of business who oppose London's excesses. It won't do for His Majesty's Governor to be tied to such people. James De Lancey was too powerful for me to oppose him head-on. But Cadwallader Colden, oh yes, yes, yes! A pot waiting to be stirred. Even without whatever choice bits this blessed letter provides.

Half an hour later she'd finished reading.

Plans to meddle with the system of trial by jury. Plans to increase the fines for trading with the enemy in the West Indies. Plans to prohibit the issuing of paper money anywhere in the colonies. Plans, God help them all, to impose a direct tax. It would no longer be enough merely to import the colonials' raw materials at a price infinitely more favorable to England than to America, or to sell the colonists every manufactured thing required for daily life at exorbitant prices and forbid them to make what they needed here or buy it elsewhere.

The King is advised to levy a Duty on all Paper and Paper Products. A Stamp will be required to be affixed to such prior to every Sale. Monies paid to purchase the Stamps will go directly to the Royal Treasury for Maintenance of the Troops.

Squaw DaSilva paled beneath her veil. London dipping directly into the pockets of the colonials. Here was mischief beyond anything she had ever contemplated. If George III followed such advice, God help England as well as America. The king would be kindling a fire that would incinerate them both.

Book Six

The Path of Flames

JULY 1765–DECEMBER 1765

Some fires are sacred. Their smoke carries the prayers of men to the Great Spirit. Other fires are evil, set when the bad manetuac *tempt men to do things that hurt the People. Such fires are made by those who carry vengeful thoughts in their hearts.*

The fires of vengeance plant the seeds of hatred.

The sacred fire purifies.

Chapter Eleven

IT TOOK ALL Caleb Devrey's strength to remain upright. The pain sent him out walking night after night, prowling the dark city, avoiding the watchmen and the curfew, though that was little enforced these days.

The thing in his belly was always with him. Sometimes it slept, a snake coiled, waiting to strike. When it did it could double him in two with a savage attack, or, as it did tonight, gnaw away at his intestines in a steady, fiery assault. God-cursed pain, eating him alive. He was always hot on the inside and freezing with cold from the skin out. High summer, the middle of July, and he couldn't do without his cloak.

"Psst, Dr. Devrey. Over here."

Caleb stumbled, nearly went into the drainage gutter. "Who's there? What are you after?"

"Don't be meaning ye no harm, Doc. Name's Vrinck." The man emerged from the shadows, put out a hand to steady Devrey. "Petrus Vrinck I be. Been lookin' all over for ye."

A seaman, from the look of him. Devrey drew away from his touch. "What do you want with me? I don't see patients at this hour."

"I don't be sick. Got something to tell ye. There's a slop shop down the road a bit. We can talk there."

"It's not my custom to drink with tars in a slop shop. You can come to my rooms tomorrow if you wish to consult me."

Vrinck moved closer. He was short and stocky, with massive arms and legs; one eye remained half closed and stared away from the other. He shoved his grizzled face so near to Devrey's they almost kissed. "Be worth yer time to talk to me," he whispered. "Swears it on me mother's grave, I do."

Most of the man's teeth had rotted away and his breath stank of putrefaction. Caleb pulled back. "In God's name, why?"

"'Cause I know things. 'Bout the *Fanciful Maiden*." Vrinck paused. "That be getting yer attention, don't it, Dr. Devrey?"

"You're imagining things. I've no interest whatever in privateering."

"That ain't what it be these days. Scavenging, more like. Gulls on a dungheap the privateers be. Ain't no prizes worth takin' anymore. Ain't been none for nearly six years."

"That's as may be. It's no concern of mine. So if you'll let me pass—"

"Wait. Ye ain't heard me out yet. Was on a real privateering run I was. In 'fifty-nine, with Morgan Turner. On the *Fanciful Maiden*. That's what I want to talk about. Lots o' things on that voyage weren't like folks said they were. Not like Turner said they were neither."

Sweet piss on the grass. He'd never thought to have another bite of that cherry. Not after all this time. Sweet piss on the grass.

Vrinck saw the light of greed in the other man's eyes and turned, jerking his head toward the far end of the road. "Follow me."

The room was barely big enough for ten, and there were at least twice that many crammed into it. Devrey drew his cloak tight to him and followed Vrinck, who was elbowing a path through the crowd. Noisy sods. Snatches of their talk were audible as Devrey passed by. Going on about how they'd never use stamped paper or pay taxes levied in London. How all the kings on God's green earth couldn't make them do it. The mob had been mouthing the same rubbish for weeks. Treasonous rabble.

The landlord waited at the back of the slop shop, next to a small door set into the rear wall. Vrinck drew even with him and pressed a coin into his hand. The landlord opened the door. Vrinck lowered his head and scurried through. Caleb hesitated a moment. Hell, he'd come this far. And whatever else this might be, it was a distraction from the pain.

He had to crouch to get through the door. Little space to stand upright once he was inside. The ceiling barely cleared what was left of his red hair. "What is this place? Feels like a damned cave."

Vrinck had moved deeper into the gloom. They were alone in this dank, dark place. Caleb felt a sudden chill of apprehension. "Look here . . . Vrinck, you said your name was, right?"

"Aye, Petrus Vrinck."

"I've no money on me, so you won't—"

The sailor laughed. "Don't be stupid. Didn't bring ye here to rob ye. Why would I do that when I could o' taken anything ye might have out on the road where none had yet seen us together?" He patted the hilt of his cutlass. "Easy that would o' been. Lot easier than this. Sit ye down, Dr. Devrey. Landlord's left us a jug o' grog."

A tin pitcher and two tin mugs stood on the battered wooden table. There were two short stools as well, and a small grate, but no fire this July night. Caleb hesitated, then squatted on one of the stools and poured himself a drink. Even cut with hot water, the rough rum burned his throat going down. Gut-rotting stuff, not imported from the islands but made in one of the local sugarhouses. His belly objected with a long, twisting jab; then the rum won. The snake went back to sleep. "Very well, Vrinck. Tell me what we're doing here."

"I already did. The *Fanciful Maiden*. She be what we're doin' here."

"As I said, why should a privateer mean anything to me?"

"'Cause ye was robbed o' what was comin' to ye. In 'fifty-nine, like I said."

Sweet Christ, did the whole world know he'd bought shares in that God-cursed voyage? Despite the proxy? And if everyone else knew, how was it that Morgan Turner and his bitch mother didn't? They couldn't have, or they'd never have allowed him to invest. "Nothing to me, as I said. But go on. I'm listening."

"That story they be tellin' back then, end o' that poxed voyage," Vrinck said softly, "'bout how the *Maiden* didn't take no prizes and came home empty? It be a lie."

Caleb shook his head. "I saw her when she came into port. The whole town did. The *Fanciful Maiden* was in disgraceful condition. There was no cargo. Every one of the investors went aboard and checked the hold, and came out saying—"

"Oh, the part 'bout her comin' home with her belly empty, that was true enough." Vrinck tossed back a long swallow of grog and wiped his mouth with the back of his hand, smiling meanwhile at the black-clad wraith across from him. Pissing himself with curiosity the frigging gentleman was. Hangin' on every word. "Afore she got here? Well, that last voyage in 'fifty-nine, richest the *Maiden* ever made, it be. I be aboard and I know. We took three prizes. Spanish ships. Stuffed to the gunnels with slaves, indigo, sugar . . . And a king's ransom in gold besides."

"So what happened to the cargo? And the money?"

"I'm tryin' to tell ye. Morgan Turner sold his cargo on Bahama Island and paid off the whole crew. Seventy-five fighting men we was, 'n we got four hundred pounds each. In bullion, if ye don't mind." Vrinck folded his arms and enjoyed the look on the other man's face.

"Four hundred to each member of the crew. Sweet piss on the grass, man, that means the total prize was . . . fifty thousand pounds. The dung-eating son of a bitch! Morgan will hang for this. It's a gallows offense!"

"Yeh, they tells me it be that." Vrinck took another swig of the grog. "But I'll wager any sum you care to name Turner'll swing to hell and back and never tell where the treasure be."

Reality damped Caleb's initial astonishment. He shrugged. "Six years have passed. If he ever did hide a treasure, he's long since claimed it. And there's no proof of what you say. None."

Vrinck shook his head, fixed Devrey with the one eye he could focus. "Forget about provin' nothin'. Ye wants Turner dead, ye has to do it for yerself. Can't depend on no magistrates and courts to do it for ye. Not here in New York. Me, far as I'm concerned Turner can die in his bed with his boots polished for the mornin'. It be the treasure what matters."

"It must be gone," Devrey insisted. "Long since. The bastard will have claimed it by now."

"No, he ain't done that. Too soon it be. Too many folks what would remember what happened in 'fifty-nine. 'Sides, I knows a tar as has sailed with the *Maiden* these past five years. She ain't never been near the Caribbean. Morgan Turner don't need any readies, does he?" Vrinck leaned forward, turning his head so he could fix Devrey with at least one eye. "Morgan Turner can put a treasure o' thousands wherever he thinks it be safe, and bide as long as he needs afore he goes and gets it."

A few seconds of silence passed. Devrey poured himself a second mug of the fiery grog, sipping it slowly this time. "What about you? How come you waited so long to do whatever it is you plan to do?"

Vrinck shrugged. "Didn't suit me to do nothin' sooner. Been in the islands. Enjoyin' meself. Didn't suit me to come north and shrivel me balls in one o' the freezin' winters ye be having up here."

"It's not winter now," Devrey said softly.

"No, it don't be. And I plans to get what I came for and go afore it do."

Returning now was an impulse, most likely. Essentially what he'd expect of this sort of creature. Half animal, like most of his class, incapable of forethought or planning. But Morgan Turner was something very different. If that bastard had laid himself open to a charge of common piracy—and lying about a prize was exactly that—it had to be part of a well-thought-out scheme. Not necessarily his scheme, but Squaw DaSilva's. The bitch whore. Anything you cared to wager said her plan was aimed directly at Caleb Devrey. Somehow she'd known about the proxy.

A stab of pain to the gut took his breath. Caleb nearly tumbled into the black pit that loomed before him each time the snake struck and the agony became too much to bear. Death was at the bottom of that hole. He saw it plainly, smiling up at him, inviting him to let go and plunge.

Slowly, Caleb fought his way back, chest grinding and bowels on fire. Better now. He could breathe. "Say you're right." His voice was hoarse with exhaustion and effort, and his face dripped sweat. "Say it's true. If Turner hid such a treasure, where is it?"

"If I knowed that, would I be sitting here?"

Fair enough, but the treasure's whereabouts was not the only question. "Why are you telling me all this?"

"'Cause yer a gentlemen, ain't ye? Someone as can get money when ye needs it."

Caleb leaned backward until his head touched the damp stone wall of the small room. For the moment he was weak from the struggle, but free of the pain. At sweet times like that, nothing else seemed important. He chuckled softly. "I'm a gentleman, perhaps, but I'm not the one who ever saw four hundred pounds in bullion. Sweet piss, Vrinck, you know every other cursed thing, you must know I haven't got two coppers to rub together."

"Yer a gentleman," Vrinck insisted. "Someone as can get money when he be needing it."

"A common misconception among the laboring classes. It's not true."

"Yer brother Bede, he be rich as can be."

And fed up to the teeth with paying my debts. But that's none of your bloody business. "What happened to your portion of the *Maiden*'s wealth? And the prizes you probably shared in before that. Drank it all, did you? Gambled and whored it away?"

Vrinck turned around and spat into the fire.

"Yes, I figured as much." Caleb put down his mug and started to rise. "Not my place to lecture you. Done my share of the same, as you probably know."

Vrinck jumped up, placing himself between the door and Devrey. "What kind o' man ye be? Got piss for blood that ye'd let that whore's son take what's comin' to ye?"

Indeed. That whore's son. That whore. The part-savage bitch who married a Jew and turned herself into the richest woman in New York while he struggled to survive. Caleb settled himself on the stool a second time and peered at Petrus Vrinck. A low creature, but he might be useful. "Say I could get some money. Not a lot, mind you, but some. How would that help?"

Vrinck returned to the table, took his seat and leaned forward, clasping his mug of grog with both beefy hands. "Back in 'fifty-nine, when he dumped the most of us in the islands, Turner couldn't bring his ship back alone. Five men sailed home with him. None of 'em was seen after the first night they made port, but I'd wager my soul they was in a dozen taverns 'n' grog shops afore they disappeared. Talked to plenty o' tars they must have. That be what sailors do. I need to send the punch bowl around in as many taverns and slop shops as tars be known to do their drinkin'. Sooner or later I be finding someone as knows somethin' 'bout where the treasure be hid."

"And if you did find such a person? It's six years ago, man. Morgan Turner's been sailing for most of it. I still say, whatever he hid in 'fifty-nine—if he hid it— it's long gone."

Vrinck cut him off with a stubborn shake of his head. "No, it don't be gone. I told ye, the *Maiden*'s been over in Europe all this time, takin' what French and Spanish prizes she can find off the Guinea coast. Ain't no point in any privateer sailin' in the Caribbean these last years. Navy's sent all the enemy merchant ships to the bottom o' the sea. Wherever Morgan Turner put that treasure in 'fifty-nine, it still be there."

"Idle hope," Caleb said quietly, the excitement he'd felt dying in him as he spoke the words. "You are deluding yourself, Mr. Vrinck."

"I kin find someone as knows," Vrinck insisted. "Might take a time. But I visit enough alehouses and slop shops and taprooms, sooner or later I be finding someone as knows somethin'."

"It's not a bad plan," Caleb conceded. "But why do you need me?"

"Has to stand me rounds o' the bowl I does. Takes a bit o' money."

"How much?" A waste of time as well as money, even presuming he could squeeze one more loan out of Bede. Utterly stupid. "How much would you need?"

"Three shillings a week, maybe." Vrinck didn't look at him. "For a month, maybe two. Like I said, tars come and go."

Sweet Christ. A pound or two to secure thousands. "And if I were to agree, and—an even more unlikely possibility—you were to discover something, how am I to know you won't take what information you have and run off with it? Why should you share whatever profit you stand to make?"

"I be needing a ship, don't I? Morgan Turner hid his treasure somewheres in the islands. I knows that for certain. Be needin' a ship and a crew to go get it. That costs some."

Ah yes. A ship. Not a couple of pounds but many thousands. A somewhat different matter. "I could never get that much money. It's an idle fancy, Vrinck. Put it out of your mind."

"A fancy, be it?" Vrinck stood up. He looked like a bent tree trunk when he leaned forward, supporting himself on his two thick arms, and pressed his knuckles into the scarred wood of the table. "It don't be fanciful that you don't be the only loser. And them other investors, at least some of 'em still be rich, don't they? For all they was cheated out o' what was rightfully theirs, same as yerself. Ye goes to 'em, tells 'em they can get what was comin' to 'em since six years past. They be puttin' up the stake we need to get a ship and a crew to sail her, sure as God."

Caleb stared at Vrinck. Little warning prickles were racing through his gut. The pain was alive, inside him, taunting him with the fact that in the end, whatever he did, it would win. God-cursed bitch and her God-cursed son. All their fault. Maybe he could live long enough to see them pay.

Vrinck was waiting. Caleb nodded.

October twenty-third in this year of grace 1765. Twilight. A cannon boomed twice from the direction of the harbor, signaling the arrival of the frigate *Edward* under the protection of two men o' war. The *Edward*'s hold was stuffed with stamped paper.

The guns of Fort George had been repositioned on the northern wall and trained on the Broad Way, on the people of New York. The cannon of the Battery had been spiked. Even if the citizenry managed to overpower the redcoats and gain control, the guns couldn't be turned on the fort. Governor Colden's orders.

Fog rolled in off the harbor, muffling the tramp of boots and shoes and clogs on the cobbled streets of the court part of town. An army was assembling. Marching without drill, not entirely in unison, but with a single purpose. They were determined the Stamp Act would not be enforced.

More than two thousand came and stared down the barrels of the guns.

"That bastard Colden's to blame for this."

"Aye. But he's only licking the hind ends of his London masters. Sons o' bitches would make us all Negroes. Here take these papers, give 'em to all you know."

The man who blamed Cadwallader Colden for the tax that would make him a pauper took the papers eagerly. "They be saying this can't happen, right? That it won't happen."

"Here, I'll read you what they say. 'The first man that either distributes or makes use of stamped paper, let him take care of his house, person and effects.' Plain enough, ain't it?"

It was no night to try and get through the town in a carriage. Squaw DaSilva walked. She'd never before been in the new neighborhood that had grown up on the west-facing land that had once been Trinity Church Farm. The dirt streets of the new section hadn't been included in the Council's latest municipal improvement: whale-oil lanterns on the city streets and official lamplighters to tend them. Neither, apparently, did the people of the district follow the old custom of a candle lantern hanging from every seventh house. The dark was absolute.

The fog made it worse. She was chilled to the bone. She pulled her long black cloak tighter against the sharp wind. One good thing, the bad weather might help disperse the mob that had gathered on the Broad Way. Then again, it might not. Sweet God, men were such flaming fools. And kings were the worst of all.

She hadn't been easy in her mind about leaving the house, not with so much obvious trouble brewing at her front door. But she'd had no choice. She'd summoned three of her strongest barkeeps and left them on guard. That would have to be enough.

The wind was sharp as glass. Despite all the years she'd lived in the whorehouse beside Hudson's River, she'd never become accustomed to the gale that almost always blew on this side of the city. Small wonder few wanted to live over here on the Church Farm. But offer a laboring man a lot for an annual rent of two pounds and he'd be bound to take it. Not that two pounds a year was as easy to come by now as it had been. Not for laborers and artisans.

England had taken Canada. France had given up her claim to all land east of the Mississippi, except for the enclave at New Orleans. Not satisfied, England moved on the French possessions in the Caribbean. When Spain indicated that she might assist the French, England, the strongest nation on earth, declared war on Spain as well. All that bluster and triumph had been a disaster for New York.

War and the wealth created by war had moved on. The city was left with inflation, unemployment, debt, and faltering trade. Not even privateering was a sure source of profit any longer. The Royal Navy had driven almost all French and Spanish shipping out of local waters. Most of the men-o'-war sailing under letters of marque rode at anchor in the harbor. But not the *Fanciful Maiden*.

Damn you, Morgan, why must you be as stubborn as I am? Six years. I'm fifty. Healthy so far, but who knows how long I have left. Morgan, oh, my boy.

She heard the snuffling of a pair of wild hogs rooting through the garbage that clogged the ditch down the middle of the road and stopped moving, trying to tell from the sound exactly where the pigs were and how to navigate around them. It was hard to believe Jan Brinker had settled here after he could afford so much better. Same as when he insisted on staying up at the bawdyhouse in the woods, whatever other accommodation she'd offered. Stubborn little freak.

"Mistress." The voice was very quiet and very close. She gasped, then held her breath. "Don't be feared, mistress. It's me, Rudolf. I'll take you to him."

The arrangement had been made that afternoon in the market on the ground floor of the Royal Exchange on Broad Street. "Tonight," the big black carriage driver whispered without seeming to look at her. "At an hour before midnight, on Little Cortlandt Street. I'll show you where he is."

"Tonight may not be convenient." She'd known then it would be no evening to move about town. She'd already had word that the stamps would arrive in a matter of hours. "I can reward your trouble if we do it next week."

"Tonight," the coachman insisted. "Has to be. He doesn't have much time left."

She had to see with her own eyes. Nothing else would satisfy her. Not after everything that had happened. "Tonight," she'd agreed.

Now the black man led her through a maze of streets she knew she'd never remember. She wouldn't get out of this cursed neighborhood unless this Rudolf brought her out.

A final turn and they were in a narrow alley. Rudolf stopped walking. She sensed rather than saw him push open a door. It moved silently on well-oiled hinges. "He's in there, mistress. May be that he's sleeping."

He held the door open for her to enter. She turned to him. "Wait," she whispered anxiously. "However long I'm in here, you must wait. An extra shilling if you do."

"Don't worry, I'll be waiting."

She hesitated a moment, then stepped inside. Rudolf pulled the door closed behind her.

There was a small lantern flickering in one corner. It cast long shadows across a surprisingly large square room with a good-sized fireplace on one wall. The bed had been drawn close to the warmth of the glowing embers. Jan Brinker's little form barely disturbed the coverings.

He wasn't sleeping. "You came," he said. "I hoped you would."

"Of course I came, old friend. I'd have been here a lot sooner if you hadn't waited so long to send word you were ill." She took off her cloak as she spoke, hanging it on a peg beside the door and moving closer to the dwarf. "Can I get you anything? Will you take a drink?" There was a jug of ale on the bedside table, and a pewter mug.

"Not now," Brinker said. His voice was weaker than she'd ever heard it.

"Are you getting any nourishment?" she asked. "And what about treatment for your illness? I can send Phoebe."

"The girl, Roisin, she simples as well as any apothecary alive. She takes good care of me. And Rudolf and old Martha Kincaid besides, though Martha won't be long joining me on t'other side. I be well looked after, mevrouw. Don't trouble yourself. It's only that I be wanting to see you again. Once more before I be going."

"Ah, Jan Brinker, what a long road we've traveled." She drew a chair close to the bedside and sat down and took his hand. "I've missed your company these past eighteen years."

"Nineteen," he corrected. "Nineteen years since we be doing all that shouting and screaming in the bordello, loud enough so's any could hear."

He chuckled at the memory and she laughed with him, until he started coughing and spewing up phlegm. Squaw DaSilva held a cloth to his mouth, supporting his small, thin shoulders with her arm. Finally he settled back on the pillows. "You must rest, Jan. I should go."

He pretended he hadn't heard her. "Remember when you be moving to your big fancy house on the Broad Way, mevrouw? Finer than anything you had over on Nassau Street it be, don't it?"

"Oh, yes, Jan. Much finer."

"And you be sending me off to Chappaqua to brew beer."

"That turned out a good plan, didn't it? It made you rich."

"*Ja*, mevrouw." Richer than them *Jesu Cristo* sons of bitches what be wanting to put me in the stocks again. "Rich as a king I be. All 'cause redcoats be so thirsty. But I always be missing you and the old days, mevrouw. And the whores, truth be telling. For all it's them what gave me the French disease be killing me now."

She wanted to say she'd never realized you could lick a dose of the French disease from between a whore's legs as well as get it in the ordinary way, but she didn't. That would be too forward even for Jan Brinker, who knew better than most what she was capable of saying as well as thinking. "I missed you, too, Jan. But it was wise. For both of us. I always knew the time might come when I'd need you, and that it would be best if no one suspected we were still friends. I was right."

"You be right most times, mevrouw. Sometimes being right be hard."

"Yes, sometimes it is." Still, she had no regrets about most of it. Far better for dear Cuf to believe he'd taken his freedom than that she'd given it to him. As for Roisin, her plan had been simply to get her out of Morgan's sight as well as his bed. One of the bordellos where he could find her at will would have been no answer at all. Of course she could never have known that the girl would become Cuf's woman, and that Morgan would leave so it didn't matter.

Jan Brinker saw her tremble. "You be too cold, mevrouw." He reached out a hand. "Where's me little bell? If I ring it Rudolf be coming to put another log on the fire."

"No, that's not necessary. I'm fine. But I wish you'd let me get you something."

"Ain't nothing I be needing, mevrouw." She had the veil in place but he could tell she was grieving. No good at all being the richest woman in New York when you had so little of what mattered. Jan Brinker licked his parched lips.

"Please," she said, leaning toward him. "You must drink something." She poured a little ale into the tankard. A fine tankard it was, beautifully made. If things were different she'd have been asking him where he got it, craving something the same for herself. "There, that's better," she said when he'd drunk a bit. "I should go, Jan. I'm tiring you."

"Be plenty of time I'll have to rest when I'm in me grave. Soon enough now. Stay a little, mevrouw." *Jesu Cristo*, how much should he be telling her? And what chance was there she didn't already know? Didn't matter. Not now when he was so close to the end. "Mevrouw, the girl, Roisin, she has a daughter. Five years the child be. Name's Clare." He tried peering through the veil.

"Yes, I heard about Cuf's child. Is Clare white or black, Jan?" Her voice sounded unconcerned, but then it always had.

"White skin, mevrouw. But she have black hair. Black as Cuf's." And as straight and shiny as Mistress Jennet's had been when she was a young beauty and he'd rescued her from the howling mob heading down Nassau Street. But if she wanted to know that she'd know it already. "Not much you don't be hearing, is there, mevrouw?"

"Not much, Jan." She'd known about the child for years. Everyone said the girl was Cuf's daughter. It must be true. If the likes of Roisin Campbell had birthed Squaw DaSilva's grandchild she'd have been knocking on the door demanding money before she was out of the borning bed. Besides, it was common knowledge the whore knew how to rid a woman of a child she didn't wish to bear.

Sometimes when she closed her eyes she could still feel herself thrusting the wooden stick into Ellen, trying desperately to find a way into the uterus. "Roisin is a clever healer, isn't she, Jan?"

"The best. So many women be going to her it be a wonder no magistrates be coming to find out why."

She knew he was probing because he already suspected the truth. Ah well, all these years, so much loyalty, she owed him that. "Don't worry, Jan. I see to it that the authorities cause Cuf and Roisin Campbell and their child no trouble. I always will." And so she would. For Cuf's sake. And because Morgan cherished the man who had been the companion of his childhood.

"*Ja,* mevrouw. I be thinking you be doing that."

Weariness overcame him. Jan Brinker closed his eyes. After a few moments he slept and she tiptoed to the door and reclaimed her cloak and stepped into the street.

The bright red glow in the sky was unmistakable. "Dear God, fire."

"Yes, mistress." Rudolf came out of the shadows. "Fire. Just got going right and proper."

"At the Battery?"

"No, right close by here. A bonfire. Not to worry, mistress, I can take you back without going near it."

"No." She drew her cloak closer. "I want to see."

"Mistress . . ."

"Take me there."

The blaze was on a hill. It rose ten feet high, sparks shooting into the night. Truly amazing, particularly now, when the price of firewood had tripled in the last few years. There was talk of the poor freezing to death this winter, and there were more poor than ever before in the city. Every ship that docked in New York brought new immigrants. Most wanted land and immediately went west, but many stayed and added to the numbers scavenging for the limited work available. Not to mention the numbers ready to stand around the flames of a wasteful bonfire and scream curses into the night.

Fools, Squaw thought. They did the same thing every November on what they called Pope Day. Official New York said it was Guy Fawkes Day, and that it commemorated saving the Houses of Parliament in London from a papist plot to blow them up. By long tradition the governor gave a ball and a fancy supper, but the laborers and craftsmen living here on the Church Farm had no interest in Parliament. Each year they burned a likeness of the pope and screamed out their hatred of Catholics.

Twice fools as far as she was concerned. Once for wasting the firewood. A second time for thinking any religion made a difference. Protestant, Catholic, or Jew, if there was no work they all went to bed with their bellies empty.

But it wouldn't be Pope Day for nearly a week.

The mob had built a scaffold a little distance from the blaze. A pair of scarecrows hung from the gibbet. They represented the devil whispering into the ear of the lieutenant governor.

The effigy was only a rough likeness, but she easily recognized Cadwallader Colden. She'd seen him just once close up, but it had been a memorable meeting that took place within days of his becoming governor. She had asked three things: for Caleb Devrey to be removed as physician overseer of the almshouse hospital. For the job to be guaranteed to Andrew Turner whenever he returned from Edinburgh. And for Luke Turner to be paid a pension for life equal to four-fifths of his former salary. Every one of her demands was met.

At the height of his power Cadwallader Colden had been then, but he'd been no match for her. He still wasn't. Andrew had arrived from Edinburgh two weeks past, and immediately put in charge of not only the hospital but the Bedloe's Island pesthouse. Luke was still collecting his pension. Meanwhile, Caleb Devrey scurried around the town like a black cockroach afraid of the light.

A low rumble began, like the sound of distant thunder. The crowd spraying its collective venom. "It be bad, mistress. Best we go."

"Yes, Rudolf, we will. Only a moment more."

They were at the foot of the hill, on the fringe of the activity and hidden by the shadows, but it was possible to see what was happening merely by looking up to the crest. The frenzied mob had converged on the gallows and were rocking the structure back and forth. The effigies swung wildly. In seconds the whole thing crashed into the heart of the bonfire.

The flames soared still higher, piercing the night, and the horde howled in an ecstasy of hate. She touched Rudolf's arm. "We'll go now. There's nothing more to see."

When she got home she learned that Colden had taken refuge on a man-o'-war in the harbor. The stamps had been unloaded under cover of darkness and locked away in City Hall. Somehow the mob found out and rampaged through much of the town, ripping up gardens, breaking lamps and windows, and threatening to pull down houses. Not hers. It hadn't been touched.

And still more news. In the midst of the chaos the *Fanciful Maiden* had slipped quietly into New York harbor and dropped anchor.

II

The pesthouse stood by itself fifty yards back from the shore, the only structure on Bedloe's Island. It was two stories high, each floor lined with wooden bedsteads topped with straw. The only partition was at ground level, where they'd built a half-wall to separate the attendants from the patients.

"Good Christ," Andrew muttered, "it's a death sentence."

"Begging your pardon, sir?" The man who was showing him the second institution the city had made over to his care was stooped, one leg was considerably shorter than the other, and he walked only with the help of a stick. "Was you speaking to me, sir?"

"No, I was not. But I am now. Johnson—that's what you said your name was, right?"

"Right, sir. Harry Johnson."

"And you're in charge of this . . . what are we supposed to call it? House of Quarantine?"

"That's right, sir. S'posed to look after any tars as is brought here 'cause they's poxed. From the ships what come to the harbor, sir."

And any New Yorker with the same misfortune, according to the law. "Tell me something, Johnson, why did you take this godforsaken post?"

"Didn't have no choice, sir. Not me nor any of the lads. Got here only an hour afore you did, sir. Took us out o' the jailhouse this morning, they did. Brought us straight here. But leastwise they say the grub's better."

Good Christ. "Johnson, have you been variolated?"

"No, sir. Never, sir. Never done nothin' but stole some candles."

"Variolation's not a crime, man. Whatever they tell you. It can save your life."

"Gives you the pox, don't it, sir?"

"A mild case. Then you can't get it again. Have you ever had the pox, Johnson?"

"Not me, sir. Crispin, he's one of me mates, sir. Came over this mornin' same as the rest of us. He had it. Got the pockmarks all over him, Crispin does."

"So you say. I want to see for myself. You, Crispin, everyone, I'll see you next door in that little room." There were three patients upstairs. All stinking to high heaven and at death's door, their variolae dried up and fallen off along with most of their skin. Never mind, he'd find enough live serum to serve the purpose. "I'll be ready in half an hour."

"You makin' that be an order, sir?"

His first instinct was to say no, that it was entirely up to them. There was some risk to variolation, after all. But without it the verdict was certain. "It's an order, yes. Every single one of you. In half an hour."

There were five men altogether. They'd been taken from the New Jail on the Common that very morning, to replace the last group that had drawn this cursed duty, and—Andrew would wager his last shilling on it—had died of the pox. Johnson and two of the others showed no evidence of having had the disease.

The job was finished in ten minutes. "You'll feel poorly for a day or two," Andrew told them, wiping his lancet on a rag. He remembered the story his grandfather had told about Cotton Mather and invisible worms that crawled around spreading the disease. In Christopher's notes, the ones that had been given to him along with Lucas Turner's journals, there was a note about wiping a scalpel or a lancet after use. To protect against the possibility of the invisible worms. "May be that you'll raise a fever. And certainly a few pox. Don't be frightened. You'll recover."

Please God, let it be so. He'd been extremely cautious about how much pus mixed with their own blood he gave them. A stint in one of His Majesty's prisons didn't leave you with much health to fight off even the mildest case of the pox. "Until you feel perfectly well, you don't set foot out of this part of the pesthouse. Not a single foot, do you hear me? The pair of you who've had the pox, you'll have to see to the patients by yourselves for the time being. And look after your mates."

There was nothing else he could do here. Andrew packed up his instruments and prepared to leave. "Johnson, signal a boat to come and pick me up."

"That means I have to put me foot outside this part of the pesthouse, don't it, sir?"

"Yes. It does. Don't worry. Going outside is no danger. I meant you shouldn't go on the wards."

The rules of quarantine on Bedloe's Island required vessels of any size to stand off. Only small boats could approach, and only if they were bringing patients or had been summoned to carry away a passenger.

Johnson waited with him by the landing. A lighter pulled rapidly toward them, rowed by four men. Andrew knew how much they hated the task. Bedloe's Island was the most feared place in the province.

"Begging yer pardon, sir."

"Yes, Johnson, what is it?"

"Over there, sir, by that big boulder. Me and the lads, sir, we be looking at it earlier."

"Looking at what?" The freezing November wind blew across the water, whipping his fair hair back from his forehead, feeling like iced darts on his cheeks. There was the smell of early snow on the air. Andrew drew his heavy gray cloak tighter around his tall frame.

"If ye'd jus' come and take a look, sir . . ." The man had no jacket and was dancing up and down, but it wasn't the cold. It was agitation.

The boat had almost reached them. Reluctantly, Andrew turned his back on it. "Very well, show me."

Johnson led him to an immense granite outcropping ten yards from the south wall of the pesthouse. "There it be, sir."

"It's a boulder, man. And no surprise the workmen didn't try and move it. It's huge."

" 'Tain't the stone, sir. What's puzzling me and the lads . . . It's them, sir." Johnson used his stick to point at a series of holes.

Andrew took a step closer. The holes were scattered around the perimeter of the boulder, apparently at random. Freshly dug, every one of them. A dozen by rapid count, only the width of a single spade, but each one something less than two feet deep.

"What ye be thinking, sir?"

"Good Christ, man. I've no idea."

"Think it be ghosts, sir? The ghosts of 'em as was poxed and died here? Digging 'emselves up from under the earth?"

"No, I do not."

"Ahoy! Dr. Turner! We're ready to take you aboard, sir!" The lighter had reached the landing and upped its oars. An officer was standing in the prow, hands cupped to his mouth, shouting against the wind. "Ahoy! Dr. Turner!"

Andrew turned and began hurrying toward the shore. "No ghosts, Johnson. Anyway, no one's buried here. Didn't they tell you what to do with the dead?"

Johnson was racing to keep up with him, hopping along on his one usable leg and his stick. "Didn't tell us nothing, sir. Only as the grub'd be better."

"The dead are to be wrapped in canvas, Johnson. You'll find plenty of it in the stores. Tight shrouded and bound with hemp, then thrown into the ocean off the other side of the island. No one's buried here, man, so they can't be digging themselves up."

"Where are you living?" Luke asked.

"Aboard my ship for the moment." Morgan tried not to see the double bulge below the blanket that covered his uncle's lap, but he couldn't seem to look elsewhere. The rounded stumps were like a pair of dueling pistols. Pointing at him.

"With a full crew?"

Morgan shook his head. "Only a couple of men to look after things. I let the others go."

"That sounds as if you're planning to stay awhile."

"Hard to say. But . . . I think perhaps I've come home permanently, Uncle Luke."

"I'm glad to hear it. Look, I suppose nothing I can say will make you settle the trouble between yourself and your mother."

"Forgive me, sir, but no, nothing."

Six years had added weight to Morgan. Not just physically; the boy was entirely gone and the man had taken his place. Luke studied his nephew, wondering how much to say. Or ask. Morgan spoke before the older man could make up his mind. "Will it offend you if I ask what news there is of Caleb Devrey?"

"No, it won't offend me. He's no longer in charge of the hospital. Dirt poor, or so the story goes. But of course, he has both his legs."

"Sir, I—"

Luke raised his hand. "Be quiet, Morgan. There's no reason to discuss what can't be explained. Fate or luck, what you will, it dictates what we do and mostly we have few choices. There's nothing more to be said about it."

"I would have pulled you free if I could have, Uncle Luke. Circumstances prevented me. I hope you believe that."

"I do, lad. Ah, I can't call you that any longer, can I? Not now you're twenty-nine."

"Old enough to take it as a compliment," Morgan said.

His pirate grin was as winning as ever, Luke thought. However notorious he might be, the women of New York would all go into heat at the sight of him. "Let's see, what more can I tell you about dear Cousin Caleb? Last I heard he was pickling himself in brandy and living alone in a room at that new tavern's been opened in what was old Etienne De Lancey's house. Man named Sam Fraunces is the landlord. Came recently from the Indies. Apparently he was prepared to let to Caleb since he knew nothing about him. Now he can't get rid of him. Still too much Devrey influence in this town for one of 'em to be tossed into the street. But Caleb's said to be thin as a scarecrow and possibly ill. That should make you feel better. Are you planning to take up your mother's old battle, lad?"

"No. I just wondered."

"My battle, then? Or what you think to be my battle?" Luke gestured to the half of him that was not there.

"Not that either, sir."

It wasn't a lie. The battle that concerned him was his own. Six years he'd seethed with the knowledge that it was his fault his uncle was legless. He'd returned to settle the score. He had other business in New York, but he would also take back what he'd had no right to give: Caleb Devrey's worthless life for Luke

Turner's legs. Devrey's death wouldn't make his uncle whole again, but at least Morgan might sleep without nightmares.

Luke chose to take him at his word. "Very well, let's talk of other things. You've picked an exciting time to return. How do you read what's going on in the city?"

"If you're referring to this infernal Stamp Act, I think it means trouble. Possibly serious trouble."

Luke nodded. "Yes, I agree. Compounded by the fact that London's lately passed a quartering act. We're now directly responsible for providing shelter and supplies for English troops. Is that what brought you home, Morgan? A liking for trouble?"

"Some would call it that."

The door to the small front room clattered open and banged shut, bringing in the chill of the outside. They heard Andrew before they saw him. "It's freezing out there. Starting to snow. Much too early for it, but there you are." He walked in slapping his gloves against his palm, shaking off a few large flakes. "I couldn't get— Cousin Morgan. You're a surprise." Andrew swung off his cloak, dropped it on a chair, and took a step closer to the fire. He didn't extend his hand.

"You look well, Andrew. Edinburgh must have agreed with you." Morgan crossed the room with his hand outstretched.

Andrew looked at him for a long moment. Finally, conscious of his father's eyes on him, he shook his cousin's hand. "I'd heard you were back."

"This always was a town for spreading news quickly. I heard you were back as well. And that you're to have a Scottish bride."

"Old family tradition," Andrew said, glancing at his father. "Meg arrives next month."

"Glad to hear it. I shall look forward to the wedding."

Luke knew how much his son wanted to say he'd as soon invite the devil as Morgan Turner. "Pour us all another tot of brandy, Andrew. And tell us how you found things on Bedloe's Island."

"Infernal," Andrew said quickly, grateful for the change of subject.

"How so? The plans were for a modern quarantine hospital. So we'd stop allowing the poxed to die like dogs and pigs in the sewer ditches."

"Once you weren't in charge, they did everything in typical Colden fashion, as cheaply as possible and with minimum consideration for the public good. Needless to say, they don't variolate the prisoners they send to look after the patients."

"Variolation," Morgan said. "Is that old war still being fought?"

"Not with quite as much passion," Andrew told him. "Grandfather had some influence over the years. Even the quacks sometimes variolate, and no one stops them. Of course, being untrained, they get the dose wrong more often than not, so they kill more than they save."

"The real reason the issue's gone quiet," Luke said, "is that we haven't had a bad siege of smallpox in New York for seven years. Not since they started inspecting ships that come into the harbor. In fact that's what gave us the idea of building the House of Quarantine in the first place."

"Well," Andrew said, "if the infernal pesthouse can keep New York free of smallpox, I'll drink to it, however hellish it is."

Morgan sipped his brandy, his glance darting from his cousin to his uncle. Hard to miss the fondness between them, or the general peacefulness of the scene. The opportunity was as good as he was likely to get. And it was, after all, Andrew who had brought up the subject of the pesthouse. "All the changes in your plans, Uncle Luke . . . I hope they at least put this quarantine hospital where you decided it was to be."

"I heard they did," Luke said, looking to his son for confirmation.

"Yes, it appears so. At least, according to the plans you showed me. Then again, they pretty much had to, or move it to another section of the island altogether. There's a boulder right beside the building. Biggest stone you ever saw. They'd have to dig to China to get the thing out of the way."

Morgan's stomach began to unknot. "That's good then, Uncle Luke."

"About that rock," Andrew put in. "Here's a puzzle for you. The new crop of attendants arrived an hour before I did. There are only three patients in the pesthouse just now, all at death's door. And God knows, no one goes to that poxed island if they can stay away. Nonetheless, someone has been digging holes around the boulder. I counted a dozen, freshly dug. What do you make of that?"

"You there." Morgan stepped up to an old man selling roasted chestnuts. "I'm looking for a Negro named Cuf. Ever heard of him?"

"Don't pay mind to no one's business but me own, sir." The man squatted and poked at the embers of the small fire he'd built on the hard-packed dirt of the road. "Care for some chestnuts, sir? A penny for ten. Best and biggest in the city, sir."

The delicious smell of the roasting nuts was making his mouth water. "Yes, indeed I would." Morgan fished a penny from his pocket and untied his neckerchief. He gave the old man the coin and held out the cloth to receive the nuts. "I don't mean this Cuf any harm. I just want to speak to him. I'm told he's often in this neighborhood."

The chestnut seller hacked and spit into the dirt. Weren't many in New York wouldn't recognize Morgan Turner, but hard to think of any as would welcome a few words with him. Least of all a runaway slave. 'Course, he didn't know the runaway part for certain. Some said Cuf was the slave of the woman called herself Mistress Healsall. All the same . . . The man hacked and spat again. "Over there," he said finally, "at the sign o' the Fiddle and Clogs. Them folks be the ones ye should ask."

It was midafternoon. The taproom was quiet, and fairly dark because no candles had yet been lit. He could just make out a large sign over the bar that offered boiled squirrel for threepence and another that said oysters were twelve for a wooden penny, fourteen for a copper. Things couldn't be as bad as he'd heard if the common laborers of the old Church Farm could still afford boiled squirrel for their dinner, or pay a penny for oysters harvested by others when they could row into the harbor and harvest their own for free.

"Afternoon, sir. What be yer pleasure?"

"Information." Morgan took a seat on the nearest bench. "And a mug of your best ale to go with these nuts."

"The ale's the easy part, sir." The barkeep went to the long, narrow counter that held the kegs and drew a tankard of frothing brew, and carried it back and put it on the table in front of Morgan. "Don't know 'bout the information, Captain Turner."

He could never make up his mind if it was a benefit being recognized wherever he went. "I think you may be able to help me. At least, that's what I'm told. I'm looking for a Negro named Cuf."

The man turned away, using a dirty rag to polish the same bit of rough wooden table over and over again. "There's plenty of Negroes about in the city, ain't there?"

"Hello, Morgan."

Morgan turned. "Hello, Cuf."

"I heard you were back. What brings you here?"

"You do, Cuf." Disappointment dropped like a cold stone in his belly. Cuf's eyes were wary. For the first time.

"Well, it appears you've found me. But I'm not going back, Morgan. Not even if you kill me." Cuf nodded at the cutlass.

"I have no interest in taking you back. Though I wonder why you couldn't wait a few years to—" Morgan stopped speaking and glanced toward the barkeep. The man had withdrawn as far as the narrow room allowed, but he couldn't hide his keen glance. "Not here," Morgan said. "Where shall we go?"

Cuf considered his two choices. He could draw Morgan away from the Fiddle and Clogs and put off the moment when Roisin saw him, or he could seize the chance to be there when the meeting occurred. "Come upstairs," he said after a moment. "We can talk private there."

The same gossipmongers who told Morgan he'd find Cuf out at the old Church Farm had said he was living with a white woman. "Story is he's her slave. A quack she be. A good one. Calls herself Mistress Healsall and cures most anything. But there's some as say she lays with that light-colored nigra. Even that she had a little girl with him."

So much talk had prepared Morgan for pretty much anything. Except Roisin.

"Hello, Morgan." She took no more than three seconds to regain her breath. He stared at her, speechless. "Sit down," she said. "I'll get you some ale. Or would you rather tea?"

His heart was pounding. He needed rum or brandy; not likely he'd get it here. The room was tiny, tucked up under the rafters in the tavern's attic. Very clean and neat, but certainly not luxurious. One corner was filled with what looked like the trappings of an apothecary. "You're the healer," he said, hating it that his voice was so hoarse. "You're Mistress Healsall."

"Yes, I am. Tea or ale?"

"I should have guessed. The first night, you told me you were a healer."

The blood rose in her cheeks and she blushed almost as red as her hair. It was the mention of their first night, he realized with a surge of satisfaction. He hadn't meant to embarrass her, but now that he had he was glad of it. She must remember everything, just as he did. God knew he'd replayed the scene often enough these past six years. Roisin on his lap, entirely naked, utterly beautiful, and him deep inside her, his hands circling her narrow waist.

"Mama, I'm thirsty. Can I have something to drink?"

The child appeared from the shadows where she'd been sleeping on a rug on the floor. Roisin drew her protectively close, one arm around her shoulders. "Morgan, this is Clare, my daughter. Mine and Cuf's."

"Why, Cuf?" Morgan asked.

"Why what?"

They were alone in the little room under the rafters. Cuf had told Roisin and the child to go. Cuf giving orders rather than taking them. A lifetime Morgan had thought of the other boy—God help him, the other man—as a slave. Cuf was no more a boy or a slave than he was.

"What are you asking me?" Cuf pressed the question. "What did you come here for?"

"I . . . There's something . . ." Jesus God Almighty. Roisin. With Cuf. And the little girl. Clare. Nothing of the Negro about her, not to judge by the quick look he'd had. Her face had been flushed with sleep below her mobcap, but the glow didn't hide skin as pale as Roisin's. Had she red hair as well? The mobcap hid most of it. Jesus God Almighty. "Bedloe's Island," he said, struggling to take control of his thoughts. "That's what I came to talk about."

Cuf had sent Roisin away before she could pour the ale she'd offered. Now he fetched a pair of tankards. "Here. The way I remember it, you're always thirsty."

Morgan took the drink. "Thanks . . ."

"Bedloe's Island."

Morgan nodded.

"If that's what you want to know about, why come here? I'm told your cousin Andrew has returned from Scotland and that he's been put in charge of the pesthouse."

"You know that's not what I mean."

"I know." Cuf drank, watching Morgan over the rim of the pewter tankard. "First time," he said.

"For what?"

"First time you're drinking my ale."

"Yes," Morgan said, starting to realize what a remarkable day this was. "I hadn't thought of it, but you're right."

"We're both to be thirty on our next birthday. We were suckled by the same wet nurse, grew up in the same house. But this is the first time we've sat together and I'm not your slave and you're not my master. That's how it is now, Morgan. I'll never go back to the old way."

"It was never like that for me, Cuf. I never thought of you like that."

"Maybe you didn't. But that's how it was."

"Not for me," Morgan insisted. "I have always thought of you as my friend. Always, Cuf. Until—"

"Until what? I ran away from your mother's house and stopped being her property?"

"I haven't seen my mother in six years. She has nothing to do with my being here."

"So you said. But she's the one who sent me to Bedloe's Island, and gave me the gold horse's head in the box, and had me bury it."

"Yes, I know. That's why I came. To ask if she's the one sent you to dig it up."

He waited, but Cuf said nothing. "Andrew told me yesterday about the holes in the ground near the big boulder. He had no idea what they meant, of course, but I did. I rowed over to Bedloe's Island last night. The holes were still there. One was in exactly the right position and it was empty. Apart from me, only two people in New York knew where the horse's head was buried, Cuf. You and my mother."

"I'll tell you this only once, Morgan. It's the truth, but you'll have to decide for yourself whether to believe it. I haven't seen your mother since the day I walked out of her house. Six years ago, same as you."

The years at sea had taught Morgan something of how men acted under stress. There were certain statements that could not be false. This was one of them. "Very well, I believe you."

"Good. We've eliminated one possibility. Another, of course, is that I went to Bedloe's Island and dug up the box for myself. Tell me something, Morgan, if I were going to steal whatever it is I buried on that cursed island, why would I wait this long to do it?"

"I don't know. That's one of the things I came here to find out."

"Damn it, man! I could have taken it that first night."

"I know."

"Morgan, I haven't any idea what's in the damned horse's head. There's something, I know that—why else close up the bottom with sealing wax? But what? I don't know. And I don't give a bat's fart. Freedom, Morgan. That's what I care about. For me and Roisin and our daughter."

Morgan lifted his tankard, took another drink, and set it back on the table. "How did all this come to be?" He waved his hand, indicating the small room and its contents.

"It came to be because we wanted it to," Cuf said wearily, exhausted by the accusations both spoken and silent. "Me and Roisin, we decided nobody was going to own us." He watched Morgan, as aware of his reactions to her name as he'd been to the look on Roisin's face when she caught her first sight of the man who had taken her virginity and never once considered that he might be doing so. She'd told Cuf everything—how she'd come to be on the street and in the pit, and how she'd never been with a man before Morgan Turner claimed her. But it was her secret, her story, and not his to share. "Me and Roisin, we decided we'd had enough of being bought and sold."

"It was different for her, she was—"

"An indenture," Cuf said. He couldn't let Morgan call her a whore. If he did there would be no choice but to fight him, and Morgan could easily kill him. Then who would look after Roisin and Clare? "She had nearly ten years to serve. It was too long, Morgan. Too much hell to live through for the crime of not having enough money to pay your passage to a new life."

Morgan nodded. "Yes. I know. But how did you come here?"

"Jan Brinker," Cuf said. "He became rich brewing beer for the redcoats. One day he found me and suggested he'd set me up in trade if I ran away. You know how things were between him and your mother. I think he did it to get back at her."

"The dwarf!" Morgan was genuinely astonished. "Where is he? How did—"

"He died a few days ago. The French disease killed him. Roisin did all she could, but it wasn't enough."

"I'm sorry I missed him."

"He'd have been sorry as well."

"Rich, you said."

"Very rich. He owned this public house, for one thing."

"Jan Brinker a landlord. Sweet Jesus, who'd have thought it."

"Here's something else you'd not have thought." Cuf lifted his ale. "These tankards, yours and mine: I made them."

"You! When did you learn to smith?"

"When you first went off to be a pirate."

"Privateer," Morgan said, for the first time betraying the edges of a smile.

"Very well, a privateer."

"I always wanted you to come with me, Cuf. You know that."

"Yes, I know. But I hate the sea. Which is one more reason I didn't go rowing back to that poxed island after all these years to dig up your damned horse's head."

Morgan leaned back in the chair and narrowed his eyes, waiting. "There's something else. Say it."

"The Fiddle and Clogs is mine now. Jan Brinker left it to me."

"Sweet piss on the grass." Caleb stared at the thing in Petrus Vrinck's hand. "Where did this come from?"

"Ain't no reason ye has to know that. I said I'd get it, and I did."

Vrinck was holding a gold horse's head. Caleb had seldom seen anything so exquisitely made. "The eyes," he said softly, "they're rubies."

"Aye, that be what I thought. Rubies." The jewels winked in the firelight.

"Give it to me." Caleb snatched at the bauble. Vrinck let it go without a struggle.

Incredible. Caleb turned it over a few times, examining the remarkably lifelike face of the animal. "There's sealing wax around the neck."

"Aye. Horse's neck be sealed when I found it."

Caleb put his finger in the hollow interior. "To protect whatever was inside," he said softly. "Which isn't there now." He raised his head and looked steadily at the other man.

They were in Caleb's room on the third floor of Fraunces Tavern. A fire burned in the grate, and a candle was on the table between them. The double glow made even Vrinck's sallow skin look ruddy. He was grinning, his head slightly turned so he could fix his good eye on the other man. "I got it," he said. "What was inside that there horse's head, I got it. Never no fear 'bout that."

"And the way you're smiling, whatever it is, it's what you were looking for."

"Aye. It be exactly what I was looking for."

"Very well, tell me."

Vrinck chuckled softly. "What be the matter with ye, Dr. Devrey? Don't be a gentleman's way to act so impatient, do it?"

"Three months it's taken you, Mr. Vrinck, and five pounds of my money."

"Yer brother's money."

Caleb shrugged. "That's not your affair. What matters is that it took a lot longer than you estimated."

"Been sick," Vrinck muttered. "Couldn't help that anymore 'n you could."

"No, none of us can. But you won't get any better, Vrinck. *Mal aria*, isn't it? The shaking sickness. I recognize the signs."

"Shake sometimes," Vrinck admitted. "Ain't like you."

"That's true enough. You're not at all like me. But as you pointed out at our first meeting, if you're to get this treasure"—Caleb raised the horse's head on one long finger, wagging it in the air in front of Vrinck—"If you're to find what Morgan Turner hid, find it in time for you to get any pleasure out of it, you require more of my aid. To get a ship and a crew. That's what you said, Mr. Vrinck. Is it not still the case?"

Vrinck waited a few moments, enjoying the last seconds of being the only one who knew. Besides that God-cursed bastard, Morgan Turner. Then he reached into the pocket of his short jacket and brought out the slip of paper and laid it on the table. "Here it be."

Caleb glanced down. The piece of paper was approximately six inches long and two inches wide, heavily creased. "Ah, yes," he said softly. "As you say, Mr. Vrinck. Here it is."

He laid the horse's head on the table beside the strip of paper, then got up and went to the chest in the corner. He came back with a silver-topped carafe and two glass snifters. "Brandy, Mr. Vrinck. Sipped from a goblet. A gentleman's tipple." Caleb poured while he spoke. "Is that what you aspire to be, once you're rich? A gentleman?"

Vrinck grabbed the glass and drank the brandy in a single gulp. "Ain't no business of yours what I be doing with me share o' the treasure. Fought for it, I did. Killed for it."

"That's not exactly accurate, Petrus Vrinck. As I recall, you got the share you fought and killed for. Four hundred pounds in bullion might have kept some men going for a dozen years, even a lifetime. But then . . ." Caleb shrugged and let the words trail away. "To business, Mr. Vrinck. What does that paper tell you? Where's the treasure?"

"Seventy-four-thirty." Vrinck spat out the words. "Twenty-four."

"That's gibberish, you God-cursed fool. What does it mean?"

"Means what I said." Neither eye was looking at him now. "Seventy-four-thirty and twenty-four."

Caleb snatched the paper. Vrinck didn't try to stop him, just poured himself a second brandy and waited.

Caleb's sight was poor these days. He had to lean so far toward the candle it almost singed his hair. His hands were trembling. He squinted at the writing. Clear enough. Formed with a quill in a steady hand, and the black India ink hadn't faded. Still the numbers jumped out at him first. They'd been impressed with more firmness than the rest. "Seventy-four degrees thirty minutes west of Greenwich," he read under his breath. "And . . ."

"And what? What be the rest of it? There's more. What's it say?"

Caleb looked up. Vrinck was leaning toward him, the half-closed left eye peering at him from under the drooping lid. "What's it frigging say? If ye tries to cheat me, ye God-cursed blighter, I be—"

"Sweet piss," Caleb said, unable to keep back a smile. "You can't read. That's what's kept you honest—you can't read."

"Numbers," Vrinck admitted. "I can read numbers. But I can't read words."

Caleb folded the paper and slipped it into the pocket of his black undercoat.

Vrinck had drawn the cutlass from his waist. He leaned forward across the table. The tip of the weapon was inches from Caleb's throat. "Ye be cheating me 'n yer life not be worth a wooden penny, ye God-cursed—"

"God-cursed blighter. So you said. I have no reason to cheat you, Mr. Vrinck; nor much reason to fear your slitting my throat. I'm dying, you ignorant fool."

"If ye be so sure yer dyin', why is it you be helping me?"

"It's not the money I want. It's too late for that. It's the pleasure of seeing Morgan Turner in the dock on a piracy charge. And watching his mother the day he swings. You can have my share of the money, Mr. Vrinck. Just prove that the treasure exists and that Morgan Turner cheated the men who'd invested in the last voyage of 'fifty-nine."

"Have to know what the paper says," Vrinck muttered, sheathing the cutlass. "Can't get the God-blasted treasure unless I know what the paper says."

"So you shall, when you need to know. And you'll have a ship, and a crew to sail her."

Vrinck's original plan was crude, but still the most effective Caleb could think of. Four of the other investors were still alive, and still stinking rich. They would put up the money for the voyage to reclaim the treasure. And their combined power would make it impossible for Petrus Vrinck to simply sail away and forget them once he found what he was after. He'd never be able to sleep in peace if he did that. No, he'd come back to New York and be hailed as a hero. And Morgan Turner would be hanged for the pirate he was.

The horse's head still lay on the table. Caleb drew it close and covered it with his hand. "I'll keep this. And the paper. Come back in a week and I'll have word of the ship."

"A week be too long. Three days."

Caleb shrugged. "Very well, three days." He didn't get up when Vrinck did.

The seaman started for the door but turned once to look back at Devrey. "Three days."

"Indeed. Now get out."

The door closed with a decisive thud. Still Caleb didn't move. The pain was preparing to attack him again. He'd sit right here and wait for it, endure until it was past. When he felt better he'd go find the men he was about to enrich by considerable thousands of pounds. They'd agree to his plan, and not just for the money. When the other investors learned what Morgan Turner had done, they'd hate the bastard as much as he did.

Caleb took the paper out of his pocket, laid it on the table, smoothed it, and drew the candle close so he could read it. He spoke the words aloud, enjoying the sound of his voice. "Seventy-four degrees thirty minutes west of Greenwich. Just south of twenty-four degrees north." He squinted hard at the third sentence. "Twice around and thrice back."

The first part of the message contained the coordinates. Caleb knew little of navigation, but he understood that with those numbers and a sextant, any competent captain could sail to a precise spot on the map. But twice what around? And thrice what back? He had no idea. And no reason to think that an ignoramus like Vrinck would— Ah, sweet Christ.

The pain enveloped him and he gave himself to it: he had no other choice. Sweat poured off him. He moaned softly, gritted his teeth, and waited. Bede's son, Caleb's nephew Samuel Devrey, had come back from the medical college in Philadelphia without a single new idea about treatment. The only thing he'd been able to suggest for Caleb's agony was cupping and bleeding and purging. Useless, all of it. For months now Caleb had been praying to die. No longer. Now, by Christ, he wanted to live.

He would live long enough to be there when they marched Morgan Turner to the gallows. She'd be in the crowd, that was certain.

Oh, Sweet Christ . . . Oh God. Worse than ever he remembered it. He was trembling like a leaf in a gale. He lifted the decanter to his mouth and managed to swallow a few drops of the brandy, though most of it sloshed over his chin and down the front of his shirt.

A few minutes more and then it was gone. He felt strong, a strength born of something he hadn't known in years. Hope. Goddamn it! He had to live. Whatever was required, he'd do it. Andrew Turner was also back in New York. An Edinburgh-trained medical man, and said to be a brilliant surgeon as well. According to the talk around the city, Andrew was better with a knife than even his grandfather had been.

The Turner gift. What would it take to get young Andrew Turner to carve open his belly and cut out whatever it was caused the pain?

It was madness. It had never been done.

I can do magic with these hands. That's what Jennet said that day a million years ago, when they stood by the stone bridge and watched the sunshine glistening on the harbor. . . . *magic with these hands . . .*

Even if Andrew had enough skill, what about the pain? The knife slicing open his gut. Could he stand it? If it meant he could live to see Morgan Turner swing, he could endure anything.

But why should Andrew Turner help him? For the chance to open a belly and perform a surgery never done before. For a share in the treasure. And Andrew knew. He knew that Morgan could have saved Luke but had chosen Caleb. He did it for her, of course. Because she wanted to keep her enemy alive so she could watch him suffer.

Well, two could play at that game. After he'd made the arrangements for the ship and Vrinck was on his way to get the money, maybe then he'd see if young Andrew had the lust for using the knife that possessed most surgeons. And the lust for riches that possessed most men.

III

Morgan had never been a regular at the Dish of Fry'd Oysters. Still, the tavern was huddled close by the waterfront, and most of the men drinking in the square, low-ceilinged room were tars. They all knew Morgan. Not a few lifted their tankards in his direction as he passed. There were nods and muttered greetings. He acknowledged as few as possible. Tonight it wasn't drinking companions he was after.

He made his way to the far end of the bar and the man standing beside a keg of ale. "Good evening, landlord. I believe I'm expected."

"Aye, Cap'n Turner. So ye be. Upstairs." The man gestured with the wooden mallet he held. "First room on the right."

Morgan climbed the stairs and paused by the closed door on the right. He pressed his ear to the paneling and listened to the quiet hum of voices until a burst of cheers from belowstairs drowned them out. The landlord must have tapped the new keg. A moment later the tumult stilled and he heard again the talk in the room behind the closed door. Morgan turned the knob.

Three men turned to look at him, their faces lit by the candles on the table, dark shadows hiding their eyes. Alex McDougall and Isaac Sears had captained privateers of their own. They'd made fortunes, though neither had brought home as many prizes as the *Maiden*. Both had left the sea some years before to become West Indies traders. The third member of the group was a different breed. Marinus Willet was a cabinetmaker, about Morgan's age. They had nothing else in common, except the reason for this meeting.

Sears and McDougall stood to greet Morgan. Willet stayed in his chair. Morgan ignored the slight, strode into the room, swung a chair around, and straddled it. "A good evening to you, gentlemen. Are we all here?"

"All as'll be here this night," McDougall said. "Though there's plenty of others be with us in spirit."

Holy Savior. McDougall wore a yellow cutaway coat trimmed with yards of gold braid and very large gold buttons. His undercoat was cream-colored satin. The lace ruffles on his shirt were threaded with yet more gold. His curly wig must have cost more than most men spent to feed their families in a year.

What justification could he claim for spending time with this popinjay while someone had the directions he'd hidden in the horse's head? In God's name, what was he doing here when so many other things remained to be done?

Marinus Willet seemed to pluck the question out of his mind. "Let's get to the heart of it. What are you doing here, Turner?"

"I might ask you the same question."

"No, you might not. There's nothing surprising about my standing against thieves and idol worshipers."

"Idol worshipers," Morgan said softly. "An interesting charge. Put it this way, Mr. Willet; if you've come to complain about anyone's religion, you're right: I have no place here. I don't care who worships what or in what manner. My understanding is that we're here to talk about the laws of these colonies."

Willet made no attempt to conceal his contempt. "Spoken like a Jew."

McDougall and Sears gasped and drew back slightly, leaving Morgan in a circle of light with his challenger. Willet wore homespun and carried no weapon. Morgan's cutlass was in place, and he had a pistol tucked in his waistband. He needed neither.

Morgan turned his back on the cabinetmaker and reached for a shiny apple from a basket on the windowsill. "You do me too much honor, sir. As I expect you know, I can claim only half a blood link to that ancient, honorable, and wise people."

"Honorable? The Jews murdered our Lord and Savior!"

"Enough!" Sears jumped to his feet and pounded his fist on the table. "It's Pope Day tomorrow and ye'll have yer chance to burn the Catholic whore of Satan, Marinus Willet. Just like ye does every November. And after we be settling this business, maybe we can find a day each year when ye can get the poison out o' yer system as regards the Hebrews and any others don't worship same as yerself. Right now, do ye wish to do something about this stamped-paper abomination, or do ye not?"

"That's why I'm here. I'm asking why he's here." A bony finger pointed at Morgan.

"Christ Almighty save us," Sears whispered. "He's here because me and McDougall asked him to be. Same as yerself."

Morgan took another bite of the apple and chewed thoughtfully. "Let me put it still more plainly, Isaac, so Mr. Willet is left in no doubt. I'm here because I oppose the notion of quartering, and of stamped paper, or any other direct tax on colonists by men who don't live among us and whom we have no say in choosing." He leaned forward and very deliberately dropped the apple core in the tankard in front of Marinus Willet. "One thing more, sir. I was invited because I have money to contribute to the inevitable expenses of any society we create. Substantial sums, Mr. Willet. Can you match me? Guinea for guinea?"

"You know I can't. I've not had a mother who—"

Morgan grabbed the front of Willet's homespun shirt and bunched it so close to the other man's throat his voice was choked off. "No more, sir," he said softly. "Not another word. I have no particular wish to cut out your tongue and bung it in your asshole, but give me an excuse and I'll do it." The men stared into each other's eyes, then Morgan released him. "Now, gentlemen, shall we get on with our business?"

An hour later and the state of the problem had been clarified. The Stamp Act had become effective on the first day of November, but the stamped paper had still not been distributed. Colden was yet living on the Royal Navy's warship *Coventry*, in fear for his life. It was rumored that a royal governor was about to arrive in the city and take over the rule of the province. Meanwhile two hundred of the city's most important men of business had signed a nonimportation agreement, swearing they'd buy nothing from the mother country until this matter was settled.

"Och, 'twas a bonny thing the laddies did. Bonny and brave besides." McDougall had come to the colonies from Scotland as a young boy. His burr got stronger the more ale he drank. "Och aye, bonny and brave. But it won't be enough to put the English devils off their high horses. Nothin' puts Sassenachs off once they got folks under their thumb." The Scot ground his own large thumb into the table to make his point.

Sears had been born and raised in Connecticut and still spoke with the flat Yankee twang, though he'd lived in New York for many years. "There's truth in that. But are we all prepared to follow where such thinking leads?"

Alex McDougall jumped to his feet and leaned forward, pounding his fist on the table this time. "Och aye, laddies! Och aye!"

Marinus Willet nodded and muttered something about God's providence.

Morgan said nothing. Upward of twenty thousand pounds in *daalders* and *louis d'or* and guilders and guineas, a king's ransom. And quite possibly someone else was on the way to get his treasure before he could sail south and move it. Holy bloody Savior.

The others were staring at him. "Captain Turner," Sears said softly.

Morgan hesitated a moment more. Then he stood up and reached for the pitcher of ale in the middle of the table and filled all their glasses. "Gentlemen, please be upstanding. I propose a toast." The three men rose, though Willet refused to look at Morgan. "To us," Morgan said. "And to those who will join us. To patriotism, gentlemen. To the sons of liberty."

"I want to talk to you, Cuf." Morgan moved closer, lowered his voice. It was just after the three o'clock dinner hour. The taproom was full of local men playing at cards and dice, drinking, laughing, talking. Mostly white faces, but a few that were black. No one paid any mind to Cuf or Morgan.

"We said everything we had to say two weeks past."

"I don't think so."

Cuf raised his cup of punch and took a sip. "Very well, talk."

Morgan glanced cautiously around. Crowded though the room was, there was a bit of space in their immediate vicinity. "How many of them know you own this place now?"

Cuf shrugged. "A few. Not as many as know the reputation of the mighty Captain Morgan Turner."

"Not so mighty these last few years. There weren't many prizes to be had off the Guinea coast. Not like the old days in the Indies."

"Things change," Cuf said.

Cuf had changed as well. His leather breeches were unpatched and his coat was wool, not flannel. There was something else though, an air of confidence. A half-black man of property. Not a rarity in the province, but still not the ordinary way of things. "Yes, things change. They're changing here in America, Cuf. If there's something . . . If something as yet unthinkable was to happen, would you consider joining rather than opposing it?"

Cuf cocked his head, and narrowed his eyes. "It's not possible to say yes or no when you don't know what you're being asked."

Morgan glanced over his shoulder. No one seemed to be listening. "These men," he said softly. "They drink here regularly?"

"Most do."

"So you pretty much know their sentiments?"

"Pretty much."

"How do they feel about stamped paper?"

"The way everyone else in the town feels about it. It's an abomination." Cuf nodded toward a table where a group of cribbage players were tossing cards and pegging at fantastic speed. A handful of onlookers roared with approval as the lead went first one way then the other. "The most of that lot are cobblers and bootmakers, except for the big fellow at the end. He's a cooper. Craftsmen who have to pay all the expenses of their trade. Put a tax on every bill they tender, two-thirds won't be able to afford to come here any longer."

"And that won't be good for your business."

"No, it won't. I'm no more in favor of stamped paper than anyone else, Morgan. Is that what you came to ask?"

"Not exactly. I'm asking what you're willing to do about it."

Cuf leaned back in his seat, lifted his punch glass. "I've heard stories, of course. Like everyone else. I can guess what's on your mind. But I've a woman and a child who are dear to me." He lifted his chin to indicate the room in the rafters above the alehouse. "I'll not be putting them in danger with any wild schemes."

"Danger comes whether we want it or not, Cuf. Sometimes we have to decide to meet it rather than wait for it to arrive."

Cuf didn't answer. The bowl of punch was making the rounds. Someone from the nearest table brought it over and set it down between them. Morgan ladled another portion into his cup and reached into his pocket for a penny to put on the table. Cuf waved the gesture aside. "Don't bother. Landlord's privilege." He filled his own cup and motioned someone to come and move the bowl on.

"Are you smithing much these days?" Morgan asked.

"Not as much as I'd like. Taking over here, it's kept me pretty busy."

Morgan nodded. "I can see as it would. But before you became the landlord here, did you know many in the smithing trade?"

"A few."

"Any from Massachusetts?"

"Ah," Cuf said with a sigh of satisfaction. "I expect you're talking about that firebrand, Revere of Boston."

Morgan smiled. "So you've met him? Do you know where Revere stands?"

"I've met him once or twice, yes. His business brings him to New York often. There's a taproom over by St. Paul's church, the Silver Hen and Her Chicks. A number of smiths drink there."

"So I'm told. And also that Revere brings news as well as business on these journeys. I'm told he's a patriot."

"A very vocal patriot," Cuf agreed. "You're not long home, but you're well informed, Morgan."

"I came home to be better informed. Cuf, listen to me. If they try to enforce this stamped-paper curse, or if the quartering becomes too much of a burden, men won't sit idly by. Some will choose to act. According to Mr. Revere, that's as true in New England as in New York. How about you, Cuf? How will you choose?"

"Morgan, look at me. What do you see?"

"A man. My oldest friend."

"A man who is not white. Not exactly a Negro either, but definitely not white."

"What's skin got to do with it, Cuf?"

"Everything. I have no choice, Morgan. Not the way you do. My skin chooses for me. I must do everything I can to protect myself and mine. And believe me, I will."

The taproom had been dark and full of smoke. Coming outside into even the weak sun of the dying winter afternoon made him blink. Morgan passed a hand in front of his eyes, waited until he could focus, then looked around. Not such a bad place, this Church Farm district. Not as fancy as the court part of town, but the men here would be as anxious to preserve their way of life as any in the city proper. They had wives and children, and few would have Cuf's particular concerns. Hard to fault Cuf for feeling as he did. Being a black man, even a mulatto, meant it wasn't easy to feel otherwise.

A group of children playing in an open field beside the alehouse caught Morgan's attention. One little girl stood apart from the others. Clare. Yes, he was sure it was she.

Clare was scratching with a stick on the bare dirt, singing something to herself. Pretty child. Looked a lot like Roisin. He moved closer.

"Poxy-island-over-the-sea, / Dig-a-hole-up-to-your-knee, / Seven-paces-east-and-nine-paces-north. / Poxy-island-over-the-sea, / Dig-a-hole-up-to-your-knee, / Turn-to-the-boulder-and-lie-down." She was humming the words as if they were a rhyming song, matching her actions to what she said. While Morgan watched she lay down on the ground, banged her heels, then jumped up and began mimicking digging motions.

Holy bloody Savior. It wasn't possible, but he'd seen and heard it for himself. "You there, little girl."

The child looked up. "I'm Clare Campbell. Who are you?"

"Morgan Turner. I'm an old friend of your mother's. And your father's," he added.

She stared at him and nodded.

He took a step closer.

The girl pulled back. "Go away. I don't want to talk to you."

"I just want to ask you a question." Jesus God Almighty. There was no end to the questions he wanted to ask her. "How old are you, Clare Campbell?"

"Five."

"Five," he repeated. "A big girl. And I'll bet you're very smart. That song you were singing, how does the rest of it go?"

"It doesn't go any special way. It's just a song. I made it up."

"Did your father teach you that song, Clare? Did Cuf teach you about the poxy island and seven paces east and nine paces north?"

She shook her head so hard a strand of dark hair escaped from her mobcap. Not coppery red like Roisin's, or dark and curly like Cuf's. Black and shiny and straight, like Morgan's own. "I made it up," the child said. "It's just a song."

"Tell me the rest of it then. After you lie down near the boulder. What comes next?"

She cocked her head and looked at him. Her eyes weren't green like Roisin's or brown like Cuf's. They were dark blue, knowing eyes. "You gonna give me a penny if I tell you?" she asked.

"I might. If you tell me everything your father taught you."

"The other man gave me a wooden penny. Will you give me a copper?"

Holy bloody Savior! "What other man?"

He grabbed for her, but she was too quick for him. "I don't like you. I don't want to tell you anything about my song. Go away."

She started running toward the alehouse. Morgan ran after her, conscious all the while that if he didn't get her on her own he'd get little more information from her. "Stop, Clare! I mean you no harm. I'll give you two copper pennies if you—"

She was quicker than he imagined. She ran around the building and up a flight of steps. He pelted after her. "I only want to talk to you, Clare. Three copper pennies."

Roisin appeared on the landing at the top of the stairs. "Clare, what's wrong?" She saw Morgan running behind the child. "Get inside. Stay there." Roisin shoved the little girl through the door and pulled it shut. "What are you doing here? What do you want with my daughter?"

Dear Holy Virgin, make her heart stop beating the way it was, as if it would thump its way out of her chest. Every time she saw him it was the same. All these years she was sure she'd hated him, that she'd done the right thing by choosing Cuf and rejecting Morgan Turner the pirate. But from the first moment he'd returned she'd had to face the truth. And now, the way he was looking at her with so much knowing in his eyes . . .

"She's my daughter, isn't she?" Morgan hadn't realized how sure he was until he spoke the words.

"She's Cuf's child. We've been together since the day we walked away from your mother's house. Clare is Cuf's daughter." She had to keep saying that. He had to believe her. Cuf had risked everything for them. Dear Lord Jesus, there were times he'd gone hungry himself to see that there was food in her mouth and in Clare's. Didn't that make him the child's father?

"She's my daughter," Morgan repeated. "Her hair and her eyes, she's Turner stock, there's no doubt. But I don't understand why you never went to my mother. You must have known she'd pay well to see her granddaughter properly cared for."

"How dare you! My daughter is properly cared for."

"I didn't mean that." He shook his head. "I'm sorry, Roisin. I mean you no harm, nor the child. Why should I?"

"She's Cuf's child."

Something about that stubborn insistence moved him more deeply than anything else. Though everything about Roisin Campbell still moved him. God, she was beautiful. More lovely than ever, now that she was a woman rather than a girl. "I have to speak with her."

"You have no claim on either of us, Morgan Turner. None." Holy Virgin, how her heart was pounding. He must hear it. "After six years—"

He shook his head. Fighting with her was the last thing he wanted to do. "Let me come inside, Roisin. I swear to you, I won't hurt you or the child. But I must speak with her. It's important. Besides, we'll attract attention standing out here. Cuf's in the taproom at the moment. He won't trouble us unless we draw notice to ourselves."

She hesitated a moment more, then opened the door and stepped away from it.

Morgan brushed past her. He made himself ignore the warmth rising from her flesh, the way she was only inches from him. Right now only one thing mattered.

Clare was sitting beside the hearth. She'd wrapped a shawl around her small shoulders, though it wasn't cold in the small room. In fact, it was extremely pleasant. There was the faint scent of roses and medicaments, and a lingering echo of whatever good stew they'd had for their dinner. A black cast-iron kettle hissing steam hung over the fire.

Roisin closed the door and came into the room behind him. She went immediately to the fireplace. "I was making a tisane." She moved the spit arm and swung the kettle away from the heat. "Put your cap back on, Clare. We have a guest. It's not fitting."

The child had pulled off her mobcap. She held it in her hand and her hair hung down to her shoulders. Lustrous, dark, silky smooth. Turner hair. There could be no doubt. Morgan squatted beside her. "Three copper pennies, Clare. I promised and I'll keep my word. Just tell me who was the other man who paid to know the rest of your song."

Roisin put her hand over her mouth to keep back a gasp of surprise. Holy Virgin, what was Morgan talking about? What had he come here to do to their lives, the peace she'd purchased against all the odds? Whatever it was, Clare held the key. Roisin put herself between the child and Morgan, staring into Clare's blue eyes. "What song, darling? What man? Tell Mama, Clare."

"I made it up." The child was looking over her shoulder at Morgan. Roisin felt his eyes staring at both of them. "I did, Mama. I made up the song."

"Very well." Morgan moved so he could see the child more clearly. "If you say so, Clare, I believe you," he said. "Only tell me who asked you about it?"

Roisin put her hands on the girl's shoulders. "Wait. Don't answer him, Clare. Answer me. What song?"

"'Poxy-island-over-the-sea, / Dig-a-hole-up-to-your-knee, / Seven-paces-east-and-nine-paces-north. / Then-turn-to-the-boulder-and-lie-down, / Dig-a-hole-up-to-your-knee.' I made it up, Mama. I did."

Roisin hung her head for a moment, then drew the child close, wrapping her in her arms. "Cuf talks in his sleep," she whispered. "He has ever since I lay with . . . Since I've known him. That's where she learned those words. I've no idea what they're about. But he says them all the time."

"I know what they're about," Morgan said softly. "What I need to know is who she told them to."

Roisin pushed the little girl far enough away so she could look into her eyes. "Tell Mama, Clare. You must. Who was it wanted to know about that song? Besides Captain Turner here."

"The bad smelly man with the funny eyes."

Morgan couldn't suppress an impatient sigh. Half the men in New York smelled bad. And what did funny eyes mean? "Did he tell you his name, Clare? When he gave you the wooden penny, did the man tell you his name?"

The child shook her head.

"Where did you see him, Clare?" Roisin smoothed the hair back from her daughter's forehead. "Was he downstairs in the taproom?"

"No. He came up here first. Then I saw him in the field."

"You mean he saw you playing in the field? Like Captain Turner did?" A nod this time. "And before that he came to consult me, to ask Mistress Healsall to help him get well? Is that what you mean?"

Clare nodded again.

Morgan started to say something, but Roisin lifted a hand to stop him. "Did the man come just once or did you see him many times?"

"A few times, Mama. You made him a tisane to drink."

"Which tisane, Clare? You know I've told you to watch me, that you have to learn everything I know so when you're a big girl you can be a healer, too. Now show me which tisane I used for the bad-smelling man." Clare hesitated. "Go on," Roisin urged. "Show me."

The little girl got up from the hearth and ran to the shelves in the corner. She stood on her toes, reached up, and unerringly took a pewter flask from the top-most shelf and ran back to her mother.

"Cinchona bark," Roisin whispered, taking the flask in her hands. "For the ague that comes with *mal aria.*"

"The shaking and sweating sickness?"

"Yes. Tars get it often. The last patient who came for the tisane was a tar. His eyes aren't straight, so he can't look at you directly."

"I've known more than one man with crooked eyes. Do you remember his name?"

"I think so. It was Dutch. Petrus something."

"Petrus Vrinck," Morgan said quietly.

Roisin nodded. "That's him."

Holy bloody Savior. Why wasn't he surprised? "He sailed with me for two voyages back when the *Maiden* was taking prizes down among the islands. A good fighter but a bad sailor. And a worse man. Not to be trusted."

Morgan moved closer to the fire. Roisin still knelt by the hearth. Clare stood beside her and Roisin put a protective arm around the little girl's waist. Roisin was beautiful. And the child—his child—would be equally beautiful when she grew up.

"Cuf's not like your Petrus Vrinck," Roisin said softly, her green-eyed gaze fixed on his face. "Cuf's a good man. He loves us, Morgan."

"I know."

"Promise me you'll do nothing to disturb his peace of mind. Promise me, Morgan. You didn't know what you took from me, but you're in my debt."

God. So lovely. He stretched out a hand, wanting to touch her, but dropped it quickly. "What did I ever take from you? I saved you from the whipper and I offered to take you with me when I left. You're the one who—" He broke off, knowing he'd said more than he ever meant to say, more than he'd admitted to himself these past six years.

Roisin dropped her head, refusing to look at him. "I know you rescued me from the pit. I've always been grateful to you for that, Morgan. But I was no . . . no doxy." Oh, God, why was it so important for him to know that? Why had she had a thousand dreams in which she told him the truth and made him believe her? And always woke up to the fact that dreams were false and Cuf—lying beside her, loving her and loving her child—Cuf was true.

Morgan wanted to argue. He wanted to tell her he'd never held her past to be anything to shame her. But there was so much he didn't yet understand about his own feelings. And the matter of Vrinck was urgent. He bit back the words and squatted so he could look into the child's blue eyes. "Clare, tell me when the man asked you about the song. When did he give you the penny?"

She shook her head. "I don't remember."

"You must."

"Clare, tell Mama about the penny. Do you still have it?" The child nodded. "Where is it?"

Clare darted a glance to the hearth. "Under the stone," she murmured.

Roisin sighed and released her hold on the little girl. "She means here." She bent and pried up a single brick at the corner where the hearth met the floorboards. "I put a bit of money in there now and again to have it by for an emergency. Clare's seen me do it. I removed the last coins I had in there three days past. Look."

She pointed to the scooped-out hollow below the loose brick. The hiding place contained one wooden penny. "Sometime in the last three days, then," he said. Roisin nodded.

"Thank you, Clare." He stood up, reached into his pocket, and extracted three copper pennies. "I keep my promises."

Suddenly shy, the little girl nodded but didn't look at him, and didn't stretch out her hand. Morgan allowed the coins to drop into the hiding place beneath the hearth. He considered offering Roisin more—it seemed incumbent on him to do that under the circumstances—but he knew she wouldn't thank him for it. "About Cuf," he said instead. "Don't worry. I shan't make trouble."

Morgan knew Petrus Vrinck to be a typical tar. He drank like a fish and did it where he could be with others like him. Morgan visited every slop shop and tavern along the waterfront.

There were dozens. Some he'd never been in—the Pine Apple, the Dog's Head in the Porridge. Others, like the Dish of Fry'd Oysters, he'd visited once or twice. Still others—the old Blue Horse, the Split Mizzen, the Five Fish on a Spit, and the Fighting Cocks—were places where he'd once been a regular patron.

Everywhere he went he followed the same pattern. He'd put a shilling in the barkeep's hand and tell him to send the punch bowl on a free round. Morgan followed the bowl, asking the same question of every man who lifted a mug to his health. "I heard that the Dutchman Petrus Vrinck was in town. He sailed with me on the *Maiden*. Have you seen him?"

Many of the sailors said they had, that for a time Vrinck had been a regular. "Bought plenty o' drinks he did, Cap'n Turner, for all as would sit down with him," one said. "And asked a few questions besides."

"What questions?"

"'Bout poor old Tobias Carter, mostly. And any as came drinking with him that last night afore he was killed."

"And do you know what answers he got?"

"None from me, Cap'n Turner. Never saw old Tobias that night. Leastwise, I don't remember if I did. Been six years . . ."

Two days and two nights. Always the same. No sign of Vrinck for nearly a week, they all said. Sick maybe. Had the *mal aria*. Though he'd found that quack Mistress Healsall and she was helping him.

It was close to midnight on the second night when Morgan finally asked the right question. "Must have been expensive for Vrinck to be standing good the drinks for all. Any idea where the money came from?"

"None. 'Course, he'd gone privateering for years 'n' years. But ain't been much profit in that lately. As none knows better'n yerself, Cap'n Turner."

"I do. So where do you think he got the money?"

"Hang on. Old Jack over there, he might know."

The man called old Jack was summoned to the table, and Morgan bought him a draught of rum. Jack held the tankard in his left hand. His right was missing and had been replaced by a fierce-looking hook. "Be me as sent Vrinck to Mistress Healsall. Helped me a lot she did when this was first done." He waved the hook in the faces of Morgan and the sailor who'd called him over. "Pain was fierce until she started giving me some o' her potions to drink. Best quack in the city, is Mistress Healsall. The Dutchman, he be suffering with the shivering sickness. Sent him to see Mistress Healsall, I did. Knowed if anyone could help him she be the one."

"Does she charge much for her healing?" Morgan thought of Roisin's little room and her shelves full of cures. She could be a rich woman if she was as good at her trade as she was claimed to be. Obviously that wasn't her aim. "Where did Vrinck get the money to pay her?"

"Oh, that don't be a problem with Mistress Healsall. Pays what ye can afford with her. But he was standin' the cost o' a mighty lot o' drinks, Vrinck was. Afore the shivering sickness got bad."

"Again. Where did the money come from?"

"Can't say for sure, Cap'n Turner. But first time I mentioned Mistress Healsall, the Dutchman, he said he had a friend what was a regular doctor. Said if it was medicine he needed he could get it fast as could be from this doctor friend. 'Course I said weren't no point in that. All them doctors does is cup and bleed and purge. If it's a cure ye wants, somethin' as will take the pain away, it's a quack ye needs. And in all New York ain't none better'n Mistress Healsall."

It was not yet December, but the first snow of the season had started in earnest. Thick sheets of white obscured the corner of Broad Street and Pearl. Except for the sign swinging over the front door, Morgan could barely make out the redbrick structure that had once been the De Lancey house, called Fraunces Tavern now.

He strode forward. Another man loomed in the blinding snow. They had nearly collided before Morgan saw him. "Andrew! Bloody Savior, what are you doing here?"

"I could ask you the same. But I think I can guess. We're neither of us come to sample the landlord's punch, are we?"

"No, I expect not. He's mine, Andrew. Whatever you think of what happened that day, Caleb Devrey's life belongs to me."

"Good Christ, man, I'm not . . . God Almighty, it's impossible out here. The cold takes your breath away. Come inside."

Morgan's cloak was soaked through and his shoulders were thick with snow. Andrew had the barest dusting of white on his collar. That could mean only one thing. "You were leaving, weren't you?" Morgan asked. "You've been here for some time and you've already seen Devrey."

The night was too foul for most men. There were just two drinkers in the tavern, sitting at a table in the far corner nearest the fire. The landlord stood beside them. Andrew pitched his voice low enough so only Morgan could hear. "I've seen him."

"By Christ, Andrew, if you've taken it on yourself to end Caleb Devrey's miserable life, I—"

"I'm not in the killing business. If I were, it's you I'd want dead."

"I don't blame you for thinking what you do about that day at the almshouse. Or about what's happened to your father. But you're wrong if you think I had a choice. You can believe me or not."

"I'll never believe that."

Morgan shrugged. "Then blood ties or no, we'll remain enemies. Not without example in this family, as we both know. Now, if you'll excuse me, I've business upstairs."

"No," Andrew said quietly. "You haven't. Caleb Devrey's dead. I was on my way to inform Cousin Bede."

Morgan's heart began to pound and his bowels churned. "Are you telling me . . ." The words came out in slow, measured tones, forced beyond the tide of rage that threatened to sweep all words, all reason, away. "After you said you weren't—"

"I'm telling you only that Caleb Devrey is dead. Get hold of yourself, man. You look as if you're about to follow him to hell." Andrew turned. "Landlord! Brandy!"

The drinks came quickly. Morgan gulped his, grateful for the warmth that flooded his belly. Andrew sipped the fiery spirit, studying his cousin over the rim of the goblet. "Better?" he asked after a few seconds.

"If you took what was mine by every right," Morgan muttered, "by God you'll pay."

"How many times must you be told the same thing? I didn't kill him. I came because Caleb sent for me. Too late, as it turned out. He was dead when I found him." And truth to tell, Andrew was bitterly disappointed. A man at death's door, whose problem was quite probably a seepage of blood in the belly—Christ, he would have been justified in trying the transfusion, the way Grandfather had written about it. The way he did it with old Red Bess. From Andrew's own arm directly into Caleb's. But he'd been too cursed late.

Andrew glanced toward the landlord. He was eyeing them warily now, obviously afraid of trouble. Probably recognized Morgan, so it was a natural assumption. "I believe it best to tell Cousin Bede before letting Mr. Fraunces here know what's transpired on his property," Andrew said, his lips barely moving to form the words.

Ice had replaced the fire raging in Morgan's belly. "If not you, who killed him?"

"Not who, what."

"Very well, what?"

"It's impossible to be certain without performing an anatomy, but my guess is that he had an ulceration of the liver, perhaps the bowel. If I'm right he'll have been in great pain for some time. I suppose that gives you a degree of satisfaction."

"Not nearly enough," Morgan said. "Tell me something, if he'd called for you earlier, would you have treated him, made him well?"

"Yes. Of course. At least I'd have tried. Not, I assure you, out of any love of Caleb Devrey." Because he lusted to try blood transfusion. "Because I took an oath."

"So did I," Morgan muttered. "God help me, so did I."

Andrew tossed back the last of his spirit. "I'm leaving. Are you coming with me?"

Morgan shook his head.

He watched Andrew go, then stared for some moments into his empty glass. Finally he stood.

"Good evening. Captain Turner, isn't it?" The landlord had finally decided to approach. He was doing his best to sound pleased with a visit from the most notorious privateer in New York.

"Morgan Turner it is. And I've come to see my cousin, Caleb Devrey. I'll take myself upstairs. No need for you to trouble."

"Dr. Devrey seems to be very popular with his cousins this evening."

"Yes, well, that's how it is among us, Mr. Fraunces. We Devreys and Turners love each other dearly."

He'd seen many dead men. The look on this one's face said he hadn't gone quietly. Caleb's eyes were open and staring and his mouth was twisted in a grimace of agony. "May you rot in hell," Morgan whispered, staring at the corpse for long seconds.

He began his search with the body. The pockets of Caleb's dank and musty black clothes yielded nothing. He moved to the bed linen. Nothing there either. Finally he started on the room, conscious always that he hadn't much time. Bede's Wall Street residence was a short walk away. He and Andrew would be returning any moment.

The room was small and the furnishings limited. It took less than five minutes to examine everything. Nothing. He'd have to search Caleb's offices on the ground floor of the Devrey house. Perhaps the best time to do it was after Bede and Andrew came back to the tavern.

Holy bloody Savior. Right there on the mantel, under a turned-up mug, was the gold horse's head. But the wax seal had been broken and the bauble was empty.

Morgan let himself into the grand mansion on the Broad Way with his own key. He'd kept it all these years knowing that one day he must return and confront her.

It was after eleven at night. The house was quiet, blanketed in sleep and snow. Morgan climbed the stairs to the second floor. Her parlor door was closed, but there was a thin seam of light above the threshold. He pushed the door open.

"Morgan! Oh, thank God . . ." Squaw DaSilva was fully dressed and veiled, sitting at her writing table. She jumped up when she saw her son, extending both her hands. "Thank God! I'd almost given up hope that you'd understand."

"I haven't come out of duty. Or because I feel any affection. Or because I've changed my mind about what you did."

Their words could be heard quite clearly in the attic room above their heads. *Press down on the floor. Lie over Jennet. Like the old days. Listen to the voice of her son. Not his. Solomon DaSilva had no cock, so he couldn't have a son.*

Morgan made no move to take his mother's outstretched hands. She dropped them. "I did what I had to do. To protect you and protect the treasure."

"You had five men murdered who were completely loyal to me. For no reason except that they might have interfered with your scheme to make your enemy grovel in the dust at your feet. I've come here tonight because I wanted to be the one to bring you the news. Caleb Devrey's dead."

She put a hand to her heart. "Dead," she repeated as if she didn't know the meaning of the word. "Caleb's dead?"

"Yes. So that crusade will have to end." He took a step closer to her, trying to see beyond the folds of the veil. Her eyes were blue, like his and the child Clare's. "There are other reasons for my being here as well."

"Caleb Devrey is dead," she repeated as if she hadn't heard him.

"Of some kind of ulceration in his belly. Or so Andrew says."

She had been staring at the floor; now she lifted her head. "Andrew? Was Andrew treating Caleb?"

"More perfidy real or imagined for you to become obsessed by," he said wearily. "And you've given me the same contagion. But as it happens, tonight was the first time Caleb had sent for Andrew. I'm sure you can get all the details from him. My second reason for coming is that you have the best web of spies in the city."

Spies. The Huron had spies. They watched while white men rode unsuspecting through the woods. Then they took the guns and ate the white men alive. Piece by piece. Starting with the cock. Maybe Jennet's whore's son, Morgan, was a spy for the Huron.

"Caleb's dead," she whispered yet again. As if he'd said nothing else.

Morgan was nearly overcome by despair. As long as he lived he'd never be free of what she'd made him, or of the hatreds and jealousies she'd put into him. "Holy Savior, can we talk of nothing but Caleb Devrey? Listen to me, damn it! It's important. Are your spies as good as they were?"

Caleb Devrey. Jennet had been going to marry Caleb Devrey. Until Solomon DaSilva stole her away. Clever Solomon made her his, taught her to spread her legs and welcome him, and cry out with delight when he took her. No more. He had no cock so he couldn't possess her. Maybe Caleb Devrey had fathered the bastard on Jennet. The bastard couldn't be his. Solomon DaSilva had no cock.

"My spies," she said, sinking into her seat. She looked up at her son. "What is it you wish to know, Morgan?"

"The whereabouts of a tar named Petrus Vrinck. I can probably find him myself if I keep looking, but if you have as many informants as in the old days and as well placed, you'll do it faster."

"And why do you care about this . . . Petrus?"

"This is why." He took the gold horse's head from his pocket and dropped it on the writing table.

She stared at it for some time. Then she reached out and fingered the hollow neck and the remains of the red sealing wax. "It's empty. I put the piece of paper you sent inside, but now it's empty."

"Indeed."

"And this Petrus Vrinck, you think he has the directions? He knows the whereabouts of the treasure?"

"Exactly."

Ah yes, treasure. He knew all about treasure. Ducats and pieces of eight and guilders and cruzados. Treasure is what kept you safe. Wealth was what made you certain of going to bed with a full belly. Money meant you wouldn't die in the alleys of São Paulo or the gutters of New York. The Huron wouldn't get his treasure. They could take his cock, but his treasure was here in New York, in the little room below the whorehouse near Hudson's River. No one would ever find his treasure. Certainly not Jennet's son. He wouldn't let the bastard boy get his treasure. That's why he kept this knife beside him. They didn't think he ever went out of his room, but they were wrong. He could go wherever he wanted. At night when they all slept. Down the stairs. Like now.

"Does the money matter so much, Morgan? More even than the hatred you feel for me?"

"The treasure has a purpose. It's the one thing I've been sure of these past years. The whole mad scheme was yours, but what comes of it will be something better and more noble."

He paced as he spoke; his emotions seemed to flash in the air between them, like lightning on a summer's night. "Tell me how you know all this," she whispered, desperate to renew the bond between them. Her fingers went almost of their own accord to the tarnished horse's head that represented so much past joy and present pain. "Where did you get this? How?"

Morgan shook his head. "It's too long a story, and unimportant. I need an answer. Do you still have spies, and will you set them looking for Petrus Vrinck?"

"A noble cause, you said. Tell me what you mean."

To finance the Sons of Liberty, wherever their path led. It was the one decent thing he could do to redeem the years he'd been a captive of the schemes that possessed his insane mother. "The *Fanciful Maiden* belongs to me. The treasure is mine. It doesn't belong to Petrus Vrinck. I have plans for it. Will you help me?"

"Morgan, I can't."

"Is that your answer? You can't?"

"No. It's just that I don't understand. Why can't you explain to me what you mean to do?"

Easier to hear standing like this, with his ear pressed to the door. Right beside them, and they knew nothing. Because he was smarter than Jennet or her bastard boy. Smarter than all of them. The Fanciful Maiden. *Belonged to Caleb Devrey's bastard son, the* Fanciful Maiden *did. Caleb Devrey had made Solomon a cuckold and there was nothing Solomon could do about it because he had no cock. The* Fanciful Maiden. *A ship. He knew. Flossie had told him. Down the stairs. Out the door.*

"I won't explain because it's none of your infernal business! All my life I have marched to your tune, now I'm going to follow my own. With or without your assistance." Morgan turned and started for the door.

"No, wait! Morgan! Please, don't go like this. I'll help you. I'll give you anything you need!"

He turned and strode toward the door. "Keep your help. I was mad to ask for it. This is my affair, not yours. Stay here with your lunatic hatreds and your unrelenting grievances. There are more important things to fight for in this world. For my part, they're what I choose."

"Morgan!" This time she couldn't let him go. She'd made that mistake once before. She wouldn't make it again. "Morgan! Wait, I'm begging you."

She ran into the hall. Morgan was already halfway down the stairs. She started to go after him, then paused to pick up a white square of cloth, thinking it was something Morgan had dropped. But no, it could be nothing of his. She tossed it aside. "Morgan, please. Wait! We must talk more. I can help you. Whatever you want, I can help you get it."

He didn't answer, just went out into the street, allowing the door to bang shut behind him.

The snow had stopped falling and the air was still. New York wore a white shroud. Near the harbor the spotless pall reflected the terrifying crimson of hell.

"Holy bloody Savior! That's my ship!" Morgan had been striding in the direction of Burnet's Key at the foot of Wall Street, only half aware that his were not the first footsteps to mar the virgin perfection of the snow. Now he broke into a run, slipping and sliding on cobbles slick with snow and ice, seeing only the red glow of the thing every sailor feared more than eternal damnation, a shipboard fire. "My ship! No!"

The *Maiden* was anchored in the roads, some distance from the wooden wharf. Morgan had left two crewmen guarding the vessel. One must be burned to death or gone over the side, because only one man was running back and forth, obviously trying to fight the blaze and failing to have any effect on the speed with which the flames traveled.

Others had seen the red glow in the sky and come out of their houses to watch the fire. They were crowding in on the dock. "It's the *Fanciful Maiden!*" someone shouted. "That's your ship, ain't it, Cap'n Turner?"

"Yes. I need a boat! For God's sake, man, get me a boat."

"Morgan! No. Don't go out there. There's nothing you can do. I beg you, don't go!"

Squaw DaSilva had followed him all the way from the house. She had neither cloak nor shawl, and her dress was soaked through as a result of the many times she'd fallen in the snow. Her hat and veil had been lost some time back. She seemed unaware of the fact that she was baring her face in New York for the first time in thirty years. "Morgan, for the love of God! There's nothing you can do."

He ignored her. He spotted a dinghy tied by the wharf and ran to it, slipped the moorings, and jumped in. There was only one oar. An old trick when someone left a small boat like this without guard. "I need another oar! For sweet Christ's sake, someone toss me an oar!"

"Here you go, Cap'n Turner. Look sharp."

A man carrying an oar rushed to the edge of the jetty and tossed it toward the dinghy. "No!" Squaw shouted. "Don't give it to him! Don't go, Morgan. Listen to me!" Her screams pierced the night, louder even than the crackling sound of flames gorging on timber and pitch and resin and canvas.

"Morgan!" she cried. "Look!"

Almost in spite of himself he turned to follow her pointing hand. Someone stood high in the rigging of the mainmast, a man dressed only in a nightshirt that billowed in the wind. His white hair streamed behind him like trails of cloud. The creature clung to the lines with his one arm. His mouth was open and he appeared to be screaming, though his voice couldn't be heard above the roar of the fire.

Holy Savior. The flames were racing along the upper deck from the direction of the stern, climbing the mizzenmast, eating the halyards with jagged crimson teeth. The mainmast would be next. Then everything was lost.

Morgan stood up and stripped off his cloak, tossing aside his cutlass and his pistols. He dove into the icy water, not allowing himself to feel the shock tear the breath from his lungs, conscious only that if he didn't get to the *Maiden,* if he didn't raise her anchor and head her out to sea, every ship in the harbor could go down with her.

"Morgan! No!"

Her voice came to him over the waters even as he swam toward the blazing inferno that had been his ship. A deep rumbling and shaking began below the sea; he felt it before he heard it. The fire had reached the munitions store. A heartbeat later, with a thunderous crack like the roar of a hundred cannon, the *Fanciful Maiden* blew apart, her two halves rising out of the water and spreading open like the petals of a terrible and deadly blossom.

The man who had been clinging to the rigging above the deck was thrown high into the air. The last thing Morgan remembered was seeing him fly through the reddened night sky, his single arm outstretched, like the swift descent of a wounded eagle, still swooping down on its prey because that was the only thing it knew how to do.

"He's passed out!" the man who hauled Morgan out of the sea shouted to those waiting onshore. "But he's alive."

His mother sank to her knees, heart thudding, her hands covering her face.

War Path

AUGUST 1776–MARCH 1784

Better to die in war, the Canarsie people said, than to dry up and blow away because your hunting grounds have been stolen and your fields cursed so nothing will grow.

In war you die with the sound of the drums in your ears, and the memory of a woman, and the sweet smell of your enemy's blood in the air.

Chapter Twelve

"INTROIBO ad altare Dei." *I will go unto the altar of God.*

The priest was gray-haired, thin, and stooped. Roisin had expected someone young and vigorous. Instead it was a dried-up old man who had dared to slip into New York now that all the talk was of war.

"Ad Deum que laetificat juventutem meum." *To God who gives joy to my youth.*

The altar boy was Josie Harmon's nephew. Fourteen, with a squint and a face full of pimples. Tall for his age, his head almost touched the rafters in this attic room of Josie's grand house on Wall Street.

Ah, to see Clare living in a house like this someday. If Josie Harmon—who had been Josie Ryan before she married fat old Leominster Harmon, who'd become rich turning sugar into rum—could make that kind of match, why not Clare? Probably Josie was pretty once. But she couldn't have been as beautiful as Clare, with her lustrous blue-black hair, her pale skin, and her enormous blue-violet eyes. Clare's eyes were closed now. The girl was praying as if she went to Mass every week, for all this was only the second she'd ever heard. Fifteen years old, and a true Woman of Connemara. A healer, devoted to the Virgin and the Church.

Roisin shifted slightly. Kneeling on the bare floor was making her knees ache, and apart from the priest and the server, there were eleven people squeezed into the hot, stuffy little room, seven women and four men. She knew them all at least by sight, had treated a few of them, but in truth they had only their forbidden Catholicism in common.

Roisin kept her head bowed but let her lidded glance wander left. Josie Harmon was madly fanning herself, her face flushed and dripping with sweat. Three years Roisin had been treating her with a tincture of dittander and pepperwort to dry the humors that drenched Josie in perspiration much of the time. Didn't help much. Her ankles were still swollen to twice their normal size, despite the tisane of monk's rhubarb that Roisin prescribed, and smoking her with a mixture of liverwort and mustard had done nothing for the way Josie huffed and puffed at the least exertion.

"Adjutorium nostrum in nomine Domini." *Our help is in the name of the Lord.*

The priest was a Jesuit, Mr. Steenmayer. Josie said he'd come because he knew their great need for the comforts of religion now that there might be war. Nonsense. Roisin had heard it said often enough in the old country. If there was a chance to grab power, the Jesuits took it. Ah, what difference did it make? The man was a priest, Jesuit or no. He could give them the sacraments. Seventeen years she'd been in this city, and only twice had she been shriven and heard Holy Mass.

If the rebels, God bless them, defeated the English (though Dear Lord, that would take a miracle) Catholics would be free to worship openly in New York along with everyone else. Didn't the grand Declaration they'd read aloud the month before say as much? All that wonderful talk about men being equal and having a right to . . . what did it say? "Life, liberty, and the pursuit of happiness." Except for Negro men, apparently. The Declaration didn't say a thing about Cuf having a God-given right to be free.

"Mea culpa, mea culpa, mea maxima culpa." *Through my fault, through my fault, through my most grievous fault.* The priest bent forward, beating his chest over his dried-up Jesuit sins.

Anytime she wanted, that bitch Squaw DaSilva could claim Cuf back and have him flogged. Both of them, if it came to that. Squaw knew where they were. Hadn't she seen Roisin once in the Fly Market? She turned away and acted as if she hadn't see her, but Lord, didn't Roisin know very well that she and Cuf were free only as long as the bitch chose to let them be free? Ah, Holy Virgin, I know it's stupid to worry about the veiled witch after all these years, and stupid to argue with Cuf about putting himself at risk for the rebel Declaration that clearly didn't mean to include him.

Three years Cuf held out against Morgan and the Sons of Liberty. Until the English taxes were stealing the bread from our mouths. It was the English drove Cuf into Morgan's secret society. Though the truth was, he wanted to join from the first. Anything to be in the same place as Morgan Turner, to be Morgan's equal. Dear Lord, that's an itch never goes away, no matter how much poor Cuf scratches.

"Kyrie, eleison. Kyrie, eleison. Kyrie, eleison." *Lord have mercy. Lord have mercy. Lord have mercy.*

On us all, Lord. For the Blessed Virgin's sake . . . Look at Josie's nephew, trying to seem so holy and sanctified when he makes the responses. The Jesuits won't get him. The lad knows what the thing between his legs is for, else why was he watching Clare the way sometimes Cuf watches me? Especially if Morgan's about. Oh Cuf, Cuf, it's true, I love him with every breath that's in me, but don't you know I'd never betray you? Not after everything you've done. You must know. But that doesn't matter, does it? Not when however many years pass, you still measure yourself against Morgan Turner.

"Credo in unum Deum, Patri omnipotentem . . ." *I believe in one God, the Father Almighty . . .*

There were no guards, only a single red-coated clerk behind a desk made of a trestle and a couple of planks. About a dozen black men crowded into the canvas tent. Waiting, and sweating in the intense August heat, jostling for position, each eager to be the next to put his mark on the document that made him a member of the loyal forces of His Majesty, George III.

Cuf let himself be shifted by someone determined to sign before he did. Then, when the man was in position, he asked, "You certain they say you can be free after?"

The man's face was thin, with a high-bridged nose and high-ridged cheekbones. Cuf had seen other black men with that same look. It meant their people came from a particular part of Africa, a particular tribe. He didn't know where in Africa, or what the tribe was called. Neither did the man. All their history, who they were, where they came from, had been stolen from them.

The redcoat sitting at the table was holding a cloth to his nose, as if black sweat stank different from his own. And the black men were ready to accept that. Anything, long as they could get back what belonged to them. Never mind if it was the English Royal African Company first loaded their people on the Guinea ships, yoked and chained like cattle. In August 1776, the British were promising to make black men free. "You sure it's true?" Cuf asked again.

The other man nodded. "It be a promise. Any slave as comes and fights for the King, soon as the rebellion's put down, he be free."

"What about that Declaration everyone was shouting about last month?" Cuf demanded. "You heard what it says?"

"I heard."

"So?"

"So it don't say nothin' 'bout the slaves bein' free, does it?" the thin-faced man said. "Way I sees it, that be a white man's freedom Declaration. Negro man, he be best helped by these English soldiers right here."

"What happens if the rebels win?"

The other man chuckled. "Ye ain't seen much o' this here Staten Island, has ye?

There be thousands of redcoats dug in over here. Redcoats springin' out o' the ground like stalks of corn. Rebels ain't gonna win."

They'd moved ahead while they spoke. Cuf's companion was next, and Cuf right after, unless he found another way to delay. The milling crowd offered plenty of opportunities to fall back and let someone else take his place. Except that just then a second red-coated clerk sat down beside the first. He glanced up at Cuf. "Runaway slave?"

Nothing for it now. "Aye, sir, I be that." Hanging his head, using the speech that was expected of him.

"What's your name?"

"Cuffee, master."

"Who owns you?"

"Nobody." Softly, looking directly into the soldier's eyes. "Nobody owns me. I took my freedom."

The soldier shrugged and put a crumpled cloth to his nose. "Put your mark right here." He shoved a paper in Cuf's direction. "Soon as the rebellion's over you'll be a legally free man. General Howe's word on it."

Cuf hesitated. The soldier held out a quill. Cuf took it and leaned down. Resisting the urge to write his name with a flourish, he marked an "X" on the document.

"Hoc est enim Corpus Meum." *This is my Body.* The scrawny, gray-haired priest lifted the consecrated wafer above his head, and Josie Harmon's pimply-faced nephew, looking more than ever as if he thought he was the focus of everyone's attention, rang his little silver bell three times.

And yet. And yet. It didn't matter how unlovely any of them were, not the priest or the altar boy, or Josie or any of the others. However stained they were with sin, Jesus Christ his very self had come to them in the most blessed sacrament of his Body and his Blood.

Roisin was trembling when she knelt to receive Holy Communion and the priest put the wafer on her tongue. Not an hour since she'd made her confession in this very room, taking her turn to come in alone and kneel beside the old Jesuit, who kept his face turned to the wall and his eyes closed.

"Bless me, for I have sinned. It's been five years since my last confession." She didn't have to tell him about Cuf or Morgan, or that Clare had been born a bastard. She'd been shriven of those sins in '68, the last time a priest came to New York. Of course that priest told her lying with Cuf was a sin because she wasn't his wife, and that she had to promise to do it no more if she wanted absolution. And she had assured him she understood, knowing all the time that she'd made a separate arrangement with the Holy Virgin. The Virgin understood Cuf's need for her, understood what a good man he was. *If it's all right for me to go on giving myself to him, Blessed Lady, make it be that his seed never reaches my womb. Then I'll know.* The Virgin had given Roisin the sign she asked for: Cuf's child never grew in her. So Roisin knew it was permitted for her to not mention again the sin of lying with a mulatto man to whom she was not married.

This time she confessed to impatience and vanity—didn't she on occasion wash her hair with a decoction of sumac to cover up any strands of gray that were showing themselves in this her thirty-second year—and to having aborted a woman who had quickened.

"You're speaking of the grave sin of murder, child. You do realize that?"

"I do. But the Holy Virgin be my judge, the woman told me she was in her ninth week, and I believed her. That early and the thing's not ensouled."

"You believe that, child? Truly?"

"Indeed. Most truly. With all my heart."

"No soul until quickening? The blessed Saint Thomas Aquinas considered the possibility. Of course, he was a Dominican, but perhaps . . . You think the babe had grown beyond the ninth week?"

"Yes. When I saw the thing as I scraped out of her"—Roisin was whispering; remembering the horror of it made her shudder even now—*"I was sure of it."*

"Murder," the priest said. *"The sin of Cain. But if you honestly didn't know she'd quickened—"*

"I swear I didn't. By the Holy Virgin."

He paused. *"Where did you learn your healing arts, child?"*

"From my mother, sir. And I've taught them to my own daughter as carefully as I can. That's the way with the Women of Connemara."

The priest's eyes remained shut, but he'd nodded knowingly. *"Yes, the Women of Connemara. I thought as much. I trust you do more good than harm, child. And if there was murder committed, it wasn't your intention and the blood isn't on your hands. For your penance say the litany of the Blessed Virgin a dozen times. . . ."*

So now, clean of any sin, she could open her mouth and receive her God. And with the wafer melting on her tongue and her whole body singing with the joy of it, beg Him to keep Cuf safe. *He's a good man, Lord Jesus, kind and strong and loyal. Protect him.* And then the prayer she almost felt ashamed to pray, the one dredged from the depths of her secret heart. *And please, Lord Jesus, please keep Morgan safe as well. Let Morgan Turner live, because if I can't see him even occasionally the way I do, from a distance or with Cuf in the Fiddle and Clogs, I shall die, Lord. I know I shall.*

The new recruits to the King's army were sent to sleep in a Staten Island field. There were few guards. There was no need for them; the black men had yet to be issued weapons. Besides, most had risked everything to get here. Over on Manhattan, on the rebels' side of the line, they were runaway slaves, subject to flogging or worse.

There was only a sliver of moon. Cuf managed to position himself at the edge of the clearing. Then, when everyone was asleep, it wasn't difficult to crawl into the trees and disappear.

The Mass was over. Nearly everyone had left Josie Harmon's Wall Street house, slipping into the night in twos and threes, careful to let a few minutes pass between each departure. The English opposed the Catholic Church for reasons of politics. The American rebels had no official quarrel with the True Faith, but there were plenty whose heretic hearts burned with hatred of it.

After twenty minutes only Roisin and Clare and Josie were left in the attic room. The priest had been escorted downstairs by Josie's nephew. "Well," Roisin said softly, turning to her daughter, gently pushing a strand of hair off her forehead. "What did you think of the second Holy Mass of your life?"

"It was beautiful." The girl's eyes were full of tears. "I felt the Virgin so close to me."

Ah, whatever else she'd done, she'd done that much right. "I'm glad. And I hope you prayed with all your might for the rebels to win. Then we can have Mass and the sacraments without hiding."

"Clare"—Josie leaned forward, still fanning herself, sweat making grimy tracks down her pudgy, powdered cheeks—"go downstairs and see that Mr. Steenmayer is given a mug of the best ale as soon as he's finished his devotions."

"Surely your nephew will see to that." Roisin made the protest without much attempt to sound convincing. Josie clearly wanted an opportunity to speak with her alone. Very well, but she suspected she knew what her hostess had in mind. Better to start the discussion from a position of strength, not weakness.

"You know how boys are, don't you, Clare, darling?" Josie's smile didn't reach her eyes. "They forget the most ordinary things. Go on. Off with you. Your mother and I will be down in a moment."

Clare kissed her mother's cheek, curtsyed to her hostess, and left. Roisin folded her hands in her lap and waited. Josie didn't speak until the sound of the girl's footsteps had faded. "Now," she said.

"Yes, now." But not now. Whatever it is, you can choke on it for a time. "Your eyes don't look well, Josie dear. Have you been bathing them with feverfew the way I told you?"

"Every day. Exactly as you said."

Feverfew or no, Josie's eyes bulged out of her head. The symptom went with the swollen ankles and the shortness of breath. The flux it was, and though she administered all the classic treatments, they didn't seem to do much good. Or maybe they did. The flux, if it had its way, was a killing disease. Josie was still alive, able to delight in gossip and plots and plans.

"I have a proposition for you, dear Roisin. It's about Clare."

Roisin knew what was coming. Though she hated the thought she couldn't afford to dismiss it out of hand. "She's as sweet and good as she is bonny," Roisin said, pretending ignorance. "I hope she hasn't offended you in any way."

"Oh, no. Of course not. And she is pretty, I'll grant you that. Even though . . ."

"Even though what, Josie?"

"Even though she's part Negro."

It was the price she paid for the peace and protection she'd bought for them. She'd always known it would be so, only she hadn't thought hard enough that it was Clare would be paying the price. "A very small part," Roisin said softly. "You know how small, Josie."

"No question how light Cuf is." The fan was waving faster than ever, creating a small storm between them as they leaned toward each other, taking each other's measure. "But I remember Phoebe before she died two years past. She was his mother, after all. And black as pitch Phoebe was."

"If you think Clare is black as pitch, you need a new treatment for your eyes, Josie dear."

"Of course I know that the parts of her I can see aren't black. But if we were to make an agreement . . . Well, I'd have to see all of her before I could let it be official."

"An agreement about what?" The idea was repugnant to her. But if it was Clare's only chance . . .

"Mr. Harmon's nephew. Mr. Harmon and I, we're the dear boy's guardians now that his parents are gone."

"Yes, I know."

"The lad has a boyish interest in your Clare. Of course, young as he is, it's entirely innocent. But the years fly by, as we both know, and in a short time he'll be sixteen—"

"Clare's nearly a year older." Don't give her any weapons she can use later, any way that if things change she can say you fooled her about something like Clare's age.

"Oh, yes. I know. But surely a single year isn't important."

"Oh, no, Josie. I agree. You're entirely correct about that. A year isn't important at all, compared to the truly important things."

"Exactly my point. There's the matter of their being attracted to each other, for one thing."

As if a treasure like Clare could ever be attracted to that boy. But he wouldn't be pimply forever. And if she could make Clare see the other virtues, the good that came with prosperity . . .

"Of course, God having given us no children of our own, my husband sees the dear boy as his heir. Such a generous man, Mr. Harmon."

Roisin nodded her head. "Generous to a fault," she said. Last time she suggested to Josie that she have a few more treatments with monk's rhubarb, the woman burst into tears and said her husband wouldn't let her spend a wooden penny more for her treatments, no matter how much better they made her feel. "A fine and generous gentleman, Leominster Harmon," Roisin said. "Everyone knows as much."

"And devoted to the True Church," Josie added. "Though he couldn't be with us to hear Holy Mass today. Such a grave risk for someone in Mr. Harmon's position. Still, to have a Catholic bride for his dear nephew . . ."

The thing Clare offered that, coupled with her beauty and the boy's lust, was the reason they were having this conversation.

"You understand, Roisin dear, that's something that would make my husband and me forget about a dowry, or social standing. As long as we could be sure that Clare was as white everywhere as the parts we can see."

"I absolutely understand, Josie dear. But do tell me, would Mr. Harmon need to see all of Clare as well? Or would he take your word for the whiteness of the rest of her?"

"Oh, my word would be more than adequate, dear Roisin. You can be certain of it."

"Indeed. Well, in that case . . ."

"Yes?" Bending forward. Causing a gale with her fan.

"In that case I'll discuss it with Cuf. He's her father, after all."

Oh, Lord, forgive me. Right after receiving your Body and Blood in communion as well. But I couldn't resist, Lord. Making her swallow it like that. Accept it and swallow it. And wouldn't I go to my grave before anything would make me tell her it wasn't true? As if Cuf weren't worth six of her, and a dozen of Leominster Harmon. And eighteen more of their pimply nephew. But if she married him, Clare would never have to worry about anything again. She'd never have to lift the stone from the hearth and see how many pennies she'd managed to put by to keep them fed.

The smoke was thick in Bolton's Tavern on William Street. Worse than in most of the alehouses and slop shops of the city, because Bolton's was where the town's doctors drank. They wouldn't have the windows or doors open no matter how hot it might be, or how many of them were crowded into the taproom puffing on their pipes. "Foul humors in the night air," the men of medicine said. "Brings disease."

Andrew Turner had never developed a taste for tobacco, but that wasn't the reason he didn't feel entirely at ease in Bolton's. Luke had been a regular, but after Andrew cut off both his father's legs and went to Edinburgh, the talk was that Christopher Turner's grandson was a surgeon at heart, like his grandfather before him.

Andrew felt their eyes on him as soon as he came in. "Well, well," someone murmured. "Look who's here. Don't see you often, Dr. Turner."

"A hot night," Andrew said. "I'm parched with thirst." He fished a copper from his pocket and took a place at the nearest of the long tables. The men already there quickly made him room, but no one spoke.

Andrew reached for one of a stack of pewter cups and tapped his penny on the table to let it be known he wanted punch. The bowl started to head his way. Without an accompanying song for once. New York had given up singing. There were two British men-o'-war and two dozen British frigates moored in the harbor. The invincible Royal Navy had its guns trained on Manhattan. For the moment, the redcoats had left the island, but no one doubted they'd be back. With fixed bayonets.

"Evening to you, Cousin Andrew."

"And to you, Cousin Samuel."

Sam Devrey had come from the other side of the room to offer his greeting. There were a dozen men at Andrew's table. They quickly rearranged themselves so Devrey could sit facing his cousin. The mood in a taproom could never be so grim that the drinkers wouldn't relish an opportunity to witness a fight.

The tension between Andrew Turner and Samuel Devrey had surfaced five years earlier in 1771, when some of the town's doctors began saying New York should have a private hospital, like the Pennsylvania Hospital down in Philadelphia. "Been going for sixteen years, the Pennsylvania has. Started as Mr. Franklin's idea, naturally enough, but the medical men took it up. Excellent place to observe disease, and test treatments."

"Strict rules, mind. I hear that in Philadelphia they admit no one with stubborn fevers."

"Aye, none who can't be cured."

"What about lunatics? They can't be cured, but the Pennsylvania takes them in. Went down and saw with my own eyes."

"Only such as they can make a bit more calm," someone else insisted. "And if we've any sense at all we'll be taking subscriptions to build exactly the same sort of hospital right here in New York."

Andrew had shown up at Bolton's a week later, as soon as he heard about the plan. "We already have a hospital here in New York, the City Hospital. And we could do a lot more with it if private funds were available."

"Not a proper hospital, Cousin Andrew." Sam Devrey it was who had made the argument. "I know you prefer we call it the City Hospital, but the truth is it's an almshouse ward for the sick indigent, society's dregs and malcontents. That's not the same."

"The Pennsylvania Hospital treats the poor, same as we do."

"Not the same as we do. They don't let sick women bring their children in with 'em, and they turn away any with contagions unless they can be put in a separate room. You have any separate rooms for the fevered up in your almshouse hospital, Cousin Andrew?"

"Not now. There's no space." Andrew had turned away, appealing to the other doctors present. "But if you gentlemen cared to contribute to the building of an extension we could take such patients in."

"Apart from anything else, your City Hospital is too far from the center of things," Samuel Devrey said. "You must admit, you're fairly isolated up there on the Common."

"Absolutely," the others agreed. "The Common's much too far north of the city. Inconvenient." And that settled it.

Andrew wasn't surprised by Samuel's opposition. More of the traditional Turner and Devrey rivalry. The new hospital Sam proposed would be a perfect counter to Andrew's lifetime appointment as head of the almshouse hospital and the pesthouse on Bedloe's Island. Besides, Sam had studied at the Medical College of Philadelphia. He was always singing the praises of the place. The only thing that brought him back to New York was Bede's insistence that all his children settle nearby if they wanted their inheritance, and the fact that Samuel's twin, Raif, was an incompetent oaf who couldn't be expected to look after their father's affairs when Bede died.

Now, five years since Sam insisted a new hospital must be built, Bede Devrey was seventy-four and still entirely capable of handling his affairs to suit himself, whatever Samuel thought. Meanwhile, what they called New York Hospital had yet to admit a single patient. First it burned down just before it was ready to open. Then, with Sam Devrey spurring them on, the doctors rebuilt on the original site, which had turned out to be on the Broad Way even farther north than the almshouse. Price had won out over convenience, and they'd built their damned hospital up near Rhinelander's sugarhouse, in a spot so bloody isolated it was used for duels. And though it was finally ready to open, no one was interested. On this August night of 1776, New York was busy preparing for war.

"Warm night, isn't it, Cousin Andrew?"

"Very warm, Cousin Samuel."

The punch bowl had finally reached him. Andrew ladled himself a portion, put his copper in the dish in the center of the table, and pushed the bowl to his left.

Sam was puffing hard on a pipe. He leaned forward and spoke through a haze of smoke. "We missed you at today's meeting, Cousin Andrew."

"Oh? What meeting was that, Cousin Samuel?"

"Meeting to discuss a medical department for Washington's army. Sixteen men agreed to serve. At least a dozen are surgeons."

"Well, that's what's needed in war, isn't it? Surgeons. Muskets seldom finish the job."

"Exactly my point. Your skills with the scalpel are much celebrated, Cousin Andrew. Have you no intention of offering General Washington your services?"

Andrew took a long swallow of punch before he answered. "I've a crippled father, a wife, and three young children, Cousin Samuel. Were I a bachelor like you, perhaps. Now, I thought we came to Bolton's to talk of medicine, not war."

"These days everything, especially medicine, involves war." Devrey's voice rose so all could hear. "No man can avoid choosing a side. Not even the acclaimed Dr. Turner. So tell us, my dear cousin, are you a patriot or a Tory?"

Every man in the place was watching him. Bolton's was no different from the rest of the New York alehouses and taverns, full of hotheads preaching independence despite the overwhelming forces marshaled against them. Andrew put down his cup and stood up. "I'm on the side of defeating illness and disease, gentlemen. Wherever and whomever it attacks."

He turned and walked out, conscious that they were all watching him, but most of all feeling Sam Devrey's eyes on his back.

It took Cuf better than six hours to make his way over the heavily wooded hills to the east side of Staten Island. The sky was flushed with dawn when he got to the place where they'd told him he'd find the Indian canoe. It was there, thank Christ, but the morning was too far advanced to risk setting out. He waited for night, then rubbed dirt on his face to darken his skin and smeared some on his shirt as well. He remembered Morgan's final words: "That's the biggest danger, Cuf. If you're found out and you're not in uniform, the rules say they've every right to claim you're a spy and hang you without a trial. Our side would do the same."

"Then the trick is to make sure they don't find me out."

Poxed sea. Much as he hated it, it always seemed to be part of his life. No moon at all this night, and thick clouds. Please God there would be fog as well. He'd need it. He had no choice but to paddle directly into the thick of His Majesty's poxed navy.

The fog Cuf prayed for took a long time coming. He was through the Narrows—the straits between Manhattan, Staten Island, and the long island—and into the outer harbor when the first wisps of moist gray air began weaving a protective blanket around the slim, swift canoe.

Cuf got through the fleet by hugging the towering sides of the various British ships and seldom letting his paddles touch the water, mostly moving himself along hand over hand, using the sides of the vessels for purchase. He could hear the footsteps of the sentries and lookouts many yards above his head, and the guttural mutterings of the fighting men in the holds, a plank's width from the palms of his hands.

II

"My best estimate, there's over nine thousand redcoats. Dug in here, and here, and here." Cuf used a stick to draw a quick outline of Staten Island on the dusty summer ground. Morgan and another man squatted beside him, examining the makeshift map with its indications of troop placements. A third man sat on a tree stump copying the information into a sketchbook.

"And the promise to runaway slaves?" Morgan asked.

"Exactly as we heard. Join George's army, soon as the rebellion's put down you're a free man."

"A little late in your case," Morgan said with a smile.

Cuf shrugged. "The officer I talked to didn't seem to care."

"Holy Savior, you spoke with them?"

"Had to. They shoved a paper under my nose and told me to sign it."

"But—"

"I only made my mark," Cuf said softly. "They didn't expect a proper signature and I didn't supply one."

"All the same, if you're ever caught, they could say you were a deserter. That means—"

"A noose. Better than being starved out of my livelihood by their greed. Listen, I had to come right through the fleet. Luckily there was some fog. Good cover, but it may have distorted sounds. Thing is, I think I heard men speaking something that wasn't English. German maybe."

"Hessian mercenaries," the man with Morgan said. "We hear there are thousands of them aboard the frigates."

The man who was taking down Cuf's information made a few more marks, then closed his sketchbook and stood up. "I'll be going, gentlemen. General Washington needs this by noon."

The head of His Majesty George III rode atop a pike outside the Blue Bell Tavern near the newly built Fort Washington in the upper reaches of Manhattan.

A little over a month earlier, in July when the Declaration was read to the town, the Sons of Liberty led a mob that toppled the Bowling Green statue of the king, sawed off his royal head, and hauled the rest of him to Connecticut to be made into musket balls. Soon after that most of the liberty boys, like Cuf and Morgan, joined Washington's army.

The hastily assembled force was nearly twenty thousand strong, over half of it encamped on Manhattan. The talk in every alehouse and slop shop was of tactics. Not the why of independence; the when, where, and how of it.

"If the British take the city they'll not only control the finest harbor on the coast." The speaker drew his finger through the moisture on the table of the Pig and Whistle Tavern in Hanover Square. His listeners bent closer to study the relative positions of the rebels and His Majesty's forces sketched in spilled beer. "They'll close the Hudson–Lake Champlain corridor, and divide the New England hotheads from the rest of the colonies."

"Hotheads, you call 'em? I say they be patriots."

"Exactly my point." Major Aaron Burr was only twenty. The brass buttons on his blue and gold uniform gleamed with newness, but he spoke with a natural authority. "Without New England to stiffen their spines, the others will roll over and wait for old George to scratch their bellies."

Burr's listeners nodded solemn agreement.

Washington and his generals were of the same opinion. New York was vital. The Continental Congress had given orders to hold the city, and the rebels had ringed the island with batteries of cannon and dug themselves in at Fort Washington. And on the Common. And across the East River, on the slopes above the Brooklyn ferry landing.

American troops were quartered in the Manhattan country houses of the Morrises and the Bayards and the Stuyvesants and the De Lanceys. James De Lancey's eldest son had been head of the clan since his father died. As soon as he heard the Declaration he left the Bouwery Lane estate and joined the crowds of Tory supporters of the crown fleeing to England. Going home, they called it.

Other Tories chose to stay and fight. Not just the aristocrats; ordinary people who thought this lust for independence was treasonous or mad. Nearly the entire Staten Island militia joined the British army. Every day scores of men and boys from New Jersey and the long island slipped through the American lines to increase the manpower aboard the English fleet.

When the Declaration was proclaimed, Oliver De Lancey had retreated to his country residence, his great estate in Bloomingdale Village on the west side of upper Manhattan. "Until the madness passes," he said. "After they've tasted some British shot." Two weeks later, rebel soldiers arrived to chop down Oliver De

Lancey's wood lot. They said they needed it for fuel. De Lancey fired a musket into the air in protest. In reply the rebels hacked down his orchards and ornamental gardens as well. Oliver took a ship for London. That left his eldest son—also named Oliver—to look after the family fortunes in New York.

The Tories weren't the only ones fleeing the city. A few months earlier, the population had been twenty-five thousand. By early August it was down to five thousand. "There's streets in this here place looks like the plague's been at 'em," a rebel soldier from Virginia muttered. "Every house be empty."

"Can't blame 'em for goin'. 'Tain't a city no more. It's a battleground."

On August 17 more English ships arrived. They brought some fifteen thousand additional men.

"I reckon that makes it twelve hundred cannon, say a bit over thirty thousand regimental troops, and thirteen thousand seamen available to take New York for the crown, sir." Morgan Turner was with Washington in the fort.

"You're sure of the numbers?" Washington's eyes were red with fatigue.

"As sure as I can be, sir. It's an estimate, but not a wild guess."

"Nearly fifty thousand fighting men . . . I'd wager that's the largest expeditionary force Britain has ever assembled."

"I think it is, sir. At least I've never heard of anything remotely close."

"Must have cost the better part of a million pounds, wouldn't you say?"

"I would, sir."

"Staggering." Washington leaned back in his seat, long legs stretched out before him. He was a remarkably tall man. Had an inch or two on Morgan when they stood side by side. "What wouldn't I give for a proper navy to put you in charge of, Captain Turner." The Continental Congress had voted to have a navy but provided no money to create one. A couple of ships, the *Alfred* and the *Providence,* were commanded by a renegade Scot who called himself John Paul Jones, but they were staying clear of the massed fleet in New York harbor.

"A proper navy," Morgan repeated. "I'd give a lot for that myself, General."

"Yes, I'm sure you would. Even five or six frigates could make all the difference."

"With respect, sir, in the present circumstances I'd choose schooners and brigantines. Fast ships with mobile firepower and a shallow draft. We could hide in the coves along the coast and come up from behind to harry them. I'm not saying we'd sink the British navy, but we'd give them something to think about besides shelling the city."

"A few sloops and a brigantine or two. Good God, Captain Turner, it doesn't sound like much, does it?"

"No, General. Not much."

"Certainly it's not hard to come by ships like that or the crews to sail them. Not in New York."

Ah, yes. Morgan knew what he was being accused of, however subtly. A number of the city's most prominent shipowners and merchants had watched the rabble-rousing tactics of Turner, Sears, McDougall, and Willet and decided that taxes imposed by London were bad, but independence in a world run by the liberty boys meant chaos and an end to profit. Besides, damned few of the shipping kings thought the rebels could win. That was the real reason they hadn't rushed to donate a navy for Washington. They'd privateer for him, but as and when they chose. Putting vessels at Washington's command was another matter. "Ships can be had, General. With money."

"Indeed." Washington stood and looked across the seemingly placid Hudson to New Jersey. The gun emplacements he'd set up on the Palisades weren't enough. Too little firepower, too few men. Then there was the so-called Continental Congress, which couldn't stop arguing long enough to vote any bills of finance for its army, and had no standing treasury if it did. "Money."

"I did tell you, sir—"

"That there's an excellent chance you could get a large sum," Washington interrupted. "If I could find you a single ship and a crew, and spare you for a couple of months. Yes, you told me, Captain Turner."

"With luck, no more than six weeks, sir. Have you considered the idea?"

"I have. Bearing in mind as well that you told me there's no guarantee the treasure remains where you left it."

Morgan wondered if someday he might regret being as frank as he had. No, not with Washington. Not after he'd made it a matter of confidence. "No guarantee," he said again. "Though the one other person who might have found it didn't do so."

The older man's eyes narrowed. "You're certain of that, aren't you?"

Morgan nodded. Eight years ago. His own two hands around Petrus Vrinck's miserable neck had choked the truth out of him.

"Didn't get nothin'. I swears it. Never had no chance. God-rotting Caleb Devrey died afore he got me a ship."

"Where's the paper, Vrinck? The instructions you took out of the horse's head, where is it?"

"Yer chokin' the life out o' me. I told ye. Only saw it that once. Then that poxed Caleb Devrey took it. I ain't never seen it since."

Soon after that Vrinck had died of stab wounds sustained in a scuffle on the docks. Morgan had seen the body with his own eyes. Petrus Vrinck and Caleb Devrey, partners in hell. "I'm certain, yes, General."

At least a dozen times he'd thought of getting a ship and a crew and going south after the hoard. He knew he could do it. He'd written the directions down and buried them for fear he might forget, but he never had. *Seventy-four degrees thirty minutes west of Greenwich. Just south of twenty-four degrees north. Twice around and thrice back.* He could still find the treasure. For a time he'd considered moving it, but the past ten years had not been ordinary times. He was needed where he was. Besides, he'd never found the money to finance such an expedition. God knows, he'd rot in hell before he'd ask his mother to pay for it. Now he'd gladly turn over the treasure to help insure the success of the rebellion.

"I can't swear the money is still there, General Washington. But I can give a reasonable assurance. Better than a seventy-five-percent chance, I'd say. Bullion and coinage, sir. Instantly usable." Everyone knew Washington was a gaming man, quick to calculate the odds and place a wager. Incredibly lucky, they said. That was rubbish. Brains and daring, had nothing to do with luck.

The general stood with his back to Morgan for some moments more. When the answer came it was the same as it had been the two previous times the offer had been made. "I can't spare you, Captain Turner." Washington swung around and faced him, the tired eyes alive with conviction. "You're among my most valuable officers. Money is important—but fighting experience, that's vital."

                                        III

By day the American rebels made brave noises. In the dark they pissed themselves with fear. "Soon," Washington promised. "War will come soon and the waiting will be over. That's the worst part, the waiting."

On August 17 notices were posted warning that the attack was near and every civilian should get out of the city.

Flossie had died in her sleep three years earlier. Squaw DaSilva was a vigorous sixty-one, but she hadn't left her house since the night Solomon set Morgan's ship on fire and left her to deal with his legacy of hatred. Solomon DaSilva had given her everything she valued in this life, and in the end, bit by painful bit, had taken it all away. Now there was nothing for her outside the four walls of her grand mansion on the Broad Way.

It was up to Tilda to tell her mistress what they were saying in the streets. "Gonna be a battle. We best be goin'."

"Nonsense, Tilda. We're safe here. No one has troubled us so far, have they?"

Squaw DaSilva's house was exempt from quartering, and guarded by half a dozen well-armed American militiamen. It was full of whores. She had brought a choice handful of the women who worked for her to live under her private roof, and she made them available only to American officers above the rank of lieutenant.

"Be so many masts in the harbor, looks like trees be growin' there," Tilda said stubbornly. "Never seen so many ships. Rebels be going to lose this fight."

Her mistress nodded behind her veil. "Yes, Tilda. I think that's likely."

"Well?"

"I believe British officers also have appendages between their legs, Tilda. And frequently require a place to put them."

It was a little past midnight. The August air soft and warm, with that sweet, clean smell that follows a summer night's rain. Six of His Majesty's warships moved into position on the ocean side of the Narrows. Under that guard, the oars of dozens of barges and longboats made a constant rippling across the surface of the calm water. Dawn was a faint pinkness when the first of the redcoats disembarked in Brooklyn.

Two hundred rebel Pennsylvania riflemen were stationed by the beachhead. Their captain squinted into the dark and assessed the strength of the troops pouring onto the long island. After a few minutes he raised his arm and silently waved his men back into the hills.

Half an hour later, hidden by the dense woods of Brooklyn Heights, Major Aaron Burr snapped his glass shut and turned to his commanding officer. "Looks like that's the last of them for the moment, sir. By my count they've landed some fifteen thousand men."

The general was from New Hampshire. He'd taken over the defense of Brooklyn less than a week earlier and his bowels had been pure water ever since. He required a few seconds of clenching his buttocks before he could be sure he wouldn't shit himself when he spoke. Nonetheless, he said: "We're ready for 'em." At least, he hoped they were. He'd never been in this poxed colony of New York before. Didn't know a damned thing about the lay of the land. The job was his because no one else was available.

They were dug in on Brooklyn Heights, and farther back along the heavily forested and mostly impassable Heights of Guan. A fighting man's dream of a defensive position. Except that he had perhaps five thousand men with which to hold the bloody Guan Heights against some fifteen thousand lobsters.

The odds got worse. The British sent additional redcoats and moved five thousand Hessians into the village of Flatbush. Their offensive line now stretched in a four-mile arc along the southern tip of the long island, or Nassau Island as they still insisted on calling it. Washington sent his New Hampshire general every live body he could spare, three thousand additional men.

When the maneuvering was finished seven thousand American rebels faced twenty-one thousand soldiers fighting for the British.

There was another force opposing the rebels, a termite burrowing from within. Kings County on the long island was a hotbed of Tories.

"Someone to see you, sir. A local."

The man who came into the British command tent had to bend to keep his head from hitting the ridgepole. A farmer, by the look of him. Big like so many of these colonials, and stinking of manure. Fellow wasted no time speaking his piece. "Be four roads through the Guan Heights." The farmer ticked them off on his fingers, speaking slowly as if he thought the English colonel might be either stupid or deaf. "The Gowanus. The Flatbush. The Bedford. And the Jamaica."

"Yes, I know." The colonel tapped his finger impatiently. "Get to the point."

"There be no rebels guarding the Jamaica pass."

"Good God! Are you sure?"

"Dead certain sure. Not one. Some so-called general from up New Hampshire way, he be the one organizing things for the poxed rebels. Ain't never been here afore and don't know the ground."

At sundown the word was passed along the line of ten thousand redcoats. "Not a sound. Not if you want your balls to continue to hang where the Almighty put 'em." They were ordered to leave their campfires burning. "So's any rebels as is watching won't be scared of the dark." Young Oliver De Lancey brought up the rear of the two-mile column, in command of a pair of companies of the long island's Tory militia.

By morning the redcoats and their allies had traveled unopposed through the Jamaica pass. Once they'd cleared it, half the British fighting force was behind the American lines. They fired two signal shots to say the rebels were surrounded.

The Hessians attacked first. Five thousand of them fell on eight hundred Yankees. The rebels broke cover and tried to run. The Hessians stuck most of them to the trees with their own bayonets. The general from New Hampshire attempted to lead his men in a retreat to safety. The maneuver failed and his troops were massacred when they tried to surrender, hacked apart by Scottish broadswords as well as Hessian sabers. By midday Brooklyn reeked of blood and dung and terror. The screams of the slowly dying made an echoing dirge in the hills.

At the Gowanus pass, four hundred men from Maryland tried to hold the high ground long enough to let their comrades escape. They held out for two hours against a hail of British grape and chain. Washington was on the long island by then, close enough to watch the Marylanders die, but he had no troops to commit to save them.

The British general in command of the expedition was William Howe. He watched as well, along with Generals Cornwallis and Clinton. "A few hours more," Clinton said snapping his glass closed. "By then every rebel's back will be to the East River."

Howe didn't answer.

"He's right." Cornwallis fished the most recent dispatch from his pocket. "Latest estimates are they've lost a thousand men, possibly twelve hundred. At least that many are wounded. And we've taken plenty of prisoners."

"Not that many prisoners," Howe said through clenched teeth. The bloody Hessians were animals, and the Scots Highlanders no better.

"It won't take much longer. We'll drive the last of 'em into the river," Clinton said again.

Howe ignored him and turned to Cornwallis. "What about our losses?"

"Sixty dead. Three hundred wounded or missing."

Sweet Christ. Head-on slaughter, and the damned colonials fighting for every inch of ground. It would be carnage, like Bunker Hill up in Boston the year before. Most nights Howe relived that battle, waded ankle-deep yet again in spilled guts, the way he had that June morning. He took the hill, but only after his entire personal staff had been killed, along with forty percent of his men. The rebel officers were prepared to fight to the last drop of blood. Their raw troops were less likely to wait patiently for death. "We'll sit tight," he said. "See how much time they need to stare down our guns before they turn their britches brown and run for the hills."

"General Howe, I promise you, sir, there's no—" Clinton couldn't speak for sputtering.

"Now's the time," Cornwallis said. "There's no reason to stop the attack!"

Howe turned and waved a subaltern forward. "Lieutenant, pass the word. We'll stand as we are for the time being."

Washington smelled that decision. It came to him over the hills on the blood-soaked wind. He knew what Howe was doing before the reports of the lookouts arrived. "They're digging in, sir. Seems they've decided to put us under siege."

"No," Washington whispered, more to himself than anyone else. "I think that is an invitation we shall not accept."

Two days went by. Pouring rain soaked the ill-equipped rebels to the skin and ruined what remained of rebel powder. There were a few skirmishes, but nothing serious.

When the third night came and darkness fell, Washington waited for Morgan Turner. It was a little after eleven when he showed up. "Everything's ready, sir."

Washington looked grave. "You're sure there are enough of them?"

Morgan nodded. "It will be tight, sir. But we'll make it."

Washington nodded grimly. "Very well. Pass the word."

Morgan stepped outside the tent. "Tell the men to form up and move out. General Washington's orders."

The rebels crept silently down from the Heights to the Brooklyn ferry landing.

A flotilla of small craft was waiting in the East River, protected from the eyes of the lookouts aboard the British fleet by the twin land bulges known as Yellow Hook and Red Hook.

What was waiting for them wasn't exactly the navy Morgan Turner had promised to finance with his secret treasure. There were rowboats, barges, sloops, skiffs, canoes—anything that could float, and none of it carrying so much as a single cannon. A regiment of fishermen, all volunteers, mostly from Salem and Marblehead up in Massachusetts.

By dawn what remained of the American army sent to defend Brooklyn— ninety-five hundred men—was back on Manhattan. They had left thirteen hundred rebel corpses behind.

It was eight-thirty in the morning before Howe knew the Americans had gotten away.

But not all of them. Washington ordered General Woodhull, once commander in chief of the long island's militia, to stay behind and drive all the cattle he could find deep into the center of the island, out of reach of English bellies. Two days later, purely by chance, Oliver De Lancey found Woodhull in an inn about two miles east of Jamaica.

De Lancey's men surrounded the two-story building. Woodhull watched from the taproom window as the Tories took up their positions. He walked back to his table, lifted his tankard and drank the last of his ale, then nodded to the innkeeper. "It's all right, man. Don't look like that. I'm not going to let them burn you out."

Woodhull walked to the door and opened it. He and De Lancey looked at each other across ten yards of open ground. "Quarter, sir?" Woodhull asked.

"Of course. My word on it. As one gentleman to another."

Woodhull drew his sword from its scabbard, let it hang by his side, and walked toward De Lancey. Oliver slid down from his horse and went forward to meet him.

The Tory militia moved in to surround them. By the time Woodhull and De Lancey met in the middle of the open ground, they were encircled by armed men. Woodhull snapped a quick bow, then raised his head and with two hands offered his sword. De Lancey took it.

One of the militiamen had yet to be blooded. The thought was eating at him, a cancer in his belly. Three days. The miserable revolution was all but over and he hadn't killed a single stinking rebel. "Bastard!" He swung his short sword and connected with Woodhull's right arm. Two others felt the same. Besides, once they'd been under Woodhull's command, and they had scores to settle. They lunged, swords flashing.

Woodhull didn't make a sound, only kept looking at De Lancey. Twice Oliver opened his mouth to call the men off, but no words came. His pulse raced and his blood sang. It did something to him, watching men die like this. As slowly as possible. Made him hard as a rock. His glance flicked to the inn. Could be there was a woman in there. . . .

Not all the Tories were part of the attack on Woodhull. Some stood back, watching their commander. They'd heard the rebel ask for quarter, and they'd heard De Lancey's reply. He felt their eyes, knew what they were thinking. He was half Jew. That was why he couldn't be trusted. All his life the son of Phila Franks De Lancey had heard the silent voices that reminded him he was half Tudesco Jew.

"Enough!" Oliver meant to shout the word, but it came out a croak. He tried again. "Enough! Stand off!" Better. More like a man, less like a frog. "This officer's a prisoner. Take him to the church in New Utrecht. Leave him with the rest of the wounded."

IV

It was five days since the battle for Brooklyn. The putrid stench of gangrenous flesh permeated the air of the church that sheltered wounded captives.

Andrew held a cloth over his nose as he walked along the rows of bodies. Once in a while he stopped and pointed to one or another of the men. "That one's dead. Get him out of here." Sometimes he wasn't entirely sure until he knelt and pressed his ear to a heart. Four out of five times he was right. Dead. And dead. And dead again. "Bury 'em," he ordered. "Quickly and deep." God knew what poxes might be loosed on them by the bloated and rotting corpses.

The detail of rebel captives assigned to orderly duty looked at him with hatred in their eyes. His accent gave him away as a colonial. That he was here meant he was a Tory. They would have torn him apart with their bare hands if not for the half-dozen redcoats on guard.

An hour went by while he separated the dead from the living, and those who might recover from the majority who were simply marking time until they were finished. The patient with a general's markings on his shoulders was the last man in the next-to-last line. "Who's this?" Andrew demanded.

None of the rebels would answer. One of the redcoats stepped forward. "I believe his name's Woodhull, Dr. Turner. General Woodhull. Captured in Jamaica Town. Wounded while resisting."

"Yes," Andrew muttered. "That's what rebels do, isn't it? They resist." He dropped to his knees. The man was looking at him. "I'm a doctor," Andrew said. "I'm going to take a look at your wounds."

Woodhull nodded.

He didn't require much time to make a diagnosis. "The arm's turned poisonous," Andrew said. No point in being delicate. This wasn't some damask-curtained bedside in the court part of town. "It has to come off at the shoulder."

Woodhull shook his head. "No."

"Don't tell me no, sir. You've no choice if you want to live. Sweet Christ Almighty, I've never seen such a hacking. Like a side of mutton . . ." He stopped speaking, looked at the patient. Woodhull looked back and said nothing. "Orderly!" Andrew barked. "Ale."

A boy with a bloody bandage tied around his head passed Andrew a canteen. He sniffed at it. The ale had been cut with brackish well water. Never mind. It was liquid. He held the canteen to Woodhull's mouth, lifted the man's shoulders slightly so he could drink without choking.

"Thank you."

"I'll make a good job of it, I promise you," Andrew said.

"I'm sure. And I thank you, sir. But no."

"You'll die."

"Sooner or later," the general said with a weak smile. "That's certain. But with both arms."

Andrew shrugged. "As you wish." He glanced over his shoulder. The rebel orderlies were still watching, but none of the redcoats seemed to be paying close attention. "Is there anything you want to tell me?" he asked quietly. "I can pass a message on. To your wife, or anyone else who's . . . important to you."

Woodhull studied him closely. "Turner," he murmured. "An old New York name."

"Yes. One of the first families in the province. I can be trusted, sir. I guarantee it." He was intensely conscious of the gaze of the young rebel who'd given him the canteen of ale.

"Oliver De Lancey," Woodhull murmured. "Any as want to know . . . say he bears watching."

"I can believe that. I'll pass it on. Anything else?"

"My wife. Tell her I send my respectful greetings."

Seven hours later, when after half a dozen amputations Andrew was so tired he could barely stand, it was the rebel orderly with the bandaged head who brought him hot tea laced with rum, and a fresh biscuit. "It's from the women of the town, Dr. Turner. They've been seeing to us."

"Smarter than we are, the women." Andrew took a long, grateful sip of the tea. "They don't choose up sides."

"Some don't," the rebel boy agreed. "My mother and my sister, they support the cause of independency same as me."

The two men were pretty much alone in the field where Andrew had set up his surgical theater. The soldiers were standing some distance apart. Most had no objection to blowing a man's head off with a musket, but the controlled savagery of surgery had proved too much for them. They'd withdrawn before the first operation was finished. "I see," Andrew said. "Independency. But the women don't have to kill for it, do they? Or be killed. What's wrong with your head?"

"Caught the edge of a bayonet on the Gowanus road."

"Shall I take a look at it?" Andrew reached forward to remove the bandage. The boy yanked his head away. "It's all right," Andrew said. "I'm a real doctor, whether I'm Tory or rebel."

"That's as might be, sir. But me head's fine now the bleeding's stopped."

"Very well."

"Can I ask you somethin'?"

"Ask away."

"What are you doin' here?"

Andrew smiled. "I've been asking myself the same thing," he said. "I suppose the answer is that the patients in my hospital, the almshouse hospital over in the city, were all sent to Poughkeepsie for the duration. Everyone in the almshouse, in fact. Washington's orders. So I came here."

"General Washington's orders," the boy corrected, emphasizing the rank. His face burned with defiance.

"Very well, General Washington. A field officer of Virginia commissioned to serve His Majesty's interests. Some years back, I believe. Which makes him doubly rebellious." Andrew had finished the tea. He broke the biscuit in two and offered half to the orderly. "Hungry?"

The boy shook his head. "I don't eat with Tories."

"Well then," Andrew said, taking a large bite of the biscuit and jerking his thumb toward the contingent of redcoats at the far end of the field, "you'll be going without for some little time."

Over on Manhattan the rebels left their sopping gear spread on the cobbles to dry. Washington gave orders that every man who still had a musket was to put it back in working order or face a court-martial. Few complied. Why bother? There were damn few musket balls left. Damn few muskets, come to that. Many of the survivors had dropped their weapons when they turned and ran.

"There's a lot of 'em would be deserters if there was anywhere to go," someone said to Morgan Turner.

"Then thank heaven we're on an island."

Morgan didn't mention that thousands of the militiamen had left anyway. They'd simply commandeered rowboats or canoes and set out for home. Once they were beyond the American lines they had little to fear. The British left them alone as long as they were headed away from New York.

As for General Howe over on the long island, he knew there was no hurry. He took nearly a month readying his pursuit. On the morning of September 15, he ordered his brother, Admiral "Black Dick" Howe, to shell the upper half of Manhattan. Five warships anchored in the East River poured a continuous barrage onto the American positions. Meanwhile, under the covering fire, dozens of longboats ferried British troops over from Brooklyn.

Four thousand British soldiers were set ashore at Kip's Bay, nearly halfway up the east coast of Manhattan, far above the populated city. The first to be landed were a contingent of Scots pipers, who began to play the moment they arrived and didn't stop for the better part of two hours. The Kip family was intensely loyal to the crown. It wasn't long since they'd seen the backs of the rebels they had been forced to quarter in their deep country retreat. Now, thank God, here were the victorious redcoats.

"Refreshments, gentlemen? Please, it's an honor."

Howe and Cornwallis and Clinton, along with a number of their senior officers, sipped sherry and ate sweet biscuits while the endless line of fighting men disembarked on the small beach between the surrounding cliffs, the bagpipes played, and Black Dick's ships belched dragon fire.

Finally the army moved again, a slow, steady westward march that would cut the island in two. No need to hurry; the enemy had been all but beaten. Reports were that the rebels were running in every direction, throwing down their arms as they went. One advance party reported that General Washington himself had failed in an attempt to rally them in a nearby cornfield, and that fearing his capture his officers had rushed him north to the rebel fort.

"Captain Turner? Is that you, sir?" Aaron Burr slid into the muddy trench beneath the dripping trees.

"It's me. What news?"

"They're finished at the bloody Kips's and moving again, sir. Towards Hudson's River."

"Logical."

"They mean to trap us down south in the city, don't they, sir?"

"What's left of us down there, yes. About thirty-five hundred troops are still in the city, aren't they?"

"Yes, sir, I believe so."

"I believe the very same, Major. So trapping them like hares in a burrow sounds like a sensible plan to me." Morgan was retying his neckerchief as he spoke, trying to find a dry bit to place next to his skin. A futile exercise. "If you were General Howe, wouldn't that be your plan?"

"Yes, sir. It would."

"Agreed. Mine as well. Holy bloody Savior, what did we do to deserve all this bloody rain?"

Burr pulled his own jacket tighter in an attempt to gain some warmth. "It might slow the English down some, sir."

"Yes, it might. But not enough. Now, my young friend, listen very carefully." Morgan hesitated. Burr was smart and loyal. Most important, he was available. "I want you to get down to the city as fast as you can. Faster. Rally the troops and lead them north to Harlem Heights."

"Up the west side of the island, sir?"

"Exactly. Up the road to the village of Greenwich. Tell the men they're to join General Washington in the north at the fort. Tell them it's about speed, not fighting. If they stay where they are they'll all be slaughtered, or worse, made prisoners on those stinking, God-cursed ships." Morgan jerked his head to indicate the frigates anchored in New York harbor.

The men the British took alive in Brooklyn, that's where they were. Stuffed into the holds of a couple of prison ships like live wares from Guinea, but of much less value. Living on quarter rations, the story went. Ships from hell, and every man, woman, and child in New York knew as much.

"I'll tell them, Captain Turner."

"Good. That should be enough to move their sodden arses."

"Captain Turner, sir . . . what will you be doing meanwhile?"

Morgan stood up and clambered out of the scant protection offered by the ditch. "I, Major Burr, am going to purchase you and the others some time. Before Howe can cut you off he has to pass Murray's farm. I know Mistress Murray well. A charming lady. I'm sure she can be persuaded to offer some of our famous New York hospitality to the glorious British victors."

"Leave," Cuf told Roisin. "You can hear it, can't you?" The sound of the bombardment was audible even as far as the Fiddle and Clogs over west of Trinity Church. "You've got to take Clare and get out."

Roisin busied herself with flipping the last of the johnnycakes frying on an iron griddle suspended over the fire. Wasn't that exactly what a man would say? Pick up and go. Never mind that her life was here. She was to take her daughter and leave, while Cuf was off to do what men did in wartime. Kill as many of the enemy as he could manage before they killed him. Might be he wouldn't even have time to eat these johnnycakes she was making to send with him. "And where would you have us go?"

"Anywhere that's not New York. The ferry across the Hudson to New Jersey is still running. I'm told it will be for another few hours. Get on it."

"New Jersey." She'd never been in New Jersey, and she wasn't going now, though the very floorboards beneath her feet were quivering. Cuf said the shells were landing up the island a ways, not on the city. Holy Virgin, what would it sound like if they were shelling the Broad Way? "What would you have us do when we get to New Jersey?"

"Same thing you do here." Cuf finished pulling on his boots and stamped about to make sure they still fit properly. He'd come home last night with them soaking wet and caked with mud. Roisin had cleaned them and dried them by the fire. Then she lay beside him, and he'd waited until he was sure Clare was sleeping, and taken her the way he always did, in silence, with her lying still and soft and pliant beneath him. Never was a time Roisin didn't spread her legs for him if he wanted her. And never a time when he knew what she was thinking or feeling while he had her.

He didn't know what she was thinking now, only what she had to do. "Take your simples." Cuf nodded in the direction of the shelves. "And you and Clare get over to New Jersey. With your skill and a stake, they'll make you welcome." He pulled a small pouch from inside his shirt and handed it to her. "You two will be safe. And I'll be able to do my soldiering and not worry."

The pouch was full of coins, and they weighed too much to be pennies. It had been years since the Fiddle and Clogs was prosperous enough to yield such profit. "Where did you get this?"

"It doesn't matter. I didn't steal it, and it's meant for you and Clare. That's all you have to know."

"You got it from Morgan Turner." Roisin wanted the words back the moment she spoke them. She'd spent the ten years since Morgan returned avoiding any discussion of him. Now this terrible war had addled her brain. She couldn't still her tongue. "Morgan Turner gave you this money, didn't he?"

"That's not your affair." He had hated taking the money, even from Morgan. Most of all from Morgan. But he wouldn't let his pride stand in the way of Roisin's safety or Clare's. If anything happened to them, nothing he was fighting for, nothing the rebels might accomplish, would be worth a thing to him.

"All you have to do is what I'm telling you. Get your things together and get out of here." He grabbed her canvas satchel from a peg on the wall and tossed it to her. "Swear to me you'll go, Roisin. I can't wait any longer if I'm to be where I'm supposed to be while I can still get there. Swear you'll go."

She didn't look at him. "Very well, I swear." Cuf wasn't a Catholic. He knew nothing of the ways of the True Church, much less the Women of Connemara. He didn't know it wouldn't count if she didn't swear by the Holy Virgin or her precious Son.

❧

Howe rode at the head of his troops, looking from side to side. The city was criss-crossed with rebel fortifications, trees cut down to barricade the streets, earth-works thrown up everywhere. All were deserted now. The city was an empty, silent shell. The view changed when they reached the southern end of the Broad Way. Not much sign of war there. Simply fine houses and stately trees, their leaves on the turn now, glowing in the late-afternoon sun that had dried the ravages of the week of rain.

Bloody stupid rebels. Much of New York must have looked like this before they brutalized it with their futile defenses. Why start a fight they couldn't win? Why not negotiate their way out of whatever complaints they had? Because so many of them were fanatics, prepared to fight to the last man.

He raised an arm to signal the pipers to stop playing. There was something eerie about the music echoing in the empty streets. He needed to hear whatever the calm and the silence were hiding. They were almost at the fort now. If a last-ditch battle was planned, that's where it would be.

"See that house there?" It was General Clinton, come up beside him, pointing with his baton at a grand Broad Way mansion facing the Bowling Green and hard by the official governor's residence. Clinton didn't seem worried about a surprise assault from the fort.

Howe looked to his right. "I see it."

"The biggest whoremistress in the city lives there. Made a fortune out of her husband's bordellos, and moved in beside us before anyone knew what she planned."

Of course. Clinton had grown up in the New York governor's residence. His father had been the royal governor well into the early fifties. No governor in the place now. Eighty-eight-year-old Cadwallader Colden had fled to the long island before Washington and his troops took over the city. Word was he was dying. "A whoremistress, eh?" Howe said with a grin. "Knew her well, did you?"

"Some of her employees, certainly. But there's more to the tale. They call her Squaw DaSilva because she's said to be part savage. Always wears a veil and widow's weeds. Her husband was a gunrunner captured by the Huron. Indians cut off his cock and ate it, then sent him back to her. Still alive, mind you. They say she kept him locked up in the attic after that."

They were a few yards past the house now. Howe had to turn to squint over his shoulder at the top-story windows winking in the westering sun. "Good Christ, is he still there?"

"The cockless husband? No, I hear he died some years ago. Set fire to her son's ship and went down with it. Son goes by the name of Turner, by the way. Morgan Turner. Time was when he captained one of the most successful privateers afloat. Supposed to be a rebel now."

"Sounds like a bloody astounding tale. I'd like to know more of it."

"Over a brandy some night," Clinton promised.

They were nearly there now, and every door on the Broad Way yet closed. "Good Christ," Howe muttered. "Hail, the conquering heroes." He glanced up. The ensign flying from the pole beside the fort was the rebel standard. Howe turned to bellow a command at his subaltern, but the words froze in his mouth. The door to the whoremistress's house had opened.

A woman stepped into the street. Her voice rang out with the clear tones of a striking bell. "Good afternoon, gentlemen. Welcome to New York."

Christ knew she wasn't young, but there was something arresting about her even now. That blue-black hair perhaps, pulled back from her face and secured with jeweled clips that sparkled in the afternoon light. But no veil.

"I am Mistress DaSilva, gentlemen. Squaw DaSilva, as the town would have it. And this"—she pulled a girl from the shadows of the house into the sunlit street—"is Amarantha. Lovely, isn't she?"

A blonde doxy appeared, wearing a blue gown cut low enough to show off a truly delicious pair of tits. Prettiest thing he'd seen since leaving London, parading her painted face on the same street that housed the mansion of the Royal Governor.

"I see we've neglected one of our duties in welcoming you to our city, gentlemen." The whoremistress shoved Amarantha forward. For a moment Howe thought she was going to fondle one of his officers right there in the street. Holy Christ, maybe even himself!

Instead Amarantha lifted her skirts high enough to show off her delightful ankles and ran in front of him, flashing a gorgeous smile. Straight to the flagpole.

They'd obviously rehearsed this. In seconds the girl had hauled down the rebel arms. One of Howe's men started forward to take the thing from her, but the general raised a hand. "Let her be. They've planned this little drama. Let's watch it all."

The older woman stepped into the middle of the cobbled road and took the bit of cloth from Amarantha. At that moment one of the horses cleared his bowels. Squaw DaSilva walked over and dropped the rebel standard on the pile of steaming manure. Then she handed something to Amarantha. The girl hurried back to the flagpole, fixed the new flag in place, and quickly hoisted it. A breeze snapped into position the arms of His Majesty, George III.

"Now, gentlemen, you know you are indeed welcome. May I invite you into my home for refreshments, General Howe? And any of your officers who care to join you, of course."

"On behalf of my men and myself, I must refuse your kind hospitality for the moment, mistress. There's much to be done. But may I assume we'll be welcome another time?"

Squaw DaSilva dropped a deep curtsy. "At any hour of the day or night, General. My house is yours. And its amenities, of course."

Howe swept off his hat and bowed elegantly, though he was still astride his horse. "Indeed, Mistress DaSilva. His Majesty's gracious reign is restored. *Toujours la gaieté,* mistress, *toujours la gaieté!*" He turned in the saddle, raised the hand that still held his gold-braided hat, and waved toward the musicians. There was first a loud drumroll, then the pipers began to play.

One after another the doors of the Broad Way houses were opened and the residents stepped into the street.

Squaw waited until she was sure all her highborn fancy neighbors had shown themselves and gotten the good look at her she knew they craved. Then she slowly turned and walked back to her house. Head high. Her naked face, lined and ravaged by time though it now was, raised to the sun.

V

Holy bloody Savior, it was hot, an October Indian summer with a vengeance. Despite the heat, Morgan wore a heavy ankle-length cloak over his blue uniform. Without it he was in peril for his life. As he'd told Cuf, get caught out of uniform and you'd be hanged for a spy. Rules of the game.

He was full of advice. So damned smart. Captain Morgan bloody Turner. Knew bloody everything. Howe would trap the rebel troops like hares in a burrow, he'd told young Burr. Well, Burr had gotten the troops safely out of the city to Fort Washington. Now Morgan Turner was the hare. By choice. Because someone had to see what was happening, and no one knew New York better.

Over a week now he'd been living in darkened doorways down by the docks, hiding among the empty ale kegs outside the taverns and slop shops. Calculating every step before he dared take it. There was no one in the city he could truly trust. Not now.

Just about everyone who supported the rebel cause had fled New York the moment Black Dick's bombardment began nearly a week before. Once Howe and his troops were landed, Tories from every colony had rushed to the city to take the place of the departing rebel patriots. As for the redcoats, they'd quickly settled into the finest houses and buildings of the town. Howe was living in the governor's mansion. City Hall on Wall Street was his administrative headquarters. King's College, over on Park Place, had been turned into a military hospital.

Morgan had spent a couple of hours the previous afternoon watching the British wounded being moved into the college, making deductions from the last numbers he'd given Washington, and conscious all the while of Andrew. His cousin had been everywhere, checking each stretcher as it was carried inside, directing the entire operation. Andrew Turner, a bloody Tory. Morgan's mother as well. So be it. As he readied the oil-soaked rags Morgan told himself he didn't feel concern for either of them.

The old Fighting Cocks tavern on Whitehall Slip had been turned into a British amenity along with so much else. Squaw DaSilva had filled the Cocks with common whores, a bordello for ordinary seamen and soldiers. The doxies in her house—the house he'd grown up in, by God—were the youngest and prettiest. Reserved for His Majesty's officers.

The thought made Morgan tremble with fury, but when he forced himself to be calm he judged the availability of whores for both officers and troops a good thing. Protected the decent women from the appetites of the victors. Not that there were many decent women left in the city. The day before the assault on New York began he'd spoken to Cuf about Roisin and Clare and made Cuf take a bit of money to help them get out of the town. They must be gone by now. Cuf was cautious by nature.

Morgan poured the last of the whale oil over the rags along the base of the old timber-framed building. He'd siphoned the oil out of a number of the streetlamps that lined the city. It hadn't been difficult. The lamplighters, like most of the laboring people of New York, were rebel supporters. They were long gone, and Howe had yet to appoint replacements. The oil-filled lanterns were easy targets after dark. As for the rags, he'd scavenged them from the rubbish that lined the roads.

The last of the oil dripped onto the bits of linen and wool and homespun. The building would go up like tinder. This was his great contribution to the noble and just cause of independence: burning the city he'd been born in. Scorched earth had been the policy of every retreating army since Julius Caeser, Morgan knew, but it didn't make him feel any better.

He paused for a moment, then lifted his face to test the wind. Coming from the southwest. Excellent. All he had to do was start the job and the wind would finish it. Take out all the most important buildings and make New York a lot less comfortable for the bastards.

His grandfather's old house would go as well. No way that could be avoided. Hall Place was little more than a long spit from the Fighting Cocks. Never mind. His maiden aunts, Wella and Cecily, had gone north to join their sister in Boston some months before and the empty house had been taken over by redcoats. As for Uncle Luke, his Ann Street house was three-quarters of a mile north. Besides, Andrew was free as a bird, riding high on the Tory wave of victory. He'd look after his wife and children and his legless father.

Morgan kicked the last of the rags into place and headed for the doorway across the road where he'd hidden a tin box that held a glowing coal cadged from a street fire made by some English marines cooking their supper. The box still felt uncomfortably hot. Thank Christ, the coal hadn't died on him.

Morgan had started back across the road when he heard the raucous singing. He jumped back into the shadows, one hand still holding the hot box, the other beneath his cloak on the hilt of his cutlass.

Three marines turned the corner. The town was full of the bastards. Black Dick must've given them all shore leave. This lot were stinking drunk, arms linked and singing at the top of their lungs. Something about Mistress McGowdy's twat. No prize for guessing where they were going. Bloody holy Savior. Why now?

"This be it." One of the marines stopped walking and brought his companions up short in the middle of the street. "The Fighting Twats, as we be callin' it now."

"Hell with that. I want to fuck 'em, not fight 'em."

"C'mon, then. They ain't comin' into the street and bending over to offer their backsides. 'Ey, what's this?" The marine prodded the line of rags with the toe of his scuffed boot.

One of the others bent closer to see. "Don't be nothin'. Jus' some protection against drafts is all. C'mon, you want to inspect the facilities or put yer tool in somethin' is wet and warm?"

The marines went inside. Morgan darted across the road and flung the coal into the rags. He watched the flames travel the length of the oil-drenched line, then begin licking at the wooden walls of the tavern. When he was sure the fire was well started, he disappeared into the waterfront shadows.

There were no trained firefighters to bring out the pump wagons and organize the bucket brigades. Rebels every one, they'd left the city with Washington's army. Within minutes sparks from the blazing roof of the Fighting Cocks tavern ignited one of the old Dutch houses on nearby Hall Place, then leapt across the road to devour the barber pole erected over a hundred years earlier by Lucas Turner. Soon the old house was burning. In some mockery of politeness the flames started at the front door and moved through the entrance hall. Marit Graumann's picture was consumed first, then Lucas's portrait crashed to the ground and became ashes.

Hall Place, Bridge Street, Beaver Street: the flames demolished entire blocks. Within two hours most of the houses built when New York was Nieuw Amsterdam were gone. Great numbers of women and children perished in the inferno. The alarm bells and church bells had long since been taken by the rebels to be turned into musket balls, so there was no way to warn the sleeping town. Those who were roused in time ran screaming into the streets, fighting their way through the smoke and the hail of cinders, mostly heading north toward the Common, with the flames licking at their backs.

A little after two in the morning the wind shifted. South by southeast now, and almost gale force. A storm of fire attacked the old Church Farm neighborhood, where all the houses were made of wood. The Church Farm houses were consumed in a quarter of an hour. The fire, strengthened, moved on.

All night the sky was ablaze, lit by the flames of the burning city. On the high hills of northern Manhattan and across the Hudson on the New Jersey Palisades rebels stood cheering as they watched. When the steeple of Trinity Church, that bastion of the aristocratic colonials who had never stopped calling England home, crashed to the earth the American observers whooped and howled in joy.

In the choking smoke and fierce heat of the city streets the enraged redcoats took their revenge. The soldiers and sailors had been sent to fight the blaze, but houses in the path of the fire were first looted, then left to burn. Dozens of locals were slaughtered as they ran for safety.

At three in the morning the Fiddle and Clogs yet stood. Roisin and Clare were part of a line of neighbors moving buckets of water from a nearby well to the tavern and the houses in the immediate vicinity. Clare lost count of the times she used her bare hands to beat out embers that landed on her skirts.

When other hands grabbed her from the rear and pulled her out of the line she thought it was someone stronger wanting to take her place in the bucket brigade. "No, please, I'm all right. I can go on. I only—"

"Shut up, bitch! Wanted to burn us out, did ye? Torch the town if yer precious Washington couldn't hold it. We'll give ye something to remember for yer pains."

There were six of them, British sailors. They dragged her away from the tavern, into the field where she'd played as a child, and systematically, one after another, they raped her. The fifth man was the worst, the most savage. He bit her left nipple almost entirely off. But it was the sixth who when he was finished with her drew his cutlass, and the one who'd bitten her so badly who dragged him away.

The two men were the only ones left in the field. The others had gone in search of more loot. "No, leave her be," the biter said in a harsh whisper. "We've given her something to remember us by. Let the bitch live and remember it."

"She can say it was us. If Black Dick has an inquiry she'll tell. Staring up at me she was, all the while. She'll know it was me."

"Well, if that's all yer worryin' about . . ." The sailor who wanted Clare left alive pulled his dagger from his belt and turned to where the girl still lay on the ground. "It's only her eyes as can make trouble for us. And they'll come out easy enough."

Morgan had reached the edge of the field not seconds before. He was still running when he drew the dagger from his boot and threw it. The blade buried itself between the shoulder blades of the attacking sailor and the man dropped in his tracks. The other saw what had happened, howled, and turned, searching for the enemy. Morgan was already behind him. He grabbed the sailor's hair, yanked his head back, and with one savage swipe of the cutlass slit his throat.

The second dead sailor fell to the ground. Morgan kicked his corpse aside, then knelt next to Clare. "Oh, God . . . I'm so sorry. Here, lass, let me get you to safety." She said nothing. He whipped off his cloak and covered her with it. "Clare, it's Morgan Turner, your father's friend, I want—"

The roof of the Fiddle and Clogs imploded, and the great crash cut off his words. The bucket brigade had lost the battle. Flames leapt from the building and reddened the sky. "Clare, where is your mother? Where's Roisin?" Morgan's voice was harsh with terror and urgency.

Clare scrambled to her feet without answering. She wrapped his cloak tight around her and began running in the direction of the blazing tavern.

"Clare! Wait!" He started after her, cursing the war, the fire, the redcoats, the madness that had made him think it was justifiable to put the city to the torch. "Clare!"

Another voice was shouting the same thing. "Clare! Over here!"

He saw Roisin, backlit by the flames, running toward her daughter. She put an arm around Clare and led her away. In seconds the smoke hid them both. Morgan took a step toward where he'd last seen them, then realized he could bring them nothing but more grief.

He was a known rebel, wearing the uniform of Washington's army. The mad impulse that made him come looking for them had served its purpose. At least he'd saved Clare's life. Now the best he could do for Roisin and Clare was to get as far away from them as he could.

Morgan stripped one of the dead sailors of his coat and breeches and put them on over his own. Then he ran.

Ann Street was as yet untouched. Hidden in the doorway of a coal shed a few yards from his uncle Luke's house, Morgan watched the dawn arrive. Andrew was nowhere to be seen, but his two young sons had managed to carry their grandfather into the street. Moments later, Meg joined them. It required both her and her small daughter to drag an oiled-cloth bundle tied with rope; no doubt the things Meg imagined she couldn't do without. If they had to flee she'd forget about them soon enough. The sun was up; Andrew's family waited. Morgan as well. It was his fault Luke couldn't run from the fire. He had to be sure his uncle was truly safe.

The sun's rays pierced the smoke. Now the noise seemed louder, but it wasn't just wordless screams of horror and fear. Morgan heard voices shouting commands. English voices. Their officers were bringing the rampaging British troops under control, and finally setting them to fighting the fire. Andrew's family also heard the sounds of the British finally restoring order. The boys carried their grandfather inside, and Meg and the little girl followed. Thank Christ.

Morgan felt his legs start to tremble. The exhaustion of the last few days was catching up with him, but he couldn't give in yet. He'd been a rebel all his life, but this time he had a purpose. This time he was for something, not against someone. Burning the city had been his duty and he'd done it. But Holy bloody Savior, at what a price.

He had to get back to Fort Washington. No better time to make a break for it then now, while there was still so much confusion. Except he had one more place to go. Covered with soot and wearing the uniform of an English sailor, as he was, no one would pay him any mind.

It was relatively easy to get to the court part of town. The mob was heading the other way, north in the path of the fire. The old fort was still standing, as were the governor's mansion and his mother's house. And most of their neighbors. All were pristine and unmarked in the early morning sunshine. Even the wind knew these were the privileged people, the leaders of charmed lives.

"You there, sailor! Pick up a shovel and get moving."

The officer who shouted the command looked at him only once, then wheeled his horse in the opposite direction. "All of you, get going," he bellowed over his shoulder. "You've got your orders. Bury the dead wherever you find them."

Morgan picked a spade out of the pile of digging tools that had been dumped in the street and fell in line behind the other English troops.

He lost count of the days, slept only a few hours at a stretch, taking cover among first one group of British sailors then another. The chaos protected him up to a point, but he was still in the city.

Holy Savior, he was hungry. He'd survived on the bits of food he could scavenge from the streets. A feast of charred pig meat once, but that seemed a long time past. He didn't dare get in line when grub was doled out to the troops in the work details. In the few minutes' respite while they ate they'd have time to look at him and ask questions.

All he needed was a few hours' more luck. A little more time to get past the city's defenses. Once he was in the woods he'd be unstoppable, at least by any bloody Englishman. Not one of them knew the paths through the trees and streams of Manhattan the way he did.

He wasn't sure if it was the second or the third day since the fire when he saw his chance. It was midafternoon when Morgan slipped through a momentarily unguarded gate in the wall that had been erected north of Partition Street, and left the city for the Rutgers estate. Careful to avoid the house—English officers were sure to be quartered there—he made his way across Division Street onto the De Lancey property he knew so well.

Bouwery Lane would have been the most direct route north, but he'd heard the sailors talking about General Cornwallis setting up headquarters in the De Lancey house. Morgan went northwest by another smaller lane and crossed the churning canal that drained what had been the Collect Pond when he was a lad. Most called it the Fresh Water Pond these days, but it seemed much smaller than he remembered. Back then everything around here had been wild and wooded. These last years—typical De Lancey greed—more and more of the old pond had been drained and filled.

What was left was turgid, murky, and covered in a slick of green. He knelt, pushed the scum away, and scooped up the first drink he'd had in many hours. Not as sweet as it used to be, but not brackish. He still had his canteen and filled it, remembering the stories his grandfather had told of boyhood swims in the Collect Pond, and of a wooded paradise where lovers met in secret. Not anymore.

North through the fields now, staying parallel with the Boston Road, but avoiding it. Once in a while he heard the tramp of feet and the clatter of hooves on the cobbles. Reinforcements being brought down to the city, most likely. An army of occupation feared confusion above all things. If they caught him and suspected he'd been the one to start the fire, drawing and quartering would be considered too merciful.

After a time he stopped long enough to take off the soot-blackened sailor's clothes and bury them. He went on in the tattered remains of his American uniform. If he was unlucky, there would at least be a military court, a trial of sorts.

There were fortifications everywhere. Many had been built by the Americans in the months and weeks leading up to the battle but were guarded now by men in red coats. He was slowed by the need to climb the rugged hills rather than take the roads that skirted them. It made for an exhausting journey, and he hadn't slept properly in days. Late the first day, after a feast of juicy plums from a tree on a long-abandoned farm, he crawled into the remains of an old root cellar and closed his eyes, telling himself he'd take only a brief rest. When he woke it was a gray dawn and a whole night had passed. He ate more plums, shoved still more into his pockets, and went on.

He heard the drumroll when the sun was high overhead. The drummer was bloody close, maybe a few yards away, no more.

Morgan reckoned he was about a mile north of Turtle Bay, on a stretch of level ground leading inevitably to the next Manhattan hill. He stopped where he stood, closed his eyes, tried desperately to remember the lay of the land beyond the stand of maples immediately ahead.

The artillery field. The great cleared space where in the spring he and a few others had been training boys of thirteen and fourteen, newly arrived from Virginia and Carolina, to load and fire cannon.

He took a few cautious steps. The trees gave way to a hedgerow of thorny wild roses studded with the bright red hips of autumn, and prickly twisting vines for which he had no name. On his belly, peering through the gnarled and heaving roots of the shrubs, he saw the field. The cannons were gone. He had no idea if they'd been captured or saved. In their place, on a raised dais of raw planks, there was a gallows.

Another drumroll, this one longer than the first. Holy Savior. It was a hanging.

Morgan had tied his neckerchief around his head to absorb the perspiration. It was only partially effective in the intense heat. He had to rub his eyes to clear them of stinging, salty sweat. Finally he could see.

The man the redcoats were leading to the gallows was a civilian, with his hands roped behind him. Any farmer left in these parts was probably a Tory. So what had this one done?

Sweet Holy Savior! The man had been turned around, made to stand with his back to the gallows and facing the hedge. Nat Hale. But out of uniform. Oh, Jesus God Almighty.

"Nathan Hale, though you claim to be a captain in the army of rebellion now unlawfully marshaled against his Most Gracious Majesty, George III, you were captured wearing the dress of an ordinary citizen." The man who spoke was a red-coated colonel, reading from a paper he held about a foot from his nose, his head drawn back so he could see the words. For his part Hale stared straight ahead, stony-faced, saying nothing.

"You admit to being in the City of New York with the intention of gaining information about His Majesty's loyal and lawful forces, and carrying same to the renegade and treasonous General George Washington. Therefore, Nathan Hale, you are judged to be engaging in the detestable and cowardly act of spying. By order of General Howe you are to hang by the neck until dead. Sentence to be carried out immediately."

Morgan's hand was on the hilt of his cutlass. It was the only weapon he had. In addition to the colonel who had read the charge there were eight redcoats in the field, and the black-masked hangman. Terrible odds. That didn't stop him from inching forward, squirming through the hedge until he reached a place where he could launch himself into the field in one thrust.

"Prisoner, do you have anything to say?"

"Only, sir, that I regret I have but one life to give for my country."

The colonel motioned the hangman forward. The man picked up the noose, testing it for strength. Damn him for a fool, Morgan thought. From this distance, with the knife that usually lodged in his boot, he could easily have killed the hangman. But he'd bloody left it between the shoulder blades of the sailor who had raped Clare.

His gaze went to the handle of the short sword of the nearest redcoat, just a tantalizing few feet away. He could grab it, toss it to Nat. They'd be two against nine then.

The plan was a jumble of thoughts that were rejected in the time it took the hangman to satisfy himself that the noose was serviceable and drop it around Hale's neck.

Now or never. The bad plan was the only one he had so it would have to do. Morgan inched forward on his belly. Closer. Close enough. He reached for the guard's sword. A hand grasped his hair, yanking his head back. He stared up into the lined and grizzled face of the redcoat who had blindsided him.

"I say, look what's come crawling on its belly to join the party. At least one of them play soldiers isn't spendin' all his time runnin' away."

In one motion the guard hauled Morgan to his feet and whipped his hands behind him. At that very instant he heard the trapdoor open and the snap of the rope. When he looked toward the gallows it was the tips of Nat Hale's boots that were level with his line of sight.

VI

"Who did this?" Andrew looked up from the examining table.

Roisin stood across from him, holding her daughter's hand. "Doesn't matter who did it. It's done. Can you stitch it back on?"

Andrew looked again at the girl's left breast. The marks on the soft flesh were starting to scab over, but they were recognizable as bites. As for the nipple, it was connected with barely an eighth of an inch of *membrana adiposa*. The wound, however, had been carefully cleaned and packed with fresh lint.

"Stitch it back," he murmured. "Yes, probably I could. But even if I do, and if the wound closes properly with no poison entering the blood, she'll still not be able to suckle a babe at that pappe."

"So be it. I don't want her scarred." Josie Harmon must find no imperfection when she inspected Clare. Apart from that, the wound wasn't important. There would be no child as a result of this outrage, Roisin would see to that. As for the future, you could feed a babe with one pappe if needs must. Besides, Clare was going to be rich. She could afford a wet nurse. "Can you make it look as if nothing has happened?"

Andrew never had a clue what went on in the heads of women. He knew he hadn't a prayer of making sense of the thoughts of this devilishly attractive redheaded creature. Looked as if she should be a sister to the girl she said was her daughter. And if she really was the girl's mother, couldn't she see there was more to be concerned about than a wounded breast?

The girl hadn't spoken a word since they arrived. She moved like a puppet, with jerky unnatural motions, and stared glassy-eyed at the ceiling. "The wound's been carefully dressed. I can see that. How long ago was the . . . the accident?"

"Nine days past. The night of the fire." Roisin adjusted the bodice of Clare's dress now that Dr. Turner seemed to have finished his examination. Morgan's cousin, she knew, though he didn't look a bit like Morgan. As fair as Morgan was dark. "I can keep the poison away from the wound. Leastwise, I can if I'm able to find a few simples now that everything's burned. But I'm not skilled with a knife or a needle. You are. That's why we've come." She lifted her face and looked straight at him. "The only reason, to be frank."

He saw the contempt in her face. Only her daughter's need had brought the woman to his Tory household. "I'll stitch it, if you like. But it won't—"

"No." The girl jerked away from her mother's touch and spoke her first words in his consulting room. "I want it left as it is."

Roisin tried to put her arms around Clare. The girl shrugged her away. "Ah, darling child, you're making a huge mistake. It will be a sadness to you all your life. Let Dr. Turner stitch it back in place. He's brilliant at such things. The whole town says so."

"No."

Andrew cleared his throat. "Perhaps you'd rather I simply cut it off altogether. That's possible if you—"

Roisin gasped, but it was Clare who answered. "No. I want it to stay as it is."

"You'll do as you're told," Roisin said, her patience worn thin by the terrors of the past days. She nodded to Andrew. "Put it back."

He turned to get a needle and a fresh ligature. Out of the corner of his eye he saw the girl reach up and draw her mother's face toward hers. The older woman stayed bent over the younger, listening to the girl's urgent whispers. Andrew busied himself with the strand of sheep's stomach.

A moment later the redhead gasped and pulled back, her hands clasped over her mouth as if to stifle a scream. The girl returned to staring at the ceiling. Andrew lifted the threaded needle so they could both see it. "Am I to proceed, mistress?"

"No." Roisin's voice was a whisper. "No, that's all right. We'll leave it be. The way she wants."

Andrew put down the ligature and helped the girl off the table. "I think it best . . . Perhaps your daughter can wait outside with my wife, mistress, while you and I discuss the care of the wound."

A moment later he'd turned Clare over to Meg—who was, as always, hovering in the hall in case he needed her—and closed the door. "Mistress Healsall, isn't it?" He'd been treating the burns of British soldiers and sailors for days on end, with almost no sleep. Otherwise it wouldn't have taken him so long to figure out who she was.

"Mistress Healsall, yes."

"And you live over on the Church Farm."

Roisin nodded.

"The destruction was worse there than anywhere. How are you getting by?"

"Same as everyone else." They had managed to secure two of the blankets being distributed by the charity circle of St. Paul's—the Anglican chapel over on the Broad Way and Fulton Street hadn't been touched by the fire—and they'd made themselves a nest of sorts in the burned-out ruins of the Fiddle and Clogs. "With pain and difficulty. Like all the rest who haven't kissed the British backside." Dear God, was she mad? She'd heard that Andrew Turner was doctor to General Howe himself. He could have them locked up, or worse, with a single word.

"It's not politics saved my house from the fire," Andrew said softly. "All Ann Street was spared, Tory or rebel. The wind doesn't blow at the bidding of the English, whatever you—or they—may think."

"It's what you think that matters, isn't it, Dr. Turner?" Holy Virgin help her. She couldn't help herself. It was the bones of the dead that did it. All the flesh burned off them, scattered on the streets of the town as if Satan himself had ridden through New York. As well he might have done.

"What I think is of very little importance. I'm a doctor. I help who I can where and when I can."

As he spoke, Andrew opened the door of a cabinet and began taking out various jars and flagons, lining them up on a small table. "Witch-hazel water, tansy, stanching powder, extract of peppermint, some poppy syrup," he recited. "I presume you lost your stores in the fire."

"Every scrap."

"I thought as much. Take these. Your neighbors will probably be glad of some Mistress Healsall care."

"Thank you. I can pay." The pouch full of coins was still in the pocket of her underskirt, saved only because it had been on her person since Cuf gave it to her.

"That won't be necessary. Here"—he took down a small vial from the top shelf—"you can—" He broke off. "But this is antimony. I'm told you don't approve of it."

"I do not. It purges the good along with the sickness."

"And no tartar emetic, no mercury . . . ?"

"None. I use only herbs and seeds and leaves."

"And seaweed." He spoke with his back to her.

Ah, she might have guessed. Like most men, he couldn't stand the notion that a woman might stop their seed from growing. Forced it in wherever they liked, then hated for it to be scraped out and thrown away with the slops. "Seaweed's natural," she said.

Andrew's flesh crawled. Filthy business, abortion. But in the case of the daughter, for example. . . . Raped, no question about it. Andrew put the antimony back in its place. "The quacks and their vegetable wars," he said evenly. "I'd forgotten. But I've seen the results of your treatments more than once. Quack or no, you do good work, Mistress Healsall."

She couldn't choke out another thank-you. Not to the devil. "My daughter," she said, taking a step toward the door.

"Meg will look after her. My wife can be trusted, I assure you. She's totally without political sentiment."

Roisin hesitated a moment more, then went to the table and began filling her pockets with the medicines. "I can ease the hurt of quite a few with these." Not a proper thank-you, but the best she could do.

Andrew watched her. Once or twice she seemed unfamiliar with something and pulled the cork and smelled it, then nodded and tucked the remedy away somewhere on her person. She definitely had knowledge. Different from his, sometimes possibly better. God knew she was right about the antimony—it forced everything out of both ends of the patient. And he'd never been entirely convinced about purging, whatever they'd told him in Edinburgh. Himself, his professors, sweet Christ, sometimes he didn't think any of them knew a thing.

All those burns. Most of the victims died in a matter of hours after unspeakable suffering and screaming. But some lived on and suffered on. There was so damned little he could do. Truth was, the longer he practiced medicine, the more sure he was that surgery was the true healer. Skill with the scalpel could be measured. Except these last days. What surgery was there for the victims of the fire? The only thing he could do was cut away the worst of the charred flesh, then wait to see if poisoned blood followed. As it usually did.

"Mistress Healsall." She stopped squirreling things away, looked at him. "Many of your neighbors . . . I'd venture they've been burned." She nodded and he could see their agony reflected in her eyes. "If you could have one thing to treat the burns, what would it be?"

Holy Virgin. A man, the most famous doctor and surgeon in New York, asking her. He truly wanted to know; she could see that in his eyes. There wasn't a Woman of Connemara would believe it. "Honey," she said.

"Just ordinary honey?"

"Yes. Though I've heard it's best if the bees come from a hive near where sage is growing. But any honey will do. Mixed with powder of balsam, if possible."

Andrew considered for a moment. "You're sealing the wound so the air doesn't get in."

Roisin nodded. "I expect that's what is meant to happen. My mother taught me my cures. And her mother taught her. That's all I know. Honey for a burn. With balsam to cleanse the humors. And for the pain, a tea made of willow bark."

Sweet Christ. Willow bark. Like animals in the woods. Honey, though, that might not be as mad as it sounded. "Thank you. I shall try honey. And look"—he nodded toward the now empty table—"if you tell me where you can be found, I'll see you get more remedies of the type you approve. And a supply of honey."

"I can be found where I've always been. The Fiddle and Clogs. Only there's but a few sticks left of it now."

"You'll have more supplies by tomorrow afternoon," he promised.

"I'd be grateful, but I wouldn't suggest you . . . What I mean . . . It would be best if you don't bring them yourself, Dr. Turner."

Andrew managed a smile. "Or the locals will tear off my legs and twist them around my throat. I know. Don't worry, I'll send someone who won't attract attention." She started for the door. "Wait," he said. "Don't go yet. I need to ask you one thing more."

She turned back to him.

"Prisoners," Andrew said. "Rebel soldiers. The ones who aren't sent to the prison ships . . . There's talk that they'll be lodged in various parts of the town—" He broke off, seeing the way her shoulders had stiffened, the way she was looking at him.

"And?" Roisin said. "Do go on, Dr. Turner."

Andrew shook his head. "There's no point in our arguing, mistress. I was simply wondering if you might visit the prisoners occasionally. Not on the ships, that wouldn't be safe. But if any are kept here in the city, as I expect they will be, perhaps you could go in occasionally. See if there's anything to be done for their wounds. I can't do it myself," he added softly. "I'm charged with looking after the British officers, and I'm to see to the British troops if any time is left. You understand."

"Indeed." Perhaps she did. The way he was looking at her . . . Her palms were suddenly sweaty. Roisin wiped them on the skirt of her dress. The only one she owned now, stained with soot and singed along the hem. "As for visiting any rebel prisoners there might be, I'll go gladly. If you can arrange for me to be allowed to do so."

"I think I can. If there are any. That's why I suggested it."

Holy Virgin, he must be living in the very pocket of General Howe. "Then of course I'll go. Gladly."

"Good. Should the need arise, I'll send word. And you'll have more medicines tomorrow." Then, as she was leaving, "Mistress Healsall, I knew Cuf most of my life. He was my aunt's—"

"Yes. I know."

"I haven't seen him anywhere. He didn't join the British forces like most of the Negro slaves, did he?"

She was on her way out, and her back was to him by then. She didn't turn around when she spoke. "Why should he? If you know Cuf, you know he's no one's slave."

Andrew moved the lace curtain slightly aside and watched Mistress Healsall and her daughter hurry away, looking like a pair of waifs in their soot-stained, scorched clothing—particularly on Ann Street, where it seemed as if nothing whatever had happened. No foolhardy Declaration. No disastrous one-sided battle over on the long island. No bombardment, no occupation, and no fire. Everything on Ann Street looked exactly the way it had been. But everything was changed.

Except him. He wasn't changed. He was here doing what he'd been doing for the ten years since he returned from Edinburgh. Looking after the sick. And wondering.

Christ, the redhead was beautiful. He'd heard she was. Some said she was Cuf's woman, some said he was only her slave.

Jesus God Almighty. Andrew had always found Cuf pleasant enough. But a white woman lying with a Negro? That couldn't be right. On the other hand, it might not be true. They said Mistress Healsall had a daughter by Cuf, but if so, it wasn't the girl he'd just seen. Those dark blue eyes, those were Turner eyes. Could be she was Morgan's daughter. God alone knew how many bastards his handsome cousin had scattered about the city. A rebel now, if he was still alive. Given the numbers of dead and wounded in Washington's army, there was no way to know.

The secret drawer in Andrew's desk was opened by pressing a lever that could be reached only when the middle drawer was entirely removed. Even then, if you didn't know the lever was there you wouldn't see it. The Scots carpenter had been that clever; every desk he made was different, he'd promised. So at least this side of the ocean, Andrew was the only person alive who knew how to find the hiding place in the desk he'd had shipped over along with his Edinburgh bride.

Andrew slipped out the drawer, then reached in and located the lever by feel. The secret compartment swung into view. And the piece of paper he'd found clutched in Caleb Devrey's dead hand was on top, carefully folded along the original creases. *Seventy-four degrees, thirty minutes west of Greenwich. Just south of twenty-four degrees north. Twice around and thrice back.*

There was only one thing it could be: a sailor's navigation guide. At least the first part was. He was certain beyond any hesitation that Morgan Turner was the sailor in question. And the only reason Morgan or any other sailor would write down something so obscure and terse—twice around and thrice back of what?—was to protect a treasure.

So in Christ's name, after all these years, why hadn't he gone after it? Because he wasn't a sailor. Because he'd have to find someone he could trust to take a ship to wherever it was. And do whatever had to be done to find the treasure. And because the only way he could be sure of getting so much as a smell of the booty—if it was still there—was to go along on the journey. And these last years, with his legless father to look after, and Meg pregnant so much of the time (though only the two boys and their sister had survived infancy)—well, he'd been busy.

He was busy still, with things more important than buried treasure. However much Morgan owed his family for that day outside the almshouse.

Andrew carefully refolded the paper and put it on top of the other things he kept in the secret compartment. Lucas Turner's journals, tied together with Christopher Turner's notes on little worms that might carry disease, and on the art and science of blood transfusion.

The day Andrew heard the Declaration he had gone home and taken the journals and the papers from the shelf and hid them in the desk. As if he didn't want his forebears to watch him do what he knew he must.

Bede Devrey was seventy-four years old and shaking with palsy. He said that was why he hadn't left the city along with the rest of the men of property who shared his view that independence was bad for business, and treason besides. Bede stayed on Wall Street, though he'd sent his ships to ports in Virginia. He said it was to be sure the rebels couldn't use them. That had been before the battle of the long island, when a British victory was likely but not entirely assured. And the way things were, well, it was hard to get word to his captains to take their vessels out and privateer in the British cause. There was a war on, hell damn it!

"Hell damn it, Andrew! You're hurting me! Can't you find anything better to do for this hell damn it shaking!"

"No, Cousin Bede, I cannot." The cut he'd made in the vein at the crook of Bede's right arm was swift and deft; it bled instantly in a steady stream. Meanwhile four large and hairy black leeches were attached to the old man's left wrist. "Please try and be calm. The leeches drink best and deepest when the patient isn't agitated."

"Weak as a kitten I am afterward. No wonder I'm agitated. Hell damn it, boy, it's a wonder I've any blood left."

"Didn't Samuel bleed you when he was treating your palsy?"

"'Course he did. That's all you doctors do, isn't it? Bleed and cup and purge. S'pose that's what Sam's doing now he's gone off to be a rebel. Making Washington's soldiers shit out their watery insides."

"Probably," Andrew agreed. "Helps sometimes."

"Doesn't stop me shaking, though."

"No. Bleeding's best for that."

"But afterwards, I can hardly move."

Andrew watched the flow from the right arm slowly fill a glass flagon with measurements etched on the side. "I haven't bled you in over a week, Cousin Bede. We can take two pints today with no undue effect."

"No hell damn it effect on the bloody palsy, either. And what are you giving me now?" Bede nodded toward the crate of bottles that Andrew had carried in with him. "Another of your filthy drinks? Enough there to see me in my grave from the look of it."

"Nothing in that box is for you." The first of the four leeches tumbled to the bedclothes, fat and sated with blood. Andrew scooped it up and returned it to the jar he used to transport the creatures. "The box is for Mistress Healsall."

"The quack from over the Church Farm way? The one who's supposed to be the almighty glorious looker ran off with Squaw DaSilva's slave Cuf?"

"The very same. She came to consult me this morning."

"She never. Pair of tits could launch a ship, I hear."

"She has. And she did. Come to see me, I mean. Brought her daughter to consult me, to be entirely accurate." The second leech had sucked its fill and let go. Andrew recaptured it. He could easily have effected the entire treatment by cutting, but one of his professors in Edinburgh had speculated that some exchange between the leeches and the patient had a salutary effect in certain instances. Andrew hoped that might be the case with Bede's palsy, though as yet there was no evidence of it.

"What's wrong with her daughter?"

"Mistress Healsall's daughter?"

"Of course, bloody damn it! That's who we're talking about, isn't it?"

"Yes. There, that's the last of them." Andrew scooped up the third and fourth leeches. "I think she was raped. Night of the fire. Left her in a terrible state of shock. One of her nipples was bit nearly clean through."

"Sweet Christ. Makes me sick to think of the number of British bastards there'll be in this town in nine months. I hear Squaw's got another brothel ready for the sailors. None too soon. Useful in many ways."

Andrew looked up. Their eyes met for a moment. "Sure to be useful," Andrew said.

"You can count on it. I'm told that little blond Amarantha lives at Squaw's place is Howe's favorite. Clever lass, Amarantha. Good head on her. Though that's not what interests Howe. Enough said, lad. Now tell me what all that clabber is for, if I'm not to drink it or bathe in it or put it on my bread."

"It's simples, from Craddock's house."

Bede snorted. "How is he, the old bastard? Didn't get burned out, did he?"

"No, Pearl Street was spared. Craddock's the same as always. Doddering about the house talking to himself and drooling."

"But he let you take those stuffs, did he?"

"I didn't ask. Just gave him a sleeping draught and helped myself. He's no use of them now that Phoebe's gone and the apothecary shop is closed."

"It's all closed, in a manner of speaking," Bede said softly. "Nothing will be the same after this war."

The old man's eyes were full of tears. Andrew felt like crying as well. "My grandfather's old house burned to the ground," he said softly. "There's nothing left of it. All Hall Place has pretty much disappeared."

"Shame that is. I always admired Christopher," Bede said. "We were never friends, couldn't be, the way things were with my feckless brother. But I know you were fond of him."

"Very. I spent many happy hours in that house, and he taught me more about medicine than I ever learned anywhere else."

"When to stop as well, I hope. That's bloody enough, Andrew. I feel quite lightheaded."

The blood was edging up to the flagon's pint and a half measure, and the leeches must have taken almost a pint more. "Yes, plenty. I agree." Andrew whipped a leather tie around Bede's right arm just above the elbow and tightened it. Almost instantly the flow of blood stopped. "I'll take a stitch to close the wound. And I'll remove the cups soon as I'm done."

He'd cupped Bede's legs while the bloodletting was going on. The blisters proved to be quite satisfactory, covering both shins from the knee to the ankle. Andrew finished treating his patient and began packing his instruments into his black satchel. "I'll tell the servants to bring you some tea on my way out."

"Tell Nancy to come herself." After forty years Bede was still devoted to his wife. "Tell her I want to see her."

"Very well, I will." Andrew snapped his bag shut. "Cousin Bede, there's one other thing. I daren't show my face around the Church Farm. Can you get someone to bring this box to Mistress Healsall in what's left of the Fiddle and Clogs?"

"Of course. I'll send Raif. No one's likely to blame him for anything. Good or ill."

Raif Devrey, Sam's twin, looked nothing like his brother. Raif stood a bit over five feet, he was fat, and his vision was so poor he had to squint to see anything more than ten inches away. Sam had always refused to marry, but years ago Bede had managed to find a bride for Raif. She died birthing his first child. The babe, a boy, died a few hours later and was buried in his mother's coffin. At thirty-six, Raif had been a widower for twelve years. Also unlike his brother, Raif had no interest in politics. Tory or rebel, it was all the same to him. Raif still lived under Bede's roof and ran any errands his father set him.

"I take it you're Mistress Healsall?"

"No, of course I'm not. I'm her daughter, Clare."

"Oh, I see." The exertion of clambering over the charred remains of the Fiddle and Clogs made Raif's breath come in noisy gasps. "Mistress Healsall," he wheezed, "where is she then?" All the while squinting mightily and staring at Clare.

"Seeing a patient. What do you have there?"

"Simples and such. My father sent them." The darkest blue eyes he'd ever seen. A few strands of hair black as ink peeked out of her mobcap.

"Very well. You can leave them with me."

"I can carry them inside, if you like." He looked around, squinting into the middle distance to see where a door might be.

"I'd like it quite well. But there is no inside. This is where we're living now." Clare indicated the two blankets that hung from the blackened stumps of a pair of beams that once supported the roof of the taproom.

Raif tipped back his head. "The blankets are only horsehair. They won't help much if it rains."

"No, I expect they won't. You can put the crate down over there." Clare pointed at a large flat rock that had once been part of the taproom's foundations.

Raif did as he was told, then looked up, squinting more fiercely then ever so he could take the measure of the expanse between the burned-out roof beams. "I'll be back tomorrow," he said after a few moments. "With enough canvas to make this space waterproof."

"Canvas is hard to come by. General Washington's soldiers emptied all the stores."

"Yes, I know. But I'll get some."

Clare nodded. "Fine. If you can, that would be very nice."

"Yes, it will be," he agreed. "Very nice indeed. Wonderful, in fact."

Raif Devrey had looked into Clare Campbell's blue-purple eyes and his world had stopped, then started to turn in a different direction.

He was back the next day with three huge sheets of well-oiled canvas, and he stayed long enough to help Roisin and her daughter rig a waterproof tent in which to live.

"Moves about a whole lot better than you'd think he might," Roisin said after he left. "Fat as he is, Raif Devrey's light on his feet."

"And kind," Clare added.

"Very."

Roisin heard something in Clare's voice. Not something new, something old.

Two days earlier, in Andrew Turner's consulting room, when Clare whispered that if her mother thought to marry her off to Josie Harmon's nephew she might as well know that Clare would slit her own throat on her wedding day, she'd sounded like someone already dead, a spirit returned from the grave. Now, because a funny little fat man who must be twice her age had brought them a gift—in addition to the wonderful simples—Clare sounded like the girl she'd been. Roisin couldn't fathom why, but she was grateful.

Two months later Clare and Raif were married. The ceremony took place in St. Paul's Chapel. With Trinity a charred ruin, St. Paul's was the most fashionable church in the town. Roisin was intensely conscious of that as she stood and watched her daughter, gowned in exquisite blue satin and elegant black lace, vow to love, honor, and obey Raif Devrey. Clare looked entirely calm and self-possessed, but Roisin felt as if she must pinch herself to be certain she wasn't dreaming.

"You're sure, child?" she had asked a few days before. "Rich as he is, and kind as he is, Raif's old enough to be your father."

"He's thirty-six."

Roisin gasped. Older even than she'd thought. "Clare, you're only sixteen."

"I'm going to marry Raif. If you say no we'll run away."

Ah, Holy Virgin, who was she to stand in the girl's way? There was no passion in it, of that Roisin was quite sure. But what was passion worth to a woman? Hadn't she denied her own passion existed until it was too late, and following her heart would have meant breaking the heart of the best man she'd ever known? "Kindness counts for much," Roisin had said. "As long as you're sure, darling girl."

"Very sure."

And so Clare was. "I do," she said firmly when the vicar of St. Paul's asked if she took this man to be her lawfully wedded husband. Indeed, she repeated it a second time. "I very do." Clare was entirely sure of her decision, but not for the reasons her mother imagined.

"I want to show you something," Clare had told Raif at the end of the first month she'd known him, when he'd come to the Fiddle and Clogs every single day on one or another pretext. "Let down the flap."

Raif's first instinct was always to do exactly what she told him, but that time he'd hesitated. It wasn't seemly. It might lead to his being forbidden to come again. "Your mother," he said. "Mistress Healsall, she might be near."

"She's gone to the court part of town to treat a patient has boils and doesn't want a barber to lance them. Mama will apply mustard and mint plasters to draw the poison. It's a slow business, another hour at least. Go ahead, let down the flap."

Raif did as he was told. Clare struck a spark and lit the stub of a candle—another of Raif's many practical gifts—and in its glow she beckoned him closer. "Come near enough so you can see without squinting," she told him. "There, that will do."

Without another word she unlaced her dress and pushed her bodice down to her waist. Raif wanted to ask what she was doing, but he couldn't speak for the burning. Not just between his legs; all of him was on fire. In an entire lifetime he had never felt as he felt now. Certainly not with his wife, or with the whores who serviced him before his brief marriage, or with those he'd occasionally visited since. Nothing ever had been like this.

When Clare pulled her chemise over her head, her mobcap came off as well. The long black hair fell free and made a curtain that reached to her waist. Clare lifted both hands and pushed it back so it would conceal nothing. Her breasts rose when she moved, defining themselves above her long, taut midriff. Small breasts. He knew they would be firm if he touched them, like a pair of pink-flushed apples. Tart and yet sweet. Delicious to the tongue.

"Do you see it?" she demanded.

"See . . ." He couldn't get the words out. He had to swallow a few times and try a second time. "See what?"

"The nipple of my left pappe. It's crooked. Bend down and take a good look."

He bent his head until his lips were a few inches from her flesh. She smelled of the eau de Cologne he'd given her. She smelled like sweet and endless summer. "Yes," he whispered finally, observing the skewed angle of the small brown stem of the apple. "I see it."

"The wound's healed over now, but the nipple will always be crooked like this. An English sailor did it. I'm not a virgin. Six sailors raped me the night of the fire." Clare spoke the words with no emphasis and no emotion. "One of them did this to my tit." She put her hand under her breast and lifted it even closer to his mouth. Then she put her other hand behind Raif's head.

He dared not move. Her smell was overwhelming him. Her fingers on the back of his neck singed his flesh. He craved to tongue the crooked nipple, desired it more than he'd desired anything in his life. But he knew that if he did not do exactly what she wanted when she wanted, she would send him away and not let him return, and what he'd so recently found to cherish of life would be over.

"No English bastard grew in my belly," Clare said. "My mother used her arts to open me up and scrape their seed out before a bastard could take form." She dropped her hand. Her fingers no longer touched him. Yet his flesh continued to burn. "Now that you know all that, and you see how I'm misformed, do you still lust after me, Raif Devrey?"

"I worship you," Raif whispered. "I love you more than my own life."

Clare backed away. Raif made a sound in his throat, an inarticulate groan of loss. His declaration had revolted her. He should have expected as much. It couldn't be otherwise with someone as beautiful as she and a fat, ugly toad like himself. Tears rolled down his cheeks.

Clare walked backward as far as the horsehair blankets that were folded away in one corner of the makeshift tent. She was still looking at Raif when she lay down on them and lifted the hem of her dress so she was as exposed below as she was above, the cloth of her dress bunched around her waist. "Come here and stick your thing in me."

"What? I don't . . ."

"You heard me. You want to do it, I know you do. I'm saying you may." She spread her legs. "Come lie on top of me and put your cock in my twat. Come ahead and do it. Quickly. Before my mother comes home."

She heard the way he was breathing, as if he was gasping for air. It took him an age to fumble open his trouser buttons and free himself. When he finally managed it and she saw the thing that stuck out in front of him, Clare considered jumping to her feet and telling him she'd made a terrible mistake. But she did not.

She had thought about this for days, knew exactly what she was doing and why. "Come ahead," she encouraged, half sitting up, supporting herself on her elbows. "Do it quickly."

He stumbled forward, shivering with want. Her thatch was as dark black as the hair of her head. He put out one tentative finger and touched it. Like velvet. Like the softest wool of a newborn lamb.

"Come on then," she said softly, lying back and lifting her hips toward him. "Time's wasting." She opened her legs wider. The black thatch parted slightly and he glimpsed the sweet, moist pinkness within.

Raif made a sound between a sigh and a groan. He got to his knees beside her, then lay over her, between her long and tapered thighs, and used his own hand to guide his tool into her. After that, for a long moment, he remained absolutely still, savoring his joy. Simply by uniting himself to her, he had taken possession of her beauty. He wasn't short and ugly Raif Devrey any longer. He was a king, a prince of heaven and earth. Finally, when he could wait no longer, he stroked in and out. Two, maybe three times. Then it was over.

"Are you done?" she asked. He must be. He'd shivered a bit. Now he lay un-

moving atop her, his face squashed up against hers. His cheeks were wet . . .
Maybe tears. First time she'd ever seen a man do that. "Well, tell me, are you finished?"

"Yes, I am. Clare, beloved, listen . . ." He lifted his head and tried to look into
her eyes.

She turned her face away. "If you're done, get off me."

He rolled away and restored order to his clothing. Clare jumped up and allowed the skirt of her dress to fall back into place. She was busy pulling her
bodice up and tying the laces. "Clare," he said again.

"No, don't speak. Listen. I had to know if I could bear it."

"Bear it? Every man, and every woman for that matter, has need of—"

"Don't talk to me of need. Each thing that has been put between my legs has
caused me pain and suffering. I could not face a lifetime of the same. But
you . . ." He was looking at her the way a puppy dog might, his eyes begging her
for something. "You were gentle," she said. "I thank you for that. Will you promise to always be so?"

"I would die before I would hurt you in any way." His tone made the words a
solemn vow.

"Yes, I believe you. Very well, Raif Devrey. I'll wed you. You want to wed me,
don't you?"

He could only nod.

"Fine. Then that's what we'll do. But there's one condition. You can only put
your cock in me . . ." She considered. "Once a month. I'll say when. Do you consent?"

He nodded again.

"Swear it."

Raif swore and the bargain was made.

So they were standing in St. Paul's being married. With no fuss. Another of
Clare's demands. Bede and Nancy said they were too old and ill to attend the ceremony. They were quite overcome with surprise at the fact that Raif had decided
to marry again; they tried to tell themselves it didn't matter that the girl was a
pauper and had a share of Negro blood. Not when compared to the fact that they
might yet have a Devrey grandchild to carry on the name. After the ceremony,
when Raif brought Clare home to Wall Street, they greeted her formally, then
fled to their private rooms.

"Now we're married," Clare said as soon as she and Raif were alone. "Tell me
what you're good at."

"I don't know. How do you mean, good at?"

"Things you do best. I can simple. And cook. And play a bit on the dulcimer.
What can you do?"

He shook his head. "Nothing. I've never been good at anything."

"Nonsense. You help in your father's business, don't you?"

"Well, yes. At least, I did. These days there's not much to do in his business. He's sent all his ships to Virginia."

"When there was much to do, what were you best at?"

Raif thought for a moment. "Figures," he said finally. "I guess I was best at doing the calculations. For the manifests and the like. I'm quick at that."

Clare clapped her hands. "Excellent! Figures are very important. And I know something else. You're good at getting things that are hard to come by. Such as the canvas, and the candles, and eau de Cologne. Right after the fire, when there was nothing to be had anywhere."

He was good at that because those things were for her. He didn't say so, simply wondered if tonight was going to be the once a month she'd promised. If she was true to her word, it might be. The count should start from the day they were married, shouldn't it? And he hadn't touched her since that first time when they became betrothed. Sometimes he thought that had been a dream. "I can find things if they're important," he said.

"We'll need a great many important things. A place of our own, for a start."

"To live in?"

"Yes. And to open our shop."

"What kind of shop?"

"An apothecary. But different," Clare said.

"There's a shop in the Rhode Island colony called a pharmacy," Raif said. "Leastwise there was, before the war. I saw it in Newport once when my father sent me to the town on some business. Owned by a Dr. Hunter; he makes that Number Six Cologne everyone's so mad for."

"Excellent," Clare said, again clapping her hands. "We shall open a pharmacy."

"But we don't have any Number Six Cologne. What will we sell?" She was a marvel. He'd given her money to buy a dress for today, and she had gowned herself in the same color blue as her eyes. That seemed wondrous to him.

"We'll trade in simples. And powder for wigs. And eau de Cologne. Things like that."

"I see. Clare, is tonight to be—"

"Where are we to sleep?"

"In my room. It's up those stairs. I had them put fresh linen on the bed for you."

She tingled at the thought of sleeping in a proper bed with fresh linen. "I'm tired. Let's go up this very minute." When they were halfway up the stairs—Clare leading, as if she were the one born in this house rather than he—she turned and whispered over her shoulder, "If you promise to be quick, you can do it to me tonight."

Chapter Thirteen

"*TOUJOURS LA GAIETÉ,* Mistress DaSilva. *Toujours la gaieté.*"

Exactly what General Howe had said to her in '76, and here it was 1780. Four years and Squaw was hearing the same words from Howe's replacement, General Clinton, who'd been put in charge when London tired of Howe's dithering and delay. And of the fact that New York City was a sink of corruption. General Clinton was not simply a better tactician, they said, he was a man of rectitude.

Henry Clinton visited her house every blessed night he was in New York.

She raised her red lace fan to her lips so he wouldn't see her smile. "I entirely agree, Sir Henry. *Toujours la gaieté.*"

The long room was warmer than she liked it to be, though every window was open to the June evening. Perhaps the heat came from the eight young women present, along with Henry Clinton and six British officers. These days ladies stuck out behind rather than at the sides; the wide skirts over wire panniers that were fashionable when she was young had given way to a craze for crimped and ruched bustles. Made it a little easier to move around. Sitting was more difficult, but given that the girls insisted on wearing three-foot-high wigs, they were better off standing. At least supporting such creations showed off their posture.

Her own red brocade dress had a fine big bustle. She had given up her widow's weeds and her veil the afternoon Howe and his troops rode into the city, when she realized what would be required of her. Now the mantua-maker called regularly—Squaw still never left her house—and everything she owned was the latest fashion. But she refused to subject herself to the weight of a three-foot wig. At sixty-five she wore her yet entirely black hair in the simpler style of noncourt ladies, drawn into a tight roll over either ear.

She fluttered her fan and studied her guest. Sir Henry was craning his neck, examining the faces below the towering powdered and decorated wigs. "I see Amarantha's not here this evening."

"Amarantha's a bit under the weather, Sir Henry. But have you met Gwendolyn?"

Amarantha was upstairs, eating her way through a pound of sugared violets, and devouring the latest pattern books from London. The girl had done her bit. She'd been Howe's favorite for the two years he was commander in chief. He couldn't get enough of her. God only knew how many times Amarantha had gone to Roisin to abort a Howe bastard. And through it all she kept her looks. Well enough so she became Sir Henry's choice from the day he took over. Clinton, however, had a taste for spanking before he fucked. The man had blistered poor Amarantha's backside fourteen nights running. Time to get him interested in someone new.

"Gwendolyn, come and meet the man we can rely on to keep New York a haven of civility despite this dreadful and endless war."

"I am charmed, Sir Henry. Truly charmed."

Her curtsy was perfect. Her tits were divine. And when Gwendolyn took off the powdered wig topped with a wooden ship under full sail, Sir Henry would find her dark chestnut hair a nice change from Amarantha's blond curls. Most important, her buttocks were luscious, two halves of a perfect peach. Squaw DaSilva had carefully inspected all the girls' backsides before deciding that Gwendolyn would take Amarantha's place. As yet Sir Henry didn't know what delights awaited him. He continued to look a bit petulant.

She leaned toward him, whispering behind the cover of her fan. "Lovely, I know, but you wouldn't believe what a naughty lass Gwendolyn can be, Sir Henry. I do think she needs a firm hand. Perhaps a strong man like you could teach her better behavior."

At that moment the young woman playing the hammer dulcimer struck up a lively reel. Gwendolyn put out her hand. "I am most forward, Sir Henry. I know I am utterly reckless and headstrong and require discipline, but I cannot help myself. Will you partner me?"

"With the greatest of pleasure, Mistress Gwendolyn."

Squaw watched for a moment as six other couples followed them to the dance floor. What a good and clever girl Gwendolyn was. What good and clever girls they all were. She had a feeling the night would prove useful. Yes, exceptionally useful. She was sure of it. No one was paying her any mind. She gathered up the train of her gown and slipped out of the long room.

The sprightly notes of the reel and the sounds of dancing feet followed her out the door. For a moment she paused, looking at the ebony walking stick that stood in an urn beside her front door. She'd had the gold horse's head with the ruby eyes remounted some years earlier. All during this miserable war it had stood where it was now, her single reminder of who she truly was. And who she had been.

As if she didn't know. She was a foolish old woman, one who still thought of calling Tilda, though the dear creature had been dead three years. Or Flossie. Dear God, wouldn't it be wonderful to summon Flossie? Ah, she would have made a remarkable ally in this business. Hard to imagine a more passionate patriot than old Flossie; anything that discomforted the English would have thrilled her Irish soul. But Bridget Hagen was also from Dublin, and entirely committed to the cause.

The Irish woman had been born with a grotesque red and puckered gash separating her face from nose to chin; her only speech was a series of grunts, and no one had ever bothered to teach her to read or to write. Bridget Hagen was the last person any English official would suspect of treason. It wouldn't occur to them that she had wit enough for it. She had wit enough to hate them, however.

Bridget was waiting for her mistress in the kitchen by a basket full of soiled petticoats.

"Wash two black and one white tonight," Squaw DaSilva whispered. "Hang them out to dry at first light."

Bridget's disfigured face twisted into a smile, and she selected two black petticoats and one white from the basket. When she hung them in the drying yard at dawn they would signal that there was information to be passed along, and when she went to the meat stall in the Exchange Market on Broad Street, the butcher's wife would be certain no one else waited on her.

Bridget would point to the haunch she wanted and pay for it after it was trimmed and trussed. Prices were exorbitant these days. Food cost eight times as much as it had before the British occupied the town. A whole handful of coins was needed to buy a bit of mutton. Impossible for anyone watching to know that one of the coppers Bridget handed over was specially made to divide into two flat halves concealing a hidden space, or that inside were the notes carefully written by Squaw DaSilva with the finest of quills on the thinnest of paper, after her girls had reported what they referred to as the useful pillow talk of the night before.

Later, because two black petticoats and one white had been hung in the drying yard behind the most fashionable whorehouse in the town, old Nancy Devrey—a widow these past ten months, but done with her mourning and remarkably full of appetite—would send her cook to the meat stall in the Exchange Market. The butcher's wife would serve her as well. And the specially designed copper would be in the change Nancy's cook brought home.

Still later, a pauper woman—never the same one twice—would show up at the kitchen door of the Devreys' Wall Street house and inquire as to whether there was any charity to be had. And so the hollow penny would pass along a chain of women, until it reached the rebel lines. And in a matter of days it would find its way back by the same route, ready to be used again.

So far this particular network hadn't been detected, but none of the women was in any doubt about the risk. Being female wouldn't protect them. Another ring of spies had been discovered a few months earlier; two of its leaders were women. A week after their capture they were trundled through the streets in an open wagon so everyone could see they were half dead from torture, then sent to the prison ship *Jersey*.

Squaw hadn't set foot outside her front door since the moment she'd dropped the rebel standard on the pile of steaming manure and invited General Howe to sample her hospitality, but once a month when the moon was full she climbed onto her roof through the hatch outside Solomon's old room, and using the powerful spyglass that Howe himself had given her when he left New York—*A token of my esteem, Mistress DaSilva; sometimes it can be quite jolly to see close up what's happening through a keyhole, can it not?*—she stood staring at the silhouettes of the prison hulks anchored across the East River, lying off Brooklyn in Wallabout Bay.

All night she kept vigil. Sometimes, if the wind was right, when the sun began to rise she would hear the shouted command that started each day in hell for those aboard: "Prisoners! Turn out your dead."

Morgan. Oh, God, Morgan. If there is any mercy left in heaven, don't let my son be alive to suffer such torment. Let Morgan be dead rather than on one of those ships. Or best of all, let him be alive, fighting with Washington. Free.

Dear heaven, why did she do it? There was no reason to think Morgan Turner was on a prison ship, even if he'd been taken. Captured rebel officers were permitted to rent rooms in the taverns and boardinghouses of the town. Why then did she come up here and stare at the *Jersey* and the others? And why, in her heart of hearts, was she sure Morgan was there, right across the river, suffering unspeakable torment?

Because for four years she had not heard his name.

Just about every British officer serving in the colonies had passed through her long room. Each one, before he fucked his brains out upstairs, told tales of glorious exploits against the Americans. Not a detail was neglected in those swaggering stories, yet not one had mentioned Morgan Turner as being among the rebels defeated, killed, or even met in battle. It wasn't natural. Not to anyone who knew the man her son had been.

She'd gone as far as she dared first with Howe, now with Clinton. Further. "My loyalty to His Majesty is absolute, you know that, Sir Henry. But I am only a weak woman and a mother. Can you give me any news of Morgan Turner?"

Lately she feared she'd asked too often. Clinton had begun to look at her with doubt in his eyes. Particularly after his lusts were satisfied and he was leaving. They'd met in the front hall a few weeks past, in the wee hours. He had stood his ground and she'd stood hers, and she'd seen the way his glance traveled from her to the rooms above where his officers were dallying. Ever since, she'd been having nightmares about the cellar on Little Queen Street where they said the women spies had been tortured. The neighbors all whispered stories about hearing their screams. And she had a feeling her house was being watched. Especially by day, when no British officers were present. Nonetheless, she went on doing exactly what she had done from the beginning. As did they all.

The morning after Gwendolyn's first encounter with Sir Henry she confirmed Amarantha's stories. Clinton liked the girl he was about to paddle to give him the wooden spoon herself, and kiss his hands and beg him to punish her. And she must always be smiling through her tears.

II

They ferried Andrew across the river in an eight-oared longboat. He could smell the prison ships while he still had to shade his eyes and squint into the distance to distinguish their shapes. The stench was of excrement, vomit, and rotting flesh, undercut with the foul reek of the mudflats of Wallabout Bay. "Christ," Andrew whispered. "Sweet Jesus Christ."

"That's the *Jersey,* sir." The midshipman standing beside him in the longboat's bow pointed to the nearest of the hulks. The four men doing the rowing turned their heads away as they moved up on her. Andrew forced himself to look.

The hell ship was splintered and rubbed gray with time and neglect, but her painted waterline was still visible a few feet above the muddy shallows. There were three decks above that, and a fourth structure of some kind had been built on the topmost. "How many men aboard?" Andrew asked through clenched teeth.

"Can't say, sir." The midshipman's voice was neutral. "Hundreds, I expect. They've hollowed her out, of course, to make room for more rebels. She'll never be seaworthy again. None of them will, for that matter."

Over the years there had been as many as twenty of the floating charnel houses anchored off Brooklyn. He counted fourteen today. Moored fore and aft with chains, barely moving, riding, it seemed, under their own death cloud despite the bright afternoon sun. Thousands of men and countless corpses tossed overboard. Nameless, faceless, unrecorded, mourned only by families who never knew their fate. And probably better that way.

He was close enough now to see they had fixed a floating dock and an outside stair broadside of the *Jersey*, and that a guard stood on her forecastle. Andrew wondered what you had to do to draw such godforsaken duty. On the other hand, he'd heard stories about the men who guarded the prison ships. Terrible stories. The rowers, he noted, continued to look away, and a couple of pairs of shoulders were heaving at the stink. For his part, he'd thought his profession had made him immune to any stench, but he couldn't resist covering his nose with his hand.

"We'll be upwind of her in a moment, sir," the midshipman said. "The *Laurel*'s anchored at the head of Bushwick Creek. C'mon, lads, put your backs into it. The doctor's a busy man."

The pace picked up and they rowed past the prison ships. Andrew couldn't help himself. He had to turn and look back. God in heaven, what cause could justify such horror?

"There she is, sir." Pride in the midshipman's voice this time. "There's the *Laurel*."

Andrew faced forward. The contrast was extraordinary. His Majesty's ship-of-the-line *Laurel* was a two-masted, double-decked third-rater that carried a crew of seven hundred, and sixty-four heavy cannon. Her paintwork gleamed, but it was outshone by her brass. The red ensign fluttered gaily at the bow, above a laurel-crowned figurehead carrying Britain's orb and scepter. The air around her offered only the tang of fresh brine. "Sweet Christ," Andrew muttered.

"Beautiful, isn't she, sir?" The midshipman was grinning with pleasure. Andrew didn't reply.

They lowered a ladder for him and he climbed it without once looking down. He'd never had a head for heights. If he could have, he'd have refused this summons, but there was no chance of that. They called the tune and he danced. That was the life of a high-placed Tory. When a pair of strong seamen reached down to haul him the last few feet he surrendered gratefully to their grip.

"Dr. Turner, is it? Welcome aboard the *Laurel*. I'm Captain Gregory." Andrew shook hands with a short, swarthy man who even when he stood still seemed to be strutting. Another man approached. Taller, more dour, bit of a scarecrow. Full black beard. Obviously not interested in fashion. "This is Mr. MacAllister, the ship's surgeon," Gregory said. "He'll look after you while you're with us."

Andrew nodded a greeting, noting that MacAllister's smile didn't reach his dark eyes. Small wonder. It couldn't have been his idea to bring a land-based doctor aboard, much less a colonial. He was civil, though. And making the best of it.

"Yer patient's below," MacAllister said as he led the way aft along the planked quarterdeck. His Glasgow burr was faint. "Mind yer head on the ladderway."

Andrew's heart sank, but it was not, thank God, another ladder, merely steep and narrow stairs. He picked his footing carefully, hanging on to the polished brass handrail, aware that the mahogany walls on either side had been buffed to a high waxed sheen, and that nowhere was there a speck of dust. "Runs a slick ship, Captain Gregory does," MacAllister said.

"So I see."

"Aye, I expect ye do. Here we be. Patient's in the Captain's day cabin." The surgeon swung open a door and led Andrew into a space some eight feet by ten, with a parquet floor and paneled walls painted gleaming white. There was a round oak table with four chairs in one corner, and a many cubbyholed desk in another. Between them was a hammock slung from ceiling hooks, making crowded what would have seemed, for shipboard, a spacious area. "Only other place to put the lad was in Captain's sleeping quarters. This seemed some better."

The head of the figure in the hammock was bandaged, and the eyes closed. Sleeping or unconscious. He'd soon know. Andrew began unbuttoning his coat. "A ship this size, I'd have thought there were plenty of other places to put an injured man."

"Every bit o' space on a ship's accounted for, Dr. Turner, however big or small it is. I promise ye that. Me and t'other officers sleep in the wardroom, and there's twenty midshipman in one cabin on the orlop deck. Crew does everything but shit where they're stationed, next to the guns. Crammed in like fish in a barrel, we all are. I've me infirmary, if that's what yer thinkin', but t'wouldn't do for the likes o' this laddie."

Andrew glanced once more at the patient. Still no movement. "And why is that, Mr. MacAllister?"

"'Cause he's a prize rebel, he is. For the moment, at least."

"Rebel? I never thought—"

"Most important man in the bloody war, to hear 'em talk. For all he ain't a man but a boy." MacAllister pulled one of the chairs forward and sat stiffly, both feet planted firmly on the floor. Obviously he intended to be no part of the examination or the treatment. "At least he's important for the next five minutes. That's how military men are, Dr. Turner. And why an ordinary ship's surgeon wasn't good enough."

"It wasn't my decision to come aboard your ship, Mr. MacAllister. These days I follow orders. So tell me who he is, and your diagnosis."

"Last part's easy. Lad got hit in the head. Brain's addled. I trepanned three places. Didn't help none. Been bleedin' him o' course. That ain't helped much neither. Least not so's ye can see. As for who he is, name's Edward Preble. Father was a general. Potato farmer now, they tell me, but General Preble fought beside Wolfe on the Plains of Abraham afore all this rebellion rubbish. Didn't teach his boy a lot about loyalty, for all that. Young Edward here was captured off a rebel frigate."

"I see. And why did they bring Edward Preble here when they captured him?"

"Didn't. Put him aboard the *Jersey*."

Andrew froze in the act of rolling up his sleeves. "And how long, Mr. MacAllister, did they keep him in that hellhole?"

MacAllister shrugged. "Couple o' weeks. Maybe a month. I've nothing to do with the *Jersey* or any o' the prison ships, laddie, so ye can get that look off yer face. First thing I knew o' this boy Preble was when they brung him aboard the *Laurel* and Captain Gregory said I was to look after him. Keep him alive as long as he was needed."

"Needed for what? It's painfully apparent that the men sent to the *Jersey* are required by no one but Satan."

The Scot shrugged. "I expect that's why this one's no longer there. He's to be exchanged. General Preble's son in return for the son of a loyal British general, I'm told. Don't know which one and don't much care." MacAllister nodded toward Andrew's battered old pigskin satchel. "I see ye has yer own things, but if there's anything o' mine ye can use, just say so."

"Thanks. I'd be grateful for some water. Fresh, not salt."

"'Course. I've me own supply o' that commodity, Dr. Turner. Collected from the steam o' the cooking fire down below. Sweet as ye likes. Very efficient, His Majesty's navy is. I'll be off and get ye a couple o' quarts o' me fine Adam's ale. Won't be long."

MacAllister left. Andrew crossed quickly to the boy in the hammock. Definitely unconscious rather than sleeping. The stubble covering his cheeks was more fuzz than beard. Christ. He couldn't be more than sixteen, and not likely to see seventeen from the look of him. Breathing so shallow his breast hardly moved. And his skin was cold, clammy.

Andrew reached below the blanket and extracted one limp arm. The fingernails were blue, indicating advanced shock, and the crook of the elbow was hatchmarked with small cuts left from the number of times MacAllister had bled him.

He let go of the boy's hand and adjusted the covering to keep him warm. Then, listening for MacAllister's step, he crossed to the desk.

He might have three, maybe four minutes, and the likelihood of there being anything of value in the cubbyholes that were in full view was all but nil. Andrew tugged at the drawers. There were two on either side and they were locked, but the center drawer slid out with no effort. Nothing inside except a few penwipes, a number of nibs, a bit of sealing wax, and sundry other supplies.

At least a minute gone. Not enough time left to work on the locks of the drawers. Andrew turned and looked back at his patient. No change. Jesus God Almighty, he couldn't let an opportunity like this slip away. He made up his mind, pulled the center drawer out entirely and set it aside, then dropped to his knees.

Dust in the cavity. Slick ship or no, this particular spot wasn't often examined.

Every secret drawer might be different, but the principle of the levers that activated them had to be the same. And in the past few years there had been a huge vogue for the damned things.

He ran his fingers along the slides that held the center drawer in place. Nothing. And no joy from the ledge that marked the division between the desk's top and sides. Two minutes at least gone by. A trickle of sweat rolled down his back. Four years he'd been at this. You'd have thought by now it wouldn't make him shake like a leaf in a gale, but it always did, at least on the inside. And the stench of the prison ships lingering in his nostrils didn't help. No, he shouldn't let that worry him. Spies were hanged, without benefit of a trial.

The ridge of beautifully sanded and smoothed wood that marked the mortise joint in the rear left of the drawer cavity yielded to the pressure of his fingers, and the sprung compartment opened soundlessly to his right. It was smaller than the one in his own desk, and shallower. Just big enough for a slim booklet with a dun-colored leather cover, some four inches wide by seven or eight long. He slipped it into the front of his shirt and pushed the secret drawer shut, then stood to replace the desk's center drawer as he heard MacAllister's step in the companionway.

He'd never get it done if he didn't stop trembling. Jesus. Have to get both sides in place at the same time. There. That did it. Just time to turn around and face the hammock.

The door opened. MacAllister held a tarnished copper bucket with a brass handle. Wisps of steam rose around his beard. His eyes measured the space between Andrew, standing with his back to Captain Gregory's desk, and Edward Preble's hammock. "Treatment from a distance," he said softly. "That's yer style, is it, laddie?"

"Sometimes," Andrew said. "When I'm calculating the pitch that's to be needed."

"Needed for what?" MacAllister set the bucket of hot water on the table, but he never took his eyes off Andrew.

"For whatever treatment I decide is called for." Sweet Christ, he sounded like a blithering idiot, and the Scot was nobody's fool. "Of course, in a case like this . . ." Andrew began.

"And just what is the case? Have ye decided that, Dr. Turner?"

"Definitely. The boy's in shock, Mr. MacAllister. He won't live out the night if we don't do something."

MacAllister nodded. "So far I've no cause to disagree," he said softly. "I'd have given him not much more than a couple o' hours meself. So what is it yer proposin' to do, Dr. Turner? What's the treatment that needs to be 'calculated' from over by Captain Gregory's desk?"

"Blood transfusion, Mr. MacAllister." He didn't know he was going to say it until he did. "You've heard of it, I expect."

"No, I can't say as I have. I told ye, I've already bled him. Took a pint mornin' and night since they brung him aboard."

"Yes, I know. Now we're going to put some back. That is, if you're willing."

MacAllister's eyes narrowed. "Put some back? Never heard o' such a thing. 'Course, it's nothing to do with me. Yer the one's in charge o' the lad's care now. If he dies, he does it on yer watch. Captain Gregory's orders. And his came from the admiral."

"Yes, I know. But the real object of this exercise is to save him, and I can't do that without your assistance, Mr. MacAllister. And first we have to push the desk a bit closer to the hammock. Can you help me do that?"

"Push the— I don't understand what yer thinkin', laddie."

"Ah, but you will, Mr. MacAllister. I promise. Come, help me move the desk. We want it a foot or two closer to the hammock. There, that should do it."

MacAllister stepped back and waited and watched. Andrew grabbed his bag, blessing the fact that it had once belonged to his grandfather and that he had never removed the transfusing equipment that Christopher had designed and always carried with him, though as far as Andrew knew the old man hadn't used it again after Red Bess's death. "Would you mind sitting here on top of the desk, Mr. MacAllister?"

"What's wrong with the chairs?"

"Nothing, but I need you a bit higher than young Mr. Preble here. To direct the flow. Yes, exactly like that. Now, we'll roll up your sleeve—"

"I can look after me own shirtsleeves, thanks very much. And I dinna see what—"

"Roll it right up, please. Above the elbow." His hand was shaking when he reached into the special compartment where the brass pipettes, the valve, and the hollow needles were to be found. It was fine. Everything was there.

Bloody hell. He'd never done this before, only heard his grandfather describe it and read the old man's notes. Whatever it was that Captain Gregory had put in his own secret drawer moved beneath his shirt. Sweet Christ, what if it fell out? He turned aside and pretended to cough. The move gave him time to readjust the position of the dun booklet.

"Dr. Turner, I dinna see what yer proposin' t' do here." Like most Scots', his burr got heavier the more agitated he became.

"I'm proposing to save this boy's life, Mr. MacAllister. And since I cannot do so without your active cooperation, we shall be equal heroes when the job is done." Andrew reached into his bag and grabbed a strip of leather, which he wrapped tightly around the other man's arm.

"But in the name o' Almighty God, what— Ow!"

He hadn't been gentle with the lancet. The whole point of using MacAllister's blood was to get the other man so involved in the procedure he'd forget the suspicions that had been apparent when he walked in. "Sorry," Andrew murmured. "Had to be done. Now, we shall simply insert this hollow tube in the incision. There, perfect. Would you mind holding it in place while I prepare the patient, Mr. MacAllister? Thank you. That's fine."

He applied a tourniquet to the boy's arm. A vein popped up, blue and pulsing. He used the triangular blade of the lancet to make an opening and insert another hollow needle. "Now, will you lean forward a trifle, Mr. MacAllister? Yes, exactly like that. Just enough for the other end of the pipette in your arm to reach into his. There. Everything's ready. I'll just release your tourniquet first . . . Now his—"

"Och, laddie, yer as mad a bugger as ever I've met," MacAllister said softly, studying the apparatus that linked him to the unconscious patient. "Madder." MacAllister's eyes were wide with astonishment.

"Not a bugger at all, sir. I assure you. I've a wife and three children to prove it." Sweet Christ, what if young Preble died? Like Red Bess. Grandfather never had the faintest notion why that happened, only the conviction that it had nothing to do with the blood transfusion. *The transfusion would have saved her, Andrew. I'm sure it would have, if the cancer or the surgery hadn't killed her first.*

MacAllister slowly shook his head. "Mad as a hatter," he whispered. "There's some would call this witchcraft, laddie. Ye knows that I suppose. He's a colonial, by God. A rebel to boot. And I'm a Scot. Ye canno'—"

"Yes, I know. But I must. What we have here, Mr. MacAllister, is a patient who is in shock, as we both agree. You have trepanned and bled him, yet he gets worse. Logic suggests the opposite treatment may make him better. Consequently, blood transfusion."

"If that were true, laddie, d'ye not think— Holy God Almighty."

Edward Preble had opened his eyes and was looking at them.

"Here, take a look. Getting it brought me this close to a noose." Andrew held up a thumb and forefinger that almost touched.

Sam Devrey took the dun-colored booklet and flipped it open. He held it closer to the moonlight penetrating the chinks in the rocks above their heads, and studied the first page. "Holy God Almighty! It's the flag code for the bloody English fleet, that's all! I don't believe it. Bloody marvelous, Andrew!"

"Keep your voice down. The redcoats are right above us."

The cousins were in the old storage cellar below the remains of Christopher Turner's house on Hall Place. The house was a charred ruin, but the fire had not touched the meat storage room that Ankel Jannssen had dug below his butcher shop over a hundred years before.

The dark was filthy, rank with the smells of rats and June heat, and with the fear neither man could entirely suppress. They had made their plans back in '76:

"One to side with the British and take every advantage doctoring allows. The other to join Washington's army. Are we agreed?" Sam had asked.

Andrew had hesitated only a moment. "We're agreed."

It was three days after the Declaration had been read, and they'd been in a slop shop where neither was known. It was Sam who had called the meeting, but it was Andrew who flipped the Connecticut penny that would decide the matter, and Andrew who called the toss. "If it lands with the writing uppermost, I take the British part."

The copper landed on the table between them. Neither man had to lean forward to read the stamped words, *I am good copper.*

"Sweet Christ," Andrew had said, staring at the coin. "So I'm to be a Tory, as well as the man all my colleagues most love to hate. I didn't think I'd mind so much."

"Don't mind. Remember what's really behind the ill will of our distinguished medical brotherhood. Hell, Andrew, they're so envious of your skills they piss green when they hear your name. There's not a man among them has a quarter of your reputation for healing, and they know it."

"I just wish—"

Sam had touched his arm. "We all wish a lot of things. Now's not the time. We'll get the job done first."

"I shall do it to the best of my ability," Andrew had promised.

And he had done it as well as he knew how: played out the charade with Sam that night in Bolton's, after he was practically the only doctor in New York who didn't volunteer to serve with Washington's army and every gossip in town called him a coward or a traitor. Swallowed every instinct that made him despise the role of Judas, never letting on to anyone what he really believed. Not Meg. Not his children. Not even his aging, legless father. Except for Sam Devrey and George Washington, there wasn't a human being alive who knew that Andrew Turner was as passionate and committed a rebel as any man in America. "Yes, flag code," he said now. "That's why I sent for you."

Their meetings were arranged by James Rivington, the printer of the weekly *Gazette.* Every issue of the paper bore the king's arms on the masthead, but when the third word of the second paragraph on the paper's front page was "come," Sam Devrey knew he must sneak into the enemy camp and meet his cousin in the old meat cellar. The number of paragraphs in the first column of the next page told him the number of days to wait before making the attempt. The time of the meeting was always the same: midnight.

Rivington had started out a true Tory, but he'd come over to the rebels within six months of the start of the occupation. He didn't, however, know who else in New York was spying for the rebels. Better that way, they all agreed. What you didn't know you couldn't tell, however much you were tortured. Rivington collected his instructions for the secret codes from prearranged hiding places that varied according to the week of the month.

"Absolutely worth coming tonight." Sam flipped the pages of the booklet Andrew had discovered aboard the *Laurel*. "Listen to this, 'Private Signals by Day for the Ships of His Majesty's Line,' and these pictures below . . ."

"I know. I studied it well."

The booklet was full of sketches of flags, carefully divided into segments and colored red and blue, or left natural to indicate white. "The meaning changes according to whether it's Monday or Tuesday and so forth," Andrew said. "Also, whether it's night or day."

"But now that it's been stolen, won't they change the code?"

"I'm betting they won't. For one thing, I don't think this was a booklet in daily use. I think it's some kind of fallback copy the *Laurel*'s captain put by for himself. For another, if he did discover it was missing, I'm guessing he's not the sort of man could bring himself to own up to losing it."

Sam shook his head in wonder. "It's a bloody marvel, Andrew. Worth every risk you took."

As if Sam's risk didn't matter. Or Rivington's. As if what any of them were doing was simple.

Sam put his hand on Andrew's shoulder. "Stop looking so grim. We're going to win, you know. And already . . . You wouldn't believe how things are outside the city, Andrew."

"I would. I hear they're terrible. Bands of runaway slaves preying on the patriot farms. And that half-Jew wretch, Oliver De Lancey . . . I'm told he's head of something he calls Refugees. Marauders, more like. Causing all kinds of mayhem."

"Worse," Sam said, closing the booklet and tucking it inside his tattered shirt. His face was blacked with dirt, he wore clogs rather than boots, and a clever artifice made him look hunchbacked. "Much of that part is worse than anything you've heard. Especially now Ben Franklin's wretched Tory son's put together his Associated Loyalists. Animals, all of them. But there's nothing new about rape and murder and pillage, cousin. Wars have always been the same. What's new is that we've a constitution for the State of New York. The State, mind you, not the bloody king's province. Constitution says there's to be elections for governor, not royal appointments. And they're to be decided by secret ballot, mind you. No more lining up in a field where everyone can find out what you think. And jury trials, same as back in London. No religion to be official, but all comers free to practice whatever mumbo jumbo their superstitious beliefs demand." Sam grinned, and in the moonlight his teeth gleamed white against his blackened skin.

"You think that's better? Everyone choosing his own God?"

"'Course it is. Who's to say the King knows any more about the hereafter than the rest of us do?"

Over their heads the footsteps of a redcoat patrol could be heard marching by. "There they go," Andrew said when the sound faded. "And us right after. Who's to leave first?"

"You go," Sam said. "Hurry home to your pretty wife. There's no one waiting for me. Only . . ."

"Yes. What?"

"Blood transfusion," Sam murmured, tapping the part of his shirt that covered the codebook. "God, I can hardly believe it. Just like Christopher Turner did with old Red Bess?"

"The very same."

"But she died."

"Believe me, I thought of it all the while I was on that miserable ship. Edward Preble, however, thrived. It was truly like watching a miracle, Sam. A minute and a half, no more, and he opened his eyes. And second after second, he just kept getting better. Two hours later, by the time I left their poxed ship, he was sitting up and eating his dinner."

"Amazing. What's the explanation, do you think? For him living and Red Bess dying, I mean."

"No idea. Except that we all know treatments work sometimes and don't work others."

"Indeed. Well, I'm glad the gods smiled on you, Cousin Andrew. Would have been a pity to lose such a gallant ally."

"I rather think so myself, Cousin Samuel." Then, just before he climbed up to what had once been the alley behind his grandfather's Hall Place house, and was now simply a passage through the scarred remains of the old Nieuw Amsterdam neighborhood, Andrew paused. "Sam, tell me something. When this is all over, when we've won—"

"We will win, you know." Devrey patted his chest again. "This will help ensure it."

"I know. And you and I will be back drinking in Bolton's before you know it."

"Exactly."

"So tell me, when that happy day arrives, will you still support two hospitals in the city?"

"Of course."

"But why? It doesn't make sense. All along I thought you were only doing it because of your opposition to me."

"I was."

"Then why pick me to be part of this scheme?"

"Because I knew you not only had the skill for the job, you had the guts. Doesn't change the fact that after we've whupped their arses I shall go back to pissing green whenever I'm told what a magnificent doctor you are."

III

Dawn of the following Tuesday. The wooden wagon piled high with bodies arrived on Duane Street just as Roisin did. She ducked into the shadows of a door across the road from the Rhinelander sugarhouse, clinging to her basket, not wanting to see but unable to look away.

Just as Dr. Turner had predicted, when the prison ships were full, captured rebels were kept in the city. The New Gaol on the Common, the Middle Dutch Church on Nassau Street, and the North Dutch Church on William had all been pressed into the filthy service, and three of the town's ten sugarhouses as well. Each day the dead cart made the rounds.

Two red-coated guards swung open the wide doors once used for rolling out kegs of rum. Five new bodies were added to the heap on the wagon. It was the prisoners had to bring out any who had died during the night, otherwise the corpses were left to rot where they lay. Holy Virgin, help them. The way things were inside, it was a wonder any of the men were strong enough to do the hauling and tossing.

"God damn you to everlasting hell, Joshua Loring." Roisin whispered the same thing a dozen times a day as she went about the city. "May devils burn out your eyes and put hot pokers in your flesh. May you suffer eternal torment."

Joshua Loring was the Boston Tory in charge of providing for the prisons. Two years before, in '77, all New York heard how Loring offered his wife to General Howe in return for a blind eye where certain business dealings were concerned. They all knew Howe had accepted the bargain. Nothing had changed when Clinton took charge; must be he got a share of the profit. Didn't the Holy Virgin herself know Loring had made a fortune twice over supplying the black market run by the quartermasters and barracksmasters of the poxed British army? Meanwhile, once a day, guards tossed a few hunks of salt beef crawling with maggots, and some loaves of bread covered with mold, on the floor of the prisons. It was up to the men to fight over them.

"Unending hellfire, Joshua Loring. Forever and ever, amen." Roisin whispered the prayer aloud and openly sealed it with the sign of the cross. Hatred had made her that bold.

"Any more to come?" the driver of the dead cart shouted.

"No more until tomorrow. On your way." The redcoats swung closed the sugarhouse doors. The driver clucked a signal to his horse and the wooden wheels clattered off over the cobbles. Roisin waited until the wagon had turned the corner, then pasted a smile on her face and crossed the road.

"Good morning, Mistress Healsall. Come to look after your charges, have you?" She was a regular. None of the guards demanded to see her pass.

"I have."

"Then in you go. And mind you, lift your skirts and show off your pretty ankles. That way the hem won't turn brown." He guffawed when he said it. Same as he'd done every time for the last four years. Stupid bloody man. Wicked. They were all wicked. The devil was in them. Eternal hellfire wasn't near bad enough.

The stench was appalling. The sugarhouse was five stories tall, each floor a cavernous open space built for storing vast quantities of sugar and turning it into rum. Now it was crammed with men—no, half-starved skeletons—who lay in their own excrement and vomit, sometimes scratching a final message on the stone walls with their fingernails before they died.

She did what she could. God knows it was little enough. "Mostly," she'd told Andrew Turner, "I just let them know there are still human beings in the world. A smile's as much as I can provide, more often than not."

She couldn't help feeling sorry for Dr. Turner as well, even though she despised his Tory ideas. The war had made him gaunt-cheeked and stooped. And hadn't his fair hair turned white, and weren't his eyes always shadowed black with fatigue? Andrew Turner seemed weighed down with despair. Still, every time they met she railed at him because there was no one else. "And there's nothing you can do? You're Clinton's private physician now, as you were Howe's. Surely you can tell him the prisoners must have decent food. They're starving. Dying like animals, without even fresh air to breathe."

Usually she'd break off about then because of the way he looked at her, his eyes begging to be spared more details. And because sometimes she entertained the notion that Andrew Turner wasn't what he seemed.

The idea had come to her the day she brought Clare to his surgery, and she'd never entirely gotten it out of her mind. If she was right, there was no way he could argue on behalf of the prisoners. There was too much at stake. And the truth was that nothing Dr. Turner could say would change anything.

"If there's any that could be helped by surgery," Andrew sometimes offered, "perhaps I can manage to—"

"Ah, wouldn't that be a waste? You doing something to put yourself in bad with the almighty British. And for what? The condition those men are in, Dr. Turner, they could never survive any surgery. The best you or I can do is let them die in peace. Help them to die in peace if we can."

Thank God and the Holy Virgin she had a reasonably steady source of laudanum. Clare was making as much as each summer's harvest of poppies would
yield. Dr. Turner had given her the receipt. Found it in the old Pearl Street
apothecary, he said, in '78 after Dr. Craddock died. Written in the hand of Sally
Van der Vries herself, Dr. Turner thought.

Mistress Van der Vries, Red Bess, and Tamsyn and Phoebe after her, they'd all
called it Health-Giving Tonic. "Elixir of Well-Being," Clare labeled the tiny vials
she sold for tuppence each in her Hanover Square Pharmacy. Elixir of health-
giving nonsense, as far as Roisin was concerned. She'd never seen laudanum cure
anything, but it gave the worst off a brief period of ease, so she had no hesitation
in using it.

Weak as they were, most of the men knew to open their mouths when she
crouched beside them. Her basket was always full of johnnycakes. She stayed up
half the night making them. It was Raif got her the Indian meal, God alone knew
where. She'd feed each prisoner a bit, watch the man chew and swallow, then, as
long as her supply lasted, Roisin dropped a dose of laudanum onto the man's
parched tongue and laid a cool hand against his hot forehead.

"Thanks, Mistress. God bless."

"And you, soldier. God grant you peace."

Often they asked about the progress of the war and she would whisper what-
ever news she had. Always the truth, whether it was pretty or not. It seemed to
Roisin to demean their suffering and their courage to tell them lies. *We won at
Trenton. Princeton is ours. Brandywine was a disaster for us. The British have
Philadelphia. Burgoyne's surrendered at Saratoga, a great victory for us. Ben
Franklin's in Paris and the French are said to be ready to come in on our side now.
We lost over a thousand men at Germantown. They say conditions for the Ameri-
cans are terrible at Valley Forge.* But year after year, no matter how discouraging
the news, she ended the same way: "Washington fights on. We shall win, you
know. In the end we shall win." The soldiers always smiled.

"Mistress Healsall, come . . ."

The hoarse plea came from some ten feet away, from over where the skeleton
of the huge old wooden still made the shadows deepest. "I'm coming as fast as I
can," she called out. "If I don't make it today, I promise I'll start at your end when
I come next."

"Roisin, please . . . You must . . . Please . . ."

She froze. For long seconds she couldn't breathe. Finally, steeling herself, she
stumbled to her feet.

"I don't understand. The rules say . . . It can't be you, but it is." Rebel officers
were never put in the prisons. They were permitted to rent rooms in the town.

All the same, here was Morgan Turner, lying next to the old still, so weak he could barely lift his head.

"Rules . . . suspended," he muttered. "No rules for me."

She crouched beside him. "Ah, dear God, what difference does it make now? Here, I've a bit of johnnycake left. Open your mouth."

His lips were cracked and they bled when he opened them. She dabbed at the wounds with the corner of her sleeve and put a small portion of the biscuit on his tongue. Holy Virgin, please stop my hands trembling so. It was as if the man she'd known had been sliced lengthwise, and this sliver of him tossed onto the sugarhouse floor. Oh God, oh God. She could count every one of his bones.

"Good," Morgan whispered. "Very good. Best johnnycake I ever tasted." He struggled with the words, but speaking seemed to increase his strength rather than sap it. She'd seen that happen before. Speaking reminded the prisoners they were men. "More," he demanded.

"I've only a bit left. Here." She fed him the last few crumbs, blinking furiously to keep back her tears. She had a few remaining drops of laudanum as well. "Open your mouth once more. I've a simple will help."

"Where's Cuf?" he whispered hoarsely. "How long do we have?"

Ah dear Holy Virgin. He thought they were trysting. "Ssh. Cuf's fine. He's not here. Don't try and say so much now. We'll have time for more later."

She tipped the last of the golden laudanum into her dosing spoon and let him lick it when the syrup was gone. "That will help a little," she promised, taking his hand. He was burning with fever. She felt for his pulse. Weak and erratic. "Morgan." She put her face close to his. He had a full beard, filthy, crawling with lice like the rest of him, but still solid black. Many of the men went white after a few months, if they lived. "How long have they had you?"

"I don't . . . What day is it?"

"Tuesday." Holy Virgin, calm the trembling. He mustn't feel her shaking like this. "It's Tuesday," she whispered.

"Friday when they caught me. I think. I'm not . . ." His words faded and died.

Dear God in heaven. He had not become what he now was in a matter of days. "What month, Morgan? Friday of what month?"

"Foolish Roisin." A laugh in his voice, as if he were wooing her. "Sweet Roisin. It's October. And Howe's come across with his troops, and the ships in the river are blasting away. And they've caught poor Nat Hale. . . ." The words left him and he closed his eyes.

Roisin rocked back on her heels. It couldn't be true. He was describing events that had happened in '76. Four years. It wasn't possible. Her mouth was parched; her tongue felt like emery paper. Still she leaned close and whispered. "Where have they kept you, Morgan? Since they caught you? You weren't here, or I'd have seen you before now."

"We're on the *Jersey,* Roisin," he muttered. "But be strong. They won't finish you unless you let them break your spirit. We're on the *Jersey* . . . No, can't be. I'm dreaming. Roisin, where's Cuf? In the taproom?"

"Ssh. Don't try and talk more now." She put a gentle hand over his eyes so he wouldn't see her tears. "Rest. Only a little time more, then I'll be back."

Roisin knew where she was going the moment she walked out the door of the sugarhouse. Making herself look calm, giving the guards no hint that anything was wrong. Even though her heart was pounding, and blood was ringing in her ears, and she felt as if at any moment her legs must give out.

She kept up her slow, measured stroll as long as the guards could see her. Then, when she turned onto the Broad Way, Roisin picked up her pace until she was almost running.

Duane Street was at the very edge of the city, farther north even than the Common. The only other building this far out of town was the supposed-to-be New York Hospital some of the town's doctors had been building before the war. A barracks for the Hessian troops it was now. Roisin slowed when she passed it, feeling the eyes of the sentries boring into her back.

A few minutes more and she drew level with the almshouse. Sometimes British troops were put in the almshouse hospital; Dr. Turner might be there. She glanced up at the sun still barely clearing the treetops. No, it was too early. Anyway, she couldn't be sure about Andrew Turner. Not absolutely sure.

The farther south she went, the more people were about. Blacks mostly. Crowds of them there were in New York these days, thousands, folks said. Some were runaway slaves, some slaves turned loose by their masters when there was no more money to feed them. All come to Tory New York, where, unlike in places held by the rebels, Negroes were permitted to have a trade.

Dear God, was it any wonder they sided with the British? Those black brigades—the Pioneers and the Guides and the Royal African—that spent all their time terrorizing the patriot farms up in West Chester, or in New Jersey, or over on the long island, could you blame them? Getting their own back, they were. Only Cuf, it seemed, was prepared to die for the rebel cause. Six months since she'd seen him.

At last, the court part of town. Roisin made herself slow to a sedate walk. A few minutes more would make no difference. Holy Virgin, don't let him die. Not now. Not after four years. He's survived so long, don't let him die now.

She was within sight of the Bowling Green. In a few hours, fashionable ladies would be sitting on the benches taking the sun. Tory bitches, every one. This part of town stank of Tory. Whores, the lot of them, whether or not they were paid for their favors. Not a few of the women from these fine mansions had come to her and spread their legs and begged her to rid them of an English bastard. She always shoved the pessary in hard as she could, and next day when she scraped them, she made no effort to be gentle.

Squaw DaSilva's house looked just as it had the first time she saw it, when she drove up with Morgan and his mother and had no idea who they were, only that they'd saved her from the whipper and the pit. She hadn't seen the place since the day she and Cuf ran away, but it looked exactly the same, the yellow brick facade and the double doors just as grand and imposing.

She half expected Mistress O'Toole or Tilda to come to the door. Instead it was opened by a woman with a hideous harelip. Her mother always said a babe was born so because the devil and an angel fought over it, pulled it in two directions. That's why there was no cure. *If heaven and hell couldn't settle the matter, there's nothing to be done.*

"I want to see Squaw DaSilva."

The woman grunted something and shook her head. She tried to shut the door, but Roisin put all her weight against it. "Don't you dare turn me out! Get your mistress. Tell her Roisin Campbell has news of her son."

"It's all right, Bridget. Let her come in." The voice came from the top of the stairs.

Bridget stopped struggling with the door. Roisin nearly lost her footing and stumbled into the hall.

Squaw DaSilva hurried down the stairs, emerging from the shadows into the greenish light that came from the two long stained-glass windows either side of the entrance. "What do you want here? Do you know something about Morgan?"

It wasn't yet nine in the morning, in a house that did not go to bed until dawn. Squaw DaSilva had thrown a silk wrapper over her nightdress when she heard the commotion at the door. It was the first time Roisin had ever seen her without the veil and the black dress. Holy Virgin, the Squaw's eyes were exactly like Clare's. No wonder Morgan had guessed as soon as he saw the girl.

Roisin's heart was pounding as if it must come out of her chest, and she was shaking so she couldn't hold her basket. She let it fall and pressed her hands to her breast. She was sure she was going to faint.

Squaw DaSilva put an arm around her shoulders. "Here. Come inside and sit down. Bridget, bring sack." She wanted to shake Roisin, but there would be no information until the wench had regained her wits.

The long room was only half cleaned. Bridget's brooms and mops were standing beside an open window and the smell of last night's Tokay and tobacco lingered. Squaw sniffed. Her visitor was no more pleasant. The few weeks she'd lived in this house Roisin had been fastidious. Today she smelled as if she'd waded in a sewer.

Bridget brought the wine. Squaw took the glass and held it herself to the other woman's lips. "Here, drink some of this. It will help you regain your senses." Roisin took a few sips. Some of the color returned to her cheeks. "Now tell me about Morgan. For the love of God, you've a child of your own. Have a mother's pity. Tell me."

"He's in Rhinelander's sugarhouse up on Duane Street."

"He's alive! My son is alive!"

"Yes, but—"

"Tell me!"

"Morgan says . . . He's addle-minded, not all his wits are in place. He says . . ."

"What? For God's sake, don't keep me in suspense!"

"He says"—she couldn't get her voice to rise above a whisper—"Morgan says he's been a prisoner on the *Jersey* these past four years."

Squaw couldn't repress a groan. "Four years. It's not possible. No one could live four years—" But dear God, hadn't she known all along? When she stood on her roof and stared at the devil ships, hadn't she known? "How is he?" She was screaming now, digging her fingers into Roisin's shoulders. "Tell me the truth! How is my son? What have they done to him?"

"I came here to tell you the truth. Morgan's alive. But only just. If we don't get him out of that place, he won't last the week."

As instructed they brought the carriage as far as the corner of Warren Street and the Broad Way and waited. The night was black, the streets silent. Twenty minutes ticked by. Half an hour. Squaw's hands were clenched so tight her nails dug into her palms. Two days it had taken to make the arrangements to free her son, the first few hours spent in deciding how to go about it.

Every instinct drove her to run at once to Sir Henry Clinton and either throw herself on his mercy or threaten to expose his relationships with Amarantha and Gwendolyn. But she was sixty-five years old. She had learned well the lessons Solomon set out to teach her all those years ago. Battles are won by the clever, not merely the powerful.

If Henry Clinton had an ounce of mercy in him there would be no more prisoners on the *Jersey*. As for the threats, no wife of any serving British officer would be shocked to know her husband visited doxies. Mrs. Clinton was probably grateful it was the whores' backsides he reddened rather than her own. And Henry Clinton was commander in chief of the British forces in America. Anyone with authority over him was in London, not New York. No scandal made by the most notorious whoremistress in New York could touch him.

No, this problem could be solved not with influence but with money. In New York, freedom, like everything else, could be bought. Not from Clinton. He was already too rich. The redcoats guarding the sugarhouse, they were the most likely to sell. But they would be taking a considerable risk. She'd have to make it worth their while.

It was a delicate calculation. She settled on fifty golden guineas, about equal to what her house earned in a week, and a fortune to an ordinary soldier. But not so much as would make him think the prize to be so valuable he'd gain more by reporting the offer than taking it up.

They decided Roisin would make the approach. Easier for her, since her presence at the sugarhouse was expected. Fifty golden guineas for the man lying next to the still on the ground floor. The one with the black hair.

"And why's he so valuable, then?"

"'Cause I say so, that's why."

"Not good enough. Not if I'm gonna be putting me neck in a noose to help."

"A noose for a half-dead rebel prisoner? Give over! Besides, it's not me you're helping. It's yourself. Fifty guineas. What'll that buy when you go home?"

Jesus bloody Christ. What wouldn't it buy? His own forge, for a start, in the Somerset village where he'd grown up. "Where you gonna get fifty golden ladies?"

"That's not your business, neither. All you has to know is that I got 'em." Roisin stepped closer. "Put your hand down my bodice," she whispered. "Pull out what you find."

They were alone in the clump of trees by the edge of the Common where the guards went to relieve themselves. All the same, the redcoat glanced over both shoulders before accepting her invitation.

Nice pair, even if she weren't all that young anymore. But tits were easy to come by; money was something else. He felt a leather pouch and yanked it free. "This here ain't heavy enough to be fifty guineas."

"'Course it ain't. What kind of fool do you take me for? That's a bond, like, they call it. There's fifteen guineas in that pouch. Bring me the man I want, tomorrow night, you'll get thirty-five more."

The redcoat considered for a few seconds. Finally he'd nodded and shoved Squaw DaSilva's pouch of coins down the front of his trousers and turned and left.

It was at least half an hour past midnight. Dear God, Roisin thought, if she had to fight back her tears, how terrible must it be for Morgan?

She had whispered the plan into his ear earlier that day. "In the middle of the night. A big guard with great broad shoulders and fair hair. He'll carry you outside. A carriage will be waiting."

"What about the others?" Morgan was more lucid, as if conspiracy revived him. "Will any raise the alarm?"

"No," she'd whispered. "There's plenty as are taken out of here in the middle of the night. I promise you, it will cause no astonishment."

Holy Virgin, who would believe she'd find a reason to be grateful to that devil incarnate, Provost Marshal Bill Cunningham? Walking about the prisons cracking his whip, known to have men brought to him at any hour a sadistic whim moved him. Said to quietly hang them when he was done.

"Don't worry about anything." She'd breathed the words into Morgan's ear, stroking his forehead. "Rest now. Wait. The guard will come for you." All day and half the night, believing his ordeal was almost over. How bitter Morgan's disappointment? Her own, terrible as it was, could be nothing by comparison.

"Look!" For the dozenth time Squaw DaSilva had moved aside the curtain of the coach and peered into the black night. A shape was moving toward them, barely discernible in the darkness.

Roisin pressed her face to the window of the carriage. "It's him!"

The older woman threw open the carriage door, leaning forward. "Morgan," she called softly into the night. "Morgan."

"Ssh!" the guard hissed, and when he was close enough so they could hear his whisper, "Keep yer mouths shut. Cunningham came to call tonight. He's still in there. That's why I'm late."

Squaw barely registered his words. She reached out her arms for her son, but the guard ignored her and without releasing his grip on Morgan shoved his face toward Roisin's. "Gimme me money."

"It's here." She thrust the pouch at him. Better if it came from her, they'd decided. Best would have been if Squaw DaSilva waited at home, but she could not bring herself to do so. "It's all there," Roisin said. "Thirty-five golden guineas. I swear it."

He hesitated. Roisin knew he wanted to go off and count the coins before giving Morgan up, but he couldn't risk being gone a second longer than necessary. "Here. Take him. Good riddance."

The guard slung his burden onto the seat next to Roisin. Morgan's eyes were closed. He didn't move. They were too late. They'd claimed a corpse.

"Morgan." His mother spoke her son's name aloud. She slipped to her knees between the seats of the carriage and pressed her ear to his heart. "He's alive," she whispered. "We can—"

"Hush!" Roisin whispered urgently. "Listen!" Hoofbeats. Coming toward them.

"Get out!" Squaw flung open the carriage door. "Climb up with the driver."

Roisin understood at once. No way on God's earth the carriage could outrun a rider on horseback. She jumped to the ground, hoisted her skirts, and used the spokes of the tall front wheel to clamber up to the driver's perch. "Quick! Put your arms around me. Someone's coming. We must look like trysting lovers."

She tossed her red hair into disarray and tore at the laces of her bodice as she leaned toward him. "For the love of God, man, what are you waiting for? Put your arms around me!"

She'd only had an instant's glimpse of the coachman when the journey began. He was clad in black breeches and a black jerkin and his face was shadowed with a broad-brimmed black hat. He kept the hat on when he turned toward her and put stiff arms either side of her waist. "Heaven help us," Roisin said. "You must be the most awkward lover ever— Dear God."

She was staring into the face of Squaw DaSilva's maid. Bridget.

The sound of the horse's hooves grew louder. Roisin closed her eyes and wrapped her arms around the other woman's neck and pressed her mouth against Bridget's deformity.

The hoofbeats were a drumbeat of terror. Only a few seconds more; then he'd have passed them by. But the sound of the horse's hooves didn't fade away as she expected it to; they stopped abruptly. There was silence, then: "Well, well. What have we here?"

She knew the voice. All New York knew the voice. And the crack of the whip.

Roisin didn't let go her grip on Bridget. She put her face over the other woman's shoulder. Bill Cunningham's pockmarked face was barely visible in the faint starlight. "How about it, gov?" she called gaily. "Care to be next? Won't be a long wait. This one's almost done. Sixpence for a fine-looking gent like you. A bargain."

Cunningham didn't answer. Just sat on his horse and studied them. The woman, the coachman, the impressive black carriage. "Well," he said. "Well."

Roisin took some comfort in the fact that he didn't get off his horse. Gossip said it wasn't women gave Bill Cunningham a hard dick. Maybe it was true. If it were not, and if she had to, she'd lie with him. "How about it, gov?" she asked again.

"Fine carriage," Cunningham said. "Remarkable. Count the folks in New York City has a carriage like this on the fingers of one hand."

She couldn't think of anything else to say or do. Her arms were still around Bridget and she could feel the other woman trembling. Maybe she should get down and let Cunningham get a good look at her.

Suddenly, without another word, the provost marshal dug his spurs into his mount's sides and snapped the reins. The horse reared, then wheeled around and galloped into the night.

Inside the carriage Squaw held her breath until the sound of hooves had entirely died away. Then she put down the pistol she'd taken from the folds of her bustle.

She'd been pointing it at Morgan's heart.

He had regained consciousness and was watching her.

These past two days she'd tormented herself thinking that four years on the *Jersey* must have made him mad. They had not. They'd confused him, perhaps, but the look of loathing in his eyes told her he was basically sane. "I'd have shot you myself," she whispered. "In an instant. Anything rather than let them take you back into that torment."

"Canvas Town, most folks call it." Roisin kept talking while she tried to make him comfortable. The escape had left him weaker than he'd been before, though she wouldn't have thought it possible. His breathing was shallow, and when he exhaled she heard a terrifying rattle in his chest.

"We're better off than many. We've plenty of sailcloth. Enough for both roof and walls. 'Course it's not so grand as your mother's house, but we couldn't take you there. Not after Bill Cunningham saw her carriage."

"Where's Cuf?" He was straining to sit up.

"Not here, Morgan. Cuf's not here. You remember, he's with General Washington's army. I haven't seen him in three months, not since we won at King's Mountain down in Carolina. Cuf sneaked home for a few days after that. He said the French were the reason we've— Ah, God, you don't know about Lafayette and the French, do you? I'll tell you the whole story. But not now. After we get you well."

She was brewing a tea of willow bark while she spoke, heating the kettle over the makeshift fireplace of stones and rubble. Twice the normal strength she made it, because sure God, he had to be free of the pain if he was to make any progress healing. And how much pain must he have? She had examined him all over when she laid him on the blankets in the corner, felt the remnants of at least a dozen old fractures. "No end to the beatings," the prisoners sometimes whispered, staring into her eyes when she fed them, grabbing her arm in their urgency to communicate. "Over and over again they beats ye. Till ye can't do nothin' but pray to die." At even her lightest touch Morgan winced.

"Here we are." Roisin added a heaping spoonful of honey to the willow bark brew and stirred it until it was entirely dissolved. Nearly the half of what honey she had, but never mind. Raif would get her more. Amazing Raif. He could find anything, though God alone knew how.

"Here, let me put my hand behind your head so you can drink this." She lifted him slightly and held the cup to his scabbed-over lips. A thin china cup, such as the gentry drank from. The only one she had, and she couldn't remember where she'd found it. Only thank God she had, because it was easier on Morgan's wounded mouth than pewter would be. "Good. Very good. You've drunk the whole thing. Rest a moment, and I'll get you something else."

She let him lie back and foraged through the hole in the ground that passed for her larder. "I'll send food and drink and everything you might need immediately," his mother had said when they parted.

"Send nothing," Roisin insisted. "It's too dangerous. I'll meet her"—nodding toward Bridget—"tomorrow morning. Outside the Exchange Market. She can give me a few things. Only as much as will fit in my basket, mind."

Squaw DaSilva knew Roisin was right. "Very well. Enough for a day or two. Then you'll meet again."

But Roisin wouldn't meet Bridget until tomorrow. Tonight she had only her own resources. "I've a bit of johnnycake." She unfolded the square of cloth she'd wrapped it in. "And a sliver of rabbit." She turned to smile at him. "It's a supper of sorts."

"Your hair," he whispered. "You're not wearing a mobcap. Not when you came to . . . to that place either. I thought I'd dreamed it. All your red hair showing."

"And don't you sound more like yourself by the minute? As for my hair—" Roisin pushed her curls back. "Mobcaps are out of fashion. No one wears them these days. Now, your supper."

She fed him the tiny quantity of food slowly, making him chew each bite, and not giving him the next bit until he had.

"I haven't . . ." Morgan whispered. "All the while, on the *Jersey* . . . never tasted any meat."

"Tomorrow," she promised. "You'll have more. Your mother will get us some." His eyes turned cold. "Ah, dear God, let it lie, Morgan. No quarrel with her means anything now. Anyway, it's not just the Squaw who'll get us things. Clare's married now, these past five years. Wanted me to live with her, leave this place. But I couldn't do that. Not while the British are here. Have to protect Cuf's—" She saw the way he looked when she mentioned Cuf's name and broke off. Foolish to remind him of all that.

"Clare has a set of fine twins, Molly and Jonathan they are. Two years old. Only she never bred except that once. Popped out a boy and a girl in one go and must have decided that would do her. She hasn't gone back to the birthing bed since." Morgan smiled and it joyed her heart. "'Course Clare always does exactly as it pleases her to do. Her husband lets her lead him around by the nose and loves it. He's a funny-looking little fat man. Cousin of yours, Raif Devrey. Do you remember him? A wonder for coming up with what's needed no matter what. Here, the last of the johnnycake. Chew it well."

"Never had anything to do with the Devreys," Morgan said. "Except—" He broke off, looked agitated. "Except— What's his name, Roisin?"

"Hush, Morgan, hush. You've been through a terrible time. Later you'll remember everything. Now you'll rest."

Rest. How long since he'd rested in a place that didn't stink. Smelled like Roisin, this place did. Sweet. Must be that little room above the taproom where she and Cuf . . . Cuf. Roisin was his. Cuf's woman. Cuf was fighting, she said. With Washington's army.

"*I am a captain serving in the army of the Continental—*"

"*You're a vertiginous rebel and you turn my stomach.*" *General Howe staring at him with such hatred as he'd seldom seen. And the ashes of New York not yet cold.* "*And you are quite probably an arsonist.*"

"The rules," Morgan muttered. "I told him about the rules."

"Ssh, Morgan. It's all right now. We're safe. There are no rules here. Sleep." She stroked his hollow cheeks. "Sleep."

"*There are conventions, sir. A captured officer is permitted to find quarters in—*"

"*Not you, Captain Morgan. Not bloody you. I am well acquainted with your exploits. You're a pirate, Captain Morgan, so we'll put you back on a ship. I've a fine one for you. We call her the* Jersey."

Thought I'd die on the Jersey, *didn't you, General? Might have, except for the fact that one of the guards had served with me aboard the* Fanciful Maiden. *Turned Tory, but didn't forget the old days. Extra food sometimes, a little ale . . .* "He helped, Roisin. Helped for a long time . . ." "*Got a chance to get you off this hell ship, Cap'n sir. Overcrowded we is. Though how they'd decide so in a place like this I can't be saying. Anyway, they's movin' some of the prisoners to jail on the morrow. I'm gonna put you in with 'em, sir. Live through the journey, maybe you'll have a chance.*" "God bless his soul, Roisin . . . Helped me . . ."

"Then God will surely bless him. Odd, isn't it, how sometimes there's more help than you think. Andrew Turner now, you may not believe it, but I think . . ." She let the words trail away. The willow bark tea and the food had done their work. His eyes were closed and she could tell from his breathing that he slept.

Roisin took up the single candle she'd lit earlier and carried it a few feet away to the far corner of the tented space. One thing she'd resisted was sleeping in the same dress she wore by day. She had only one frock, but she aired it overnight and slept in a homespun shift and a woolen shawl. She draped herself in the shawl now, then slipped the dress off underneath.

There was a well not far away, and each morning Roisin drew a bucket of its brackish water and stored it near the flat rock that served for a table. Now she took the small square of homespun that was her washing cloth, dipped it in the bucket, and sponged all parts of herself, afterward rubbing her skin dry with a corner of the shawl. *Holy Virgin, if this war is ever over, let me live long enough to have at least one more proper hot bath beside a proper fire. And if I could have a piece of scented soap, I'd count myself ready to die and go to heaven.*

"Roisin."

She heard his whisper and turned to him, clutching the shawl over her nakedness. "I thought you were sleeping."

"I was a bit, but I woke. I . . . Please, the water . . ."

"Ah, it's not fit to drink. I've a few swallows of ale. Or I can make you a tisane."

"No, I don't mean that. I . . . Could I wash a bit?"

"Holy Virgin, I never thought . . . Of course. Of course."

She grabbed the bucket of well water and carried it to where he lay and knelt beside him. "That first night I ever saw you," she whispered while she dipped the washing cloth and rung it out and sponged his face and hands and arms. "Mistress Flossie told me how you liked nice things, clean things. Nearly scrubbed the skin off me while she did it."

"That's good," he murmured. "The water on my face, it feels so good."

"Tomorrow, if you like, I'll get hold of a blade and shave off that filthy beard."

He lifted his hand to it. "Yes, I'd like that." Then, sounding suddenly more like the man she'd known than anytime in these last miraculous and terrible few days, "How beautiful you are. Still."

The shawl had slipped off her while she cared for him and she had completely forgotten that she was naked. "Not like I was," she whispered, looking down. "It's all sags and droops now." She reached for the shawl and wrapped herself in it once more.

"Beautiful," he said again.

Roisin had planned to sleep across from him, near the tent flap, so she'd hear if something untoward happened. But the idea that anyone would miss a prisoner from one of the sugarhouses, much less come looking for him here, was preposterous. Then again, so was everything that had happened these past few days.

So was the notion that she had some kind of propriety to maintain in the face of so much loss and misery.

"Here," she said, lifting the blanket she'd spread over him. "I'll help to keep you warm."

Morgan turned to her. Unthinking, with nothing but instinct to guide him out of the fog that much of the time gripped his brain, he pressed his mouth to her breast, closing his bruised lips around the nipple.

So they passed the night.

The whip cracked for the seventeenth time. "Talk, ye bloody bastard. Talk!" Cunningham wiped the sweat from his face and turned to the boy who was watching. A soft-faced boy, too young for even a proper beard. And terrified. It showed in his eyes.

"More salt," the provost marshal said. "Get it from out back." The boy ran to do as he was bid and Cunningham leaned down, closer to the naked man fixed to the long bench. "Not much skin left on this side o' yer frame. And when the next lot o' salt comes and I drizzle it over them wounds . . ."

The man groaned, but so quietly it almost couldn't be heard.

"And when that's done, we'll undo them chains and roll yer wretched self over. Interestin' what a whip can do to a man's prick and balls. Very interestin'. This, this ain't nothin'." Cunningham raked his fingernails down the flayed flesh of the victim's back.

There was another sound, not much louder than before. Big the bastard was, broad-shouldered and fair-haired. From Somerset he said. A stalwart type. But they were all stalwart. For a time. "'Course, it don't have to be so hard. Ye wants this to be over, only thing ye has to do is tell me why Squaw DaSilva's bloody great black carriage was outside Rhinelander's sugarhouse this night. Yer the chief guard, ain't ye? Ah, here's the lad back. With the salt."

It took ten minutes more. After the salt on his back, followed by a dozen lashes on his chest and his belly. Then, after the first one that landed on his privates, the groans turned to screams. "Enough! Enough! I'll tell ye!"

"'Course ye will, boyo. 'Course ye will. Sing sweet as a bird, won't ye? They al'ays do."

Cunningham flung the whip aside. It satisfied him only up to a point, and the point came more and more quickly these days. Soon as he broke 'em, he was bored by the effect of the lashes. Except that this time there was a reason for it. "I'm waitin', boyo. What was Squaw DaSilva's carriage doin' up there near Duane Street?"

"Don't know nothin' bout her. It was . . . Jesus God Almighty . . . Can I have some water? I can't—"

Cunningham dropped to his knees and took hold of the guard's fair hair, yanking his head back so the eyes, glazed with pain, were staring straight into his. "Ye thinks ye've felt the worst of it, ye bloody son of a bitch, think again! Next thing I'll give ye water up yer nose and up the hole in yer arse, until ye blows up and bursts like the bag o' shit ye be. Now talk!"

"She wanted a prisoner. Had to bring him out."

"Squaw DaSilva? Wanted one o' them half-dead bags o' lice and stink? Which one?"

"Don't know. Lying by the still, she said—" The words were replaced by gurgling in the man's chest. A trickle of blood began from the corner of his mouth.

"Talk to me, ye son-of-a-bitch whore!" Cunningham roared. "Squaw DaSilva, who'd she want?"

"Golden ladies . . . Fifty of 'em. Enough for me own forge back in Somer—"

Blood poured from both sides of the guard's mouth this time. Then the silence of death and the stench of excrement as the corpse's bowels emptied.

"Bloody son of a bitch! Bag o' shit!" Cunningham's chest churned with rage. A torrent of sweat poured off him. He knew the man was dead, but he banged the head on the wooden bench until the skull split and the brains oozed. "Bloody useless son-of-a-bitch whore!"

The boy saw the whole thing. He was a bugler. Twelve years old and served a year already. Been up at Stony Point and seen how terrible it was when the rebels won. Him sounding the retreat the way they told him, and the redcoats goin' on gettin' killed anyway. Nothin' like this, though. Never seen nothin' like this.

The guard's head was mush. The provost marshal staggered to his feet, heaving with rage. Squaw DaSilva. As powerful a woman as could be found in New York. Had the ear of those in charge in the city. So why would she pay a guard to . . . ? Jesus bloody Christ, Morgan Turner! Somehow or other, she'd found out her son was in Rhinelander's. Not something the Squaw would talk to Clinton about. She'd talk to him, though. To keep anyone from looking for the escaped rebel prisoner, she'd definitely talk to the provost marshal o' the whole poxed city. Fifty golden ladies, eh? Ten times fifty. Squaw DaSilva could afford it.

Cunningham turned to the boy cowering in the corner as if seeing him for the first time. "Looks like a little rat, ye does, boyo. Well, ye ain't had nothin' to be feared of, not yet. Come here."

Cunningham was naked from the waist up. He yanked at the buttons of his breeches and let them drop. "On yer knees," he told the boy, grabbing the sides of his head. "And if I feel a single one o' them sharp little teeth, I promise ye I'll knock every bloody one of 'em out o' yer bloody mouth."

Chapter Fourteen

CUF RODE alone down the Broad Way, wearing the flannel jacket, homespun shirt and leather breeches that had been his particular uniform through most of the rebellion. He attempted to keep his eyes only on the road ahead of him. As for the other people milling about the town, none paid him any mind. Too preoccupied with their own griefs and worries.

The date of the official British evacuation of the city was set for November 3, 1783. Two days to go, but a great many patriots, the New Yorkers who'd fled the occupation, hadn't waited. They'd been flocking back for weeks now. And sweet Christ in heaven, look what they'd found.

The streets were strewn with garbage and a fecal stench hung in the grayed autumn air. Houses had been used for stables—or worse, privies—and birds and rats nested in ruins no longer fit for human habitation. Most of Manhattan's trees had been dug up, even on much of the Broad Way. Used for fuel mostly, or as here at the corner of Maiden Lane, cut down to make a barricade that was still in place because no one could be bothered to remove it.

Cuf turned his horse east. He had to go as far as the river before he found a way to turn again toward home. For a moment, before he put it behind him, he stared at the wreckage that had been the landing of the ferry to Brooklyn over on the long island. First day he ever lay with Roisin, they'd taken that ferry. A penny each for the ride. And he'd made her pay so everyone would assume he was her slave. Not far wrong.

He shivered as he did every time he thought of that Brooklyn beach. He could still remember how it had felt, lying over her in the sand that first time, knowing he was opening a door he'd have better left shut, but powerless to do anything but what he did. Mostly he didn't regret it. More than twenty years they'd been together. But during the last seven of them—him off with the army, seeing her so seldom—he'd lain with a few others. Black women and white, moving between two worlds the way he always had, never one thing or the other, despised by both. Mostly, it didn't matter. Mostly, the women didn't matter, either. Only Roisin.

The shore each side of the ferry landing was a string of neglected, crumbling wharves. Seven years of misery and cold and semistarvation, fighting and risking and daring, insinuating himself where white men couldn't go. He was never suspected as a rebel because of the color of his skin. For what? To come home to this desolation. And all the while remembering the general's farewell. Two years back, after the siege of Yorktown, when Cornwallis finally surrendered, Washington had grasped his hand.

"It isn't over yet, Cuf. I'm asking you to remain with General Lafayette and the French forces. They have need of someone who can go among the enemy with relative ease. Will you stay?"

"Yes, sir. If those are your orders, sir."

"They are, Cuf. But I'll never forget you. Your country owes you much."

His country. Perhaps. Only back home, in Virginia, the general owned Negro slaves. Was it their country, too?

He wheeled the horse around and rode west on Wall Street to Trinity Church. It was a burned-out hulk, brooding over the remains of what had been the busy Church Farm district. That was Canvas Town now, a place of suffering and want.

He knew his bit of canvas from the rest only by the mark he'd made on his last visit, nearly three years past, after the campaign of the Carolinas. They sent him sneaking back into New York for a day or two, and he managed to spend one night with Roisin. He'd used his knife to scratch the words on the charred beam in front of her hovel: "The Fiddle and Clogs Taproom. Cuf, Proprietor and Landlord."

There was a small lad sitting in one corner, with fat rosy cheeks and red curls. Couldn't be more than a year or two. "Clare's boy?" Cuf asked.

Roisin shook her head.

"Whose, then?"

She turned away from him. She'd touched him only once since he had come home. One quick kiss of welcome, and kind words about how glad she was to see him. Many kind words. Now she spoke only two. "He's mine."

"But not," Cuf said softly, "mine."

Sweet Jesus. Where had those words come from? He wanted them back. "Not mine," he said again, the voice rising out of pain somewhere deep in his gut.

She was crying without making a sound; tears were rolling down her cheeks. "No, Cuf," she whispered. "He's not yours."

Cuf thought he couldn't breathe. Stupid, he told himself. Bloody stupid. Seven years and he'd been home to her four times all told. So maybe once she'd lain with someone else. Maybe even twice. That wasn't unforgivable, considering all the things that marked their lives together. Except . . . "You didn't have to bear him and shame me, did you? You know how to end a breeding. That's what the sea gift is for, isn't it?"

"I didn't think you remembered. About the sea gift."

"I do. I remember everything about that day on the beach. So this boy, you needn't have—"

"I wanted him." Roisin went to stand beside the child and put her arm around him. As if Cuf might try to take him away.

The gesture made him angrier than her admission of lying with someone else. "I'd never hurt him. Christ Jesus, Roisin, don't you know I'd never hurt a child?"

"I know." Talk of something else, she told herself. Anything else. Anything so he doesn't ask the next question, the hardest one. "Cuf, are you hungry? Thirsty? I haven't much, but—"

"I want nothing. What's his name?"

"Joyful Patrick."

"It's a strange name."

"Maybe. Joyful for how I felt, and Patrick for the Irish in him." She touched the lad's red hair.

"That's all? Just Joyful Patrick?"

Holy Virgin, help me not to be such a coward. Cuf deserves better. "Joyful Patrick Turner," she whispered.

A long moment passed when the world stopped and his heart stopped and there was nothing except rage and pain. "Morgan's boy," Cuf said finally.

He looked at her, waiting for her to say "No, not Morgan's child." Even though he knew she'd be lying, he'd believe her. Because he wanted to. Like always.

"Yes," she said. "Morgan's son."

He'd never hit her. It was unthinkable. But God forgive him, how much he wanted to. Cuf balled his big hands into fists and fought to draw one normal breath. One cool breath of air that would stop the roiling in his chest and bowels.

But this time it wouldn't stay down, buried in his gut the way it always had. Not now. Not when he looked at Roisin with her arms around Morgan's son. "Clare's not mine either, is she?" The words burned in his throat. "Clare . . . all these years. Clare's not my baby girl, is she?"

"No, Cuf, not the way you mean. But she loves you as if she were."

"She's Morgan Turner's child. That day in Brooklyn . . . she was already there, growing in your belly. Both your children, they're Morgan's."

"Yes, but— Cuf, for God's sake, don't look like that! It's not the way you're thinking. After Morgan left, all those years, and after he came back— I was true to you, Cuf. Always. I swear it."

"True to me? You were true to me? In your heart as well, Roisin? Or only true between your legs? Except, of course, when you lay with Morgan Turner and let his seed grow in your belly again."

"True in every way, Cuf. Every way that matters. You're the best man I've ever known and I never cheated on our bargain. Not once until . . . Never before. I swear it."

"Then why"—he was amazed at how soft his voice was when he wanted to shout at her—"why is it you never bore me a child in all these years we've been together? How many times have I had you, Roisin? How many times have I put my half-black cock in you? And no babe of mine ever grew in your belly. How come only Morgan's white children were good enough for your breeding, Roisin? Not Cuf's part-Negro children. Every time one of them started in you, you made sure it didn't grow. Isn't that how it was?"

"Oh, Holy Virgin, no. I never did that, Cuf. As God is my judge, I never did. In all the years we were together, no babe of yours bred in me. I swear on my mother's— I'm telling the truth, Cuf. I swear it." But it wasn't the whole truth. That was why she couldn't truly swear on her mother's soul. There was her bargain with the Holy Virgin that no babe of Cuf's beginning meant it was all right to lie with him though they weren't married. "I'm telling you the truth."

The child sensed the tension between them and whimpered. Roisin hugged him to her hip, smoothing his hair and making a gentling noise.

Cuf shook his head. The rage was draining away, leaving numbness behind. And when the numbness went, he knew, there would be emptiness and pain. Nothing, nothing could ever put back what he'd lost. "I thought Morgan was dead," he said. "We all thought so."

"All but dead," she said. "He was a prisoner four years, on the *Jersey*. Then they moved him to Rhinelander's. I found him there and his mother bribed a guard to let him out. After I got him well enough, he went back to serve with General Washington. Oh God, Cuf. Sit down. You must. You look as if—"

"I don't want to sit down. You haven't answered my question. Where is my old friend Morgan Turner now?"

"Dear God, Cuf, you wouldn't do anything foolish? Promise me you wouldn't. The British nearly killed him."

Cuf took a step closer to her and the child. "Thing I don't understand is, Morgan Turner's a rich man. How come you're still living in here?"

"Morgan wanted to find somewhere else for us, but I refused, Cuf. Same as refused to move in with Clare and Raif after they got their place in Hanover Square. I had to stay here and protect what was yours. All the patriots coming back, saying this or that is theirs, grabbing whatever might have belonged to a Tory or someone they think might have been a Tory, they haven't gotten the Fiddle and Clogs. I stayed and protected it. This place is still yours, Cuf."

"Nothing's mine," he said. "Not a thing worth having. What I did have, you've thrown it in the mud and trampled it."

November third came and went. The redcoats didn't budge. Everyone knew it was simply a matter of time, but in Squaw DaSilva's long room the officers spoke of how they wouldn't go until the last Tory who wanted to leave had done so.

"And what of you, Mistress DaSilva? The rebels will be after blood when they come back. Wouldn't you be wise to go home?"

"But this is my home, gentlemen. Where else would I go?"

"To London. Now there's a thought! Love to be able to visit you in Mayfair or Piccadilly, Mistress DaSilva. All the rage you'd be, with your New York ladies."

"That's exactly the point, gentlemen. We shall miss you, of course, but we're New York ladies." And when they looked disappointed, or pretended to, she waved her fan and said, *"Toujours la gaieté, gentlemen. Toujours la gaieté."*

On November twenty-third Squaw went up to her roof with the spyglass Howe had given her. A few rotting hulks remained in Wallabout Bay, but she'd heard they were empty now. Anyway, she wasn't looking at them. She was watching the streams of redcoats marching down the Bouwerie road and marshaling at the end of Queen Street, waiting to be ferried out to the ships waiting in the harbor.

She'd been poorly all the previous day, but felt better now. Indeed, she felt marvelous. Dear God, dear God . . . After everything, despite everything, they had won. She had won. Morgan was alive and well. He still hated her, or so he said. But Roisin insisted he didn't mean it. She said now that the war was over she could make peace between them. And if she didn't, there remained Joyful Patrick, the most adorable child in the world. Her darling grandboy. Roisin brought him whenever she could.

She snapped her glass closed. The last of the British soldiers were getting into the last of the longboats, which meant General Washington would soon arrive. According to the *Gazette*—and it was only last week that that wretch James Rivington had given up plastering the royal standard on his front page—the general was waiting just north of the city. He would make a triumphal entry on the heels of the redcoats. It was time to prepare.

Squaw stepped to the edge of the parapet. She'd had a pole erected there a few days before, in preparation for this very minute, and she had sewn the standard with her own hands. Her magic hands, as Mama used to call them, back when she was a girl named Jennet and her needlework was so much admired. Another life, that seemed, as if it had all happened to someone else.

She'd torn up two frocks to get the fabric she needed—a red one and a blue one—and three white petticoats. She hadn't actually seen the thing before, but she knew how it was to be made. Thirteen alternating red and white stripes, and thirteen white stars on a blue field. The Continental Congress had voted the design official six years ago, in '77, but this was the first day the American flag would fly over New York City. And hers, by heaven, hers would be the first of the first.

She ran the standard up the pole and a breeze came along as if on command, whipping the flag stiff. Squaw pressed her hands to her chest. No wonder her heart was beating so fast. Who wouldn't be excited after so much worry and fear and risk? But they had won. Thank God. Thank God.

"Mistress! Bit bloody in advance o' yerself, ain't ye?"

Squaw looked down. William Cunningham, wearing a wig and a splendid scarlet coat, looked up. She stared at him a moment, then went down.

"Left it rather late, haven't you, provost marshal? I believe the last longboat has already left."

Cunningham stood beside the front door of the mansion on the Broad Way and studied the woman in front of him. Bloody Squaw bitch. Women disgusted him. This one worse than most. "I got me own arrangements. Meanwhile, I came for a final payment."

"A final payment? Do you honestly think I'm likely to pay you any more money? Now? Today?"

"Sure I do. Way I see it, all them rebels is comin' back now, takin' whatever pleases 'em. How's it gonna be if the like o' me hangs about long enough to tell 'em the place where His Majesty's officers got the most o' their recreation while they was here? Best ye be payin' me and I be leavin' without talkin' to no one."

"No, Mr. Cunningham, that most assuredly is not best. And while we're about it, I'll inform you of something else, you bestial excuse for a man. I've paid you these past few years only because it was the easiest thing to do. I knew full well you had no idea where Morgan really was or you'd have gone after him, however much I paid."

"Ye didn't know any such thing."

"Oh, but of course I did. And you might care to know that it's been extraordinarily useful having His Majesty's officers visiting my home nightly. How better to keep General Washington informed of their most personal and private thoughts?"

"Bloody savage bitch. I al'ays thought ye was a traitor."

"Indeed. I'm everything you thought. And more. Much more, Mr. Provost Marshal. Remember that when you're rotting in hell, as you surely will be." Her heart was thudding so it must break out of her chest, but she didn't care. This thing standing in front of her wasn't a human being. He was an abomination. The suffering he'd caused was beyond measure. It demanded vengeance.

The ruby eyes of the golden horse's head winked at her. She grabbed the walking stick and lashed out.

"Bloody whore bitch!" Cunningham snatched at the end of the ebony cane and missed. "Lift yer hand to me, will ye! I'll see ye stripped naked and marched through the streets for the spying, lying—" The walking stick swiped his cheek. Cunningham felt the blood start from his nose. "Bitch!" he roared. "Jezebel! I'll see ye in hell!"

Her strike at his ugly, pockmarked face had split the ebony walking stick in two. Squaw lunged with the jagged end of the piece still attached to the horse's head. "I'll gouge out your eyes, you devil! Blindness is only a tenth what you deserve. I'll get your—"

The pain came in one single wave. She waited for it to crest and ebb as all pain must, but it did not. Instead it went higher, reaching from her chest into her head, stabbing her behind the eyes, taking her vision and leaving only a crimson haze. She cried out, staggered back, and fell against the stairs.

Cunningham leaped forward. Bound to be plenty worth taking from this place. Probably she had money on her as well. He was interrupted by the sound of bugles and fifes and drums. And cheers. Not very far away. Bloody hell. That bloody whore's son Washington. Not wise for William Cunningham to be in New York when George Washington arrived. Not wise at all. He turned and ran, leaving the door open behind him.

A ray of midday sunshine found its way into the front hall of New York's finest bordello, and the ruby eyes of the golden horse's head sparkled in Squaw DaSilva's lifeless hand.

II

December fourth. More than a month since he'd been home. Cuf didn't know how most of the days had passed, how he'd eaten or where he'd slept. He couldn't remember. He'd been drunk much of the time, and God knew how long since he'd washed. He smelled like a mule.

"Come in. I be all ready for ye."

The woman was black and big and everyone called her Jessie Jump Up. "Used to be I was al'ays ready to jump up and dance and sing," she'd told him the first time he'd come to her little house in an alley off Nassau Street. "But I don't be doin' that no more. Too old and too fat. Ought to call me Jessie Clean Yez Up these days. But folks ain't got that much sense."

Jessie's place was snug and warm; in her front room she took your measurements with a length of twine, and afterward sewed you clean clothes that fit proper. In her back room Jessie Jump Up had a big copper tub sitting beside a fire that always seemed to be blazing. So before you changed into your new clothes you could have a real bath, and Jessie would even trim your hair and blade your face clean if you asked her.

Seemed as if all the horrors of the war and the redcoats hadn't touched Jessie Jump Up, though in fact they made her business possible. The American soldiers coming home looked like urchins; not a proper uniform among them. First things they wanted were clean clothes that covered their bones, and not to smell like a pig been wallowing in slops. Jessie Jump Up served their needs and didn't charge too much.

"Fine mornin' it is," she told Cuf when he appeared at her front door. "A fine early mornin'." It wasn't yet seven, and the weak winter sun was barely up.

"You have my things?"

"Sure I do. Got yer clothes all ready. Only ye got to pay me rest o' what ye owes 'fore ye can have 'em."

Cuf took a coin pouch from his pocket. A French colonel had given it to him. "Your wages, Monsieur Cuf. For extraordinary service." He hadn't expected anything; most of Washington's men weren't paid, because there was no money to pay them. But later, he counted what was in the pouch: ten guineas. And later still he learned that to raise the money the French officers had taken a collection among themselves. Because they believed that without Cuf many of them would not have survived.

He opened the pouch and counted out three shillings. "There, with what I paid before, that's five shillings altogether."

Jessie Jump Up took the money and tested each coin between her teeth before she nodded agreement. "That be fine. Ye can go in now. Bath's waitin'. Ye wants me to come along and scrub the back o' ye?"

"No, thanks. Are the clothes in there as well?"

"Yes, did everything just like you be saying. Do a lot o' sayin' how ye wants thing, don't ye? A mighty lot for a man ain't exactly one color or t'other. Where you gonna go once ye shined up yer mulatto self?"

Cuf pushed past her without answering. "I'll be out in an hour. Maybe less. You keep your distance until I'm done."

He shut and barred the door behind him. That was one thing that had convinced him to make his arrangement with Jessie Jump Up: when he inspected her facilities he saw that he could bar the door against any intrusions.

The water was steaming hot—he'd insisted on that as well—and he settled into it with a sigh of satisfaction.

There was only a sliver of rough brown soap, with abrasive bits of ash left behind from the making. Not like the sweet soap Roisin used to make. Clare made it now. He knew because he'd gone to her shop in Hanover Square and seen her standing beside a counter piled high with all manner of things, including squares of the sweet-smelling soap her mother had taught her to make.

Clare had seen him as well. She'd glanced up and smiled a big smile and hurried to throw open the door. Cuf hadn't gone inside. He'd run away down the cobbled street instead. Backward, so he could keep looking at her. And she'd looked at him and called out, "Papa! Papa!" but he didn't answer. She must know he wasn't her papa. Deep in her bones, same as he always had.

The bath was cold by the time he got out and dried himself beside the fire. The clothes Jessie Jump Up had made for him felt good when he put them on. Not Negro slave clothes like he'd been wearing all this time: a linen shirt, not homespun, a jacket of wool, not flannel, and woolen britches, not leather. Finally Cuf tucked the dueling pistol into his waistband, made sure it was hidden by the coat, and unbarred the door.

Cuf got to the corner of Broad Street and Pearl at nearly eleven in the morning. Fraunces Tavern looked as fine as ever, having survived the destruction of the last years. Folks said Mr. Fraunces still set a fine table upstairs in his long room. Certainly there had been more than one celebration held in his tavern in the week since General Washington had marched into the city in triumph. Now the general was going home to Virginia, and he'd invited those of his officers who remained in New York to drink a final toast with him before he left.

The whole town knew about it. That's why so many were on Broad Street, waiting to bid Washington a safe journey. Cuf stood behind a group of men who had taken a place across the road from the tavern. He kept his hand tucked inside his coat, on the hilt of the pistol. It was primed and ready to fire. *Dear God, Cuf, you wouldn't do anything foolish? Promise me you wouldn't.* Roisin's voice, living in his head the way it always had.

Had to be that Morgan Turner was over there in Fraunces's place with Washington and the rest.

Ten minutes went by. Twenty. The crowd was quiet until someone murmured, "They're coming," and the door to the tavern opened. Men began filing into the street, and the waiting people began to clap.

You'd think they'd have had enough of beating their hands together these last few days, but seemed as if they hadn't. Plenty of will and strength for one last round of applause. Sounded as if it might never stop.

Cuf didn't clap. He took the pistol from his waistband and let it hang by his side, knowing that everyone in the street was too intent on Washington and his officers to pay him any mind. He recognized a few faces immediately—Alexander Hamilton and Philip Schuyler and Richard Varick—but some he expected weren't there, like Major Burr. Must be true that Burr had left the general's staff because he was jealous of how much Washington relied on Hamilton. No sign of Morgan, either. Not until after Washington himself came out the door.

The shouts began as soon as the general appeared. Washington raised his hat, turning this way and that to acknowledge the greeting of the onlookers. Morgan had followed him into the pale morning sunlight. He was standing some five feet behind the general, not intruding on the homage the crowd was paying its hero. All the same, it was impossible to get a clear shot at Morgan while Washington was acknowledging the people's cheers.

Dear God, Cuf, you wouldn't do anything foolish? Promise me you wouldn't.

Foolish was what he'd been doing, not what he was going to do. Foolish was all the years when he'd known the truth and let it fester in his belly. Foolish was allowing Morgan to steal everything he valued. Foolish was acting as if nothing had changed, as if Morgan was still the master and Cuf was still the slave. As if he had no right to avenge himself for the theft of his honor. That was foolish.

Washington turned and said something to Hamilton. The younger man waved his hand and someone brought a horse; the general mounted and set off up Broad Street toward the Broad Way. The tumultuous crowd surged after him. Cuf stayed where he was.

So did Morgan. A few of the others turned to him and shook his hand, and one or two clapped him on the back. Not Hamilton, Cuf noticed. There didn't seem to be any affection between Alexander Hamilton and Morgan Turner. All the same, Hamilton was standing near enough to spoil Cuf's aim.

Then another man came up to Morgan, one Cuf didn't know. And after that a third. Each of them blocked the line between his pistol and the evil heart of Morgan Turner.

A couple of times Cuf actually raised the weapon. Once he came within a single breath of firing it. Then something else happened to distract him. Cuf wasn't sure what. A bird, perhaps.

Dear God, Cuf, you wouldn't do anything foolish? Promise me you wouldn't.

Finally everyone was gone and Morgan was crossing the street and coming toward him. "Morning, Cuf."

Morgan walked with a limp. The British had nearly killed him, Roisin said. That had to be why he needed the stick. And why one of his eyes didn't seem to be entirely open, and why his left arm hung at his side. Not that any of it had kept him from lying over Roisin and planting his child in her belly. His second child.

"You going to use that or not?" Morgan was standing a foot away from Cuf now, looking straight at him. They were the only people left outside the tavern. Morgan nodded toward the pistol in Cuf's hand. "I've been watching you and wondering, so you may as well tell me. Do you mean to kill me or don't you?"

"I mean to."

"Yes, that's what I thought. Are you going to do it?"

Cuf didn't answer.

"Will it make any difference if I say I'm sorry?" Morgan asked.

"Not much."

"I know. But Roisin and I, we both are. If the war hadn't happened, we'd probably never . . . When I came back that first time, Cuf. When I realized she was your woman, I had no intention of trying to get her back. And she wouldn't have come if I had. It was just—" He broke off and shook his head. "The war," he said finally. "It's not an excuse. Only a reason."

"How old's your son?"

"Eighteen months. Joyful Patrick. Mighty strange name, but Roisin insisted."

Cuf nodded. The pistol was still hanging heavy by his side.

"I hear your mother died."

"Yes. The day the redcoats evacuated." Morgan held up his walking stick. The wood was new, but the fancy top was not. "Recognize this?"

"The horse's head I buried on Bedloe's Island."

"The very same. Cuf, did you ever know what was in it?"

"Some kind of paper, I figured. Didn't weigh enough to be anything else."

"But you never looked at it?"

"Never did. Back then I believed in getting the promise."

Morgan smiled. "Too bad. If you'd read it and remembered what it said, we might both be some richer."

"You wrote down what was in there, didn't you? The directions for burying it, seemed to me they had to come from you."

"They did. And you're right, I wrote the note. But it's gone, and these days"— Morgan gestured toward his own head—"I don't remember things as well as I once did."

"Anyway, with your mama dead you're already a rich man. You going to move into her house? You and Roisin and your boy?"

"Never. I'm never going to live there again, Cuf. Roisin, either. I've let it to Isaac Sears. You remember Captain Sears."

"From the Sons of Liberty. Of course. So you and Roisin, where are you—"

"Not the Fiddle and Clogs, Cuf. It's your property. In fact, we won't be in New York but a few more weeks. We're going to China."

"China?"

"The West Indies are finished for New York trade. The British plantation owners won't buy our goods. But the East India Company can't keep our ships out of the Orient now we're independent. Some of us have gotten together and outfitted a three-masted merchantman, a real beauty. *Empress of China,* she's called. Loaded to the gunnels with pelts and some root called ginseng. You can dig it up in the woods down in Virginia and Pennsylvania. Roisin doesn't know much about it, if you can imagine that, but the Chinese think it cures just about everything. Pay a fortune for it, they will. We're sailing for Canton soon as the Narrows and the harbor are free of ice."

Poxed pistol was weighing down Cuf's arm. *You wouldn't do anything foolish? Promise me you wouldn't.* He was stupid. Standing here talking when he should be taking the vengeance he was owed. "So you're to be a sea captain again."

"Not exactly. I'm taking the owner's cabin." Morgan made an awkward movement with his bad arm. "Can't con a ship when you're not in top form. But you, Cuf, you've come out of the war looking as fine as I've ever seen you. Are you—"

"You and Roisin, you going to be married?" She'd never married Cuf. She couldn't have, of course. There were laws against a white woman marrying a mulatto.

"We are married, Cuf. Been so for more than a year."

Holy God Almighty. Cuf felt the bile rise in his throat and feared he was going to puke up his guts right here in the street, make himself ashamed. Holy Jesus Christ.

"There's a Jesuit priest in New York," Morgan said. "Going to be a Catholic church, too, I'm told. Anyway, this Mr. Steenmayer, he married us. It's Roisin's religion, but it seemed all right to me. Cuf, give me the pistol." Morgan stretched out his undamaged right arm. "Someone comes by, sees you holding it . . . There could be trouble."

Because after all this bloody war, after all the killing and dying, there were still slaves and still masters. And everyone knew which was which. Cuf didn't hand over the pistol, but he turned away and started walking.

"Cuf, wait. Where are you going? I don't—"

Cuf raised the hand holding the weapon and fired it off straight over his head. Over both their heads.

"Cuf!"

Cuf heard steps coming after him. Uneven, off-balance steps. Morgan Turner could never catch him if he didn't want to be caught. Morgan was a cripple. Cuf could take some satisfaction in that, maybe. But not much. Crippled or no, Morgan had Roisin.

III

March, three months after Evacuation Day, and the almshouse was chock-full. A few weeks after the British left, a new Assembly had been voted in, and a mayor elected to preside over a new Common Council. Soon the basic services were restored. Anyone who knew how to run them was expected to do the job. Andrew reckoned that was pretty much the reason he was still in charge of the City Hospital in the poorhouse. He was available and he knew how. And God knew there were plenty of sick poor.

Poverty and filth and disease: they seemed to go together. All those people crammed into Canvas Town, it was as if they passed their contagions and illnesses among themselves. Invisible worms. Maybe so.

A short time before he'd taken Lucas's journals and Christopher's notes out of the secret drawer in his desk and returned them to the bookshelf. The only thing in the drawer now was the paper he'd taken from Caleb Devrey. Andrew was still certain it contained directions for finding a treasure. Maybe someday he'd make the journey. Meanwhile, as soon as he had a few hours clear, he planned to read the medical material again from start to finish. The boy Preble, the way he'd revived after the blood transfusion, though Red Bess had died after the selfsame treatment . . . There was a good deal yet to learn.

"Here's the last of them, Dr. Turner." The man assigned to the orderly's job pointed to the woman in the last bed. She'd been sent up to the hospital from the almshouse carding and weaving room, he explained. "Got a fierce throat, she has, and I expect a fever. And she can't work the loom for the coughing as sets her shaking from head to toe." As if to prove his point the woman began another siege of hacking and shivering.

Andrew could feel the heat radiating from the woman's body before he touched her; nonetheless he put his palm against her forehead. A raging fever, as the orderly said. "You were re—" He broke off, hearing screams and shouts. "What's that damnable noise?"

The orderly held a heavy tray containing Andrew's instruments and supplies. He shifted from foot to foot. "Coming from outside it be, sir."

"On the Common?"

"Aye, sir. Be a number o' folks down there."

"You don't have any windows open, do you? The foul humors—"

"No windows open, Dr. Turner. None. Like ye always says."

Andrew grunted approval. "Then how come the rabble on the Common can be heard up here?"

"There be a fair number of 'em, sir."

"Yes. Must be." He dismissed the noise and returned to his patient. Her lungs were filling up with fluid, he'd take a wager on it. He and his grandfather had opened dozens of corpses that demonstrated the fact. "Tartar emetic," he said, reaching for the bottle and the dosing spoon. "Open your mouth, mistress. I'm going to help you bring up the sickness." She'd vomit until her stomach was empty, and empty her bowels of everything they held. Tomorrow he'd bleed her. If she lived, she might recover.

"Grandfather, why can't we open the chest while patients are alive? The way you do after they're dead."

"And do what, boy?"

"Suck the fluid out of the lungs."

"Yes, I suppose that might help. But what you see me do here in this little dissecting room, peeling the skin and the muscles back from the rib cage, cracking the sternum to see better, no one could endure such pain and live, boy. Remember what Lucas Turner said, no such thing as painless surgery, so we'll never open a belly or a chest."

"But if we could, Grandfather . . ."

"If we could, Andrew, we might save many lives."

Andrew turned and replaced the tartar emetic on the orderly's tray. "You'll have to spend the next few hours with her." The man looked pained. "Better than going back to work breaking stones, isn't it?"

"She be going to puke and shit for hours, that's what you reckon, Doctor?"

"That's what I reckon." Andrew lifted the bottle he'd just used and checked the level. "In fact, most of them will."

"Then I don't be so sure it's better."

"Andrew Turner." The voice came from a man standing in the doorway of the ward, holding a cloth over his nose against the stench of illness.

Andrew turned. "I'm Dr. Turner. Do I know you, sir?"

"Don't matter if ye does or not. Yer to come with me."

"On whose authority?"

"Theirs." The man turned as he said it and motioned two others forward. They were armed with muskets and carried short swords at their waists.

"Bloody hell," Andrew said softly. "I thought the army was gone."

"Redcoat army is. Now we're getting rid of the poxed Tories was brazen enough to stay behind."

There had to be a hundred people on the Common, wedged into the flat stretch of meadowland between the powder house and the rear of the prison and the almshouse. No wonder he'd heard their shouts and screams even with the ward's windows shut.

"Exactly what are you doing here? What do you want with me?"

They'd tied his hands behind his back and were pushing him forward. "Ye be seeing soon enough. Going to get the same as all them other Tories."

He knew he should tell them that he wasn't a Tory, that he never had been, but the words stuck in his throat. Bloody animals. Seven years in hell, risking his life, and the lives of his family, dragging his honor in the gutter doing the dirtiest job in the war, for what? So a horde of maniacal lunatics led by the same rabble-rousers who'd been in charge of the Sons of Liberty could take over the city and attack every decent principle that gentlemen defended. Hell would freeze over before he'd befoul himself by making explanations to such vermin.

Besides, they wouldn't believe him.

The men with the muskets shoved him through the thick of the crowd. Hands grabbed at him, struck him, ripped at his clothes, and tugged at his hair. A few spat in his face. Screaming furies, they all were. Sweet Christ, as many women as men, and apoplectic with rage, most of them. Oh, Jesus God Almighty.

Straight ahead of him was a stake and beside it a roaring fire.

Andrew's bowels churned and his heart thumped in his chest. He wouldn't beg. They'd all grow horns before he'd do that. It was a filthy way to die. Filthy. But he wouldn't beg for mercy, because he knew there was none to be had.

"This one's next!" someone shouted.

Andrew stiffened himself and willed himself to walk upright to the burning place. Nothing happened. No one shoved him forward. Next didn't mean him. It was an elderly man with thinning hair and a paunch, and clothes that had been fine until shortly before, when they were splattered with excrement and dirt. The man's forehead was badly cut. A thrown stone, no doubt. Blood was dripping down his cheek.

It took Andrew a moment to put a name to the terrified figure. Yes, of course. Leominster Harmon. One of the sugar kings. Had a fine house on Wall Street. Thrived during the war, made a fortune supplying the British navy with rum. The poor benighted bastard. Should have had the sense to get out while he could. They all should have.

Harmon was roped to the stake. One of the men who seemed to be in charge of things went over to the fire. Probably to get coals to set the victim alight. The screams of the crowd were deafening. Harmon was moving his mouth as well. Praying, maybe. Yes, of course, Leominster Harmon was a Catholic, that's why he'd stayed. Nothing could be worse than being a Catholic in Britain, except maybe being burned alive right here in New York. Oh Jesus God Almighty, give me the strength to die well. So when they hear about it, Meg and the children and my father, they can be proud.

The crowd grew silent. Andrew closed his eyes.

Harmon screamed. A long, sustained howl of pain that remained echoing in the air.

The mob moaned its collective satisfaction. Andrew could feel their pleasure writhing around him, like a whore lusting during sex. "There! Ah, yes! That's right it is!"

He opened his eyes. Had to. Couldn't refuse to be a witness to—

To something different than his worst fears.

They were pouring buckets of liquid pitch over Harmon Leominster, and some of the women were dashing forward and flinging handfuls of feathers.

"Ye can go back to yer fine mansion now, ye blackhearted Tory traitor. And take her with ye!"

Two men dragged Josie Harmon toward the stake. At first Andrew thought they meant to tar and feather her as well. Then he realized they'd already done worse. The rear of her bustled frock was hitched up to her waist, and from the way she was being pulled across the still-frozen earth it was clear she couldn't have walked if her captors allowed it. The backs of her fat legs were bloodied and she was sobbing with terror and pain. Sweet Christ Almighty, they had hamstrung her, cut the tendon that made her legs work. She'd never walk again.

Animals. Seven years of hell for animals like these.

"Papa! Papa! Let me through, you evil bastards! Papa!"

"Lucas! Get out of here. Go home. Your mother needs you. Go home!" Lucas was eighteen, his eldest son. If he was to be crippled or blinded or worse by these swine—

"Andrew! It's me, Sam. Are you all right?"

Andrew had no chance to speak for himself. The man who'd come up to the hospital ward and dragged him down to the Common answered for him. "He be fine for now. But he won't be so fine in a minute or two. Stay and watch, why don't ye?"

"I'll watch you on trial for bodily assault is what I'll do." Sam Devrey's voice cut through the noise. His words were spoken distinctly and carried absolute authority. "Moreover, I'll personally testify that you dared to interfere with the liberty of an American hero."

Sam had pushed his way through the crowd by this time, young Lucas right behind him; they were even with Andrew and the men who held him prisoner. "Let him go," Sam said. "Immediately."

"Hero, ye says? No disrespect, but are ye mad, Dr. Devrey? He be right here all the while ye was looking after our boys. He coulda done that as well. Instead he—"

"Instead he stayed here," Devrey boomed, silencing the other man with the volume and conviction of his voice. "In the lion's den. Surrounded by the enemy.

Risking his life every single day by transmitting information to General Washington."

"He never did!"

The crowd had gone silent and was hanging on every word of the exchange.

"How in God's name do you dare to say that to me?" Sam demanded. "He never, did you say? But you are wrong, sir. You know who I am, don't you?"

"'Course I do. I already said so. Only this time yer out o' line."

A voice from the crowd shouted him down. "It's Sam Devrey what's talkin'. Saved my boy's life at Trenton. Let him speak."

"I've already said what I came to say. Dr. Andrew Turner is a hero of the war for independency. If you want a letter from General Washington that says the same you have to give me a couple of weeks to go to Virginia and get it. But if instead you want to cover yourself with shame this very afternoon, you'll go on with your vicious attack on a man who repeatedly risked his life for all you cherish."

There was silence while the crowd struggled to come to terms with the news. Finally a woman's voice shouted, "Let him go."

"Aye, do that," someone else said. "Free him. Free Dr. Turner. Real hero, he is."

The man who had taken Andrew prisoner sputtered a few words about Turner doctoring for the British, whatever else he might have done, and then slunk off. The men with the muskets untied Andrew.

"Come on," Sam said in a low voice. "Let's get away from here. Quickly, before we're challenged for proof."

"We can't," Andrew said. "There are others. Terrible things are happening. Wicked things."

Sam grabbed his arm. "Don't argue, damn it! Come!"

"Papa, please come away."

Andrew looked into young Lucas's eyes and saw the terror there. His own bowels were still churning. All the same . . . "I'm sorry," he whispered. Then he turned back to the crowd.

"Listen, all of you. What you're doing, it's—" Andrew stopped. There was no need of his words. Sam's accusations had deflated the crowd. The change in the atmosphere was discernible. People were drifting away. Two men had begun pouring sand on the fire they'd made to heat the pitch. Someone else was starting to take down the stake.

"Come," Sam said again. "Meg's waiting."

"How did you know?" Andrew asked when they were on Ann Street. Meg had given them tea and biscuits, and young Lucas poured Madeira for his father and Samuel Devrey, who was his third cousin once removed, and who had never before set foot in this house. "How did you know what was happening, Lucas? And how in God's name did you know to get Cousin Samuel?"

"I was in town at the Dish of Fry'd Oysters and I heard about a riot on the Common. Tarring and feathering Tories, they said. I knew you were at the hospital, so I just assumed . . ." The boy shrugged and let the words trail away.

Andrew nodded, took a sip of the wine, and blessed the way it calmed his still-churning gut. "Very well. But you knew to go to Cousin Samuel? How—"

"He did indeed know," Sam said. "Arrived at my front door in a tearing hurry and yanked me out before I'd time to brush away the crumbs of my dinner. Obviously not a moment too soon. You were next, weren't you?"

"Yes. But that doesn't explain— Lucas, I want the truth. How did you know?"

Lucas wasn't as tall as his father, and he was dark, not fair, but he had the direct way of speaking that marked so many of the Turner men. "I followed you about," he said. "All those years, when you went out late at night and left messages at various places. I followed you."

"I see." The thought of the danger his son had been in, that he himself had put the boy in, made Andrew sick at his stomach, even now. "And when Cousin Samuel and I met, you were nearby then as well?"

"Yes, sir. If you mean near the old cellar at Hall Place, I mostly was."

"You might have been seen, Lucas. It would have been the end for Cousin Samuel, and for me and for yourself. Not to mention a wicked blow for General Washington."

"I know, sir. I didn't think about it at the time, though. All I wanted was to be sure you weren't what they said you were, a Tory, Papa, who was committing treason against independency. I had to know that."

"So, Sam."

"So, Andrew."

It was after eight. Lucas had left and the cousins were alone. "I owe you my skin," Andrew said. "Maybe even my legs. Did I tell you they hamstrung poor old Josie Harmon?"

"You told me."

"Christ, Sam, what did we do it all for?"

"I can't believe you don't know the answer to that."

"I thought I did. For the right to govern ourselves, not be tormented and taxed and dictated to by men thousands of miles away with not an idea in their heads about the way of things here in America. But what have we got? They're cattle, Sam. They've no sense of what is fitting, no respect for private property. They mean to sell off all the lands that belonged to the better class of people. The De Lanceys are—"

"To be first," Sam finished for him. "Hell, they're easy targets since young Oliver took off for London."

"A pox on him. I hold no brief for any De Lancey, God knows. It's the principle I'm weeping for, New York's chance to come back and be a decent city again. I'm told they're making a grab for Trinity's lands as well. The Church, Sam! The radical fanatics that have been elected to the Assembly and the Council mean to rob the Church. What next, for God's sake?"

"So you side with Hamilton. Forgive the Tories because they're useful, and get on with the business of business."

"What else should we do? Look at the crowd that's piping the tune. Those black-clad holier-than-thou types preaching no drink or dance on Sunday, but on Monday catch whom you will and tar and feather and hamstring them, and do Christ knows what else. What's the point of it, Sam? What did we accomplish?"

Sam helped himself to another glass of Madeira and sipped it before he answered. When he did he spoke quietly, pretty much anticipating the reaction he'd provoke. "Way I see it . . . the point's democracy."

"Democracy! Rule by any scoundrel can muster the votes of the ignorant rabble? Sweet Christ, I hope not."

The Path of Dreams

JUNE 1798

The Canarsie People said the knowing belongs to the old and wise, but the unfolding is in the keeping of the young. The old prevent the young from straying off the path of wisdom. The young yearn after the path of dreams. Between the two there is truth.

I

The second week of June 1798, a few days out of Canton. The sea was calm, the wind fresh. His father's words repeating themselves over and over in his mind. "Remember this: New York's about get rich and the devil take the hindmost. Always was. Always will be."

Not for him. For Joyful Patrick Turner, not quite seventeen, it was about becoming a doctor.

"Holy bloody Savior," Morgan said when he heard about his son's ambition. "You're a true Turner, even if you have been raised in Canton. A doctor, eh? Not an apothecary like your mother? God rest her beautiful soul."

"Not exactly like her, Papa. Though I do want to heal."

Morgan had fixed his one good eye on his son. "It's what she said to you that last afternoon, isn't it? It's what Roisin said is sending you back there."

"Yes, but it was in my mind before that."

Mama, holding his hand, lying in the big bed in the house on top of the Cantonese hill, sweet breezes blowing the curtains, her whispering so he had to lean over to hear. "I know you, Joyful. I know what's in your heart. Be a healer. Make folks well. It's what you want. Do it. But not here. Go home. There's loose ends need weaving, you go pick them up. New York's where you'll do your magic."

"Very well," Morgan said when Joyful told him. He was sixty-one, devastated by Roisin's loss, and past arguing. "Very well." Quietly, not letting his feelings show: "Go back then, with my blessing and hers. I won't go with you. Going to stay here and be buried beside your mama when my time comes."

"Papa, I—"

"No, don't fret. It's fine. I'll write to my cousin Andrew. He was a great friend of your mama's during the war. He'll help you for her sake if not mine. See you into that medical school he's part of at . . . What do they call it these days? Columbia College. Used to be King's. Changed a lot of the old royal names, I'm told, and good riddance to 'em. But you remember this, boy, New York's always been about money. Always will be."

His father's words in his head were so loud Joyful almost didn't hear the voice of the man who came to stand beside him in the prow of the merchantman. Someone else who didn't mind the sting of the salt spray and the slap of the waves, and the low persistent hum of the wind in the taut canvas overhead. "Fine afternoon, isn't it, young Mr. Joyful Patrick?"

"I suppose it is. Mighty fine."

"And how are you keeping after last evening?"

Joyful turned away, ashamed to meet the other man's glance. A right fool he'd made of himself the night before. Four men, all passengers, all getting giddy from sniffing at that strange gas. And him, the youngest and the giddiest of all. "I'm well, thank you." Damn! he could feel his cheeks reddening. He hated that he blushed like a girl. Hated hearing the soft chuckle and knowing his companion had noticed.

"Don't look like that," the man said. "It's not important. First time you're on your own, every young sprout gets carried away."

"Do they all fall on the floor senseless?" Joyful asked. "Listen, I never thought . . . I've had rum plenty of times before. And brandy. I never expected—"

"'Course you didn't. The gas is different. As I told you. Amazing stuff. All the rage at parties in London these days. Makes everyone into laughing fools."

Joyful put a hand to his forehead. The place where he'd cut himself when he fell still throbbed beneath the bandage applied by the ship's surgeon. The wound had been deep enough to require stitching. "I didn't feel it," he said. "Nothing. I didn't know I was hurt."

"No, so you said last night. You just wanted more of the gas."

Joyful blushed again. "Amazing stuff, as you said."

"Indeed."

"Tell me something—if they have such remarkable things in London, why are you going to New York?"

"Good Christ, man, why does anyone go to New York? To make my fortune, of course."

II

After so much desolation and ruin and evil, still the same dream. Get rich. Get rich.

In the end, despite bitter opposition, that was surely why the merchants of Manhattan prevailed over the rural Antifederalists in the rest of the state. In July 1788, at a raucous convention in Poughkeepsie, New York, the last of the hold-outs—having been assured that individual liberties would be protected by a Bill of Rights—had agreed to ratify the Constitution. New York would throw her lot in with the others. They would be the United States of America.

As a reward New York City was made the seat of the new federal government. City Hall would become the capitol building and the new country would be run from Wall Street. "Entirely fitting," the merchants of New York said.

On April 30, 1789, George Washington stood on the second-floor balcony of the building that had been transformed from City Hall to Federal Hall. The new seat of power.

Washington looked south toward what had been the court part of town. Toward the old Stadt Huys where they'd had the ducking stool that so terrified pregnant Sally Turner. Toward the fort with the ancient gibbet where the physician Jacob Van der Vries, his dead body covered in pitch, hung twisting in the ocean breeze.

Standing on the balcony of Federal Hall, Mr. Washington of Virginia needed only to turn his head east to look down on the spot where New Yorkers had broken Robin on the rack, and gibbeted Kinsowa, and burned Quaco and Peter the Doctor in a fire so slow it took them ten hours to die while Amba sang. The place where they put little Jan Brinker in the stocks and dislocated both his shoulders. And hanged God knows how many. Right there on Wall Street, where the nation's first president swore the first oath of office.

New York had no time for old nightmares, or even old dreams. New York was a place of the new. New York rejoiced. Being the capital was excellent for business.

The moneyed men, they were called. The richest of the rich. Because of them, a never-ending stream of immigrants arrived, many with cash and connections, some with only hope. Soon over thirty thousand were crammed into the city that had spread itself two miles up Manhattan, as far north as what had been James De Lancey's extensive farm.

What they called Delancey Street (being too much in a hurry to give it the old two-word pronunciation) wasn't the countryside any longer. Neither was Grand Street, or even Oliver Street. They were thoroughfares created to make room for new houses for the new rich.

Thomas Jefferson, Virginia aristocrat that he was, couldn't bear this throbbing, thriving, thumping place called New York City. He summoned two other influential men of politics to his house on Maiden Lane, and he and James Madison and Alexander Hamilton worked out a compromise. They would make a new capital in a neutral place. Never mind that it was a swamp at present. They'd drain it. Meanwhile they'd leave this hellhole of Manhattan and take up residence in Philadelphia.

The three prevailed. "I suppose we must go," Abigail Adams sighed to John. "I shall make the best of Philadelphia, but it will never be Broadway."

Seven years into independency, the Broad Way had become Broadway. In New York, faster was important. The quick get rich faster. It wasn't unheard-of to have fifteen kinds of wine with dinner, and after the cloths were removed, the best bottled cider and every kind of ale.

However fast it might be, the creation of such wealth was never easy. Slaves helped. Pennsylvania, Connecticut, Massachusetts, Vermont, and Rhode Island had all abolished slavery. In 1798, as Joyful Patrick Turner sailed homeward, there were three thousand black folks in New York City. Four of every five were slaves.

Meanwhile, most of Manhattan was still the wilderness it had always been. Above North Street (later called Houston), the countryside began. The woods were thick, and the path that led to the East River shore was twisting and narrow and uneven, littered with rocks that had slid down from the hills, particularly after so much spring rain.

The slave called Laniah, usually so sure-footed, stumbled once or twice. The third time she actually fell, tearing her calico dress, skinning her knee and bruising her cheekbone. She paid the injuries no mind. "Don't you do nothing foolish, Mistress Molly," she muttered to herself. "Nothing stupid. Leastwise not until I find you." Laniah spoke the words over and over, whispering them into the quiet, humid warmth of the June afternoon. "Nothing foolish, Mistress Molly. Not until I gets to you."

She heard the voices before she saw anything. Not her mistress's voice nor Molly's, men calling to each other.

"Put in here. Mind the rocks."

There was the slap of oars cutting through the water, and someone yelling to someone else to catch a line. "Need to build a mooring here, Dr. Turner. Somewheres we can tie up to. Things would go a lot faster if you did that."

The faster Laniah ran, the louder the voices became. She heard Lucas Turner's answer as clearly as if he were speaking to her.

"This hospital is a temporary arrangement. We're only here until the yellowing fever leaves the city. There, that's your line secure. How many do you have?"

The tree-shaded path ended abruptly. Laniah was in a clearing, half-blinded by the bright midday sun.

"Got me four, Doc. Lyin' here half dead, they is. And nine more back on the packet what ain't in much better shape."

Laniah's vision cleared in time for her to see a man jumping out of a rowboat into the shallows. Two other men appeared at the same time, though not from the direction she'd come. From the big house set back a ways from the shore, divided from it by a sloping green lawn. "House is almost full, Dr. Turner," one of them called out. "We cleared floor space for two more, but that's rightly all."

"Sweet God in heaven. Then we've taken in what? Seventy-five patients since Sunday?"

"Ninety-four, sir."

"And the Bedloe's Island pesthouse is full as well." Lucas knew because he'd sent word to Andrew to send any extra bedding he had available, and gotten his father's message that there was none. "Sweet Christ."

The man still clinging to the prow of his rowboat motioned to the men from the house. "C'mon, lads, get these sick blighters out o' me boat. I've two more trips to make," he added, nodding toward the small single-masted sloop lying off in the middle of the broad river.

"You can't bring me more patients," Lucas said. "You heard them. We've only room for two of these."

"I've four aboard," the boatman insisted. "And nine to come off the ship afore sundown."

"Impossible."

"With due respect, Dr. Turner, it has to be possible, on orders from the mayor and the council. If they don't get them what's got the jaundice out o' the town there'll be a panic. Like last year."

"Bloody fools." Lucas wasn't sure if he meant the politicians or the ordinary town folk, but he wasn't asked to clarify. "Very well, you can offload these poor buggers you've brought today. But tell your captain to tell the mayor and the council we can't take more unless they send canvas, and a few strong men to erect some tents along the shore. Tell them the house is full to bursting."

Lucas turned to go back to the makeshift hospital. That was when he saw the black girl standing in the clearing. He squinted a moment, recognized her, and strode in her direction. "Laniah! It is you, isn't it?"

She stood her ground, too shy to go forward and meet him. It wasn't like when she sometimes served him at the pharmacy in Hanover Square. Everyone knew Lucas Turner went there 'cause he was courting Mistress Molly, for all he was twelve years older and had already been married once. When he was on the other side of the counter at the pharmacy he wanted something, and it was almost as if Laniah was in charge. Not here. "Yes, it's me, Dr. Turner. Master Raif's Laniah."

"So I see. What are you doing here?"

She'd already made up her mind how she'd answer that. "Mistress Molly, she forgot something." Laniah raised the drawstring bag she carried.

"Molly? But, Laniah, Molly had the yellowing fever last year. Both twins did. Mistress Molly and Mr. Jonathan. So why should she be here today?"

"Dearie my soul, you be having to ask her that, Dr. Turner. I only come to bring Mistress Molly what she left behind."

Lucas shook his head impatiently. "You're talking in riddles, and I've no time for that today. You heard what those men said, didn't you? I've a houseful of patients to look after."

"Mighty big house," Laniah said, gazing toward the redbrick structure with its broad veranda. "How many rooms there be in a house like that?"

"Fourteen. We've four laundresses and three cleaners living in the place, as well as the patients, and the family members who come to look after them. So we're stuffed to the rafters, as I said. Tell your master, why don't you? Mr. Raif might be interested in sending someone up here with cures and simples. I warrant a number of them would be sold."

"Dearie my soul, Dr. Turner, ain't no simple as cures the yellowing fever. You gets well or you don't and that's it."

Lucas sighed. "I know. But people like to think otherwise. I doubt Raif Devrey would hesitate to profit from their hopes and fears."

"After I find Mistress Molly, talk to her, then I promise I be going back and telling Master Raif what you said." She took a step toward the house.

"You can't go in there, Laniah. There's no reason for it. I already told you, Mistress Molly isn't here. I don't know what made you think she would be."

Laniah thought so, because she'd already checked the City Hospital and the New York Hospital, and her mistress was in neither of them. So she could think of no alternative but this pesthouse for them as had the yellowing fever. Only place left. Not that Mistress Molly liked being where Lucas Turner was. She said he wasn't really sweet on her. According to Mistress Molly, when Dr. Lucas looked at her he saw a big strong woman could take care of his house and his three motherless children. "I can have a look, can't I, Dr. Turner? Wouldn't hurt none if I had a look."

"It's a waste of your time, Laniah. As I told you."

She had taken a step toward the redbrick house; now she stopped. "You absolutely sure, Dr. Turner? These things Mistress Molly forgot—" She raised the drawstring bag again.

"I'm certain, Laniah. The house isn't as big as it looks. It wasn't even the main house when the Kip family lived here. Only part of their farm. It's called Belle Vue. Because the view's so pretty," he added. "Don't you think it's pretty?"

Laniah looked at the expanse of river, and the green hills and trees of the long island on the opposite shore. "I s'pose it is. Dr. Turner, you're absolutely sure, right? Mistress Molly, she don't be in there?"

"I'm positive, Laniah. Now go home. And don't forget to tell Mr. Raif what I said about selling things up here. He'll count you a clever girl for making the suggestion."

Laniah chose a different path back, cutting across the Post Road and making her way south through the woods on the west side of the island. Sun would be going down soon. Had to be close to seven at night.

"Here in this place, Lucas? Must we bury . . ." Marit nodded toward her drawstring sack, Lucas's leather pouch. "We have had so much joy here, it does not seem . . ."

The third trip from the town to the Voorstadt and beyond. Each time they had moved deeper into the Manhattan wilderness, leaving a trail of the body parts of Ankel Jannssen, carefully scuffling the top of each fresh hole. Now they had reached the Collect Pond, shimmering in the heat of midday. The sounds of buzzing insects filled the air.

"Here," Lucas said. He turned his back to the pond, chose a place beside a bramble thicket, took the trowel from his bag, and began to dig.

Mistress Clare would flog her for being gone so long and coming back so late. Laniah felt the tears start. Made it harder than ever to see. She reached up to wipe them away and wiped her nose as well. Stupid to get all snot-nosed and soaky-eyed over what you couldn't change. Weeping only made things worse. Oh, dearie my . . .

Laniah stopped short. She was at the edge of a clearing, near what was left of the old Collect Pond. Someone else was there. His back was to her, but she knew instantly who it was. She'd wanted Mistress Molly, but she'd found Mr. Jonathan. Heaven only knew what he'd—

Her gasp of surprise had given her away. The figure whirled around. "Laniah! What are you doing here?"

"I was looking for Mistress Mol— Oh, my. I thought you was Mr. Jonathan. But you ain't."

Molly Devrey put her hand to her head. Her hair was her best feature, Mama always said. *You're no beauty, Molly Devrey, but that red hair will catch you a man if you let it do its work.* Now she'd cut it off. Most of it, anyway. "Did I make it too short, Laniah?"

"I can't say, Mistress Molly. Too short for what?"

"For what I'm supposed to be, damn it!" That was the first time she'd said it aloud. Damn. The way a man did. "Damn it, Laniah, tell me. Do I look like a him, or just a her with ugly short hair?"

"I thought for sure you was Mr. Jonathan, Mistress Molly. Before you turned around, I was certain. Them clothes . . ." She gestured toward the broadcloth breeches and the linen shirt. "Them's Mr. Jonathan's clothes for sure."

"No, they're not. They're mine." Molly raised her hand and pointed to a small leather satchel. "I've another set in there, and my coat's ready to put on. In fact, I shall do that just now. Come over here and you can help me."

Sweat ran down Marit's face. The bodice of her frock was soaked with it. Lucas's shirt as well. The heat of the summer day. And the labor.

"We are almost done," Lucas said, continuing to dig the fourth hole he had made in this place. "Afterward, if you like, we can swim."

How many times they had come here and frolicked like children in that cool, fresh water, and she had given herself to him with such perfect joy, such abandon. Now, it seemed to her, rivers of Ankel's blood must travel under the ground and flood the pond. "I do not think I will swim," she whispered. "It is not like before."

Lucas stopped burrowing into the earth long enough to look up at her. "It will be better than before. Much better."

She had done it for him. And because Ankel Jannssen was a monster who did not deserve to live. He would never allow himself to think otherwise.

There were two more closely wrapped packages in his bag. A hand. And the monster's head. Lucas reached for the hand.

Laniah dropped the drawstring bag she'd been carrying all day and jumped to pick up the coat lying neatly folded on the grass. She held it open the way she often did for Master Raif or Mr. Jonathan, and Mistress Molly slipped her arms inside and shrugged it comfortably onto her shoulders. Just like Master Raif or Mr. Jonathan, that was. Exactly like.

"How do I look?"

"Like a him," Laniah conceded. "Like Mr. Jonathan."

"Good. Now you go on home and don't you dare— Laniah, stop that weeping. I can't stand it when you weep. And what have you got in there, anyway?" The girl had stooped and picked up her drawstring bag. She was hugging it to her as if it were her last hope on earth.

"It be my things," Laniah said. "Only mine. I didn't take nothin' didn't belong to me."

"Your— Laniah, what are you doing? Are you running away?"

"I been running after you, Mistress Molly. All day. I went to the City Hospital and New York Hospital and even up to that new pesthouse in the woods, that Belle Vue. I asked, but—"

"Did you talk to him? To Dr. Turner?"

Laniah nodded.

"And what did he say?"

"Nothin'. Only that you didn't have the yellowing fever so you weren't in his Belle Vue pesthouse."

"Bloody fool." Oh, that felt good. Bloody. Another word she could say when she wore breeches and never if she had on a skirt. "He doesn't know anything about me. Why should he? He didn't guess why you thought I'd be in any of those places, did he, Laniah?"

"No, ma'am."

"Say 'sir.' Say, 'No sir,' Laniah. Look at me and tell yourself I'm a man and say, 'No, sir.'"

"No sir, Mistr— Mr. . . . I can't say Mr. Molly, can I?"

"Of course not." Molly reached into the pocket of her coat and pulled out a letter. "See this. It's from my grandfather Cuf."

"The one up in Nova Scotia? The grandfather ain't never be seeing you?"

"That's right. My mulatto grandfather, Laniah." Her voice softened. It was always hard for her to understand how her mother could let her father buy slaves when Mama was a little bit Negro herself. And Laniah . . . It was hard to understand why Laniah should belong to anyone except herself.

The oiled cloth wrapping came apart as soon as Lucas took the head from his bag. It was an awkward package. He had not removed the cleaver from the skull. He could not bring himself to do so now. Jannssen's pig-eyes looked up at him. By the time Lucas had come upon the corpse the eyes had been death-frozen in that wide-open stare, and he could not brush them closed.

He heard Marit retching in the bushes, swallowed his own bile. A murdering animal who deserved exactly what she did to—what he got.

"Stay there," he called softly. "Don't turn around. I will be done quickly."

He looked for a suitable burying place. The thing was heavy, the presence of the cleaver meant it must go into a large hole. Very deep. Unless . . .

People said the Collect Pond was deep as the ocean. In the old days, when he and Marit swam naked here, as soon as they were a few feet from shore they could not touch the ground.

This time he went fully clothed into the water, holding the last of Ankel Jannssen above his head. When at last he dropped it, weighted by the heavy cleaver, it sank without a trace.

"We will not swim," he told Marit when he rejoined her. "Not today."

She nodded in agreement, trying not to look at the pond.

"My grandfather Cuf," Molly said again. "He's written to me twice. And do you know what, Laniah? He thinks it's Jonathan he's writing to. 'Dear Boy,' that's how he starts the letters."

"And what does he say?"

"He says that there's plenty of people need a surgeon in Nova Scotia," she whispered. "He says if Jonathan wants to come to Nova Scotia and practice surgery there, then he'll be happy to welcome him."

"Oh, dearie my soul. That's what you're going to do, ain't it? You're going to be a surgeon in that Nova Scotia place."

"Yes, Laniah. That's what I'm going to do. Because I must." Molly held up her big, strong hands. Nothing feminine about them. Never had been. And they were as steady as any man's. When she started practicing with the scalpels she snitched from the pharmacy—on corncobs and apples at first, later on Laniah and a few other black folks who couldn't afford to visit a proper surgeon—she had been astonished at how right the knife felt in her steady hands. "I'm going to Nova Scotia and live with my grandfather Cuf and be Jonathan Devrey the surgeon. You going to tell on me?"

"'Course I won't do that. You know I never tell on you."

"I know. But you've got to go home now, Laniah. Mama will take a switch to you if it gets any later."

"She be doing that already." Laniah glanced at the sky. The sun was a fiery red ball, shooting its last rays at what was left of the old Collect Pond. "Been gone all day. She be taking the switch to me for sure. You got to let me go with you, Mistr— Mr. Jonathan. That's what I been looking for you all day to say. You gotta take me with you."

Molly who was Jonathan didn't pay much attention to the request. She had dropped to her knees beside the pond, bent over it to see if the setting sun would show her herself as she was now. Transformed. "I can't do that, Laniah. You'd slow me down. And you might— Oh! Oh God!" She jumped to her feet and took two backward steps, hands pressed to her mouth as if she wanted to stifle a scream.

"What is it?" Laniah demanded. "What you be seeing in that water?" She ran past Molly and knelt at the pond's edge. "What you— Oh, dearie my soul . . ."

"You see it, too? I wasn't imagining it?"

"You weren't imagining nothing. It be there all right. Plain as it can be."

The skull had worked its way from the depths to the shallows as a result of all the draining. The meat cleaver that had split the head in two was still in place.

"Who is it?" Molly demanded.

"I don't be knowing that." Laniah stumbled to her feet and made the sign of the cross. Mistress Clare, she'd made them all be Catholics just like she was. That was the one thing Laniah figured she had to thank her mistress for, making her a member of the true Church so when she died she'd go to heaven. "I don't know who that be, Mr. Jonathan. See, I remembered."

"So you did." Molly who was Jonathan took a step closer to the water and looked again at the death's head and the cleaver. Harder to see now that the sun was almost entirely gone. "Been dead a long time, it looks like," she said. "Don't you think so, Laniah?"

"I expect."

"And whoever did it, do you think he was ever caught?"

"Might have been a she what did it, mightn't it?" Laniah asked.

"Yes, of course. It could have been a woman. If she were really strong." Molly who was Jonathan held up her hands. "You never know what you're going to leave behind, do you, Laniah?"

"No. I guess you don't. Or who's going to find it. You planning to leave me behind, Mr. Jonathan? To get switched by your mama? Won't be no one to speak for me now you're not going to be there."

One more glance at the thing in the remains of the pond; then Molly who was Jonathan, prepared to be Jonathan for the rest of her life as long as that meant she could practice surgery, picked up her satchel and began to walk. She felt the incredible freedom of the breeches, the blessed lack of a skirt and petticoats. And without actually realizing that she'd made up her mind, she tossed the words over her shoulder, "Come on, Laniah. Look sharp. You and me, we've a long way to go."

A SCRIBNER PAPERBACK FICTION
READING GROUP GUIDE

City of Dreams

Discussion Points

1. The novel spans more than 130 years of early American history. How does the author effectively blend together the leaps in time? Aside from family trees, what historical or social links unite each section? Which of the generations did you find most compelling? Why?

2. Lucas Turner sets the stage for the rest of the story when he promises his sister's hand in marriage to Jacob Van der Vries. Do you believe he thought it would benefit Sally, or was he acting purely out of self-interest? Considering what he had to gain and the social structure of the time, would you have made the same decision?

3. Many of the characters' decisions and actions have long-term, far-reaching ramifications. Aside from Lucas's agreement with Jacob Van der Vries, which single decision had the most impact on the story and the characters' lives? How did the consequences differ from what he or she intended, if at all?

4. The story begins at a time when the practice of medicine is slowly evolving. Discuss the risks involved in the earliest surgical procedures and the superstitions attached to them. What factors play a role in the gradual acceptance of certain medical procedures? In what ways is medicine different (and unchanged) at the close of the book than it is at the beginning?

5. How does each generation pay for the feud initiated by Lucas and Sally Turner? How often do the successive generations question the reason for the feud, and how often is it taken for granted? Which characters had the best chance of overcoming the past bitterness and reconciling, and why?

6. Put yourself in Morgan's shoes when he chooses to save Caleb instead of his Uncle Luke. What factors made Morgan the type of person capable of making that decision? Would your choice have been the same? If not, why not?

7. Jennet believes that "Amba always managed to make it seem as if the white people were the slaves and she the owner." How does Amba manage to do that? How do the other African-Americans deal with being enslaved? White characters exhibit various ways of treating and relating to slaves. How did the author use this issue to define her characters?

8. Women were forbidden from practicing certain skills, like surgery. Were you surprised by anything the women were allowed to do? What do the women in the book use as leverage for power? How effective are they? Does the behavior of the story's women in any way foreshadow the eventual gains made by women in modern societies? If so, how?

9. Of all the factors that severely limited people in earlier history—gender, race, religion—which seemed to be the most restricting in this story? Think of at least one instance in which gender, race, or religion caused a character to do something they might not have done otherwise.

10. What grievances did the people of early New York have with the British? Several characters spent time in Europe being schooled, such as Andrew's experience at Edinburgh. How were those characters perceived by other colonists?

A CONVERSATION WITH BEVERLY SWERLING

Q: Where did the idea for *City of Dreams* come from and how did the project evolve?

A: *I had always wanted to do a book about the beginnings of Manhattan. It's an incredible metropolis and compared to most of the world's great cities, its history is much more accessible. Ten years ago my husband and I had an apartment in SoHo. Nearby was a small patch of ground some local people had turned into a "timescape." It was planted with species indigenous to the island, and landscaped to resemble lower Manhattan before Europeans arrived in the early seventeenth century. It was fabulous. You could almost envision the native population around every tree. I began thinking about a novel set in the early city, but I couldn't find a peg on which to hang such a story, so nothing came of it.*

Some years later we moved to an old brownstone in Murray Hill, not far from Bellevue Hospital. I was having dinner with my literary agent one evening and he said he'd love to have a book about the development of a hospital like that. It struck me that a history of Bellevue might parallel a history of the city. . . The two ideas came together and this book was born.

Q: What sort of research did you do for *City of Dreams*?

A: *For the historical novelist, New York on New York is as good as it gets. I spent countless hours in the city's numerous specialist libraries. The book I wrote was not the one I first thought I was writing—it isn't about the growth of Bellevue, only about its earliest beginnings—but I didn't know that until later, so I began with research at the NYU Medical Center library, which has the Bellevue hospital archives dating back to the early days in Nieuw Amsterdam. Then the NYU librarian told me about the*

New York Academy of Medicine, which turned out to be a wonderful resource. The Academy's rare book collection is rich in breathtaking seventeenth- and eighteenth-century medical and surgical texts. All, needless to say, in the public domain. I hand-copied numerous descriptions of old surgical techniques (putting the books in a photocopy machine would put too much strain on their ancient spines) and they became the excerpts from Lucas Turner's journals interspersed throughout City of Dreams. *That's why they so accurately reflect the medicine of the time.*

Q: What happened when you discussed some of those medical techniques with modern doctors?

A: *They were astounded. In one case, I described the stone cutting technique Lucas Turner used on Peter Stuyvesant, which was taken word for word from an old surgical textbook, and the doctor told me it was basically a technique that could still be used today—albeit with anesthesia and sterile instruments. I also had a fascinating talk with my own gynecologist. I was checking to see how long it would take to die from a botched abortion, how long it would take a woman to bleed out. No time at all she said, and she mentioned that when she was a medical student she'd heard about a particular type of seaweed that was once used to dilate women preparing for abortions. That's what led me to create the Women of Connemara, the ancient healing society, that is so important in the second half of the book.*

Q: What surprised you most as you conducted your research?

A: *I was totally astonished by the degree to which the New York economy depended on slavery. Unlike Boston, Providence or Philadelphia, which were founded on high-minded theological principles, New York was always about making rich men richer. The Dutch originated the idea, but it was the English who perfected the process, and one way they did it was through slavery. New York was the only city in the colonies governed directly from London, and it became the linchpin of the British slave trade. I had certainly known before that slavery was not confined to the south, and that much of New England's shipbuilding wealth came from building vessels to transport slaves, but that's different from finding out that slavery and trading in slaves permeated every aspect of New York life. Or that the first slave uprising in the colonies took place in New York in 1712. Or that Wall Street served as the home of the biggest official slave market in the north. All of it was fascinating and all of it became part of my* City of Dreams.